I0719039

MOUNT FITZ ROY

Also by **Scott Sigler**

NOVELS
Infected (Infected Trilogy Book I)
Contagious (Infected Trilogy Book II)
Ancestor
Nocturnal
Pandemic (Infected Trilogy Book III)
Earthcore

THE GENERATIONS TRILOGY
Alive
Alight
Alone

THE GALACTIC FOOTBALL LEAGUE SERIES
The Rookie
The Starter
The All-Pro
The MVP
The Champion
The Gangster

THE GALACTIC FOOTBALL LEAGUE NOVELLAS
The Reporter
The Detective
Title Fight
The Reef
The Rider
The Stone Wolves

ANTHOLOGIES & COLLECTIONS
Blood is Red
Bones are White
Fire is Orange
Hunter Hunterson & Sons War Journal Vol. 1

MEDIA TIE-INS
Aliens Phalanx

MOUNT FITZ ROY

SCOTT SIGLER

MOUNT FITZ ROY
December 2021

This is a work of fiction. Names, characters, places and
incidents either are the product of the author's imagination
or are used fictitiously. Any resemblance to actual persons,
living or dead, events or locales is entirely coincidental.

ISBN: 978-1-939366-05-4

Book design by Donna Mugavero at Sheer Brick Studio
Cover design by Scott E. Pond at Scott Pond Design Studio

Published in the United States of America
by Empty Set Entertainment

This book is dedicated to my friend John Vizcarra,
the Siglerverse Continuity Czar, who makes my work better.

ACKNOWLEDGMENTS

A big thank-you to the following consultants who helped make this story as real-world accurate as it could be:

Joseph Albietz III, MD
Andrew Allport, Engineering
Daniel Baker, PhD, Pharmacology and Toxicology
Jeremy Ellis, PhD, Developmental and Cellular Biology
Chris Grall, US Army Special Forces (Ret.)
J.P. Harvey, Colonel, US Air Force (Ret.)
Daniel Joll, Mountain Climbing
Alex Kent Kendrick, PhD candidate, Geophysics
Joseph Meert, PhD, Geology
Phil Plait, PhD, Astronomy
A B Sigler, Publisher

Author's Really, Really, *Really* Important Points Before You Begin Mount Fitz Roy

THIS STORY IS THE SEQUEL to the novel *Earthcore* and features some of the same characters. If you haven't enjoyed *Earthcore* yet, I strongly advise you do that first, then come back and serve yourself up a heapin' helpin' of *Mount Fitz Roy*.

This story also mentions the events of other books in the Siglerverse continuum. In particular, characters in *Mount Fitz Roy* reference a global pandemic that occurred in the Infected Trilogy, which consists of the novels *Infected*, *Contagious*, and *Pandemic*. You do not need to read those novels in order to enjoy *Mount Fitz Roy*, but be aware that the lethal pathogen was of alien origin, which made most people on Earth conscious of the fact that we are not alone in the universe.

Several characters from my other previous novels are mentioned in *Mount Fitz Roy*. As with the Infected Trilogy, you do not need to read these works in order to enjoy this story. However, if you are a big reader and want the full, unadulterated, integrated Siglerverse experience, here is the suggested reading order of my modern-day novels:

Infected
Contagious
Ancestor
Nocturnal
Pandemic
Earthcore
Mount Fitz Roy

Finally, a personal request from me, the author: We live in an interconnected world. If you discuss *Mount Fitz Roy* online, in reviews or on social media, please try to avoid spoiling the major plot points and big reveals. Other readers only get one chance to absorb this story for the first time, and I hope you can respect their time by letting them see the twists and turns for themselves.

Thanks,
—Scott

MOUNT FITZ ROY

PROLOGUE

August 28

SHE WATCHED ON her phone.

A larger screen, like her computer, or the TV in her office…a bigger picture would make it more real.

Barbara Yakely didn't want it to be real.

He couldn't be gone.

He couldn't.

No volume on the video—a newscaster's voice would do her in. The picture alone carved at her being, painted a horror story she'd already lived through twice.

Could she survive a third?

She didn't know.

Alone in her Republic Plaza office, Barbara watched.

A mountain range, hazed in a pallor of thin clouds. A peak that had been tall and green and brown was now far smaller, and black. The peak gave birth to whitish-gray smoke that billowed up, and to rivers of orange and yellow that flowed down.

The lava streams followed the range's gullies and depressions. Around these rivers, wide shores of pitch black—scorched earth and new volcanic rock. In hundreds of spots, thin plumes of white smoke marking the flaming death of grasses, bushes, the few scrubby trees that had tried to carve out a life on the slopes of the Wah Wah Mountains.

In one spot and one spot only, rising black smoke.

That smoke came from the last dying embers of man-made material. From sheet metal buildings and the equipment, furniture, and gear held inside. From burning jeeps, trucks and mining vehicles. From the clothes—and bodies—of the people who had worked for her.

From where the EarthCore camp had been before lava covered it.

Text scrolling across the bottom of the small screen. She couldn't block that out.

VOLCANIC ERUPTION IN UTAH MOUNTAINS
USGS SEISMOGRAPHS PINPOINT ERUPTION AT NOON, MT
CASUALTIES REPORTED
TOXIC FUMES PRESENT, AVOID THE AREA

The time on her phone read 3:43pm. Three hours since the ground had opened up, swallowed one mountain, and started another.

She'd told her assistant to hold all calls. All, except for calls that came from the personnel at the EarthCore facility in Utah.

The time changed to 3:44pm.

Still no word from Connell Kirkland.

He couldn't be gone.

He couldn't.

The phone buzzed in her hand, making her jump, making the image disappear, showed the ID for her assistant.

This was it. Confirmation.

She watched the phone, felt the buzz of each ring. She felt a pain in her chest. Maybe she'd die before she heard the news. That would be just fine.

She answered.

"Yes?"

"Missus Yakely, I have a call from Sonny McGuiness."

"Put him through."

Barbara looked to the wall, to the framed photos of her husband, Rocky, and her son, Charles Junior, both long since dead. Maybe she'd commission paintings of them, hang them in the same place. Paintings were classier. She wondered why she hadn't thought of that before.

A clicking sound on the phone as the new call came through.

"This Yakely?"

Barbara closed her eyes. "Is Connell dead?"

A pause. Long enough to realize that McGuiness was looking for the right words—she had her answer before he spoke.

"Yeah," Sonny said. "Him and a lot of other people."

"I don't give a fuck about other people." That wasn't true, but grief and anger had taken over. "Are you *sure*? Did you see his body?"

Another pause.

"No, I didn't," McGuiness said. "You watched the news? That whole peak went down."

She knew what he would say next. She wanted to hang up, go back to pretending this wasn't happening.

"Yes," she said. "I saw it."

"Connell was in there. Down at the bottom. A mountain fell on him. He's gone. Now, can we talk about the fucking people who survived? They work for you, too."

That pain in her chest…biting…deep. Heart attack? She hoped so, but she knew she wouldn't be that lucky—there was still a business to run.

"How many survivors?"

"Three," Sonny said. "O'Doyle, Lybrand and me. That's it. And before you ask if I'm sure, I'm fucking sure. I'm at Utah Valley Hospital in Provo. O'Doyle and Lybrand are in the ER. I'm a big-time donor here, enough so that they were rushed in. They'll live, but they're messed up to the point where people are going to ask questions. O'Doyle told me to tell you these aren't the kinds of questions you want answered right now. He said you need to put a lid on this, fast."

Put a lid on it. What was the point? Connell was gone. The camp was gone. Her investment was gone.

But O'Doyle…Connell had said he was a good man, a loyal man. If Connell liked him…

"I'll take care of it," Barbara said. "Don't talk to anyone."

She hung up. Maybe Sonny had more questions. She didn't care. She wasn't the one who was going to solve his problems.

Harvey would.

On the phone, Barbara called up her favorites, tapped Harvey's name.

He answered on the first ring.

"Missus Yakely, let me say how sorry I am to see the news. It doesn't look good."

"Because it's not," she said. "We have three employees at Utah Valley Hospital. Your point of contact there is a man named Sonny McGuiness."

She heard the faint sound of a pen flying across paper.

"McGuiness," Harvey said. "Got it."

"Make sure my people get VIP treatment and are left alone. Spend whatever you have to spend to make it happen."

"Yes ma'am. Do you want me to interact directly with them, or handle this in the background?"

McGuiness and O'Doyle didn't need to know Harvey. Not yet.

"Background," Barbara said. "I don't want any calls from you, Harvey. You understand? I pay you to take care of things."

"Yes ma'am, Missus Yakely. Call me if you need anything else."

Harvey hung up.

Barbara set her phone facedown on her desktop. She couldn't watch any more.

She again looked to the photos of Rocky and Charles Jr. She would need to add a third—one of Connell Kirkland.

Barbara opened a desk drawer, pulled out a bottle that had been in there for a long time. She wiped dust off it. Pappy Van Winkle Bourbon. It had been her husband's favorite. When he and her son had died, she'd sat at this same desk, not knowing what she would do without them, and had drunk an entire bottle.

She'd replaced the bottle. Could she still drink the whole thing?

She was about to find out.

BOOK ONE
STRUCTURE

UNPRECEDENTED ERUPTION CONTINUES TO CLAIM LIVES

By ELIJAH BENSON
The Salt Lake Tribune

MILFORD, UTAH—A film of dust and ash still hangs in the air above southwestern Utah, the remnants of yesterday's unexpected volcanic eruption in the Wah Wah mountain range that has left five people dead and at least another 50 missing and presumed dead.

According to officials from the United States Geological Survey (USGS), the eruption was accompanied by a 3.1 magnitude earthquake, shockwaves of which were felt in the towns of Frisco, Utah, Hamlin Valley and Lund. Limited property damage was reported in those areas.

Approximately 63 injuries caused by the eruption and the quake were treated at local hospitals. The tallies of the dead and injured are likely to rise as search parties locate persons still missing following the eruption.

The Wah Wah eruption was the largest volcanic eruption in the continental United States since Mount St. Helens in 1980.

While the area is consistently monitored for tremors and other tectonic activity, the eruption came with no warning.

"We've never seen anything like it," said Lamont Plum, associate director of natural hazards at USGS. "There was no precursory activity at all, and no indicators of a potential volcanic eruption. The area wasn't even considered volcanically active."

"Wah Wah Springs was the site of a supervolcano some thirty million years ago, but in modern times the area is stable," said Brigham Young University geology professor Camille Estrada. "An eruption of this size, completely unpredicted by any supporting geological information, is quite unprecedented."

Of the deaths reported so far, three were hikers killed by carbon dioxide inhalation.

A fatal car accident on Route 21 that took two lives is being attributed to the volcano as well.

Three more hikers are currently missing.

The largest source of missing persons is from an iron ore mining site operated by EarthCore LLC, a Denver-based company. "The mining facility was in the wrong place at the wrong time," Plum said. "The camp's access road was built in a depression that led up to the adit. The adit apparently channeled the lava flow directly into the camp. We estimate the lava flow reached 40 miles per hour, possibly higher. It would have hit the facility like a tidal wave."

No bodies have yet been recovered from the mining facility. State officials estimate they will not be able to search for remains for weeks, or possibly months, until the flows have completely cooled and hardened all the way through.

Representatives of EarthCore would not go on record regarding the incident, but did say that they are fully cooperating with officials to provide information about the employees at the site.

"We're fortunate the area of the eruption is so remote," Plum said. "Had it been closer to more densely populated areas, we would have seen far more damage, injuries, and deaths."

Plum was asked if EarthCore's mining activity could have caused the eruption.

"It is basically impossible for a manned mining operation to reach the depths necessary to encounter magma."

Lamont Plum, associate director of natural hazards at USGS

"Highly unlikely," Plum said. "There have only been three instances in which drilling hit magma, and those were geothermal drills that were meant for research, not for removing ore from the ground. It is basically impossible for a manned mining operation to reach the depths necessary to encounter magma. This was a freak occurrence. Mining is common in Utah. The presence of a mine near the eruption site is an unfortunate coincidence, no more."

1

August 30

HE PRESSED THE buzzer button.

He'd never known such pain. Had anyone? *Ever?* Maybe some torture victim, somewhere, if an enemy had wanted that person to suffer for a long time.

The copper wire … the rusty pliers … that woman …

He tried to bite back the pain. He had to focus. He had to get out of here before O'Doyle came for him.

He pressed the buzzer button again. And again. And again.

A nurse came into the room — the wrong nurse.

"What's wrong, Mister Doe? Do you remember something?"

They called him *John Doe*. What else would they call him? He hadn't given them his real name.

"I want to see Alice Linton," he said, forcing the words through his mangled mouth, one tooth broken, one gone altogether. "I saw her…yesterday, maybe."

The nurse checked his vitals, a process as automatic and familiar to her as breathing. She looked like she hadn't slept in days.

"I'm your nurse, Mister Doe. I'm sorry things are taking so long, but we have far more patients than we can handle."

A wave of agony swept over him, seemed to bounce from his broken hand to his broken leg, to his smashed face, to his busted mouth, to his broken arm and back again.

"Oh, dear," the nurse said. "You've refused pain meds, Mister Doe, but I can get them for you."

"No, you stupid cunt—get me Alice Linton!"

The nurse's face shifted from caring to blank; the instant, emotional armor of a person who has to deal with difficult people day in and day out.

"Please try to be quiet," she said. "There are other patients in this room."

He blinked, lifted his head. Three other hospital beds, every corner of space taken up. What a shitshow. At least the other patients were out cold. Maybe they had the good sense to partake of pharmacological wonders. He could not…he couldn't risk giving his real name while in a drug-fueled haze.

He couldn't risk saying, *I'm Angus Kool.*

"Just get Alice," he said. "I saw her before. When I did…I thought I remembered something."

The nurse left the room.

Angus laid his head back, tried to cope with the pain.

What if O'Doyle is in one of those beds?

His head snapped up, the sudden movement bringing more agony. He looked at the other patients again, one after another. No O'Doyle.

That crazy bitch hog-tying him with wire.

The gag ball: the taste of rubber, the grit of sand against his tongue, the snot pouring out of his nose onto his lips and chin.

The pliers. The sound they made when she opened and closed them, a high-pitched squeak like that of a baby bird begging for a meal. He remembered her chipped red nail polish. He remembered the feel of those pliers clamping down on the base knuckle of his pointer finger.

He remembered the *crack*—he'd *heard* his bones break before the pain actually hit home, before it exploded through his hand.

After that, most of the ordeal was a blur.

More broken knuckles.

O'Doyle looking like he was on death's door. Lybrand, looking like she'd already stepped through it.

O'Doyle, condemning Angus to death: *I'm taking your suit. If you fight me, I'll kill you.*

The brute taking the suit off Angus, peeling it away like it was a skin and Angus was a dead animal to be dressed and butchered.

Then, the *heat*.

The higher you go, the cooler it gets, O'Doyle had said. *You want to live? Run fast. I see you again, and I kill you.*

Naked, Angus ran. Despite his wounds, despite the scorching temperatures, despite the feeling of his skin bubbling like bacon and his lungs baking from the inside out, despite fighting his way up a nearly thirty-five-degree incline, he ran faster than he ever had in his life.

It had been a close thing, but O'Doyle was right: by the time Angus's tolerance and endurance had all but given out, the temperature began to lower.

Angus would never know how he made it to the top of the Linus Highway. In his swirl of partial memories, he had almost seemed to float there, to almost teleport from the fire to the frying pan to the plateau in an instant.

The cuts and second-degree burns on his feet told him that teleportation was nothing but a heat-stroke-fueled fantasy.

Yes, he'd made it out of the tunnels, but his ordeal had only just begun. The mountain had trembled beneath him. Boulders tumbled down the slopes. He'd known it was only a matter of time before the entire peak collapsed, so he'd run, *down*hill this time, bare feet on sharp limestone. A new sprinting speed record.

Call Guinness: this white boy be fast as hell.

He'd fallen more times than he could count. Sometimes he was able to bring his hands and arms up in time to block his fall—to which his broken right arm and cracked left elbow could attest—and sometimes he wasn't able to do so—as evidenced by his laundry list of injuries: fractured cheekbone; swollen-shut left eye; broken rib; a hundred and forty-two surgical staples spread across five lacerations; cracked left canine to join the missing left incisor knocked out by the crazy bitch's rifle butt.

Running/tumbling down the slope, into the foothills, and then the entire fucking mountain had exploded. Rocks falling like head-sized hail. A swirling hot fog of choking ash. Lava blobs arcing high into the air, the outside cooling into black glass before the volcanic bombs smashed into the ground and erupted like brittle water balloons of death.

A couple of those bombs had landed close enough to splash him — tiny third-degree burns, one on his right shoulder, one on his lower back, one on his left thigh. That last bit of scorching delight had singed away not only flesh but a chunk of muscle as well. Angus had used a sharp stick to dig the still-smoking bit of volcanic rock out of his leg.

And still he'd run on.

He'd headed north, desperate to avoid the EarthCore camp and anyone in it. He'd known his only chance at survival was to reach Route 21 and hope that someone would stop.

The wind had been southwesterly, carried the ash plume away from him. One fluke of many that had kept him alive.

He'd stumbled, limped — and even crawled, at the end — for five miles.

Or was it six?

When he finally reached Route 21, he saw not one but *two* vehicles full of dumbshits who had pulled over to the shoulder to watch the spectacle of ash spewing into the air. One of the cars — a Jeep, maybe — had driven to him. Angus couldn't remember what the driver looked like. Someone had put him in the back seat. Someone had held him.

The people drove him to Milford Valley Memorial Hospital. The same hospital where Angus and Randy had pretended to go after their "lab accident." How ironic.

This time, though, Angus had been hurt for real. As had twenty-odd other people injured by the volcano in one way or another: ash inhalation, CO_2 poisoning, broken bones and concussions from falling debris, a couple of hikers who had also suffered the hell-shrapnel of volcanic bombs, and a handful of local yokels who had crashed their cars while gawking at magma spewing thousands of feet into the air.

Calling Milford Memorial a "small-town hospital" was generous to begin with. The place was not suited as a triage center for a natural disaster. Wounded everywhere, in all the rooms, in the halls, in the waiting area. Chaos ruled. There was so much going on that when hospital staffers asked him who he was, and he pretended to remember nothing at all, his affected amnesia fell far, *far* down their list of priorities.

He'd accepted pain meds that first night. Anyone would have. After that, however, he'd endured. Serious fucking *agony*, and he'd endured. He had to stay sharp. If doctors, nurses, cops or anyone else found out who he was, word might get out.

If it did, Patrick O'Doyle might find him.

That scarred freak-and-a-half and his gorilla-titted linebacker factory girlfriend might be in another room.

By the second night, as Angus fought a constant battle to keep from screaming, people who had been treated for minor injuries began to leave the hospital. The place was still over capacity, but things were calming down. His *I don't remember* ruse wouldn't last much longer. By day three, he knew, the cops would be there, trying to learn his identity so they could seek out someone who gave two wet turds about him.

The joke's on you, coppers: ain't no one left who does. Randy was the only one.

Randy. Angus's best friend. Possibly his only friend. Slashed up by a silverbug. Paralyzed by fear, Angus had stood and watched.

No…not *paralyzed*…Angus had run. He'd run without even trying to help save his friend.

But what could he have done? If he'd tried to help, he'd be just as dead as Randy.

Angus didn't want to think about it. There was something vastly more important to focus on—Argentina. The Chaltélian culture discovered by Veronica Reeves. Platinum knives, just like the ones found in Utah.

There was another ship. Location: somewhere near Cerro Chaltén, also known as *Mount Fitz Roy*.

He concentrated on the obstacles, tried to prioritize what he had to do. Problem-solving. One of his specialties. What were the main obstacles to finding that ship?

Money, first and foremost. He had money put away, but it wasn't nearly enough, and could he even access it if he wanted the world to keep thinking he was dead? He had to acquire big-time financial support.

Second: immobility. His body was ruined. Months before he could walk on his own, most likely. For a full recovery, returning him to his pre-accident abilities, he was looking at *years* of therapy.

Third: guns, and lots of them. How could he get military support?

Fourth: he—

Angus groaned as a fresh bolt of pain lanced up his broken hand. Hurt so bad, so hard to think…

He took a slow, deep breath. Focus. He had to focus on something other than the pain.

Where was he?

Oh, yes…

Fourth: he had to figure out how the mountain had blown up, and also figure out how to stop that from happening at Fitz Roy. Had the rocktopi done that? The silverbugs? Had Connell or Veronica or O'Doyle done it?

The door to his room quietly opened. In walked a fat woman with a beehive hairdo and oversized horn-rim glasses complete with a blue plastic chain—Alice Linton.

She approached his bed, annoyance on her face. Then, she saw him. She recognized him. Behind those ridiculous glasses, her eyes grew as wide as pie pans.

Alice turned and reached for the door.

"I'll tell on you," Angus said.

A ridiculous thing to say, but it stopped her.

Alice's wide body slowly turned. She glanced at the other patients, her experienced eye evaluating if they were truly asleep. She hesitated a moment longer, then walked, silently, to Angus's bedside.

"The FBI came looking for you," Alice whispered. "You could have told me you were a felon, you know."

He ignored the idiocy of the second half of Alice's statement, focused on the first half. Why would the FBI come looking for him? They wouldn't. So, who had?

His smarts might be dulled by pain, but he was awful smart to begin with. He quickly put the pieces together.

"Let me guess," he said, forcing the words past broken teeth. "The FBI agent was a woman? Tall? Dirty blonde hair?"

Alice nodded. "Agent McGuire gave me her card. She told me to call her if I saw you."

Angus had no doubt that *Agent McGuire* was the same woman who had somehow acquired a KoolSuit, walked down the Linus Highway, hit him in the mouth with a rifle butt, hog-tied him, then broken all the knuckles on his right hand with a pair of rust-speckled pliers.

After that lovely little afternoon delight, the psycho woman had left him there and gone further down the Linus Highway, which was the only way in or out. Even if she'd survived the glowing monsters and the silverbugs, even if she'd somehow avoided O'Doyle, she probably hadn't had time to make it out before the mountain turned into a jacuzzi of boiling rock.

"Go ahead, Alice. Call her. Right now."

Alice hesitated.

"*Call her,*" Angus said. "She wasn't FBI. I worked for a mining company. She worked for a rival company. She was out to steal our secrets. She…she wanted to kill me."

Alice's lip quivered. "I don't want to get in trouble."

"Then you—" the words froze in Angus's throat, trapped there by a random nuclear explosion going off in his mangled, crippled hand. He got control of the pain, pushed on. "Then you shouldn't have taken a bribe from me. What would your supervisors think of the scam you helped me pull?"

The big doe eyes widened even further, then narrowed.

"We'll see about that, Mister." Alice pulled a cell phone from one pocket of her scrubs, a business card from the other. Right there, in front of Angus—who was powerless to stop her—Alice Linton dialed.

She held the phone to her ear. She said nothing. After a moment, she lowered the phone, double-checked the number on the card, and dialed again. She stared at Angus as she waited.

Alice lowered the phone, ended the call.

"Let me guess," Angus said. "No answer?"

Alice shook her head. "That seems strange."

"You think? If you want, look up the number for the local FBI bureau office. You can ask them if they have an Agent McGuire there, but I wouldn't recommend it."

Alice frowned. She shifted her considerable weight from foot to foot.

"Why not? What could that hurt?"

"Caller ID," Angus said. "Once you call them, it goes into the Delta System. The system's bifurcated analytical algorithm will search for all calls made by your phone. You'll be marked by the FBI. They may even start investigating you."

Alice stopped shifting. "Investigate *me*?"

Angus had never considered taking a nursing exam, but if this lady had passed it, the bar must be exceedingly low. Hopefully, he could remember the spur-of-the-moment bullshit phrase *bifurcated analytical algorithm*. He could probably use that on stupid people from any walk of life.

"You're probably not the first person this *McGuire* contacted," he said. "Her name will be watched by the FBI, and if you call them and ask about her, *you* will be watched by the FBI. She's not from the government, Alice—she wants me dead. If she finds me here, she'll know that you know about me, which means after she gets rid of me, she will have no choice but to get rid of *you*."

He was making things up as he went, the look on her face told him his story was hitting on all cylinders.

"She scared the poo out of me," Alice said. "I don't want her thinking I'm a witness to anything. What are we going to do?"

That lovely word: *we*. As soon as someone uses it, you know they will do what you want them to do. Go team.

"Get me out of here," Angus said. "I never gave my name."

Alice shook her head. "I can't do that. You're a patient."

"If I'm here when McGuire comes back, that's it for you and me both."

The woman's lip quivered. "I could get fired."

"Better than being murdered."

Alice shook her head.

He almost had her. How to push her over the edge? Of course: *greed*.

"I'll triple what I paid you before. Please, Alice…I don't want to die. And I don't want *you* to die."

With those words, something in her expression changed.

"I'll get you out here tomorrow morning," she said.

"No, *now*. We have to go now!"

"Shhhhh!" Alice glanced to the other beds, scowled at Angus. "Leaving now will draw too much attention. I've worked here for twenty years, I know what I'm doing. You need to sleep. Can I give you pain meds?"

He shook his head. "I...I can't risk it. I might talk, say who I am."

Alice stepped closer, put her hand on his forehead. Her skin felt soft. Soft and cool. Maybe he had a fever.

"It will be all right," she said. "What I give you will put you out cold. You won't say anything. You need your rest for tomorrow. All right?"

Compassion. He'd judged her too easily. Was she taking his money? Yes, but that didn't mean she couldn't also be nice about it.

"Okay," Angus said.

He closed his eyes. He hurt so bad. He wasn't sure if she put a new needle in him, or if she did something with his IV—the pain faded, and he was gone.

2

August 31

"CHRIST, YOU'RE A big fucker," Sonny McGuiness said. "I hope this wheelchair has heavy-duty suspension."

Patrick O'Doyle let the insult slide. Sonny had saved his life. Not just his life ... Bertha's, too, which meant that Sonny could say whatever the hell he liked.

The hospital hallway seemed oddly empty. Quiet. Sonny pushed Patrick along — Bertha's room was around the next corner.

"How is she?"

"I ain't a doctor," Sonny said. "She's awake. She's talking. I think she's going to be okay. But her face is ... ah ... never mind."

Her face. Her hand. Her arm.

The silverbug had sliced Bertha up. Patrick had all but carried her out of the mountain. Then she'd carried him. Or maybe it was the other way around. He wasn't sure—a lot of that bonkers escape remained a blur.

Connell Kirkland was gone.

So, too, was Veronica Reeves, Sanji Haak, Mack Hendricks, Randy Wright and Angus Kool. And everyone else in the EarthCore camp, apparently. Death abounded, plenty for all.

But Patrick and Bertha had survived.

Thanks to the man pushing the wheelchair.

Sonny could have just left. When the earth trembled, when magma pulsed into the air, when lava bombs dropped all around and ash choked the sky, he could have saved his own ass. Instead, he'd risked his life to drive a Land Rover up the side of a dying mountain. He'd rescued Patrick and Bertha. Without Sonny, their long fight through the tunnels, the terror of the Dense Mass Cavern, and the limping race up the Linus Highway wouldn't have mattered—one way or another, they would have died.

"Sonny...I owe you."

"Goddamn right you do. That was some hellacious driving, if I do say so myself."

"I'm serious," Patrick said. "I won't forget what you did for Bertha and me. A guy like me...well, I'm a good friend to have."

But he hadn't been a good enough friend for Connell, had he? Connell was dead. Patrick's job had been to protect the man.

He felt Sonny's small hand pat his shoulder.

"Let's not worry about who owes who what," Sonny said. "Not right now. Your girlfriend wants to see you. Focus your energy on that."

Girlfriend.

Patrick hadn't had a "girlfriend" in...well, in decades. Not since Skylark. Plenty of dalliances, sure, but most of those had been the for-hire kind. Women who sold themselves, which made them just like him.

"Here we go," Sonny said.

The older man stopped the wheelchair at a room. He slid open the door, rolled Patrick in.

Bertha lay in the hospital bed, an IV running into her right hand. Bandages covered her head, most of her face, her left hand and arm. She looked like a mummy. Her eyes were closed.

"Hey there, lady," Sonny said. "I brought you a little something. Well, a *big* something, anyway."

Bertha's eyes fluttered opened. She saw Patrick, smiled a sweet painkiller smile.

"You're alive," she said.

He nodded. "I'm hard to kill."

She blinked slowly. "Thank God for that."

Sonny pushed the wheelchair up to the bed.

"I'll leave you kids alone," he said. "Be as noisy as you like. I think we have this whole wing to ourselves, courtesy of Barbara Yakely."

Bertha's dreamy eyes turned to Sonny. "Yakely is here?"

"No, but her money is," Sonny said. "Private hospitals are the only way to fly. I'll be right outside."

Sonny slid the door shut behind him.

Patrick stared at her. Bandages covering the stitches on her face, the stubs of her severed fingers. What little exposed skin she had looked red, as if she'd fallen asleep on a beach while the sun slowly cooked her.

So much damage. A lesser person wouldn't have survived.

Bertha noticed him looking at her; her smile faded. With her right hand, she felt at the bandages on her face.

"How bad are the cuts?"

"Don't know," Patrick said. "I haven't seen them yet."

She looked away. "It's okay. It's not like I was pretty to begin with."

He gently took her right hand. "You are to me."

She met his eyes, held his gaze.

"You mean that," she said. "You really mean it."

"I do." He turned his head to give her a clear view of the scar tissue that was where his ear had once been. "Besides, you'll never be as ugly as me."

She let go of his hand. She reached up; her fingertips traced his scars.

"Patrick, I can't imagine someone more handsome than you. I can't."

He was a twisted freak. He knew it. Fat. Old. Wounded. And yet, her words rang as true as his had.

"Me … *handsome*," he said. "Whatever painkillers they got you on, I want some, because it's got to be the good shit."

She laughed, winced against the pain the laugh brought with it.

"Morphine goggles," she said, smiling. "Everyone should try them."

She turned her right hand, her fingers cupping his, brought his hand to her mouth, kissed his fingertips. She closed her eyes, leaned her cheek against his palm.

"We almost died, Patrick."

"Almost only counts in horseshoes and hand grenades."

Her skin against his. That simple contact soothed him in a way he'd never known, eased a balled-up knot of frustration and fury and fear that had lodged in his chest for so long it seemed he'd been born with it.

Bertha opened her eyes. The eyes of a warrior. He'd never seen any as beautiful as hers.

"I want you to know I'm sane," she said.

"Why would you tell me that?"

"Because what I'm about to say will sound crazy."

"Crazier than glowing aliens hiding three miles underground in a platinum spaceship that's older than all human civilization?"

She nodded. "Even crazier than that."

"Then this must really be something. Shoot."

Bertha took a long, slow breath.

"I love you," she said. "Life is short. Wanna get married?"

He stared at her.

"What?"

"Married," Bertha said. "You and me."

Did she have any idea what she was asking?

"Maybe we can talk about this when you're not on painkillers."

"Stone-cold sober, I'll want the same thing."

Yes, she did know what she was asking. She wanted to marry him. *Him*. Scars and all. Tattoos and all. Brutal killing history and all.

Did he want to marry her? The answer came instantly, and surprised him—*yes*, he did. He'd never wanted to be married before. Not even to Skylark.

But he was damaged goods. She had to know that. Bertha deserved better than him. Far better.

"I'm too old for you," he said. "It would be like some silly Hollywood movie where the hot young actress gets paired with the crusty old has-been."

She kissed his knuckles.

"*Hot young actress.*" She smiled. "With two missing fingers and a face full of scars. That's sweet. I'm not some dumb girl with stars in her eyes, Patrick. I'm thirty-two. I've served my country. I've *killed* for my country. We just lived through some seriously hairy shit that we should *not* have lived through. It changed my perspective on life. I won't wait around thinking about what could be. I don't have time for that. I'll say what I want and let the pieces fall where they may. Do you get it? I don't care about your age. All I know is there will never be another man like you. Never. If you don't want to marry me, that's cool, I'll take whatever I can get. I want to be with *you.* Only you."

She was right about one thing, at least—they had lived through some seriously hairy shit. Did she have the right idea? Live for the moment and let the pieces fall where they may?

He loved the sound of it.

He loved *her.*

"Yes," he said. "I'll marry you."

Ignoring the pain in his body, he awkwardly leaned over and kissed her. He felt the Vaseline on her lips, the cracked skin beneath it.

Patrick sat upright.

"Holy crap," he said. "We're engaged."

Her nod was so slight it was almost imperceptible. "We are."

They sat in silence for a few moments. He'd survived close calls with death before. More than he could count, really. When the grim reaper came calling and you, somehow, managed to keep him at bay a bit longer, the little things—like breathing, like sitting quietly and just *being*—became things to savor.

"Oh, one thing," Bertha said. "I'm not taking your last name."

Patrick shrugged. "I don't care. Do you want a big fancy ceremony?"

She shook her head. "Something simple is all I need. Happen to know anyone who can marry us?"

He did know someone. Someone he hadn't spoken to in a long, long time. Someone who probably never wanted to speak to him again.

"Patrick?"

"Huh?"

"You blanked out there for a second. You okay?"

"Yes, I'm fine. It's just…"

Sleepy was still alive. He went by *Douglas,* now, of course. Who wanted the old nicknames anymore? Patrick certainly didn't. He'd seen Doug's sermons online, even listened to his podcast a couple of times. Not for the Bible-thumping bits, but rather just to hear the voice of a man who had once been a friend. A blood brother.

"I do know a guy."

"Want to ask him?"

Patrick hadn't spoken to Sleepy—to *Douglas*—in, what…twenty years?

"I don't know if he'd be down."

"Only one way to find out," Bertha said. "Go for it."

Go for it. Could things really be that simple? Yes. Yes they could.

"Let the chips fall where they may, right?"

"That's right," she said. "Hell, I tried it and it worked on you, so why not this guy. Who is he?"

Doug Rapson. *Sleepy*. A man who—like Patrick—should have died a dozen times over.

"A guy I served with."

"So ask him," Bertha said. "All he can do is say no."

He could say more than that. Quite a lot more. And none of it good. Maybe a direct approach wasn't the right thing…maybe Sonny could give Doug a call, and—

"Patrick?"

"Huh?"

"You did it again."

"Oh, sorry," he said. "You know what? You're right. Let's give it a shot."

"Kiss me first. But on the cheek, please, I think it's the only spot that doesn't hurt."

3

September 1

PATRICK O'DOYLE SMILED at him.

"You're a funny guy, Angus. That's why I'm going to kill you last."

Angus crawled backwards, his hands, naked feet, and bare ass sliding across the rock-strewn dirt, dirt so hot it burned his skin.

O'Doyle came forward, a yellow behemoth dressed in a KoolSuit, his face a grinning, bloody mess, his giant knife glinting and gleaming.

He reached out, grabbed Angus's shoulder. He slid the knife point under Angus's chin.

"Come on, Angus," he said. "Let's party!"

Angus slapped at the hand on his shoulder.

"Be still," a woman hissed. "You'll wake the others!"

Angus stopped struggling. He wasn't looking at O'Doyle … he was looking at Alice Linton and her big-ass horn-rimmed glasses.

His heart hammered. It had been so real. Angus knew he'd heard those lines in an old movie somewhere, but that didn't change the terror of it.

"Get me out of here," he said. "He'll find me."

"*He?* You told me you were afraid of a woman."

Was he? Well, the more the merrier, it seemed.

"She doesn't work alone," Angus said. "You really don't want to meet her friends."

Alice quickly glanced around the hospital room.

"Keep quiet," she said. "It's almost time to go. I brought you clothes."

She set neatly folded clothes on the side of his bed: jeans, a button-down flannel, a windbreaker, sneakers that looked two sizes too big.

He tried to sit up. Her hand on his chest told him to wait. After the automated system recorded his blood pressure, she put his pulse oximeter and blood pressure cuff on the sleeping patient in the bed next to him.

"I already took out your catheter," she said.

How wonderful—she'd had her hands on his junk. Helluva way to start the day.

Alice held his shoulders as he slid his legs over the side of the bed. He felt so weak. She helped him dress. The shoes weren't two sizes too big—they were *three*. At least. Clown feet.

"Go slow," Alice said. "Can you walk on your own?"

Angus had managed five or six miles on his own before he'd been driven to the hospital. Even in the shoes, though, each step was agony on his ruined feet.

"I don't think so. Any chance for a wheelchair?"

"A man walking out on his own won't be noticed," Alice said. "A man in a wheelchair will be stopped every time."

"Then I'll walk."

"Go out the hospital's front door. Go left on Main. When you get to Five Hundred North—that's a street—turn left. I'll pick you up at the corner of One Hundred East. Got it?"

"What about cameras?"

"No one watches them," she said. "This isn't a high-security prison. I've been here twenty years—you won't be the first person to walk out of the hospital. Based on how crazy things are, it will be hours before you're missed, then hours more before anyone checks the video recordings.

I know your feet hurt, but it's important you move *normally*, not limp or do anything that will draw attention. You need to go now, right now. Can you do that?"

If it got him out of here, away from where O'Doyle might come looking, Angus was willing to jog on broken glass and whistle *These Boots Were Made for Walking* while he did.

"Yeah," he said. "I can do that."

ANGUS STEPPED INTO the hall. Doctors, nurses and techs moved from room to room. Family members of the various wounded lurked as well, taking up space, asking questions, fetching soft drinks or coffee from vending machines for their loved ones.

He did the best he could to walk normally. No one gave him a second glance.

At the front desk, the sight of two exhausted Utah State Troopers made him pause. Ash streaks on their brown uniforms. They weren't looking at him, didn't even notice him.

Ignoring the pain flaring through his feet, Angus walked out the front door. Had it snowed? No…that was ash, curls of it marking the slight breeze. Cars packed the small parking lot. Beyond the lot and the two-lane road that ran past it, an expanse of scrubland, mountains in the distance.

Ash hung in the clouds, casting the afternoon in a dull haze. He looked to the west, expecting to see a column of ash rising into the sky, but there was none. He could see the ridgeline of the Wah Wah Mountains, yet he had no idea which peak he'd almost died under.

Correction—he had no idea which peak was *missing*.

Angus Kool mustered his strength and walked south, toward the tiny excuse for a "town" that was Milford.

Fifteen minutes later, Alice's blue Subaru picked him up at the corner of 500 North and 100 East.

Even the street names had no imagination.

She helped him get into the passenger seat. Her glance flicked this way and that, probably looking for the mythical pseudo FBI agents that she now believed would kill her if they saw her with him. She shut the car door. Whatever meds she'd given him were finally tapering off. Angus did his best to push the pain down. He didn't realize he'd closed his eyes until the car drove on. Through half-lidded eyes, Angus watched the town of Milford pass by. Not a three-story building in sight, and the few houses with a second floor looked like the height of local luxury.

He thought of the steps he needed to take to go after the fortune waiting somewhere beneath Mount Fitz Roy. First and foremost: *money*.

"I'm going to need a phone," he said.

"You can use mine."

Jesus Christ she was stupid. Hadn't he already covered this?

"I told you about their bifurcated analytical algorithm. My voice on your phone will bring them running. They have computers that monitor all the lines."

"They do?"

He didn't even know if there still was such a thing as *phone lines*, but it sounded legit, so he ran with it.

"I need a burner phone, Alice. Something from a drug store, with pre-paid minutes."

"Pre-paid? I'm not made of money, you know."

He wanted to scream. From the pain? From her stupidity? Probably both.

"I'll reimburse you. Three times what you pay. Use cash, no credit cards. All right?"

She glanced from the road to him, back to the road.

"I suppose so," she said.

He'd reached his limit. The tiny town faded away behind them. He closed his eyes and tried not to cry.

Maybe a half hour later, they reached her small house in Minersville. The last of his energy had vanished. It took all of his focus just to keep from screaming.

She helped him inside. She undressed him. She made him take a few pills. He didn't know what kind.

Once his pain subsided, he found he didn't really care what kind they were at all.

4

September 3

TIM FEELY HAD once been chased by a hoard of man-eating monsters.

He knew they were *actual* man-eating monsters, because he saw them eat an actual man. That particular adventure had ended with him soaked and freezing, his leg broken, his odds of survival maxing out at around ten percent, and without an ounce of booze, drugs or trim to be had.

A few years later, he'd wound up in an even worse situation. He'd been in Chicago during the outbreak, dead center in a city filled with mutated psychopathic killers. Yes, his *second* experience with man-eating monsters, although at least this bunch would have the decency to kill you before roasting you for dinner. Tim had been shot at, hunted, had to dodge debris from a collapsing skyscraper. He'd killed people. While he couldn't say for certain exactly how *many* he had killed, he knew of one, for certain, because when you use a piece of broken concrete to smash in a human skull, you know for sure that bastard isn't going to bother anyone ever again.

Both of his life-altering situations had been horrible. Beyond description, really.

And yet, facing what he now faced, doing the job that was his and his alone, Tim Feely almost saw those experiences as the *good old days*.

"I don't care if the Secretary of Defense is golfing," Tim said into the phone. "I don't care if he's getting a hummer just off the ninth tee and is about to hit a birdie and then roll into a greased-up orgy in the clubhouse with a trio of nubile Eagle Scouts, you get him on the phone to talk about Incident Forty-Two. And about the budget cuts. If you don't, I promise you I will lose my fucking mind and there will be an *Incident Forty-Three*. You got me?"

The person on the other end of the phone said she would see what she could do.

Tim hung up on her.

"Asshole," he said. "Mike?"

The young assistant appeared at Tim's office door as if he'd been standing there all along, masked by some cloaking device.

"Yes, Director?"

"Schedule a lunch with Senator Billings," Tim said. "Insinuate that if he doesn't do something about SecDef cutting off my budget ballsack and telling me I should be grateful to be rid of such a pesky burden, then maybe I have to apply my shrinking resources to something *other* than the Swinestine issue that is rutting up his home state."

"Mild insinuation, or strong insinuation?"

"Insinuation on so many steroids its pee glows green," Tim said.

"Got it."

Tim wasn't sure if he just blinked, or maybe dozed off for an instant, but Mike was there one second, gone the next.

Senator Billings was a self-serving prick. All politicians were, really. Evil, soulless skanks to the last. At least with man-eating monsters and alien pathogens, Tim had known where he stood.

Tim wanted a drink. That was nothing new, of course. He'd wanted a drink every day—perhaps even every hour, if not every minute—since he'd given up the sauce.

Sobriety was a real motherfucker.

He also wanted to pop a benny, but since that substance also fell under his pledge of sobriety, he popped two Tums instead.

Incident Forty-Two was giving him fits. Incident Forty-One had been put to bed—thanks to several hundred tons of still curing concrete in a large pit somewhere in the Mohave desert—but Incidents Thirty-Seven through Forty, along with the ever-present Incident Twenty-Two, were still afoot.

Six cases open.

His budget cut forty percent, after it had already been cut thirty percent.

How was he supposed to solve problems when they didn't give him the tools?

Oh, he'd had a big budget once. After Detroit, Chicago, the Pandemic, he'd had the cash to do whatever needed to be done. Then came a new administration. The incoming president felt strongly that the Pandemic had been a *one-time fluke*, and that *God will not let that happen again.* Tim had brought up the rather obvious question of why "God" had let it happen in the first place, but his sarcastic argument had fallen on deaf ears.

New president, new priorities, budget slashed. The world wanted to move on, didn't want constant reminders of the largest loss of life in human history.

A knock at the door. Mike was there again. Mike only knocked if Tim had a visitor.

"I don't have time," Tim said.

"I'll clear your schedule." Mike's tone spoke volumes. "The NSA director is here to see you."

Tim leaned back in his chair, confused. "Admiral Tenner is here? Why?"

"Not Tenner," Mike said. He raised one eyebrow. "The *real* director."

The bit of cold that washed through Tim's body brought with it a shiver.

"Vogel?"

Mike nodded. "In the flesh."

Tim sniffed, sat forward.

"Send him right in."

Mike ducked out.

Tim felt annoyed at his inexplicable burst of anxiety. Vogel ran F6—the CIA and NSA's combined "Special Collection Service" of high-tech spies—but he was all right. Tim had met him in person once, at a Senate Appropriations subcommittee closed-door meeting. Vogel had seemed personable enough, even though every hall he walked through seemed to generate whispers about how connected he was, drew hushed warnings to not cross him, no matter what. After that, Tim had talked to Vogel on the phone, when the man provided critical intelligence on Incident Forty-One.

There was no cause for concern. Was there?

Well, maybe. People called Vogel the *NSA Director* because he was supposedly the guy that actually ran things, who had been with the department for almost twenty years as "official" DIRNSAs, all admirals or four-star generals, came and went.

The head of a classified department had come *here*, to see Tim.

Alright... maybe there *was* cause for concern. Concern over exactly what, Tim had no idea.

André Vogel walked into Tim's office. Tim came around his desk, shook hands.

"André, how are you?"

"I've been better. From the bags under your eyes, I imagine you're in the same boat."

The best thing about Vogel was his size; he wasn't one of the countless Tall Old White Dudes that populated DC's positions of power like cockroaches in a White Castle dumpster. Vogel wasn't tall. He also wasn't white.

Tim sat behind his desk, Vogel in the chair before it.

"Quite a surprise," Tim said. "A personal visit."

"Things going well for you, Feely?"

Tim shrugged. "Swimmingly, old chap. Apparently there is a strain of feral pigs in rural Georgia that are so smart they not only cover their own tracks, they can smell people from miles away, know how to camouflage themselves, and have, quite possibly, taken to predating on lone hikers, runaways, and even armed hunters. It's my job to find the piggies soon, because if they are like most ferals, they're breeding like wildfire. So that is a source of joy in my life. And dare I speak of the sheer bliss of the reports of monsters of all shapes and sizes in San Francisco? Yes, the life of the Director of the Department of Special Threats is an interesting one. If only it were better-funded, I'd truly be living the dream."

"Ah," Vogel said. "I thought you were a breath of fresh air in the world of bureaucracy, yet here you are angling for money like an old pro. Don't you have a black budget?"

Tim smiled. "Some blacks are bigger than others."

"Hmmm. You know, I'd assume that was either a joke about my size, the length of my genitalia, or about African Americans in general, but then again I assume you know better than to poke fun at someone who, with the click of a button, can look up every email you've ever sent. Not to mention your internet history, which I gather is impressively diverse." Vogel made a show of looking left, then right, then he leaned closer. "Spoiler alert, I may have already seen said internet history, as part of your confirmation process. *Vinyl Vendetta Vixens* seemed like a particular compelling storyline."

A flush of embarrassment. Well, when you become a high-ranking member of a department that doesn't exist on paper, you can't really think a $50 anti-virus program is going to keep your naughty secrets safe.

"You win," Tim said. He gave his best *you're the boss* smile. "I will cease and desist with all jokes. Honestly, though, it's good to see you again. How can the DST be of help to the Special Collections ... excuse me, to the NSA?"

Director Vogel tugged absently at his earlobe.

"I have something unusual," he said. "I don't know what to do with it, so I thought I'd come and explain it face to face."

Translation: Vogel didn't want anything documented in an email. Or on paper. Or have a phone call secretly recorded and stored away on a server somewhere. Vogel was an old spy, but to get where he was — and stay there for two decades, across multiple presidents — he was a spy *and* a politician.

Something that looked and smelled like a turd was about to dropped in Tim's lap.

At least this meant his office wasn't bugged. Always best to look on the sunny side of things, was it not?

"Hit me," he said.

"Couple of days ago I got a call from a former operative of mine.

She said she was gathering evidence of a new species. A new, *sentient* species."

"She leave the NSA to go into biology, or something?"

Vogel huffed. "Doubtful. This woman was a psychopath. She hid her tendencies from us during initial evaluation, and for several years' worth of fieldwork. She was good ... perhaps the best operative I ever had. But, eventually, her tendencies came to the fore. We had to dismiss her. After we did, she worked as a freelancer. Digging up dirt on people, competitive intelligence for the corporate sector, and so on. One of the companies she worked for was EarthCore."

The name rang a bell.

"EarthCore ... the company involved in that freak Utah volcano?"

Vogel nodded.

Looked, smelled, and *tasted* like a turd.

"You're not telling me your agent, the company, and the volcano are connected, somehow. Are you?"

"I don't know," Vogel said. "What I do know is that I received a call from a former agent who claimed she was gathering evidence of a new sentient species. That kind of thing belongs to the Department of Special Threats, so I'm passing it on to you."

A new sentient species? Yeah, unless that sentient race was beaming signals from across the universe—in which case NASA had dibs—that kind of thing did belong to the DST.

"Did the call come from Utah?"

"It came from *nowhere*," Vogel said. "Nowhere and everywhere. The former agent is a specialist in signals intelligence."

The director of (or *head of* or *commissioner of* or *motherfucker in charge of*, or whatever the hell Vogel was) F6 was sitting there, in Tim's office, saying a call couldn't be traced. The woman must be talented indeed.

"Is she running a con or something? Do you trust her?"

Vogel huffed. "*Trust* her? If you knew the things this woman had done, you wouldn't ask that question."

"Let me rephrase. Do you *believe* her?"

Vogel leaned back, slapped his knees, sighed. He seemed conflicted, uncomfortable with the conversation.

"She wanted back in the NSA," he said. "She thought the

information she had was so powerful that I would accept it as … I don't know … as the equivalent of blood money to forgive and forget her past sins. She knew damn well I'd come close to having her cut off. She knew that contacting me might put her back on my radar, might make me re-think my decision to *not* cut her off. That means she thought she had something *staggering* to offer me, to offer the United States. Do I believe her? She didn't give me any details on what she'd found, but I know she wouldn't have made that call over some triviality."

Tim tried to keep the smile plastered on his face. Every day of this job brought new wonders about how the government truly worked.

"And by *cut her off*, you mean?"

"Don't be naive, Director Feely."

Vogel said that casually, as if discussing the illegal assassination of a US citizen was no more or less interesting than a baseball score. Tim made a mental note to never again joke about Vogel's dick.

"So what was this species she found?"

"She didn't say," Vogel said. "Something distracted her. She became angry and cut off the call. I haven't heard from her since. I had my people look into what she'd been doing, which is how we found the EarthCore connection."

"Your people find anything else?"

"They're still digging."

This already had the earmarks of a long, complex, budget-chewing incident. And since Vogel was here, quietly handing it off, saying "no, thanks" wasn't listed on the menu.

An offer Tim couldn't refuse…

"Let me see if I have this straight," he said. "You have an ex-NSA operative, a *psychopath*—your word for her—that fucked up so bad you almost had her, um … *cut off*. She calls you, tells you she found a sentient species. She has no evidence to offer, doesn't give you any details, *and* you haven't spoken with her since. Now you want me to make time to look into her claim?"

Vogel thought for a moment, then nodded.

"Precisely," he said. "Yes, she was a psycho. She was also one of the smartest people I have ever met, and in my career I have met a great many extremely smart people. If she said she found a new sentient species, then she believes it."

Tim didn't know Vogel well. They weren't friends. And yet Tim could see that whoever this woman was—or had been—she scared the living hell out of the man. Vogel feared her, and he respected her. A powerful combination.

"The EarthCore connection," Tim said. "Anything more on that?"

Vogel stood, shook his head. "No, but we're looking into it. I don't have anything concrete for you yet, but I will soon. I just wanted to give you a personal heads-up."

Tim stood, momentarily enjoying the fact that, for once, he could look someone in the eye without having to look *up*. He offered his hand. Vogel shook it.

"We'll get to work," Tim said. "Please let me know when you have more info for me."

"Thank you. This one is all yours. I'll support it fully, because of our wayward operative. You'll keep me informed of everything that you find."

"I'm sure I'll sound rather childish when I say, *you're not the boss of me*. DST does not report to the NSA, André. Or to … well, to whatever department you work for."

Vogel's glare came instant and powerful; this was a man who was not often told *no*. Then, just as fast, the expression faded.

"Then kindly keep me informed as a personal favor," he said. "The woman's name was Kayla Meyers. Known aliases included Carrie Thomas, Harriet McGuire and Miriam Van Doren. Any info you find about her, let me know. She's dangerous."

"As in, dangerous with a capital-D?"

"As in, *all-caps* dangerous," Vogel said. "Dealing with people like her is not what the DST does. Fair?"

"Fair. Now, since you're here and you know many things about many people, what can you do for me about this budget bullshit?"

Vogel smiled. "You're in the big leagues now, Director Feely. I can help you with that, but you'll owe me a favor. A big one. Do you want to owe me a favor?"

Tim looked at Vogel's all-knowing smirk, at the gleam in the man's eyes.

"No," he said. "I don't want to owe you jack shit."

Vogel nodded. "Smart. You have yourself a nice day, Director."

He left the office.

Tim sat, rested his face in his hands. Did the very definition of *shitshow* mean *more shit all the time*? It had to. Shit in all-caps, apparently.

"Mike!"

"Yes?"

Tim jumped in his chair, looked up, saw that Mike was already standing there, *must* have been standing there before Tim even called for him.

"Mike, you're a spooky fuck, you know that?"

The younger man nodded. "I've been told that once or twice. What did you need, Director?"

"I need to research a company called *EarthCore*."

"A little research, or a lot of research?"

"All the research," Tim said. "Get me everything there is to know."

THE PHONE VIBRATED on her nightstand, waking her.

Samira Jabour opened one eye, saw the phone, then hid her face in her pillow. The call buzzed and buzzed until it went to voicemail. She was just falling asleep again when it vibrated anew.

Whoever it was would not leave her be.

She reached out, picked up the phone: a video call request from Ramiro Chus.

His smiling profile pic stared out at her. Same pic she'd had for him since before they started dating.

It was **3:32am**. What the hell could he want at this hour?

Sam thought of texting him that she would call back later, after a shower and a coffee, after she looked presentable, but Ramiro had seen her barely open morning eyes more times than she could count. He wanted video? Fine, he could have it.

She held the phone up over her face, tapped the icon to let the call through. Ramiro looked tired. His black hair hung rumpled and wild in front of his eyes.

"It's early," Sam said. "Are you just home from a goth rave or something? Decent folk are trying to sleep."

She waited for the inevitable crude joke, but for once, she didn't get it.

"I've got some bad news," he said.

Ramiro looked visibly upset. Hurting. Sam sat up, pushed her back against the headboard.

"Okay," she said. "What's going on?"

"Have you seen the coverage on that Utah volcano?"

"Of course I've seen it. Everyone has seen it."

His lips quivered. He blinked, trying to find the right words.

"Veronica was there," he said. "She was doing consulting for that mining company, EarthCore. She's missing, presumed dead."

Veronica Reeves? *Dead?*

"That can't be. She stayed in Argentina."

Ramiro sniffed. "In her infinite wisdom, apparently, she left and went to Utah."

"What the hell was she doing helping a mining company?"

"EarthCore put out a press release that said she was on-site in case they found evidence of indigenous cultures. To respectfully manage any artifacts that might turn up. That kind of thing."

"But she hated mining companies," Sam said. "She was *helping* one?"

"I have no idea what she was actually doing there. Making some money, probably. For herself. Not like it's anything new for her to jet off without tell us what's up."

Wasn't that the truth. Veronica was the leader of the Chaltélian project, the *face* of the project. *She* got flown to various cities around the world. Not Sam and Ramiro. *She* got the honorariums, the stipends, the speaking fees, the per diems. Not Sam and Ramiro. Veronica had gone to the dark side to work for a mining company? A temp gig to rake in the big bucks of the private sector? Come to think of it, that didn't seem so far out of character at all.

"I don't know what to say," Sam said.

Ramiro shrugged. "Me neither. I don't know if there's a funeral planned or anything."

"We could call her dad."

"Sanji was with her," Ramiro said. "He's also missing, also presumed dead."

Maybe that explained things. Veronica didn't like people—Sam and Ramiro included—but she adored Sanji Haak. A chance for father and daughter to spend some time together, *and* get paid? Kind of nice, when one thought about it.

"I don't think she had any other family," Sam said. "At least none that she talked about."

Ramiro rubbed his bloodshot eyes. Had he cried over Veronica? The two hadn't exactly been best friends. But Ram had spent the last four dig seasons with Veronica, as had Sam. You don't have to *like* someone to be sad at their passing. Sam suspected her own tears would come eventually.

"More bad news," Ramiro said. "I found out about the press release from Osmond Dex at NatGeo. They're ending our grant."

Ramiro handled Veronica's grant applications and management. He was better at it than Sam was. Veronica always seemed to be too busy to do anything other than rubber-stamp the approved grants, then go flash her famous face in meetings to seal the deal.

"But that was our last grant," Sam said, as if Ramiro didn't already know. "How are we going to fund this season?"

"We're not. It's over, Sam. Without Veronica, we're done."

Sam's sympathy for Veronica was replaced by anger. Veronica was the project lead, sure, but Sam and Ramiro were also well-qualified to carry on the work. Why did the fucking world only give a shit about Veronica Reeves?

"We're not done," Sam said. "Did you finish that new cooling gear you were working on?"

"Almost. But now there's no point."

The deeper the team went into the Chaltélian tunnels, the hotter it got. They'd reached the limit of how far a human being could go. In the middle of the dig season, Veronica had sent Sam and Ramiro back to Michigan—Ramiro to upgrade the cooling gear, Sam to use the University of Michigan's high-powered computer cluster to help crack the impossible code that was the Chaltélian written language.

Veronica Reeves was dead. Hard to accept, yes, but that meant she wouldn't be calling the shots anymore.

Sam would.

"Finish the upgrades, Ram. We need that gear."

"I told you, we're *done*."

"And I told you we're *not*. We can apply for new grants."

He tilted his head a bit to the left, like he always did when he was annoyed, like he'd done so many times when they'd been married.

"What, you're going to show me how easy it is to get funding? Should I tell you how to better analyze the glyphs? How's that coming, anyway? Any breakthroughs in the Chaltélian language I could add to these mythical new grant proposals?"

Three years earlier, Veronica had assigned Sam to do detailed analysis of the images found in the caves. Some images were easy—it wasn't hard to recognize crude paintings of a grasshopper, animals or plants. The culture's glyph language of circles and various types of wavy lines, however, continued to frustrate her. She knew she could crack the code, at least partially, but only if she could find more symbols.

To find them, she had to go deeper.

"That's a low blow, Ram. I've done all that can be done with what we have."

"I know that," he said. "You know how I know that? Because you have more experience with those glyphs than anyone else. Just like I have more experience getting grants for the Chaltélian culture dig than anyone else. Sam, listen to me—there won't be any more money. It's *over*."

Veronica had been working alone when she'd uncovered the massacre site at Cerro Chaltén, when she'd found the tunnel entrance, the first few glyphs, and the first double-crescent knife. When that work graced the cover of *National Geographic*, her career took off.

Young, attractive, whip-smart, witty on camera, Veronica Reeves became a science rock star. She did talking-head stints on news shows, was featured on CNN, sat in the guest chairs of shows like *Good Morning America* and *Joe Rogan*. U of M was the first to fund her research, which allowed her to hire Sam and Ramiro.

Back then, getting grants had been easy.

Over the last four years, though, most of those grants had run their course. Veronica's initial research created quite a splash, but "publish or perish" remained the law of the land. They found two more knives, some more undefinable glyphs, but that was it. The tunnels' heat barrier prevented Veronica, Sam and Ramiro from going deeper. They didn't find anything *new*, and as a result, the grant money started to dry up.

Veronica could have acquired corporate funding in a snap—from mining companies. All she'd had to do was reveal the knives were made of a platinum alloy. But she refused that option for fear of capitalists tearing the priceless archaeological site apart. Only four people knew of the knives' composition—Veronica, Sanji, Sam, and Melissa Askew, VP of Development at U of M.

Not even Ramiro knew.

And now Veronica and Sanji were dead.

Veronica had been just as careful about hiding the location of the Chaltélian tunnel system. Other than her, only Sam and Ramiro knew where it was.

Was Veronica paranoid? Yes. Did that paranoia turn out to be foresight? Absolutely, especially when the pyramidology set got involved, when Graham Hancock tried to connect the Chaltélian culture to Atlantis.

More absurd claims followed. The internet pseudo-history crowd postulated wild theories tying the Chaltélians to the Seven Cities of Gold, to the absolutely ludicrous concept of Agartha, and—of course— to alien intelligence. Veronica clammed up even further, afraid that adventure tourists, artifact hunters and selfie-crazed "influencers" might start combing the area, looking for that perfect photo that would generate millions of likes.

TV programs, documentarians and internet shows sent requests for access to the Chaltélian caves, or at least for decent video footage. Veronica said *no*.

News sites and blogs asked for access to shoot photos and do on-the-scene reporting. Veronica said *no* to those requests as well.

And *everyone* seemed to want to get their hands on the knives: museums, archaeologists, historians, TV show producers, and on and on. Veronica always had the same answer: No.

Without visuals, no coverage. Without coverage, interest in the Chaltélian culture ebbed from the high-water mark. Funding dried up. Only the National Geographic grant had remained.

Now that was gone as well.

"I'm not giving up," Sam said. "Get me a meeting with Osmond. I'll convince him to help us get the grant back."

"The only reason we still had that was because of Veronica's brand name. Without her, there's no chance."

He was wrong—this was a *huge* chance. A chance for Sam to step out of Veronica's shadow. A chance to lead.

"I can take her place," Sam said. "I can do what she did. Now that she's gone … I mean, well, it's tragic that she's probably dead, but I can do everything she did."

Ramiro stared out from the phone.

"Maybe you can," he said. "But you can't be *her*. Whatever *it* is, she had it. You don't."

That was bullshit. Sam had *it*, whatever the hell that phrase meant, but how could she show *it* when Veronica had always hogged the spotlight?

And if the Chaltélian dig was really over, Ramiro would move on. For good. Sam wasn't ready for that. Divorce or no divorce, he was still her best friend.

"The rental cabin is already paid for," Sam said. "So is storage for the truck. You finish your cooling gear, then all we have to pay for is travel and food, right?"

His eyes narrowed, not in anger but in thought.

"Yeah, I suppose that's true."

She could sway him. She'd always been able to talk Ramiro into doing whatever she wanted—everything except *not* getting divorced.

"You and me, kid," she said. "One more shot at the title. You know damn well your new gear will let us go deeper. We'll find something huge. I can feel it."

His lips twitched to the left side of his mouth, something he did unconsciously when he was thinking.

"Is this really about the science, Sam? Maybe you think it's your turn to be the face of the franchise, so to speak."

He saw through her. She could lie to him, but he knew when she was lying. He'd always known.

"It's about both," she said. "Come on, it's just a couple of months more. We don't find anything, you go on with your career."

And probably never see me again, which will kill me, because I brought this on myself.

"I supposed you want me to plan it," Ramiro said. "Do the budget and everything else?"

"You did it for Veronica."

"Veronica's gone."

"All I'm asking is that you have my back like you had hers."

Ramiro sniffed, rubbed his right eye.

"Let me think about it," he said.

And with that, she knew he was in. He knew her better than she knew herself, no denying it, but the inverse was also true.

"That's fair," she said. "If you hear anything about a memorial service, let me know."

"I'm sure U of M will have one. They'll be celebrating her life and all of that jazz. I don't think it's hit home for you that she's actually gone, Sam. When it does, call me if you need me. I'm still here for you."

She started to say *thank you*, but he disconnected before she could speak.

He was still there for her. Why? She really had no idea. Had their positions been reversed, she would have probably never wanted to see him again. But he wasn't her; Ramiro was different.

He would back her play.

Sam knew it.

5

September 4

ON HOLD, SONNY sat alone in the hospital's private waiting room. The padded leather recliner felt lovely on his old bones. No back-breaking lobby chairs in here, thank you very much, not for the people who contributed big bucks to the place. Critics could say what they liked about the American medical system, but for those with enough money to become a hospital patron, the care is always first-class across the board.

As he waited for the woman on the other end of the call to take him off hold, he watched a video of a puffed-up bleach-blond preacher delivering a fire-and-brimstone-and-give-me-your-money sermon.

"And the Lord sayeth-*ahh*," the man hollered to the adoring, boisterous congregation, "that no man is free from sin *save through him-ahh!* Isn't that what the Lord sayeth?"

The audience shouted out affirmations. Some waved their hands. One fainted.

"Reverend Rapson," Sonny said. "Proof of at least one universal truth—there's a sucker born every minute."

Sonny watched Reverend Doug Rapson stalk the colorfully lit stage like a hyena waiting for a wounded animal to die. White suit so perfectly tailored it barely rumpled when he waved his arms, or when he reached to the heavens and bounced on tiptoes. The guy wore more rings than even the most flamboyant escorts Sonny had hired over the years. White patent leather shoes that gleamed so bright they left little tracers of light as he moved. Bright yellow shirt. White tie fastened with a thick diamond tie-tack, matching diamond cufflinks on his yellow cuffs. Hell, even his *socks* matched—yellow just like the shirt.

"You look like a pimp," Sonny said. "And not a good one at that."

O'Doyle and Lybrand were getting married, and O'Doyle wanted this prancing peacock to perform the rite? No accounting for taste. O'Doyle had asked Sonny if he'd make the call, fight through whatever phone tree existed to speak with Rapson.

Sonny had agreed to help. He still didn't know why. It wasn't like him.

He was doing a lot of things that weren't like him. Case in point— why had he driven a Land Rover up the side of a fucking *volcano* to save two people he barely knew?

Maybe Funeral Mountain had changed him. Maybe watching that psycho supermodel kill Cho Takachi had changed him. Sonny couldn't say.

Once away from the mountain—away from the spewing lava, the burning ash, the falling rocks, and the worst of the ongoing tremors— Sonny knew he had to get O'Doyle and Lybrand to a hospital. He could have taken them to that speck-of-shit hospital in Milford, maybe should have, considering their wounds, but he'd asked them both if they could hold on for a few more hours, enough to get far away from Funeral Mountain and the media and law enforcement attention the volcano would soon bring.

As messed up as they were, both O'Doyle and Lybrand had seen the need to tough it out for a little while longer, to get away from curious eyes.

During his mining career, Sonny had repeatedly been flat broke and stinking rich. When rich, he tended to spend wildly on himself and give generously to charities, a combination that inexorably led to him being poor once again.

His favorite two charities: Brigham Young University and Utah Valley Hospital. The former because it gave him access to BYU's geology department staff and school records, useful tools in his constant search for new deposits. The latter? Because he was old. Because he needed medical care more often than he had in his past. Because one thing remained true from the time before the pharaohs right up to modern-day internet tycoons—rules don't apply to the rich.

If Sonny had been some Joe Schmoe who pulled up to the emergency room entrance with a pair of half-dead people in tow, there would have been questions. Forms. Waiting. More questions. At Utah Valley Hospital? None of that. Not for "Mister McGuiness." For him, there was access to the small private wing.

His money had got O'Doyle and Lybrand in, but it wasn't enough to keep everything truly quiet, not with the laundry list of injuries the two had sustained. *Yakely's* money, on the other hand? The brand-new donation to Utah Valley—made in Sonny's name just a few hours earlier—ensured O'Doyle and Lybrand would get the best of the best, and get it quietly.

Money. It was always about money.

The whole Funeral Mountain affair should have set Sonny up for life. He'd been *rich* before, several times, and had spent each fortune. This dig was the one that would make him *wealthy*—so "rich" that he would have had to hire a financial strategist to find creative ways to actually spend it all.

But he wasn't wealthy. He had a million bucks in the bank, thanks to his deal with Connell Kirkland, so Sonny was still *kinda* rich. That barely bottom edge of seven figures didn't exactly put him beyond the dreams of avarice. Instead of a perpetual percentage of an endless fortune, Sonny had barely escaped with his skin.

"Mister McGuiness, is it?"

On the phone, a man's voice. Deep and resonant—the same voice Sonny had heard from the puffed-up peacock strutting across the stage.

Sonny let the video play as he talked. "That's right. This Doug Rapson?"

"I prefer *Reverend* Rapson."

Oh for fuck's sake—he was one of *those* guys.

"Of course, Reverend."

"I usually don't take direct calls, but what my assistant said…who asked you to call me?"

"Patrick O'Doyle."

Silence.

"Reverend Rapson? You there?"

"Yes," Rapson said, his voice a tight monotone. "I'm here. I just…I haven't heard that name in a while. What does that mother… what does O'Doyle *want*? If he's coming for me, you tell him I'll be ready."

Coming for him? A man of the cloth about to drop an F-bomb? Rapson and O'Doyle must have some history. Sonny glanced at the video—on the screen, white-and-yellow-clad *Reverend* Rapson was bouncing in place, one hand holding the mic, the other reaching up to JEE-sus-*ah*.

"He wants you to marry him and his fiancé," Sonny said.

More silence.

"I see," Rapson said. "That's…I guess I never expected to hear that. I assumed he was dead."

"He ain't. He'd like you to officiate. You up for it?"

"No, I'm not up for it," Rapson said. More punch in his voice now, but still a shell of his on-stage performance energy. "Tell him I'm happy he's alive and I wish him the best. Can you do that for me?"

"I'll make it worth your while," Sonny said. "A nice donation to your church."

"How big of a donation?"

Of course. Rapson was a businessman-*ahh*.

"Twenty grand," Sonny said. With a million bucks in the bank, he could splurge a bit for two people who'd been through hell. "I'll cover flights, of course, and put you up in a swanky hotel. You fly in, do the ceremony, head home. No drama."

"If I'm going to perform a wedding ceremony for that man, it will cost a hundred thousand dollars."

Rapson was a send-me-your-money type, granted, but a hundred large for *one day's* work? Sonny wasn't going to give up a tenth of his net worth for a fucking wedding. And he wasn't going to ask Yakely for it, either. Maybe she could afford that, but it was the principle of the thing that mattered.

"The budget won't cover that, Reverend."

"Then I'm afraid I have to pass. Mister McGuiness, how well do you know Patrick O'Doyle?"

A question Sonny had been asking himself. "Call us co-workers. I've known him for a few weeks."

"You sound like a nice enough guy," Rapson said. "I'll give you a little unsolicited advice—when you're in his orbit, be careful."

When you're in his orbit? Who the fuck spoke that way?

"Maybe you could be a little more specific, Astronomer Rapson. What do you mean by that?"

"I mean people around him have a tendency to die."

Based on the events of the last week, truer words had never been spoken.

"I'll keep that in mind," Sonny said.

"I said *no* to your offer, and if Ender is still the same man, he'll want to call me himself to talk me into it. Or order me into it, if he still thinks that will work. Please inform him that unless he's got six figures for me, I'm not interested. I've got a church to build. Goodbye, Mister McGuiness."

Rapson hung up.

Ender? What the hell did that mean?

Sonny put his phone in his pocket. He leaned back in the recliner, his right hand encircling the bracelet on his left wrist. The feel of the Sikyatata's cool metal always helped him think. His fingertip traced the whirling long image engraved in the silver, a symbol most people mistook for a swastika. Sonny enjoyed when people did that, when the image of a black man wearing "Nazi" confused the ever-loving fuck out of them. Plus, the thing was older than he was, which always made him feel grounded in a way that nothing else did.

O'Doyle's guy was a money-grubbing dick? Well, so what, so was Sonny.

It didn't matter. If O'Doyle and Lybrand wanted to tie the knot,

Sonny knew a few people in Provo who could sling a wedding ceremony like nobody's business.

"All right, you crazy kids." Sonny pulled his phone out again, scrolled through his address book. "Let's hope you don't object to being married by a Mormon."

6

September 6

ALICE HELD a sippy cup in front of him. A pink cup, with a yellow lid. Angus drank from the blue straw. The cold, watered-down juice felt amazing on his tongue and sore throat.

"Thank you, Alice. You're a godsend."

"Don't you try and butter me up." She scowled at him—angry, but also enjoying the power structure. "If you think I'll forget about you paying me for this, you're crazy. Take one more sip, peanut."

Peanut. She'd started using that nickname the day before. Angus sipped, watched her smile as she did, and wondered if she'd ever read Stephen King's novel *Misery*.

Hopefully she didn't have a wooden block and a sledgehammer lying about.

She set the sippy cup on the bedside table. "I can't have you here much longer. Is someone coming to help you, or not?"

His first reaction was to say something insulting, to be a smart-ass, but his normal instincts had faded away when it came to Alice Linton. She had saved his ass. In her home, he felt *safe*.

At least for now.

"I think people will come," he said. "It can't be much longer. Maybe today."

She put the back of her hand on his forehead. She pursed her lips. She took his left hand, the motion wobbling the blue plastic chain of her glasses. She pressed her fingers into his wrist, stared at a wristwatch.

He waited patiently while she took his pulse.

"No sign of a fever," Alice said. "Pulse is normal. You may be a scrawny little thing, but you're healthy as a horse. Aside from your injuries, I mean." She gently put his wrist back down to his side. "I'm going to make you some lunch. Do you like tuna?"

Again the urge to make a crude comment, and, again, that urge evaporating.

"Yes," he said. "Thank you."

A blast of pain ripped through him, coursing from his ruined right hand, under the cast covering his forearm, all the way up to his broken cheekbone.

"Oh, Peanut—are you sure you don't want more pain meds?"

Did he *want* more? No. Did he *need* more? Fuck yes, he did.

"Please," he said. "But I need to stay sharp for this."

She reached into a pants pocket, pulled out two plastic vials. She shook out a pill from each.

"Ten milligrams of oxy for the pain, ten of Adderall to help keep you alert," Alice said.

She handed him the pills. He swallowed them, chased down by another drink from the sippy cup.

Alice adjusted her glasses on her nose.

"We're going to have to measure the meds out carefully when I go back to work tomorrow," she said. "I've used four sick days to care for you. You'll need to pay me for those as well. You know that, right?"

Angus smiled. "Happy to do so. And, like everything else, triple what they're worth."

She smiled a smile of greed. She left the bedroom, leaving Angus Kool alone with his agony.

He wasn't worried about paying her. When his contacts came through, he'd have so much money that what he owed her would be an infinitesimal fraction of his net worth.

This room of hers. Pink blankets. Fluffy pillows. Wallpaper of pale-pink stripes and light-blue flowers. An overweight black cat sitting quietly on a white dresser, staring down at him. Hard to imagine a bedroom more diametrically opposite to his tastes; also hard to imagine appreciating any place more than he appreciated this one.

Compared to the nightmare he'd endured, this overly feminine cat lady's bedroom was an absolute dream.

He'd spent five days here, in and out of sleep. Alice fed him. She helped him to the bathroom and back. The *Patient With No Name* had vanished from the hospital, she'd told him. Local police had canvased Milford and nearby towns, looking for a small, injured man in a hospital gown, checking to see if any homes or businesses had been broken into.

Yes, people had looked for him. They just hadn't looked very hard.

Hopefully, they wouldn't find him until he had enough wealth to hire his own fucking army.

So many variables. Veronica's probable location lay in a region with an unclear national border. If the Mount Fitz Roy ship was like the Utah ship, it was three miles below ground—that far down, people could drill in at an angle from a long ways off. Expensive, yes, time-consuming, yes, but worth it to many who had the kind of resources needed to get that done.

That meant there was probably no way to make a clean deal with the Argentinians or the Chileans. This wasn't just some potential mineral deposit. This was beyond even the gold rush that had turned the West Coast into a land of money and power, that had turned San Francisco from a sleepy port into one of the world's great cities—this would change the world's economy, forever.

In Utah, he'd missed much of what had happened after he faked his lab accident. He didn't need to see data, though, to figure out the basics. Somehow, the rocktopi had lifted up an entire mountain and set the massive ship beneath it. What they'd done in Utah, they had most likely done in Argentina.

The Utah ship had been four miles long, a half-mile wide. As long as nineteen Nimitz-class aircraft carriers stacked end-to-end, almost as wide as ten Nimitzes laid side-by-side. It was impossible to accurately calculate the weight, but Angus had ballparked it so many times it might as well have been a brain tattoo. The Nimitz was 101,600 tons, made primarily of steel.

Angus was the only person alive who had studied the alien platinum-iridium compound. The few samples he'd brought up from beneath Funeral Mountain showed an engineering marvel—despite being a tenth of steel's density, the Pt/Ir compound was nine times stronger.

If a Nimitz had been made from the alien metal:

$$101{,}600 \; / \; 10 = 10{,}160 \text{ tons of platinum-iridium}$$

But the math fun didn't end there. Oh, no sir, not at all. It would take approximately *1,492 Nimitzes* to equal the Utah ship.

$$10{,}160 \times 1{,}492 = 15{,}158{,}720 \text{ tons of platinum-iridium}$$

More math? Sure, sounds great! One ton equals thirty-two thousand ounces.

$$15{,}158{,}720 \times 32{,}000 = 485{,}079{,}040{,}000 \text{ ounces}$$

The last multiple, well, that one was a doozy. That one was the big-titted bimbo bouncing into the room in a skimpy dress, screaming: *Hey, boys, lookit me!* That last multiple was the current value of the platinum-iridium compound, which Angus approximated at $950 per ounce.

$$485{,}079{,}040{,}000 \times \$950 = \$460{,}825{,}088{,}000{,}000$$

The Utah find had been worth $460 *trillion*. Enough to pay off the US national debt nearly twenty times over. Hell, there were only $1.5 trillion US dollars in circulation.

That wasn't just a mineral deposit, it wasn't just a gold rush, it was the kind of money that would start wars. At the very least, a war between

Argentina and Chile as each country fought to establish a defined border that would include Mount Fitz Roy. Would the conflict stop with just those two countries? No way of knowing. Would Brazil get involved, perhaps backing Argentina to have easier access to the treasure trove? No way of knowing.

And then, of course, there was the United States. That kind of world-changing resource in America's backyard? Uncle Sam would dive in head-first, backing one side or the other. There was so much wealth to be had that China, India, or Russia might back the other side, trying to get the bigger piece of that tasty platinum pie.

That would be bad. Not for the lives lost, or the damage done, but because if nations found out about the platinum, the country that wound up controlling Mount Fitz Roy would take ownership of the find, possibly kick out whatever company Angus enticed to locate the damn thing in the first place.

If that happened, Angus would lose his shot at becoming the richest person in history. He wasn't going to let that happen.

Suck a bag of dicks, Jeff Bezos.

Deals would be made. Very *quiet* deals. Deals that would make everyone involved filthy rich.

That much platinum, of course, would lower the price-per-ounce significantly — it would be worth less than tin. Although, even if the price of platinum dropped to twenty-five cents an ounce, the find would still be worth $121,269,760,000.

Not bad at all.

But Angus had no intention of allowing the price to drop so low. To keep prices up, whoever controlled the site would need to create artificial scarcity, become an instant cartel dictating the price of platinum (and iridium, for that matter) all across the globe. Just as OPEC had done with oil for half a century. Just as DeBeers had done with diamonds for a *full* century.

So why not Angus — and his partner-company-to-be — with platinum?

He was getting a little ahead of himself, though. He knew it. He had to land a partner first. And basing his numbers on the Utah ship was a best-guess scenario. The Fitz Roy ship might be much smaller — the size of one 101,600-ton aircraft carrier instead of over a thousand of them, for example. Or it could possibly be even *bigger* than the

Utah ship. There was no way of knowing. In fact, there was no way of knowing if there was a Fitz Roy ship *at all*. A single knife and some bumbling kid archaeologists finding a few shitty cave drawings proved nothing.

Except…Angus *knew* there was a ship. He knew it like he knew his own name.

It was there, he just had to figure out a way to get at it.

Alice came back into the bedroom. "Someone is here to see you."

Thoughts of wealth vanished, replaced by thoughts of the smiling, glowering Patrick O'Doyle.

Angus pulled the covers up to his chin. "Is it a man? A *huge* man?"

She frowned. "No, silly, it's not that man you see in your nightmares, or the lady who told me she was an FBI agent. Your visitor is a young woman."

Angus pushed himself up in bed. Alice moved quickly, tucked pillows behind his back so he could stay sitting up.

The pain had ebbed somewhat; the extra oxycodone going into effect. The Adderall made him feel on-edge.

"She's very pretty," Alice said. "Why do attractive women come looking for you, I wonder?"

A hint of jealousy in her voice.

"Alice, come on, you know you're the only girl for me."

She stopped fluffing the pillows. She glared at him, her eyes only inches from his.

"Don't play with me," she said quietly. "It's not fair."

She walked out, leaving Angus with a new emotion. Was it…*guilt*? Did he actually feel *bad* for upsetting Alice?

He didn't have time to analyze his thoughts, though, because a stunning woman walked into the bedroom. Brown pantsuit. Briefcase. Gleaming red hair pulled back into a tight bun.

"Doctor Kool, I presume?"

"That's me."

Green eyes and red hair. If there was a combo that invariably put his pecker at attention, that was it.

She walked closer, gently sat on the bed. "I'm from BHP Billiton. My name is June. June July. Yes, for real. Blame my hippie parents. And, yes, I've heard all the one-liners."

Her words came out with well-rehearsed ease. That kind of name, it was like the female equivalent of *A Boy Named Sue*.

"All the one-liners," Angus said. "As in, *hey, Calendar Girl?* Heard that one?"

"Maybe four or five hundred times."

"How about, *say what you may, June July?*"

She tilted her head. "I've only heard that one a hundred times."

"How about—"

"Doctor Kool, can we please get on with it?"

Angus winced at a surprise stab of pain, but he couldn't let the wordplay go.

"Jeez, lady," he said. "What's the matter? That time of the months?"

She opened her mouth to speak, closed it. She smiled. "That one I have *not* heard before. Well done."

Angus closed his eyes and dropped his head back against the pillow. Just talking to her was tiring—coming up with more zingers would exhaust him to the point of death.

"Doctor Kool?"

"I'm listening," he said.

"You need to *talk*, not *listen*," June July said. "We know who you are, obviously. Stealing you away from EarthCore would be a coup all by itself, but you know that's not why I'm here. When you called, you said you could give us—" she opened her briefcase, pulled out a piece of paper "—I quote, *the biggest fucking find in history, man, like bigger than a Brontosaurus schlong.* End quote."

Perhaps he'd still been on painkillers when he'd made that call…

"While I've never *seen* a Brontosaurus schlong, Doctor Kool, the description paints a rather grandiose picture. I'm ready for you to elaborate. In accurate terms, if you don't mind. I'd rather not hear additional comparisons to paleontological genitalia."

Paleontological genitalia. If only he were a musician, that would be the perfect name for a punk band…

"First," he said, "you'll want to get survey teams out to take samples of the volcanic rocks thrown off by that volcano. Get them out there as soon as you can. Keep it quiet."

"And what are they looking for?"

"A platinum-iridium compound. Got a pen?"

She opened her briefcase, offered him a pen and her notepad. Angus instinctively reached for the pad with his right hand. He saw his mangled fingers anew. He wouldn't be writing with that hand anytime soon, if ever. He'd have to do something about that—he already had ideas.

With his left hand, he set the pad on his lap, took the pen and scrawled out *Pt60Ir12* in shaky, child-like writing. He handed the pad and pen back to her.

"Get your hands on volcanic rock that fell in the area," Angus said. "Examine it for traces of that compound, then you'll know I'm telling the truth. There were literally *millions of tons* of it right above that new volcano's main vent. I'm sure a significant amount melted and was blasted out with the magma."

June's eyes narrowed. She twisted her head a bit to the right as people sometimes do when their bullshit detector goes off.

"A million tons of platinum would be about… oh, five hundred times the total amount ever mined."

"Platinum-iridium," Angus said. "And I said *millions* of tons. You seem educated—one would think you'd understand the concept of *plural*."

Her head twisted a little more, so that it looked like she could see him only with her narrowed right eye.

"Just so we're clear, Doctor Kool, you're telling me a volcano went off in an area that had zero active volcanic activity, and you're telling me that said volcano erupted under a deposit consisting of millions of tons of platinum-iridium?"

"Bingo. Give the lady a prize."

Her head snapped back to center. She shrugged.

"The area is completely compromised," she said. "It's now an active volcanic area. Nobody can dig there, for years to come, most likely, so could you kindly tell me why I traveled from the delightfully metropolitan city of Houston to the itty-bitty backwater village of Minersville, and I'm here listening to a man make bad jokes about my name while an overweight black cat sits there and judges me?"

Angus glanced to the dresser. The cat did look a bit judgmental, he had to admit.

He looked at June. Christ on a pogo stick, she was hot.

"You're here because I know of another deposit. It's just like the one that was torched by the volcano. There is so much ore that whoever controls it will have to hoard the platinum, otherwise it will be worth less than lead. You might say this location holds a rather *august* resource."

June's eyes burned with annoyance at yet another play on her name, and, unmistakably, with pure *hunger*. She wanted this to be true. Who wouldn't?

"What's to stop us from buying up all the land around here and mining that?"

"First, because you can't fence in thousands of square miles," Angus said. "Once word gets out, amateur prospectors will flood the area. You can't stop them. And second, because mining an active volcano is beyond even my rather considerable skills. The ore deposit was extremely concentrated—whatever wasn't kicked out by the eruption has sunk to the bottom of a lake of magma. It will never be recovered."

"So you're saying the location you're offering is somewhere other than Utah."

"*Very* other," Angus said. "And I will keep said location secret until I know my interests are covered."

"And how much to cover your interests?"

"For starters, an unlimited research and manufacturing budget with a minimum of fifteen million dollars."

June July laughed. He couldn't deny that he liked the way her little mouth crinkled at the corners, or how her matte red lipstick complimented the color of her tongue.

"I came to the middle of nowhere expecting at least a charade of believability," she said. "Fifteen million *minimum*? Do you think we're made of money?"

"I'm actually a little surprised you don't shit Benjamins and piss compound interest. BHP earned four *billion* in profit last year. Just *profit*. You can afford what I'm asking. In return, you have a shot at becoming the richest company in the history of mankind."

He saw cracks in June's aloof demeanor. Running a minimum budget of fifteen mil up the corporate flagpole would bring great risks.

"Cut to the chase," she said. "What's your projection for BHP's total investment?"

Angus closed his eyes, ran through the numbers. *Money, immobility, guns* and the *doomsday device*, the big four problems he had to solve to pull this off. June represented the money, but would she and BHP be willing to shell out what was needed?

"To fabricate the necessary equipment, outfit the expedition, and locate, secure, and mine the deposit, I expect BHP will shell out at least thirty million before an ounce of ore is extracted."

"*Locate.*" She shook her head. "So you don't know where it is after all?"

She was fixated on that, but the phrase *thirty million* didn't seem to bother her in the least. Interesting.

"I know where to look," Angus said. June rubbed at her eyes. "This sounds like a wild goose chase. If you actually had this info, you'd give it to EarthCore."

"EarthCore thinks I'm dead. And I wouldn't work for those fucksticks again if you paid me *sixty* million. Did you not hear the part where I said I would make BHP the richest company *in the history of mankind?* You'll be able to buy a company like Apple and wipe your ass with it."

June July had the look of someone who was out of her element. She'd been sent here, probably, because she was young and mid-level; decision-makers didn't make a trip like this.

"Come on," Angus said. "Make this deal happen, play your cards right, and you'll shoot straight up the corporate ladder."

Still, June hesitated. Yes, an opportunity for her, but if Angus's story turned out to be bullshit, it would set her back. Corporate politics were far too easy to predict.

Angus winced as a blast of pain roiled through his hand. He'd had enough of this woman's indecision. He reached to the nightstand, picked up the burner phone Alice had given him. He held it up for June July to see.

"Tell you what," he said. "We can have a race. You call your bosses. At the same time, I'll call a few other companies—Anglo Platinum, Implats, and Lonmin PLC, to be precise. I'll sell my information to the highest bidder. I'm guessing BHP might win that auction, but you'll wind up paying a helluva lot more than I'm asking for right now. Ready? *Go.*"

He didn't have any of those phone numbers memorized, but he started dialing anyway.

June reached out, put her hand over the phone.

"How about you give me a ten-minute head start so I can call my bosses first?"

She offered her best smile.

He offered one of his own, showing his battered teeth.

"Ten minutes," he said. "The clock is ticking, Calendar Girl."

7

September 8

EVEN AS A DREAMY teenage girl, Bertha had never really put much thought into what kind of a wedding she might someday like. She knew some girls did, and that was fine, it just wasn't all that important to her. And since she'd never really thought about a wedding, she'd never thought at all about a honeymoon.

If she had thought about one, though, she doubted she could have ever dreamed up one more perfect than this.

"This is just amazing, Patrick. Amazing."

His arms were around her, her back against his chest. They soaked up the hot tub's heat. They gazed over the tub's edge, past the wooden deck's log railing and out across the mountainside. Plenty of pines up here, their color a gorgeous, dark green, but more than a few leafy trees blazing with fall colors. Across the valley, on the slope's far side, a sea of yellow turning to orange turning to red. Within a week, maybe, most of the leaves would fall, but now, here, she found herself in the midst of staggering, colorful beauty.

"It is at that," her husband said. "More scotch?"

She nodded, felt his body move as he turned to fill her glass. She had a good buzz on, one magnified by the heat, enriched by the steam coming off the water, electrified by the stunning view.

He handed her the tumbler. She liked it with a couple of cubes of ice, which he already knew. He took his neat. They clinked.

"Here's to you, wife," he said.

She adored his voice. Deep, husky. He sounded like her drill sergeant from basic, only … *nicer.*

"And here's to you, hubby," she said.

They clinked again. She took a sip. As she lowered the glass, she noticed anew the stitches on the stumps of her fingers. More stitches on her face, from above her left eye, down across her nose to the right corner of her mouth. Ugly stitches that would leave an ugly scar.

But you know what? Patrick didn't care. And if he didn't care, why should she?

Bertha settled into him once more, rested the back of her head against his chest.

The wedding ceremony had been simple: a preacher at the hospital chapel, not even ten minutes from start to *I now pronounce you man and wife.* Tying the knot marked the end of their week in the hospital, then they were out the door and into a waiting limo. Bottles of booze inside. They'd told the driver to stop at the first tattoo parlor he saw. Bertha couldn't wear a ring, not with her severed finger, but she wanted everyone to know she was Patrick's, so she had his name inked around the stump—that had been one painful tattoo. When it was done, they got back in the limo and the drinking began—they'd chugged one bottle of champagne even before they'd reached Provo's outskirts, and another as they headed north, into the mountains.

"They have that movie thing around here," she said. "Don't they?"

"You mean Sundance? Yeah, I think."

She sipped her drink, feeling the comforting presence of his big body. Bigger than hers, by far, which was nice. She'd been with men smaller than her, had no problem with that, but there was something about the sheer mass of Patrick O'Doyle that made her feel … feminine. She'd never really *felt* feminine before. Not with anyone. Only with him.

She liked it.

"I got to be honest with you," he said. "We fuck again and I might die."

Bertha laughed, nodded. "Baby, we shouldn't have fucked *at all*. Neither one of us are in good shape. Once was plenty. I'm happy."

Sex had been a check mark, but they'd gotten the job done. What a clumsy affair it had been, with her battered hand still horribly painful to the touch, her skin still blistered, the stitches on her face aching and stinging. He wasn't much better off than she was. But like the two old soldiers they were, they'd found a way to get the job done, with more than a few yelps along the way, laughing the whole time at their combined infirmities.

There would be plenty of time for sex—far better sex—when they had a few more weeks to heal up.

"Sure is beautiful up here," he said, and kissed the back of her head.

She nodded. "Imagine that some people get to live like this all the time. Kind of amazing, isn't it?"

He didn't answer for a moment. She took another sip, wondered how much the Scotch had cost. Probably expensive stuff. Sonny had paid for it, and the limo as well, and maybe for the rental of this cabin, although that might have been Yakely's doing. Bertha didn't know. She didn't care. There would never be another moment like this in her entire life, she knew, so she meant to soak up every last second of it.

"I've been thinking about that," Patrick said. "About how other people get to live. And I'm thinking maybe that should be us."

Bertha laughed again, waved her tumbler above the water, barely keeping the expensive booze from splashing over the side.

"Yeah, that's us," she said. "The fanciest grunts this side of the Pecos. Or … what mountain range is this?"

"The Wasatch, I think."

"Fanciest grunts this side of the Sasquatch."

She giggled at that. The *Sasquatch Mountains*. Sounded like a great title for a horror movie.

"I'm serious," Patrick said. "We could be rich. You and I. Richer than Sonny. Richer than Yakely. Maybe richer than all the people on this mountain combined."

That was a silly idea—he had no idea who lived around here.

"And how, exactly, could we be that rich? We can sell our bodies, baby, but I think we'd wind up on the scratch-and-dent lot."

"We don't have to sell anything," he said. "The money is there for the taking. It's in Argentina."

She grew suddenly cold, for some reason, as if she was in a tub of ice.

"Mount Fitz Roy," she said. "You want to go *there?*"

"I got the idea from Sleepy. Well, from thinking about Sleepy, anyway."

"Who is Sleepy?"

"Oh, sorry. Doug Rapson. The man I wanted to marry us. Sonny said Doug asked for a hundred grand to do the ceremony. I was offended at the time. But since, I've been thinking. If money was no object, I would have paid him that much without batting an eyelash, because it would have been special to have him do it. And that got me thinking about the others, about Worm. Skylark. El Gato. Hatchet and Curveball. Mullet. All the NoSeeUms that might still be around."

How much had *he* had to drink?

Bertha slid forward, turned, set her drink on the edge of the hot tub.

"Patrick, are you having a stroke?"

He grinned as if he knew there was a good joke but he didn't quite get the punchline.

"I feel fine," he said. "A little drunk, but, no, I'm not having a stroke. Why?"

"Because you're babbling nonsense. Worm? No-see-ums? Curveball? You *sure* you're okay?"

"Oh, right." He sipped his drink, nodded. "Some people I used to work with, you might say."

"Work with where?"

He opened his mouth to answer, then shut it, teeth clacking together.

"I can't tell you," he said. "It's … it's classified."

She hadn't known him all that long, but she knew him well enough to understand his tone of voice. *It's classified.* He wouldn't say something like that unless he meant it.

"Classified from when, exactly?"

"When I was in the service."

She looked at the tattoos of flags on his arms, on his chest, water and sweat making the faded colors gleam. Dozens more on his back. A tattoo for every country where he'd killed someone. He didn't talk about his past, and, frankly, she'd kind of forgotten about it. Patrick—her *husband*—didn't seem like the kind of person who'd killed dozens of human beings, perhaps hundreds of them.

But he *was* that kind of person.

He'd told her that because he'd wanted her to know who he really was, even though he'd said right up front that he couldn't tell her details, could *never* tell her details. Even though his country had fucked him over, he still took his oath very seriously.

"We're married now," Bertha said. "And you still can't tell me?"

She knew the answer. She still had to ask.

Patrick smiled a sweet smile, sweat beading on his forehead, trickling down his temples.

"You know I can't," he said.

She knew no such thing. Yes, he took his oath seriously, but now didn't he have another oath? An oath to *her*?

"You don't tell me about your past," she said. "I assume there's stuff that is *not* classified. You don't tell me about that, either."

He glanced off, stared out, blinking. A strange expression for a man who always seemed so sharp.

"The stuff that's not classified…that's thirty years in the past," he said. "Hard to remember. I guess I'm really good at blocking it out. I've had to…train myself to do that. Honestly, babe, once something is in my past, I just don't think about it."

Patrick paused for a moment, leaving only the hot tub's bubbling hum and the sound of wind through the trees. Bertha waited for him to continue, hoping that he might finally open up.

"And, anyway, there's not much to talk about," he said. "My parents died before I joined the military. No brothers or sisters. High school was boring. I was a nobody. When they brought me into the NoSeeUms, they erased my past."

His avoidance was starting to chip away at the moment, at her delight in being with him here, now.

"They can't just *erase* someone, Patrick."

He laughed. "Don't be naive, babe. The US government can do damn near anything. I got to keep my name, but I had a new social security number, made-up high school transcripts, that kind of thing. So I'm not being flip when I say that I don't really *have* a past before the military—that Patrick O'Doyle is dead."

Bertha's home life had been a train wreck, but at least it was hers. What they'd done to Patrick seemed … unbelievable.

"Why would they do that to you?"

"In case we were killed *or* captured. When we were operating in that unit, we had no connections to the US military. None. We sourced our own gear. We operated like a mercenary squad, even though Uncle Sam was telling us where to go and what to do." He stared out at the sprawling view. "Some of the things I've done, the things I've seen … it's amazing I don't have nightmares. But maybe that was part of why I was recruited in the first place. They only took people with no family connections, people who fit a certain psychological profile. I satisfied both categories. And in my former line of work, a short memory was a good thing to have."

So short that it was already blocking out the terror of the rocktopi? So short that he wanted to go to Mount Fitz Roy and possibly face those creatures again?

"We're lucky to be alive," Bertha said. "Think of all the people who aren't. Maybe we should just leave things alone."

He looked out across the valley.

"Or maybe I've left enough things alone for far too long. Maybe I've taken orders from other people for far too long. Where has it gotten me? I don't even know if we have jobs with EarthCore anymore. If not, there goes our healthcare. I've got like fifteen grand in the bank. That's all I have to show for giving twenty years of my life to my country. Aside from you, I have nothing."

Aren't I enough? she wanted to ask. But she did not. Maybe because she had less in the bank than he did.

"We'll never have another chance like this," he said. "Aside from you, me, Sonny and Yakely, I think everyone else who knew about the platinum in Utah is dead. One other person, maybe—Herbert Darker, who analyzed a dust sample from Sonny's initial find. Darker knew nothing about the larger operation, though. He didn't know Connell hired Veronica Reeves. Once Connell brought her in, he kept her from contacting anyone outside the camp."

Patrick sipped his drink, seemed to choose his next words carefully.

"Reeves didn't go deep enough in the Mount Fitz Roy tunnels to learn about the ship there. That means there's a *trillion dollars'* worth of platinum in Argentina, and no one knows about it but us."

Bertha looked at her missing fingers, then dipped her hand beneath the roiling surface.

"But the monsters," she said. "The silverbugs. We got lucky. We might not get lucky again."

He drained his tumbler, set it down, picked up the bottle. She thought he would refill his glass, but instead he held the bottle by its narrow neck.

"We didn't know what to expect," he said. "We weren't armed correctly. We weren't prepared. The people we had with us … I'm sorry those guys are gone, but they weren't cut out for what we faced. My old friends … they're a different story."

"Keyword *old*."

He squinted at her. "What's that supposed to mean?"

"It means you're almost fifty years old. I assume your buddies are about the same?"

He smiled, took a drink from the bottle.

"Don't worry about them," he said. "If I can get them to do this, each one is worth a dozen men half their age. I can't tell you what we did, but I can tell you these people were the best in the world at handling unusual situations. And at dealing out violence, if it came to that."

He took another drink. He squeezed the bottle neck so tight his knuckles looked white. No more smile on his bruised, stitched face. His eyes … the way they burned, just like they had down in the tunnels.

"This isn't just about money," she said. "Is it?"

His lip twitched into the briefest of sneers.

"They don't belong," he said. "Connell Kirkland saved my life. When push came to shove, I couldn't save his. He died so you and I could survive. He's not the only victim. Good people died because of those fucking things. They're killers, Bertha. Killers."

Then how are they different from you and I? she wanted to ask. But she did not. Maybe because she hated the rocktopi just as much as her husband did.

"You've said you've got fifteen grand," she said. "Gonna take a whole lot more money than that to mount an expedition to Argentina. Where are we going to get that kind of bank?"

Finally, his smile returned, but it wasn't a smile of love.

"We get it from a rich person." He reached out with the bottle, filled her glass where it sat at the side of the hot tub. "The richest person we know."

8

September 10

SAMIRA AND RAMIRO stepped inside the one-room cabin and shut the door against the cold. The place looked almost identical to the way they'd left it months before. And the year before that. Tiny, barely big enough for bunk beds and the one twin bed, a battered old desk and a kitchenette with a yellowing sink and a rust-speckled faucet, a chipped Formica table with four plastic chairs.

"Home sweet home," Sam said.

Ramiro shrugged off his backpack, set it on the bottom bunk. "For the next month, anyway."

Did he have to remind her of that at every opportunity?

"We're going to find something," she said. "And then we'll get a new grant. Count on it."

She'd read a couple of books on leadership. *Projecting positivity* was one of the keys, the books had said. She was trying to do that—it wasn't working.

Ramiro said nothing. Instead, he hopped up onto the top bunk and lay on his back.

"I assume you want the twin," he said. "Since you're now the boss of this outfit."

The twin. Veronica's bed.

Sam sat on the edge. Kind of silly how she and Ramiro—two years divorced—had slept in bunk beds like little kids at a sleepover. But no one cared; the less money spent on housing, the more could be spent on research efforts. It was no different from archaeologists the world over.

"Not holding my breath on the grants," Ramiro said, laying his forearm over his eyes. "But I'm here for you, kid. Who knows? Maybe you're right and we'll find something Veronica couldn't get too. One can always hope, right?"

Hope. A simple word, yet it pissed Sam off because she knew what Ramiro really meant—without some blind luck, they were finished.

He was wrong. This was *her* time. Things were going to change for Sam, and in a major way.

"Get up," she said. "We should get into town and get some groceries."

Arm still on his face, Ramiro shook his head. "We just traveled our asses off. I'm unpacking the truck, then taking a nap. A big one."

His words seemed to usher in a wave of lethargy. She *was* tired. So much flying. Detroit to Miami, then the all-nighter from Miami to Buenos Aires, then to Bariloche, and finally to El Calafate. There, they'd picked up the old truck from storage—and the gear they'd shipped—then driven the three-and-a-half-hour, 215-kilometer drive from El Calafate to El Chaltén.

All told, she and Ramiro had been traveling for thirty hours to get here.

"Maybe you're right," she said. "A nap would be a good idea."

Ramiro didn't answer, because he was already asleep.

One would think that sharing a tiny cabin with one's ex-husband might lead to impulses of shenanigans, but Sam had no illusions of that happening.

The first year of marriage, they hadn't been able to keep their hands off of each other. The sex had been passionate, intense, and inventive—everything a couple could want. But somewhere around thirteen or fourteen months in, her desire for Ramiro started to fade.

Perhaps he'd gained some weight. Perhaps he'd stopped taking care of himself as much. Perhaps he'd lost the urge to make himself as attractive as possible for her. At the time, she blamed him for those things—and many, *many* more, so that she didn't have to admit it was her fault—but in retrospect she knew the truth was that she'd simply grown bored.

When they'd dated, she'd been the initiator. She'd pursued him. Getting Ramiro in the sack had been a challenge. Sneaking away from digs for any private (and some not-so-private) moments they could get, their sex life had been *muy caliente.*

Once they were married, though? No challenge at all. Sex was available anytime she wanted it. A helluva time to find out it was the challenge that turned her on more than the man himself.

The second year of their marriage had started bad, ended worse. His lust for her never faded, yet the death knell of their union manifested itself in an obscenely simple concept—she didn't want him anymore.

At first, she didn't realize it was happening. He'd made some tentative comments about needing to improve their sex life. She'd responded with anger instead of with kindness, or with understanding, or with a desire to figure out how to meet his needs.

That's when he started keeping a calendar.

Her friends often asked her about her sex life with Ram. She told them that while it wasn't as hot as before they were married, they were still knocking boots one or two times a week. Pretty healthy, right?

The morning after their second anniversary (and they didn't have sex that night, either, because she "wasn't feeling it," something that she now looked back on with embarrassment, because who *doesn't* fuck on their anniversary?), he showed her the calendar: In their entire second year of marriage, they'd had sex four times.

Four. Once every season, it seemed, whether they needed it or not.

Leave it to a scientist to make his point with cold, hard data.

She vowed to do better, to try different things. They both knew it was her desire—not his—that had flagged. Wasn't it supposed to be the man who got bored? Even so, he agreed to try different things, to do his part in rekindling that spark. He read books, watched videos, tried hard to implement ways to spice things up. He started working out again. He made dates where they met at bars and pretended to be different people. Ramiro was committed, creative, caring, and kind.

And it still didn't work.

Then, something else happened that the man was supposed to do: infidelity.

She met Julius Marcon, of all things, in the grocery store. He'd hit on her, offered her his phone number. Why had she taken it? She'd asked herself that question at least twice a day, every day since Ramiro found out.

She still didn't have an answer, and the *why* no longer mattered.

Julius had been a fling, nothing more, yet that fling destroyed her life. Ramiro had filed for divorce. Sam hadn't fought it. They decided they made far better friends than spouses. That much, at least, had stayed true. He could have left the project, but instead he stayed, promised to do all he could to help Sam's career—just as he'd done before they were married, just as he'd done *while* they were married.

But was that, too, coming to an end?

Two months before the tourist season began, before the rent for this shitty cabin went up by a factor of five. Two months before hikers, tourists, and climbers flocked to the area around Cerro Chaltén. Just enough people that Sam and Ramiro didn't dare go to the cave mouth, even in the dead of night, for fear it would be discovered and then become public knowledge.

Before an endless stream of self-serving idiots trampled on the history of, quite possibly, the human race's oldest civilization.

Sam had held out hope that Veronica might still be alive. She was listed as *missing* or *presumed dead,* after all. That hope was now gone. Two weeks since the volcano eruption. State and Federal authorities had scoured the area around the mountain, looking for additional survivors. They'd found no one wandering around aimlessly. No comatose survivors in the hospital. Everyone who'd reported to area hospitals had been accounted for, except for one patient, apparently, who had claimed to have amnesia and then walked away from the hospital never to be seen again.

That patient had been a man.

Sam jerked her head up, blinked madly—she'd almost nodded off, almost fallen from the edge of the bed.

She stood, whacked Ramiro on the thigh, startling him awake.

"Let's unload the truck," she said. "If someone steals that gear, it's not like we can just order more."

He blinked, raised his eyebrows as he did, nodded. "Yeah, you're right. It's going to be so much fun hauling the new coolers up the mountain."

It wouldn't be fun at all. It would suck with a capital S, but it had to be done. The gear would provide extra range, and the extra range would result in Sam finding something truly significant.

And finally let her step out from the shadow of Veronica Reeves.

9

September 11

"IT'S ALL YOURS," June July said. "Sixty thousand square feet."

Angus winced as he turned in his wheelchair, trying to take it all in. Whitish floor and walls, scuffed with thousands of blackish marks made by careless factory workers of old. Battered fluorescent lighting fixtures overhead; most of the parallel bulbs glowed brightly, although a few were dead and gray, and two flickered in that annoying way dying fluorescent bulbs did. Empty metal racks along the west walls. A few old cardboard boxes scattered across the floor, the remnants of the former occupants. Along the east wall, five pallets topped with shrink-wrapped boxes—the property of the *new* occupants, soon to be assembled and put to work.

"You already ordered the equipment, I see."

"Most of it," June said. "The rest will be here later today."

Two days earlier, BHP's investigators had acquired volcanic rock kicked out by the Utah volcano, confirmed it contained the platinum-iridium compound Angus had told them they would find. Once that happened, June and her bosses had signed off on Angus's initial budget. They thought it was the *whole* budget—better to get them invested now and make them fear the loss then tell them his real amount and scare them away.

"What about my direct reports? They should be here already."

June came around to the front of the wheelchair.

"If you think hiring people away from Boston Dynamics, Prox, and Google is cheap, you're horribly uninformed." June flashed a sex-on-wheels smile. "We're moving quickly, Angus, because we believe in you."

That smile was likely well-practiced and deployed tactically, as needed. Maybe she was flirting, trying to gain an advantage with him, but Angus knew her kind—women who looked like June July only wanted men that looked like professional athletes or movie stars.

Women who looked like June July did *not* want five-foot-six guys with broken bones and missing teeth who rode around in wheelchairs.

Angus didn't know what the old factory had once made. It didn't matter. Maybe the company had been bought out, the manufacturing jobs shipped to Mexico or overseas. People had probably lost jobs. *Boo-hoo-hoo*, the world was an unfair place.

He'd seen uniformed security guards on the drive in, and there were a few standing near the pallets. They looked alert, attentive. Guards, yes; workers, no—Angus needed to get this show on the road.

"Well, don't just stand there, lady," he said. "Wheel me around."

"I have someone else to do that for you."

June raised a hand as if she was hailing a cab. One of the security guards approached. Like the others, he wore a tan shirt and pants, black tie, a black police duty belt with sidearm holster and various pouches, and a tan, wide-brimmed Stetson-ish hat with a black band. This one also wore mirrored aviator sunglasses, for fuck's sake, perched over a broken-several-times nose and a salt-and-pepper mustache.

"Angus Kool, meet Donnie Graham," June said. "Donnie is the commander of the G4S guards we hired for you. He's worked with us before and has experience in the field."

The word *guards* was a bit generous. *Mercenaries* was more accurate.

G4S was a massive company, providing security services all over the world. Over half a million employees. Most were probably typical rent-a-cop bumpkins, but Donnie and his men were from G4S's off-the-menu options of actual, *shoot-you-in-the-fucking-face* mercs.

Angus looked up at Donnie. "Experience where, exactly?"

"South Africa, mostly," Donnie said, his gruff voice a perfect match with his mustache and nose. "Also Zimbabwe and the DRC."

The Democratic Republic of the Congo. A few small platinum deposits there, Angus knew, but it wasn't the kind of place you could set up shop and not be bothered. Mercenaries were used as proxy armies to drive people out of their lands for mineral exploration, or to outright steal existing operations.

"Miss July has informed me that you expect potentially violent resistance from an as-yet unnamed force when you locate your deposit," Donnie said. "She is also concerned about the possibility of industrial espionage at this site. I am here to address both issues. My men and I will ensure security at this facility, and when the time comes to secure the area of the deposit, I'll be leading that effort as well. The global resources of G4S provide us a significant amount of latitude in moving men and equipment. I'll be your main point of contact, Mister Kool."

The man talked in sharp, short syllables—a machine gun in the form of a human voice.

"It's *Doctor* Kool, thank you very much."

"Are you telling me you didn't spend six years in evil medical school to be called *Mister?*"

Ah. The man thought he was funny. Angus so loved it when the hired help thought they were funny.

Things were coming together. Well, they were *beginning* to come together, but it was a great start. *Money*: June had come through. *Immobility*: With funding secured and this building acquired, he'd begin work on that tomorrow. *Guns*: Donnie Graham and his G4S merce-naries. *The doomsday device*: That part Angus had not yet figured out.

But he would.

"I suppose this building is adequate," he said. "Not that we have much choice at this point. What about security on the grounds?"

"The property covers four acres, all fenced-in," Donnie said. "There's not much around here, other than the distribution center on the other side of the train tracks, but BHP bought that as well, so there's no legitimate reason for anyone to come to this area who is not part of your operation. Authorized personnel only from here on out. I have men patrolling the perimeters of both properties."

Angus looked Donnie up and down.

"Are all the guards dressed like knock-off state troopers?"

Donnie nodded once. "Standard G4S kit, Doctor Kool. They're carrying AR-15s. Don't worry, they all have CCW permits, and Utah is an open-carry state. Perfectly legal. It's better for my guys to present in *do-not-mess-with-me* gear then have a bunch of civvy-looking dudes walking around with sidearms. Who knows what the locals of Ephraim might think? In my experience, for situations like these, it's better to have uniformed guards."

BHP Billiton's endless resources were an ever-unfolding Swiss Army knife. Donnie and his G4S goons. This place, just a two-hour drive from Minersville. That was helpful, considering that Angus was still considered "missing," so he wasn't about to go near any airport. The company had also found out which EarthCore employees survived the disaster. Not counting Angus, only three had: Sonny McGuiness, Bertha Lybrand, and that big ol' barrel of joy Patrick O'Doyle.

Angus had mocked the guards' uniforms, but perhaps he'd been too hasty. He liked the idea of being protected by G4S's off-the-books operatives, by former soldiers and experienced killers, because as long as Patrick O'Doyle remained alive, Angus knew he would never be truly safe.

"I'll be on my way," June said. "Angus, more of your equipment order will arrive later today. Your first subordinates arrive tomorrow. Costs are already high, so I trust you'll have the actual location for us soon?"

"Why, June, the way you say that, it's almost like you don't think I have the location."

Which Angus did not. Not yet.

June smiled. "Your words, not mine. Good day, gentlemen."

She walked off, her heels clicking a bit too loud, her hips swaying a bit too much.

"She's a peach," Angus said. "Don't you think, Donnie?"

"If I hadn't attended several mandatory sexual harassment seminars for G4S, I might tell you that Miss July is not the kind of woman I'd kick out of bed for eating crackers, but since I did attend those seminars, I would never use those actual words."

A mercenary's version of political correctness? Interesting.

"The upstairs office," Angus said. "Is it ready for me?"

Donnie moved to the back of the wheelchair, pushed Angus along.

"It is," he said. "A crew is installing an elevator later this afternoon, so for now I'll have to carry you up. Sorry."

Well, wouldn't that be humiliating? All that jostling on his broken body. Good thing he had plenty of meds.

"The secure internet acccss I asked for, that's set up as well?"

"It is," Donnie said. "Let me get you up there."

Donnie rolled the wheelchair toward the building's south end. There, above the former factory's open floor, was a wide, square window. The office of the former manager or owner, most likely, which had let him look down upon his toiling minions. Not so ironically, a role that Angus himself would soon mirror.

While at Alice's, he hadn't dared do a deep dive into research about Veronica Reeves and her discoveries in Argentina. For people with enough money, internet searches could be bought and sold on a whim. BHP had enough money. They'd probably already greased a few palms to buy the internet history from Alice's IP address—BHP would love to get any clue they could to the location of the new platinum-iridium site. Angus knew this, because had he been in their shoes, he would have done the same. Why pay the farmer for the milk when you can put the cow on a truck and drive it back to your place? So to speak.

With the equipment he'd ordered, he could obfuscate any internet search done from this building. Well, he *probably* could. At any rate, he couldn't wait any longer.

Knowing that Mount Fitz Roy was the likely target peak helped some, but that was akin to knowing the specific blade of bluegrass you wanted was located somewhere in the infield of Yankee Stadium. *Mount Fitz Roy* wasn't a precise X-marks-the-spot; it covered a massive area. One couldn't just start sinking three-mile-deep holes through solid granite and hope for the best. On top of that, it was very possible that Veronica had lied about which peak was involved. Snooty academics did shit like that, wasting their precious energy trying to preserve elements of long-extinct cultures.

Such a waste of time.

Donnie rolled Angus toward the battered metal stairs that led up to the office. Normal industrial stairs, but in Angus's condition, the ascent might as well have been Mount Fitz Roy itself.

"Miss July told me to prep a budget and an operations plan," Donnie said. "She told me that you said we might be facing armed resistance, but added that you wouldn't tell her exactly who that armed resistance might be. I'll need to know what we're up against."

His comment caught Angus off guard—he hadn't thought about what to tell the men that would be going into the tunnels. Could he tell them about the rocktopi, the silverbugs? No, not really, not unless he wanted the information to get out.

"Don't worry about it," Angus said. "Your men will have guns, right?"

Donnie stopped the wheelchair in front of the stairs. In places, red paint had peeled off the metal steps.

"That's not how this will work, Doctor Kool. Before we go in, you're going to tell me everything you know. I need to ensure project success, and I need to ensure my men have the best chance possible of coming out of this alive."

How many men would they take in? What would they be armed with? What could they know ahead of time, and, correspondingly, what could wait until they were in the tunnels?

"Your men will be fine," Angus said. "I'll be designing some of the gear myself. I take it a guy like you knows how to acquire military hardware?"

"A company like mine does, anyway. Trust me, Doctor, if the money is right, G4S can acquire anything you want. I'm under the impression this operation involves a *lot* of money."

A lot of money, yes, but not his. Not yet.

Angus looked up the stairs.

"Any chance the office up there has a pisser, Donnie?"

"No bathroom in the office. But if you need to drain the lizard, you let me know and I'll bring you down."

Sure. Why not? What was yet one more humiliation between new besties?

"Carry me up, please."

Donnie didn't bother lifting Angus—the man picked up the entire chair, tiny damaged genius and all.

Yes, Angus had to do as much research as he could on Veronica and her findings, but that wasn't the first thing he'd use the internet for.

He was going to buy some goddamn crutches.

10

September 14

GUM CLINGING TO the bottom of a plate. Some food stuck in it. Eggs? Yes, eggs. *Chewed* eggs.

"Lovely," Tommy Strymon said.

He pried the gum free. He put it in the garbage can at his side, but the sticky mess clung to the plastic liner, which lifted when he tried to pull his hand free. Tommy set the dish in the metal sink, next to a hundred other dishes, used the liner to pinch the gum off his skin.

"Where there's a will," he said.

He wiped his hands on his pants, which were already soaked through with dishwater, already splattered with bits of food. The radio sitting on the metal shelf above the sink let out the keyboard and bass opening tones of Bon Jovi's "Livin' on a Prayer."

Tommy turned it up.

Every time he heard that song, he thought of hanging out in the high school parking lot with his buddies, or goofing off in shop class, building whatever he wanted instead of what the teacher required. Oh, for the power to send a message back in time to that idealistic young Tommy, a message that said something like: *boring is better; adventure ain't all it's cracked up to be.*

If he'd studied hard back then—what he was supposed to study, anyway—would things have turned out different? He could have been an engineer, maybe. He could have spent his years *making* instead of *destroying.*

Tommy scraped food off the stack of plates to his right, dipped them into the soapy water of the right-hand sink, scrubbed them, dipped them into the cleaner water of the left-hand sink, then put them on the rack on the sink's left-hand side to await a final rinse.

"Mister Strymon, Joe says we're running out of clean dishes."

Tommy glanced back to see Sally Carson, a stack of dirty plates in her hands. He hated that she still called him *mister.* Sally had strawberry blonde hair, just like he did. He kept his short. Hers was long, beautiful even though she kept it back in a ponytail.

She was just the kind of girl Tommy would have hit on back in the day. Joe made his waitresses wear blue dresses and white aprons, an old-timey look that fit the diner's retro style. Sally's apron hugged her waist and flared at the hips, in the way it could only for a teenager with a flat stomach.

Had Sally been from a small-town in the Midwest, she would have unquestionably been the homecoming queen. A girl with looks like that gets what she wants in high school. But here, in Los Angeles, she was just another pretty face, and nowhere near the prettiest at that. LA was a magnet for beautiful people her age, all coming here to try and make it in one entertainment industry or another.

"I'm going as fast as I can," Tommy said, returning to his work: *grab, scrape, dip-right, scrub, dip-left, rack.* "The dishwasher's broken."

"Again?"

"Again."

"You fixed it last time," Sally said. "And the time before that."

Tommy shrugged. "That was the macerator, then the drain impeller. Easy fixes. This time the whole pump is shot. I told Joe it was gonna break."

"He's so cheap," Sally said, quietly. "Still, I bet you can fix it. You fixed that old vintage cassette thing."

Vintage? Tommy looked at the radio, a beat-up Lasonic TRC-935 boombox he'd found at the Salvation Army. It hadn't worked, which is why it had cost him all of five bucks. He'd had one in high school. They didn't make 'em like that anymore.

"It's so retro and cool," Sally said. "Is it playing a cassette now?"

Both cassette trays were empty.

"We're listening to the radio, Sally," Tommy said, returning to his work.

"Oh. My dad does that. He likes oldies stations, too."

Tommy stopped in mid dip-right. "*Oldies?* Come on, kid, this is eighties rock."

Sally smiled. "I was born in 2000. The eighties seem pretty old to me."

I was thirty or thirty-one when she was born. Jesus. Tommy tried to wipe the image of her curves from his mind.

"Don't be a smart-ass," he said. "It doesn't become you."

Sally laughed. No matter how old a man gets, the sound of a young woman's genuine laugh will always raise his spirits.

He tried to remember where he'd been in 2000. Herat? Tarnikot? No, those had both been in 2001. Shahi-Kot Valley, then? Maybe. Tommy's ability with raw numbers operated outside of his conscious thought, which made it ironic that he had so much trouble remembering what had happened on particular dates. Well, maybe not all that ironic, considering the number of places he'd been, considering the number of bodies he'd left behind.

Hard to remember the details.

"I got to put these somewhere, Mister Strymon," Sally said, lifting the pile of dishes a little higher. "Where do you want them?"

The small counter area to the right of the sink was already a teetering mass of food-smeared crockery. The rack to the left of the sink, the one that held his clean dishes, took up all the available space there.

Joe stormed into the dishwashing nook, a wobbling, furious human egg with stubby legs and fat arms.

"Sally! Orders are up! The fuck are you doing back here?"

Sally froze, a proverbial 17-year-old deer in the headlights.

Joe stomped to the sink, slapped at the boombox. Jon Bon Jovi, unperturbed by the assault, mentioned that Tommy had his six-string in hock. Joe slapped the radio again; Jon, Richie, Tico and the gang fell silent.

"Strymon," Joe said, "how about you leave my waitresses alone and put some fucking motion in the ocean? How about that?"

Tommy didn't mind being yelled at, but there was no need to curse in front of the young woman.

"Dishwasher's broken," Tommy said. "Again."

"So fix it."

"Can't this time. It's fifteen years old, Joe. When are you going to get a new one?"

Joe sneered. "When the Money Fairy falls out of the sky, hikes up her skirt, and pays me cold hard cash to fuck her rotten, that's when."

Tommy felt his temper stir. He immediately shoved it back into the armored lockbox deep in his soul where it belonged. He wished he could have forever eliminated that temper, destroyed it, banished it to the Phantom Zone, but that was impossible, because pure evil can't be killed.

Tommy tilted his head toward Sally. "Easy on the language, all right?"

Joe glanced at the girl. His concrete-hard face softened a tad. Joe was at least a decade younger than Tommy, which meant he was still two decades older than Sally.

"Sorry," Joe said to her. Then the ever-present scowl returned. "Your food is up, Sally. You wanna keep this job? Then *move it.*"

Sally's eyes went wide. Tommy didn't know her details—she talked about her limited past about as much as he talked about his extensive history, which was to say, not at all—but everyone knew how much she needed the job.

"Yessir," she said, then stepped forward and dumped her armful of plates into the right-hand sink. A wave of dirty water splashed up, splattering Tommy and cascading over his just-cleaned plates. A bit of damp toast clung to one. A soaked, lipstick-stained napkin clung to another.

"Oh my god," Sally said. "Mister Strymon, I'm sorry, let me help clean this up."

Joe pointed a finger to the kitchen. "You are fired in five, four…"

Sally was gone before Joe said *three*.

"You're an asshole, Joe," Tommy said. "You know that?"

Joe huffed. "Kids these days. They got no discipline at home. You got to have discipline."

Tommy's temper fought to slither out of the lockbox, a rattlesnake hunting for an exit, fangs dripping with poison.

Joe pointed to the sink. "Get these goddamn dishes done, and get them done *fast*. You got me, Strymon? I know you're a vet and all, but I got wetbacks lined up around the fucking block ready to take your job, and they get paid under the table."

Tommy eyes lingered on Joe's neck, on the slight *bump-bump* of the blood coursing through his carotid artery.

Such a tough guy Joe was, bossing around teenage girls.

Such a dictator Joe was, lording over his ten-table empire.

"You pay *me* under the table," Tommy said.

"I pay you to *wash the fucking dishes*, not flirt with my waitresses, not to sit on your ass on the back patio and read goddamn kids' books."

"Kids' books? They're classics."

"Books about spaceships and aliens and magic and shit are not *classics*. Those are for children."

Tommy smiled. "All right, Joe. Name one *classic* book."

"*Gone with the* Fucking *Wind*. How's that, smart-ass?"

"I've read it," Tommy said. "Have you?"

The look on Joe's face told Tommy he'd gone too far.

"Wash the goddamn dishes," Joe said. "Get your ass moving or the beaner parade will do it for you. You get me?"

Maybe Tommy hadn't made the best choices in life. That was inarguable. Still, though, it was hard taking this kind of shit from a man you could kill in three seconds.

But Tommy didn't do things like that. Not anymore. Not after his stint in Allenwood.

"I get you, sir," Tommy said. "I'll work faster."

Sir. That word alone took the edge off Joe's expression.

"Good," he said, nodding. "And Hernando called in sick, so you're working a double shift today. Don't make me come back here again. You get me?"

People could say what they wanted to about prisons. They could say that convicts never really got rehabilitated, that they were destined to be repeat offenders. People could say that, but not Tommy. He wasn't going back.

"I get you," Tommy said. "No problems. I need the money anyway."

Joe wobbled out of the dishwashing nook.

The snake inside Tommy. It writhed. It hissed. It thought of Joe's neck.

Tommy fed it memories of the things he'd done in Hirat.

Or ... had he done those particular things in Venezuela?

The snake didn't care about accuracy. The snake calmed down, coiled up, and fell quiet.

He turned the radio back on.

You live for the fight when it's all that you've got.

He didn't even have the fight anymore. He had nothing.

Tommy picked up the rack of formerly clean dishes. There was no room on the right side of the sink, so he set the rack on the floor in front of it. He pulled the plug on both sinks, watched the water drain.

He would start over.

11

October 3

"AND THAT'S EVERYTHING, ma'am," Bertha Lybrand said. "That's what happened."

Barbara Yakely looked at Bertha, then at Patrick O'Doyle. Their story was utter madness, and yet facts seemed to back them up. Five weeks since the volcano erupted, and still no one could explain it.

No one except for O'Doyle and Lybrand.

But…a buried spaceship? *Aliens?*

If it was a lie, the couple had gone through pretty extreme lengths to make it believable. Lybrand's two missing fingers. The stitched-up slash across her right cheek and upper lip. O'Doyle, stitched up as well, fading yellow and purple bruises discoloring a face that had already been through years of violent abuse to begin with.

Just seeing them made her think of Connell. That was a lie—everything made her think of Connell.

Barbara noticed her cigar. Still in her hand. A curl of smoke rising up from the ash. She'd lit it just before O'Doyle and Lybrand entered the office. She had yet to take a drag off of it.

Their story…so goddamn unbelievable. The platinum, not ore at all, but rather a massive buried spaceship. Angus Kool going rogue. Farm Girl showing up armed for bear, chasing Connell, possibly killing him before dying herself. Even if she hadn't killed him, he would have died in the heat of an erupting volcano.

Or, he would have died at the hands of alien *monsters* that had poured up from the depths of hell, that had murdered the only family she had, murdered the man she'd thought of as a son.

"So these…*things*…they killed my Connell?"

"Yes ma'am," O'Doyle said. "They were responsible for his death, although, as I told you, he sacrificed himself to save Bertha and me."

Connell died a hero. So fucking what. Was Barbara supposed to be proud of that? She would have taken a living, self-serving, manipulative coward over a dead hero.

She raised the cigar, bit lightly, absently, on the butt. A wave of anger—why did *these two* survive when her Connell had not? Barbara lowered the cigar, glared at the two battered survivors.

"Your story sounds like science fiction bullshit. How convenient there's no evidence of any kind. No way to find any evidence, either. Other than your face and her missing fingers. No offense."

Lybrand sat up straighter, like she wanted to say something, but O'Doyle lightly touched her back, stilled her.

"I wasn't exactly a male model before this shit happened," he said. "All the burns didn't help—thanks for noticing. Our story does sound like bullshit. No argument there. But we didn't make up a new volcano. You've seen the news coverage, the pictures. And what's more, you strike me as the kind of person who can spot bullshit a mile away. Tell me, do you think I'm lying?"

She *wanted* him to be a liar. But she'd read his file. What little of it there was, anyway. Connell had trusted this brute, this mystery man, this supposed killer with no past, with no records of any kind outside of the few shreds Farm Girl had dug up.

It wasn't just that Connell had trusted him. Barbara saw the hurt in O'Doyle's eyes. Hurt that mirrored her own. She didn't know how tight he and Connell had been, but there was no question that O'Doyle had considered Connell his friend.

Patrick O'Doyle was a lot of things. A reliable head of security. A dedicated, creative employee who had done wonders for EarthCore. And, yes, supposedly a killer, part of a team of government assassins that didn't exist.

One thing Patrick O'Doyle was not? An actor.

"No," Barbara said. She set the cigar in an ashtray, rubbed at her eyes. "No, I think you're telling the truth."

She looked at the folder on her desk. O'Doyle had brought it in with him. Inside, two pieces of paper. Not even stapled. His *business plan*, he called it, although it was more akin to a *mission briefing*.

A very expensive mission briefing.

Barbara picked up the folder, held it without opening it.

"You're *sure*," she said. "You're sure he couldn't have made it out alive?"

Lybrand nodded. "Yes, ma'am. No one was behind us, and there was only one way out. The mountain collapsed. If that didn't kill him, the lava would have. He's gone."

O'Doyle wasn't an actor. Neither was Lybrand.

For a moment, Barbara teetered at the edge of existence, balanced on the precipice between the all-powerful will to live and the hopeless acceptance that there was no point in living at all.

Connell was gone.

She had no one.

No … that wasn't true.

She'd dealt with unimaginable loss twice before. Both times, one thing had been her life preserver, one thing had kept her from slipping below the surface of sanity and never again drawing a sane breath.

That one thing?

EarthCore.

Barbara couldn't bring back the dead, but she could honor them. EarthCore had been her husband's creation. It had been her son's dream. It had been Connell's entire life.

For them, for all three of them, she would do as she'd always done—she would make the company flourish. She would bury her existential crisis, and her grief, make those things just as dead as the three men she'd loved with all that she was.

Barbara Yakely focused on O'Doyle. She sniffed.

"All right," she said. "He's gone. And now you want, what…*revenge?*"

O'Doyle nodded. "That's right."

What he proposed wasn't just outlandish, it was illegal. O'Doyle was experienced, of that Barbara had no doubt, but he wasn't exactly a spring chicken. O'Doyle seemed like a man who had made his living doing physical things that came easy to the young, and now his youth was a thing of the past.

That thinning blond hair. One ear nothing but a mass of scar tissue. The bags under his eyes, the pallor of his skin, the bruises, the stitches…

Hell, Barbara knew she was twenty years O'Doyle's senior, and at that moment, he looked twenty years older than she did.

She leaned forward, elbows on the desk. "But *why?* Everyone in that camp is dead. You two made it out alive. Lucky, from the sound of it. Now you want to put yourselves in harm's way again? Why don't you two ride off into the sunset together? If my Connell died so that you can live, why throw that away?"

For a brief moment, he hesitated, then answered with such quiet conviction that it made Barbara's hair stand on end.

"Because Connell Kirkland was my friend. He was my friend, he's dead, and someone has to pay."

Was that his real motivation? Payback for Connell? Against literal *monsters?*

Killing those things, whatever they were, wouldn't bring Connell back, but if that drove O'Doyle, and O'Doyle would drive the acquisition of a site that would make up for the company's losses a thousand times over, then Barbara could make his hatred work for her.

She opened the folder.

"And this Argentina thing. This is how you get your payback?"

"That's right," O'Doyle said. "If there any of those creatures left, we're going to wipe them out. They don't belong here, ma'am. We're going to make them extinct."

She flipped to the second page. His budget estimate: a hair over two million.

"This looks expensive," she said. "Is it dangerous?"

"*Very* dangerous," Lybrand said before O'Doyle could answer.

Barbara glanced over his business plan. Some of the budget was for weapons, some for *local operational costs*, but most of the budget was for *freelance operators*. Mercenaries. If what Farm Girl had said about O'Doyle's past was true, what kind of killers did this man have access to?

Two million dollars. EarthCore had already lost five times that much on Connell's folly.

But the potential payoff…

Barbara closed the folder, set it on the desk.

"I'd have to sell off several assets to fund this. I'm willing to do that, but you're talking about taking an armed force of mercenaries into Argentina. Last time I checked, that's a sovereign nation. What makes you think the local authorities are going to allow this to happen?"

O'Doyle glanced off. He rubbed at a tattoo on his left bicep: a pale blue rectangle with a horizontal white stripe, a radiating yellow sun at the stripe's center— the flag of Argentina.

"I've done business there before," he said. "I know what palms to grease."

Coincidence? No, not really. Barbara had a feeling that O'Doyle had "done business" in a lot of places.

She noticed her cigar was half burned away. A Bolivar Belicoso. Rocky's favorite brand. The smell of them always brought back memories of his smile. She took a long puff, thought of him, thought of the happy times they'd spent together while they built their company from nothing into a multi-million-dollar enterprise.

O'Doyle wanted revenge? Well, that was fine. His revenge wouldn't impact her grief one way or another, but she could feed fuel to that fire.

"A lot of people died at our mine," she said. "Not just Connell. I had to call their families, tell them their husbands, wives, mothers, fathers, sons and daughters were dead. Do you know what that's like, Mister O'Doyle? Do you know how it feels to make those calls?"

The man nodded slowly. "In my younger days, I made those calls myself. More times than I care to remember."

Lybrand sat forward in her chair, put her left elbow on the desk. She stretched out her fingers, or at least what was left of them. Horrible wounds. Two fingers gone, the stumps crisscrossed by black stitches. A dark tattoo encircled the stump of her ring finger, so new the lines were somewhat blurry. Were those tiny letters?

"I can't wear a fucking wedding ring because of what happened to me down there, but Patrick and I were just married," she said. "That's his name inked on what's left of my finger. I love him. He's going to do this with or without your support, Missus Yakely. If you fund it properly, he's got a much better chance of coming out alive."

Barbara looked away from the ghastly fingers, met Lybrand's eyes.

"You're going with him?"

Lybrand nodded. "I won't leave his side."

O'Doyle wanted payback; his new bride did not. Barbara could sense that, could recognize the expression on Lybrand's face, the emotion that expression revealed—a strong woman backing the folly of her man, because she'd back him no matter what, because she'd rather die than be without him.

Barbara knew that emotion well.

She glanced to the new paintings hanging on the wall. Rocky. Charles Junior. Connell Kirkland. All in suits and ties. The eyes of each man seemed to stare at her.

The sense of loss, of *finality*, it grabbed Barbara and threatened to overwhelm her again, but she'd slain that dragon enough times in her life that the battle didn't last long.

Money. Did this really come down to money? Did money even matter?

What about love?

O'Doyle and Lybrand loved each other. It didn't take ring tattoos to see that. The way they talked to each other, looked at each other. Even though they were both hard as coffin nails, they couldn't hide their feelings. And why should they? Newly married. So many years ahead of them. Years *together*.

Barbara could find another way to make EarthCore flourish. She could try, at least, try to give these two the chance she herself would never have again.

"I'll pay you *not* to go," Barbara said, her voice an unintentional whisper. "I'll give you a million dollars if you leave this madness behind and start your new life together."

O'Doyle shook his head as if the offer of a million dollars was somehow annoying.

"Thank you, ma'am, but we're going. Nothing can change our minds."

Barbara felt a hint of tears, the last gasp of the dying dragon. She wiped them away. She nodded.

"I knew you'd say that," she said. "I can see it in you, O'Doyle. Stubborn. And idealistic. Two qualities that get people killed. But…if you want this, then I want it, too. It will take me a while to raise the money."

Barbara wrote a memorized number on a piece of paper. If you wanted shady shit done, you gave the job to Harvey Dillinger. She stared at the number. Dillinger…was he her version of Farm Girl? Would Dillinger someday betray her the way O'Doyle said Farm Girl had betrayed Connell?

"Call this number in the morning," Barbara said. "My man Harvey will handle things from here on out. You don't call me, you don't come here, ever again. None of this can be traced back to EarthCore, you understand?"

O'Doyle nodded. "Of course, ma'am."

Time to end this. End it, then cut off all contact with these two until they located the deposit—no, the *alien ship made of platinum*—and Barbara could cut a deal with the Argentinian government.

Cigar in hand, she gestured toward the door. "Thank you for the visit."

The two battered soldiers stood. O'Doyle opened the office door, held it as Lybrand walked out. Something about the gesture seemed simultaneously romantic and ridiculous, yet it touched Barbara.

Rocky had always insisted on holding the door for her.

The dragon stretched its wings.

"O'Doyle?"

He looked back at her. "Yes, ma'am?"

Her tears came again, and this time she couldn't stop them. She wanted to break things, to *throw* things, to smash whatever she saw.

Connell was gone.

The bottom line ruled all. Her company was all she had left. Money mattered, but maybe this wasn't only about money. O'Doyle wanted payback?

So did she.

"I want you to kill them all," she said. "Kill every last one of those motherfuckers."

O'Doyle nodded. "That's what I do."

He left, shut the door behind him.

Barbara sat there, alone. She realized she'd made fists so tight that she'd unknowingly smashed her cigar between her fingers, spilling ash and tobacco on her desktop.

She closed her eyes, and for one gutting instant, the smell of cigar smoke made her think Rocky was in the room with her.

"THAT WENT WELL," Patrick said. "Better than I expected. Yakely is solid."

Better for him, maybe—it hadn't gone the way Bertha had hoped at all.

She eased the rental car out of the Republic Plaza's parking structure and into Denver's afternoon traffic. She was trying hard to control her annoyance. Trying hard, and failing.

"Head back to my apartment," Patrick said. "I need to put some things together."

"Got it."

She worked the car through downtown Denver. Traffic wasn't that bad for early afternoon, a rare and appreciated occurrence.

"To be honest," Bertha said, "I wasn't expecting her to get behind it."

To be even more honest, Bertha had spent the last three weeks working on the business plan with Patrick, assuming Yakely would shoot the idea down. What kind of a person loses dozens of employees in a scenario straight out of a science fiction film, then turns around and authorizes *another* round, where *more* of her employees might get killed? It didn't make any sense. How could people be like that?

Not for the first time, Bertha realized she didn't know jack shit about how most people thought.

"Well, she's definitely behind it," Patrick said. "She's going to fund the whole thing. She didn't even push back on the budget. I need to get my people together. That's going to take a bit of work."

He sounded so ... *excited.*

Had he sounded that excited when they'd gotten married? He had, but maybe not in the same way. This was different. Maybe this was the excitement of someone who thought he was owning his own future, instead of leasing it from someone else.

Bertha felt foolish. She'd helped with the business plan, asking dummy questions because sometimes a dummy comes up with a possibility the smart person is *too* smart to think of. She'd wanted to support Patrick in any way she could—but she hadn't thought this would actually *go* anywhere.

"Your people," Bertha said. "You mean the people you served with."

He nodded. He didn't elaborate. Still? Money was coming, which meant this had gone from a pipe dream to pending reality. Her frustration grew. She needed more information—how could he not see that?

"Are you going to tell me about them?"

"I can't," he said. "It's classified."

The car in front of her stopped short at a red light; Bertha had to hammer the brakes to stop in time. She wanted to take a crowbar to that car, smash the shit out of it, maybe put the fear of god into the driver.

Just her annoyance, fucking with her.

She wanted to be patient with him. Her own memories of war, they haunted her. *Stalked* her. The look in that man's eyes when she'd driven her blade into his chest. One tour, one kill, and she could barely deal with it. How many tours for Patrick? How many kills? They'd been through wild shit together, *impossible* shit, and they'd killed so many rocktopi, but that was different—they weren't *people*.

How many *people* had Patrick killed?

She wanted to be patient, *needed* to be patient, but at the back of her thoughts, a nagging voice grew in intensity: *is he* EVER *going to tell you, is he* EVER *going to let you in?*

"If all goes well," she said, "I'm going to meet them soon. Are you going to pretend I'm not allowed to know when I'm side-by-side with them?"

He glared at her out of the corner of his eye.

"Just leave it alone, babe. Okay?"

They drove the last two miles in silence. She found a surface parking spot right in front of the apartment building. She tried to hold her tongue, but when the elevator door slid shut, she couldn't hold her feelings in check any longer.

"I'm not just some person on the street," she said. "I'm your wife."

She felt ridiculous saying that. His wife, yes—for just over *three weeks*. Tying the knot wasn't some punch-card that gave you access to a person's entire past. She knew that. And yet, it was already starting to get to her, to fuck with her mind, that he might never tell her about his past.

He said nothing as they walked into his apartment—now *their* apartment. The door closed behind them. She thought he might yell, or that, even worse, he might speak to her in the same soft, low growl he'd used when he spoke to Angus Kool, there at the end of it all.

Instead, Patrick gently took her wounded hand. He held it. His calloused thumb ran slow circles over her wrist. Most men would be disgusted by her disfigured fingers—hell, *she* was disgusted by them—but Patrick didn't seem to care.

"Tell me," she said. "If we do this, I need to know way more than some numbers on a spreadsheet."

"We're going to be billionaires, and you're worried about—"

"I don't *fucking care* about money! I care about you. About *us*! Your past is a part of who you are. I want to know all there is to know about you."

He held her shoulders, looked into her eyes. So much damage to his rugged face—much from Funeral Mountain, far more from battles long past.

"Some things I'm just not ready to talk about yet," he said. "Some things, I *can't* talk about. I took an oath."

An oath. Patrick O'Doyle, man of honor.

"An oath to who?"

"The United States of America." Not a shred of irony or contempt in his voice.

How could he still be so idealistic?

"The same country that cut you loose? The same country that abandoned you?"

His eyes narrowed slightly. He didn't like it when people pointed out logical flaws with his worldview.

"It doesn't matter if the people I worked for didn't live up to their word," he said. "I live up to mine. *That* is what matters."

"And now you're going to gather up a bunch of people just like you? People the country used up and tossed away? And they're going to help you?"

He shrugged. "Maybe. I doubt they'll pass up the money we're offering."

"Are they your age?"

His eyes narrowed again. So proud, this man. Why couldn't he understand? He was too old for this. Even if he wasn't, he shouldn't be doing it anyway.

"That again? You mentioned that when we were in the hot tub, but you haven't since. You never mentioned my age while we were working on the business plan."

Because I didn't think I needed to, because I didn't think Yakely would go along with it.

"Someone has to tell it like it is," Bertha said. "You barely made it out of Utah alive. We *both* almost died. I'm sure you ate iron and shit nails back in the day, but that day has *passed*."

He stared at her for a moment, then let go of her shoulders. A normal movement, yet it instantly made her panic, made her think he was about to abandon her.

"Patrick, I—"

"I'm doing this. Decide if you're doing it with me or staying here."

I'm leaving—the same thing her father had said to her mother, when Bertha had been a little girl. Patrick hadn't said those words, but that was what her soul heard. *I'm leaving*. She couldn't be without him. She couldn't.

"I'll do it," she said. "I'll go with you."

He regarded her for a moment, as if trying to decide if she meant what she said. He was going to walk away from her. She was going be alone again.

Alone.

Then, he leaned close, kissed her on the forehead.

"Thank you," he said. "I wish I could tell you what it means to me that you're coming with me, but … well … I'm not so good with words."

A flood of relief, so strong she almost cried. She'd go with him. She'd watch out for him. He would survive. When this was over, they'd spend the rest of their days together.

She felt an urge to soothe him, to reassure him that she truly was on his side. He didn't want her to ask about his past, but he liked it when she asked about the plan, when she tried to poke holes in it. Questions like that sometimes made him think of things he'd missed. He loved that.

"Have you stayed in touch with the people you want to bring in?"

Patrick glanced off. He touched the stitches on his forehead, scratching at them absently.

"I haven't talked to them in twenty years. But I know how to find them. I know a guy. A guy who owes me."

Something about Patrick's expression frightened her. Whoever this man was, he owed Patrick far more than money.

"Did you work with this man, too? Was he a NoSeeUm?"

"The NoSeeUms worked *for* him," Patrick said. "I worked for him."

He wanted to contact someone who'd been part of erasing his past, someone who sent him all over the world to kill, to murder.

"We don't need him," she said. "We can find them with Facebook, Google, that kind of thing."

"They're not dumb enough to be on Facebook, or any social media. Except for Doug, I'm sure they all think the same way I do—keep a low profile, stay off the grid as much as possible. That's the best way to stay alive."

To stay alive? Maybe his oath to his country wasn't the only thing keeping him from talking about his past.

"I've looked here and there over the years," he said. "Just to check up on them, see how they're doing. No trace. I found an article on Worm when he went to prison. I thought about reaching out to him, but that might have drawn more attention to him. I wouldn't have been surprised if they'd taken him out while he was in Allenwood."

Patrick sounded like he'd worked for the mob or something.

"If who had taken him out?"

"The government."

Was he paranoid, or was this real? She thought of all the flags tattooed on his body.

"You mean *our* government?"

He nodded.

"That doesn't happen," she said, even though she wasn't sure she believed her own words. "The government can't just kill Americans, Patrick."

He stared at her with a look that was both understanding and patient, the look a parent might give a child when the myth of Santa had evaporated and it was time to know the truth.

"If the US government wants you dead, you die," he said. "Full stop. I can't tell you how I know that, but I know it firsthand."

He lifted her hand to his mouth, kissed knuckles still marred by scabs.

"Someday I'll tell you about my past," he said. "I promise. Someday, I'll tell you everything. I can't now. Not yet. Please be patient."

Bertha knew she was ugly. Even before the slashes on her face, before the missing fingers, she knew she had been as ugly as ugly gets. Boys, men, other women … enough people had told her over the years that it had to be true.

But she wasn't ugly to *him*.

Yes, you are. He thinks you're horrible, just like all the others do, because you ARE.

His eyes closed, he held her hand to his cheek.

"I love you," he said.

Those words, they shut her down.

No one had ever said them to her before. Not her pitiful excuse for a mother. Not the father she barely knew. Not the boys she had fucked, not the men in the service who had used her even while she was using them. No one had said it.

No one except Patrick.

"I love you, too," she said.

He kissed her gently. She felt an easing in her chest, like she'd held her breath for years and was finally drawing in air. She wanted that kiss to go on forever.

It did not.

"It will take me some to track down the guy who owes me," Patrick said. "If he's still alive, that is. I better get started."

12

October 10

"YOU IDIOT," ANGUS said to the engineer. "Do you have *any* coordination in those sausage fingers of yours? Because it'd be a fucking *miracle* if you could even grab your ass with both hands at the same time."

The engineer stared back, part angry, part crestfallen.

"I do not have sausage fingers."

"Get cracking, fuckwit," Angus said. "We need this interlined system active *and shielded* against everything I've listed. I want it done by tomorrow, or you're gone, and you can forget the bonus. I'll have you out of here so fast your dick won't know a socket from a sprocket."

The engineer—Blankenship was his name, or something like that, anyway—started to stammer a response. Angus didn't bother staying around to listen. He had too many people to supervise. Too many parts to make. Too many machines to coordinate.

Too many fucking hobbling steps with these stupid fucking forearm crutches. At least he could hold a crutch with his right hand, thanks to the bulky glove he'd had fabricated. The thing looked as clumsy as the big-ass hand Hellboy had in those movies, but with it, Angus could pick things up, grip the crutch handle, even write. That crazy woman had ruined his hand—his own brilliance brought it back. Mostly, anyway.

The next version of the glove, already in production, would be much smaller, about the size of a ski glove. It would utilize a new type of artificial muscle inspired by the black material he'd seen when he and Randy had dissected a silverbug.

Randy.

Angus's physical pain ebbed away, finally, replaced by that strange nagging feeling about the man's death. Could Angus have done more? No, that was ridiculous—alien robots with knives for faces weren't something that could be *stopped*, they could only be *avoided*. It had been every man for himself.

Angus pushed the thought away. He had more important things to worry about.

The glove was only the first step, a proof-of-concept for a larger, full-body augmentation exoskeleton. When he built that puppy, he could ditch the stupid fucking crutches for good.

All over the factory, a dozen teams worked on as many projects. Some of the best engineers, technicians and fabricators in the world were hard at work on Angus's designs. BHP had thrown gobs of money at these people, and gobs more on the latest and greatest equipment they needed to get the jobs done. Things were coming together. Not as fast as Angus would like, but pretty damn fast.

Water might be the universal solvent, but cash was the universal *lubricant*—it made all wheels turn faster.

A crash of metal—at one of the team stations, people scattered away from a workbench upon which a four-legged metal frame kicked and bucked wildly, like a gazelle fighting against a lion's throat-crushing bite. The robotic beast-to-be thrashed so hard one of its legs ripped free of the socket and shot across the factory floor, trailing multicolored wires in its wake. The now three-legged machine kicked again, tumbled off the workbench, hit hard and twitched once more.

A curl of smoke rose up from its hips. Or were those its shoulders? Hard to tell without the head attached.

Angus glared at the technicians who had fled the station.

"*Du verdammte idiot,*" he shouted at them. "Säubere diesen Müllhaufen *und erledige den job!*"

Fucking Germans. When it came to engineering, they always thought they were the shit. If they made the best stuff, then why had they gotten their asses kicked in the Big One? German engineers never liked answering that question.

Angus hobbled toward the next station, hating the way the crutches' forearm rings ground his shirt against his skin. A venomous twinge of pain shot up his leg, stopping him cold. He breathed in slow, trying to cope with the agony rather than will it away, because he had learned that willing it away did jack shit.

On the ten-point pain scale, his normal level ranged between three and four. Bursts would hit, though, cranking that number to seven, eight…maybe even nine. With his jacked-up feet and leg, he could stand for only about two hours before he had to sit down. No more wheelchair, no way—he wouldn't let these people see him rolling about like some mad scientist out of a James Bond flick.

And no more Donnie Graham or his goons carrying him to the bathroom every time the Piss Fairy made a call.

He'd have to up the oxy. And, of course, the Adderall to mitigate the drowsiness. There was no time for naps, no time to lose focus. The oxy was starting to make him queasy. And constipated, which was *so* fun.

On top of the pain factor, Angus's muscles *ached.* Too many days in Alice Linton's far-too-feminine bed, too many days in that goddamn wheelchair. His physical conditioning was shot to shit. He couldn't exactly run laps or hit the weight room. As for spelunking again, any normal human being would have known that was impossible, known that the days of exploring tunnels and caverns were gone forever.

But Dr. Angus Kool wasn't a normal human being.

He still hadn't found the location of the second buried rocktopi ship, but he *would* find it. When he did, the augmentation suit would let him be a part of that expedition—if, that was, the inept, Cro-Mag fuckstick engineers he'd hired could get things right.

Even if the suit turned out perfect, even if it gave him full freedom of movement, it wouldn't take away his pain. That didn't matter. Angus had yet another chance to be the first human being to set foot in virgin tunnels. Whatever it took, however hard he had to push himself, whatever pain he had to endure, he would get the job done.

Angus shuffled around the factory, giving his personal brand of encouragement to the various teams. They'd all signed ironclad NDAs that, if broken, were a professional and financial death sentence. He could fire any of them on the spot. They knew that, knew there was nothing they could do about it.

He criticized the team making the BlackBugs.

He yelled at the team making the ButterKnife.

He positively *screeched* at the team making the Wolves and BaDonkeyDonks.

Barely literate idiots, that's what these people were.

Angus saw June July walking toward him across the factory floor, Donnie Graham at her side, still in his uniform and hat, still wearing his ridiculous sunglasses. June wore a tight maroon skirt and a black button-down open to the sternum. Her red hair was pulled back in a ponytail, with one lone strand—*accidentally*, Angus was sure—dangling down the right side of her face. A typical *business casual* look for a super-hot chick that would strut her stuff and shake her ass, then turn around and bitch to the world that men were ogling her, and—*gosh darnit!*—why couldn't men just treat her like an equal?

"Hello, Doctor Kool," she said. She looked down at his right hand. "Nice glove."

Angus plastered a wide smile over his pain. "Well, if it isn't June July. Been a minute since I last saw you."

"A month," she said. "One month since you started this…" she gestured to the stations, to the factory space "…what do you call it again?"

"An R&D lab." Angus nodded toward the severed metal limb still sitting on the floor. "You know, R and D, as in *robot dicks* all over the place."

"That would be an *R-D* lab," Donnie said. "No ampersand."

Angus shifted his weight on the crutches. At first glance, June appeared to be the same polished, had-her-shit-together businessperson Angus had seen last time, but up close, he saw more. She was nervous.

Very nervous. Trying to hide it, sure, and doing a decent job of it, but that look on her face, the fear in her eyes, these things showed the true story.

She was scared. Angus knew why.

"So, Donnie," he said. "How's the next round of asset allocation coming along?"

"That's why I came," June said. "I needed to talk to you in person, Doctor Kool. The assets you asked for … are you looking to start a war or something?"

"I'm sure this isn't the first time G4S has been asked to obtain that kind of hardware," Angus said. "Right, Donnie?"

Donnie gave his single nod.

"Much of the equipment on that list is my suggestion," he said. "Since Doctor Kool still won't give me details about what kind of opposition force we might be facing, I think it's best to go in prepared."

June's eyebrows rose. "*Prepared*? That's what you call it?"

"Yes ma'am," Donnie said. "We'll need to move a significant number of men and materiel, as well as likely offer bribes to get them where they need to go. I've been assured by the G4S upper management that if BHP increases our funding, we can deliver the necessary equipment and manpower anywhere in the world. In short, we have guns and will travel."

She crossed her arms. "And the last item on that list, Mister Graham? Was that yours?"

"No ma'am," Donnie said. "If it had been mine, most likely I would have chosen a code name other than *Dirty Randy's Money Shot*."

June stared at Angus.

"Mister Graham," she said, "would you give us a moment?"

The big mercenary spun on one heel and walked off.

Two of the German engineers picked up the severed robot limb and carried it back to their station. A Dutch team was arguing, loudly, about programming protocols for the BlackBugs. The R&D lab sang with the sound of whirring machinery, intense discussions, and an occasional old-school clank of metal.

"Tell me why you need it," June said.

For fuck's sake, was she going to waste his time with this crap?

"You'd be better served just signing off on what I ask for," Angus said. "Don't worry your pretty little head about it."

A perfectly shaped eyebrow went up. "Excuse me?"

Oh, she was going to be all sensitive now?

"Maybe you should just let me talk to your boss," Angus said. "It's about time we cut out the middlewoman, don't you think?"

June smiled. Not the practiced, sexy smile she'd used on him before—this was a predator's smile. Her *real* smile.

"I don't *have* a boss," she said. "Not anymore. The company made a new subsidiary company for this project, due in no small part to your recent hardware requests. You might say their faith in you isn't quite as high as mine. Oh, and by the way, I run the subsidiary. If things go south, my bosses are insulated. I take the fall. So, while I don't have a boss, it seems that you do—that boss is *me*. Got it?"

Angus hadn't seen that coming. He didn't appreciate her attitude. He couldn't go over her head? Fine, maybe he'd try another company. He glanced around the R&D lab, saw the engineers hard at work bringing his visions to reality. Finding another company would take time. He'd have to start over. He had a hunch there wasn't enough time for that.

"Yeah, I got it," Angus said.

For now, anyway.

"I asked you a question," June said. "Why do you need it?"

He couldn't tell her the real reason. She still didn't know the full story, didn't know about the big-ass wrecked spaceship buried somewhere beneath Mount Fitz Roy, or the rocktopi and silverbugs that might be down there. If his hardware requests made her *former* bosses nervous, Angus could only imagine what the concept of ancient aliens would do for their already shaky confidence.

"We might need to move a significant amount of earth," he said. "*Significant*. That item will get the job done and help us speed up extrication of the ore. Everything we do will be far below ground, June. Nothing will be traced back to BHP. I promise."

She stared, thinking, her expression hard. Angus wished she'd flash her fake sexy smile again—at least that was pleasant to look at.

"The answer is *no*, Doctor Kool." Angus felt a twinge of pain in his ruined hand.

"It's not an option," Angus said. "If you want to control the site, fully control it, I need it."

"Then find another way. You're a genius, right? Figure out something else. The answer is *no*. You are already far, *far* over budget. We don't need more risk." June glanced around the factory, taking it all in. "To think this might turn out to be all smoke and no fire. You still don't know the exact location. Right?"

Angus bristled. He'd tried to find it, but so far, bupkis. Some things, shockingly, couldn't be found with Google maps. Veronica Reeves had covered her tracks well. Angus had read every paper she'd published on the Chaltélian culture, consumed every article written on her, watched every interview she'd ever done—not one clue as to the actual location of her mysterious tunnel entrance. He'd also read every metallurgical analysis about Argentinian mineral deposits conducted over the past decade. Very little platinum mining in South America, none in Argentina or Chile. As a last resort, he'd powered through all the documented tribal history of the Patagonian region.

In short: Veronica had never revealed a thing. Nor had her team members Samira Jabour and Ramiro Chus. Angus would start on them next; hopefully O'Doyle or McGuiness hadn't gotten to them already. If O'Doyle or McGuiness located Veronica's caves first, Angus still had one trick up his sleeve, but hopefully it wouldn't come to that.

Location, location, location. That was all that mattered, really. He'd toyed with the thought of having BHP reps, even June herself, talk to Veronica's team members, but if he did that he risked the company double-crossing him. If BHP got the location before Angus could control it, June and her superiors might try to cut him out of the operation altogether.

That was unacceptable—he had to get to Jabour and Chus first.

"I told you there would be traces of platinum-iridium in the Utah volcanic rock," Angus said. "I was correct. So it stands to reason that when I tell you I'll get the location, I *will* get the location."

She gave him a disapproving look, a look probably as well-rehearsed as her other mannerisms.

"Perhaps you don't understand how much money you have already spent," she said. "It's been five weeks since you signed on with us. You can't burn through money forever, you know."

"Actually, it's been four weeks and six days."

She rolled her eyes. "Jesus Christ, are you really going to mansplain the calendar to a woman named *June July*?"

Angus tried to dismiss her comment with a casual wave, but lifting up one crutch almost threw him off-balance.

How he *hated* being a cripple.

"Think *profit*, not *investment*," he said. "You could maintain this burn rate for years and the expense would still be a hundred thousandth of a percent of the profit you'll make."

June's stray hair drifted across her left eye—she blew it clear with a sidelong puff of breath.

"You don't have years," she said. "You told me McGuiness, O'Doyle and Lybrand don't know anything about this new site, but you can't be sure of that. As far as I know, they're looking for the same thing you are."

O'Doyle and Lybrand knew plenty about Veronica Reeves's discovery in Argentina. The trailer-trash couple hadn't sold their underground aliens story to the *Weekly World News*. They'd kept quiet, which made it possible they were looking for the new site. Were they still working with Yakely and EarthCore? Maybe, but if not, there were many other outfits that would be happy to help them get rich. And then there was Sonny McGuiness. That man had spent decades in the mining business. He had contacts, knowledge, and a reputation for delivering, which made him a far more likely spoiler than O'Doyle and Lybrand.

Angus felt a fresh wave of pain radiate from the burn wound on his leg. He'd have to sit down soon. The longer he gave June a hard time, the longer he'd have to stay standing.

"Trust me," he said. "You *will* get the location."

She again flashed that heart-melting, dick-stiffening smile.

"We better. BHP's checkbook will eventually run out of checks."

Angus knew he had to go after Veronica's team members, and fast. They were probably just as stupidly idealistic as she had been, but even idealistic morons tend to have practical bosses.

"Speaking of checks," Angus said, "I need BHP to write me one for a million bucks."

Her eyebrows rose. "Oh, is that all?"

"It's part of acquiring the location."

"You've got to be shitting me, Kool."

He'd had just about enough of her attitude.

"There are plenty more companies out there that would love my information," he said. "If Billiton won't butter my flagpole, Rio Tinto will grease it up real nice. Or Anglo Platinum. Or Aquarius Limited. Hell, Freeport McMoRan Copper & Gold would raw-dog a rabid wolverine to learn what I know."

"Now you're making threats?"

"Give me the fucking funds I need to do this job right, or they won't be just *threats*."

And then June did something that surprised and infuriated Angus—she reached out and patted the top of his head.

"I think you'd be hard-pressed to make *any* mining company take your call."

Her tone, so calm, so assured; it made him nervous.

"What do you mean by that?"

June again gestured to the activity on the factory floor. "While you have been a busy little beaver, enjoying the graciousness of my company, I might have fudged a cardinal rule of business and revealed to the competition how much we've already spent on this project."

A flush of fear, a feeling of helplessness, all taking the form of Patrick O'Doyle coming for him.

"You … you told people who I am?"

"Not yet," June said, clearly enjoying the moment. "The world thinks you're dead, so you'll stay dead—until we want people to know that you're not."

"You wouldn't do that."

"We have to protect our investment. Turns out we had a—" June made air quotes "—*leak*. I'm afraid our internal communications security wasn't up to the task, and it's slipped that we've spent millions on a particularly risky project, and that—so far—we have absolutely nothing to show for it. Should you choose to court other companies, *more* information might leak. Your name, for instance. And the fact that we, admittedly, made a *huge* mistake and fell for your ruse."

"You won't do that," Angus said. "Your stock price would tank."

June tilted her head left, then right, pretending to think over his words.

"*Tank* might be a tad strong," she said. "*Dip* is more accurate, I think. It will dip, then recover. We'll be fine. You, on the other hand, are a different story. Do you think any company will hop into your

Hobbit-sized bed with you when they learn you bilked BHP for millions, and that we generated zero revenue? Or never even got a *location?*"

His mouth felt dry. His hand *hurt*. He needed to sit down.

"It's there," he said. "I'm telling you, it's there."

June shrugged. "But where is *there?* You don't even know yourself."

"I'm doing my best to get the location. You…"

He trailed off. He had to get hold of himself. She was running circles around him. *He* was the one with the power here.

Wasn't he?

"I need that money, June. Please."

The tiniest hint of a smile—perhaps her *real* smile—played at the corner of her perfect mouth.

"There, Doctor Kool, now was that so hard? I'll get the million for you, but it is your *last* advance. Agreed? You need to produce results for us, and soon."

He hated her in that moment. Angus felt ashamed and humiliated that this stupid woman had somehow taken control of the situation.

"I'll produce results," he said. "I promise."

June July patted him on the head again, then she walked away, swishing that ass of hers, but not so much that it looked like she was trying to swish it.

"Fucking bitch," Angus said, but not quite loud enough for her to hear.

13

October 11

MURRAY LONGWORTH STEERED his boat northwest, along the forested coast. It was overcast, with intermittent drizzle. The chill air somehow slipped through his insulated clothes, feasted on his aching muscles and old bones. Most people would call the day "miserable," but not Murray.

Because the worst day of fishing is better than the best day of work.

And since he didn't work anymore, that meant every day on the water was a day stolen from the inevitable death that would eventually drag him down. Every day on the water was pristine, perfect—even the days where he was wet, cold and shivering.

He'd only been on the water for two hours and he'd already landed a redfish, two stripers, and three croakers. The croakers were his favorite.

He heard them in the live well, croaking away with their mournful, frog-like, *please release me* noises.

He'd release them all right—in the frying pan.

The actual fishing was the best part of his day, but what came next would be almost as satisfying. He'd probably get the boat back home around noon, clean his catch, then fry up the redfish and the croakers for a well-deserved meal that would chase the cold away.

Hell, he already had a freezer full of filets—maybe he'd call the neighbors over and make it a lunchtime feast. The Johnsons had just moved in. Nice couple. Both retired schoolteachers. The Browns, Rob and Suzanne, had been coming to Florida for years, traveling from Missouri. Murray wasn't great friends with them by any means, but they were decent enough people. He would enjoy sharing his bounty.

His boat wasn't anything special, just an old sixteen-foot MirroCraft he'd picked up for a song, but it was his and he loved it. Plenty of scuffs and scratches in the paint, plenty of dings in the hull, plenty of crusted-up bits of seaweed clinging to the surfaces. The boat sparkled in places, from old fish scales that avoided notice until the sun hit them just so.

In a small tray on the console, just above the steering wheel and to the right of the fish finder that hadn't worked for a year, Murray's cell phone rang, the vibration rattling plastic against plastic. Probably Rob Brown, already sniffing the air, detecting a future fish fry like a hungry Spider-Man detecting danger.

Murray answered.

"Yellow?"

"Hello, sir."

Murray Longworth's bladder let go.

That happened from time to time. He could read all the literature there was about how it happened to many men. He could listen to doctors telling him there was no shame in it. None of the well-wishing dulled the humiliation, though. And it never would.

Murray Longworth: taker of lives, both in person and from a distance.

Murray Longworth: former Deputy Director of the CIA, former director of the DST.

Murray Longworth: consultant to not one, not two, but *eight* presidents of the United States of America.

Murray Longworth: a man who had played an instrumental role in saving the life of everyone on the fucking planet.

That was the old Murray. The new version? Murray Longworth … a geriatric wreck who pissed himself often enough that he had to wear a goddamn diaper.

If getting old is a bitch, prostate cancer is a strap-on-wearing dominatrix who doesn't bother asking for consent before she bends you over and drives it home. Murray had survived cancer surgery, of course, just like he'd survived so many other things in his life. *Should* he have survived it? Maybe. Maybe not. Pissing one's self was a definite mark in the *not* column.

Age with dignity? Not for him.

Sometimes Murray pissed himself because he'd had too much to drink. Sometimes because he was too far from a restroom when the urge hit. Sometimes for no reason at all other than that his body hated him.

This time, however, he had a much better reason—the sound of that voice.

"Ender," Murray said. "Jesus Christ."

"Is this line clean?"

Of course it was clean. Murray was retired. No one gave a damn what he did anymore.

"As far as I know," he said.

"Good. I prefer it if you didn't call me by that name anymore. How about you call me *Pat*."

"Pat," Murray said, the single syllable slipping out of its own accord. *Pat*. Nope, that wouldn't work. A *Pat* was the kind of guy you got drunk with, gambled with, but who had a tendency to go all-in on a pair of sevens, counting on the river card to deliver the goods. A *Pat* got drunk and sometimes passed out on your couch during the Steelers/Ravens game. A *Pat* would watch your dog for a few days while you took a well-deserved trip.

In short, a *Pat* was not the kind of guy who had over fifty confirmed kills.

"How did you get this number?"

"Doesn't matter," O'Doyle said. "I got it."

What was it … *six years* since Murray had heard that man's deep growl? The past had returned and brought fear along for the ride.

Chest-gripping, intestine-pinching fear. Because if this man, Ender or Patrick or O'Doyle or even fucking *Pat*, if this man wanted Murray dead, then Murray was dead.

"I'm old," Murray said. "I've already had a couple of brushes with the Grim Reaper. Even so, I have to know … are you coming for me?"

There was a pause. Maybe O'Doyle was considering it.

"No," he said.

A flood of relief. Some days — most days, perhaps — Murray Longworth wished for death. He'd lived a long time. He'd done and seen it all. Now his body was failing him, one part after another. People weren't supposed to live this long. Dying wouldn't be so bad.

Or so he'd told himself, before death itself gave him a ring-a-ding on the cell phone.

"What do you want?"

"A favor," O'Doyle said.

"What kind of favor?"

"Ever see the movie *Blues Brothers*?"

Such a strange question. Part of a normal conversation, almost, the kind of conversation you might have with "Pat" over a couple of beers in a corner bar. This wasn't normal, though. This was about as far from normal as one can get.

"Sure," Murray said, "I've seen it. Why?"

"Because I'm putting the band back together. I need you to find the other players for me."

Other players? The guy had been fired from the Department of Special Threats. He'd been a pariah there. No one had liked him.

"What the fuck do you want with the DST, *Pat*? I don't work there anymore, and you certainly aren't welcome back."

"I'm not talking about the DST."

Then what did he …

A flood of faces that Murray had spent twenty years trying to block out: *Sleepy, Landslide, Skylark, Curveball, Hatchet, Knuckles, Swampy, Bookworm, Mullet, El Gato,* and, of course, *Ender.*

"I'm retired," Murray said. "Have been for three years. I can't find those people anymore."

"Of course you can."

"Listen to me. I am *out*. What part of *retired* do you not get? They gave me a gold watch and a slap on the ass, not a security clearance to be named later."

"You're so full of shit I can smell you from miles away," O'Doyle said. "You got *old,* you didn't *mutate.* You're the same guy I knew way back when. I'm calling in a favor from you. That means you call in favors from someone else. You still have connections. Use them." A pause. "You used *us,* right?"

Murray closed his eyes, as if that might stem the tide of heat rising to his face.

"I did," he said. "I absolutely did."

"You will do this for me."

This wasn't a favor; it was an *order.* Murray would obey, just as O'Doyle had always obeyed.

It was the least Murray could do.

"I'll get right on it."

What O'Doyle wanted was no simple request. His team members didn't exist. Their pasts had been erased. It was like they'd never existed. That was the prerequisite for joining a squad that did very illegal shit. A squad of assassins that killed Uncle Sam's enemies. Or, sometimes, a *potential* enemy of Uncle Sam. Or, sometimes, the enemies of Uncle Sam's pals.

Back then, Murray had believed in the job. In the cause. Now? Maybe not so much. How many deaths had he ordered? Because of him, how many men and women never got the chance to retire, to buy an old fishing boat and shiver in the misty cold of dawn, watching the sun rise day after day?

"Murray?"

"Yeah. I'm here. I'll get you what you want. This will square us."

Then, a sound even more frightening than the voice of Patrick "Ender" O'Doyle—his laugh.

"Not even close, old man. Not even in the *ballpark* of square."

"That shit wasn't my fault," Murray said, anger lacing his words. Anger at the past. Anger at the present. Anger at a life that seemed more and more empty every morning that death had the fucking utter lack of courtesy to come a-courting.

"Maybe," O'Doyle said. "Maybe the powers that be took the decision completely out of your hands."

They didn't, Murray old sport, and you know they didn't. You could have done something, but you wanted to be done with it all. You wanted O'Doyle and his team of psychos to just go away…

"That's not why you owe me," O'Doyle said. "That's not why you owe *us*. Even if you had nothing to do with it, you could have checked up on us. We went to the wall for you. Many times. We got thrown to the wolves—you got to be the Deputy Director of the CIA. You could have kept in touch. You could have seen if your people were okay. You didn't. We weren't. *I* wasn't."

Pissing one's self was humiliating. Thinking about what Murray had done—or *hadn't* done—was worse.

Far worse.

O'Doyle and his team, the "NoSeeUms," they called themselves, had once worked for Murray. He had sent them all over the world. Covert missions to dozens of countries. Full deniability if they died, because the men and women that made up the NoSeeUms had no records of any kind. No ties to America. Murray had made those histories vanish. *Poof*, a cloud of smoke, your past life is gone. Maybe that couldn't be done nowadays, what with the digitization of every fucking thing there was, but back then, it was possible.

The NoSeeUms had worked for him. They had killed at his command. They had *died* at his command, too.

Murray had run a department that did not exist. The NoSeeUms were that department's primary operating unit. Things started out fine; kill a dictator here, eliminate a war criminal there. But the team had been too good at their job. Within a year, Murray was getting can't-be-denied requests from other departments. A monster had been born, and everyone and their cousin wanted to use that monster for their purposes.

Then Bandah happened.

Bureaucracy tends to move at an agonizing, glacial pace. When the shit hits the fan, though, and things need to be quickly and efficiently swept under the rug, bureaucracy can put the proverbial pedal to the metal. The department that did not exist was shut down. Those that did have power—like Murray—pulled strings, made arrangements, cut deals. Murray found himself in a new position with the Department of Special Threats. Those that had no real power—like O'Doyle and his squad mates—were quietly left with a choice: keep your mouth shut, or someone would shut it for you. Permanently.

After Bandah, when things had been shut down, Murray had been glad to wash his hands of it all. Shit happened, right? He'd done good work for the country, right? He'd *earned* a better position, right?

He'd moved on. He hadn't looked back.

And therein lay his shame.

Murray had continued his climb up the CIA's promotion ladder, eventually becoming Deputy Director. He'd even had a shot at the top spot in the CIA, but that hadn't happened. He'd been offered a far more challenging role instead—Director of the Department of Special Threats.

He'd taken that position. And after a few years, he'd hired Patrick O'Doyle.

Other than O'Doyle, Murray hadn't checked in on the other NoSeeUms. He hadn't reached out to see if they needed help. He wasn't *supposed to* contact them, of course—his orders were to leave them be.

He wasn't supposed to, but he should have.

His people.

He'd left them behind. For good. For the simple reason that they scared the living fuck out of him. Assassins. Each of them with multiple unofficial kills to their name.

The most frightening of them all? Their boots-on-the-ground leader: Patrick "Ender" O'Doyle.

"I'll do my best," Murray said. "I really will."

"Good. And do it fast. I'll call you at this number in twenty-four hours. You will answer, won't you?"

For the second time in mere minutes, Murray Longworth's bladder let go. Not as much piss this time, of course, but enough to bring embarrassment.

"I will," he said. "I will."

"Good. Talk to you then."

Patrick O'Doyle hung up.

Murray had pissed himself the second time because his brain, experienced in the ways of the NoSeeUms, had instantly put some pieces together. *Their* pasts were erased—*his* was not. O'Doyle had called

Murray's personal phone, which meant it would be child's play for the big man to find out where he lived.

So if Murray didn't do what he'd been asked to do …

He pushed the thought away. A touch less than twenty-four hours to go.

Time to make some calls of his own.

Murray pushed the throttle forward, and the fishing boat shot across the water, headed for the docks.

14

1,886 Feet below the surface

OCTOBER 12

Switchback after switchback after switchback. Descend a 12-degree decline for 40 meters or so, turn 180 degrees to the right, go down another 12-degree decline for another 40 meters or so, then repeat 112 times just to get down to sea level, which they referred to as "the surface" for purposes of depth measurement.

From the surface on down, things got really steep. Slope declines doubled to 24 degrees. The small cavern they'd set up as their basecamp was 925 feet below the surface, which meant traversing fifty-seven of the steeper switchbacks. Descending was murder on the knees, ascending always made her legs scream, but that was the price of admission to ride this ride.

The constant hiking didn't get *old*, exactly, but it had a tendency to put her in a zone where she wasn't paying close attention to her surroundings. It didn't help that she'd made this same trip down … was it fifteen times now? Sixteen?

It was worth it, though. The more they made the trip, the better they knew their footing on the cave floor, the better they knew each hidden rise of jagged stone beneath the fine silt. Each trip was a little faster than the one before. And with Ramiro's new cooling gear, they were farther down than anyone had gone before. Including Veronica. *Especially* Veronica. Only a few hundred feet further, but that extra distance had produced a reward: a new glyph.

Sam's hardhat lamp lit up the image on the tunnel's pale granite wall—a rough circle with six waving lines radiating from it. Drawn *thousands* of years ago in reds and yellows and blues, forever frozen in this place that had no wind, no rain, no moisture. Four smaller, colorful symbols beneath it. She recognized two of them, although she didn't know what they meant. The other two symbols she'd never seen before.

No one had.

New characters notwithstanding, it was the circle itself that sparked curiosity and excitement. While it looked similar to ones she'd seen elsewhere in the tunnel complex over the last four dig seasons, this one had a variation unlike any she'd seen—white chalk marks slashing through the red and yellow lines.

Sam rubbed her eyes, her face and fingers slick with sweat.

"Sam, you okay?"

She nodded. "I'm fine. It's just this *heat*."

Something tapped against her shoulder: a water bottle.

"Here you go," Ramiro said. "Enjoy a nice mouthful of my warm fluid."

Sam sighed. Six years she'd known this man—two of those as husband and wife—and still he made the same tawdry jokes he'd made when they met as undergrads.

The tunnel was wide enough for them to walk side by side, but they usually moved single file. Ramiro preferred to put his feet where she'd put hers, reducing the variables of walking in this ancient place.

"Seriously, *drink*," he said. "Dehydration is the killer."

She took the bottle, drank. Water and bottle alike were hot, just like everything else down there.

"Thaaa*aaat*'s it," Ramiro said. "Swallow it all down like a champ."

Sam groaned, turned to him, careful to keep her helmet lamp aimed just left of his eyes, just as he kept his helmet lamp aimed just left of hers.

"*Swallow it like a champ?* Jesus, Ram, grow up."

"Where's the fun in that?"

He smiled, but it was the kind of smile that looked like it had taken some effort. Sweat covered his face, the only part of him exposed to the tunnel's blistering geothermic heat. His half-lidded eyes revealed his exhaustion. He'd lost weight—as had she—in the week they'd spent at their basecamp, which was at a depth of 925 feet below ground. The constant marching up and down the steep tunnel. Eating nothing but meal bars and vitamins for days at a time. The hours spent in temperatures of 100 degrees Fahrenheit, sometimes even hotter.

All of it combined to take a harsh toll.

He held out his hand. "Gimme back my rigid, girthy cylinder."

She rolled her eyes, handed him the water bottle.

Considering it was sex (and/or the lack thereof) that had doomed their marriage, it was actually kind of cool that he was comfortable enough with her to make bawdy jokes.

Time heals all wounds, as they said.

If so, she was grateful for that time.

Hard to believe that over a year had passed since their divorce. They'd both decided to stay in the project. The dig season that followed the divorce…that had felt like a constant emotional assault. When Ramiro spoke to her at all, which wasn't often, he'd addressed her in clipped, perfunctory tones. So much tension. So much bitterness. By the end of that stretch, though, before the tourist season began and they returned to Michigan, Ram's heart had begun to thaw. He accepted that he and Sam weren't meant to be married, that they had taken a deep, lifelong friendship one step too far.

They'd spent the summer apart, trying on their new lives for size. They hadn't seen each other at all until they'd once again joined Veronica for this year's long trip back to El Chaltén. Right from the start, Sam and Ramiro had worked together almost as well as they had before the divorce. The bad jokes had returned, as had the easy laughs that came with them.

They'd become good friends again. As good as they'd been before the doomed marriage? Probably not, but Sam loved him and was grateful to have him in her life.

"You look like half-cooked spaghetti," he said. "How are you holding up? Tell me the truth."

She knew better than to lie and put on a brave face. "Not that great, I'm afraid."

He gently took her arm, looked at the readout on her computer.

"Ninety-eight point nine," he said. "The ice in your pack is probably almost gone. The water is warming up some, but that's to be expected."

They'd started using cooling gear earlier in the season. Just a heavily insulated vest then, a vest that circulated water cooled by an attached, ice-filled backpack.

It was a simple process, albeit a laborious one. They'd hauled two Yeti coolers up the mountain, along with dozens of water bottles. The mountain's cold froze the water solid. One cooler stayed just inside the tunnel entrance. Ramiro carried the other cooler, filled with bottles of ice, to the basecamp cave. Those bottles provided the temperature control for his coolant suits. When that ice melted, he and Sam returned to basecamp, then Ramiro—or Sam, sometimes, if Ramiro was too wiped out—would haul the Yeti up the twelve-degree slopes to the tunnel entrance, swap it for the other one, then come back down to basecamp.

Simple, primitive, yet it was the only way. They couldn't exactly haul a generator up the mountainside, let alone the fuel needed to run one, so they could create the electricity needed to power a freezer, which they couldn't haul up in the first place.

While basic, Ramiro's suits kept a person's internal temperature mostly normal, even when geothermal energy cranked the heat to insane levels.

The gear had allowed Veronica, Sam and Ramiro to stay in the tunnels an extra hour, allowing them to penetrate deeper down the steep slopes than they'd ever gone before. But that hour was all they could get. And seeing as every step *down* necessitated a laborious step back *up*, the vests only allowed them another twenty minutes of actual descent time.

Ramiro thought he could work with university engineers to modify the system, add legs, sleeves and a faceless hood, creating a suit that covered almost everything. The extra coverage, he'd hypothesized, would add an additional hour of descent time. Once he pitched that to Veronica, she'd sent him back to Ann Arbor to do the work, had sent Sam home as well to try and make progress on the glyph language.

And while they'd been in Michigan, Veronica had gone to Utah and gotten herself killed. Someday, hopefully, Sam would understand why.

This wasn't the time for thoughts of Veronica, not when every minute mattered. The suit kept her body cool, but Ramiro had yet to figure out a way to properly cool the air they both breathed.

"It's my *lungs* that are getting to me," Sam said. "I feel like I'm inhaling a hair dryer."

"What's your body temp?"

She looked at the small computer strapped to her forearm. Ramiro had built it, and one like it for himself, as most off-the-shelf electronics wouldn't work in this high heat. The cell phone-sized device had a small keyboard below an industrial screen that showed black data on a field of green. It measured air temperature, body temperature, depth, kept various timers going, and even had a camera.

"For shit's sake," Sam said. "It's *a hundred and thirty-five* degrees down here. How much longer do we have?"

Ram stepped to her side, poked at the keys of his computer.

"The water and ice still in our backpacks should stay under a hundred degrees for about another ten minutes," he said. "I've got one ice refill for each of us left. We're thirty minutes below the safe temp level, so as soon as we change out the ice we need to head back up."

Just ten more minutes?

"That's not enough time," she said.

"It is, unless you want heat stroke. And if I have to haul your ass up this slope, we'll *both* end up dead."

How could she argue with him? He carried ice bottles in his bigger backpack, enduring the extra weight so she didn't have to. He also carefully tracked their time—when Ram said it was time to go, it was time to go.

She nodded, knelt in the cave's fine silt.

"Get shots of this glyph," she said. "A bunch. It's important."

She wished she had time to sketch it. By force of habit, she still carried a sketch pad and thick charcoal pencils in her backpack everywhere she went, even down here, when there was no time to use it.

Sketching helped her lock in details, helped her puzzle out possible meanings. Back at base camp, she would look at the digital picture and make a drawing of it anyway—a photo helped, but was never quite the same as drawing something from real life.

Ram knelt down next to her, slid his small computer out of his forearm strap.

"Keep your headlamp on it," he said. "Keep it steady."

She did as he asked. He worked quickly, taking photos up close, farther back, from different angles.

"It looks like the other glyphs," he said. "Their sun god. But you're so pumped. Why?"

Sam pointed, careful to keep her gloved hands from touching the drawing.

"See the white chalk marks? Those are new."

Ramiro leaned in but didn't touch. "None of the others had those?"

"No, they're new."

Sam peeled off a glove, wiped sweat away from her face, but was alarmed to see there wasn't as much sweat as she'd expected. *Dehydration is the killer*. She put the glove back on.

Ramiro slid his computer back into its strap. "What do you think the glyph means?"

"Can't say right now. Maybe the chalk lines are some kind of modifier. Like…punctuation, perhaps. Like an exclamation point, drawing extra attention to whatever meaning is in these particular radiating curves."

"Like a warning sign?"

A warning sign. Where had he come up with that? Out of nowhere, and yet, it felt right. Maybe she should have thought of it, but it was so hard to think in this *heat*.

"I'm calling it," Ramiro said. "We need to change out the ice and head for the surface, and then it's back to El Chaltén."

She couldn't stop now. She couldn't. They'd finished their last meal bars that morning, which meant it was time to return to El Chaltén. It was a six-hour hike from the tiny town to just the *base* of Cerro Chaltén. No roads out here, not even any two-track trails that might support a good off-road vehicle, which they didn't have in the first place. Once at the base, it was still a three-hour climb to the hidden tunnel entrance, and *then* two more hours in the tunnels to reach their base camp cave. That was why, when they came here, they hauled as much food as they could carry, so they could spend a week at a time operating from base camp instead of making the long trek back to the small town.

It was a horribly inefficient system, but what choice did they have? Without ice, they couldn't survive the geothermal heat. No electricity out here. They couldn't haul big solar panels up to the mountain, couldn't run some non-existent extension cord hundreds of meters to a non-existent freezer.

"What if we go back up to base camp now, get some sleep," Sam said. "Then we get more ice, come back down later? One more descent before we head back to town for resupply."

He made that face that she hated so much, part sneer, part *oh my god how stupid are you?*

"We're out of food," he said. "And, no, we are *not* going to keep going without a meal. Gambling with our calorie intake adds to the danger. Safety first. By tonight I'll be at Glaciares, pounding Quilmes and eating a burger, or at least something other than fucking calorie bars."

If they headed up now, if Ram insisted they return to El Chaltén, Sam wouldn't be back to this spot for four days, maybe five.

"Not yet," she said. "The big discovery could be just ahead of us."

"We're in the temperature red zone. We keep going and something unexpected happens, we won't make it back to the safe zone before our coolant runs out. If that happens, it's lobster-boil time for both of us."

She gripped his arm. "Just a little farther. *Please.* Two more switchbacks. We can do it."

The condescending expression she hated so much shifted into one she had always loved, the face he'd made when they'd been married and he'd caved into one of her needs, caved simply because he loved her and wanted her to be happy.

He glanced down the tunnel, his headlamp beam playing off the granite edge of the next switchback corner. She knew he was thinking of how tired they both were, how the never-before-trod footing could result in a fall. This far down, at this heat, a simple injury might prove lethal, more so when they were nearly out of ice.

Each inch, each *centimeter* of walls and ceiling and floor—none of it had been seen by human eyes for thousands of years. Possibly *ten* thousand years, maybe even more. She was the first modern person to see any of it.

"Five minutes more," he said. "That's it, no matter how far we do or don't get. Give me your word."

"Word given. Come on."

She continued on down the tunnel. Ramiro, as always, followed.

They turned the switchback corner and her persistence was rewarded, instantly, by more white-slashed, colorful sun god symbols painted on the walls. *Dozens* of them, drawn much closer together than the symbols higher up the incline. Sam was simultaneously thrilled to be the first to see them, and sad that Veronica wasn't here to do the same. What if this collection of symbols was some kind of Chaltélian Rosetta Stone, or at least missing pieces that would help her unlock more of their written language?

She turned back to Ramiro. "Get as many pics of these as you can."

"On it," he said, pulling his computer free. "Three minutes left. No fucking around, Sam."

She nodded, wondering if she should try to use the limited time to see the symbols in context, lock in the overall image of how they might relate to each other, or to walk as fast as she could to the next switchback corner, only fifteen-odd meters away.

She had to know what lay beyond it.

"One more corner," she said, and started down.

She tried to move carefully, but the burr of seeing the next thing was already under her saddle. She slowed only when her left foot slipped in the silt and she almost fell.

Sam turned the corner—ten meters or so down the tunnel, a bit of blackness in the floor that ignored her headlamp's glow. What the hell?

She moved closer. A hole, irregular, almost as wide as the tunnel itself.

Her heart sank. How far down did that hole go? And how stable was the ground beneath her feet?

"Ram, come here, quick, and move carefully."

He was there in seconds.

"Possible cave-in," she said, pointing "Maybe another tunnel undercuts this one."

Ramiro's headlamp beam joined hers, played down the tunnel, past the black spot. Then, his beam flicked slightly right—and came to rest on the wall, almost to the next switchback edge, on a small, roughly carved alcove that flashed with bright reflections of metal.

Her beam joined his.

"Holy shit," he said.

She started to nod, which made her beam move, then held her head still.

"Yeah," she said. "Holy shit."

Three double-crescent knives. *Three.*

The knives were the hallmark of the Chaltélians, the thing that set them apart from all other primitive cultures. Their level of metalworking mastery predated anything even remotely close by five thousand years.

"Three," she said. "This is big. *Big.* Let's grab them."

Ramiro put his hand on her shoulder. "We have to be very careful of that hole, we—"

His computer beeped an alarm. He shut it off.

"Time's up," he said. "We have to move."

She brushed his hand away, shook her head.

"They're *right there*. It will only take a couple of minutes."

"We don't have a couple of minutes," Ramiro said. "We'll get them on the next trip."

"Ram, *please*. They're twenty meters away. Help me grab them, then we'll head right up. Three knives will change everything. They'll land us the grants. Please."

He stared down the tunnel, hesitated.

"We'll have to move fast," he said. "Even so, the ice will be gone before we get to the safe zone. We'll both be a little crispy around the edges, but—"

click-click, click…

Sam froze.

Ramiro's headlamp flicked about the tunnel. "You hear that?"

She nodded. "Yeah, I heard it. Small rocks falling from the ceiling, maybe?"

A dual-edged comment—if it was falling rocks, even small ones, this entire tunnel could collapse at any second. If it *wasn't* falling rocks, what could it be?

Something is down here with us something is down here with us …

"Bad news if it's falling rocks," Ramiro said, his voice level, calm. "Even small ones. We need to back out of here, real slow."

click

The sound again, tiny and … *closer* … than it had been before.

You know that's not falling rocks, that's metal, *what could it be what is down here with us what is—*

Sam shut her eyes and shook her head. The heat hit her anew, and with it came Ramiro's reminder of their limited time frame.

The knives. Without them, would this be the last time she saw this place? No, she'd be back—the new glyphs, the pictures of the knives … it would be enough.

And if it wasn't enough? Dead people didn't fill out grant applications.

"Let's get out of here," she said. "As fast as we can go."

For once, her ex-husband didn't argue.

15

October 13

IT WAS SO CLICHÉ it was funny. A covert meeting in a diner? Straight out of a bad gangster movie.

Patrick O'Doyle sat a in a booth in the rear corner of a Denny's, his back to the wall. His position offered him a full view of the front door. The kitchen was a few steps away, which meant a back door was a few steps away. He knew how to hunch in on himself to hide his size. His jeans: well-worn, but no holes, no discerning marks. His windbreaker: plenty of bulk-concealing space, but not baggy. A black beanie that hid the scars on the side of his face, because a man with scars for an ear is quite memorable. His clothes were his camouflage, designed to let him blend in, to hide in plain sight, to be seen but not remembered.

The restaurant wasn't that busy, which was good. Two tables and one booth with families: people with kids were rarely a threat, as few operatives went so far as to incorporate children into the act. An old man at the table to Patrick's left: maybe seventy, by himself, his face half-hidden by a menu. Patrick would keep an eye on that one. The table in front of Patrick's: three teenage girls, all staring at their phones while talking to each other with enough volume to draw occasional glares from the families and the old man. A booth by the far wall: a woman in a pantsuit sitting across from a man in a shirt and tie, both with open laptops, both with a cup of coffee. The woman had a small purse on the seat beside her. Probably too small to hold a weapon, but both of them had computer bags. Could hide a big-ass handgun in one of those and no one would be the wiser.

The business couple was the most likely threat, which was to say, not much of a threat at all. Patrick had chosen this restaurant only fifteen minutes ago. Even if his burner phone was tapped somehow, these patrons had already been in their booths before he'd made the call. He was more worried about people who'd come in after him, but so far they'd been seated in other areas.

Harvey Dillinger entered the restaurant. O'Doyle knew him on sight, from Harvey's own description: *I look like a used Q-tip*, he'd said on the phone, and he'd been right. Tailored brown suit. New shoes, gleaming. White shirt, wrinkle-free. Pale skin. A too-thin neck topped by a big head with a puffy, curly brown afro. French manicure.

The hostess said something to him. Harvey looked around, saw Patrick, then smiled at the hostess and walked over. He slid into the booth opposite Patrick.

"Good afternoon," Harvey said, taking a menu from the condiment rack at the table's back edge. "Don't know why I bother to look at this, I get the same thing every time. Nothing quite like a Moons over My Hammy." He glanced up, smiled, spoke softly: "Doesn't it strike you as a little cliché to have a covert meeting in a diner?"

Patrick shrugged. "Hadn't crossed my mind."

Motion from the nearby table: the old man putting down his menu, giving his order to the waitress. No weapon. No phone. Patrick mentally moved the man down to *non-threat* status.

"Sweet Jesus," Harvey said. "Look at this monstrosity. *Salted Caramel & Banana Cream Pancake Breakfast*? Are the Denny's overlords trying to kill the world via a massive, global coronary? Oh, and where's your partner?"

"Making sure you weren't followed."

"Hmmm," Harvey said, and continued to scan the menu. "Should we begin without her?"

"No."

A waitress came. Patrick ordered two coffees. Harvey ordered the Moons Over My Hammy, opting for fruit instead of the hash browns. He also ordered a coffee, asked the waitress to leave the pitcher.

Patrick watched the front door. A couple entered. They went left instcad of right, which took them to the other side of the restaurant. An old Latina woman, mid-60s, came in next; the hostess sat her in Patrick's section. He kept his eye on her but didn't think she was a threat.

The waitress delivered the coffees. And the pitcher.

"Thank God," Harvey said. He drained his first cup in one pull.

Patrick put one sugar and a little cream into Bertha's coffee, pushed it aside. He preferred his black.

The front door opened again; Bertha walked in.

She was dressed in a similar fashion to Patrick. Nondescript clothes, neither too baggy nor too tight, no exterior branding. Blue ballcap, no patches or insignia. No identifying elements. She walked to the booth, casually checking out the families, the loud teenage girls, the old man, the old woman, the business couple.

Patrick stood. She met his eyes, shook her head—*no one following*—then slid into the booth. He sat down next to her.

"Ah, Bertha," Harvey said, quietly. "Nice to meet you."

Her answer was a cursory nod. She took a sip of the coffee that had been waiting for her.

She smiled at Patrick. "Coffee's just the way I like it. Thank you."

That smile. Bertha didn't smile often. When she did, it gave Patrick a sense of peace, of accomplishment. He was going to find ways to make her smile more. So many ways.

Harvey picked up the pitcher, poured his second cup. "Aren't you two just the cutest thing ever? Congrats on your nuptials, by the way."

Patrick glanced at his wife, expecting to see her smile again. She did not. She stared hard at Harvey, probably trying to determine if the *cutest thing ever* comment was actually an insult, his way of calling her ugly. Bertha tended to see the worst in people.

She was sensitive about her looks. Patrick could admit that maybe she wasn't beautiful by the traditional definition of movie stars and super-models, but she was the most beautiful thing he'd ever seen. He knew he could count on her, even in the worst possible conditions. Bertha was *solid*. Reliable. She had a good heart. She loved him, of that he had no question. As far as he was concerned, her scars made her all the more attractive, because those badges of courage showed the world that she could take whatever came at her and spit it right back.

"Thank you," Patrick said to Harvey. "It's been a wild ride, but when you find the right person, you know it."

Harvey laughed. "I've found the right person four times and counting." He raised his coffee cup. "Here's to your marriage lasting longer than all of mine combined."

Patrick raised his own cup. He noticed Bertha relax; a slight lowering of the shoulders, the suspicion leaving her eyes. She raised her cup and the three of them clinked.

Harvey drained his coffee in one pull, immediately poured himself a third cup. He glanced side to side, finally taking a moment to examine the people around him. He leaned closer, spoke softly.

"Barb told me quite a tale. I won't lie and say I believe all of it, but at the same time I'm not going to tell you I *don't* believe it, either. What she told me fits what we know to be real. And she's the boss. She told me to get you whatever you ask for, so that's what I'll do. Where do we start?"

There was so much ground to cover, but as with most missions, Patrick wanted to make sure he and his people would be properly equipped. That meant he started with the fundamentals: weapons, ammo, tech, supplies.

"When we were in Utah, we had specific hardware," Patrick said. "Connell asked me for a list of what we needed. Were you the one that acquired the items on that list?"

Harvey nodded. "Those items and everything else. Fulfilling all of Doctor Kool's requirements—and Kirkland's, and yours, and purchasing the land, and getting the right permits—that was all my doing. I'm good at my job, Mister O'Doyle."

"Don't call me *Mister*. I work for a living."

Harvey smiled, shook his head. "I should have known that was coming."

Bertha leaned forward. "You have military experience?"

"Me? Good God, no. My dad was a career sergeant in the Army. I grew up an Army brat. I've heard all the lines. So, what do you need?"

Patrick pulled a folded piece of paper from his left pants pocket.

"We need all of this."

Harvey took the paper, unfolded it. He studied the list, nodding slowly.

"A bit more extensive than last time, but shouldn't be a problem. I can make it happen."

"How soon?"

"Shouldn't take long," Harvey said. "Three or four days, if my supplier is properly motivated."

That was fast. The list included serious hardware, as well as high-tech solutions that would solve some of the problems Patrick had encountered in the Utah tunnels. If Harvey Dillinger could obtain everything in less than a week, he was a valuable asset to have on the project.

"I also need you to recruit specific personnel," Patrick said, passing over another folded piece of paper. "Names, addresses and contact information. I'm afraid they're quite dispersed."

Harvey unfolded the paper. Patrick noticed Bertha scowling slightly. She hadn't seen that list, and he knew that bothered her. She'd learn plenty about those who chose to join the mission. Any that didn't join, however...she didn't need to know anything about them, and they didn't need to know anything about her.

Harvey frowned as he read the list. "When do you want these people assembled for the pitch meeting?"

"Yesterday," Patrick said.

"Then you'll be very disappointed. Five people, four in different states and one in Bogotá? I can make the calls, but since I don't know them, I—"

"No calls," Patrick said. "You need to see each of them *personally*. We can't risk any electronic communication."

Dillinger glanced off, thought for a moment, nodded.

"I suppose I can see your point," he said. "Farm Girl did raise a number of problems. Isn't she dead, though?"

Patrick saw the waitress coming, tray in hand, waited to answer. She put Harvey's plate on the table. He rubbed his hands together in anticipation.

The waitress walked away. Harvey ate the two strawberries in his fruit before touching anything else.

"Farm Girl is dead," Patrick said.

"*Probably* dead," Bertha said.

Harvey looked from Patrick to Bertha and back again.

"We didn't see a body," Patrick said. "But there's a lot of bodies we didn't see, and none of those people have showed up. Yeah, we can assume she's dead, but what we *can't* assume is that she worked alone. We're not taking any chances, Mister Dillinger. Especially with the people on that list."

Harvey took a big bite of the scrambled egg and ham sandwich.

"I'll work as fast as I can," he said as he chewed.

A huge task had been set before him, yet the man wasn't making any advance excuses. Patrick was beginning to like the guy.

"The last thing is a base of operations," Patrick said. "I'll need to put the team through training to make sure they're ready. Find me a place with room for five to eight people, creature comforts, a good distance away from any towns or villages."

"But you don't know exactly where the deposit is," Harvey said. "Right?"

He drained his coffee, poured more. Maybe his stomach was lined with asbestos.

"Right," Patrick said. "But we're probably close enough for government work. We think. We have someone working on the location."

Harvey picked up his second half of the sandwich. "And that someone is McGuiness?"

Patrick nodded.

"Mister Dillinger," Bertha said, "something is bothering me. How do we know you're not selling our information to other companies? To the highest bidder?"

"Simple," Harvey said. "Barb offered part ownership."

He bit off a big bite.

"*Part ownership*," Patrick said. "Of what?"

Harvey held up a finger as he finished chewing, draining the coffee cup to help wash it down.

"Of EarthCore," he said. "She knows she won't live forever. No children, no nephews, no nieces, no relatives at all to which she might leave her company. Kirkland was supposed to take it over, but—" Harvey shrugged "—that didn't work out. Barb wants to make sure her employees are cared for in the long run. So, if you two and your pals succeed in this operation, she's leaving the company to me. You might say that makes me *extremely* motivated to support your efforts."

Bertha leaned back in her seat. "You're our boss, then?"

Harvey shook his head as he poured his fifth cup. Patrick wondered how long it would be before the man raced off to the bathroom.

"Barb is old, but she's still going strong," Harvey said. "I have a lot to learn from her before I become the boss."

Patrick had a vision of this frizzy-haired fancypants whispering in Barbara Yakely's ear, lying to her, manipulating her. As soon as the vision appeared, however, it vanished—Yakely did not seem like the kind of person who could be manipulated.

"There is no amount a rival firm could offer to get me to switch sides," Harvey said. "Are you two familiar with the band Rage Against the Machine?"

Patrick nodded. Few soldiers his age didn't know of the band's aggressive music.

"They have a song called *Down Rodeo*," Harvey said. "It has one of my favorite lines ever—*fuck the G-ride, I want the machines that are making 'em.* Understand what I'm saying?"

Patrick didn't, but Bertha nodded.

"You don't want money to buy things made by others," she said, "you want to own the factory so you make money from other people buying *your* things."

Patrick glanced sideways at his wife. She'd picked up that much meaning from a simple song lyric?

Harvey grinned. "Close enough. Say what you will about Barb, but she's been a successful owner for decades because of one thing—she *gets* people. She wanted my utter loyalty, so she bought it by offering me something no other company *could* offer." Harvey pushed his empty plate aside, rested his elbows on the table, leaned close.

"If your project is successful, and after Barbara is gone, I won't just be *rich*, I might very well be the richest person in the world. In *history*."

Patrick had no desire to be that rich, but the concept of someone he worked with possibly attaining such heights seemed pretty cool.

Bertha leaned back, crossed her arms. "That seems unfair. I mean, it's people like Pat and I that face the danger, that get shot at, get cut—" she held up her hand, drawing attention to her two missing fingers "—get parts of us chopped off, and *you* might become the richest man in the world?"

Harvey grinned, shrugged.

"My dear Bertha, forgive me if I don't want to get drawn into a debate that involves your life decisions as compared to mine. There is no such thing as *fair*. There never has been, never will be."

"Meet the new boss," Patrick said. "Same as the old boss."

Harvey smiled. "Ex*actly*. People on the frontlines die, people behind the lines get paid. It's as true in this endeavor as it was when you served, as it was for the Roughriders, as it was for the Greeks and the Romans." He spread his hands. "Don't hate the player … hate the *game*."

Bertha started to talk, but Patrick put a hand on her arm. There was no point in arguing over facts.

Harvey put the lists in an interior jacket pocket. The same hand came out with a one-hundred-dollar bill.

"Breakfast is on me," he said. "I'll have some gear sent to your apartment this afternoon. Use that gear and that gear *only* to stay in touch with me. Nice to meet you both."

Patrick and Bertha watched him walk out of the restaurant.

"You like him," Bertha said.

Patrick shrugged. "You saw how tricked out the Wah Wah camp was. He put all that together. He knows what he's doing."

"You *trust* him?"

Patrick wasn't sure. It was easy to say you'd be rich in a possible future, then choose instead to take the known present and whatever cash came with it.

"We don't have a choice," he said. "The cat's out of the bag, babe. Harvey knows everything. If he's going to fuck us, he's going to fuck us."

He felt her hand squeeze his knee under the table, slide up his thigh.

"Speaking of fucking," she said softly. "Let's get out of here."

Patrick would have said *check please*, but the bill had already been paid.

"I like your way of thinking," he said. "Race you to the car."

16

October 14

FROM BEHIND THE *headboard slipped a tiny hunter-seeker no more than five centimeters long. Paul recognized it at once—a common assassination weapon that every child of royal blood learned about at an early age. It was a ravening sliver of metal guided by some near-by hand and eye. It could burrow into moving flesh and chew its way up nerve channels to the nearest vital organ.*

The seeker lifted, swung sideways across the room and back.

"Tommy?"

Joe's voice. Tommy hated being pulled away from a book. He read to escape, to go to a place where pain and suffering happened only to imaginary people. Maybe if he ignored that overly important shithead, Joe would go away.

Tommy sat at the tiny round picnic table in the break area behind

Joe's Eats. Overfull dumpster on one side. Parking lot on the other. Patio umbrella lined with white lights above.

"Uh, Tommy?"

Tommy finally looked up from his book. Joe the Asshole stood in the diner's back entrance, waiting for Tommy to respond.

"On break, Joe. Still got ten minutes. First time I've sat down today other than to drop a deuce."

The human egg nodded. He even smiled.

"Yeah, that's cool. There's someone here to see you. Listen, let's double your break, okay? On account of you working those extra shifts. Take another thirty minutes. And … if you need some time off, no problem, your job will be waiting for you. Gotta support our vets, right?"

The fat man slid back into the diner.

Time off? What the hell did that mean? Even curiouser, Joe was being … *nice?*

Tommy glanced up to see if there was a full moon, but the umbrella blocked any view of the LA night sky.

A man stepped through the kitchen door. Brown suit, perfect fit. New shoes, gleaming. White shirt, wrinkle-free. Puffy, curly brown hair.

"Mister Strymon?"

Tommy's internal calendar rolled backward at high speed, the automatic reaction of an ex-con. He scanned backward three months in a blink, wondering what he'd done wrong, wondering who he had *hurt*, before he remembered he didn't have to go to parole meetings anymore, before he remembered that he truly was a free man.

This wasn't a cop. Wasn't a parole officer. Just some guy.

"Yeah," Tommy said. "That's me."

The man tilted his head toward the table. "Mind if I have a seat?"

Tommy closed his paperback. "It's a free country."

"Yeah, and I've got a bridge to sell you," the man said. He sat, offered his hand; the man's French manicure seemed even more out of place here than his sportscoat. "I'm Harvey Dillinger. I know, I know, crazy last name, right? But it's for real, and no, I'm not a descendant of the famous John. Wish I was. Wouldn't that be a great story to tell at cocktail parties?"

The mini speech flowed out smooth and refined. Dillinger had said those same words many times.

Tommy shook the offered hand.

The man reminded Tommy of something. He couldn't put his finger on what, though. The curly fro, his too-thin neck … something.

Dillinger glanced at the book on the table.

"*Dune?* Never read that one."

"Your loss."

The man gave the novel a judgmental look, as if the novel somehow might give a shit about his opinion.

"You like that sci-fi stuff?"

"I like political commentary," Tommy said. "Especially when it's served up with a healthy dose of social metaphor."

Dillinger's eyebrows rose up over his thin frames.

"Not exactly what I'd expect to hear from a line cook."

"Sometimes I have to get on the grill in a pinch, but I wouldn't recommend you eat what I cook," Tommy said. He shrugged. "I'm just a dishwasher."

Dillinger grinned. "We both know you're more than that, Tommy."

With those words, Tommy understood. Understood, and felt like an idiot for not seeing it immediately.

"I *am* a dishwasher," Tommy said. "That's my job. That's my *only* job now."

That cheesy grin widened. "Franky, I don't care about what you do or don't do. Your business is your business. I was paid to deliver you a message. I'm delivering said message."

He reached his hand into his brown coat.

Tommy's hands shot out, his left wrapping wound Dillinger's neck, thumb on the windpipe, right sliding into the coat and locking on Dillinger's wrist.

Dillinger made a noise, perhaps trying to say something—words couldn't escape Tommy's power. The man recovered from his instant shock, tried to grab at Tommy with his free hand.

Tommy squeezed harder. "Stay still."

Dillinger did.

Tommy slowly pulled Dillinger's hand out of the coat, found that the hand wasn't holding a gun, or a knife, or even a *gom jabbar,* for that matter—it held a white number ten envelope.

Reality washed back, an almost out-of-body experience where

Tommy saw a man dressed in filthy, wet, white kitchen clothes, a man who was a mere iota of pressure away from taking yet another human life.

Tommy let go.

A moment of stillness. Perhaps Dillinger would never breathe again, perhaps it was already too late, and *Hello, Allenwood, I missed you so*— then the man sucked in air in a heaving gasp. Dillinger put one hand on the table to steady himself, rubbed at his neck with the other.

"Fuck," Tommy said. "Mister … I'm sorry."

Tommy hadn't *thought*—he'd *reacted*. Muscle memory. The snake that lived inside Tommy had slipped out, pulled the puppet strings, and Tommy had moved.

Harvey Dillinger rubbed his neck, winced.

"My … fault." He coughed, cleared his throat. "I should have thought of how that might look to someone … someone of your skills."

Tommy stared at his hands. At the scars. At the calluses.

Dillinger cleared his throat again. "Never seen anyone move that fast."

Tommy laughed, a small laugh birthed from darkness.

"I'm forty-seven. You should have seen me in my prime."

"From what I've heard, I wouldn't have wanted to." Dillinger nodded at the envelope on the table. "If I pick that up, are you going to use the five-point-palm exploding-heart-technique on me?"

Dillinger was making jokes? Tommy had damn near killed him, and the man was shaking it off as no big deal. Tommy's opinion of Dillinger ticked up a few notches.

The thin neck, the curly brown hair …

"Anyone ever tell you that you look like a dirty Q-tip?"

Harvey laughed, shook his head. "No, never heard that one."

He reached out—slowly—and slid the number ten envelope across the table, leaving it in front of Tommy.

"It's funny," Harvey said.

"What is?"

"I've had more than a few times where my mouth wrote checks my body couldn't cash, but this is the first time it happened delivering an actual *check*. Open it."

Tommy didn't want to. He wanted to read *Dune*. He wanted to go back to listening to '80s hits and washing dishes, to bitching about the broken dishwasher. What he did *not* want to do was see what was inside the envelope, because men like Harvey Dillinger worked for other people.

Serious people.

"It's all right," Harvey said. "Honestly, that incident was my fault. I'm not calling the cops. You're not going back to jail. But I will have bruises on my neck tomorrow. Delicate skin. Dad was a linebacker for Alabama, and I get my mom's Jew genes? Life ain't fair. So, since you marked me with your Kung Fu Grip, how about you see what's in the envelope and we call it even?"

The envelope wasn't sealed. Tommy flipped it open. Inside, ten twenty-dollar bills, a first-class, round-trip ticket on United—from LAX to DEN—and an unsigned check from "Titan Drilling" for twenty thousand dollars, made out to *Thomas Strymon III*.

Tommy looked up. "The fuck is this?"

"Your flight leaves in two hours," Harvey said. "Should be enough time for you to shower. No offense, but you smell like the fryolator's grease trap. When you land in Denver, a car will take you to a meeting."

A plane? Tommy hadn't been in an airport in, what, six years? No, at least seven—he hadn't flown since he'd gone to jail.

"I already told you *no*," Tommy said. "You work for Academi? G4S? Triple Canopy?"

Harvey smiled. "Not familiar with those firms. Are they in the drilling business?"

"They're mercenary outfits. Private armies." Tommy glanced at the dumpster, wanting to look anywhere but at the used Q-Tip who wanted to drag Tommy back into a life he'd long since left behind. "Doesn't matter. I'm done killing people."

Dillinger cleared his throat, winced a little this time. He turned his head, spit—a glob of blood hit the dirty concrete.

"Look, Tommy, I know about your record. I know that's made it hard for you to find work. All you have to do is hear a sales pitch. Then the check gets signed. I promise you, this isn't about killing *people*."

An emphasis on the last word, as if it was a punchline. The guy thought he was being clever.

"What is that supposed to mean?"

"Does it matter? You don't have to do anything you don't want to do."

Dillinger looked around the break area, eyes lingering on the dumpster that almost touched the picnic table. "How many hours you think you'd have to work here to make twenty grand?"

"One thousand, nine hundred, thirty-two hours, twenty-one-and-a-half minutes."

Dillinger blinked. "That's a weird thing to have memorized."

"Wasn't memorized." Tommy shrugged. "I'm good with math."

"A skill that comes in handy for washing dishes."

"It's an honest job, okay?"

The man nodded. "If you like, you can have your *honest job* back when you return from Denver tomorrow. I gave that loudmouthed boss of yours a little something to make sure of that."

No wonder Joe had been so nice.

Dillinger stood. "One meeting, Tommy. Twenty grand. And I promise you, if you like what you hear, there's more than the twenty large. A *lot* more. Your call."

The man walked to the kitchen door.

"I'm not going," Tommy called after him.

Dillinger waved without looking back, and then he was gone.

Tommy stared after him for a bit.

Didn't have to kill *people*?

What the ever-loving fuck did that mean?

Tommy looked at the unsigned check. Something on the top right corner…gum. Must have been some left on his thumb or something.

Used, filthy, dirty gum. On a check for twenty thousand dollars.

One thousand, nine hundred and thirty-two hours. Forty-four weeks' worth of work.

"Dammit," Tommy said.

He picked up his copy of *Dune* and walked back into the diner.

ANGUS FELT ITCHY.

The goddamn oxy, he knew. His mouth felt dry, too. Was that from the oxy, or the Adderall? It didn't matter. Whatever kept the pain away, whatever kept him working.

With all the money he had spent in the last two weeks, he probably should have thought about ergonomic office furniture, something that was more comfortable for his ruined body. In truth, though, he kind of liked the old Steelcase desk and the worn '70s-era wooden chair, lacquered finish craquelured with age. The desk had been left here when the previous company had abandoned the factory. The laptop sitting on its surface seemed somehow out of place, like a far-future prop left behind after a movie shoot.

He rested his crutches against the desk, eased himself into the old chair. He stared out the rectangular window. Down on the factory floor, his teams were hard at work on their various projects. That part of things, at least, was coming together nicely. New patents up the wazoo. June July thought the patents were going to her shiny new subsidiary of BHP Billiton, since the company's money was paying for the work. A couple of patents would go there, for sure, but Angus had quietly submitted ten times as many in the name of his own company, which was still running along fine without him.

Soon he would have the location of the Fitz Roy tunnel system. June had come through with the million bucks, which Angus had immediately offered to the University of Michigan's archaeology department. So far, the university hadn't heard back from Samira Jabour or Ramiro Chus, but Angus had a feeling that Melissa Askew—the university's VP of Development—would track them down toot sweet.

Want a million-dollar donation? All you gotta do is pony up the location of Veronica Reeve's Chaltélian tunnel system.

Simple, right?

Hopefully. If the donation didn't work, he was screwed. Absolutely screwed. For starters, June July would hang his ass out to dry. The world would know he was still alive. No one would hire him. He'd have to make his living with his own company, which he'd set up years ago, but that was doomed as well—BHP Billiton would choke him with legions of lawyers and layers of lawsuits. His new patents would be worth a big stinky pile of shit. He'd have to sell off his old patents to pay his own legal fees. The law favored those with money, and BHP Billiton had a whole heapin' helpin' more money than he did.

Worse, though, would be knowing he'd lost out on seeing that tunnel system, on being the first one to the bottom of it. Oh, and he'd miss out on becoming the *richest person in human history*, too. But no big deal, right?

A knock on the glass of his office door—Dimwit Donnie Graham stood outside.

"Come on in," Angus said.

Donnie entered, shut the door behind him.

"I can get you what you want," he said.

Angus leaned back in the chair. "A blowjob from Betty White? Damn, Donnie, you're one connected motherfucker, you know that?"

"Not a Betty beejer," Donnie said. "I can get you the last thing on the list—I can get you the money shot."

Angus sat up. It was funny that no one wanted to use the actual word for it. He was no exception—even saying the word out loud made him nervous.

"For real?"

Donnie nodded once. "I told you G4S is global. We have people in Bulgaria. It's said you can get anything in Bulgaria—all it takes is money."

Angus scratched at his itchy neck. "I'm afraid I don't have any more. June July has cut off my financial nuts."

Donnie walked to the desk, sat on the edge. Looking up at him, Angus was reminded anew of the man's bulk.

"But you *will* have money, if this works," Donnie said. "I've been around the mining industry for a while. I see how June reacts to all of this. I see the kind of coin BHP is dropping, and they're barely asking questions. That tells me you're after the mother of all motherlodes. BHP thinks you can get it."

Angus had a quick vision of Samira Jabour and Ramiro Chus hearing about the million-dollar donation, falling all over themselves to cooperate. Shit, the phone might ring at any moment.

"I can," Angus said. "I will."

Single nod. "That's what I was hoping to hear. How about you and I make a little side-deal, Doctor Kool? I get you the hardware you asked for. June doesn't need to know. In return, you cut me in for five percent of whatever you make, you tell me exactly what we're up against, and you tell me *why* you need that hardware."

Angus laughed, scratched at his itchy chest.

"You're a fucking comedian, Donnie! *Five percent*? Sure! And while I'm at it, why don't I just tell you everything I know so you can try and cut me out altogether? Sounds like a plan!"

"Let me rephrase," Donnie said. "First, if I don't hear what's going on, and I mean *everything* about what we might face, you're not going into those tunnels even if you do find them. I will call my bosses and tell them this op is too risky. They'll call June and cancel the contract. Once they do, my guess is BHP walks away from all of it. They might try to retain another merc outfit, sure, but as twitchy as June is right now? My guess is *her* bosses shut everything down. You'll be back to square one, Doc. Good luck coming up with the millions you need to keep this project going—word is that June is waiting to piss in the punchbowl of your career if you screw this up."

Angus wasn't laughing anymore. Half of him wanted to shoot Donnie Graham in the face. The other half of him knew he *needed* Donnie.

"Two percent," Angus said. "And I've told you we might be facing armed resistance. That's all you need to know."

"With the weapon you want, you think I don't need to know every-thing? We're going into a tunnel system. You're bringing in all kinds of hardware, including your hauler robots, your BlackBugs and the rest. Untested gear, untested systems. The lives of my men will be on the line."

Angus huffed. "*Your men*. They're mercenaries, for fuck's sake. Pretty sure they know the risks. It's not like they're fighting for god and country, right?"

"Dead men can't spend their paychecks," Donnie said. "It's not just the tunnels and the big unknown, Doc. I'm sure you won't be surprised when I tell you that G4S has the resources to look up the service record of any soldier anywhere in the world. We looked up Bertha Lybrand. Army. She served in Afghanistan as a truck driver. She has combat experience, including a confirmed hand-to-hand kill. She suffered from acute PTSD. The Army rotated her out. I know her serial number, her social security number, and every phone number she's ever had. I know her bra size. I know her marksmanship scores—she's quite good with a pistol. You understand what I'm telling you?"

Angus shook his head. "I understand that I have no idea why you're telling me you know everything about Bertha Lybrand."

"Because I don't know *anything* about Patrick O'Doyle. The same system that let me look up Lybrand? It doesn't show diddly-squat about

O'Doyle, except for one thing—he's on the *do not hire* list. It's a helpful little unofficial list that the US, the Russians, the Chinese and other countries use to block former soldiers from serving with most security companies. If G4S hires anyone from that list, G4S stops getting government contracts. You get me?"

Angus had known O'Doyle had a secretive background, but he didn't know what the man had done. Military something-or-other. It hadn't mattered. Apparently, it mattered now.

"You're a badass, Donnie," Angus said. "I'm sure you're bringing badasses with you. You afraid of Patrick O'Doyle?"

"Let's say I'm superstitious. I'm afraid of *ghosts*—that's what O'Doyle is. There are enough variables here that I'm thinking of pulling the plug. So you need to decide how bad you want this, Doc. You tell me about Utah. You give me *three* percent, and you tell me what you saw there that makes you want to bring an army with you this time."

Could Donnie take his ball and go home, and in the process ruin the entire game? If he rocked the boat, would that be it for June's patience? Angus had no allies, and was realizing he didn't have the power he'd thought he had. Maybe Donnie could give him both things.

"If I tell you, are you going to blab about it to June? To G4S?"

"I know you're keeping this secret so you don't have to face competition. I agree with that strategy. Only you and I will know the whole story until we get into the tunnels themselves. At which point, I'll disseminate the information to my men on an as-needed basis. These are mercenaries, Doctor Kool, but they are still human beings. They need every chance I can give them to come out of this alive."

So was Donnie doing this for more money, or because he actually cared about his people? Probably both.

Without Donnie, Angus had new problems to solve. There wasn't time to solve new problems. It was a risk, but all told, Angus knew he didn't have any choice—it was Dimwit Donnie, or nothing.

"You should go get a chair," Angus said.

"Why's that?"

"Because this is going to take a while, Donnie, old chum. It's quite a story."

"AND THEN I CRAWLED away," Angus said. "Several miles to a nearby hospital, where they checked me in as a John Doe."

He left out the part about the Jeep driver picking him up. Sounded better that way.

Donnie Graham sat for a moment, thinking, occasionally smoothing out his salt-and-pepper mustache.

"I believe you," he said.

Angus felt surprised. He'd expected those three words, but with a *don't* included.

"Now I believe I understand the need for the equipment you want," Donnie said. "You told me this expedition will be going deep underground. How deep?"

Angus didn't want to tell Donnie anything, but if Donnie could provide, that was worth some level of risk.

"At least a mile and a half," Angus said. "Probably more like three miles. It's so far down that no one will ever know."

Donnie thought on this for a moment. Angus had a feeling the man didn't just believe Angus, he *wanted* to believe.

"And this hardware, you need it to kill the … what did you call them again?"

"Rocktopi," Angus said. "It's a stupid name, but it's stuck in my head, so screw it. Unless you want to see Mount Fitz Roy wiped out—possibly with you and I in it—the rocktopi gotta go. We need to kill anything that moves inside that mountain."

Donnie stroked his mustache.

"Crazy shit," he said. "Crazy and dangerous. But if the payoff is as great as you think it will be, it's worth the risks."

Angus had low-balled the projections, telling Donnie the find was worth billions, not *trillions*. The numbers were still large enough to light a fire of greed under the man's ass.

"Three percent," Donnie said. "That's our side deal. You pay me three percent of what you make?"

Could this man really come through?

"I can do three percent of net."

Donnie smiled. "The deal is three percent of what *you* make. Don't play bookkeeping games with me, Doctor. Every time you get a check, a stock option, assets, *anything* related to this dig, you cut me in for three percent of the value that same instant. You get paid, I get paid. You seem smart—smart enough not to back out on a deal with a man who carries weapons for a living. So, going into this, know that I will be checking up on my investment regularly. Do we have a deal?"

Donnie offered his hand: his *left*. He knew enough not to offer to shake Angus's ruined right hand. A small touch, but a nice one.

Did Angus have to get into bed with this troglodyte? If he wanted to get to Mount Fitz Roy before anyone else, then, yes, he had to make this happen.

"We have a deal," Angus said.

The two men shook hands.

17

"HERE'S TO THE NEXT big thing," Ramiro said. He raised his bottle of Quilmes in salute, tilted it toward Sam.

Her head was still killing her. Dehydration headache. Or was it from general exhaustion? Or, probably, from the constant stress of knowing she had to produce on this trip or it would be her last.

I'll take ALL OF THE ABOVE for $200, Alex.

With the headache, the last thing she needed to do was get drunk, but she was already well on her way.

"Whatever," she said, and clinked her bottle against his.

They drank. Ramiro loved toasts. He made them all the time, for just about any reason that kept the people around him drinking and happy.

He started to put his bottle down, seemed to think the better of it, took another pull, then leaned back in his wooden chair. He looked around.

"Place is damn near empty."

Sam nodded. "It'll be full in a couple of weeks."

During the height of the tourist season, the tiny Glaciares Bar was packed with adventure-seekers from all over the world. Americans, sure, but also twenty- and thirty-something hikers, climbers, backpackers, hitchhikers, campers and outdoorsy types from all over South America, Europe and more. They came for the mountain trails, the glacier lakes, the glaciers themselves, and—the true adrenaline junkies, at least—to climb Cerro Chaltén, known in some parts of the world as Cerro Fitz Roy or simply *Mount Fitz Roy*.

Glaciares was a picture-perfect image of what one might expect from a bar in Patagonia frequented by outdoorsy tourists. From the outside, it was a spartan, teal shoebox with few windows. Inside, everything was wood, from the bar to the tables to the chairs to the peaked ceiling above. Kind of a low-rent Swiss chalet decorated with faded Argentinian flags and soccer scarves, dartboards and cork boards half-covered with handwritten ads selling tents, hiking gear and the like.

There were maybe ten people in the place, wearing attire typical of the clientele: jeans, T-shirts, sweaters, sweatshirts. Sam knew all ten people here. Delfina working the bar. Santiago, sitting alone at a table as he always did this time of year, getting hammered and remembering how his climbing partner had fallen to his death nine or ten years earlier. Alfonz and Luciero, locals who lived in El Chaltén year-round, taking the winters off, making all their money as hiking and climbing guides during the warm months.

Sam rested her beer on the table, pulled her sweater tighter.

"Freezing in here," she said. "We should be drinking something hot."

Ramiro shrugged. "Quit your bitching. I'll fire up hot chocolate when we're back in the cabin. Snow predicted for tonight."

This was her fourth year as part of the Chaltélian project, yet the flip-flop of seasons still messed with her head. Back home in Michigan, fall was on the way. In a few weeks, the trees would explode with color. When winter sat its big fat ass down on the state, Cerro Chaltén would be enjoying "Patagonian summer," with eighteen hours of daylight and highs in the mid-sixties.

"Sucks being here without Veronica," Ramiro said. "She loved this place."

Sam smiled. "Remember that first year? What a disaster."

They'd come in May, at the height of winter. Almost *nothing* had been open, something Veronica hadn't accounted for. While El Chaltén had a population of around twelve hundred during the summer, in winter the town shrank to *maybe* four hundred people. Veronica, Sam and Ramiro wound up wasting three days of their limited time just to drive to El Calafate for groceries. A dumb mistake, but one that had taught them just how far away El Chaltén was from everything else.

Ramiro turned his bottle in a slow circle. "You miss her?"

"Of course I do," Sam said. "You?"

"Yeah. She was kind of a cold, selfish asshole, but she was also one hell of a person."

They sat in silence, drank, absorbed the place that had been their happy spot every "winter" for the past four years.

Hard to think of Veronica and not think of the lost grants. Funding: the fuel of science. Especially a science like archaeology, which didn't produce patents and revenue-generating technology. Move a few genes around in bacteria, and you wind up being a billion-dollar company like Genentech. Discover the oldest civilization in human history, and you go around, hat in hand, begging for money to continue the research.

"Tomorrow, we should look for another place to rent," Sam said. "I don't want to go home in two weeks. We need more time."

Ramiro's lips pressed together. "You're ruining my buzz, a buzz I have put considerable effort into cultivating."

"I'm serious." She leaned closer, spoke softly. "We're going to get those knives when we go back in. We need more time."

"It's not *time*, it's *money*. We're both already spending our own. We talked about this before I agreed to come with you. I can't afford to go any further in debt. Neither can you. And besides, you and Veronica were the ones who came up with the *no tourist season* rules, remember?"

"Screw the rules," Sam said. "And it won't cost that much more. We can make it work."

Ram closed his eyes, tilted his head back. "Why do I even bother having sincere discussions with you? You just piss all over them. You know how much time I spent planning and budgeting this trip? And now you want to wipe your ass with those plans?"

"We need more time, that's all. If Veronica had asked, you would have made it happen."

He shook his head. "That's horseshit. And Veronica doesn't matter, because she's dead. This is about you. I should have known you'd waste my time, that you'd *lie*. It's what you do."

She leaned back, away from the table, away from him.

"I … I wasn't lying."

She looked down, at nothing, just so she didn't have to look at him. She hadn't *lied*, but she had changed her mind, invalidating the hours and hours and hours he'd spent planning this out down to their last negative penny.

"I shouldn't have said that," Ramiro said. "I'm sorry."

He'd apologized. Maybe he shouldn't have.

"It's okay," she said.

Ramiro sighed, put on a fake, happy smile. This was his way—he'd hurt her and would now try to make up for it by being extra nice.

"I know you're frustrated," he said. "But honestly, Sam, we've gone about as far as the new cooling gear will let us. I'm not saying we're done *forever*, okay? We need to find better gear and a way to pay for it."

He stared at his beer bottle, started slowly peeling away the label.

"You're not telling me something," she said. "What?"

He glanced at her, smiled, shrugged.

"Is the label thing a tell?"

"Totally," Sam said. "You always do that when you're holding something back. Out with it, sir."

Ramiro sighed. "I didn't want to mention it because of the funding running out, but there's a vastly better version of our cooling gear. It's brand-new. The company's called Kool Products. I think it's a start-up. Their gear is called a *KoolSuit*. With a *K*. Costs a fortune, though."

"How much?"

He grimaced, peeled off more of the label.

Sam reached out, gripped his wrist. "Ram—*how much*."

"A quarter mil," he said. "Each."

She let go of his wrist. Sat back. "Damn."

"Now you know why I didn't want to tell you," Ramiro said.

"Yeah, but is it worth it? I mean, how much more time would it give us?"

"As much as five *days* more. According to their website, the suits are self-contained. They store the concentrated food paste that satisfies dietary needs—although even *their* site says it tastes bad. It stores a day's worth of water. Two days if you use the urine filtration system."

Sam's nose wrinkled. "We'd have to drink our own pee?"

"It's not *pee* anymore after it's filtered, you idiot," Ram said. "But it's easy to load more food and water into the suit."

Five *days* more down in the tunnels? For that, Sam would gladly drink her own pee—even the unfiltered variety if she had to.

His head tilted slightly left; he was getting annoyed with her. The more things changed, the more they stayed the same.

"I'm putting my foot down, Sam. With the gear we've got now, we can do one more trip down. If we go straight for the knives, no monkeying around looking at glyphs or whatever, I'm confident we'll have enough time to see if we can safely get to those knives. One more try, then that's it. Then we're out of here. Got it?"

She nodded. They would go down with one objective and one objective only.

"All right," she said. "We get the knives, and we head home. With the new glyphs and the knives, you can go after more grants."

He started peeling the label again.

"Jesus Christ, Ram, do I need to slip you a truth serum? Out with it."

"I'm not doing grant requests anymore," he said. "To be honest, Sam…I'm going to stay in Ann Arbor."

Stay in Ann Arbor…

"Ram, are you telling me you're done with the project? Are you messing with me?"

He shrugged. "We've put in our time. We should reap the benefits. You do the professor thing for a few years. I can finish up my doctorate, which should be a lock after all of this, right?"

As drained as she was, his words exhausted her even further.

"But the suits you found," she said.

"They're skin-tight, apparently. They'll look good on you, and whoever else you get to come with you. You'll be fine without me."

Would she? She sure as fuck hadn't been fine without him since the divorce.

"You can't quit now," she said. "Not after what we just found."

He smiled again, but this smile was different. It was the smile of a former lover: sweet, caring, yet patronizing in the *I know you better than you know yourself* way.

"You talk about *what we just found* like it's a big deal. We found three knives. So what? So did Veronica. There aren't going to be any more grants. This site is played out. There's nothing more to find."

How could he say that? "You don't think I can do it."

He shook his head. "Not without money, and the money is gone."

"I can raise more. You get the interest, I'll close, like Veronica always did."

He leaned forward, elbows on the table. "When are you going to accept reality?" He tapped the bottom of his beer bottle against the table-top to emphasize each word: "*You ... are ... not ... Veronica ... Reeves.*"

"I'm just as good as she was!"

Ramiro closed his eyes, rubbed at them. "Sam, you know I am your biggest fan. I always was, always will be, even now that we're not together. But Veronica was a star. You're not. It happens all the time in the science world, you know that."

Well, fuck you very much, Mister Ramiro Chus.

"I'll get the goddamn money." She reached across the table, gripped his hand, squeezed hard. "Believe in me, Ram. We can do this. We can keep going."

He fell quiet. The good-natured humor left his eyes. Sam felt a shiver—his expression looked exactly like it had when he'd told her he wanted a divorce.

Slowly, he pulled his hand free.

"I've made my decision," he said. "When we get back, I'm heading to Berkeley to finish my doctorate. Even if you do get funding, I'm out."

Her skin felt cold where she'd touched him. Her hand lay on the table—a gesture of solidarity rebuffed, exposed. With an instant sense that she'd been a fool, she pulled it back.

He was leaving her. Leaving completely. That was his right. Wasn't it? They weren't married anymore. He owed her nothing. He'd stood by her, even after the divorce, given her far more than most men would. Hell, then *any* man would.

So why did it feel like a wrecking ball had just hit her in the chest.

"I … don't want you to go."

Ramiro nodded slowly. "I know you don't. But it's time."

"Mind if I join you?"

Those five words seemed to be intangible for a moment, a transparent ribbon floating through the air, nothing more than lyrics from a radio, then Sam realized they'd come from a man standing at their table.

A black man. Sixty-something, with a thick white beard. Black parka. Dirt-stained, green cargo pants tattered from long use. He wore a silver bracelet and held three unopened bottles of Quilmes.

A stranger. And he'd interrupted the most important discussion of her life.

"I mind," Sam said. "We were talking."

The man held up the bottles as if she hadn't seen them.

"You sure? This round's on me."

Ramiro reached to an empty chair, pulled it out a bit.

"Sure," he said. "Join us."

The coward … he was taking the easy way out. Sure, invite a stranger to sit down and end the conversation when her whole life was falling apart.

The stranger sat. When he'd been standing, Sam hadn't realized how short he was. In the chair, though, it became clear. Probably a full head shorter than her.

"My name is Sonny McGuiness," he said. "I was a friend of Veronica's."

The last thing Sam had expected to hear.

Sonny opened the first beer, set it in front of her. He did the same for Ramiro, opened the last one for himself, then angled his bottle forward.

"Here's to Veronica Reeves."

Ramiro nodded as if those were the sagest words ever spoken, clinked bottles with Sonny. They didn't wait for Sam to join — they drank.

Something wasn't right. A stranger showing up, in the off-season of butt-fuck nowhere, saying he'd been a friend of Veronica's?

"Veronica didn't have any friends," Sam said. "Trust me, we know everyone she knows. She never mentioned you."

Sonny sipped his beer. "We worked together. In Utah."

Where Veronica had died.

Sam pointed toward the door. "Here's an idea. How about you get the fuck out of here?"

"Sam, chill," Ramiro said. "He obviously came a long way to talk to us."

Sonny held up a hand. "No, maybe she's right. I'll go, just let me say what I have to say first."

Sam sneered. "I don't give a *fuck* what you have to say. You work for EarthCore, right?"

Ramiro reached his hand across the table toward her, as if he was going to pat her arm to calm her, but the hand stopped halfway.

"Sam, calm down," he said. "You're yelling."

She was yelling. She *wanted* to yell. Losing Veronica *hurt*, and, finally, she had a target for that pain.

On top of that there was the obvious threat—a man from a mining company was *here*, in El Chaltén. Did he know about the platinum knives? He *had* to know. He wouldn't have approached unless he wanted something.

This asshole wanted the *site*.

Was it already too late to stop EarthCore or some other company from defiling the site? She had to get rid of him; she needed time to think.

"Veronica went to work for your company," Sam said. "Now she's dead. You think I care about anything you have to say?"

She heard wooden chairs scraping against the floor.

Sonny's gaze flicked left for an instant, toward the bar, then he leaned forward and spoke in a rushed whisper.

"*It's about the platinum.*"

He knew.

Ramiro whispered back: "*What platinum?*"

Sonny smiled. A tiny, predatory smile—he'd found a card to play.

"Oh," he said to Ramiro, "she didn't tell you?"

A pair of shadows fell across the table.

Sam glanced up, saw Alfonz and Luciero standing there, glowering down at Sonny.

"Hey, Sam," Alfonz said, his eyes never leaving the smaller man. "This guy bothering you?"

In a flash, she saw the scene as Alfonz and Luciero must have seen it. She'd been shouting, she'd been angry. They knew her—they didn't know Sonny.

"Never seen you before," Luciero said to Sonny. "You just get into town?"

Ramiro held up a hand. "It's cool, guys. He's a friend of ours."

In that instant, Sam felt something slip away; Ramiro wanted to hear Sonny out.

Alfonz glanced at Sam. "You sure?"

You sure you don't want me to throw this bum out on his ass?

That was exactly what she wanted, but it was too late for that.

"Yeah," she said. "Thanks for looking out for me, though."

Alfonz nodded at her, silent assurance that he'd be close by if she changed her mind. He and Luciero returned to the seats at the bar.

"Thanks," Sonny said. "That could have gone south in a hurry."

Ramiro nodded. "And it still can, so tell me about the platinum."

Sam stared at Sonny, trying to keep a poker face yet also trying to send him a clear message: *Please, don't do this.*

The tiniest tug at the corner of his wrinkled mouth told her that he wasn't about to let her off the hook.

"How long you two been working on this dig?"

"Four years," Ramiro said.

Sonny smiled at Sam. "You wanna tell him, or should I?"

Sam started to rise, to call out to Alfonz and Luciero, have them throw this old man out, but Ramiro reached out, gently gripped her forearm.

"Sam, what is he talking about?"

"I'll tell you later," she said.

He shook his head, spoke quietly but with conviction. "You'll tell me now."

Frustration overwhelmed her. After fucking up their marriage, she thought she'd had her best friend back, but her best friend was giving up on her. And now? This would change their relationship again, maybe end it for good.

She should have told him. As soon as Veronica died, she should have told him.

Sam leaned back in her chair; she felt hopeless.

Ramiro sighed in that way he did when he'd lost patience with her.

"Sometimes, Sonny, my colleague Samira has trouble sharing the truth," he said. "So you tell me."

Sonny looked sidelong at Sam. "That what you want?"

The asshole managed to say that in a gracious tone, as if he was being a *ladies first* gentleman.

Sam said nothing.

Sonny shrugged. "All right, have it your way. Those knives y'all found. Know what they were made of?"

"Steel," Ramiro said instantly. "Way ahead of their time, they…"

His voice trailed off. He glanced at Sam. She saw the betrayal in his eyes.

"Platinum," Ramiro said in a whisper. "The knives are made of platinum."

A statement, not a question, because he saw the truth. He leaned back in his chair, the disgust and anger on his face so tragically familiar.

"Start talking, Sam. Start talking or I'm taking the truck and getting out of here. You will never see me again."

Sonny sipped at his beer, waited.

She wanted to rip that bottle out of his hand, smash it over his head. She wanted to see him on the floor, bleeding. Why did he have to come here? Why *now*?

"I'm not kidding," Ramiro said.

Not telling Ramiro had been Veronica's idea. But Veronica was gone. Sam had no one to blame but herself.

"Veronica did the metallurgy on the knife," Sam said quietly. "Once she figured out they were made of platinum, she decided it was best to kept it a secret."

"But not from *you*," Ramiro said. "You and her both kept it secret from *me*."

Sam reached across the table to grab his hand. He pulled it away before she could.

"Ram, please understand," she said. "Do you have any idea what would happen to the Chaltélian site if word got out? We *had* to keep it a secret."

He nodded. The look in his eyes, it made her feel six inches tall.

"Just so I'm accurate on the timeline," he said, "you knew of this while we were married. Right?"

She felt the stinging threat of tears, fought to hold them back.

Ramiro turned to Sonny.

"So this … *material*," Ramiro said, as if he didn't want to speak the actual word. "It's a coating on the knives? Or a bit of it mixed in with other metals? Like that?"

Sonny laughed. "Afraid not, youngster. The knives are solid you-know-what."

"Solid," Ramiro said. "As in … *solid*-solid?"

Sonny nodded. "Fifteen pounds, one ounce. I know you're a scientist, but I'll save you the math — that's two hundred and forty-one ounces."

Ramiro glared at Sonny, glared at Sam, then pulled out his phone and called up a browser.

"Amazing you can get the internet way out here," Sonny said. "Ain't technology grand?"

Ramiro tapped at his phone. His eyebrows raised.

"The current price of platinum is nine hundred fifty-two dollars and fourteen cents. Per ounce." He tapped the phone again, then stopped and stared at the screen. He held the screen up for Sam to see.

A calculator: 229,465.74

"Almost a quarter mil," Ramiro said. "Per knife."

"*Per?*" Sonny said. "You make that sound like there's more than one. Have you two lovebirds found other knives?"

The pressure of pending tears vanished in an instant. *Lovebirds.*

Wrong word, motherfucker.

"McGuiness," Sam said, her voice a low growl, "you are going to leave here and never bother us again."

Ramiro shook his head. "Sam, listen—"

"*Enough*," she said.

Ramiro stopped talking.

Yes, he knew her better than anyone else. No matter how mad he was, how disappointed, he heard something in that one word that made him give her the floor.

"Get out," Sam said to McGuiness. "Get out, or I'll see to it that Alfonz and Luciero fuck you up. *Bad.*"

Sonny set his beer down, held up his hands, palms out.

"I just want you to listen for a second," he said. "The company I work for has amazing gear. I'm guessing you guys hit a heat barrier you can't deal with?"

Ramiro nodded.

Sam wanted a time machine to go back and strangle Veronica, tell her to *stay here*, to avoid Utah like the plague.

"We can help," Sonny said. "I'll let you in on a little secret, cupcake. Veronica was in Utah because we found a knife there."

He might as well have kicked the chair out from under Sam.

"Impossible," Ramiro said.

"Saw it myself," Sonny said. "Veronica said it was the real deal, made by the same culture you're studying down here. Carbon dating or whatever showed they were made at the same time, too. And it wasn't moved there, it was found deep in tunnels that went untouched for thousands of years."

In Utah. Some six thousand miles away.

Sam shook her head. "It can't be the same culture."

"Veronica told us it was," Sonny said. "She said it was evidence of the largest pre-modern empire in history. I'm not gonna pretend I know more than what she said, but she said it. There's a whole bunch more I can't tell you right now, but part of the Utah dig involved sinking a shaft to reach a tunnel system. Long story short, they went *three miles* underground."

Three miles? She and Ramiro had just set a site record by descending 4,600 feet. If what Sonny said was true, EarthCore had gone three and a half times deeper.

"But the heat," Ramiro said. "Three miles, that's deeper than any mine. How could they go so deep?"

Sonny hunched over his beer, his eyes hungry, eager.

"We've got advanced equipment," he said. "Crazy, state-of-the-art stuff. We can take you way past where the heat stopped you, and we can do it *safely*."

He was playing to their needs, as transparent as a pussy-hungry man saying *baby, you're so beautiful* over and over again. He seemed cool and confident, but he couldn't quite hide the stink of desperation.

"Let me guess," Sam said. "You didn't just show up here yesterday, right? They sent you because you know what to look for, and you *have* been looking. You didn't find shit, right?"

Sonny said nothing, but some of that know-it-all smirk faded.

Ramiro's eyes flicked from Sam to Sonny and back again.

"You need us," Sam said. "We don't need you. You want the location. If you could find it on your own, you would have already, because I know you tried."

He rubbed at his silver bracelet. Sam noticed it had a swastika on it. A black man with a swastika?

"I've found lots of stuff over the years," Sonny said. "You two seem like nice enough kids, so let me clue you in—we'll find the tunnel entrance eventually. We want to find it sooner, rather than later. We're willing to pay for that privilege."

Ramiro's cell phone buzzed. He glanced at it, absently, tapped the screen.

Again, his eyebrows rose.

"Sam, take a look at this," he said.

Ramiro slid the cell phone—facedown—across the table.

She picked it up. An email, from Melissa Askew, Vice President of Development at U of M.

SUBJECT: New donation offer, contact me ASAP
TO: Ramiro Chus

Ramiro,

We just received amazing news. A donor, who wishes to remain anonymous at this time, has generously offered a $1 million grant to continue Professor Reeves's research.

I handled this call myself. The offer comes with minor contingencies. The donor requires more information than Professor Reeves was willing to give, but I assured the donor that, with Samira taking over the project, we would be able to work out all the details.

I know you and Samira are on-site. Please contact me as soon as possible so we can coordinate the details. This is a fantastic turn of events for your research and the university.

Sincerely,
Melissa

———————

Melissa Askew
Vice President for Development, Office of the Vice President for Development

Sam read it again.

"Check your email later," Sonny said. "Let's talk turkey."

Sam put the phone facedown, slid it back to Ramiro. She sagged back in her chair.

"So you're going to help us out," she said to Sonny. "How you going to do that? A donation to the university?"

"If that's how you want it," Sonny said. "I've got a great track record for that. You can check my bona fides with Brigham Young's archaeology department. Ask for Hector Rodriguez, he'll vouch for me."

BYU. Where Sanji Haak had worked. Veronica's dad, who was just as *dead or missing* as Veronica was. Because he'd been at the EarthCore camp alongside her.

Working with Sonny McGuiness.

"We don't gotta go that route if you don't want to," McGuiness said. "You want a donation? We make a donation. You want it off the books? We do it off the books."

Sam glanced at Ramiro. He met her eyes, gave his head the slightest shake. She didn't need to hear him say it to know he agreed with her — the million-dollar offer hadn't come from EarthCore.

In the span of ten minutes, she'd gone from no chance at funding to *two* sources. It should have elated her. It should have had her jumping up on the table and dancing a jig. But she felt the exact opposite, so instantly depressed it was all she could do to keep from falling out of the chair.

EarthCore knew about the platinum.

And so, too, did some other mining company.

Ramiro had said it was over. He was right.

Somehow, word had gotten out about the platinum. If the relics of that ancient culture were to be preserved, there was only one answer—walk away from it. Forever.

"Unfortunately, Mister McGuiness, your timing sucks," she said. "Ramiro and I are all done here. We were just making plans to head home, weren't we, Ram?"

Ramiro nodded. "We were. Can't wait to get back home. Tourist season around here, you know. Too crowded, takes all the charm out it."

He was back on her side, at least for now. She would have some apologizing to do later, *genuine* apologizing for making the wrong choice, but he was putting their friendship above her mistake. That was Ramiro—when he stood by your side, nothing could move him.

Sonny glared at Ramiro, then her.

"You're making a mistake," he said. "Don't be a couple of dumbasses."

Sam shrugged. "Not as big a mistake as you'll make looking for whatever you think it is you'll find here. It's a big mountain. Isn't it a big mountain, Ram?"

"*Really* fucking big," Ramiro said.

Sam sat up straight, banishing her sadness. The game had changed. It wasn't about her anymore, it was about the find, about preserving the few remnants of the Chaltélian culture. It was about *history*.

"McGuiness, do yourself a favor and go home," Sam said. "Or keep looking and die in the mountains, for all I care."

McGuiness seemed to take it all in. He'd tried to play Ramiro against her, and he'd failed. She almost saw the thoughts ripping through his mind as he fished for a way to get what he wanted. To his credit, he didn't take long.

"Fine, fuck it," he said. "You win. You two seem like smart kids, so I'm guessing you take a sat-phone into the field with you?"

Ramiro nodded.

Sonny reached into a side pocket of his cargo pants, pulled out a business card. He set the card on the table. It was white, plain save for a fifteen-digit number.

"Keep this," he said. "It's not just about the platinum. You say you're done, and to be honest, I hope you're telling the truth. If you're lying and you go back there, if you find a way to go deeper into the tunnels, there's things down there—" he paused, seemed to search for the right words "—there's dangers you can't know. If you go back and see something you can't explain, call that number. If you get into trouble, of any kind, call that number. Yeah, the people I work for want to make money. I want to make money. But no one wants to see the two of you get hurt. Or worse."

Sam could get emotional whiplash from talking to this guy. In a blink, he'd gone from a know-it-all who thought he could push her buttons to genuinely concerned for her safety, for Ramiro's safety. McGuiness wasn't acting. He was … scared for them.

"I told you we're not going back," she said. "So take your super-spy tracking device and shove it up your ass."

Sonny laughed, shook his head. "It's just paper."

Sam smiled at him. "Sure it is."

"Then write down the number," Sonny said. "Please."

That sincerity again.

Ramiro sensed it, too.

"Just write it down, Sam," he said. "Then McGuiness will leave. Isn't that right, Mister McGuiness?"

McGuiness looked at Ramiro, then glanced over his shoulder, saw that Alfonz and Luciero were looking at him. The two men grinned, raised their bottles toward McGuiness.

"Yeah," he said. "Then I'll leave."

She pushed down the feeling that it was somehow a small victory for Sonny. She pulled her notebook from her back pocket and wrote down the number.

Sonny stood. He drained his beer, set the empty bottle on the table.

"Stay safe," he said. "We're here if you change your mind."

With that, Sonny McGuiness walked out of the Glaciares Bar.

"Good riddance," Sam said.

Ramiro stood. "Let's get out of here. You and I need to have a talk."

That sinking sensation again, but there was nothing to do about it other than face the music.

I should have told him.

18

October 16

TIM FEELY UNWRAPPED the roll of Extra Strength Tums, let the tablets drop onto his desk. He took half of them and made a neat stack that he set aside.

The rest, he scooped up and popped into his mouth.

Too many incidents to deal with. Another round of missing persons in Georgia. Were they runaways? Good old-fashioned side-of-the-road murders? Was a serial killer at work, possibly? As awful as it was to do so, he prayed for such things—and he was an atheist. He prayed for something normal, something rational, because if it wasn't any of those things, Occam's Razor pointed its sharp edge to the obvious answer: *Swinestine*.

"Such a stupid nickname," he said. "Way to go, Feely."

Of course it had been him to label the mythical wild boar. He was all about the cute and clever sayings, wasn't he? He'd used the name *Swinestine* trying to be funny. It stuck. Everyone in DST used it.

Smart pigs. Smart pigs killing people. If that didn't give a director heartburn, what would?

P.J. Colding was leading the investigation. He and Tim had been through some serious shit together. Colding was one of Tim's first hires for DST. Hopefully, Colding and his partner for the case—DST's newest hire, a woman named Lianna Wilkerson—could find more info about the beasts.

Tim's desk phone buzzed: Mike wanted him. Tim answered.

"Yeah?"

"Vogel is on line two," Mike said. "You want to take it, or do you want me to make something up?"

Make something up? That was exactly what Tim wanted Mike to do. But maybe Vogel had more info on Utah. Other than assigning people to do a deep dive on EarthCore, Tim hadn't found anything. So far, Incident Forty-Three was a big ol' *non*-incident.

"I'll take it," Tim said.

He punched the button for line two.

"Hello, Director Vogel. No personal visit this time? This isn't a long-distance dump, is it? I'm not sure my tender heart can take the drama."

"You and I are still an item," Vogel said. "So hard to keep you off my mind, Director Feely."

"How can I be of service today?"

"It's about your old boss," Vogel said. "The man who used to hold your job."

Murray Longworth. Tim hadn't thought much about the man in the last few months. When Tim had first taken over as DST director, he'd called Murray repeatedly, looking for guidance on managing the department, advice on how to navigate the internecine complexities and cutthroat politics of Washington. Murray had been helpful at first. After four or five months of taking three, sometimes four calls a day from Tim, though, Murray had cut the net and allowed Tim to flourish or crash on his own. Murray had made this clear to Tim when several desperate calls for help were answered with the simple phrase: *Fuck you, I'm fishing.*

"What's up with Longworth? He dead?"

"Still very much alive," Vogel said. "And he's been a busy boy. He contacted people still active in multiple departments. Including *my* department. He wanted info on a team of people that did work for him in a position he had before he ran the DST, even before his stint as CIA deputy director."

Murray hadn't told Tim much about his pre-DST life.

"And what position was that?"

"Know how you like to joke that the DST barely exists at all?"

Tim had a sinking feeling.

"Yes."

"Longworth's old outfit *doesn't* exist," Vogel said. "Then, or now. They were what you might call an *outsourced* unit of the CIA's Special Operations Group. The people he had working for him were serious business."

"What kind of business?"

"The *enemies of the state* business. The *cut them off* business."

Tim had a sinking feeling that his shit life was about to become a whole lot shittier.

"Did Murray get the info he was looking for?"

"He did," Vogel said. "He called in some pretty high-level markers to get it. As for who gave him that info, I will deal with that at a later time. What matters now is that the leader of this team was a man named Patrick O'Doyle."

O'Doyle. The bad motherfucker with the burned-off ear. Tim had met him, once, in a very dark time. Monsters were scary things—something Tim knew firsthand—but O'Doyle was scarier.

"O'Doyle used to work for DST," Tim said. "When Longworth ran it, back before the first big round of budget cuts."

"I'm aware. Guess who O'Doyle works for now?"

"The Lollipop Guild?"

"Very close," Vogel said. "O'Doyle works for EarthCore."

So now Murray Longworth was directly involved with Incident Forty-Three. No, Tim's life hadn't gotten shittier: it had become a full-blown diarrhea splatter.

"Normally, I'd take this up with Murray personally," Vogel said. "He and I have a history. But since I already dumped this gem of a situation in your lap, I'll leave it up to you to decide. Do you want to talk to him first, or shall I?"

Tim realized something, something he realized maybe five times on a daily basis — being a director *sucked*.

"I'm on it. Thank you for the info."

"You're welcome, Director Feely. May I rely on you to get back to me when you find out what's going on?"

Tim nodded. "Like you said, handsome. We're still an item."

He hung up. More Tums … he was definitely going to need more Tums.

TOMMY LEFT THE passenger area and headed into baggage claim. He stopped, stared at the man in the black jacket holding up a tablet. On that tablet, a name:

THOMAS STRYMON III

He walked up to the man.

The man smiled. "Mister Strymon?"

Tommy nodded.

The driver looked Tommy up and down, a fast flick that took in Tommy's combat boots, jeans, tattered hoodie sweatshirt and the small gym bag slung over his shoulder.

"Any checked baggage, Mister Strymon?"

"Call me *Tommy*."

"Sure thing, Tommy." The driver offered his hand. "I'm Bill."

They shook. The awkwardness faded, just a bit; they were two working-class guys, not a driver and some rich asshole.

"I didn't check a bag."

"I'll take you to the meeting," Bill said. He nodded toward Tommy's gym bag. "Can I carry that for you?"

Tommy inadvertently hugged it tighter to himself, realized he was doing it, and felt awkward all over again.

"I got it."

"All right," Bill said. "The car is this way."

NOT A CAR, a *limo*. Twenty grand and a limo ride. The people Harvey Dillinger worked for liked to roll out the red carpet. All this just to hear a pitch? Tommy could only imagine how much the actual job might pay.

Which didn't matter, because nothing could make him go back to that life. Not that he could go back, anyway—the agency with no name would find out if he was doing merc work and would put him in the dirt for it.

He looked out the window as the limo exited the airport. The faint glow of the coming sun brushed the distant horizon with pale orange and yellow.

"Hey, Bill? Why the hell is there a giant blue horse with glowing red demon eyes guarding the airport?"

"That's Blucifer," the driver called back. "Thirty-two feet tall. Did you know the guy who designed it got killed when a piece fell off and smashed him?"

Tommy stared at the sculpture. It looked like something out of one of his less-than-prestigious sci-fi reads.

"And, *why*, exactly, would the airport administrators put up a giant blue demon horse?"

"Because important people are fucked up people," Bill said. "Pardon my language."

"Don't worry about language around me. How long will the drive take?"

"About a half an hour. Helluva view of the mountains on the way in."

Mountains. Tommy stared down, at the toes of his boots, focusing on *not* focusing on the mountains in the distance. How many people had he killed in the mountains?

He needed to get his mind off of that, fast, before the memories pressed in.

"I'm going to read for a bit," Tommy said. "Cool?"

"Cool with me, Tommy. You want any music?"

Tommy shook his head. "I prefer silence, thanks."

He opened his duffel bag and moved aside his change of clothes (socks and underwear rolled up in a T-shirt, since jeans and the hoodie were wearable the next day). Beneath the clothes, his mental therapy for the trip: paperback books.

He'd finished *Dune* on the plane ride.

"Bill, you got a pen?"

"Look in the passenger-side door, down at the bottom in the plastic thingy."

Tommy did. Sure enough, a pen and a small pad of paper. He took the pen, opened *Dune*. On the inside cover, a neat list of fifteen dates: month/day/year. He added that day's date to mark his sixteenth read, then put the book aside.

Next up? He scanned the books he'd brought with him: *Dragonflight*, *A Canticle for Leibowitz*, *The Moon Is a Harsh Mistress*, *Nexus*, *Sandman Slim*, *The Call of the Wild*, *Relic*, and *Lord of the Flies*.

Lord of the Flies would make him think of war, as would *The Moon Is a Harsh Mistress*. Thinking about thinking about war made him, unsurprisingly, think of war.

The memories were burbling up, threatening to engulf him.

"Dragons," he said, quietly.

"Pardon me?"

"Sorry, I was talking to myself. I'll just chill here until we get to wherever you're taking me."

Tommy opened *Dragonflight* and let Anne McCaffrey's words take him away to another world.

A world where he hadn't killed anyone.

LESSA WAS RAMOTH'S *and Ramoth was hers, mind and heart, irrevocably attuned. Only death could dissolve that incredible bond.*

Tommy read for the entire ride. He didn't look up until the limo slowed to a stop.

"We're here, Tommy."

Tommy put his bookmark in the page — no dog-ears, thank you very much, and he *never* cracked a spine — then got out of the limo. An industrial park. Many cars in the lot, including three other limos. He kept his eyes mostly down so as not to get a good look at the mountain range in the distance.

Bill walked to a glass door, painted with a logo for *Titan Drilling*. He opened it, held it.

"Have a good meeting," he said. "I was told to wait for you here in case you need a ride back to the airport."

Tommy wondered if he should just get back in the limo, right now. Blood money was blood money even if you had yet to spill any blood. People didn't pay guys like Tommy unless some bad shit was going to go down.

But *twenty thousand dollars…*

It wasn't like he'd actually take the job. He would do the meeting, get the check signed, and go home.

Easy peasy puddin' pie.

"Thanks," Tommy said. "I won't be long."

Tommy entered. A typical industrial office. Clean, well-appointed but spartan, no money wasted on expensive furniture. *Sterile*, was the word. Large photos on the wall showing men in dirty coveralls working on what Tommy assumed to be drills, a few images of men in button-down shirts, ties and hard hats slumming it up with the greased-up grunts.

"Good morning, Mister Strymon." The receptionist seemed to fit the decor: nondescript, businesslike, probably efficient as hell.

"Good morning," Tommy said.

"They're waiting for you in the conference room. Can I get you a coffee?"

Tommy glanced back at the glass door. Bill was right outside, waiting with the limo.

Not too late to bail…

No, there was no point in leaving now.

"A coffee would be great. Thanks. Uh…what's this meeting about, anyhow?"

The receptionist smiled. "I'm sure they'll tell you shortly, Mister Strymon. Let me show you the way."

THE RECEPTIONIST PULLED open the door to the conference room, held it. Styrofoam coffee cup in hand, gym bag slung over his shoulder, Tommy stepped inside—he stopped cold as a time-warp vision hit him like a head-on collision.

Five people sitting at a conference table: four men, one woman. Their faces, older than before, yet the same age as he'd last seen them, because they were locked in his memories. As timeless as…

…as timeless as mountains.

At the sight of Tommy, all five faces lit up.

"*Worm!*"

They said it in a chorus, as if he was a sitcom regular walking into his favorite bar. He hadn't been called that name in twenty years.

Tommy hadn't known exactly what to expect, but he'd never expected this. These people had been with him when he'd travelled the world. He'd fought alongside them. Bled with them. *Killed* with them.

Kevin "Mullet" Bliss stood first, strode toward Tommy. Kevin still had his movie-star looks: the cheekbones, the cleft chin, the sandy-brown hair cut in what had to be the latest style. Women loved him. Tommy had often wondered if those women had any idea of how many lives Kevin Bliss had taken, any idea of the man's capacity for cruelty. If they had known, maybe they would have wanted him even more — but when it came to a guy who looked like Kevin, women ignored principles and warning signs. When it came to a guy who looked like Kevin, women were dumb as fuck.

"Tommy," Kevin said, smiling wide, shaking his head in amazement. "Seriously, you guys, am I imagining this? Is the Bookworm in the house?"

Kevin hugged Tommy tight. Tommy hugged him back, simultaneously elated to see his old friend and repulsed at the sight of him.

"Good to see you, Kev," Tommy said.

No sooner had Kevin let go then Tommy was battered and rattled by slaps on the shoulders and back — the four syncopated hands of two men that did, and *said*, everything together.

"*Tom-dog!*" Anders Keeley said.

"*Dog-man!*" Carson Wampler said.

How different they looked, and yet they still looked the same. Anders, a.k.a. "Curveball," had gained a good twenty pounds. Same shaved head, same shiny dark skin, but his thick black beard had gone gray. His eyes, though, still showed the same gleam they had a decade ago — the constant danger and brutality hadn't got to him back then, didn't seem to haunt him now.

Carson "Hatchet" Wampler's thin red hair was in the process of abandoning him, making a beeline for the back of his head. He combed some of that remaining hair straight forward. Was he trying to fool everyone else into thinking he wasn't balding, or just trying to fool himself? Hatchet's eyes hadn't changed much, either; charming and delighted to anyone who met him for the first time, but if you knew him, like Tommy did, you could see the ghosts of Hatchet's regrets, the vacant echoes of the comrades he'd lost. He always had rings around those eyes, no matter how much sleep he got.

"Curveball, Hatchet," Tommy said. "You guys are still together?"

"Yeah, we are." Hatchet's Staten Island accent hadn't changed, either. "You surprised or something? Didn't think the homos could tough it out? Something like that?"

"You're just as laid-back as ever, I see," Tommy said. "I was going to say *that's great, I'm happy for you*, but you kind of ruined it."

Anders shook his head. "Hatchet has a tendency to do that."

"Fuck you both," Carson said.

Anders pulled Tommy in for a hug. So good to see this man again, to see everyone again.

"Seriously," Tommy said, "I'm happy you guys are still a thing. Twenty years is a long time. What are you guys doing now?"

"We own a cake shop," Carson said.

Tommy blinked. "A *cake* shop? As in, a bakery?"

"That's right," Anders said.

"Isn't that a little … uh …"

Carson held up a fist. "If you say *that's a little gay*, I will lay you out, happy reunion or not."

Tommy laughed. "I was going to say *on the nose*, but I guess that's the same difference. A cake shop. You two, successful businessmen? Amazing."

"We *own* a cake shop," Carson said. Lights gleamed off his too-white head. "We didn't say we were good at running one."

"Step aside, boys. I got to say hello to the greatest marksman of all time."

Anders and Carson did as they were told; Marie Dunlop stepped in. She took both of Tommy's hands in hers, smiled up at him.

"Never thought I'd see you again, Thomas."

Tommy fought back instant tears. The last time he'd seen this woman, he'd taken a bullet in the gut. He'd been bleeding out—Marie Dunlop had saved his life.

"Skylark," he said. "I ... I ..."

Marie stood on tiptoes and kissed Tommy's cheek.

"I am glad you're alive," she said, then returned to her chair.

Only one person remained seated—Doug Rapson. Tommy almost didn't recognize him. Brown hair now bleach-blond, fatigues traded in for an immaculate white suit, purple silk shirt, purple tie. Weapons replaced by jewelry: gold tie-tack, two large gold rings, and a gold watch with a purple face. Tommy knew, somehow, that beneath the table Doug was wearing white shoes and purple socks.

"Hey, Sleepy," Tommy said. "It's been a long time."

"I go by *Reverend Rapson* now, Tommy."

Kevin rolled his eyes. "Watch out, Worm. Doug-E-Doug got hisself some religion."

"You look good, Reverend Rapson," Tommy said.

"And you look like a hobo," Doug said. "I'll say a prayer for you. Perhaps your fortunes will change."

Maybe it was an insult, maybe it was a joke. Tommy didn't care. These people, the *NoSeeUms* ... he'd been through so much with them.

"This is hard to process," he said. "I haven't seen any of you since ... since ..."

"Since Bandah," Anders said.

Tommy closed his eyes. Images of that day came flooding back. A village in the middle of nowhere. The shooting. The flames. Landslide's blood all over the place. That girl, Tommy sliding the knife into her belly, the look on her face ...

An arm around his shoulders, squeezing tight.

"It's in the past, Tommy," Kevin said. "We survived, right?"

Tommy nodded. Not for the first time, he wished it had been him that died that day, not Landslide, not the girl.

"Glad to see you remember it, Worm," Doug said. "That's where you went psycho on us."

Kevin glared at Doug. "Back off, Sleepy. No need to bring that up."

"I'll bring up *everything*," Doug said. "You were all psychos that day. All of you."

Marie crossed her arms, raised her left eyebrow—the lecturing schoolteacher look Tommy had seen more times than he could count.

"*All* being the key word," she said to Doug. "Or do you somehow think you're clean of that blood?"

Kevin leaned his fists on the conference table. "Yeah, Sleepy. I watched you literally *scalp* a guy."

Anders nodded. "Which was fucking *awesome*."

Carson nodded. "Totally badass, if you ask me."

Doug slowly stood. He smoothed the lapels of his white coat, hands automatically making sure his clothes were properly arranged, unwrinkled. He stared at everyone in turn, not backing down for an instant. Some things, it seemed, never changed.

"*If we confess our sins, he is faithful and just to forgive us our sins, and to cleanse us from all unrighteousness.*" Doug scowled at Kevin. "I've confessed my sins, Mullet—have you?"

Kevin returned to his seat. "For fuck's sake, Sleepy. You of all people, a Bible-thumper?"

"Please call me *Reverend Rapson.*"

Kevin waved a hand. "In your fucking dreams, pastor douchebag."

"Hey," Tommy said, "is El Gato coming?"

Marie shook her head. "Shot himself three years back."

"Felix is dead?" Tommy had barely thought of the man in years, yet the news hit hard. "I didn't know."

"Not like you kept in touch with us," Doug said. "but I suppose it's hard to reach out from a jail cell."

Kevin half stood, one hand on the tabletop, one finger pointing. "Sleepy, you run that sucking-Je-*eee*-sus-cock-mouth one more time and I will pimp-slap you into the middle of next week."

Doug sneered. "You think my being a man of God doesn't mean I won't put you on your ass, Mullet?"

"A hundo on Doug," Curveball said.

"I'll take that action," Hatchet said. "Mullet will whoop him."

Marie sighed, rubbed at her temples. "It's like you idiots haven't aged a day."

Tommy couldn't believe it—Felix "El Gato" Bereda, dead. The man had loved to rap, even though he was terrible at it. He'd adored breakfast cereal. Trix was his favorite, Lucky Charms a close second.

He was *gone.*

Which made Tommy afraid to ask the next question.

"Then there's only one of us missing," he said. "Is he…he…"

"I'm right here."

Tommy turned. There, in the door, stood the blocky form of Patrick O'Doyle. Black jeans. A black belt with a knife pouch and holstered sidearm attached. Long-sleeved black shirt with the *Titan Drilling* logo above the left breast.

"Ender," Tommy said.

O'Doyle smiled. "Worm."

They embraced. Tommy felt years of his life melt away as he momentarily slipped back in time to when he'd known who he was, what he had to do. When he'd *always* been in the right. And, simultaneously, to the time when a part of him knew everything he was doing, everything they asked him to do, was wrong. Back to when they'd lost Snowflake. When they'd lost Gomer. Through all those times, the good and the bad, Ender had been the team's rock.

Right up until he hadn't been—when they'd lost Landslide, Knuckles and Swampy.

He thumped Tommy on the back, then held him at arm's length.

"So good to see you, Worm."

Tommy said nothing for fear he might start crying.

"Have a seat," Ender said. "Let's get started."

Tommy knew that if he sat, if he listened, Ender might talk him into being a part of whatever this was. He glanced around the table, at these people he loved, at these people he hated. They were all killers. You gathered killers together to do one thing and one thing only—to kill.

"I should go," he said quietly.

Patrick gestured to an open chair next to Marie.

"Twenty grand just to sit and listen," he said.

Tommy shook his head. "Like I told your guy, I'm done killing people."

Doug lightly thumped a fist on the table. "Good for you, Tommy."

"You won't be killing *people*," Patrick said.

What the hell did that mean?

Ender looked Tommy up and down. Was that understanding in his eyes, or was it pity?

"No offense, Worm," he said, "but from the looks of things, seems like that twenty thou is something you could use. All you have to do is listen. If you don't like what you hear, then you can go."

Everyone waited for Tommy to decide.

All he had to do was listen. What could that hurt?

Tommy took the seat next to Marie. He held his duffel bag on his lap. She put her hand on his shoulder. It felt comforting.

Ender nodded to someone out in the hall.

"You've all met Harvey," he said. "And this is Bertha Lybrand, my wife."

Tommy's eyes shot to Patrick's hand, noticed the silver ring on his left index finger.

Harvey Dillinger walked into the meeting room. He wore a brown suit similar to the one he'd worn at the diner, although his new fashion accessory—a purple bruise running across his neck—made Tommy's face flush hot.

Dillinger was followed by a heavyset brunette wearing the same black shirt/jeans/sidearm combo as Patrick. A scar ran from above her left eye, across her nose, to the right corner of her mouth. Looked like stitches from closing up that wound had been removed quite recently. The pinkie and ring finger of her left hand were nothing but scarred stubs.

"Heya, Harvey," Mullet said. "You run into a clothesline or something?"

"Yes, Mister Bliss, after I met with you I retired to my country estate and wasn't being particularly careful when I chased the laundry wench about the grounds."

Harvey winked at Tommy, then sat. Bertha sat as well.

Patrick remained standing.

"Bertha served two tours in Afghanistan," he said. "She was on staff for the project that led to you sitting here. I know you've all seen the shit—I was there with you for most of it—but she's seen things that would make even *your* heads spin. She stayed cool. She delivered. She's as good an operator as any of you. Understand?"

Around the table, everyone briefly studied Bertha Lybrand, then nodded. Tommy did the same. Bertha seemed uncomfortable with the attention, but she kept her back straight and met everyone's gaze in turn.

Ender's body had changed. He'd gained a few pounds, his blond buzz cut had thinned a bit, but his words, as always, carried serious weight. He vouched for Lybrand. Did he think she could operate alongside the NoSeeUms, a group that had worked together so well for so long? Probably not. Maybe Bertha's *part of the project* meant administrative duties, or backside support.

Not that her role really mattered to Tommy—he wasn't taking this gig.

Kevin leaned back and put his worn brown cowboy boots up on the table.

"So, you've got a choice mission," he said. "Can't wait to hear what you've got in store for a bunch of old farts like us. I mean, what's our average age? Forty-five?"

"Forty-four years, three months, six days," Tommy said. The words came out without him thinking.

Curveball elbow-nudged Hatchet.

"Tommy and that numbers shit," Curveball said.

Hatchet nodded once. "Still trippy."

Sleepy—*Reverend Rapson*—pushed his chair far enough back from the table that he could cross his right leg over his left—yep: white shoes, purple socks.

"Ender," he said, "at the risk of taking the lord's name in vain, could you get to the goddamned point? What did you bring us all here for?"

Marie sighed, shook her head. "You always were an asshole, Sleepy."

Ender crossed his thick arms. Brow furrowed, he stared down at the center of the table. Tommy felt like he'd stepped back in time—Patrick "Ender" O'Doyle was trying to parse the information that he had, trying to ascertain what he could and could not tell his team. Even now, in the private sector (at least Tommy assumed this was a private-sector enterprise), the ever-present *need to know* reared its ugly head.

"I can't tell you everything," Ender said. "Not yet."

"Color me surprised," Sleepy said.

Bertha Lybrand leaned forward.

"You got a mouth on you," she said to Sleepy. "How about you keep your mouth shut and let Patrick talk?"

Sleepy stared at her, then he smiled. That smile made Tommy's skin crawl. He'd seen that particular smile too many times.

Like in Afghanistan … and that awful summer in Venezuela …

"Bertha," Patrick said, "I'll handle this."

She glanced up at him, annoyed, then leaned back in her chair, arms crossed.

"The job is in the Patagonian region of the Andes mountains," Patrick said. "Near the border between Argentina and Chile."

"Those countries have dictators?" Kevin grinned. "Been a damn long time since we took out a dictator."

"You mean *murdered*," Sleepy said. "The verb is *murdered*, and the subject is *sovereign leader of a foreign nation*."

"The subject is actually the pronoun *we*," Tommy said. "*Sovereign leader* is the object, and—"

Patrick again held up a hand. Tommy fell silent.

"We can argue grammar later," Patrick said. "We're not taking out a dictator. Think of this as a ..." he crossed his arms, thought, again wondering what he could and could not say "... think of this as a geological recon expedition."

Curveball laughed. "Then I guess we better go back to school. Need to get our geology degree."

"We'll take night classes," Hatchet said, nodding. "Be all you can be, right?"

Marie rested her elbows on the table, laced her fingers together.

"We're not geologists," she said. "We were killers. We were good at killing."

"We were also good at infiltrating foreign nations," Patrick said. "We were exceptional at getting in fast and silent."

Kevin raised his pointer finger. "*Used* to be good. It's been years, man. We'd be rusty as hell."

"Like riding a bike," Curveball said.

"Some things you don't forget," Hatchet said.

Patrick pulled out his chair and sat. He looked around the table, slowly, making sure everyone knew the time for joking was over.

"What I am about to tell you doesn't leave this room."

Doug huffed. "Come on, Ender, you going to make us sign an NDA or something?"

Bertha turned to Patrick. "Why do they keep calling you *Ender*?"

The question clearly caught him off guard.

"I haven't been called that name in a long time." He looked at each of the NoSeeUms in turn. "I'd appreciate it if you'd all stop calling me that."

"A rose by any other name," Doug said. "Or to put it another way, a skunk can't change its stripes."

Kevin threw up his hands. "Jesus *Christ*, Reverend Fuck-Wit. I appreciate that you scored some great threads at the estate sale of the Artist Formerly Known as Prince, but that doesn't mean you get to be a walking jackass."

"Yeah, Sleepy," Hatchet said, "you look like a real *thriller*."

"Michael Jackson was *Thriller*," Curveball said. "Prince was Purple Rain."

Hatchet rubbed a hand over his almost-not-there red hair, shrugged. "All you black guys look the same."

"Not sure M.J. was actually *black*," Curveball said.

Harvey straightened up in his chair, cleared his throat.

"Patrick, while this gathering of old pals warms the cockles of my jaded heart, we should get down to business."

Ender nodded. His jaw muscles twitched. Not a good sign.

"Mister Dillinger is right," he said. "If you could all do me the favor of shutting your traps for five minutes, we'll get this done. Acceptable?"

He looked around the table. Everyone nodded. Even Doug.

"No NDA," Ender said. "No signing of anything, because what we're about to do isn't actually happening."

Marie sighed, slid deeper into her chair. "Just like old times."

Ender laughed, a single *humph* that snuck out of him before he could throttle it down.

"Good point," he said. "Here's the deal. I'm trusting all of you. What I say stays between us. You talk about it—to anyone—and that means you betrayed my trust. That means you are my enemy."

A chill washed through Tommy. A thick tar of tension filled the room, instantly spreading to every corner, filling up every available space. Everyone fell quiet.

Bertha clearly sensed this. She glanced at her husband, not understanding the reaction his words generated. Apparently, there was plenty that Ender hadn't shared with his bride.

Kevin raised a hand.

Ender nodded at him.

"Your *enemy*," Kevin said. "Can we assume that means what it used to mean?"

Ender nodded again.

Kevin put his hand down. "Well, then. Feel free to assume that I will keep said trap shut."

Curveball mimicked locking his mouth and throwing away the key.

Hatchet pointed to Curve. "That means he ain't talking."

"We know what it means," Marie said.

Hatchet grinned at her. "Jokes are funnier when I explain them."

Patrick waited to see if anyone else responded. No one did.

"Here's the situation. Titan Drilling is a subsidiary of EarthCore, a mining company."

"EarthCore," Kevin said. "Is that the company that caused that volcano in Utah?"

Harvey looked at his fingernails. He seemed very bored with the affair.

"The volcano was a tragic act of God," Ender said. "The company didn't *cause* anything."

Carson looked at Ender, jerked his thumb toward Harvey.

"We all came to your dance party, Ender, so why do we still need numbnuts?"

Harvey switched to examining his other hand, on the hunt for even a speck of dirt beneath his French manicure.

"I'm the guy who signs the checks," he said. "That a good enough reason?"

Kevin raised his hand, and this time he spoke without waiting to be called upon.

"Mister Dillinger, may I, for one, communicate what a fine job you've done bringing us together?"

Curveball laughed, clapped. "Damn, Mullet, how I've missed watching you kiss ass."

Kevin grinned his movie-star grin, leaned back in his chair, and again put his boots up on the table.

"I try, Curve," he said. "I do so try."

Sleepy slammed a fist on the table, making Tommy jump.

"Enough with this shit," the reverend said. "Get to the *point*, Ender.

Tell us some pretty story about how you brought a team of assassins together for some noble cause."

Ender stared at Doug. Doug stared at Ender. The room grew tense.

"Fair enough," Ender said. "I told you the target zone is near the border between Argentina and Chile. To be more accurate, the entire border area is disputed."

"*Disputed*," Marie said. "Countries still dispute borders?"

"Yes, and it complicates things," Patrick said. "Which is the first reason why our team is ideal for the job. We've infiltrated far more difficult places."

"Sure we did," Hatchet said, "when Uncle Sam paid the bill."

"Black is beautiful," Curveball said. "As are black budgets."

Harvey brushed at his jacket lapel, spoke without looking up.

"Uncle Sam isn't involved, but your Uncle Harvey is."

Tommy didn't like Dillinger. He was the kind of man who had no problem sending people to do dangerous work, when he himself had probably never been in real danger for even a moment in his entire life—except for getting randomly choked when delivering a check, perhaps.

"We're looking for a tunnel system," Patrick said. "We don't have the exact location, but we're working on that. If we find it, most of our work will be below ground."

"Gold in them thar hills?" Kevin asked.

"Something like that," Patrick said. "We suspect the tunnel entrance is likely high up a mountain. Even if the governments of Chile or Argentina find out about it, they don't have the equipment or expertise to go in."

"And you do," Sleepy said. "How convenient."

Bertha shook her head. "We work for a mining company, dipshit, so yeah, we do."

Harvey finally looked up from his nails. He smiled at Patrick.

"So sorry, Mister O'Doyle, but I have other tasks that require my attention. May I expedite this situation?"

Patrick gestured an open hand to the table: *you have the floor.*

"Wonderful." Dillinger smiled brightly. "Anyone who signs on for this operation gets a quarter mil."

Kevin's boots came off the table and he leaned forward so fast his elbows hit the table at the same instant his feet hit the floor.

"Ex-squeeze me?" He squinted and cupped a hand to his ear. "Did the fine gentleman with the pretty nails say, *a quarter million?*"

Harvey nodded.

"*Dollars?*" Kevin said.

Harvey nodded again.

"*American* dollars?" Kevin said.

Harvey's lips pressed into a thin smile.

"I'd call you an idiot, Mister Bliss, but since you could probably murder me using only your pinkie, I won't actually call you that."

Kevin nodded. "Wise choice." He let out a long whistle. "A quarter mil."

"I'm in," Hatchet and Curveball said simultaneously.

Doug looked at them, his face wrinkling with disgust. "You morons don't even know what we're up against."

Curveball shrugged. "I give zero shits."

"And I give one less shit than he does," Hatchet said.

Curveball stroked his gray beard. "Would that make a *negative* shit?"

"I believe so," Hatchet said, nodding thoughtfully. "The precise formula equals *negative one shit.*"

Marie patted the table with both palms, just hard enough to command everyone's attention.

"Curve, Hatchet, I love you guys, but shut your oozing pie holes for five fucking minutes, okay?" She turned to Dillinger. "Sleepy had a valid point. What are we up against?"

Patrick answered. "I'll tell you only after you sign on. We're treating this as a military operation. I'm in command."

Kevin nodded. "Just like old times."

Tommy found himself nodding as well, more in acceptance of the situation than in understanding. Ender always said what he meant and meant what he said. Civilian or not, the parameters were clear—there would be no walking away unless Patrick O'Doyle himself ordered it.

"Two hundred and fifty thousand dollars," Reverend Sleepy said. "That should just about cover the nice funeral we're all going to have doing whatever illegal work Ender has lined up."

"Harvey," Ender said. "Tell them the rest."

Harvey hesitated. "That wasn't pre-approved."

Ender turned his cold stare on the man. "Tell them."

"Fine," Harvey said. "On top of the quarter-mil, each of you also gets two hundredths of a percent of the find's profits."

Kevin laughed, looked around the table to see if anyone else was laughing with him.

"*Two hundredths of a percent,*" he said. "That and five bucks is enough to buy a shitty cup of Starbucks, am I right?"

Harvey's smile returned, not quite as energetic as it had been before, but also not quite as fake as it had been before.

"We have estimates," he said. "We think the deposit's value is *at least* ten-point-two billion."

The number stunned the room into silence. Even Doug's hard expression eased.

Kevin raised his hand. "Ten-point-two billion *dollars?*"

Harvey grunted. "Mister Bliss, that schtick wasn't even funny the first time."

Marie pulled out a smart phone. "I got a calculator on here."

"Two million, forty thousand," Tommy said. "Each."

Marie set her phone flat on the table. She spoke slowly, evenly. "Mister Dillinger, if this deposit is worth *at least* ten-point-two billion, what's the high-end estimate?"

Harvey hissed through his teeth. This was the *real* Harvey, Tommy thought. The smiling, smooth-talking guy was a front. Deep down, Harvey was a control freak and didn't like being told what to do.

"O'Doyle," Harvey said, a singsong lilt to his voice, "are you sure you can trust these people?"

"With my life," Ender said instantly. "Give them the real number. Stop stalling, Harvey—didn't you say you had somewhere to be?"

The used Q-Tip rubbed his palms together, let out a cheek-puffing breath. Patrick had a way of subtly getting under someone's skin. When Ender wanted to, he could push anyone's buttons.

"Fine," Dillinger said. "We're estimating a high end of 520 billion."

All heads turned to Tommy.

"One hundred and four million dollars," he said.

"Each," Patrick said.

Kevin raised a hand. "*American* Dollars?"

"And I'm out," Harvey said, standing. "O'Doyle, you can handle the rest of this on your own."

Harvey left the office.

Bertha glanced at Kevin. "You always have that kind of effect on people?"

Kevin pressed his fingertips to his chest, opened his mouth in a shocked, *Why, I do declare!* pantomime.

Marie shook her head. Her eyes squinted as if she couldn't process what she'd just heard.

"No one pays that kind of money for a normal job," she said. "Just how dangerous is this, Ender?"

He hesitated before answering. "It could be the most dangerous job we've ever done."

A strobe light of memories flashed through Tommy's mind. Images of the assassinations, the recons, the car bombs, the sabotage. The screams of the wounded. The silence of the dead. He closed his eyes as if that would chase away the visions of blood, terror and pain … it did not.

No one asked Ender if he was serious. Ender did not joke about such things.

"We were a team of assassins," Doug said. He looked around the room, locking eyes with Kevin, then Tommy, then Marie. "He claims we won't have to kill people. You think he'd go through the trouble of tracking us down and bringing us here if he didn't want us to do what we used to do?"

Ender pointed to the door. "Your opt-out is right there, Reverend Rapson. The limo is waiting to take you back to the airport."

Hatchet pointed back and forth between himself and Curveball. "Did I mention we're in?"

"So am I," Marie said. "Know what I do for a living? I teach rich, white assholes how to fly helicopters. I'm tired of rich, white assholes."

"You'll be risking your life," Doug said to her. "You *know* that."

She smiled at him. "When we were in the NoSeeUms, my top-end pay was six grand a month. How many times did I risk my life for that much, Sleepy?"

Doug glanced down, considering. "Twenty. Maybe thirty."

"Twenty-nine," Tommy said. "If we count Columbia."

Marie spread her hands: *there you go.*

She looked to Ender. "If I die on the mission, what are my assurances that the money will go to my daughters?"

"Daughters," Tommy said. "You're a mom?"

"Three times over. My girls are seven, five, and two." She looked to Ender. "Well?"

"You can list beneficiaries in your contracts," he said. "If you go on the mission, the money is *yours*."

Marie nodded. "I'll check the contract language, but if it matches your promise, I'm good with that."

"Lots of money, or a living mother," Doug said. "I wonder which your children would prefer more?"

Marie rolled her eyes. "Who is this man who speaks to me as though I need his advice?"

Doug's jaw clenched. "Ender, you've always been straight with us. You say it's dangerous. We need to know more."

Sleepy's volume had dropped, as had his challenging anger. Like all of the team, there was more than one Doug. *This* Doug was the one Tommy remembered most, *liked* the most—the soft-spoken man who, during quiet times on missions, would quietly hum Beatles songs.

Patrick laced his fingers together, rested his hands on the conference table.

"For the last time, you don't get to know what this is about unless you're in. All the way in."

Kevin leaned back in his chair, put his hand behind his head. He looked so cool doing that. He always looked cool … except for when he looked psychotic.

"I tried to use a fake name to hire on with Academi," he said. "Yeah, I know that was dumb, but it didn't matter—fucking douchebags found out I was on the no-hire list, and that was that. So I worked as a mall cop. A fucking *mall cop*. Ten fucking years I did that. Then I busted a shoplifter, maybe a little too hard, and I got fired, so I gave up on the security biz. Know what I do now? I work at a used car lot. Know what I hate more than being a mall cop? Working at a used car lot. For two million, I can retire. For a *hundred* million? I can *really* retire."

Doug stood. He buttoned his white jacket, smoothed it, tugged twice at the hem.

"Listen to me, all of you. We're middle-aged. The stuff we used to do, we're not cut out for that anymore. Maybe we aren't all best pals, but we went through difficult times together, and I would rather see you all live to a ripe old age. Marie, are you *sure* you want to do this?"

She nodded. "I trust Ender. Big risk, big reward, and I'm a big girl."

"I'm a big girl, too," Curveball said.

"So am I," Hatchet said. He grabbed his pecs and shook them. "My titties are bigger than Skylark's, though."

Marie flipped him off.

Doug turned to Kevin. "Mullet, you really *need* that money?"

Kevin affected an expression of great concentration, made a show of counting out something on his fingers. He then looked at his hands like he'd just discovered something wondrous.

"The answer, Reverend Sleepy, is, yes, *I really need that money,*" Kevin said. "It's not just the money. My life is *boring*. I never thought I'd miss our old job, but I do. I miss it bad. No one will hire me as a merc. If I can do one more run with y'all? Shit, I'd probably do it for free—the money is gravy." He smiled wide, looked up at the ceiling. "Thick, steamy, *delicious* gravy."

Tommy glanced at Ender. The team's former leader sat there, back straight, patiently waiting for his people to make their decisions.

When Tommy turned back to Doug, he found Doug staring straight at him, eyes burning with an intensity that would be right at home in a revival tent.

"And you, Bookworm? You said you don't want to kill people. You think you're here because you're well-read? You were invited here because you can put a bullet through a playing card at a thousand meters. I'm telling you right now—you do this mission, and you *will* kill people, no matter what Ender is telling you. Money like this always comes at a price."

Tommy knew that. It didn't seem possible to get millions of dollars—perhaps a *hundred* million dollars—without taking people out.

But so much money. Life-changing money.

"I … I wash dishes for a living," he said. "I spent some time in jail. I killed a guy in a bar fight. I didn't mean to do it, it just … it just …"

Tommy could still feel the man's neck under his hands, still feel the crunch of the windpipe, still see the man's shocked expression.

An argument over a spilled beer. An argument that put one man away for seven years, took away all the years the other man would ever have.

So many days and nights in that Allenwood cell, days and nights where Tommy had sworn to himself that he'd never kill again. Even when he was fighting other inmates, establishing that he was not to be fucked with, Tommy had gone easy on them, making sure to avoid lethal force.

So many ghosts in his past. So many faces of the dead. He couldn't handle adding more faces to that endless parade. He couldn't.

Tommy locked eyes with Patrick.

"Why *us*, Ender? With this kind of money, you could get real operators. Not a flight instructor, a dishwasher, a used car salesman, a couple of bakers and a born-again preacher. Why *us*?"

Ender looked around the room, studying each person for one more moment, but it was clear he already knew his answer.

"Because I can trust all of you," he said. "I know that if you give me your word, you'll keep it. The money we're talking is massive, so it should come as no surprise that there's nothing other companies wouldn't do to know what we know. I can hire active operators and teams, sure, but can I count on them to keep their mouths shut if we find what we're looking for? I can't."

He put his palms flat on the table, moved them in slow circles. He had calmly waited for his team to work things out, and now his team calmly waited for him to do the same.

"We went through hard times together," he said. "We did that for a cause. For a flag. For a concept. I don't regret it, but…well, what did we get for our sacrifices? A pat on the back and a threat to stay quiet, or else. We gave our best years to a country that spent them like gambling money. The people who made those decisions, what did they care about us? They didn't care at all. When we were dismissed, dismissed for following *their* orders, they stayed in power."

He stood. He rubbed at his forehead, then let his hands rest at his sides.

"This mission isn't just about money. Six weeks ago, friends of mine died. I want payback for them. I also want to make things right for all of you. The work you put in, the things you had to do, the shit you had to endure, and now you wash dishes and sell used cars? Unacceptable. I'm giving you one last chance to exercise those skills you developed, but this time, you get *rewarded* for it. Not with a medal you can never wear. Not with stories you can never tell. Not with a quiet nod in some general's back office. Not with nightmares you can't even share with a shrink."

He held up one finger.

"If we do this one job, this one *dangerous* job, if we put our asses on the line one last time, every one of us can live the rest of our lives the way we *deserve* to live."

The room fell quiet for a moment.

"If we survive," Doug said.

Ender nodded. "If we survive."

Kevin leaned his elbows on the table, grinned at Tommy.

"Hey, Worm … how many hours would you have to work to make a quarter mil?"

The gears clicked, spit out a number.

"Twenty-four thousand, one hundred and fifty-four," Tommy said. "At forty hours a week, that's six hours shy of six hundred and four weeks."

Over eleven and a half *years'* worth of washing dishes.

Kevin laughed, shook his head. "I love it when he does that shit. Hey, Worm … how many hours to make *two million?*"

"Cut the Rainman act, Kevin," Doug said. He took a shaking breath. Earlier, he'd had the presence of a powerful preacher—now he wore the desperation of a street beggar.

"Tommy, I can find you another job," Doug said. "If you don't like what you're doing, that doesn't mean you have to go with us."

Kevin sat up straight. "Go with *us?* Wait a minute, Bishop Bullshit, you're in?"

Doug nodded.

"I run a church." He sounded apologetic. He sounded defeated. "The Church of the Holy Signal. God guided me to founding it, to building it into what it is now. I think God put me here, too. At this moment. I can do a lot of good with that kind of money. I can help a lot of people."

"And buy more suits," Marie said. "Probably some nice cars, too, am I right?"

She meant it as a barb, but Doug shrugged it off.

"Costumes and branding matter," he said. "I'm not going to bother explaining that to you. We also feed a thousand meals to the homeless every month. We run a shelter for battered women. Job training and placement. Clothing drives. School supplies for disadvantaged kids. Do you do anything like that, Marie?"

She tried to hold his gaze, but she could not. She looked away without answering. Even if Doug did only half the things he claimed, that was *far* more than Tommy contributed to others—and the same probably went for everyone else in the room.

"I don't want to do this mission," Doug said, "but if I pass up that money…well, as strange as it sounds, I feel like that would be a sin."

Curveball stroked his beard. "Whatever justification you got to make, Sleepy, I'm damn glad you're with us."

"Fuck yeah," Hatchet said. "NoSeeUms ride again."

Marie nodded. So did Kevin.

"That leaves you, Bookworm," Ender said. "What's it going to be?"

Tommy knew people. He knew that Doug was telling the truth about using the money for good, but also lying—he wanted the money for himself as well. He knew there was far more to Marie's job than she let on. He knew Hatchet and Curveball wanted the money, knew that they wouldn't give a damn what they had to do to get it. He knew Kevin wanted excitement again, but that deep down, Kevin was also hoping to *kill* again—killing was the ultimate rush for him. Always had been.

And Tommy knew Patrick O'Doyle. For Ender, this was about revenge far more than it was about money.

It was obvious to anyone that Bertha didn't really want to go, didn't really want Ender to go. She was doing this for him. To keep an eye on him, maybe. To protect him, maybe. Ender didn't see it, even though it was right there in front of his face.

Tommy didn't just know other people—he knew *himself*. This was a chance to do the only thing he'd ever been good at. When he'd been with these people, he'd had a place, he'd had a role.

He'd had a home.

Tommy stared at Patrick O'Doyle.

"No killing," Tommy said. "You promise?"

"Like I told you, no killing people."

Tommy wanted the money. He wanted to be with his friends. But perhaps more than anything else, Tommy desperately wanted to find out what the hell *no killing* PEOPLE really meant.

"All right," he said, "I'm in."

Ender's chest puffed out. He beamed with pride.

"Exceptional. You all have fifteen minutes to call whoever you need to call, then a van will take us to a private airstrip."

Marie stood. "I assume I get to do the flying?"

"Of course," Ender said.

Everyone else stood. The air felt thick with energy.

"I need more time than that," Doug said. "I have too many things to take care of. Where are we going? What do I tell my people?"

"Tell them you don't know how long you'll be gone," Patrick said. "Tell them that you don't know when you'll be able to touch base again. And don't ask me for more information, because you won't get any until we get where we're going." He looked at his watch. "Fourteen minutes, thirty seconds."

Hands jammed into pockets. Phones came out. People made calls. The conference room buzzed with five simultaneous, hurried conversations.

Tommy just stood there, duffel bag over his shoulder. He didn't own a phone.

"Worm," Ender said, "can I have a word?"

He walked out of the room. Tommy followed.

Ender stopped in the hallway. He looked at Tommy, smiled slightly.

"It's good to see you, Tommy. Really."

"You too, man."

"I need you to give me recs on communications gear that will work in the tunnel system we need to explore."

Tommy glanced at the *Titan Drilling* logo on Ender's shirt.

"You work for a mining company. You don't have comms that work underground?"

"Not as far underground as we're going to go, no."

"How far, exactly?"

"*Far,*" Ender said. "The comms systems for mining operations require surface base stations and lots of cabling. They're designed for fixed operations. We'll be on the move, probably traversing several miles of tunnels."

"Will we have any support on the surface?"

Ender shook his head. "We will be on our own."

Far underground. Miles of tunnels. No support.

"I take it we won't be following OSHA regulations," Tommy said.

That small smile again. "We won't. When we get where we're going, it will be problematic to buy gear and have it delivered, so I need to place the order before we leave. I've done some preliminary work on systems we can use. You can review that in the van. I need you to make sure I'm not missing anything. Can you do that for me?"

Tommy had been the NoSeeUm's comm expert, but that had been two decades ago. The fact that Ender was asking him—and not an up-to-date expert—said a lot about how he wanted to handle operational security.

"Sure," Tommy said. "I'll take a look."

BOOK TWO

ARRIVAL

19

October 17

FUCK YOU, I'm fishing."

Tim Feely closed his eyes and sighed. Should he have expected to hear anything less when he called Murray Longworth?

"Not this time," Tim said. "I need to talk to you. It's important."

"Oh, it's *important*? Oh, gosh, my bad. Now that I know it's *important*, let me rephrase—I am fishing, so, fuck you *and* the horse you rode in on. I ain't got the energy to help you do your job today. Whatever it is, figure it out for yourself this time."

A reaction like that was no surprise. Not really. Not when Tim had called Murray dozens of times to get advice or guidance on various incidents from a man who'd done Tim's job for many years. But this time, it was different.

"I'm not asking you for help," Tim said. "I'm calling as the Director of the Department of Special Threats, and you are a person of interest in Incident Forty-Three."

A long pause.

Tim expected Murray to hang up. He did not.

"Well … shit," Murray said.

"I want to know about this man you talked to. Tell me about Pat—"

"*Don't* say his name," Murray said. "We both know who we're talking about. Best if we don't mention his name."

That took Tim aback. *Don't mention his name?*

"We're not talking about Old Scratch here, Murray. Or Voldemort, for that matter."

"Don't know who *Voldemort* is, but the gentleman we're discussing is worse than Old Scratch. Way worse."

Worse than Satan, huh? Must be one heckuva guy.

"I want to know everything you know," Tim said. "I want to know about this guy, what he did for you, and what he's doing now."

"Not going to happen. First of all, it would take years to tell you about my pre-DST days. Second of all, if I tell you any of it—*any* of it—you'll probably be reading my obit by the end of the week."

No hint of exaggeration. Murray was a former director of not one, but *two* federal agencies, and he thought talking about this would get him killed? He'd consulted presidents. He'd been one of the key decision-makers who had—literally—saved the world. To think that some *other* shadow agency might, as Vogel so casually put it, *cut Murray off?*

"Tell me that the obit part is needless hyperbole," Tim said.

"Have you ever known me to be hyperbolic?"

A flush of fear, of uncertainty. Was no one safe? Apparently not— Tim included. Say the wrong thing at the wrong time, and that's your ass. Maybe Tim should have put his lovely gray matter to work for the Mafia instead of the government. At least with the Mafia, you knew what could get you killed.

"So you can't tell me about the past," Tim said. "How about the present? What is this guy doing?"

"I don't know. He wanted a list of people. I got him a list of people. Case closed. How is this a new DST incident?"

"Now *you* want answers? *Now* you want to be involved in DST business again? What if I tell you I'm fishing and reference both your anus and the anus of a certain equine form of transportation?"

"You don't fish," Murray said. "Stop dicking around and tell me how this is an incident."

Tim could pretend to be indignant all he liked; the truth was he felt a huge sense of relief that Murray wanted to know more. Murray understood this business better than Tim ever would.

Tim shared what Vogel had told him about Kayla Meyers, Earth-Core, and the possible sentient species.

"Well, well, well," Murray said. "Punch me in the taint and call me Sally. Sounds like you have yourself quite a pickle."

Ah, the wisdom of the elderly. "So what do I do? How do I find this guy?"

"You have the power of the US government at your disposal. Find out where he lives and send someone to talk to him. You still have Otto working for you?"

"I do."

"Then send Otto," Murray said. "But tell him to *be careful*. This guy, he's dangerous, so make sure someone dangerous goes with Otto. You have someone dangerous working for you?"

"Yeah," Tim said. "I have someone dangerous."

"Good. But remember that no matter what badass you have lined up, he or she is an amateur compared to this guy. Tell Otto to *ask*, not *push*. It's up to Otto to learn what he can. I don't want anyone getting hurt."

"Otto is a federal agent," Tim said. "You think this guy would assault a federal agent?"

"Jesus H. Christ, are you really that fucking naive? If you want Otto to go bye-bye and never be heard from again, then tell him to be a bull in a china shop. You won't find his body. Or any evidence. Understand?"

So far, Tim's time in the DST had involved cases with monsters. Like actual *monster* monsters. Now, apparently, he was dealing with one of the human variety.

"And if we can't find this guy?"

"Feely, do you have any hair on your balls?"

Tim tapped his fingers on the desktop. He was grateful for Murray's help, but the man's brusque manner left a lot to be desired.

"Yes, Murray. I have long since hit puberty."

"Then act like it," Murray said. "Call Larry Fitch at the Bureau, tell him I told you to call. Have him find out what EarthCore is spending money on. And call Wendy Bostwick at Revenue. If you need leverage, she can make it happen."

The FBI. The IRS. With a couple of phone calls, Tim could put the pinch on EarthCore?

"Murray, is that even legal?"

A sigh so loud Tim could have heard it all the way from Florida even without a phone.

"If you can't actually grow pubes, shave your head and glue some of that hair on your sack," Murray said. "Then you can at least pretend to be a man. I'm hanging up now, Feely, so fuck you—I'm fishing."

20

October 18

That was the word. Sonny had never felt more *conspicuous* in his life. He slumped down low in the driver's seat of the piece of shit Toyota he'd bought with cash off some yokel in Tres Lagos. The beat-up Hilux truck would have blended in just fine if there were more cars and trucks around.

There weren't.

Because there weren't many people in El Chaltén. The place was damn near a ghost town. People were coming, he'd been told, when most of the hotels, bars and other businesses opened up in a few weeks for the beginning of the tourist season. With the bite of winter only beginning to release its lockjaw hold on the area, however, even the die-hard adventure seekers had yet to show up.

"Goddamn cold," he said. "Should be some penguins around here or something."

Penguins. Southern hemisphere, or northern? He couldn't remember.

Today was the day. He could feel it. For two days, those kids had dicked around their tiny cabin. Maybe they thought they were lying low, maybe they were arguing, maybe they were fucking … who knew? But Sonny had put the fear of loss in them, *deep* in them, and sooner or later they would head back to their little scientific discovery and lead him right to the tunnel entrance.

He was freezing his ass off because he didn't dare start the truck. A vehicle sitting on the side of the road at 6am, frost on the windshield? Normal. The same vehicle idling, exhaust curling out of the tailpipe, frost melted away? Not so much. Not when the smart people were tucked up in their tiny little cabins, toasty warm and sheltered from the cold. Not where everything in the small town was an easy walk and there were no jobs outside of town that required a car-warming for the commute.

Sonny checked the time: *6:07a.m.*

Same shit as the last two mornings, sitting here, freezing his wrinkled old balls off, waiting to see a light go on in the tiny house rented by Samira Jabour and Ramiro Chus. They were probably sleeping in, again. The day before, Sonny hadn't seen movement in their house until almost 11am.

Scientist types were supposed to be early risers. Veronica and Sanji Haak had been, for sure, and Angus Kool and Randy Wright slept so little Sonny still wondered if the two had been meth-heads.

Sonny had discovered the secrets of Angus and Randy by following them, which was exactly how he was going to find out the secrets of Sam and Ramiro. That snotty bitch thought she could talk to Sonny that way? Get ready to get fucked, lil' darlin', and not in the good way.

Stupid kids. Sam and Ramiro could have had a big budget backing up their little research project, but *nooooo*—their holier-than-thou pride was more important to them. They would lead him right to the tunnel entrance, and they'd get nothing for their troubles.

Such was life.

Sonny slid up in the driver's seat a little bit, stared at the cabin's door, the window. Still no sign of movement. No lights.

6:11 a.m.

He settled back down, continued to wait.

A few months back, Connell Kirkland had offered him two percent of the Utah mine. Tens of millions. *Hundreds* of millions. That opportunity was gone, blasted into bits by a goddamn volcano, but now Sonny had a second chance at the big leagues. And this time, he got *three* percent.

Would this go down like it had in Utah?

Sonny prayed it would not. That shit had been crazy with a capital "Z." So many people had died. Reeves. Haak. Angus. Randy. Connell Kirkland. And, especially, Cho Takachi. A good kid. Such a bright future ahead of him. That crazy psycho Kayla Meyers had shot Cho in the head, then hacked him to pieces with a goddamn axe.

She'd *butchered* Cho's body.

Sonny pushed the thought away. Best not to think about it, best not to focus on what utter evil *shits* human beings could be to each other.

Better to focus on the money.

Somewhere near here, maybe under Mount Fitz Roy, maybe under some other peak, there was a big-as-hell alien ship made out of solid platinum. One way or another, Sonny was going to find that ship.

He reached up, scratched frost off the driver's-side window. In the distance, a dark shadow against the lightening sky, he saw the mountain ridgeline, and in the center, taller than any other, the steep peak of Mount Fitz Roy.

"I see you," Sonny said. "I see you."

He checked his watch: *6:15 a.m.*

Any minute now. Samira and Ramiro were young enough they probably slept through the night without having to get up and pee every other hour. A full night's rest, and they were still sleeping in?

Youth was wasted on the young.

Sonny hadn't wasted *his* youth, though. Not at all. He'd found his calling early, spent his wild young years prospecting for gold, silver, beryllium, whatever mineral happened to present itself. He'd spent his late teens and twenties becoming a master of his craft, an expert in his field. He'd also drunk everything there was to drink, fought everything there was to fight, and nailed more Grade-A pussy than Hef.

Well, maybe not *Hef,* but Sonny certainly had netted his share of trim.

Back then, the ladies had all but thrown themselves at him. Those days had long since dried up for him, as they did for all men.

He knew Samira and Ramiro were divorced, but a part of him hoped they were still banging the holy hell out of each other. Samira was quite a piece. A bit smarter than Sonny normally dug, but still, that fine body, lean from rock climbing and hiking … the kind of thing that could make even an old man's divining rod seek out deep water. And Ramiro seemed like a decent enough guy. *More* than decent, really — what kind of guy *helps* his ex-wife?

Sonny checked his watch: 6:24 *a.m.*

Something was wrong. Only an hour or so until sunrise. If they were heading out, they'd want to be up, packing food, checking supplies, making sure they were out the door before dawn so they could take advantage of every minute of daylight.

And they *were* heading out. They'd said they were heading home. How dumb did they think he was? Sonny had seen that look in Ramiro's eyes when he'd learned the knives were made of platinum. Maybe he and Sam were telling the truth, maybe they were heading back to America, but before they went they would make sure they covered up the tunnel entrance so well that no one would ever find it.

And, if Sonny knew human nature, which he did, thank you very much, they would either take their new-found knives with them, or move the artifacts to a safer location.

So … where were they? What was taking them so long?

He stared hard at the front door, and saw something he'd missed — a piece of paper sticking out from underneath it.

Sonny got out of the truck. His breath billowing around him, he quietly walked to the tiny house. Yes, a piece of folded paper under the door, and on it, one word: *McGuiness.*

They'd left him a fucking note?

He picked up the paper, unfolded it.

DEAR SONNY: GFY

GFY? What the hell did that mean? Not that the meaning really mattered. What mattered was that the note had been left for him. *Specifically* left for him.

"Sonofabitch," he said.

Sonny had gotten cocky. He'd thought he could scare the birds into flight, then follow them to their nest. He'd shown up at 5am, expecting to get the drop on them, follow them to this ship's version of the Linus Highway, only to find them gone.

They'd left *hours* ago, left Sonny holding his dick.

GFY.

He stared at the letters; their meaning crystalized.

Go fuck yourself.

Sonny shook his head. They hadn't just made him look like a greenhorn; they'd rubbed it in his face.

"Sonofabitch," Sonny said. "O'Doyle is going to cut off my balls."

HIS BODY HURT all the time—did his goddamn *head* have to hurt, too? Maybe he could add some Advil to his oxy-Adderall mix. To think he'd gone most of his life without taking a goddamn thing, with barely even *drinking*, and now he was popping pills like a fucking addict.

The pressure was getting to him. Still no clue as to the actual location. Jabour and Chus, apparently, were fucking idiots who put the value of some long-dead culture above cold hard cash. And they had no idea the "indigenous culture" they wanted to protect wasn't indigenous at all. It wasn't even fucking *human*.

Infuriating.

Costs continued to climb. Angus knew he was running out of time. Soon, perhaps even tomorrow, he'd have to talk to June July about using the same search techniques he'd used in Utah: ground-penetrating radar, helicopters flying in an expansive grid pattern, lots of manpower, lots of resources.

Lots of *noise*, noise that would draw lots of attention.

If he went that route, the extra expense would likely make June cut his deal dramatically. And there were the two bigger risks—competitor companies getting word of what was going on, and BHP actually finding the location and cutting Angus out altogether.

June was cranking up the heat. She wanted results, and she wanted them yesterday.

Angus sighed. Had he actually just thought the phrase *wanted results, and wanted them yesterday?* He'd spent too much time with that corporate vampire. What was next? Maybe he'd start dreaming about *synergy* and *verticals*, or tell people his inventions combined *best of breed* solutions. Corporate speak: corn-choked turds jammed down his ear canals.

Angus groaned in pain as he sat forward, started reading emails. Eleven in the inbox. Five from June July. Two financial reports from his investments—sure, he was *presumed* dead, but he had seven years until any death in absentia actions that might liquidate his holdings. An email confirming two new patents for his company. He had to respond to that one, tell the people in his company what to do next.

When he did have to communicate to his people there, he used a fake account, pretending to be "Artemis Bulgari, Attorney at Law," the personal representative of the estate of Angus Kool. Clumsy, but everyone at Kool Products thought he was dead. They were so overworked, so in fear of the company shutting down and losing their jobs, that they weren't about to look into details.

Angus typed the response, pleased with the functionality of his fourth-generation glove. So *thin.* His hand still hurt like a motherfucker, but he could write, type, do everything he'd been able to do before that psycho woman had gone to work on him with a pair of pliers. He'd already had Artemis Bulgari, Attorney at Law, file three more patents for the artificial muscle he'd created for the glove and for the exosuit— at least chopping up that silverbug had produced *something* of value.

Three emails to go. Two were junk, because even if you hid your location and your identity, somehow junk mail *still* found its way to you.

And the last email …

A rush of excitement. A corresponding wave of doubt. The last trick he had up his sleeve … *had it worked?*

He read the email a second time. And a third.

He wanted to kiss the laptop.

"That's it," Agnus said. "That's *it.*"

He fought against the pain as he pushed himself up out of the chair.

Angus had made the G4S contracts under *his* name. Not June's. Not BHP's. His. Donnie Graham said that put Angus in charge. Was that for real?

Angus was about to find out.

EVERY TIME SAM and Ramiro went to the tunnel mouth, they took a different route. Lots of stops, lots of waiting and looking, seeing if anyone was following them. Standard procedure, really. This time, though, they took the most convoluted route they could think of. Their stops were longer than normal. Just in case.

"I still don't see him," Ramiro said. "I don't see anyone."

He was looking through binoculars, scanning the horizon, panning across the snow-speckled green scrub of the mountain's foothills.

Sam looked, too, but without the aid of binoculars. She wanted to soak up this beautiful place. Dawn breaking. A cold, brisk wind driving white clouds across the blue sky, making her jacket sleeves slap with a staccato rhythm. The green scrub brush, the clumps of white snow. And, of course, the spectacle of Mount Fitz Roy and the surrounding peaks, fists of stone stretching up to the heavens, the summit hidden in thin clouds.

No houses. No buildings of any kind. Even though El Chaltén was a few hours' hike away, this place remained as wild as it had been before the dawn of man.

Ramiro lowered the binoculars. "No way he'll find us now. We can head up."

His face red from the cold and the wind, he slid blue sunglasses on to protect his eyes from the snow's glare.

"Maybe he didn't try to follow us," Sam said.

"Of course he did. I hope he liked that note. And freezing his ass off in his car for three days. Serves him right."

Sam couldn't argue with that. She didn't want to underestimate Sonny McGuiness, but it was hard not to. Sam and Ramiro had spent enough time in El Chaltén that they were nearly considered locals. One of their friends had quietly let them know of a stranger, hiding in his truck in the early mornings. A stakeout.

She and Ramiro had waited a couple of days, hoping Sonny might give up. Besides, they'd had plenty to talk about.

Sam had spent the better part of the first day apologizing. She had no excuse for not telling Ramiro about the platinum. She could have laid the blame on Veronica, because Veronica had made that decision initially, but that would have been a cop-out. Sam had *liked* being in the know. She'd *liked* being in Veronica's confidence. And when Veronica was declared missing or dead, some weird part of Sam had *loved* knowing she was the only one on the planet with that secret.

Turned out, though, that she wasn't the only one. During her time in Utah, Veronica had blabbed. Intentionally or accidentally, it didn't matter. One more bit of hate for Sam's love/hate memories of the woman.

Ramiro had forgiven Sam, but, like with the infidelity, their relationship would never be the same. He was going to Berkeley. Sam was on her own.

At least he was still with her in spirit—they would not allow scumbag miners to find the tunnel.

People thought money bought anything they wanted. They thought that everyone had a price. Well, those people were wrong. Sam could not be bought. Neither could Ramiro. Maybe there had been remnants of the Chaltélians in Utah, and maybe not. There was only one place in the world that, for certain, held evidence of this ancient culture. Sam would go to the grave before she'd let some capitalist pig destroy it all in order to add a few more dollars to the bottom line.

"It's getting late in the morning," Ramiro said. "We better start climbing."

THE SNOWSTORM BEGAN when they were halfway up the slope.

They'd known it was coming and had tried to reach the plateau before it arrived. Maybe they'd spent too much time looking back for McGuiness. Whatever the cause, the strong wind, biting cold, and stinging bits of snow and ice made the last hour of climbing and hiking difficult, miserable, and dangerous.

Having made this ascent nineteen times together, Sam and Ramiro knew what they were doing. They took their time, carefully managing how much they exerted themselves. The trick to climbing any mountain was to stay calm, stay smooth: *slow and steady wins the race.*

They finally reached the Notch, their name for a small, uneven, snow-covered plateau within striking distance of the summit. A natural, V-shaped slot in the mountain, the Notch's tip butted up against the steep, nearly sheer wall that rose up to form the peak, while the wider end opened into an erosion runoff that led down the north slope.

Located on the west side of the Fitz Traverse ridgeline, the Notch was out of sight of most hiking trails. The only people who came here were serious climbers. The Notch marked the end of the climb, and the beginning of the tunnel descent.

The pair stood there, coiling ropes, making sure they'd accounted for each and every bit of gear. They didn't want to leave any trace of the route they'd took to reach this spot. Wind whipping at their jackets, snow whirling around them, Sam stared west across the white expanse of the Southern Patagonian Ice Field. Such a sight. They were above the clouds: below, white mist drifted lazily across the endless sea of ice and snow. Almost due west, the peak of Cordón Mariano Moreno. Northwest, the peak of Lautaro, an active stratovolcano that Sam hoped to visit someday.

No sign of civilization here. None at all.

"I've always hated this climb," Ramiro said. "But I won't lie, I'm going to miss seeing this."

Sam would, too. "Ready to go in?"

Ramiro breathed in deep, a lung-filling draw of mountain air, as if it was his last and he wanted to take in as much as he could.

"Yeah," he said. "Let's get to work. Lead the way."

Boots crunching on snow, Sam walked carefully across the angled, snow-packed field of rocks to a chest-sized boulder at the base of the Notch. She took off her backpack and slid between the boulder and the rock face, pulling the backpack along with her by its strap. At the back of the boulder, an indent in the stone gave her enough space to squat down.

There, a spot of darkness not even two feet high, just under three feet wide—the tunnel entrance.

How Veronica had found this years earlier, Sam did not know. Veronica had kept many secrets. Among them, how she had discovered this spot. Now Veronica was gone, and her untold secrets along with her.

Sam pushed the backpack in before her, then crawled into the cave. Fifteen feet in, the space opened up enough for her to squat on her heels.

"I'm in," she called out. "Come on."

Ramiro was taller than she was, and wider in the chest. It took him a little longer to get past the boulder.

While she waited, Sam started to make a pile of loose rock. When they left this place for the last time, they would use the rocks to fill the crawlspace. When that was done, they'd build a small fire and use a pot in Ramiro's pack to melt snow. It was still cold enough that water froze quickly—they would turn the pile of rock into a pile of rock and ice. After that, a day or two of the mountain's high winds and blowing snow, and no one would ever see the tiny crack of rock that allowed entrance to the Chaltélian caves.

In effect, they'd seal the cave forever.

And that suited Sam just fine.

THE SIKORSKY S-76 helicopter thumped through the storm. Every now and then, the wind would hit it hard, bounce Bertha's helmet off the back of the seat or the portside window. She sat quietly, alternating between reading about the area on her tablet sitting atop the pack between her knees and gazing out at the towering Argentinian peaks.

Maybe she wasn't hyped on this mission, but she couldn't deny that she was fascinated by the area and energized by the trip. The Fitz Traverse consisted of fourteen peaks set in five kilometers of ridgeline. Aguja Guillaumet on one end, reaching up 2,580 meters; Aguja de l'S at the other, 2,330 meters. Those peaks were nothing special, at least to her, just big-ass chunks of granite in the endless expanse of the Andes. In the middle of the ridgeline, towering above the other peaks, the iconic Mount Fitz Roy, a nearly rectangular chunk of eroded granite jutting up 3,405 meters.

The ridgeline itself was the logo for the Patagonia clothing company, although to her, one stylized mountain range looked like the next.

Except for that center peak. Except for Fitz Roy.

The sides of it, so steep they were almost vertical, then angling together to form the point.

It looked like a weathered gravestone.

The marker for her death? For the death of her husband?

Bertha was ready for death, but the thought of losing Patrick … it sent a sharp shiver through her body.

"Hey, you cold?"

Kevin Bliss sat on her right, in the middle of the bench seat. Tommy

Strymon sat on the other end. They were pressed together shoulder to shoulder. Like her, they had their packs between their knees.

On the bench in front of them sat Carson Wampler, Anders Keeley and Doug Rapson. Patrick was in the copilot seat, riding shotgun next to the pilot, Marie Dunlop.

"I'm fine," Bertha said.

Kevin nodded toward the mountain.

"Look at that beast," he said. "It's like the earth decided to give humanity the finger, you know?"

He was leaning over her slightly to look out the window. This close, she smelled his cologne, and whatever product he was using in his hair.

She decided to ask him the question that had been bugging her since they'd lifted off from the tiny Aeropuerto Internacional El Calafate, where the team had picked up the Sikorsky.

"Everyone else is wearing a helmet except you," Bertha said. "You too cool for school or something?"

Kevin flashed a smile that could wet a thousand panties, if you were into that kind of guy. Bertha wasn't. Perfect white teeth, dimples in his cheeks, laugh lines accentuated by a day's growth of stubble, and eyes that belonged on a movie screen. And yet, there was something *missing*. When Patrick smiled—which was rare, but happened often enough when she was alone with him—it was a genuine thing, a window into his damaged soul. When Kevin smiled, it was *fake*. A masterful counterfeit that would fool most everyone, but not her.

All of Patrick's former squad mates were sketchy. There was something … *off* about them. Kevin Bliss even more than the others. Something in his eyes, or maybe something *missing* from his eyes.

Bottom line: Kevin Bliss gave her the creeps.

"I'm not too cool for school," he said. "But I'm awful pretty. I know better than to cover up a work of art." He ran a hand through his sandy-brown hair. "Would you hide the Mona Lisa behind a blanket? I don't think so."

The other NoSeeUms laughed.

"Some things never change," Carson said over his shoulder.

Someone had to tell Carson about his awful hair. So thin, and—in this light—more orange than red. What kind of a conceited, oblivious douchebag combed their hair *forward* to try and pretend they weren't going bald?

Anders awkwardly turned in his seat to look back at Kevin.

"One of these days I'm going to get you drunk," Anders said. "Then I'm going to talk you into shaving your own head." He slid a hand across his dark pate. "We'll look like twins." He glanced at Bertha. "That's how Kevin got his call sign, because of that hair."

She thought back to the meeting in Denver, glanced at Kevin.

"*Mullet*, right?"

Kevin nodded. "We were out in the field for two weeks. We didn't get to bathe, let alone shower. They thought it was funny to mock my luscious head-lettuce. Joke is on them, though, because even when my hair is greasy and unkempt, it *still* looks glorious."

"Speak for yourself," Carson said without turning around. "You looked like a rag doll that had been left in the mud."

Kevin ignored him, spoke to Bertha instead.

"There's a story behind everyone's call sign. Carson's is unimaginative, just like he is—he likes a hatchet as his personal weapon. So clever, right?"

Carson kept his eyes forward as he raised his right hand and gave Kevin the bird.

Anders was still turned in his seat. Bertha patted his forearm.

"And you're *Curveball*," she said. "How'd you get that one?"

"I was in the minor leagues for two years," he said. "Back in my younger days, I had some serious heat."

"Who did you play for?"

An uncomfortable pause.

Tommy leaned forward so Bertha could see him. He held a paperback in his hand: *Stranger in a Strange Land.*

"He can't tell you that," Tommy said. "Our pasts are ... we don't have pasts."

Tommy sat back, returned to reading his book.

Don't have pasts. Patrick had told her so little about himself. She knew he'd grown up in Wisconsin, but he didn't talk about his hometown. When she brought up family, his parents, any brothers or sisters, he politely changed the subject. That had quietly infuriated her; a husband and wife were supposed to know everything about each other. She'd thought he was ashamed of his family, or perhaps they had kicked him out, as her family had done to her, but maybe it wasn't those things.

Maybe he wasn't *allowed* to talk about his past, as if doing so might put him in danger.

Or put *her* in danger.

Who, exactly, had she married?

"Then there's Bookworm," Kevin said, nudging Strymon. "Another lazy-ass nickname. Dude is always reading."

Bertha didn't bother telling Kevin that the moniker *Bookworm* was more than a little obvious, especially considering Tommy was actually reading a book at that very moment.

She reached forward, patted Rapson on the shoulder.

"How about you, Reverend Doug? How'd you get your call sign?"

He didn't answer. The other NoSeeUms laughed quietly, even Tommy, and Bertha realized why—despite the howling wind, the roar of the helicopter engine and the rough, thumping ride, Doug "Sleepy" Rapson was out like a light.

"He can sleep anywhere, anytime," Kevin said. "Always been envious of that."

It was the first time Bertha had them talking to her, and she wanted to keep it going.

"Let me guess yours, Marie," Bertha said. "Since you're the pilot, the sexist boys gave you the name of a pretty bird?"

Bertha heard Marie's laugh in her helmet's headset.

"These assholes, paying someone a compliment? I don't think so," Marie said. "When we were first assigned to the same unit, I had this old beater Buick Skylark I'd been driving since high school. Put some miles on that car, let me tell you. I did the maintenance myself, got her up to 250,000 miles before she gave up the ghost."

Kevin nudged Bertha.

"But it wasn't the engine miles that got her the nickname," he said, grinning. "It was all those trips in the back seat."

"Real classy, Mullet," Marie said. "But yeah, I nailed all the boys except Anders in that car at one time or another. I even got Carson once."

"I was confused about my sexuality," Carson said quickly. "Do we really have to bring this up?"

A few insults and retorts flew back and forth, but Bertha didn't register them. Marie had had sex with *all* the men?

Including Patrick?

Patrick, who was up in the copilot seat, sitting right next to Marie, a woman he'd fucked?

He should have shared that. He should have shared it before Bertha even set foot in that conference room. No, before he'd even had Dillinger contact Marie at all.

But Patrick hadn't done any of those things.

Because he doesn't tell you shit. These people know more about your husband than you ever will.

"That's enough chatter," Patrick said. "You all need to take a good look at the terrain. We don't know where we'll wind up, so study it as much as possible. Never know what will help."

The talking ceased. The NoSeeUms did as they were told.

Bertha wasn't a NoSeeUm.

She slunk down in her seat as much as her restraints would allow. She closed her eyes, and tried to follow Rapson into sleep.

BERTHA AWOKE AN hour later as the Sikorsky set down just south of a small, turquoise-blue glacial lake.

"Welcome to Laguna Torre and Estancia Araceli," Marie said. "We hope you've enjoyed flying Skylark Airlines. Please travel with us again."

Bertha stepped down from the helicopter; her feet crunched on rocky ground.

Either the storm had died down or they'd flown out of it. It was just a few minutes past noon. Some clouds to the northwest, but aside from those there was nothing but blue sky. The small lake—Laguna Torre— blazed with rippled reflections of the sun. At the rocky shore, the water was crystal clear; further out, it took on a blue so pure it almost hurt her heart to look at it. Chunks of ice floated in the water, the smaller pieces gleaming clear as wet glass, the larger ones blue-tinged white.

Mountains rose up all around, shimmering white striated with streaks and spots of gray. To the north, postcard-perfect Mount Fitz Roy and its sister peaks, the mountain's summit obscured by a single, thick cloud.

Bertha breathed in deep: crisp air, cold and clean.

"Rooms are assigned," Patrick said. "Get your gear stowed, get some rest. First mission brief is tomorrow, in the lounge, at oh-nine-hundred local."

On the other side of the helicopter sat a squat, clean, long house—Estancia Araceli. A vacation lodge for people who needed to get away from it all, to take in the glaciers and the mountains and the rustic splendor, but still be pampered with maid service, a restaurant, and a staff that catered to their every need. There was a road that led to El Chaltén, some six miles east, but in the mission brief Patrick had told everyone the "road" was only traversable by serious off-road vehicles—most travel to and from Estancia Araceli was done by horseback.

Or, obviously, by helicopter.

Harvey Dillinger had rented the Estancia under some dummy corporation/subsidiary of EarthCore. During the peak tourist season, a room there was about $700 *per night*—Bertha could only imagine how much it cost to rent the entire building.

The team spread out through the rustic lodge. There were nine rooms, so everyone got their own, except for Carson and Anders, who took one together.

Bertha and Patrick would stay in the same room.

Marie got her own room. Would Patrick want to visit her?

Bertha chased away the thought as she stowed her gear. She was being ridiculous. Jealous. Wasn't she? But Marie was so pretty.

Marie didn't have scars on her face.

Marie had all her fingers.

Marie didn't have a big fat ass.

Bertha found the room she would share with Patrick. She started unpacking her gear when Patrick entered, his bag slung over his shoulder, his movements sharp and quick, fueled by excitement.

"This place is perfect," he said, tossing his bag onto the bed. He opened it, moved with the same methodical efficiency that marked his every action. "No one around for miles. We can train hard, get the team back into shape. Got to do it fast, though—no telling when Sonny will find the location."

Frustration clawed at Bertha. He should have told her about his past with Marie. A lie of omission? Bertha tried to push the thought away.

"That mountain is something else," Patrick said. "Did you get a good look at it from the back of the bird?"

Back of the bird. Right, because he'd been *in front*, with *Marie*.

"Why didn't you tell me about her?"

Patrick pulled out a roll of T-shirts from his bag—he loved to pack things in rolls—and put them in a dresser drawer. "Tell you about who?"

Oh, he was going to play dumb?

"That woman you fucked and brought on this mission."

His hands froze. He squinted at her, confused.

"Are you talking about Skylark?"

"No, I'm talking about one of the other twenty women that came here with us."

"You can't be serious."

Now he was dismissing her feelings? What an asshole.

Stop it, look at his face, he's not doing anything with her, stop it…

…no, he's making a fool of you, and she's in on it, they ALL *know…*

"Don't play it off," Bertha said. "How stupid do you think I am?"

Patrick spoke in a low voice. "I haven't seen that woman in twenty years."

"Right, so it's familiar pussy and strange cooch all at the same time, right? Best of both worlds."

His left eye twitched: he was getting angry, trying to control it.

"There is nothing going on with Marie," he said. "Nor will there be."

Nor? He was fucking Shakespeare all of a sudden.

"But you *did* fuck her. Right? In the back seat of her shitty car?"

Patrick glanced at the room's open door, making Bertha wonder how loud she had just spoken. He stepped to the door, shut it.

"You should have told me about that," Bertha said.

He lifted his hands, shrugged. "You're right, I guess, but it never crossed my mind."

"Oh, it never crossed your mind to tell your *wife* that a woman you *fucked* is going to be under the same roof as us, for God knows how long? Seriously? You expect me to believe that *never crossed your mind?*"

He stared, blinked.

She crossed her arms, waited. He looked as stupid as he thought she was.

Why are you doing this? Stop speaking to him like that, JUST STOP IT, *you're ruining things…*

"It happened a long time ago," Patrick said. "In another life. Babe, listen to me—I'm not interested in her."

"Oh? Then why is she here, huh? Tell me that."

His confused look melted into one she hadn't been expecting—the face he wore when he was giving commands.

"Skylark is here because she can fly anything," he said. "She's here because she speaks fluent Spanish in a dozen dialects, can converse passably in Portuguese, and is an expert sniper. Not in Worm's league, but then again, who is? Skylark is here because she knows when Mullet is about to get out of line and how to talk him down before anything happens. Skylark is here because she saved my life *three times*. She's here because she followed every command I ever gave, and because *I owe her for her service*. She's here because the military she volunteered to serve took a giant shit on her, just like it took a giant shit on the rest of us, and this is my chance to make things right for her."

He paused, opened his mouth to say more, then stopped. Bertha hadn't really known Patrick all that long, but she knew him well enough to see when he was about to start cursing, start yelling—and he'd stopped himself from doing that.

He can stop himself, but you can't do the same? Way to go, Bertha. Say something good, SAY SOMETHING GOOD.

"Doesn't mean you don't want to fuck her."

Bertha wanted to punch herself in the face. Why couldn't she stop saying awful things?

"Keep this discussion between us," Patrick said. He spoke quietly, cold iron in his words, making her acutely aware that she'd crossed a line. "I can't have you impact team morale. Understand?"

She nodded, instantly, a reaction bred from eight years in the military rather than five weeks of marriage.

"I'll unpack later," he said, then walked out of the room, shutting the door behind him.

Bertha's face flushed with heat. Why had she kept digging at him? He'd been trying to talk to her. So *frustrating.* She felt the tears coming, fought them back.

"There's no crying on commando missions," she said, then tried to take her mind off her abhorrent behavior by putting away her gear.

She put Patrick's away as well, maybe a first, small step towards making things up to him.

21

October 19

"DON'T KNOW WHO you are that you think you can just walk into my office uninvited," Barbara Yakely said. "But unless you want a truck full of lawyers to drive a rusty Greyhound bus straight up your Hershey highway, I suggest you turn around and visit my legal department."

Two men stood in her office: one black, one white. The black man wore a brown suit; the white one, a blue sportscoat and jeans. They were both big men, both in shape, although the black man had more weight around the middle, more sag in his cheeks—he was probably ten or fifteen years older than the white guy. The white guy looked like he'd been carved out of granite.

The black man reached into his jacket, pulled out a leather badge holder. He opened it, showed the gleaming, seven-pointed gold star inside.

"I'm Clarence Otto," he said. "Department of Special Threats." He seemed to wait for something, then glanced at the white guy. "Paulius?"

The white guy twitched the way people do when they realize they've forgotten something important.

"Oh, right." He produced his own matching badge. "Paulius Klimas, ma'am—Department of Special Threats, too. I mean, *also*." He seemed to search for another word, shrugged, started to put the badge back in his jacket.

"Hold on," Barbara said. She set her lit cigar into the ashtray on her desk, curled her fingers inward. "Bring those badges over here, boys."

She had a brief twinge of concern that the word *boys* would be offensive to the black guy, but if she was calling them *both* "boys" did that count? She then remembered that she didn't really give a shit.

Both men approached her desk, showed their badges.

The matching gold stars had that air of authenticity about them: seven-pointed, with deep blue circles in the middle, DEPARTMENT OF curved across the top, SPECIAL THREATS curved under the bottom. Inside the blue, a twisted white ladder running from top to bottom—DNA.

"Never heard of this *agency*," she said, mocking the last word. "You got a big budget? I'd like to get an idea just how much I can sue you for."

"Budget cuts would get in the way of your windfall," Otto said. "We flew coach from DC. We don't have a Denver bureau, so we took a cab here from the airport."

Barbara shrugged. "I don't give a rat-fuck if you flew in on fairy wings. Get out."

Otto gestured to the chairs in front of her desk. "May we sit?"

"No," Barbara said. "You may not. Get lost. If you want something from me, call my lawyers."

The white guy—Klimas—made an apologetic little face.

"Maybe you should take a minute to do that yourself, ma'am," he said. "Before you kick us out, I mean. Might save you a little time, and a little trouble?"

Something very earnest about that one. Her instincts told her to slow down a bit, see just how problematic these two might be.

"Sit," she said, then she dialed her legal team.

Five minutes later, she realized it didn't matter that she'd never heard of the *Department of Special Threats.* Moments earlier—the timing undoubtedly coordinated to this visit—her lawyers had received a call from the Justice Department, telling them that cooperation was in EarthCore's best interest. In short: there was a new player in town. A player with significant authority.

She hung up.

"Sounds like you boys know the right people."

Klimas glanced at Otto. "Is *boys* racist if it's both of us?"

Otto closed his eyes, answered with a barely perceptible shake of his head.

"Missus Yakely," Otto said, "we have some questions about your Utah operation."

"How about first you tell me what constitutes a *special threat?*"

"Potential or actual threats of an unknown nature, primarily of biological origin," Otto said, delivering the line as smoothly as if he was asking for a cheese sandwich.

Biological. Shit…they were here about O'Doyle's little green men? How could they have found out about that?

It didn't matter. This wasn't the first time she'd faced down bureaucrats. Otto was half her age. Klimas maybe a quarter. She could manage this.

"We're in the mining business," she said.

Her cigar had gone out. She reached for the crystal lighter on her desk.

Otto nodded at the lighter. "Would you mind not smoking while we're here?"

Barbara paused in mid-reach, then made a dramatic show of looking around her desk.

Otto's smile faded. He knew she was mocking him, but he bit anyway.

"What are you looking for?"

"The company that you spent three decades building from the ground up," Barbara said. "When I find it, then you can decide what people can and can't do in this office."

The other guy—Klimas—snickered, caught himself, made his face blank again.

Otto glanced at him. "Was that funny?"

Klimas held up a finger and thumb with barely any space between them. "Just a smidge."

Barbara opened a drawer, picked up a cigar, offered it to Klimas. His eyes lit up, but he looked at Otto first.

"Might as well," Otto said. "If I'm bathing in secondhand smoke anyway, why not?"

Klimas took the cigar. He sniffed its length, smiled, nodded at Barbara.

"Thank you, ma'am."

"Call me Barbara," she said, offering him the heavy lighter. He used the built-in clipper to snip the end, then lit it. After a few short puffs, he sat back and smiled.

"Nothing like rich people cigars," he said.

Barbara nodded. "Got to spend my money on something. Might as well be on a slow, delicious death."

Otto crossed his right leg over his left. "Barbara, you—"

"I said *he* could call me *Barbara*," she said, cutting him off. "Not *you*."

Any pretense of humor left Otto.

"We have information that your people found a new species," Otto said. "Tell me about it."

Barbara rolled her cigar in her fingertips, studying it, using the motion to buy time to think. It was the little green men. Or little multicolored squids. Definitions didn't matter—what mattered was how Johnny Q. Government had found out. Was there a leak in EarthCore? No, that didn't make sense, as the only people who knew about the aliens were McGuiness, O'Doyle, Lybrand, Harvey and herself. Could it have been McGuiness? Possibly, but what did he have to gain? The man was getting three percent of the new find, same as O'Doyle and Lybrand. McGuiness didn't seem like the kind of guy who would fuck that up.

"Ma'am?"

Barbara came back to the present. Otto and Klimas were waiting for her to speak.

She'd slipped into her thoughts. That seemed to be happening more and more these days. Age was a python, its grip slow, steady, inexorable. Maybe she was headed for a nursing home and tapioca pudding three times a day.

But she wasn't there yet.

"I don't follow the day-to-day activities of a dig," she said. "If this is some spotted-grouse bullshit meant to shut down my business, you're too late—the volcano took care of that for you."

Klimas squinted. "Grouse?"

"She means *spotted owl*," Otto said. "More precisely, the *northern* spotted owl. Logging in Oregon was curtailed to protect the species, resulting in a problem for businesses."

"*Was curtailed*," Barbara said. "I like how you say those words as if some government *boys* in nice suits had nothing to do with putting people out of work."

She was trying to get a rise out of Otto, see if she could throw him off, learn more about how much he knew. He seemed unfazed. Either he did his job with machine-like indifference, or he had a top-notch poker face.

"We're not talking about an animal protected by the endangered species act," he said. "We're talking about something far more important. I wasn't sure if you knew about it before I got here, but now I *am* sure."

While she was trying to read into him, he was reading into her—and doing a helluva good job of it. Barbara felt off-center, she felt rattled. She had to protect O'Doyle's project; the company's future relied on it.

"Your agency sounds like tree-hugging lib bullshit," she said. "You think you can come in here and tell me what to do with *my* company? You aren't the IRS, young man."

Otto laced his fingers together, rested his hands on his lap. Calm, unaffected by her words or anger, by her indignation.

"We aren't the IRS," he said. "But we are working in conjunction with them. They have motions and injunctions ready to go. I'd like to tell you exactly how many motions and injunctions, but to be honest, I lost count somewhere around seventeen."

"That's a lot of injunctions," Klimas said.

Otto nodded. "It is. And, ma'am, before you tell me that *we're not the FBI*, let me say that while you would be correct, we're working in conjunction with them as well. Now I'm not a lawyer, and I don't know if the charges will stick, but I can tell you that they will be … let's see, how did you put it? Oh, yes—the charges will be akin to a rusty form of public transit driving into an anal sphincter. Do I have that euphemism right?"

Barbara grunted. "Close enough for government work. No offense."

"None taken," Otto said.

Barbara looked at Klimas. "You always let this guy run the show?"

Klimas shrugged. "Mostly I just get paid to shoot people."

She looked at Otto again, expecting a smug grin, but the stone face remained. This man didn't give a damn about anything other than the job. Barbara wondered what kind of shit he'd gone through to end up that cold.

"Here's an idea, Agent Otto," Barbara said "How about you fuck off? I'm calling my lawyer to discuss my options, and while I do, get your ass out of my office."

Otto sighed, as if he was slightly disappointed in her.

"You have *zero* options," he said. "That is, if you want to stay in business. You can call your lawyer if you like, but if I leave this office empty-handed, I guarantee you that EarthCore goes into mothballs. Not next month, not next week, it happens *today*. And between you and me, Missus Yakely, I wouldn't hold out hope that your company will ever come *out* of mothballs. Maybe your lawyers can do something about that, but by the time they do, I'm sure your sixteen-point-four million dollars' worth of debt will have come due. Your investors and creditors, you see, will *not* be mothballed."

Burning ash fell to her desk before she realized she'd made a fist, smashed her cigar right in the middle. Bits of tobacco stuck to her hand.

This fucker knew *exactly* how much debt EarthCore was carrying. The company was private, which meant there were only three ways to get that figure—from her, from her accounting firm, or from the IRS.

She doubted her accounting firm had given it up.

These two men had come out of nowhere, representing an agency she'd never heard of. Big Goddamn Government, wrapping its talons around her throat. She had lawyers—an army of them. She could hold these assholes at bay.

But if she couldn't…

Barbara had learned the rules of business from a man who had mastered them: from Rocky, her husband. Rocky's basic business philosophy hadn't come from a textbook. He'd come up with it himself, paraphrasing from an old country song that he'd loved. The phrase had helped guide Barbara's decisions during the two decades since Rocky's death:

You got to know when to hold em, know when to fold em, and know when to grab the Vaseline if you're going to get bent over no matter what you do.

"All right," she said. "They found something in Utah. Something underground. I don't know exactly what that was. Something intelligent, is all I know. Something that was already inside the mountain."

Cigar between his teeth, Klimas couldn't hide his eagerness. He was like a little kid watching his favorite TV show. Otto, on the other hand, kept the poker face firmly in place.

"Tell me more," he said.

Barbara wanted to shove the warped butt of the cigar right in his face.

"I don't know any more," she said. "In my line of work, it's important to keep a zone of ignorance about certain details."

Klimas smiled, nodded. "*Zone of ignorance.* Man, do I like that phrase. That's good."

Otto stared at her. Stared until the silence grew uncomfortable.

Barbara brushed her ruined cigar into a wastebasket, then pulled out a fresh cigar. She lit it. She spent hours a day sitting in silence, in this very office. If Otto thought his quiet, steely gaze was going to make her start babbling information, he'd be waiting a long, long time.

"I'll take you at your word," he said, finally. "For now. You have your zone of ignorance. Fine. There are two people well outside of said zone—Patrick O'Doyle and Bertha Lybrand. Where are they?"

Barbara's anger flared anew. Otto had been playing her. He'd been after O'Doyle and Lybrand all along.

"You're a rotten fucker," she said.

"Where are they?"

"I don't know," Barbara said. "And that's the truth."

Otto leaned forward. "Then give me someone who *does* know where they are. If you don't, playtime is over. I'm calling my pals at the IRS and the FBI. You spent *three decades* building this business? Watch me shut it down with a phone call."

She studied him anew, looking hard into his eyes, searching for any shred of bluff, of bullshit.

She found none.

"Klimas," Otto said, "may I please have the phone?"

The white guy reached into his sportscoat, handed the black guy a strange-looking cell phone.

"Nice," Barbara said. "Do you carry his jockstrap, too?"

Klimas laughed, handed the phone to Otto.

Otto leaned back in his chair, tapped the phone screen.

"This phone lets me ring through to special people," he said, giving it a theatric final push. "One minute to put me on a path to finding O'Doyle and Lybrand, or the wrecking balls start swinging. And once they start, ma'am, they can't be stopped."

One minute? Trillions of dollars on the line, and this prick was giving her one minute?

"Horseshit," Barbara said. "You think I was born yesterday? You need to give me some time to think about this."

Otto calmly held up the phone so she could see the timer ticking down.

"Fifty seconds," he said.

Klimas leaned forward, put his elbows on Barbara's desk.

"Babs," he said, "I know you just met both of us, but let me give you some insider info. This guy?" He pointed his cigar at Otto. "This guy does *not* fuck around. If he says he'll do it, he'll do it."

Good cop, bad cop? More like asshole cop, even bigger asshole cop.

Barbara had burned through most of EarthCore's reserves to fund the initial Utah dig, then sold off several revenue-generating assets when the project had gone way over budget. As of late, she'd had to borrow heavily to keep the company afloat, and to get capital for O'Doyle's adventure. She could manage the debt, but only if the company's remaining assets kept producing day-in and day-out. If Otto wasn't bullshitting, if he really could shut down EarthCore's operations, even if only for a few months, the company would go under.

But if she gave up O'Doyle, and these asshats got in the way of his hunt for the new motherlode, EarthCore might miss out on becoming the wealthiest company in the world.

"Twenty seconds," Otto said.

Barbara wanted to tell them to bugger each other all the way out the door, but she'd spent her adult life sizing people up, measuring a person's worth, deciding if they were real or just full of hot air. Something about these two screamed that they'd been through hell and high water yet come out alive. Especially Otto. There was a deadness to his eyes … trying to intimidate him was like trying to intimidate an alligator. A big fucking alligator that was about to eat you.

She glanced to the paintings on the wall. Rocky, Junior, and Connell. Could she risk losing the company those three men had helped build?

Her choice was simple: bend over and give up now, or gamble and possibly watch EarthCore go up in smoke.

Which meant there was really no choice at all.

"Pass the Vaseline," she said.

Otto's eyebrows rose. "Excuse me?"

"Never mind," Barbra said. "I'll give you what you want."

Barbara picked up her phone and called Harvey Dillinger.

AT OH-NINE-HUNDRED local, Tommy Strymon walked into the lodge's lounge to find the team—sans Ender and Lybrand—already gathered.

The NoSeeUms sat in chairs or on couches, except for Doug, who stood in the back corner, leaning against the wall humming the melody of "Hey Jude." Everyone held a mug of coffee. All stared out the picture window at the glacial lake, and beyond it, scrubland covered in a thin blanket of snow. In the distance, the towering peak of Mount Fitz Roy stood out among the chain of mountains.

A gust of wind picked up loose snow, carried it in a winding, roiling ghost wave across the surface of the turquoise water.

"Man," Mullet said. "There is a whole lot of nothing out here."

Mullet. Tommy was already thinking of everyone by their call signs, not by their names. That hadn't taken long.

"This place is like that one movie," Curveball said. "Y'all ever seen *The Shining?*"

Heads nodded.

Curveball glanced at Tommy. "Knowing you, you read the book."

"Seven times," Tommy said. "So far."

Curveball *hmphed.* "Of course. Well, anyway, if I see a ghost bartender or a couple of spooky little white girls asking me to *come and play,* I am so out of here."

Mullet raised an eyebrow, his *time to start some shit* grin on his face.

"What if it was a couple of little *boys*, Curve?"

Hatchet scowled at him. "Homosexuality and pedophilia are two completely different things."

Mullet turned his shit-stirring grin on Sleepy. "What's your take on that, Deacon Dickhead?"

Sleepy sipped at his coffee. "Stop trying to start trouble. This isn't the time."

Hatchet tilted his head, squinted at Doug. "I notice you didn't answer the question, Sleepy. Now that you're a man of god and all, your thoughts on Anders and me?"

Sleepy took another sip. "No comment."

Everyone went back to staring out the window.

"Ender's late," Skylark said. "Maybe he's nervous about the opp."

Mullet huffed. "The day that dude is nervous is the day I jump into a three-way with our friendly neighborhood cake makers."

Hatchet dismissed the thought with a wave. "Got no room in our bed for ugly people."

The surprise on Mullet's face made Marie and Tommy laugh.

"I'm the best-looking person here," Mullet said. "And you all know it."

Skylark smiled at him. "Once upon a time, sure, but you've gotten a bit long in the tooth." She frowned. "Say, Kevin … is your hair thinning?"

Mullet's hand went to his long hair an instant before he realized she was screwing with him.

"Fuck you, Skylark."

"Bet you got gray pubes," Hatchet said.

Curveball shivered. "An over-the-hill Lothario. Sad."

"I brought some extra Rogaine," Sleepy said. "Want to try it out?"

Tommy couldn't keep the grin off his face. So many years had passed, yet the team had quickly fallen back into the familiar old pattern of ripping on each other.

"You are all a bunch of assholes," Mullet said. "You wouldn't know pretty if it fell out of the sky, landed on your face, and started to wiggle."

Ender and Lybrand entered the room. Ender carried a large pad of presentation paper and an easel.

"Glad you two could be bothered to make it," Mullet said, obviously eager to make someone else the target of ridicule. "Busy with a quick round of pre-meeting, marital coitus? I'm guessing that only took a few seconds, right, Ender?"

"Shut up, Kevin," Ender said. "Playtime is over."

The man's tone chased away any frivolity. Ender's command voice—it had been two decades since Tommy last heard it. Like so many other things in the past twenty-four hours, it threw Tommy back to a time of his life that was both far better and far worse. By the stony expressions on the faces of the other NoSeeUms, Tommy knew they were experiencing similar sensations.

"We start mission training in an hour," Ender said. "First, though, the big picture. There is a lot to cover. When I'm finished, you get one last chance to decide if you're still with me, or if you want out. Here's the high-level info-dump—fifty-three people died at the EarthCore camp in Utah. The volcano didn't kill them. The camp was attacked. We believe that the same enemy that attacked the camp may be defending our objective here in Argentina."

You won't kill people, Ender had said. Tommy had a bad feeling that was bullshit. But then again, the man had never lied to him. Never.

"We were deep underground when they attacked," Ender said. "They destroyed the elevator that led back up to the surface. Seven other people were trapped in the tunnels with us. Bertha and I made it out. The rest died. As for the people on the surface, a man named Sonny McGuiness was the only one to survive. He's on our team."

"*Sixty* casualties," Mullet said. "Did I hear that right?"

Ender nodded. "Including twelve security guards who had military experience and were armed at the time of the attack."

Mullet gestured to the NoSeeUms. "And you're only bringing us? For what you're paying, you could hire Academi or G4S or Triple Canopy or whoever, get a full company of mercs properly outfitted. Why are we doing this with a skeleton crew?"

"A *middle-aged* skeleton crew," Sleepy said.

"A couple of reasons," Ender said. "First, the Utah camp was designed to keep out a potential handful of spies and saboteurs—not hundreds of assailants. Second, the guards on duty were not prepared for the enemy. They had no idea how to understand what they were seeing until it was too late. Now we know what to expect."

He set up the easel, talking as he did.

"Third, this time we are the aggressors. Fourth, I brought all of you into Argentina on a covert mission two decades ago. When it comes to getting a small team in unnoticed, without raising local alarms, not all that much has changed here. Bringing in a larger force exponentially increases the risk of exposure. As for importing enough military hardware for a company-sized force, or buying it locally? Forget it. There's no way to do that quietly. And as I told you in Denver, I can't risk leaks. To maximize our chances of success, we have to have *absolute* information control."

Skylark crossed her arms. "Now for the part you *didn't* tell us. Who is this *enemy*?"

Ender flipped the pad's first page over the top, revealing a detailed drawing.

"This is the enemy's primary weapon. This, and rocks."

Tommy had never seen anything like it. A heavy disk with a wide hole in the middle. On opposite sides of that disk, curved blades, thick at the base, tapering to a fine point.

"Kinda looks like a hurricane symbol," Hatchet said.

Ender nodded. "Yeah, it does. These blades will slice you open like a fish. I've seen it happen."

Lybrand's hand went to her missing fingers. She gently rubbed at the stumps.

"The blade is all curves," Tommy said. "Where's the handle? Where do you hold it? Looks pretty heavy."

"Fifteen pounds, one ounce," Lybrand said. "And they're hard to hold. By humans, anyway."

Mullet raised his hand. "A confused man says *what-the-fuck?* Is there something other than *humans* who would use that thing?"

"We're getting to that," Ender said. "First, before we reach the enemy, we will most likely be facing automated drones. Bertha and I saw them in the Utah tunnels. We call them *silverbugs*."

He flipped the knife drawing over the top of the pad. The next drawing showed a metallic ball, with four triple-segmented legs located equidistant around its equator. The first leg segment angled up, and the second down, like the legs of an insect. The third segment was actually split into two equal lengths, giving the four-legged machine eight "feet," each foot ending in a single small hook.

The metal ball also had a "head," of sorts—a small block that ended in a slightly curved, six-inch-long knife blade.

"When you mentioned *drones*," Curveball said, "I figured you meant the flying kind."

Ender shook his head. "We didn't see any that flew. We saw *thousands* of these crawling bastards. They work together, like ants, like parts of a single organism. They are our enemy's recon. Initially, they didn't have the knife-head. The silverbugs watched us, tracked us. After we won a couple of battles, the enemy reconfigured them—" he tapped the drawing's curved blade "—to be combatants."

"Or they reconfigured themselves," Lybrand said. "We're not sure about that."

The NoSeeUms traded glances, then looked to Tommy, silently communicating their disbelief.

"Robots reconfiguring robots," he said. "That would be advanced tech, way beyond anything I've ever heard of."

Ender nodded. "Agreed. There's no question we're dealing with advanced tech. They communicated via radio frequencies. Another member of the group figured out how to modify walkie-talkies to jam them, make them stumble around like they were drunk. However, the silverbugs adapted to that, and after a while the jamming didn't work. We're taking a high-powered backpack jammer with us, but all of our tactics will assume that we can't jam them at all."

A self-configuring AI swarm. Tommy had been out of the military game for a long time—maybe that level of tech wasn't as unusual as he'd first thought.

"Who made these drawings?" He asked.

Ender tilted his head toward Lybrand. "In-house talent. We couldn't risk hiring an artist or doing computer models or anything."

Something about his words embarrassed her.

"I did the best I could," she said, looking at the ground. She looked at the ground a lot.

"They're good," Tommy said.

Lybrand's head snapped up. Tommy couldn't read her expression. Had Ender not complimented her work?

"Next, I'll show you your primary enemy," Ender said. "This isn't exactly right, but it's close enough to give you the idea."

He flipped the next page.

A ball-ish shape, with what looked like pseudopods extending from it, pseudopods of different thicknesses and lengths. Like a goo-filled balloon caught in mid-burst, or like a monstrous amoeba. And its colors…electric neon oranges and reds and greens. Small, glistening black dots of varying sizes speckled the multihued skin.

Lovecraftian. The word popped into Tommy's head unbidden, yet it fit perfectly.

He felt a burst of adrenaline surge through his body: *It's an alien. Please-please-*please *let it be an actual alien.*

Skylark pointed at the drawing. "What the unholy *fuck* is *that?*"

Ender glanced at the image, perhaps trying to see it anew through everyone else's eyes.

When he again faced the team, Tommy saw his cold intensity, his grim determination. Something had changed in the man, changed because of what that drawing represented.

"We call this a *rocktopi,*" he said.

Mullet shook his head. "Color me ignorant of biology, but that as sure as fuck ain't a couple of octopuses."

"Not *OCT-o-pie.*" Ender over-enunciated the syllables. "*ROCK-toe-pie.* As in, the rocks the mountains are made of. A man named Mack Hendricks named them. These things killed him."

"This is that Pandemic shit," Hatchet said. "Right? The same shit that turned people into rioting psychos and mutated monsters?"

Tommy stared at the picture. He'd been in prison when the Pandemic had hit four years earlier, starting in Chicago and raging across the globe. The worst disaster in human history. Nukes had flown, and not just in America. By the time the Pandemic was contained, the death toll was estimated at eight hundred million people. Thirty million of those had been Americans.

Tommy—along with most of the world, probably—had been shocked to see how fast things returned to normal. Governments buried or burned the bodies. Roads and highways were repaired. Cities had been rebuilt with stunning speed, fueling a new economic boom.

Great floods, world wars, earthquakes, revolutions, famines, even a disaster of Biblical proportions caused by a microscopic bit of extra-terrestrial matter…after massive loss of life, humanity had a knack for recovering quickly.

"These creatures have nothing to do with the Pandemic," Ender said. "They were under a mountain in Utah at least twelve thousand years before it happened, and they were still there after it was contained. They attacked the EarthCore camp. They attacked us in the tunnels. Somewhere around here, there is another tunnel system. When we find it—" he pushed a finger against the drawing "—these things might be in there."

Kevin raised a hand. "Exactly how many of these *cock*-topi might we be facing?"

"We don't know," Lybrand said. "There might be none at all. In Utah, there were hundreds of them."

Skylark stood. She stepped closer to the drawing, studied it.

"You didn't answer my question, Ender," she said. "They're not connected to the Pandemic, okay, I'll take your word for it, but what *are* they? You said they've been here for twelve thousand years? Is this some subterranean species people have never seen before? What *is* it?"

Tommy held his breath.

"They are alien beings of some kind," Ender said. "Creatures from another world."

Dead silence in the room.

Tommy's heart hammered. It wasn't possible. It just wasn't. But he knew Patrick O'Doyle. Ender wouldn't bullshit, not about something like this.

If it was real, if these were actual extraterrestrials … not from a book or a movie or a TV show, but *real* … Tommy's head swam.

"Aliens," Mullet said. "Seriously?"

Ender nodded. "We saw the spaceship that brought them to Earth."

Curveball stroked his beard. "I'll go ahead and be the one to say it out loud, since everyone is thinking it. We spent a whole day traveling here. We all walked away from business, jobs, families. Yes, we got a check, but if this is just some grandiose practical joke—"

"*Grandiose* is an excellent word," Hatchet said.

Curveball bowed his head. "Thank you, I do try. If this is some grandiose practical joke, Ender, my good man, it's time to come clean. You got us. But if you try to keep stringing us along and it turns out this is bullshit? I will kill you myself."

Tommy wanted Ender's words to be true more than he'd wanted

anything in his entire life. Did the others feel the same? Did they have any idea of how momentous this was?

"You all know me," Ender said. "You know damn well I wouldn't have brought you here as a gag. Bertha and I fought these things. We got up close and personal with them. They're real. Their spaceship was a wreck, but it was *real*."

He paused, gave everyone the chance to say something. No one did. Tommy saw the expressions of his former squad mates, saw that they felt the same way he did—that Ender was telling the truth.

"Aliens," Mullet said. "Holy motherforking shirtballs."

Hatchet nodded. "This is wild, Ender. Really wild."

"Wait a second," Tommy said. "You told us the rocktopi attacked you with knives and rocks. You also said you saw their ship. Why would an advanced, sentient species use primitive weaponry? They didn't have firearms?"

Mullet made air quotes. "Or *lay-zers?*"

"Get it out of your head that this is a sentient species," Ender said. "These aren't the cuddly *E.T. Phone Home* types. They're savages. Animals. They kill anything they see. A hundred years ago, they butchered a bunch of miners who got too close to their tunnels, chopped them into little pieces. The same thing happened somewhere near here, thousands of years ago, when the aliens attacked a village. They slaughtered men, women and children."

It was too much to process. And it didn't make sense.

"Aliens with a wrecked spaceship that use knives and rocks to kill people," Tommy said. "But a mining company is funding this mission. Do the rocktopi dig for gold or something?"

"Not gold," Ender said. "Platinum. Their entire ship was made out of it. A platinum ship that was four miles long, a half-mile wide."

He paused, let that sink in.

"That's a lotta fucking platinum," Hatchet said.

Ender nodded. "It was. When we started, EarthCore didn't know it was a ship. They found a huge platinum lode, and they went after it."

"Gotta go after those huge loads," Kevin said. "Am I right, Curve?"

Curveball rolled his eyes.

"There's one more major threat," Ender said. "When we were in the ship, we saw a large metal orb hanging above a shaft. Most of the ship was beaten to hell, showing the effects of twelve thousand years of neglect, but the orb looked like it had been consistently maintained. Two scientists, Veronica Reeves and her father, Sanji Haak, were trapped underground with us. The rocktopi killed Sanji. Veronica was grief-stricken. When we were almost out, she slipped away from us. Bertha and I think she figured out how to lower the orb into the shaft and detonate it. That's probably what blew up the mountain and caused the volcano."

A bomb that created a volcano? Tommy tried to calculate how much power would be needed to punch a hole in the Earth's crust. Or, how advanced a culture would have to be to dig a hole so deep the detonation point was already close to the mantle.

"Tech of that level is vastly beyond anything humankind knows," Tommy said. "Quite a bit more advanced than rocks and knives."

Ender nodded. "Legacy tech, probably put there thousands and thousands of years ago. Trust me, the rocktopi we faced weren't capable of building it."

"So much for an act of God," Hatchet said.

Mullet raised a hand. "And you're telling us this because you think the ship we're looking for will have the same thing?"

"We have to assume so," Ender said. "Finding the ship, determining if there is a similar device, locating it and securing it is our primary objective. Once we have control of it, we'll expand the operation. But I want you all to understand the risk."

Silence fell over the room.

So much of what Ender said didn't line up logically, yet Tommy knew the man—Ender was doing this with or without the rest of the NoSeeUms. Was the payoff really worth it?

"Not an act of God, but the power of one," Sleepy said. "You all need to think carefully about the value of your lives."

More silence.

What *value* did Tommy's life have, anyway?

"Somewhere around here, there are tunnels that lead to another ship," Ender said. "We are going to find those tunnels. If there are rocktopi down there, we're going to wipe them out. Every last one of them. Once the site is cleared of threats, we will turn it over to EarthCore, and we will all become very, very rich."

The NoSeeUms traded looks. Each of them wanted someone else

to say something, but what was there to say? As bizarre as the scenario was, it boiled down to a rather simple equation: fight aliens, get paid.

An equation that seemed out of character for Patrick O'Doyle—at least for the Patrick O'Doyle they'd all known two decades ago.

"You never cared about money," Tommy said. "You cared about country. You cared about *us*. But never about money."

Ender gestured around the room, to each of the NoSeeUms.

"I still care about all of you," he said. "That's why I brought you in for this. I'm confident that with our skills, and knowing what we're going after, we can get in and out without losing anyone. You'll all be set for life."

Tommy shook his head. "Bullshit." The word came harsher than he'd meant. He softened his tone. "I mean, okay, I believe that setting us all up for life is *part* of your decision, but there's something else to this."

Ender said nothing. Tommy read his eyes. Maybe twenty years had passed, sure, but like Ender had said, he hadn't changed that much. Money or no money, there was only one real reason the man would want to throw down like this.

"You lost someone in Utah," Tommy said. "Someone that mattered to you like *we* matter to you."

Ender glanced to the window. Outside, a shifting, swirling curl of snow danced away from the shore, gleaming in the sun before it died on the surface of the turquoise lake.

"Eighteen years after we were disbanded, my life was a mess," he said. "I don't know if any of you have thought about taking Felix's way out, but I was close to it."

Suicide. The stillness in the room told more truth than all the words in existence could ever convey. The unspoken communication of soldiers who have been through hell together, the almost telepathic connection of hard-core operators who have seen—and *been*—the worst that humanity has to offer.

Ender wasn't alone; everyone in the room had thought about eating a bullet at one point or another.

Everyone, including Tommy. He had a shitty little twenty-five caliber pistol in his shitty little studio apartment. How many times had he pressed the barrel of that Raven MP-25 to his temple and thought of ending it all?

One hundred and seventy-two times.

Because a bullet would chase away the thoughts of Bandah, forever.

"I had nothing," Ender said. "No money. I was basically homeless. I couldn't get work in our field, obviously. I tried other jobs, but I couldn't seem to—" he glanced up, searching for the words "—to get them right. I couldn't get my head around them. They all seemed so… meaningless."

Tommy found himself nodding, saw Curveball doing the same.

"I was angry all the time," Ender said. "Angry, sad, confused, betrayed." He forced a smile. "And you all know how in-touch with my emotions I am, right?"

That drew an awkward but welcome laugh, a laugh that helped break the tension of the NoSeeUms watching their stoic leader talk about how far he'd fallen.

"Command cut us loose," Ender said, steel slowly returning to his voice. "After all that we accomplished, after all that we suffered, they *cut us loose*. What was our parting gift? A not-so-subtle reminder that the things we did never happened, that if we ever talked about any of it, to *anyone*, we'd wind up just like the people we'd taken out."

That memory brought a chill to Tommy's heart. He, Ender and the others had worked for a department that had no name. *Gray work*. Tommy remembered the day their boss, Murray Longworth, had left the department. His replacement told the NoSeeUms they'd been discharged. Time to move on. Thank you for your service. Oh, and by the way, if you like your skin actually attached to your body and not piled up on a dirt floor in a location where laws don't apply? Then keep your mouth shut about the things you did for your country. Don't bother trying to get mercenary work, because we've put you on an industry blacklist that no company will ignore. If you take off-the-books merc jobs? Refer back to the comment about where you might find your skin.

Dear Thomas Strymon III—you are *retired*. Permanently.

"I didn't tell you this before, so I'll tell you now," Ender said. "In 2010, I went back to work for Longworth."

"You *what?*" Sleepy's hand shook with fury. Coffee sloshed out of the mug. "You went back to work for that bastard? He cut us loose!"

Skylark turned to look over the back of the couch at Sleepy.

"He wasn't responsible for what happened to us, and you know it," she said. "He probably got shafted just like we did."

"*Fuck* him." Sleepy looked at his hand—he'd spilled coffee on it. He set his mug down, wiped his hand against his pants leg.

"I agree with Pastor Pussybitch," Mullet said. "Fuck that guy. Say it wasn't his doing, okay—he didn't even have balls to give me a call and tell me himself? He's *never* called me to check in. He call any of you?"

The silence spoke volumes.

Skylark turned back to face Ender.

"But he called *you*," she said. "With a job. Right?"

Ender nodded, guilt thick in his eyes.

"Yeah. But it wasn't gray work. Not really. He had a new gig, working for the Department of Special Threats. Biohazards, mostly, with some really weird shit I won't get into right now. Just like I've tuned out most of what we did in the NoSeeUms, I've tuned that out as well. What matters is I lasted only two years with him. When I was there, I was … I was in a bad place, mentally. He cut me loose. I can't blame him for that. Anyway, when I got canned, I thought I'd lost my last chance to do what I'm good at."

He paused, rubbed at his jaw, then, absently, at the scar tissue where his ear had once been.

Tommy wondered if Ender would tell the story of that horrible scar. He imagined not—the man wasn't the kind to talk about old wounds.

"I spent the next few years just … floundering," Ender said. "I was close to cashing in my chips when I got lucky. This woman, a former spook, I think, she somehow found out about my past, my work for Longworth. She recruited me to handle security for EarthCore. A man named Connell Kirkland was my boss. It was a big job, a difficult job. Connell gave me full responsibility to get it done right. First job I ever had where the paycheck didn't come from the government. Connell Kirkland had *faith* in me. He never knew it, but that job saved me." Ender glanced at Lybrand, smiled. "And because of him, because of that job, I met my wife."

He cleared his throat. Was he about to cry? In all the years they'd served together, Tommy had only seen the man cry twice: once when he got word his mother had died, and once after Bandah.

"Connell wasn't a soldier," Ender said. "But when we were trapped underground, he fought his ass off. Outside of the people in this room, he was the best man I've ever known." He tapped the colorful drawing of the rocktopi. "Because of these things, Connell is dead. So are a lot of other people. Is this money? Of course. Is money the only reason I'm going in? No, it's not. On most of our missions, they told us we were taking out fanatics. Lunatics. Monsters. Well, that's what these things are—*monsters*."

Tommy empathized with the man, but his story raised red flags.

"In Denver," Tommy said, "you told us you wanted payback because these things killed your friends, but you didn't tell us how deep that went. This is *personal* for you. We never did *personal*, Ender."

"Worm's right." Skylark sat back down. "We didn't do vendettas or revenge. We were professionals. We followed orders. You were the one who told us making things personal could cloud our judgment."

Ender put his hands behind his back, stood at parade rest.

"We all followed orders," he said. "Now I'm the one giving them. I made it clear from the start this is a military operation. I'm in charge. If you aren't comfortable with my leadership, if you want to opt out, speak up now."

Opt out. Tommy's instincts screamed at him to do just that, because Ender wasn't the Ender of old. He had a score to settle. That could lead to bad decisions. Bad decisions got people killed. But Tommy could barely look away from the picture of the wildly colored creature. His instant and powerful desire to see one in real life drowned out logic.

"You told us we wouldn't have to kill *people*." Tommy gestured to the drawing. "What you meant was we get to kill these things instead."

Ender nodded.

"If you're right and they really are aliens," Tommy said, "we're talking about the most important discovery in the history of mankind. And you want to go in there and slaughter them all?"

"*Hundredmillion*," Mullet said in a fake cough. "*Hundredmillion-each*."

Curveball sighed. "For fuck's sake, Worm, we've done so much killing, does it really matter if it's people or some stupid alien?"

"*Yes*, it *matters*," Tommy said, again hearing that unintentional sharpness in his voice. "This isn't some tin-pot dictator in a third-world country. And yeah, I know some kind of extraterrestrial microorganism caused the Pandemic, but this is different—these are sentient creatures that *flew here* on a *starship*. This is proof we're not alone in the universe. It changes our place in the cosmos. It changes *everything,* instantly and forever."

Mullet squinted, pantomimed masturbating. "Unnnnhh, alien life. Unnnnn*ahhhh*! My name is Tommy and I beat off to alien life!" He wiped his hand against his shirt. "Go stroke yourself somewhere else, Tommy. Aliens don't change shit, just like everything else we've seen didn't change shit, just like all the wars ever fought didn't change shit. No matter what happens, people will keep being horrible to each other. Nothing is *ever* going to change that. So if we have to live in this shitty world, shouldn't we at least be rich?"

No one argued with him. How could they not see what this meant?

"We can't just kill them," Tommy said. "We need to report this to the government. These aliens need to be protected."

"*Protected?*" Ender sneered. "They attacked us. They didn't just kill everyone, they *chopped up the bodies* and *buried the pieces*. Every time the rocktopi have encountered people—from the old west in Utah, to what we went through, to tribal civilizations around Mount Fitz Roy hundreds of years ago—they have murdered every human they've found. They cut open skulls and use those knives to stir the brains inside, just to be sure."

He jabbed a finger against the drawing, hit it too hard—the easel rocked backward, almost fell over before it tipped forward again, back into place. The rocktopi drawing rattled, swung out from the momentum, making the multicolored creature seem to move on its own.

"These things kill people," Ender said. "In a way, what we're doing on this mission is the same as all the other missions we did together."

"Only with more cash involved," Curveball said.

Mullet raised his hand. "Might I add, *a lot more* cash?"

Tommy had to get through to Ender, to everyone. How could anyone be thinking about *money*?

"No one's ever heard of these beings," Tommy said. "They're not some slavering horde rampaging through the countryside. It sounds like they kill those who enter their space—like they're defending themselves. Maybe they just want to be left alone."

"*Hundredmillion,*" Mullet coughed.

Hatchet rubbed at his face. "Tommy, Bookworm, my pal, *who gives a fuck?* We deal in death. Can you even remember how many people you've killed?"

Twenty-four. That I know of.

"No," Tommy lied.

"Neither can I," Hatchet said. "But it was a lot. If we can whack human beings for a paycheck, then why can't we whack whatever these things are for a *much bigger* paycheck? You want to sit on the sidelines for this one? Go ahead. Me? I'm in. Kill them all and let God sort them out."

"Or the Cylons," Curveball said. "Maybe the Cylons will sort them out. I'm in as well. We might exterminate some fancy intelligent race? So fucking what. I don't care."

Hatchet's take didn't surprise Tommy, but Curveball had always seemed the more thoughtful of the two. More philosophical.

"I'm in," Skylark said. She gave Tommy a sad smile. "This kind of money changes everything for my family. Forever. It's worth the risk. Maybe in *Star Trek*, humans and other races get along, but getting along won't pay my bills. The future of my children is more important than the future of your aliens."

Mullet laughed. "I got kids, too, and I could give a shit about their future. No one helped me when I was their age, so they can make it on their own. But to see an actual alien?" He looked up to the ceiling, smiling. "To *kill* one? That's the kind of story not many old soldiers can tell."

Tommy stood alone. What had happened to these people since the team had been shut down? Wasn't this far bigger than terrorists or taking out a dictator that *might* someday pose a minor threat to the US?

Or … maybe his squad mates hadn't changed at all. Maybe they'd always been this way—willing, even *eager*, to kill.

"All right," Tommy said. "What happens if I opt out?"

Ender gestured to the room, the lodge, all of it.

"You stay here until the mission is complete. Enjoy the view. Go for a hike. Read your books. Don't do anything you don't want to do. But I need an answer, Tommy, and I need it now—are you in, or are you out?"

Out. He's not the leader you once knew. He's going to get you killed. Out, out, out.

Tommy opened his mouth to say just that, but the words didn't come. He stared at the drawing. The angry, amazing, impossible drawing.

He didn't want to do this.

But if he walked away, he could never live with himself. If he passed up a chance to see these creatures, to see an actual alien spaceship, he knew damn well that in a matter of months he'd wind up following in Felix's footsteps.

"In," he said. "I'm in."

22

October 20

LOOKING AT THEM all was like looking into a time warp.

Prior to the meeting in Denver four days earlier, Patrick hadn't seen these people in two decades. They'd changed. More lines around the eyes, down the cheeks. Some were fatter, like Hatchet, some were thinner, like Worm. Gray hair in Skylark's shoulder-length black curls, and in Curveball's formerly jet-black beard. Two dye-jobs, even— Sleepy's bizarre bleach-blond, and Mullet pretending that his thinning hair was still the same brown it had been way back when.

And so many intangible signs of age, where Patrick couldn't put his finger on exactly what had changed, he just knew his friends were visibly *older*.

Faces changed over the course of twenty years, and faces also stayed the same. Patrick simultaneously saw the middle-aged people they were and the vibrant soldiers they had been in their prime: the constant hint of a smile on Skylark's mouth; the intelligence in Worm's eyes; Sleepy's intense stare; Hatchet's constant expression of suspicion, like someone was always trying to pull something over on him; Curveball's constant expression of subdued joy, like he was the guy everyone wanted to confide in.

"Ender," Skylark said. "You gonna get on with this or what?"

Patrick came back to the moment. "Sorry. Let's get to work."

He'd gathered them in the lounge again, this time to go over weapons and load-out. Bertha stood next to him, a large equipment crate resting on a small table in front of her. The NoSeeUms sat in chairs and couches.

"We were able to locally source most of the gear," Patrick said. "One of our old suppliers here was able to get us the bulk of it."

Mullet raised a hand. "Santiago's still alive?"

Patrick nodded.

"Fucker still owes me forty bucks," Mullet said. "Or was that pesos? Either way, with twenty years' worth of interest, I'm sure it's a bunch."

Sometimes, if not most times, it was better to just ignore Mullet's babbling.

"We'll all be wearing camo fatigues, black and gray to fit the tunnel conditions," Patrick said. "No insignia of any kind. Boots are provided, as are advanced combat helmets fitted with mining headlamps. You got a jumpable plate carrier rig with front and back ceramic armor plates. The rig has MOLLE webbing, so you can configure your load as you see fit. There is going to be a lot of walking—you might be tempted to ditch your plates, but I advise against it. I'll be wearing mine."

Patrick looked at each person in the room, seeing if anyone objected to the extra weight of body armor. No one did.

"You'll each carry four thirty-round mags and two V40 grenades," he said. "Everyone gets a repelling-capable rescue belt, with carabiners, ascender, holster for sidearm, and three fifteen-round magazines. You will be carrying a backpack with internal Camelback, a hundred and fifty feet of rope, a first aid kit, seven extra thirty-round mags, four extra V40s, one M112 block of C4, and one claymore."

Mullet grinned, nodded. "I *love* claymores. Not a lot of those in the used car market. Which is a shame, when you think about it. What kinda guns we get, man?"

Patrick nodded at Bertha.

From the crate, she pulled out a black, compact rifle, front handgrip folded under the frame, slim-profile stock folded against the frame's right side.

"Our primary weapon." Bertha flipped the front grip into place, did the same with the shoulder stock. "Forty-five caliber Glock 21s converted to carbines with a KPOS kit." She removed a suppressor from the box, screwed it on the end of the barrel. "Holographic sights, thirty-round mags, and a fun switch that kicks it to full auto."

She held up the full weapon for all to see.

"Fuck that shit," Mullet said. "We don't have H&Ks or something? Glocks are for mall ninjas."

Bertha snorted. "Then you'll love our sidearm choice."

She handed the carbine to Sleepy, who felt the weight, started examining it closely. From the crate, Bertha pulled out a handgun.

"Sidearms are G21s as well," she said. "Everyone carries the same ammo, all magazines are interchangeable between sidearms and carbines."

Mullet shook his head. "This is some goddamn bullshit, Ender. I've got my own weapon preferences. You know this."

Bertha sighed, rolled her eyes. "Jesus, dude, quit bitching. You point, you shoot, you make a big hole, okay?"

Mullet flipped her off.

Not even two full days at the lodge, and Mullet and Bertha were already getting on each other's nerves. Patrick understood—most people didn't get along with Mullet. Because Mullet was a dick. Bertha wasn't acting like herself, though. She seemed to be itching for a fight. Jealous of Skylark? That was ridiculous, yet very real. And there was something else going on with Bertha, something Patrick couldn't put his finger on.

"Everyone goes in with identical gear," he said. "That's the way it is."

Sleepy shook his head. "Not even a sniper rifle for Tommy? That's a waste of talent."

Patrick couldn't argue with that, but reality was reality.

"Long guns aren't feasible where we're going," he said. "We need compact weapons. There's one piece of gear we need to focus on, because if you don't use it correctly, you'll die. Bertha?"

She reached into the crate again, pulled out the yellow KoolSuit

Patrick had worn in Utah. It was dirty, burned in a few places, ripped in several others, and—across much of the surface—splattered with rusty bloodstains.

"Great," Kevin said. "I always wanted to cosplay as a banana."

Patrick took the KoolSuit, held it by the shoulders. The flaccid arms and legs dangled.

"This is an advanced temperature-control rig, known as a *KoolSuit*," he said. "That's *Kool* with a *K*, after the inventor. When we go into the tunnels, we—"

"*If* we go in," Bertha mumbled.

Patrick glared at her. She was contradicting him in front of the others? Marriage or not, she'd have to understand that—on this operation—he was in charge, and she was at the same level as the rest of the team.

"*When* we go into the tunnels," he said, "we will be descending far below the surface. Perhaps as far as three miles deep. At those depths, geothermal heat is so intense that rocks will burn bare skin. It's hot enough that without these suits, we would die even before we got to that level."

He watched his people, let that information sink in. He'd told them they'd be in tunnels, but never mentioned the insane depths they were likely to experience.

"I guess the rocktopi are tough bastards," Hatchet said.

Patrick nodded. "That they are."

"Temperatures that would kill us," Worm said. "We're talking about 160 degrees Fahrenheit and up. That about right?"

Worm knowing at least a little something about damn near everything—that hadn't changed in twenty years, either.

"We had temps of over two hundred Fahrenheit," Bertha said. "My KoolSuit got cut up. The internal fluid partially drained out. Repairing the suits is fast and easy, but if you're exposed to those temps for even a minute, you're pretty much fucked."

Skylark stood, took the beat-up yellow suit out of Patrick's hands. She looked it over. She held it up as he had, by the shoulders—the suit's feet and lower legs lay limp on the floor.

"One size fits all?" she said.

"This is the old model," Patrick said. "The V1. I wanted you to see what Bertha and I wore in Utah, and we survived. This time, we're going in with the new V2 suits. Sadly, Mullet, the new version will not support your banana dreams. Bertha?"

Skylark set the suit aside and sat back down.

Bertha reached into the crate again, this time coming out with a matte-black tube about the length and thickness of her arm. *Kool Products* was printed on the surface in glossy black letters. The tube had two sections, one that took up about two-thirds the length, and the other the last third.

She pressed a button in the middle of the longer segment, which popped open lengthwise. She took out a tightly rolled suit. With a flick, she extended the suit, held it up by the shoulders—the material was thinner than the V1, and transparent, save for a thick, rubbery, milky-white waistband filled with small but blocky bits of equipment.

"All the cooling gear is in the waistband," Bertha said.

Mullet clasped his hands together as if he was praying.

"But it's not *yellow*! I won't *look* like a banana, Ender, but will I *feel* like one? I've always identified as tropical fruit."

"Now you know how Hatchet feels," Skylark said in a deadpan.

Hatchet slow-clapped. "Wow, a fruit joke for the gay guy. That's some high-level comedy, Marie."

Curveball shrugged. "I thought it was funny."

Skylark laughed and blew them both a kiss.

Patrick nodded to Bertha, telling her to continue.

"The suits are unisex, one size fits all," she said. "Repairs are easy. This is a smart material, whatever that means, so if you have a tear, just press a patch over the top and it will seal itself up. There's some kind of chemical fluid circulating through the material that provides the temperature regulation. I won't pretend I know how the tech works."

"Neither will I," Patrick said. "But we know it *does* work. Show them the rest."

Bertha opened up the shorter section of the tube. She pulled out a hood made from the same clear material. A milky-white headband built into the hood popped into shape.

She pulled the hood on. Like spandex, the material contracted to form-fit her head, neck and chin.

"This is where it gets cool," Bertha said. "No pun intended."

She pressed the headband at the center of her forehead. A visor popped down like a sci-fi version of a Venetian blind, sealing to the hood's cheeks and chin. Once locked in, the visor had no glare and was as smooth as glass.

"There's a built-in heads-up display that gives basic information," she said. The face shield barely affected her voice. "Air temperature, body temperature, depth and compass heading, and remaining battery charge." She pressed the headband at the left temple—her face shield flooded a transparent gray. "Night vision uses active illumination. Deep down, the temperatures we'll be facing are a hundred degrees higher than normal body temperature. We're not sure how well any night vision system will work down there. The outer layer of the KoolSuit itself will match the ambient temperature, so anyone wearing one of these suits is all but invisible on infrared."

Sleepy leaned forward in his chair. "Can the rocktopi see in the dark?"

"We don't know," Patrick said. "They generate their own biolumi-nescent light. Maybe they see by that light, maybe they see some other way. They didn't seem like they were active hunters, it was more like the silverbugs made long lines that told the rocktopi where to go, where to attack."

Curveball stood, lifted the V2 KoolSuit off the table, stared through the clear material.

"Temperature control, stored air, night vision … must be expensive stuff."

"Enormously so," Patrick said. "A single one of these suits costs more than all the rest of our load-out combined. If your suit gets cut, you'll know, because the coolant is yellow, kind of runny. And, of course, you'll probably start to get hot. You will carry spare coolant and repair kits, letting you fix most tears or cuts. We will have two KoolSuits for everyone, so you have a full backup available if your primary suit is too damaged to repair. These suits used up the bulk of our budget, so learn how to use them, and handle with care."

Patrick enjoyed the fact that Angus Kool's side-company had outlived him. He hoped the people who worked there were enjoying a life that didn't involve that little prick's arrogance.

"Wait a minute," Mullet said. "You told us it's like two hundred degrees where we're going. Do we take off the suit to go numero uno and numero dos?"

Bertha winced. She didn't want to mention that part. Patrick couldn't blame her.

"That part is a little bit disgusting," Patrick said. "The suit's booty, for lack of a better word, contains some micro-machinery that removes moisture from feces, then ejects the remaining dry material."

Kevin's face wrinkled. "*What?* What happens to the recovered moisture, then?"

"I'm guessing the same thing that happens to the water vapor in our breath," Tommy said. "And our urine. It gets captured, filtered, and reused. Right?"

Patrick and Bertha nodded.

Tommy grinned. "It's like a damn stillsuit from *Dune*. Amazing."

Kevin held up his hands. "Woah, *hold on* a minute. Are you telling me that I will be drinking my own shit and piss?"

Hatchet elbowed Curveball. "Lucky Kevin finally gets to live out his fetishes."

Curveball laughed, as did Marie. Even Sleepy couldn't hide a smile.

"Fuck you guys," Mullet said.

Curveball sat forward, elbows on knees. "What about comms? The poop-suits have those, too?"

Patrick nodded. "They do, but Worm replaced the stock system with one of his own. The physical realities of underground communications constrain our available tactics. Worm?"

The skinny man stood.

"We'll be on the move, so we won't have the luxury of laying cable or utilizing surface stations to power our signals," Worm said. "We use standard headset comms in our helmets until the ambient temperature forces us to wear the KoolSuits. Once we have those on, we wear the helmet over the hood, but we switch to comms integrated into the suits' headbands. I replaced the suits' stock comms with a miniaturized tactical system. We'll have push-to-talk, and an open channel. Because our comms are inside the suits, we don't have to worry about high air temps screwing with the gear. However, once we're underground, our signals won't go much farther than line of sight, both for us and for the little hornet drones we'll be using to scout."

Mullet raised his hand. "Let me get this straight. We'll be far below ground, where it's hot enough to kill us, we may be heavily outnumbered by silverbugs and fucking aliens, and if we get too far apart, we'll have no way to call for help if we run into some nasty shit?"

Patrick nodded. "You understand the tactical landscape."

"Come on, Mullet," Hatchet said. "You wanna live forever?"

Mullet shrugged. "Oh, I'm not complaining. I'm in. I just wanted to make sure I understood how this chickenshit operation was going to work."

Bertha pointed at him, started to speak, but Patrick held up a hand to cut her off.

"Enough chit-chat," he said. "We'll cover other gear in training, including the jammer that will hopefully screw up silverbug communication. Time for us to get used to working together again. Full dress rehearsal. Get your KoolSuits on, then the rest of your gear. We'll meet out front in thirty minutes."

"I COULDN'T FIND their trail," Sonny said.

He held a coffee cup in both hands. The heat warmed his skin. It was still far too cold outside for his taste. When the "road" leading to this lodge got so bad his truck couldn't handle it, he'd had to walk the rest of the way—well over a mile, face-first into a stiff wind.

The Utah desert had never seemed so distant.

O'Doyle's nostrils flared. His face looked a bit redder than normal, increasing the contrast with the thinning blond buzz cut.

Sonny had just told the big man how Jabour and Chus wouldn't play ball. How the kids had snuck away from their cabin. How he'd been unable to spot any sign of them.

"And yet, you're in *here*," O'Doyle said. "Not out *there*, hunting."

Over the years, Sonny had faced down many angry people. Some powerful, some rich, some dangerous, even, but none of those people made him want to find a place to hide—Patrick O'Doyle did. The holstered pistol strapped to the man's right hip didn't help.

Sonny leaned back on the couch, tried to relax, or at least to make it look like he was relaxing. This big-ticket lodge, this pristine location … under other circumstances, the place would have been the ideal getaway. As things were, though, Sonny suddenly wanted to be anywhere but here.

"I spent a day trying to pick up their trail, but a storm hit shortly after they ditched me. There was no trail to follow."

"Is that the same storm that blew over yesterday?" O'Doyle shook his head. "You came *here* instead of heading up the mountain to look for them?"

Sonny was intimidated, sure, but there was only so much nonsense he could take.

"The storm didn't *blow over*, it just died down a bit," he said. "And it's picking back up tonight. Climb up after them? Has your big, dumb ass even *seen* that mountain?" Sonny pointed out the picture window. "Oh, look, there it is. That giant middle finger of granite, right out there. The mountain that experienced climbers *die on*, even in *perfect* weather. You think my wrinkled old ass wants to get caught up there when the storm comes back?"

O'Doyle stared.

Sonny barely knew the man. They weren't strangers, but they weren't friends, either. They were business partners, trying to pull off the score of the century.

"You had one job," O'Doyle said. "You see me and Bertha here doing our jobs, don't you?"

Sonny's mouth felt dry. O'Doyle looked wound up tighter than a two-dollar watch.

"The mountain range covers thousands of square miles," Sonny said. "Hard terrain. Dangerous slopes. I'm sixty-seven years old—I'm not going to go hunting for a needle in a haystack."

"You did that just fine in the Wah Wah mountains."

"Compared to Fitz Roy, those are molehills," Sonny said. "Ain't you and those scary bastards you got outside a bunch of backwoods Rambo badasses? You got to be better at tracking than me, and there's *eight* of you. Can't *you* go into the mountains and see if you can spot them coming out?"

O'Doyle started pacing. He stared straight ahead, reaching one wall, turning on a heel, reaching the other, turning again.

"A search like that could take months," he said. "We don't have that kind of time. With what this operation is costing us, we've got two weeks, max, before we have to shut it all down. Ramiro and Chus have to come back to town sooner or later. When they do, we need to throw more money at them."

"I don't think they *care* about money. Fucking hippies. I know where they're staying—maybe you and your scary buddies could go there and introduce yourselves."

O'Doyle stopped pacing. "And then what, Sonny? *Beat* the location out of them?"

That was exactly what Sonny had meant. Hearing it spoken out loud, though, made it sound like it was the dumbest idea ever.

The big man reached behind his back—his hand came out holding a knife, the edge of a ten-inch blade reflecting the sunlight that came through the picture window.

"You can borrow this," O'Doyle said, flipping the knife and offering it hilt-first. "I mean, if we're going to torture people to get the information you were supposed to get, shouldn't it be you who does the slicing?"

Sonny tore his gaze from the weapon, forced himself to look O'Doyle in the eyes.

"I didn't mean it like that."

"Yeah, you did," O'Doyle said. "You just assumed my friends and I would be down for that kind of thing."

"All right, that was asinine of me. No, I don't want to rough up a couple of kids."

O'Doyle's hand reached behind his back again, slid the knife into the unseen scabbard.

"We have to think," he said. "If we don't find that entrance, we're so screwed."

Sonny felt bad for failing. And O'Doyle was right—they had to come up with something, fast, or all of this was for nothing.

"I'm not giving up," Sonny said. "The best chance to find Jabour's trail—or even the tunnel entrance itself—is to use that big Sikorsky y'all brought out here. I've got maps of the area. Let me draw out a proper search pattern. I know what to look for. The storm will last a day or so, then we go up."

O'Doyle started pacing again, back and forth, like an aging lion trapped in a zoo cage.

"A long helicopter search will draw attention, but we don't have much choice," he said. "I'll get ready to take my people up the mountain as well. We'll start first thing tomorrow morning. One of us better find that needle, Sonny. If we don't…"

He stopped pacing. His hand made the slightest motion toward his back, as if the hand itself was thinking about the knife.

About how the knife could get him what he wanted.

The hand fell to his side, became a fist.

"We better find that needle," he said again. "Get to work."

O'Doyle left the lounge.

Sonny sat there. He stayed very still, tried not to think about how the big man's knife blade had flashed in the sun.

23

1,906 feet below the surface

OCTOBER 21

In the safety of their El Chaltén cabin, and even in the two days in the basecamp cave prepping for their ultra-fast descent, it had been easy to forget about the fear of falling rock, about that odd clicking noise.

Now, however, in the utter silence of the steep, dark tunnel, Sam could think about little else. But she had to focus—every moment counted.

"There it is," she said, her headlamp beam flicking between the hole in the silt-covered granite tunnel floor, about fifteen feet further down the tunnel, and the three double-crescent knives in the alcove just past the hole. "How'd we do on time?"

Ram checked his forearm computer display. "We did great. Even with the extra weight, we cut…thirty-two minutes off our previous time."

"Want to change coolant now?"

He thought for a moment. "Yeah, we should. That leaves us with one extra each. Sam, look at me."

She turned to face him. Her headlamp beam amplified the shadows under his eyes, revealed his *do not fuck with me* expression.

"We change and work until that ice is melted," he said. "Then we make our final change and ascend. Agreed?"

Sam nodded.

"I'm serious," Ramiro said. "No cutesy begging like last time, Sam. When I say we make the last change, we make it, and that's it."

He'd forgiven her for keeping the platinum a secret. If she wanted to keep this man as her friend, she knew she'd burned through any tolerance he had left. Even though this might be her last few hours here, perhaps forever, she didn't dare push him any further.

"I promise," she said.

He stared into her eyes, perhaps looking for the lie that would soon come. But there would be no lie this time, no pleading, no whining. He had stood by her all this time—he deserved better.

"For real this time," she said.

His stare lasted a moment longer, then he smiled slightly.

"Then let's get you changed."

She turned again, studied both the hole and the three gleaming knives as he added ice bottles to her backpack.

Ramiro tapped the keys on his forearm computer.

"Starting the timer … now," he said. "I'll tell you what, Sam, I will miss this place but I sure as hell won't miss this heat."

She wouldn't miss that part, either. Who knew? With the new knives, maybe she could get more grants. Enough to buy a KoolSuit? Well, no, those were too expensive, but maybe she could approach the company directly, convince them to donate one to her so she could continue the research and, in exchange, get the company all kinds of free advertising.

"You hear anything?"

She listened, hearing only her breath and his.

"No," she said. "Nothing."

He nodded. "Good. Let's hope it stays this way. There's enough handholds in the wall for me to go past the hole, but let's put anchors in here just to be sure. You do the left side, I'll take the right."

Sam searched the wall for a suitable crack or fissure. She found one just above the silt-covered tunnel floor. She hated the thought of potentially defacing the tunnel, even the tiniest bit, but Ramiro's safety came first.

She removed an angle piton from her belt, slid it into the crack. She used her climbing hammer to lightly tap the piton into place, making sure it didn't wiggle in the slightest. Next, she took a quickdraw from her belt, hooked one of its two carabiners through the piton.

"Here's the rope," Ramiro said.

Sam threaded the rope through the quickdraw's other carabiner.

Ramiro tied off the rope, then pulled a climbing harness from his belt.

"Help me with this," he said. "These suits are so damn awkward."

She helped him get into the harness. The suits they both wore were basically water balloons with legs and sleeves, so she was careful to position the harness so it would cut off as little water flow as possible.

He tugged on the harness, making sure it was secure.

"All right," he said. "Let's get this done."

He secured the rope to his harness. They slowly moved closer to the hole, which was right in the middle of the four-foot-wide tunnel. They let out slack as they went, staying close to the wall.

Ramiro reached out a foot, gently tapped the edge close to the irregular black spot. Silt spilled over the side, hissing as it fell.

"How's it feel?" Sam asked.

"Feels solid, but I'm not going to chance it. Here we go."

Belly to the wall, Ramiro slid his left foot forward, made sure his footing was solid. He took his time finding a secure grip with his gloved left hand, then slid his right foot in, then found a good grip for his gloved right hand. He repeated the process. Slowly, methodically, he moved down the tunnel.

"I hate touching the stone," he said. "I can feel the heat right through the gloves."

He slid his left foot forward—when he reached for a new handhold, Sam heard a crack of stone, horrifyingly loud in the tight space: The floor collapsed beneath Ramiro, the black hole widening as if to swallow him up.

Frozen in time, she waited for him to drop, but he clung to the wall, seemed to hover above the now-larger black spot.

"I'm okay," he said. "Might have peed my pants, though." He looked down, his headlamp beam piercing the blackness. "I see the bottom. Maybe twenty feet down. Silty, just like up here. I don't see any tunnels out."

Twenty feet? A fall like that could kill him if he landed wrong. He'd definitely be hurt, probably debilitatingly so—down here, that could be the kiss of death.

Suddenly the whole quest for those three knives felt idiotic.

"The area is unstable," Sam said. "Forget it. Let's head back up."

Ramiro laughed. His headlamp flicking toward her, making her squint.

"If you think I'm leaving now, you're crazy," he said. "Gonna get me them knives."

"Ram, you almost *fell*. I'm calling it. We're done. Come back."

"I'm quitting, remember?" He reached out with his left hand, found a new handhold. "That means you're not the boss of me. It's okay, Sam, there's a ton of handholds here. Hard to tell, but the footing past the hole looks stable. I'm pretty sure I can get those knives."

Slowly, he moved past the hole, one handhold at a time, one foothold at a time. Sam watched, unable to help him. Her headlamp beam lit him like an actor in a spotlight.

A good five feet past the larger hole and almost to the carved alcove with the knives, Ramiro tentatively tapped with his left toe, testing the ground.

"Seems okay," he said.

"There's too much slack in the rope. Put in an anchor."

He nodded, making his headlamp beam bounce. "I will. Should be stable right next to the wall. I need to get a foot down to get the leverage."

His left foot tap-tap-tapped. Sam held her breath as he put his weight on the foot, his gloved hands still gripping handholds.

"Yeah, it's fine." She saw his beam flick to his left, saw the knives gleam like sharp, white fire. "Look at these bad boys. Hard to believe each one is worth a quarter-mil."

"Just get the anchor in," Sam said.

He nodded again. Right hand gripping the wall, with his left he reached to his belt for a piton.

The tunnel floor gave out beneath him. He vanished in a blink, there one second, gone the next.

"Ram!"

Sam rushed toward the edge of the hole, instantly stopped herself. The tunnel floor was unstable—she had to disperse her weight as far as possible. She got down on her belly, started crawling toward the edge.

"Ram! Answer me!"

His disembodied voice drifted up from the hole.

"Um … *ouch*," he said. "That hurt."

She slid forward a heart-hammering inch at a time. She was almost to the edge.

"Are you okay?"

"No," he said. "I think … aw shit, I think my leg is broken."

A chill in her gut, spreading down to her knees. A broken leg?

Calm down. One problem at a time. Get him out of the hole. He's got two coolant spares in his rig—you have time to get him to a safe temperature level before those run out.

She reached the edge, looked down.

Ramiro was on his butt, both hands holding his left leg just above the ankle. Broken rock lay all around him, sharp and hard. His mining helmet was still on. His safety rope had only the slightest bit of curve to it—if the hole had been another five feet deeper, it would have caught him before he hit bottom.

He glanced up at her, forced a smile.

"Sorry, kid," he said. "I've put us in a bit of a pickle."

"Just your leg? Anything else?"

His face screwed tight with pain. "I … I'm bleeding from somewhere." He took one hand off his ankle, felt at his shoulder. "Yep, shoulder."

"Bad?"

"No, not bad. Good cut, but not deep. Suit's cut, though. I'm leaking water."

The chill in her gut turned to solid ice.

"Can you climb?"

Her headlamp beam lit up his left leg. Bent funny just above the ankle.

"Yeah, if you can help with the slack," he said. "We better move quick. I don't know how bad the suit tear is."

Still flat on her belly, Sam slowly pushed away from the edge. When she was ten feet from the hole, she stood. Their situation wasn't good, but it could have been so much worse. Ram was conscious. He was in pain but could still move. With the rope, she could help him get out of there in short order, then they would patch his suit, if possible, and head up the tunnel.

She reached for the rope.

click-click …

She looked down the tunnel, over the hole in the floor.

"Ram, did you just make a noise?"

His voice filtered up from the shaft. "I'm losing non-essential gear to lighten the load, maybe that rattled a bit or something."

Sam wanted to feel relieved, but she didn't. That sound, the same one she'd heard the last time they were down here. More falling rock?

click-click … click-click

Her heart thudded. Her fingers tingled. That sound, it wasn't bits of granite falling, it was more like … like metal tapping on rock.

"I heard it that time," Ramiro called up. "And it wasn't me. Sam, hurry the fuck up. There's some small holes in the wall down here … I think the sound was coming from one of those."

She grabbed the rope, pulled a few feet to take up the slack.

"Keep it tight," Ramiro said.

click-click-click, click-click

"Oh *fuck*," Ramiro said. "They're coming out of the cracks! Pull! *Pull!*"

Sam put her foot against the wall and leaned back on the rope, pulling it as hard as she could, using the carabiner as a pulley. The rope tightened in stops and starts as Ramiro worked his way up the shaft wall.

She fell backward, slammed backpack-first against the tunnel floor. Her helmet fell away, smacked against the wall. The rope was still in her hand, but there was no tension.

"*They cut the rope,*" Ramiro screamed. "Sam, *help me!*"

She grabbed her helmet and slapped it on her head as she flopped to her belly, swam more than crawled across the silt toward the shaft's edge. She wanted to turn and run; the edge was unstable, she could fall in and they would *both* die, but she had to help him, had to see what was happening.

Sam reached the edge and peeked over.

Ramiro lay there, shivering, his headlamp beam flitting around the chasm with spastic intensity.

He wasn't alone.

Metal spiders, four of them, clinging to the walls, their round bodies gleaming a reflection of her headlamp. They crawled toward Ramiro. A small crack in the wall, right at the shaft floor, and in that crack, in the darkness there, Sam saw another reflection of metal, of *moving* metal.

She flinched as Ramiro's headlamp beam hit her eyes.

"Sam," he said, his voice little more than a whisper. "*Help me.*"

The crack vomited a wave of twitching silver, liquid metal splashing out in a mercury flood of round, shiny bodies and long, thin, jittery legs.

Ramiro screamed. He tried to scoot away, but there was no place for him to go.

The metal wave crashed over him; he vanished beneath it. His headlamp blinked out, leaving only hers to light up the horror. Ramiro's hand reached up through the metal, gloved fingers reaching toward Sam, too far away to grab.

"*Sam, get them off me!*"

The flood of metal thickened. The shaft floor, gleaming and reflecting and flashing, seemed to rise up, and Sam saw the spiders climbing up the walls, climbing *fast.*

Climbing toward *her.*

She found herself on her feet, on her feet and running up the slope.

From behind her, the echo of Ramiro's terrified voice.

"*Get them off me gethemoffme!*"

Those were the last words she heard, because he started screaming, a throat-ripping sound that ricocheted off the stone walls.

Sam ran. She ran and she didn't look back.

ON THE SURFACE

Bertha and Patrick lay in bed, him on his back, her head on his shoulder, his arm around her, his hand on her ribs. They were both exhausted from the day's training.

"I'm going to be so sore in the morning," she said.

"Me too. But don't tell anyone else. I'm supposed to be bulletproof."

Bertha laughed. "I doubt your pals think a forty-nine-year-old man is *bulletproof*. Y'all aren't in the military anymore, I don't think they'll question your leadership if you show a little weakness."

She felt his body stiffen at the word. That was her man—others were allowed to be weak, he wasn't. Not for the first time, Bertha wondered at his upbringing, wondered what kind of life he'd had to make him this unforgiving of himself.

"I'll be fine in the morning," he said.

She angled her head, kissed his cheek. "I know you will."

He stank of sweat, and she loved it. She loved the smell of him, even when he was funky. He needed a shower, but that could wait a few minutes.

Was this what love was like for everyone? So overwhelming. So peaceful just to be in his arms. *Content.* That was the word, that was how she felt when she was with him and he was with her—with *her*, not plotting to conquer a mountain or talking to his team.

Or talking to Marie.

Just the thought of that woman made Bertha think of losing Patrick.

If he and Sonny and the others found the tunnel entrance, if he fought the rocktopi again, he might die.

"Pat?"

"Yeah?"

She hesitated a moment more, not wanting this perfect moment to end, then she dove in.

"Maybe we should call the whole thing off."

She felt his body stiffen again. He slid his arm off her. He sat up, feet on the floor, and stared out. The temperature in the room seemed to drop fifteen degrees.

She sat up, too, laid her head on his back.

"We don't need the money," she said. "We don't. We can find something else."

She felt him take a deep breath, felt his chest expand, then contract as he let it out. Bertha shivered. She couldn't help it. He hadn't said anything, but his demeanor had changed. Just like that, she was afraid of him, of what he might do next.

"We talked about this," he said. "When we were in Denver. I told you that if you didn't want to come, you didn't have to."

"You know I had to. No matter what. We're a team. I have to look out for you."

Some men would have laughed at that. Especially men like Patrick—highly trained, dangerous men who could take care of themselves. But he didn't laugh: *team* was his native language.

Finally, he stood up. He turned, looked down at her.

"This doesn't make any sense," he said. "We did all that planning, and you didn't object. We pitched Yakely. We got the money. Now we're *here*. As soon as we find the tunnels, we're going in, and *now* you want to quit?"

He was angry. She pulled the blanket over her legs, brought her knees to her chest.

"I just … I don't want to lose you," she said.

His expression shifted. She'd read him wrong—he wasn't angry, he was confused. With him, the two emotions looked so similar.

"What changed?" Patrick pointed in the direction of the lounge. "Because I've got six professionals out there ready to go. We've got the gear to do this right. Yakely paid millions to set this up."

"Oh, fuck Yakely! Maybe she pretended to try and talk us out of this at first, but she's just another rich, greedy asshole sending a bunch of grunts to do her dirty work."

"This was *our* idea," Patrick said. "*We* pitched it to *her*, remember?"

"Of course I remember. I just didn't think she'd say *yes!*"

The words were out before she realized what she'd said.

Patrick backed up slightly, away from her, just enough to make her heart crack.

Now he was mad. No mistaking that look on his face for anything else.

"You didn't really want this," he said quietly. "You didn't think I could do it. You were … what … *humoring* me?"

That was exactly what she'd been doing. He was so angry, talking in a low voice, clearly trying hard to control his temper. Was he angry enough to walk out on her? Angry enough to leave her here at the lodge while he and his old war buddies went out looking for the tunnels?

Angry enough to try and send her home?

"I wasn't humoring you," she said, surprised at how easily the lie came out. "I wasn't. I just…I didn't think she'd actually go for it."

A nod. "Well, she did. And now here we are, ready to make it all happen, and it turns out you never believed in me in the first place."

She pushed the blanket aside, slid across the bed. She reached out, took his hand, was surprised he let her.

"Baby, look where I am," she said. "If I didn't believe in you, would I be here? I know you can do this, I just don't know if you *should*. Why risk our lives for money and some dead man if—"

"He's not just *some dead man*."

Patrick tried to pull his hands away, but she squeezed harder, refused to let go.

"Of course Connell was more than that, but Baby, *he's gone*. Those things murdered everyone but us. Your friends are killers, yeah, but remember the rocktopi? Wave after wave of them. And the silverbugs with the knives. What other kinds of silverbugs might be waiting for us this time? If we get in the tunnels, we have no idea what's going to happen. I don't want to see you cut to pieces. Do you want to see *me* cut to pieces?"

He blinked rapidly, his anger vanishing in an instant. Had it never occurred to him that his *wife* would be at risk?

"But you won't get hurt," he said.

"You don't *know* that. Let's just leave this place. Let's start a life together. Let's grow old together."

He started to speak, stopped, as if whatever words he'd been about to say made no sense. She knew him better and better each day, saw his confusion and instantly understood it—as crazy as it seemed, maybe he'd never really thought of growing *old* at all. Patrick O'Doyle had spent his life fighting the short-term battle of the moment, perhaps at the expense of thinking of the long-term war that was surviving long enough to see the future.

Bertha took his other hand, looked up into his eyes. She wanted him to see her, to *really* see her, to understand that each day with him was worth more to her than all the platinum that had ever been mined.

"Call it off," she said. "We go back safe. Your friends go back safe. It's not too late. Call it off."

She stared into his eyes until he looked away.

"It's … it's not that easy," he said, his voice as soft as it was when he whispered in her ear in the darkest hours of the night. "We'd be letting so many people down."

"It *is* that easy, Baby. It is. We choose *us*. Your friends still love you. They'll understand."

He pulled his hand free, but only so he could run his fingertips along her jaw, let them linger on her still-healing scars.

"I never thought I'd find someone like you," he said. "Maybe we —"

The door opened. Sonny McGuiness rushed into the room wearing nothing but blue-and-red-striped boxer shorts, his eyes wide, his beard electric-white, a sat phone in his hand.

"Christ, Sonny," Bertha said. "Ever hear of knocking? Get the fuck out, we're having a private conversation."

Sonny held up the sat phone.

"She called! Jabour! Sonofabitch, *she called*. Her guy, Ramiro, her husband, I mean *ex*-husband, she said he's hurt, she needs our help!"

Patrick held up a hand. "Slow down, Sonny. Where is the hurt man? Why did she call us?"

"She called because her man is trapped in the tunnels," Sonny said. "I told her we have gear that lets us go deep in the tunnels, I told her to call me if they got into trouble. She knows we're the only ones who can get down there and help him!"

Patrick took a step toward Sonny, a step away from Bertha, and in that singular motion she knew she'd lost her chance.

"*Down there*," Patrick said. "Are you telling me you found the tunnel entrance?"

Sonny nodded madly. "She told me exactly where to go. She told me all we have to do is save Ramiro, and she'll tell us anything we want to know!"

Patrick grabbed his pants and ran out of the room. Sonny followed.

Bertha heard Patrick's voice bellow through the lodge: "NoSeeUms, get your fat asses out of bed and gear up! Get the crates into the chopper, *make sure* you load the crate with the KoolSuits. We dust off in fifteen minutes, I'll fill you in once we're in the air! *Move it!*"

Bertha stared at her hands; they were shaking. She wanted to kill

Sonny McGuiness. She'd almost gotten through to Patrick, almost had him understand what was *really* important. No chance of that now—he had the scent, and nothing would pull him off the trail.

She stood, grabbed her gear bag out of the closet, and headed to the lounge to load up with the others.

24

8,500 feet above the surface

THE SUN BROKE over the horizon just as the Sikorsky completed a circle of Mount Fitz Roy's peak. Patrick saw no climbers—probably due to the twenty-mile-per-hour winds driving snow across the granite face. No hikers, either, although there might be some brave souls down there, enduring the storm, too small to see through the blowing snow.

"Luck is with us," he said. "No one around."

Marie scoffed. "Luck? This wind is straight murder, Ender."

"You got this," he said.

Patrick turned awkwardly in his seat, looked over his team. With all their gear on, they looked like they were barely removed from their operational days. Older, yes. Fatter, yes. But still the death-dealers he had trusted his life to on multiple missions.

Black-and-gray camo fatigues and combat helmet, a mining light mounted to the helmet's center. MOLLE vests with pouches holding magazines, flashlights, grenades, other gear. Everyone held their carbines, which were attached to harnesses. Backpacks at their feet.

He was going to make all of them so very, very rich. They deserved it. They'd *earned* a life free from work and worry. Soon, they would have exactly that.

Only McGuiness looked out of place. He stared out the side window, his left thumb tracing a lazy figure-eight pattern on that weird silver Nazi bracelet he never seemed to take off.

They were older, they were *fatter*, yet the NoSeeUms followed pre-mission rituals they'd followed back in the day. Mullet, chewing gum as loudly as he could. Worm, reading a paperback: *The Call of the Wild*. Hatchet and Curveball, sitting together quietly, their shoulders pressed close. Sleepy, staring off, the praise-Jesus light gone from his eyes, replaced by the distant gaze of an experienced killer.

McGuiness looked forward, caught Patrick's eye.

"She said she's on the far side of the peak," Sonny said. "You see her yet?"

Patrick faced forward, scanned the area, feeling a twinge anxious that the call had been a trick of some kind, maybe Jabour's idea of a practical joke.

"Flare," Marie said, pointing down. "At about eighteen hundred feet elevation. That's got to be her."

The west face of the mountain—the side not seen in photos of the iconic peak—was perhaps even more dramatic than the east face. Hidden in shadow, the "backside" of the peak dropped down maybe two thousand feet in an almost vertical angle that ended at a narrow erosion plateau. Where the mountain met the plateau stood a person waving a flare, its red light reflecting pink off the snow beneath her feet.

Jabour.

Patrick felt a rush of excitement. Or was it relief? Unknown dangers awaited, but if this woman showed them the tunnel entrance, the mission became *real*.

He focused on the terrain. Where Jabour stood wasn't level by any stretch of the imagination. It angled down, the starting place of a seasonal river that carried mountain runoff down to the foothills. On one side of the narrow plateau, the towering peak, and on the other, a steep rise of rock with a sheer drop-off of at least a thousand feet.

"Put us down on that plateau at the base of the erosion area," Patrick said. "As close to that woman as you can get."

As if the fates announced they didn't much care for his plan, a blast of wind skewed the helicopter sideways.

"*Jesus*, Skylark!" Kevin, shouting from the back of the helicopter as if everyone didn't have headsets in their helmets. "When did this become amateur hour?"

"Blow it out your ass," Marie said. "And *plateau*? That spot is steep enough to be a bunny hill at a ski resort. I don't like the looks of it. The wind catches us wrong, you'll find out that in a battle of mountain versus helicopter, the mountain always wins." She looked out her side window. "Maybe we should wait for this storm to calm down."

It was a risk, but Patrick had seen Skylark handle a dozen tough landings.

"We're a rescue mission now," Patrick said. "Put her down. That's an order."

Marie sighed. "This is what I get for associating with idiots. Hold onto your jumblies, boys, we're going in."

With coordinated movements of the flight controls, she eased the helicopter down and to the right, slowly angling toward the waving Samira Jabour. Wind caught the chopper again; Marie corrected instantly. The helicopter lowered. Jabour moved out of the way, ducked down by a big boulder at the back of the narrow plateau.

From the rear of the helicopter came the sound of retching.

Snow swirled across the angled white surface. Patrick couldn't stop his feet from pressing against the floor as yet another gust of wind slammed the helicopter, drove it sideways just as the skids touched down—the Sikorsky actually slid across the snow and loose slate before it came to a hard, lurching stop, angled up as if it was beginning a shallow climb.

Marie blew out a big breath. "Lordy almighty, I still got it. Which one of you weaklings blew chunks? Mullet? Tell me it was you."

Kevin's cutting laugh. "Not in this lifetime, sugar tits."

"Sorry," Sonny said. "I wasn't ready for that."

"Everyone *out*," Patrick said. "Get the gear out. Move fast. McGuiness, you introduce me to the contact."

Side doors slid open. The NoSeeUms disembarked, started hauling out crates of supplies.

Patrick leaned closer to Marie, covered his mic. "Can we keep her on the deck?"

Marie checked a readout.

"Wind is gusting at twenty-three knots," she said. "And this isn't a level, stable surface. If the wind picks up more, it might be enough to slide the bird right down the runoff area." She lifted her visor, looked at him. "I want to come with you and see those creatures, but the smart thing to do is for me to get her out of here and stay on-station in case we're needed."

Blunt honesty, and putting the team's needs before her own. Just two of the reasons he admired Marie.

"All right, so you're the cavalry," Patrick said. "Sorry."

Marie forced a smile, tried to shrug it off. "That's what I get for being so good at my job." She reached over, cupped his chin. "Go get 'em, tiger. Make us that money."

Patrick got out. The helicopter wasn't warm, but it had shielded him from the wind, which now made him take short, careful steps lest he be blown off the peak.

Hatchet and Curveball pulled the final gearbox out of the helicopter, hauled it clear. Worm slid the doors shut. Mullet and Sleepy were kneeling on opposite ends of the small plateau, carbines in hand, scanning every which way, on the lookout for trouble. Bertha arranged the already off-loaded crates into an orderly stack.

Sonny was by the boulder at the point of the V-shaped plateau, standing with Samira Jabour, her eyes hidden by ski goggles. Sonny waved Patrick over.

As Patrick walked to them, he looked west. It was like something out of a medieval fantasy movie—ice-covered mountains as far as the eye could see. The tips of some were hidden by clouds. Not a sign of civilization. Absolutely breathtaking.

He had to force himself to look away from the grandeur when he reached the boulder.

"This is Patrick O'Doyle," Sonny said. "He's in charge."

Samira Jabour wore a blue parka that rippled in the wind. She lifted her goggles. Brown eyes, surrounded by red brought on from both the weather and from crying. She looked completely shot-out—drained by whatever ordeal she'd just been through.

"Miss Jabour," Patrick said, offering his hand.

She ignored it, looked beyond him to the team. Worm and Mullet were helping Bertha unload the crates.

"You need all that shit to save my friend? We need to move fast."

"They will only be a few minutes more," Patrick said. "I promise you we'll move fast and do everything we can to save your friend, but we won't get careless and put more people at risk. The safety of my people matters. Agreed?"

Jabour looked from them to him. Her puffy eyes blinked. She looked like she hadn't slept in a long time.

She nodded. "Okay."

"Good," Patrick said. "Tell me what happened."

Jabour talked fast, almost in a monotone. She told him about three double-crescent knives, the warning glyphs, how the floor and wall had collapsed under Ramiro, how he'd fallen into a shaft and broken his leg. She told him about a *swarm of metal spiders*.

She told Patrick how he'd screamed.

When she told him how she'd run away, she stared at the ground.

"Stop with the guilty feelings," he said. "If you hadn't evacuated, Ramiro would have no chance at all, and you might be in trouble as well. You did the right thing."

She looked up, eyes blinking against the wind.

"Do you know what those metal spiders were?"

Patrick nodded. "I do."

"Is there any chance Ramiro is still alive?"

Odds were the man was already dead, but Patrick would do everything he could to save him.

"A small chance. I won't lie to you, he's probably gone, but we will find out one way or another. If he can be saved, we'll save him. Show me the tunnel entrance."

Jabour stared at him blankly, tears welling up. She'd wanted to hear that Ramiro would make it. Better for her to get her head around reality now rather than later.

Without another word, she turned her body and slid between the boulder and the rock face. She half-vanished behind the curve, then knelt and was gone.

"Come on," she said—he heard her but couldn't see her.

Patrick looked at the narrow space. It would be a tight fit for him; he might have to take off his vest in order to fit through. Even without a vest, Hatchet would have an even harder time of it.

"Shit," he said.

He was the biggest of his team, but if he couldn't fit, Doug probably couldn't either, and maybe Bertha as well.

"Sonny, go with her," Patrick said. "Get the lay of the land. Get any info you can out of her about distances to Ramiro, any danger spots, things like that."

The old man shook his head. "I ain't going in there. You know that. You agreed to it."

Patrick pointed to the crates. "I have to get all of that—" he pointed to the narrow space behind the boulder "—in there. It's going to take a few minutes. You don't have to go down into the tunnels with us, but I need you to stop fucking around and get me what intel you can, got it?"

Sonny looked at the space behind the boulder. "I get freaked out in tight spaces. It ain't pretty."

"Be claustrophobic on your own time. You're on my clock now, so get to work."

Sonny sneered, making the white whiskers over his lip stick out like a paintbrush, then he easily slid his tiny body into the space.

Patrick was about to follow him in when his skin prickled with goosebumps—something was wrong. He brought up his carbine, dropped into a shallow crouch.

Across the plateau, without a word or a signal, the NoSeeUms reacted instantly, each of them bringing up their own weapons and scrambling for cover. In two seconds flat, six people had formed a perimeter, their backs toward the plateau and the mountain, their guns sweeping the downslope, everyone looking for danger.

Only Bertha stood there, looking around, unsure of what to do. Two seconds later, she rushed to Patrick's side.

His subconscious—a survival tool hammered, hardened and sharpened from dozens of missions—processed a faint sound before his conscious mind: the sound of a second helicopter.

Impossible to hear at a distance due to the Sikorsky's engine, but there was no mistaking it now.

"Incoming," Curveball said over the headsets. "Civilian bird, south-southwest, five hundred meters out, coming at us."

Patrick nudged Bertha.

"Find cover," he said.

She moved off, headed toward a small chunk of rock to the left.

He knelt, got as low as he could. He needed to get to cover as well, but he wanted to see what was coming first.

The unknown helicopter was coming in low, well below the peak. A commercial chopper? Military? It was coming straight in; no way to make out any insignia, not yet.

Mullet's voice on the headset: "Ender, do we take it out?"

He wanted to shoot first and ask questions later. No surprise there. Patrick pushed the plastic *talk* button on the box strapped into his vest's MOLLE webbing.

"Hold your fire," he said. "Everyone stay cool."

A small helicopter, room for a pilot and three passengers, max. A tall rotor mast rising up almost like a shark's fin. Probably a Robinson R44.

A tourist helicopter? Unlikely in this weather. No climbers to be rescued, either, at least none that he'd seen. Could it be Argentinian park rangers? Patrick had paid bribes to make sure that wouldn't happen. He'd also bribed members of the Argentinian military so they would look the other way if anyone reported the presence of heavily armed foreigners.

Chilean military, perhaps? The peak was within the disputed border area. Patrick wondered if he should have paid bribes there as well.

Or ... even worse than the military ... could the R44 be carrying people from another mining company? Had someone or something leaked about the operation? Had Harvey Dillinger sold them out despite his promises of loyalty to Yakely?

Skylark's voice in his headset: "Ender, tell me what you want me to do. I'm a sitting duck."

Only seconds to make a decision. Order the team into the Sikorsky and try to get clear? If they got off the mountain before the R44 arrived, they'd be leaving Sonny behind. The man could handle himself, stay hidden until they came back.

But the R44 was faster than the Sikorsky and had a longer range. If it was flown by Chilean military, Argentinian military or park rangers, it would follow; there was no outrunning it. Wherever Skylark set down—be it at the lodge or at El Calafate Airport to refuel—police or troops would quickly swarm in. The game would be over.

And if the R44 was from another mining company, Patrick wasn't about to give up the spoils without a fight.

There was no point in leaving.

He pressed his *talk* button. "Stay calm, people. Let's see what happens."

The R44 slowed to a hover about a hundred meters away. Red and white. "FLY WITH US" painted on the side in letters as big as the chopper itself, *Ushuaia Air Tours* in smaller letters above it.

Skylark: "Ender, they're on the horn. They asked for you. By name. They sound American. They also asked that we kindly not shoot them."

Patrick walked to the Sikorsky. He slid his combat comm rig down around his neck, got into the passenger seat. Marie handed him a headset. He put it on.

"This is O'Doyle."

"I'm agent Clarence Otto," the scratchy voice came back. "From the Department of Special Threats."

The DST. Patrick's heart sank. Motherfucking Murray Longworth had given him up.

This mission wasn't over, not yet, but the fat lady was warming up her singing voice.

"We need to talk," Otto said. "We're coming down."

Marie chimed in. "You sure your pilot can handle that? It takes some big-boy flying to land up here."

A pause.

"My pilot says he's been dying to try landing there for years," Otto said. "And we just gave him reasons to try."

"What reasons?" Patrick asked.

"Ten thousand of them," Otto said. "The green kind."

Marie flipped up a switch, silencing the transmitter. "Funny, the green kind of reasons seem to motivate people to do all kinds of stupid things."

The DST. Only one reason they would be here, now—they knew about the Rocktopi.

Patrick wasn't about to shoot down their chopper. Otto was an American, and the helicopter pilot hadn't done anything wrong.

"Turn it back on," Patrick said.

Marie shook her head, flipped the switch down again.

"Go ahead and land," Patrick said. "We won't hurt you."

He tossed the handset at Marie, then slid out of the Sikorsky. He repositioned his combat comm rig, pressed the *send* button.

"The incoming bird has at least one US government agent aboard," he said. "Curveball, Hatchet, Mullet, take positions to give me cover if things go south. Weapons *slung*, but be ready. Lybrand, Sleepy, finish unloading the crates, get as much gear and ammo as you can to that big boulder, tell McGuiness and Jabour to get it into the tunnels. *Do not stop* unloading unless I order it. Bookworm, you there?"

"Copy that, Ender," Worm said.

"You're with me. Weapons slung. Let's meet our new friends."

1,804 FEET UP THE MOUNTAIN

Atop a mountain, with the wind whipping like the lashing tail of a dragon, two helicopters sat idling on snow and rock, the tips of their rotor blades not even twenty feet apart.

Tommy Strymon stood next to Patrick O'Doyle, waiting for the R44's passengers to step out.

Ender was on edge. He got twitchy when he was like that.

"Want me to do the talking?" Tommy asked.

They had frequently done it that way in the past. Ender was a tactician, a leader, a do-er, but negotiations weren't his strong suit. If the situation required pure intimation, Ender handled it or turned it over to Sleepy's soulless stare. If charm was needed, the team always let Mullet be the mouthpiece. If the encounter required quick thinking and raw mental horsepower, Tommy usually got the call.

"I'll talk," Ender said. "At first, anyway."

Tommy nodded. Strange how after fifteen years apart, it all felt so familiar, like they'd done the same thing only yesterday. Ender would do the talking; if he glanced Tommy's way, that was Tommy's cue to take over.

Two men got out of the R44. The first man was black, middle-aged, wearing a red parka, tan ski gloves, blue jeans, and casual black boots. The parka looked too small for him. That and the jeans told Tommy the man hadn't taken time—or *had* time—to properly prepare for the mountain's cutting cold.

The second man was white or Hispanic, thirty-ish, wearing waterproof, cold-weather pants, a bulky black jacket, black gloves, and heavy hiking boots. He looked more prepared.

Tommy pegged the black guy as ex-military. The younger man was military too, maybe active duty. Special forces, probably—his gaze flicked about the mountain top, locking in for a beat on each of the NoSeeUms, who were spread around the plateau like sentries. Or, like waiting executioners.

Both men looked exhausted, like they had traveled a long way in a short time. They walked up to Ender and Tommy.

"Patrick O'Doyle," the black man said. "I'm special agent Clarence Otto, this is special agent Paulius Klimas. We're with the Department of Special Threats."

Otto stripped off a glove and offered his hand. Ender glanced at it, as if he had no interest in being friendly to these men, but after a second or two he pulled off his own glove and shook.

"We know you're fully aware of the DST," Otto said. "Tim Feely says hello."

O'Doyle hadn't heard—or even thought about—that name for a decade, at least.

"How do you know Feely?"

"He's our boss," Klimas said. "He's the DST director."

How had the little shit pulled that off? Patrick realized he didn't really care.

Both men put their gloves back on.

"The DST has no authority here," Patrick said.

Otto shivered, glanced around the tiny plateau.

"Neither do you," he said. "Nor do you have an invitation from the Argentina government to bring armed mercenaries into the country."

Ender paused. Tommy waited for his signal to step up, but it didn't come.

"Mercenaries?" Ender shook his head. "You're misinformed. We're up here on a rescue mission."

"My ass," Klimas said. "Unless your *rescue* somehow requires enough firepower to take over a small country."

A feat Tommy and the NoSeeUms had done before. Twice.

Klimas tilted his head toward Lybrand and Doug, who were quietly carrying armfuls of gear to the boulder that hid the tunnel entrance.

"Tell them to knock that off," Klimas said.

Ender ignored him, spoke to Otto instead. "Every second you two spend dicking around with us is one more second a man might die. So how about you get back in your chopper and forget this ever happened?"

"Cut the bunk," Otto said. "You work for EarthCore. You were in Utah at the time of the volcano eruption. While you were there, a former NSA agent reported information about a new, sentient species at that location. Since you're *familiar* with the DST, you know a report like that comes to us."

Ender's hands curled into fists. "Farm Girl. Fuck."

"We're looking for her, too," Otto said. "Happen to know where Kayla Meyers is?"

Patrick remembered watching Connell Kirkland lead her deep into the Utah ship, not long before the entire mountain collapsed, giving birth to a volcano.

"She's dead," Patrick said.

Otto held a hand out to Klimas, palm-up.

Shivering, Klimas reached into his pocket.

Tommy didn't aim directly at Klimas, but he moved the barrel in the man's direction enough to send a clear message.

"Easy," Otto said. "It's just a phone."

Klimas looked at Tommy, raised an eyebrow for permission.

Tommy nodded.

Klimas pulled out a satellite phone. He handed it to Otto.

Otto took it, gestured to the plateau, to all the NoSeeUms.

"Pack up shop," he said. "We talked to your boss, Yakely. She's pulling the plug on your operation. The United States Government does not want a bunch of spec-ops ghosts operating in foreign territory. The Argentinians don't know you're here. Yet. Choice A—we quietly get you off the mountain before things escalate. Then you'll contact McGuiness, get him to come in from wherever he is, then you, him, Bertha Lybrand and myself are going to sit down in that awesome lodge you rented and have a nice chat. Choice B—I call Director Feely, tell him you're being difficult, and the lot of you are in a giant heap of trouble."

The wind ebbed, for just an instant, and in that instant, Tommy heard something, something other than the idling engines of the two helicopters clogging the angled plateau. Just as fast, the wind picked up again, howling off the mountainside.

"I told you this is a rescue operation," Ender said. "You want to get me off the mountain? Shoot me. But I warn you, we shoot back."

He turned to walk away. Tommy grabbed his arm.

"Ender, listen."

The wind ebbed again, and Tommy heard it, clearly this time, understood why he hadn't been able to nail it down at first—the sound of a *third* helicopter.

He looked up, his eyes drawn to the towering pinnacle of Mount Fitz Roy, just as a bulky, white helicopter came from the west, over the ridgeline, hugging the peak. Even from underneath, he recognized it instantly as an AW109 Trekker. It roared overhead, rotors a blurry circle of gray, started to drop, to slow and turn, and when it did, Tommy saw the open side door—and the death-dealing barrel of what looked like an M240 sticking out. A man behind it, his face hidden by a blue-tinged helmet visor.

Tommy was moving an instant before Patrick screamed: *"Take cover!"*

The door gunner opened fire, the weapon's *braddah-braddah* cough barely audible over the sound of three helicopter engines. Tracer trails marked the 7.62-millimeter bullets that hammered the R44, punching holes in the white- and red-painted metal, spiderwebbing a trail across the windshield until the pilot's blood splattered the inside of the glass.

Tommy ran for the boulder at the back of the plateau. The NoSee-Ums returned fire. Sparks flashed off the Trekker's hull. The gunner fell back. The Trekker dove and banked north, quickly blurred by blowing snow.

Mullet's voice in the headset: "Fuck, here comes another one!"

A second Trekker came over the crest, this one already skewing sideways, giving the door gunner an improved angle of fire.

Bullets stitched across the plateau, lost in snow or kicking up rock, tracing a line toward the Sikorsky.

Skylark: "Shoot that motherfucker! Get him off me!"

Ender: "Skylark, get out, *now*. Everyone, to the back of the plateau, into the tunnel!"

Tommy reached the boulder. Lybrand and Sleepy knelt there, weapons to their shoulders, firing up at the second chopper as it moved past the plateau, side-gunner pumping rounds into the Sikorsky's still-spinning rotors.

Tommy pushed Lybrand.

"Into the tunnel," he said. "Now."

She obeyed instantly, slinging her carbine and slipping behind the boulder. Forcing her big body into the tight space. Tommy dropped to one knee—he and Sleepy would hold this position until the others were inside.

As the second Trekker flew off into the storm, the first one came roaring back, M240 pouring fire into the Sikorsky, tracer rounds stabbing home like lasers. Tommy saw Skylark, sprinting up the incline, Mullet at her side, Hatchet right behind them.

The Sikorsky burst into flames.

"Haul ass," Sleepy said, his voice calm and level.

Skylark shot past Tommy as if she'd slid by that boulder a thousand times and knew its curves by heart. Mullet followed her in. Around Tommy, bullets slammed into stone—he hit the deck, broken bits of boulder raining down around him.

A blast of pain in his right thigh.

He raised up on his elbows, sighted in. The Trekker was a ghostly shape half-hidden in blowing snow and the Sikorsky's billowing, madly whipping black smoke, but he fired anyway, squeezing off single shots until the attack helicopter again banked away.

Over comms, Tommy heard Ender: "Otto, Klimas, get to that big boulder! There's a tunnel entrance behind it."

He saw the two men rushing in, Ender behind them, protecting them with his own body.

Mullet: "I'm in, so is Skylark. Come on, fuckers, move!"

Otto stumbled—Sleepy caught him, steadied him, moved him into the space between the mountain and the boulder.

Ender stopped, turned, knelt, shouldered his carbine and started firing, trying to give cover to Hatchet, who lumbered up the incline, and Curveball, who stayed at his side.

Klimas knelt next to Tommy.

"Get in the tunnel," Tommy screamed at him.

Klimas held out a hand. "Give me your sidearm!"

Tommy could barely hear him over the wind, the gunfire, the burning Sikorsky, and the roar of two attacking helicopters.

Both birds banked away at the same time, instantly out of sight behind the thick black smoke and the blowing snow, but Tommy knew the respite wouldn't last long.

He drew his sidearm and handed it to Klimas.

Hatchet tried to wedge himself into the narrow space—he was too big. He stepped away, scrambled to take off his equipment-laden vest.

Curveball stopped to help him.

Hatchet slapped his hands away. "Get in there! I got it!"

Through the smoke, Tommy saw the helicopters, higher up and coming in again. This time, they'd attack together. Sustained fire from two M240s—things were about to go from bad to worse.

Ender grabbed Curveball, shoved him into the space between the boulder and the rock wall. Curveball struggled for an instant, tried to get back to Hatchet, but just as quickly realized he was blocking others— he slid in, out of sight.

"Sleepy, *go*," Ender said.

Sleepy turned and slipped behind the boulder.

Klimas took his place, dropping into a shooting stance, aiming at the incoming birds. He started firing, steady and sure. Tommy did as well, hoping for a lucky shot.

Hatchet tossed his vest ahead of him into the space between the boulder and the wall. He started to wedge his body in there, right arm first.

The first helicopter banked.

Hatchet struggled to slide through the narrow space. A line of tracer fire stitched across the plateau, dotted its way to him—he grunted, a low, long sound that made Tommy's stomach quiver. Ender grabbed Hatchet, pulled him down to the ground.

Tommy and Klimas aimed, fired, aimed, fired. Tommy pulled the trigger again, saw a door-gunner fall back.

The wind shifted suddenly as if kicked by a god. Black smoke poured toward the boulder, so thick Tommy couldn't see Klimas five feet to his left. Tommy heard bullets cracking off rocks, tried to shrink down, waited to feel a round punch into his head, his chest, his arms, his legs.

Ender: "Worm, go!"

Tommy sprang up. He was smaller than the other men and side-stepped quickly, following the boulder's curve until he felt a hand tapping at his leg.

"Drop down! Give me your gun!"

It was McGuiness. His hand reached out from a too-small dark space, a space not even two feet high.

Tommy handed down the carbine, then awkwardly bent at the knees, stone against his chest and his back. Hands grabbed at his feet, urging him to drop to his butt. He did, eased into a cramped, dark opening. A small cave, ceiling so low he couldn't stand up straight. There was enough light filtering in from the thin opening that Tommy could see a low-ceilinged tunnel leading away.

And, oddly, a closed Igloo cooler sitting against the wall.

"Keep going in," Sonny said. "Gotta make room."

"I have this position." Tommy slapped Sonny's shoulder. "Go!"

Sonny obeyed as if he was a NoSeeUm himself, turning and crouch-walking into the tunnel.

Tommy turned back to the opening, knelt and looked out, saw a pair of black boots awkwardly sidestepping along the curve. Black waterproof pants—it was Klimas.

"*Down here*," Tommy shouted.

Klimas kept sidestepping, went past the opening, and then Tommy saw why—Klimas was dragging Hatchet.

Tommy reached out, grabbed Hatchet's ankles, pulled them into the cave mouth. Hatchet's belly wedged in the opening. Tommy reposi-tioned himself, his every motion clumsy in the tight space, and yanked Hatchet inside.

Tommy had to make space. Half bent over, he gripped the back of Hatchet's collar and pulled, dragging the man a foot or so at a time into the tunnel where Sonny had fled.

Step back, pull.

Step back, pull.

In here, Tommy could barely hear the helicopters.

Step back, pull.

Step back, pull.

Light further down the tunnel, playing off the walls.

He kept at it.

Step back, pull.

More light. Tommy dragged Hatchet into a larger space, another cave.

"Carson?" Curveball's voice, in Tommy's ears as well as his headset. "*Carson?*"

Otto grabbed Hatchet's feet. "Let's get him out of the way."

Tommy and Otto moved Hatchet away from the entrance.

"Put him down," Curveball said. "Skylark! Hatchet's hit!"

They lowered Hatchet to the ground. Someone pushed Tommy aside—Skylark, med kit in hand. She and Otto went to work on the wounded man. Curveball stood there, paralyzed by fear and indecision, staring down at his lover.

Tommy took a fast look around. A couple of battery-powered lanterns lit up the cave. Piles of canvas equipment bags and crates. McGuiness and the woman cowering against the back wall. McGuiness held Tommy's carbine. Tommy took it, changed out the magazine.

Klimas stepped into cave, bloody left hand pressed to his face, Tommy's sidearm in his right hand.

The woman, Jabour, ran to Klimas, guided him to the wall opposite Skylark, Hatchet, and Otto.

Where were Sleepy and Lybrand?

Ender stepped into the tunnel, carbine hanging from its sling. He stood straight, unfolding like a hibernating bear coming out of a deep dark hole.

"I saw a third helicopter coming in, pretty sure it was a Chinook," he said. "With the two wrecks, they're going to have a hard time putting men down, but we'll have a lot of company real quick. Casualties?"

Compared to the madness on the plateau, the cave seemed disturbingly quiet, even with people working on the wounded.

"Hatchet's hit bad," Skylark said. "We're working on it."

Jabour pressed a bandage against the right side of Klimas's face.

"This man got hit with stone splinters," she said. "Missed his eye. I think he needs stitches."

Ender bent slightly, looked back up the tunnel. "Mullet, you there?"

Mullet's voice in Tommy's headset: "Copy that, Ender."

"Booby-trap the main entrance," Ender said. "Fast, before they land, then haul ass down here. Tommy, guard this room."

Tommy took up a position just to the right of the ragged entrance.

"Sleepy, Lybrand," Ender said, "report."

Sleepy: "We're moving down the next tunnel. All clear for fifty meters. Want us to come back?"

"No," Ender said. "Keep going, we'll be right behind you. Be alert— as far as we know, those same assholes may have found another way in."

Sleepy: "Roger that."

Patrick stepped toward Hatchet.

Hatchet's chest and head were hidden by the kneeling Skylark and Curveball.

A frozen moment, then Tommy saw Ender reach down, put his hand on Skylark's shoulder.

"Go up and help Mullet," he said to her.

Skylark stood, stared down for a moment. She drew her sidearm. When she turned, Tommy saw the tears on her cheeks. As she passed by Tommy, she looked him in eyes, shook her head—Hatchet wasn't going to make it.

She vanished into the tunnel.

"Worm," Ender said. "Come give us a hand."

Three steps brought Tommy to Ender. To Hatchet and Curveball— to Anders and Carson.

Anders was holding Carson's hand, black fingers tightly laced through white.

Carson lay on his back, blinking irregularly, staring up at nothing. Blood flecked his lips and chin. Skylark—maybe it had been Skylark— had opened his fatigues, sliced his blood-soaked shirt down the middle, exposing his pale, red-smeared skin.

One bullet had hit his left thigh, a black spot at the center of blood-soaked fabric. She hadn't bothered cutting the pants away. One look at his other wounds showed Tommy why—a second and third round had entered Carson's back, come out his chest along with most of his left lung.

He would be dead in minutes, if not seconds.

Anders looked up at Tommy, his eyes pleading: *Tell me all my experience is wrong, tell me I don't see what I'm seeing, tell me he's going to be okay.*

Carson "Hatchet" Wampler had survived engagements where hundreds of men died. He had taken life on three continents. He'd handled every threat the gods of war had sent his way, and, he'd laughed while doing it. Most of the time, anyway. All that risk, all that horror, and the worst damage he'd suffered had been a few bruises and scrapes.

Yet here, in a cave in a mountain in Argentina, his luck had run out.

"So sorry, Curve," Tommy said. "Say goodbye."

Anders doubled over like he'd been kicked in the stomach. His forehead rested on Carson's bloody chest. Without rising up, Anders's head rolled from side to side.

"No," he said, his voice a choked, anguished moan. "No."

He lifted up just enough to move, to lean close to Carson's ear.

Tommy saw Carson's blood gleaming on Anders's gray beard.

"Fight for me," Anders said. "Stay alive. *Fight* for me, man."

Carson started to nod, then seemed to forget what he was doing. His mouth opened, birthing a bubble of blood that popped and dotted both his face and Anders's with new spots of red.

"Anders…I…I love you."

Anders pushed his forehead against Carson's temple, kissed Carson on the cheek.

"And I love you," Anders said, his voice more wail than words. "I have for so long."

Carson gave another half-nod, blinked madly. "Can I…can I tell you something?"

Anders sat back on his butt, his fingers still locked with those of his lover, gripping tight, so very tight.

"Of course you can," Anders said. "You can tell me anything."

Carson blinked glassy, unfocused eyes.

"I hate baking," he said. "I really fucking hate it."

He stopped blinking.

Anders's body shook. He leaned forward again, pressed his cheek against Carson's. Anders stayed there, as motionless as his dead lover.

Tommy looked away, trying to give the man a moment's privacy.

McGuiness, Jabour, Otto, and Klimas—a bloody bandage on his cheek—were stuffing backpacks with ammo, climbing supplies and food. Mullet and Skylark must have already headed further down, scouting ahead.

Ender knelt near the entrance, carbine aimed out, ready to slaughter anyone who came near. While Carson lay dying, he'd put the others to work.

Mullet in the headset: "We're coming back. One delicious Claymore ready for our new pals."

Skylark: "Motherfuckers. I hope their dicks get blasted right off."

Ender stood. "Sixty seconds and we're gone." He looked at Tommy, pointed at Anders, then circled that finger in the air: *Tell him to finish up, we have to move.*

No time for mourning.

Tommy put a hand on Anders's shoulder, felt the sobs shaking the man to his core.

"Curve, he's gone."

Anders didn't rise. He still held Carson's hand.

"I'm staying," Anders said. "Gonna kill those bastards."

Tommy slung his carbine, knelt down next to the man.

"Get up or you'll die here."

Eyes still scrunched tight, Anders nodded. "Fine with me."

Snot dripped from his nose. He didn't try to wipe it away.

Tommy glanced back at Ender. Ender tapped the top of his wrist: *time's up.*

God dammit.

Tommy knew this would all become ultra-real, and very soon, knew it would hit like a tank, but for the moment he felt numb, felt the soul anesthesia that always came with combat, with killing. That blankness of emotion translated into clarity of thought. It was one of the things that had made him so good at the job.

He had to get Anders moving.

Tommy leaned in close, whispered in Anders's ear.

"You stay here, you'll kill one of the assholes, maybe two before they take you down. Ender said they're landing a Chinook. Why get just a couple of them when you can kill a whole company?"

Anders finally looked away from Carson. So much pain in those eyes, so much *hate.*

"Come with me," Tommy said. "We'll figure out how to get every last one of them. Just like old times."

Anders blinked away tears. He wiped the back of his hand across his mouth and nose, smearing snot and spit and blood across his cheek.

"Moving out," Ender said. "Now."

Tommy stood. "Come on, Curve. Time to go."

Anders lifted Carson's left hand. He pulled at Carson's ring finger: a thin circle of gold slid free.

A wedding ring. A wedding ring that Tommy hadn't even noticed.

Anders leaned close to Carson's ear.

"I'll kill them all, my love," he said. "I'll find out who ordered this. I'll make him *hurt*."

Ender reached down, grabbed Anders's shoulder, yanked the man to his feet.

"And we'll help you," Ender said. "Now get your weapon and *move*."

Anders grabbed his carbine off the cave floor, hurried to the second tunnel mouth and vanished into the darkness.

Tommy realized he and Ender were the only ones left.

"I've got the rear," Tommy said. "I'll get his gear."

Ender nodded. He grabbed the shipping crate that held the KoolSuit tubes, then headed down the second tunnel.

Tommy hesitated for a moment. He stared at Carson's corpse. The man had survived two dozen missions. He'd served his country. He'd killed for his country. He'd watched friends and squad mates die.

He had survived.

Until now.

Here, Carson Wampler had died. Died for *money*.

Tommy felt sick.

He pulled three extended magazines from Carson's belt holster, picked up the man's carbine and slung it. He clipped Carson's helmet to his webbing; with the extra people, someone would need it. Probably Klimas.

Tommy pocketed one of Carson's two grenades. He held the second grenade for a moment, then wedged it under Carson's shoulder, careful to keep the dead man's weight on the arming lever.

"Give them one for the road, Hatchet."

Tommy pulled the pin. He grabbed Carson's backpack, then ran down the tunnel.

1,804 feet up the mountain

SO EMBARRASSING.

Only a few months ago, Angus Kool could have dropped down a rope on his own and done it way faster than these meatheads.

But he couldn't manage it on his own—the meatheads had to help him.

Angus fumed, his face red as the harness dug into his armpits and crotch. A man in the helicopter above lowered him down to the plateau, where two more men grabbed his feet, reeled him in like a helpless infant.

Those men—Fuentes and Khatari, if Angus had their names right—had been assigned to him as assistants and personal bodyguards. Angus knew they hated the job. Who wanted to babysit a cripple? But fuck 'em, they were getting paid to do a job, so Angus expected them to do it.

"Hold still, Doctor Kool," Fuentes said. "We'll unbuckle you."

Angus stood there, arms outstretched, a child being undressed by his two mothers. The helicopter ride here had been less than smooth. That, compounded by the humiliation of dangling like bait on a hook, had cranked up the pain in his hand and legs. And the chafing of the harness… it made him itch worse than ever.

How long until he could take his next dose? He didn't want Donnie to see, didn't want Fuentes and Khatari to see, either.

The harness fell away. But no, he wasn't done yet, was he? Of course not. To keep from falling on his ass, he kept a hand on Fuentes's shoulder.

"Hang steady," Fuentes said, smiling. "We'll have you squared away in a second."

The man smiled about everything. And why not? His arms and legs worked just fine. Fuentes wasn't the biggest guy, but he looked like a badass. With wide-set eyes and a big nose, he was one of those mutt-faced American men who could easily pass for Italian, Arabic or Hispanic.

Fuentes wore the same uniform as the rest of the G4S mercs: tan ballcap with no insignia; thin headset over the top of the hat, with a microphone arm that angled near his mouth; tan body armor and pocket-ladder webbing over a green-and-tan camo pattern canvas jacket; tan cargo pants; heavy black combat boots. An M4 hung on his chest. All the mercs carried M4s and a sidearm of choice. Once they went into the tunnels, they would wear combat helmets.

Khatari waved hand signals up to the helicopter, which slowly lowered a net full of gear. No mistaking his ancestry, not with his black beard and the tan turban he wore in lieu of the ballcap.

The net sagged against the ground. The rope went slack. Khatari reached up and undid the hook; the net fell open, revealing the crates inside stacked on a wooden palette. The rope rose up, winched in by the helicopter's loadmaster.

Khatari pulled Angus's forearm crutches from between two crates.

"Here you go, Doctor," he said, offering them to Angus.

Angus took the crutches one at a time, cursed under his breath as he slid them on, leaned his weight against them.

"Need more help, Doctor?" Fuentes asked.

"No," Angus said. "Move those crates, then get to work assembling the BaDonkeyDonks."

The men did as they were told. Were they supposed to salute or something? Angus didn't know. Maybe he'd ask Donnie.

Fuentes and Khatari quickly arranged the crates. They opened one up, took from it the final version of the four-legged frame that the knackwurst-gargling Germans had perfected back in the R&D lab. A *BaDonkeyDonk*, about to be put to use.

Angus wondered what the two men would think if he told them what they might soon be facing. Would they flip out at the thought of fighting aliens? More likely, they'd think they were in some action movie and start gunning down anything they saw, which worked fine for Angus.

Only Donnie knew about the ship. Only Donnie knew about the rocktopi, and Angus's plan for dealing with those bastards. Here at Fitz Roy, maybe there weren't any rocktopi at all. Maybe not even any silverbugs. The ship had landed twelve thousand years ago, after all. The passengers and crew might have died on atmospheric entry, on landing, or from any number of causes over the millennia.

If the rocktopi and silverbugs were there, Donnie would have to explain it to the mercenaries soon enough.

Across the plateau, in the shadow of Mount Fitz Roy's peak, a dozen men were hard at work putting out the fire that had consumed O'Doyle's helicopter. The wind had shifted, carrying the now-sparse black smoke west, out across the glacier, where there was nothing and no one to see it. The ridgeline, the storm and the early hour had hopefully kept the smoke out of sight from anyone in El Chaltén.

Once that fire was out, the Chinook would lift the wreck and dump it somewhere on the glacier, as far away from Mount Fitz Roy as could be managed.

A second Chinook was en route, bringing more supplies and the rest of the mercs. Once unloaded, that Chinook would carry away the bullet-ridden aerial tour helicopter.

G4S had quietly given some serious money to the local authorities in Villa O'Higgins, and had set up a small base of operations at the single landing strip known as Río Mayer Airport. The base was self-contained, consisting of barrack tents, a supply depot, a field hospital, communications arrays, et cetera. Two dozen personnel remained behind there—mechanics, medics, admin staff and the like. Also, armed guards, responsible for both protecting G4S assets and making sure wounded mercs returning from Mount Fitz Roy stayed put and stayed quiet about anything seen on—or under—the mountain.

If things went well, all helicopters would depart the plateau before noon. With mercs policing the area, looking for spent shell casings or anything else that didn't belong, there would be no evidence left of the mountaintop battle. Even if someone had seen the smoke—which Angus doubted—and was skilled enough to climb the mountain to see what was up, at most the curious soul would find nothing more than a few strangely scorched rocks.

Things had gone perfectly.

There could be no trace of what had happened here.

Angus heard a muffled *whump* come from the boulder, behind which lay the entrance to the tunnels.

"Fuentes, what was that?"

Fuentes smiled, shrugged, then his head twitched slightly, like a dog who'd heard a whistle—a message had come over his headset. Angus needed to get his headset on at some point, but he didn't feel like it at the moment.

"It's Henderson, recon lead," Fuentes said. "Sounds like we have casualties."

Angus would have expected no less of O'Doyle. Good thing the G4S unit had so many men.

"Hold tight, Doctor Kool," Fuentes said. "Donnie is coming to talk to you."

Angus spread his hands to show the rocks and snow around him: *Where exactly do you think I'm going to go?*

Fuentes returned to his BaDonkeyDonk assembly duties.

Moments later, Donnie Graham strode across the plateau toward Angus, a tablet computer in his hand. A few flakes of snow clung to his salt-and-pepper mustache. He wore the same general outfit as the rest of the mercs, although he'd added wraparound sunglasses and a tan scarf.

"Bad news, Doctor Kool. Your friend O'Doyle mined the entrance. We lost two men from our recon team."

"Bummer," Angus said.

Donnie's mouth twitched. "We also have two wounded and one dead from the helicopter assault."

Angus thought of mentioning that if the helicopter assault had gone as planned, Donnie wouldn't have lost the two men from the mine, but decided against it.

"Most unfortunate," Angus said. "You knew O'Doyle was a bad motherfucker, right?"

Donnie nodded. "I did. However, we have some good news. The attack forced O'Doyle and his team to leave a lot of their supplies up here. Firearms, a case of V40 grenades, a good amount of .45-caliber ammo, food rations, a few other things. They had a jammer, but the thing took a couple of rounds. It's trashed. The attack helicopter pilots reported O'Doyle's men had personal weapons, rifles, and sidearms. Maybe they'd already taken supplies into the tunnel before the gunships closed in, but even if they did, based on what I've seen so far we'll heavily outgun them, not to mention have them outnumbered ten-to-one."

"How long until we can go in after them?"

Donnie tapped the tablet, glanced over to a team of two mercs who were lifting something out of one of the crates that had been lowered by the Chinook.

"The second Chinook is approximately fifteen minutes out," Donnie said. "So maybe … thirty minutes until they rappel down and form up. As soon as they do, and as soon as your haulers are set up, we're good to go."

"The mechanized burden units have a proper name, Donnie, and I'd appreciate it if you'd use that name."

Donnie glared. "What are you, thirteen? I'm not calling them *BaDonkeyDonks*."

"But—"

"I'll call them *donkeys*," Donnie said. "But that's as far as I go. Try to have them operational inside thirty minutes."

There were no bodies on the plateau, which meant O'Doyle was still alive. How far ahead could the big fucker and his thugs get in thirty minutes?

"I don't think we should wait that long."

"Were you not listening when I told you a mine just killed two of my men?"

"I heard you," Angus said. "So … *when*, exactly, are we going in?"

"Patience is prudent. The people who were up here know what they're doing. We flew a drone in. It missed the mine, but it got visuals. The tunnels have switchbacks. About fifty meters from the tunnel mouth, it widens into a small cave before continuing on. One prone man in there. Dead as a doornail, but after the mine, we're not going to rush things."

Angus's heart surged—maybe it was O'Doyle? Dead?

"A corpse? Can you see the face?"

Donnie tapped the tablet, turned it so Angus could see.

Naked chest. A bullet hole Angus could put his fist in. But whoever it was, it wasn't Patrick O'Doyle.

Angus felt the pressure of an invisible ticking clock, a weight bearing down on him—he didn't want O'Doyle to get away.

"Send your people in, Donnie. For fuck's sake, they're mercenaries, not momma's precious baby boys fresh off the Nebraska farm."

Donnie lowered the tablet. He walked closer, sat down on the rock next to Angus. Angus had to slide to the side to make room. Sliding to the side hurt.

"Doctor Kool, I said we are not going to rush it. These *mercenaries* are men. *My* men. One was named Luke Potter. Another was named Ty Swindon. They are dead, because they tripped a very well-hidden mine, a mine hidden by a pro. Another of my men was named Willy Ekhard. Willy Ekhard is also dead. Do you know why he's dead?"

Oh, this talking ape wanted to ask rhetorical questions?

"Uh ... because he got shot?"

Donnie nodded. "Because he got shot. By a forty-five caliber round fired from a distance of approximately seventy-five meters, from a mountain top, in a snowstorm, and also through heavy black smoke, a round that went into the open door of a helicopter moving at approximately thirty miles an hour. That is a very difficult shot, even when said shooter isn't under fire from a pair of M240s on full auto. Has anyone ever fired an M240 at you, Doctor Kool?"

Angus shook his head. He hadn't expected such intensity from Donnie, wasn't prepared for it.

"One was fired at me about ten years ago," Donnie said. "I shit my pants. That's not a euphemism. I literally filled my drawers. With that gun trying to find me, I cowered behind a wall and instantly developed a deep love for Jesus and Buddha and Allah and any supernatural being that might save me from getting my guts blown out. For someone to be facing that kind of firepower and have the wherewithal to return fire, accurately, kill Ekhard, as well as wound Harper Poole and Leo Evanson, we're talking seasoned, experienced, hardened soldiers."

Intense wasn't the word for it. Jesus Christ, Angus wanted to be somewhere else, wanted to be *anywhere* else.

Donnie leaned closer. "When one is facing seasoned, experienced, hardened soldiers, Doctor Kool, do you know what one does *not* do?"

"Um … one does not … rush in?"

Donnie nodded. "Precisely. Get the donkeys assembled. I'm ordering Henderson's recon team to stand down until your Wolf units are ready. You gave them cute little names, didn't you?"

The names weren't *cute*. Angus had to call them something, didn't he?

"Snoopy and Oberon," he said.

"Either Snoopy or Oberon will go first from now on to make sure the way is safe. Then and *only* then will *my* men enter the tunnels. You got it?"

His tirade finished, Donnie stood.

Angus felt embarrassed anew. Not at his damaged body this time, but rather that an underling—his *employee*—would speak to him that way. Angus wished he was bigger so he could headbutt Donnie in his mustached mouth, maybe break some teeth. But these soldiers obeyed Donnie's commands—Angus was in charge, but he had to be smart about things.

"Fine," he said. "Your men are important. Donkeys first."

"Speaking of the donkeys, my men had all of three hours' worth of training learning how to assemble them. Can you help out?"

It was a question that sounded suspiciously like an order. Angus hoped Donnie understood the chain of command. If not, Angus would soon have to remind him.

"I'll supervise." Angus pointed a crutch to the two black equipment cases he'd marked with Xs in blue tape. His *special* cases. "Let's make sure those come in with us. High priority."

Donnie nodded. "You've told us, Mister Kool. Several times. Now, if you could help with the donkeys, I'll manage the rest of the load-out and wreckage removal."

Donnie Graham turned and walked away, barking orders in a voice distinctly different from the one he'd just used to speak to Angus.

Off in the distance, to the north, Angus saw the second Chinook helicopter coming in low, well below the ridgeline. In it, more lovely gear, and another fifty G4S mercs.

Patrick O'Doyle had escaped, but he wouldn't live long.

Angus hobbled toward the two men who were struggling to lift the BaDonkeyDonk onto its four metal feet.

BOOK THREE
DESCENT

26

925 feet below the surface

"IT'S JUST AHEAD," Sam said. "After the next switchback."

O'Doyle glanced back, making sure Sam was right behind him. Up on the plateau, she hadn't appreciated how *big* he was. A bulging canvas bag hung from each of his shoulders, and he held an olive-green metal crate in his hands. In the narrow tunnel, with his bulk and all that gear, her headlamp beam lighting up his back, O'Doyle was like a camo-clad plunger being pushed through a stone syringe.

Ahead of O'Doyle, two of his killers—*Mullet* and *Sleepy* seemed to be their names—led the way. Sleepy was a bleach-blond with distant eyes, almost *dead* eyes. He hummed quietly, so quietly that Sam could just make out the notes of "Yesterday." Mullet had a face like a movie star, so handsome he would have been distracting under other circumstances.

Sam carried a heavy canvas bag in each hand. She was already exhausted. They'd been going as fast as they could for the last twenty minutes, descending the steep incline, switchback after switchback.

O'Doyle stopped, set a bag down, pressed a button on a black box strapped into his chest.

"Worm," O'Doyle whispered, "plant another repeater."

Sam didn't hear "Worm's" response; she wore her mining helmet, not one of the combat helmets with the built-in headsets.

McGuiness and the other two normally dressed men were close behind her. Farther back, the rest of O'Doyle's gun-toting thugs brought up the rear.

Angling her head this way and that to look past O'Doyle's bulk, Sam saw Mullet and Sleepy had reached the next switchback. As they had two dozen times already, Sleepy crouched down while Mullet stood tall. The pair leaned around the corner—*barely* around it—at the same time, looking through the scopes of their rifles. They moved like a single person. If anyone had been around that corner, they would have seen only a gun barrel, maybe *part* of a helmeted head, and that was it.

Mullet went around the corner as Sleepy flashed hand signals to O'Doyle.

"They see your basecamp cave," O'Doyle said to Sam. "You're sure there won't be anyone in there?"

How many times was he going to ask that? Only she and Ramiro had entered the tunnels. She had come out and stayed by the entrance until O'Doyle's helicopter landed.

"I'm sure," she said.

O'Doyle nodded. "Stay behind me."

He moved. She followed.

Moments later, she entered the basecamp cave, once a place of happiness and excitement. Now? This place was just as terrifying as being up in the tunnels, or up on the Notch, because anywhere she went there were people with guns. Sleepy and Mullet stood there, weapons aimed out of the cave's other entrance, the one that led down.

O'Doyle set the crate and his bags against the cave wall. Sam did the same, stacking hers on his.

"Jabour's basecamp cave is clear," O'Doyle said. "Bertha, double-time it, get everyone down here. Sleepy, keep going, two switchbacks forward. Make sure there's no one in front of us. Don't go farther. I can't risk losing radio contact with you."

The dead-eyed bleach blond quickly walked out of the cave.

"Mullet," O'Doyle said, "find some presents you can leave for those fucks if they follow us down."

The movie-star mouth smiled. Mullet opened one of the bags Sam had been carrying, started to sort through the contents.

There wasn't much to the basecamp cave. Roughly circular, maybe twenty feet across, ten feet high, chipped out of solid granite just like the tunnels were. Three bedrolls on one side, rolled-up sleeping bags atop them. Veronica hadn't taken her sleeping bag with her when she went to Utah. Now maybe it would stay here forever, just another artifact like the millennia-old knives.

Veronica had picked this spot. It was far enough below the surface's winds and storms that the cave remained a consistent 69.4 degrees Fahrenheit. It was in this cave that she, Sam and Ramiro had slept, eaten, compared notes, made plans for tunnel exploration. Along the curved walls were stacked water jugs, a kerosene camp stove, cardboard boxes of energy bars and dried food, a hand-crank generator, notebooks, pee bottles and poop kits for storing and removing human waste…the basics required for days-long stretches underground.

O'Doyle pointed to the bed rolls. "Move over there, please. Try to stay out of the way."

Stay out of the way?

"We have to go after Ramiro," Sam said. "He's dying."

If he's not already dead, cut to pieces by fucking silver robot spiders.

O'Doyle gripped her arm, not hard enough to hurt, but hard enough to commandeer her attention.

"One of ours died," he said, slowly, patiently. "I want to help your friend, but right now we have to deal with the threat at hand. I have to get my people into a defensible position, and then I have to know what's coming after us. If it's a few mercenaries, that's one thing. If it's a hundred of them, that's another. This isn't just about you and Ramiro anymore—I have nine other people to keep alive. Understand?"

Ten people besides herself and Ramiro. Ten lives. With the guns and the fear, she'd lost track of that.

"Yes," she said. "But try to hurry."

He nodded. "I will. Now, please, stay out of the way."

Sam walked to her bedroll, sat down on the rolled up sleeping bag. She was shaking. That poor man. His horrible wounds. The way he'd died. The way his boyfriend, or husband, or whatever he was, had fallen apart. Real anguish brought on by a loss of real love.

Sonny entered the cave, followed closely by the two men who weren't dressed like extras from a war movie—a white guy with blood-soaked gauze pressed to the left side of his face and a black guy guiding him along.

"McGuiness," the black man said, "I need to stitch him up. Get me a first aid kit."

Sonny said nothing. He walked straight to Ramiro's bedroll and sat down on the sleeping bag, right next to Sam. Sonny was shaking. Afraid of the fighting, or was he claustrophobic? Either way, he wasn't responding.

"I have a first aid kit," Sam said.

She grabbed it from its place along the wall. Over the last three years, how many times had she, Veronica and Ramiro used the kit to clean up each other's bumps, bruises, and cuts?

Sam handed it to the man.

"Thank you," he said. "I'm Agent Clarence Otto. This is Agent Paulius Klimas."

The man with the cut face jutted his chin forward in greeting.

Agents. Of what?

"We need access to the surface," Klimas said. "We need to call for help."

Otto held up a satellite phone. "I tried calling when we were inside the entrance, but no joy. I need somewhere I can see the sky."

"Sorry," Sam said. "You're out of luck. The entrance is the only spot."

Otto's nostrils flared. He handed the phone to Klimas, who shoved it into his pants pocket.

"I was afraid of that," Otto said. "Can you get me some water? I need to clean my partner's wounds before I stitch him up."

Sam nodded, ran to grab a water jug. As she did, the rest of O'Doyle's team poured in, all laboring under the weight of heavy canvas bags and big plastic crates. Two women, two more men, all dressed in the same black-and-gray camouflage pattern as O'Doyle, Sleepy and Mullet, all with identical, compact black guns slung on their backs or hanging from a chest harness.

Sam handed the water jug to Otto, then moved out of the way, maybe because that was what O'Doyle had asked her to do, maybe because with ten people in the small cave there wasn't room for much else.

"Listen up," O'Doyle said. "We left a lot of gear up on the plateau. I need a hard count of what we have. Worm, get a hornet up and running. I want to know what our new pals are doing."

The redheaded man moved quickly to one of the canvas bags.

O'Doyle calmly gave orders. "Bertha, check the KoolSuits."

The big woman with the facial scars nodded, moved to a metal crate.

KoolSuits ... Ramiro had mentioned those. How many suits did these people have?

"Mullet," O'Doyle said, "I need a count of working weapons. Worm, did we get the jammer?"

The redhead quickly glanced from bag to bag, crate to crate.

"No, it must be up on the plateau."

O'Doyle's lip curled into a sneer. "Fuck. Skylark, you're on food and ammo count."

The smaller woman slung her rifle behind her and ran to the canvas bags stacked on the wall.

"Curveball," O'Doyle said. "Make sure the other hornet drones are working."

There was only one person left—the bald black soldier with the graying beard. The one who had cried over the dead man. When the bald man didn't answer, O'Doyle turned to him.

"*Curveball.* I said—"

"Leave him the *fuck* alone," Skylark said.

Her anger and aggression seemed to catch O'Doyle off guard. Lybrand looked between the two.

A high-pitched buzzing sound broke the tense moment.

In his right hand, Worm held a controller, which looked somewhat like a tan pistol grip with buttons on top. A cable from the controller connected to a tan, rectangular canvas pack hanging from his neck. Part of the pack had folded down: a small video screen, facing up at him. Above his shoulder floated what looked like a tiny, palm-sized black helicopter, rotors a circular blur.

"Hornet is ready to go," Worm said. "I'll do Curveball's count, Ender. Cool?"

Worm sounded consoling, like he was trying to deflate the tense situation, but there was an edge to his voice, an edge that Sam knew was directed at O'Doyle.

"Yeah," Ender said, softly, without taking his eyes off Curveball. "Yeah, that's cool. The drone will reach all the way to the mouth?"

"Roger that," Worm said. "I put up ten repeaters. That should be enough. Roughly fifteen minutes flight time to get it back to the tunnel mouth. We'll have full visual all the way."

Curveball sat on the cave floor, rested his elbows on his knees. He stared down, utterly drained, utterly lost. A complete stranger, but Sam's heart broke for him.

O'Doyle kept staring at him.

"*Ender,*" Worm said. "You want me to send the hornet up or not?"

With some effort, O'Doyle tore his gaze away from Curveball.

"Yeah, send it. Let's see what we're dealing with."

FOUR GAPING HOLES in the thin, clear material, each one big enough for Bertha to put her fist through.

Shit.

She tossed the damaged KoolSuit aside. It crumpled on the cave floor next to the other ruined suit, like two sets of clear skin shed by some reptilian person. The holes were so big it wasn't worth trying to repair them. Maybe she could cut those suits up for patch material, if she had enough time.

They'd stored all of the black KoolSuit tubes in one shipping crate. A stupid call, in retrospect—that crate had two big holes in it, thanks to a pair of rounds taken during the helicopter attack.

Gunships. *Two* of them. Bertha had never faced fire like that before—the mujahideen hadn't had much in the way of helicopters.

She took another tube out of the crate. She had to stay cool. It wasn't easy. She'd tried to talk Patrick out of this when there had only been silverbugs and rocktopi to worry about. Now there was a well-funded paramilitary force involved?

One person dead already.

It could have been Patrick.

It could have been her.

An air of anger in the cave. Anger and sadness. These people hadn't seen each other in over a decade, yet Hatchet's death hit them all very hard. Bertha saw the dark glances the others threw at Patrick. The mission had barely begun, and he was already losing them?

Much more danger still to come. How many troops would be coming down that tunnel? Would these "NoSeeUms" continue to follow Patrick? Bertha didn't know about them. She only knew about herself—she would follow Patrick's orders. She hadn't wanted to come here, but what was done was done. If she and Patrick were going to survive, they had to be unified.

Bertha tilted the black tube this way and that. No holes, no damage. She clicked the release button, took out the rolled-up KoolSuit, unfurled it. No damage that she could see. She rolled it back up, put it in the long part of the tube, then opened the smaller end, took out the hood. She examined it carefully, saw no holes in that either.

That made ten undamaged KoolSuits, ready to go. Bertha carefully put the hood back in the black tube, set the tube on the stack of the other undamaged ones.

For the mission, Patrick had bought two suits for everyone on the team, a total of sixteen suits. Now there were four more people involved: Otto, Klimas, Sonny and Jabour. Gone was the luxury of each person having a spare.

The only real good news was resupply for water, coolant and the food gel packs. They had plenty. With the water recapture and filtration systems built into the KoolSuits, a person only needed about a liter of additional water a day. There were enough water replacement bottles to last five days, easy, probably seven or possibly eight if they pushed it. Everyone had six days' worth of the concentrated food packs that provided calories and nutrients, and enough of the tiny coolant recharging pellets to keep the suits' temperature controls working for *ten* days.

"I'm Samira."

Bertha turned quickly, hand going to her sidearm.

The scientist woman took a step back.

"I'm sorry," she said. "I didn't mean to startle you."

Bertha took her hand off the weapon. "Don't sneak up on people. Especially people with guns."

The woman nodded, offered her right hand. "Samira Jabour."

A handshake? What did this bitch think was going on here?

"I know who you are. I'm Lybrand."

Bertha picked up another tube, examined it for damage.

The woman let her hand drop. "Look, we can't just wait here. We've still got hours to go before we reach Ramiro."

Ah, so that's what this was about.

Bertha looked at the woman. "And you want me to talk to Patrick, right? After he told you we'd get to your man as soon as we could. Why, because I'm a *woman*, and you thought we'd see eye-to-eye, or something like that?"

Samira wiped away a tear, nodded. "Yes, that's what I was hoping."

Bertha opened the tube. "Forget it. I don't make the decisions around here."

I tried to do that—I got rejected, and look where we are now.

She pulled out the suit, let it unfurl, held the material close to her face as she tried to examine every little bit.

"Ramiro told me about those suits," Samira said. She glanced at the crate that held the black tubes, at the two ruined suits crumpled on the cave floor. "Sixteen of them? That's … something like … four million dollars' worth."

Bertha remembered looking over the budget in Patrick's business plan. Four million, just for the suits. At the time, the amount had seemed ludicrous, but here she was, checking gear that might, just *might*, keep her and Patrick alive.

The suit was fine. She rolled it up, put it back in the tube, then checked the hood—also undamaged. That made eleven: at least one for each of them.

"Let me take this one," Sam said, softly. "I'll go after Ramiro on my own."

"Touch any of these and I will knock you the fuck out."

Bertha set the black tube on the stack of good ones, removed another tube—a hole right through the middle. She tossed the tube atop the two ruined suits.

"I need to go after him," Sam said. "He's dying."

Those words hit home. How would Bertha respond if Patrick were in trouble?

"Stay cool," she said. "Things are bad. They're going to get worse. A *lot* worse."

Samira nodded, watched as Bertha checked the last two suits. One was shot to hell, the other appeared to be fine. That gave them twelve working suits—only *one* spare. Not good.

Bertha rolled up the last one and closed the tube when she saw Otto and Klimas approach Patrick. She set the tube on the stack.

"Don't touch them," she said to Sam, then moved closer to Patrick— Otto and Klimas both had pistols jammed into their waistbands. A line of new stitches on Klimas's left cheek, another on his left temple.

"O'Doyle," Otto said, "you need to tell me what's going on."

Patrick looked at Klimas, at his stitches.

"Strong work out there," Patrick said. "You know what you're doing. Combat experience?"

Klimas nodded. "SEAL Team Two. I know my business."

"Wow," Bertha said, "we have royalty in our midst."

Patrick flashed her a look, turned back to Otto. "How about you?"

"Rangers," Otto said. "Special forces after that, then CIA."

Bertha didn't know if she should be happy the two men knew what they were doing or worried that they did. They had no loyalty to Patrick.

"But I'm no spring chicken like Klimas," Otto said. "And he's the youngest operator here. We need to call for help, ASAP."

Patrick shook his head. "Ain't no cavalry coming. We're on our own. I'm thrilled you two know your business, but understand that I am in charge. We're probably up against a lot of people. We need to operate as one unit. You both do what I say. Understood?"

Klimas and Otto both glanced around the cave: at Bertha; at Skylark, who stared at them even as she counted magazines; at Tommy, who gave them a cold look as he worked with the drone controller; and at Mullet, who grinned at them in a way that screamed, *go ahead and start some shit.*

"All right," Otto said to Patrick. "You're in charge for now, but you need to tell me who those people are up there."

"I have no fucking idea who they are." Patrick turned away from him, stepped to the center of the cave. "Everyone gather around. That means you, too, Sonny, Jabour."

Otto and Klimas clearly wanted to say more, to ask more questions, but they held their tongues.

Patrick stood at parade rest. "Mullet, give me the weapons count."

"I must have left my extra guns in my other pants," Mullet said. "We have the personal weapons we brought down with us, plus Hatchet's carbine and sidearm. Our extra weapons are now the property of the fucksticks who killed Hatchet. Oh, Curve, I grabbed something for you."

Mullet reached into one of the bags, came out with a mean-looking black axe, maybe ten inches long, black plastic cover clipped over the thick blade. He tossed it at Curveball's feet.

"Hatchet must not have wanted it on him in the helicopter," Mullet said to him. "I figure you'd like to have it for when those assholes catch up with us."

Curveball reached out slowly, picked up the weapon. He looked at Mullet.

"Thank you."

"Back on task," Patrick said. "Otto, Klimas, give the sidearms you have back to their owners. Otto, you take Hatchet's sidearm. Klimas, you'll take Hatchet's carbine, helmet and pack. Be aware his pack has C4 and a claymore in there. Jabour, McGuiness—either of you experienced with firearms?"

Samira shook her head.

"Used to be," Sonny said. "But it's been awhile."

"Then we'll hold off giving you a piece until I know you're safe with it," Patrick said. "Skylark, how's our ammo situation?"

"Bad." The woman gestured to a stack of magazines arranged neatly atop a now-empty green canvas bag. "Fifty-one full thirty-round mags. Twenty-four full fifteen-round mags. Eleven rounds left over. We each have our claymore and block of C4. We didn't get all the food packs in—with this many mouths to feed, we've got three days' worth, tops."

That didn't sound like much, but it was more than Bertha and Patrick had had when they'd been trapped under Funeral Mountain in Utah. She hadn't really thought about food then. Three days of food could be stretched out quite a while.

"All right," Patrick said. "Let's put our cards on the table. Otto,

Klimas, maybe you know already, maybe you don't—we're here because there may be a platinum deposit under this mountain. We have killers behind us, and there's no question they're here for the same thing. I don't know how well they're armed or if they're experienced, but whoever hired them can afford to outfit a pair of helicopters with M240s. You can bet your ass we won't be going up against Cub Scouts wielding sharpened spoons."

Patrick turned as he talked.

"There's much more to the story," he said. "I'll fill you in once we get moving. We have a head start and enough equipment to make it to our destination. Jabour, any side tunnels between here and where you lost Ramiro? Anywhere we could get off this main tunnel, maybe make the enemy split their forces?"

Samira shook her head. "There are cracks in the walls here and there, but none big enough to hide in or crawl through. Believe me when I say that there's only one way in and one way out."

Patrick's jaw muscles twitched. He looked up to the ceiling. He was getting frustrated. Bertha could see that—could his old war buddies?

"Get your KoolSuits on," Patrick said. "Sonny, Jabour, Otto, Klimas—Lybrand will show you how they work. Make it fast, people. When you're done getting the suits on, pack up everything we can carry on our person. We'll march as soon as we get whatever intel we can from Tommy's drone."

27

1,804 Feet up the mountain

ANGUS KOOL WAS freezing his balls off.

But it wasn't *all* bad—a double dose of oxy (and the corresponding double dose of Adderall) was already setting him straight, getting the pain down to a controllable level.

He sat on a rock, laptop in his lap, the mountain wind seeming to hit him from every direction. He was sure he already had windburn on his cheeks and his nose. All thanks to Dimwit Donnie not letting anyone into the tunnels.

"Running system check again," he said.

He typed in command lines. The software for the Wolves and BaDonkeyDonks wasn't booting up properly. Probably because Fuentes and Khatari—both of whom, he had to admit, worked hard and tried to do everything he asked—were not trained engineers. Angus felt embarrassed he hadn't planned better for on-site variables. He'd assumed his gear would work flawlessly. Rookie mistake. A hundred men stood idle on the plateau, waiting for *him* to get things right.

"Crossing my fingers," Fuentes said. "Fucking cold out here."

Khatari frowned at him. "You think this is cold?"

Fuentes smiled at him.

Where the mountain's pinnacle wall met the angled plateau, six of his machines stood in a row like sleek, robotic Great Danes, the level back of each as tall as Khatari's hip. Quadruped robots, all six used identical metal-frame chassis, although four—the BaDonkey-Donks—were designed for hauling, and two—the Wolves—were engineered for more aggressive purposes. They all had cameras, of course. If Angus was lucky, he'd get footage of one of the Wolves killing Limpdick O'Doyle.

The programming problem impacted the machines' ability to lower their bodies. When working properly, the machines could drop down until the bottom of their chassis were only an inch off the ground, yet they could still move forward or backward. That low-profile potential was a critical design element, allowing the machines to navigate through almost any tunnel.

Angus entered a command. As one, Snoopy and Oberon—the two Wolf models—lowered in place, a synchronized dance of metal, plastic, humming servos, and messing gears. The four BaDonkeyDonks didn't lower. At all.

"Fuck," Angus said.

Fuentes tipped his head toward the plateau. "Doctor Kool, Donnie don't look happy."

Sure enough, Donnie Graham was striding toward Angus. Even behind sunglasses, Donnie looked visibly unhappy. Clearly, Angus needed to establish boundaries—*he* was the boss here, not Donnie.

"Doctor Kool," Donnie said as he came closer, "are you going to get those machines of yours working today, or should I have the men set up tents?" He stopped in front of Angus, stared down. "Here's a hint—we didn't bring tents."

Angus started a sniffer subroutine to find the problem in the BaDon-keyDonks' code.

"I don't know, Donnie," he said, "maybe if we could go *inside the tunnel* it might help with the bifurcated analytical algorithm. I think the cold is fucking with it."

Donnie shook his head. "I'm old, Doctor Kool, not a fucking idiot. *Bifurcated analytical algorithm* isn't a real thing."

More embarrassment. Maybe Angus shouldn't have expected Donnie to fall for the same gibberish that Alice had.

"The problem is with the BaDonkeyDonks," Angus said. "The Wolves are working now. You can send one in."

"Then get one moving," Donnie said. "We're burning daylight."

Angus had been the one bitching about sitting up here and letting O'Doyle get away, yet Donnie was turning that around on him? What utter bullshit.

Donnie turned to face Fuentes and Khatari. "And you two, do you have your thumbs up each other's asses? While Doctor Kool figures out what's wrong with the haulers, get them loaded up. We need to be ready to move. And don't forget the doctor's *very special cases* that he won't stop reminding me about."

Donnie strode up the plateau toward the boulder that hid the tunnel entrance.

"Fuentes," Angus said, "bring me the HUD before you start loading up the haulers."

The man brushed snow off a small case, opened it, and brought the bulky headset inside over to Angus. Angus slid it on and flipped the heads-up display screen down over his right eye. When he did, the screen blinked on, showing Angus the front-camera view of Wolf 1, a.k.a. *Snoopy*.

The HUD screen had icons along the top, bottom, and edges. Most commands were activated by staring at those icons and blinking a specified number of times—the HUD interface tracked eye direction and eyelid movement. Once one knew how the interface worked, choosing commands became fast and effortless, control at the speed of thought.

Angus looked at icons. He blinked, giving several commands at once.

Snoopy stepped forward, front-right and rear-left legs moving simultaneously, then the front-left and rear-right.

Both Snoopy and Oberon had front-facing M249 SAW light machine guns mounted inside their heavily armored chassis. Their only cargo was 2,000 rounds of ammo. They also had Angus's soon-to-be-patented "snake head" feature.

One of those Wolves would kill Patrick O'Doyle. Angus felt it in his bones.

"Kool, let's go!" Donnie, calling out across the plateau, embarrassing Angus further. That fucking guy.

With a few blinks, Angus sent Snoopy marching toward the tunnel entrance. In the HUD, Angus saw the organized platoons of mercenaries, groups of ten men kneeling together, waiting to be called into action. Snoopy marched between the platoons.

For shits and giggles, Angus called up the HUD's targeting scope and sighted the crosshairs on Donnie. Three little blinks in a row, and it would be bye-bye for the man. The Wolves could fire on their own, if so commanded, but having the ability of human targeting control was always a good thing.

Angus had given all of his robots one secret, critical bit of code. He couldn't ignore the fact that he was in the middle nowhere, surrounded by a hundred mercenary killers who had been paid with someone else's money. Donnie had cut a side deal with him; maybe he'd also cut a side deal with June July. As far as Angus knew, June had told Donnie to find the platinum source, then quietly do away with one Doctor Angus Kool. Highly doubtful she would do that, but it was a possibility, one for which Angus had prepared as best he could by embedding a voice-only command—and only for *his* voice—in the two Wolf units.

That command: *All but me.*

With those three syllables, Angus could kill everyone on the plateau in a matter of seconds—Donnie included.

Dimwit Donnie had given no sign he had backstabbing plans, but Angus would tread very, very carefully around the man.

In the HUD, Angus saw Donnie gesture to the wider space that led to the tunnel mouth—*after you, good sir.*

Snoopy was just narrow enough to fit through the gap between boulder and rock face, although it had to move slowly and methodically to do so.

Angus blinked commands, sending Snoopy forward.

28

925 feet below the surface

TOMMY FOCUSED ON flying the hornet drone. The thing operated on autopilot for the most part, avoiding walls and ceilings and floors, but focusing on it helped him ignore the thought that threatened to swallow up his mind—he'd shot a man.

Shot him, probably killed him.

Exactly what Ender had promised would not happen.

Tommy couldn't be sure, of course—the helicopter door gunner had gone down, and that was all Tommy had seen. Maybe the man was just wounded.

But maybe he wasn't.

"How much farther," Ender said.

Tommy was sitting cross-legged on his butt, the hornet pack with its little fold-down video monitor hanging from his chest. Ender was on one knee to his right. Both men focused on the screen, which showed a night vision view of the endless stone tunnel, chipped walls whipping by as the hornet ascended switchback after switchback.

The pack was a cool piece of gear. Below the touchscreen monitor hung a hard plastic case with a docking slot for each of the kit's two drones. When the slot's lid closed, the hornet protected inside recharged from the kit's built-in battery. A one-handed joystick controlled the flying units. When not in use, the controller snapped home into a form-fitting space between the slots.

"Just a bit more," Tommy said.

During the retreat, Ender had ordered Tommy to place signal repeaters, and Tommy was glad of it. On the surface, the little drones could transmit video in real time from up to a thousand meters away. In the tunnels, however, the endless granite switchbacks cut that range to a hundred meters, tops. By placing signal repeaters—tiny transmitters relaying the hornet's signals like an electronic bucket brigade—Tommy could still see whatever the hornet saw.

"Past the last switchback," Tommy said. "Coming up on that cave where Hatchet died."

Tommy kept his eyes on the screen, yet noticed Ender glance over at Curveball. Curve was in bad shape. Could anyone blame him? Twenty years with one person, and now that person was gone. Gone, killed by *people*, when Ender had said the NoSeeUms wouldn't face people at all.

Things had fallen apart. Hatchet, dead. Samira and Sonny, civilians who knew nothing about weapons or tactics. Otto and Klimas, X-factors who Tommy and the other NoSeeUms didn't know, couldn't trust, yet Ender had armed them. Curveball, zoning out, unreliable, at least for the moment.

Tommy had worn the KoolSuit for all of two hours, and already he'd almost forgotten the thing was on. A thin strip of data at the top of his vision showed him the depth, direction and air temperature—well over a hundred degrees, yet he felt neither hot nor cold. The face shield had no glare of any kind. If not for the HUD and the slight reflection of his own voice, he wouldn't have known the shield was there at all. With it extended, the suit's headband wasn't as thick; his helmet fit fine. Everyone wore their normal clothes and gear on top of the suits. Impressive tech indeed.

"There's Hatchet," Ender said quietly. "Wait, what is that?"

On the screen, a green/white view of the small cave just inside the tunnel entrance. Hatchet's body lay there, shirt still open, blood smeared on his skin. In the entrance to the cavern, the one that lead out to the mountain, something crouched down on all fours. An animal?

"It got past Mullet's claymore," Ender said. "Or someone found the mine first."

"A *mine?*" Sonny said. "You idiots would set off explosives down here?"

The old man trembled, his breaths shallow and rapid. Up on the plateau, he'd mentioned his claustrophobia. Just one more problem Tommy and the others would have to deal with.

"We're in a *tunnel,*" Sonny said. "You blow things up and that causes a cave-in, then we're *completely* fucked."

A claymore sent 700 one-eighth-inch steel balls exploding outward at a velocity of 1,200 meters-per-second, in a sixty-degree fan-snapped pattern. The balls would slam into the walls and ceiling. Could that break off enough rock to cause a cave-in?

He glanced at Ender, saw that Ender was thinking the same thing.

Maybe it was just dumb luck Mullet's claymore hadn't sealed them in here forever.

"We won't use the mine," Ender said. "For now. Try to calm down, Sonny. All right?"

Sonny slid his silver bracelet off his wrist, held it with both hands, his thumbs rubbing furiously against the metal. The man was a mess.

"Worm, I need to see more," Ender said, "Don't take the hornet any closer, but can you zoom in?"

Tommy did.

Not an animal; a four-legged machine. The size of a big rottweiler, maybe bigger. The body, a metal frame with molded plates covering most of it, was low to the ground, the bottom of its belly only a few inches above the cave silt. The front legs bent in toward the body—like any quadruped's front legs did—but the back legs bent *away* from the body. Four identical legs, the knee joints all pointing backward … it gave the machine an oddly insect-like appearance.

On top of the framework, two stacked rows of interlinked metal segments, each perhaps the size of a tennis ball. No, not two rows … one, which connected to the top front of the machine and ran down to the rear end, where it folded over on itself and stretched to the front. Like a scorpion tail, ending in what looked like a much wider version of a jumper cable clamp. On either side of the clamp, a spot of white with a dark dot inside it.

Tommy didn't think of the machine as rottweiler-like anymore. With the four back-folding legs and the molded plates that covered the frame, it now seemed insectile to him.

"Those plates look like some kind of advanced armor," Tommy said. "That ain't good."

A circular hole in the armor. He zoomed in again, thought he could see something through the seams in the plates, something black, running along the inside of the robot. Something with a barrel …

"And that *definitely* ain't good," Tommy said, using his fingertip to trace the weapon's outline on the screen.

"A fucking M249," Patrick said. "A robot with a SAW. Shit." He pointed to the clamp. "Is that its head?"

"I don't think so," Tommy said. "I don't think it has a *head*. It—"

The robot moved forward, front-left and rear-right legs simultaneously folding up and reaching forward with machine precision, followed by the same exact motion from the front-right and rear-left. Low to the ground, it crawled forward five steps, the body as level and flat as if it had been rolling along on wheels.

"It's moving toward Hatchet's body," Tommy said. "We'll see how well the armor works. I left an M40 on …" his words trailed off as he glanced over his shoulder, saw Curveball watching him. Tommy faced forward, spoke so quietly only Ender could hear: "I left a going-away present."

"Move the hornet back," Ender said. "But keep visual."

Tommy guided the hornet backward. The tunnel entrance grew smaller in the screen, a narrowing window on the scene of Hatchet's body and the insectile robot.

Could the machine hear the hornet? The hornet ran without lights. Its tiny black body would be invisible in the dark tunnel. It didn't make a ton of noise, but in those close confines the buzz would be hard to miss.

Tommy watched the insectile robot close in on Hatchet's body. The scorpion tail reached out. The clamp pinched down on Hatchet's arm, then pulled—Hatchet's body slid a foot.

The image on the screen shook, filled with static. The image stabilized, showing billowing dust that slowly thinned.

"Still standing," Ender said.

A few scratches in the curved plates, but the machine didn't seem any worse for wear. Definitely not good.

"Thing is like a little tank," Tommy said.

The clamp released Hatchet's body. When it curled back, folded over on itself and again rested on the machine's back, Tommy saw the white spots on either side of the clamp—and inside those, the black dots, wiggling.

"Googly eyes," Tommy said. "Whoever our foes are, they've got a sense of humor."

Tommy became aware that people had lined up behind him and Ender. Otto, Klimas, Sonny and Lybrand leaned down, quietly watched the screen.

Ender's jaw muscles twitched. "How many hornets do we have?"

"Four, total," Tommy said. "The one deployed, the other one in the pack I'm wearing, then two in a second pack."

Ender nodded slightly. "Worth losing one if we can find out who these oh-so-funny *foes* are. Go past the robot as fast as you can. Let's see what we can see outside."

Tommy double-checked the controls, knowing that if the insectile robot did have weaponry, he might only have one chance to move the hornet past it.

"Here we go," he said, and move it forward.

On the screen, the insectile robot seemed to rush closer. The clamp on the back moved, the thing turned, then the hornet was past. Tommy only had to tell it to keep going—the hornet managed the switchbacks on its own.

A flash of white, then the green night vision switched to a full-color, fish-eye view of the plateau.

"Fuck me," Otto said. "There's got to be a hundred men up there."

Men and equipment. Tommy wished that he could go back to that Denver meeting room and walk out, go back home and just wash dishes. He had a feeling it wouldn't be the last time he wished that.

Some of the men must have seen the tiny hornet, because Tommy saw them standing, yelling.

"There," Ender said, finger stabbing at the screen. "That guy doesn't have a uniform, close in on him, fast."

Tommy worked the controller, moving the hornet toward Ender's target. Tommy had a fast impression of a man wearing some kind of HUD rig, then the screen turned to static.

"Sorry," he said. "They destroyed the hornet." He looked at Ender. Veins pulsed in the man's temples. His skin was turning red.

"Can you show me that last frame before it was destroyed?"

Tommy nodded, worked the controls. The last frame showed a man sitting on a rock, HUD screen over his right eye. Laying on the rock next to him, a pair of wrist crutches.

"Motherfucker," Ender said. "Lybrand, tell me I'm not crazy."

Lybrand leaned over Tommy. "You're not. That's Angus fucking Kool."

"Sonofabitch," Sonny said. "The little prick survived."

Ender stood. "How did he find us?" He pressed his *talk* button. "Mullet, Sleepy, back to basecamp, now."

The gunships. They hadn't been in a search pattern—they'd flown straight in, located the NoSeeUms with pinpoint accuracy, on a mountaintop in the middle of nowhere.

"There's a transmitter in our gear," Tommy said.

He flipped his chest monitor closed and moved to the stacks of equipment.

"That motherfucker," Ender said. "I didn't even know he was alive. He must have known what we were up to when we placed the KoolSuit order."

Tommy looked at bags, then crates. His eyes fell on the stack of matte-black tubes with the glossy words *Kool Products* printed on them. He grabbed one, looked at the bottom of it, saw a dime-sized circle of black plastic, the same material as the case itself. He drew his knife, slid the point under the disk—a slight twist of the blade, and the disk popped off.

The underside of the disk was green with patterns of parallel yellowish lines.

"This is it," Tommy said. He showed the disk to Ender. "This is how he knew how to find us."

Ender's eyes bulged with rage. "What about the suits? Can he track those?"

Tommy popped open the tube, looked at the rolled-up material inside.

"I doubt it. I went over each suit when I put in the new comms gear. I just never thought of checking the damn tubes they came in. His tracking tags probably used GPS or some kind of signal triangulation. That worked on the surface, but it won't work down here in the tunnels. Maybe he could have RFID tags in the suits, but he'd have to be very close. The suits themselves are probably fine." He looked at two ruined ones piled on the cave floor. "I can take those apart piece by piece and make sure."

"Take them with, check first chance you get," Ender said. "We have to get out of here."

Otto stepped in, looked at the white disk, then at Ender.

"Who is Angus Kool? Tell me what's going on."

Ender put a hand on the Otto's chest, stepped past him to the center of the cave. Mullet and Sleepy came running in. Ender turned as he talked, addressing everyone at once.

"All right, people, saddle up," he said. "They'll be coming down. We need to move fast. Skylark, can you fly one of those hornet drones?"

She sneered. "Did the Trojan Horse have a wooden cock?"

"You'll bring up the rear with Mullet," Ender said. "Keep the drone clear of the enemy, we can't afford to lose another. Tommy, show Mullet the footage of their scout machine. Mullet, come up with something that can stop that machine."

Mullet nodded. "I will."

"We're moving out," Ender said. "Worm, you're on point. Use a hornet so nothing surprises us. Lybrand will go with you. She's got the most experience in this situation. Sleepy, Curveball, up front with Worm and Lybrand."

"Affirmative," Sleepy said.

Lybrand nodded.

Curveball didn't respond. All eyes turned to the man, who hadn't budged from his spot at the wall. He held the axe in his hand, stared at it like he didn't really understand what it was.

Ender stepped to him, stood over him.

"*Curveball!*"

The man looked up, his eyes rimmed with tears.

"Hatchet is gone," Ender said, his voice softer, more understanding. "We're moving out. You can either come with us and survive, or you can stay here and die. I need your head in the game. What's it going to be?"

The man blinked a few times. He rubbed at his graying beard, then wiped his eyes and stood.

"I heard your order," he said. "I'm on point with Worm. Got it."

Ender gripped Curveball's shoulder. It was supposed to be a gesture of support, of understanding, but Ender was terrible at shit like that. Curve just looked at the hand until Ender let go and turned back to face everyone else.

"Otto, Klimas, Jabour, you're with me in the middle so I can get you up to speed. You too, Sonny. Everyone, move *slowly*, move *quietly*. We know that silverbugs cue in on sound. We want to avoid them as long as possible. Got it?"

All around, heads nodded.

"All right," Ender said. "Let's go."

29

1,804 feet up the mountain

AT LONG LAST, the company of mercenaries began to move into the tunnel. Not a moment too soon: Angus was sure his nuts had already frozen solid and dropped off, indiscernible from the plateau's numerous rocks, and that he would only feel the pain of said lost nuts if he lived long enough to thaw out.

The mercs entered, one platoon of ten at a time. The five-man recon—well, the *three*-man team, now that a mine had killed two of them—had entered first, then Donnie had gone in with the first platoon. Angus stood there, shivering, waiting with Fuentes and Khatari and two BaDonkeyDonks, wondering at the long delays between each group entering.

"The fuck are these idiots doing?" Angus shook his head. "Why is this taking so long?"

Khatari shrugged. "Military or mercenary, it's the same as always—hurry up and wait."

"Yeah," Fuentes said, smiling despite his chattering teeth. "Hell, man, compared to the Army, this is moving at light speed."

While the G4S jagoffs took their sweet time, O'Doyle got farther and farther ahead. What if there was another way out of the mountain? What if O'Doyle found it? Angus wished, yet again, that he'd had the freedom to do a full subterranean map, like he'd done in Utah.

A different time, a different situation.

Dimwit Donnie had ordered Snoopy to operate a few hundred feet ahead of the recon group, to scout and spring any booby traps. Angus had put the machine on autopilot. If it detected any movement, it would stop and signal back.

Oberon, the other Wolf unit, was in the middle of the column, along with two haulers packed with ammo, food, equipment and medical supplies. If a fight started, Oberon was in position to rush forward or come to the rear, depending on which direction the threat came from.

Another platoon of eleven mercs went in. Aside from Angus, Fuentes and Khatari, there were only sixteen people left on the plateau.

"We're up," Khatari said. "Let's go, boss."

Boss. Nice. At least someone understood how things were supposed to work.

Fuentes watched to see if Angus needed help, but Angus ignored him and limped along on his own power. The two remaining haulers marched along behind. These two carried cases packed with Angus's inventions: the BlackBugs, the SwarmStorm, the ButterKnife, Dirty Randy's Money Shot, and the creation that would let Angus get rid of these fucking crutches for the near future.

He limped by five men who were waiting at the boulder, watching him hobble up the slope like the enabled pricks they probably were.

"These five are the rearguard," Khatari said. "They'll be in the column behind us. The other ten guys, Ninth Platoon, they'll hole up inside the tunnel, make sure no one else comes down. The lucky bastards. No climbing for them."

One tenth of the fighting men out of the game before things even got started? Maybe Donnie didn't get how dangerous O'Doyle was.

Angus chased the thought away. O'Doyle had only a handful of people. Even without the mercs who would remain behind to guard the tunnel entrance, Angus still had eighty-eight armed men—O'Doyle's team was outnumbered nine-to-one. And that didn't even count Snoopy and Oberon.

If the mercs or the Wolves didn't get O'Doyle, the rocktopi would. If there *were* any rocktopi, that was. Either way, Limpdick O'Doyle wasn't leaving here alive.

The rocktopi. Angus hadn't forgotten about those glowing, amorphous nightmares, the multicolored amoebas with their slashing, flashing knives. How *could* he forget? The savage aliens were a crazy mix between a Cthulhu acid trip and a Bob Ross oil painting bursting into a psychotic reality. He wasn't that worried about them, not with all the well-armed mercs heading into the tunnels.

The silverbugs should have been the bigger concern, but Angus wasn't worried about them, either. The machines had sliced Randy up real good. Angus felt that strange twinge again, that sense of loss at his dead friend. He'd get payback for Dirty Randy, that was for certain.

As Angus reached the boulder that led to the tunnel entrance, he stopped, took one more look around. All helicopters had departed, returning the mountain to icy silence. They'd taken the two dead mercs with them, as well as the shredded body of O'Doyle's man and the pilot from the tourist chopper. Donnie might be a dimwit, but Angus could barely see any trace of the battle that had happened here only hours earlier. The next snowfall would cover the scorch marks left by the burning helicopter. If there was no more snow, anyone who reached this spot would, at worst, think the marks had been left by careless climbers who had somehow found enough wood to make a bonfire.

To the west, Angus saw snow blowing across the unreal spectacle of a miles-long glacier, a giant white river frozen in time, and endless mountains beyond it.

"Boss, quit gawking," Khatari said.

Angus faced forward, stared into the narrow little gap between boulder and mountain. This was going to be a huge pain in the ass. Yet again he thought of opening the special cases right now, but putting that gear together would take time—the longer they were on the plateau, the higher the chance that some random flyover or plucky climber might see the mercs, might report that back to someone in authority. Or to the media. Same difference, really.

"I'll go first," Khatari said. "I'll point out any really bad footing." He turned sideways, moved into the gap a few feet, then waited for Angus to follow.

Dreading the inevitable, Angus turned sideways and started in. If he'd been fit, he would have slid around the boulder with ease.

He was far from "fit."

The crutches made it damn near impossible to navigate the narrow, curved space. He had to lurch his body sideways to move at all. He tried to shimmy along, boulder in front of him, sheer wall of rock behind, loose stones at his feet. The foot of the crutch caught against a crack—he started to fall, unable to reach out and stop himself, but Khatari stepped in and steadied him.

"You all right, boss?"

"Fine," Angus said.

So fucking embarrassing, so *humiliating*.

Khatari inched along the narrow curve, watching Angus like a parent watches a clumsy toddler. They'd gone almost 180 degrees around the boulder when Khatari squatted down, slid himself into the cave mouth. He vanished for a second, then reached out his hand.

"Give me the crutches," he said.

Khatari gripped the bottom of the left-hand crutch. Angus twisted his arm free of the forearm clamp; the crutch disappeared into the tunnel mouth. Then went the right-hand crutch.

Khatari stuck his hand out again. "Your turn, boss. Give it a shot."

This was going to suck.

Angus tried to squat down—a blast of pain up his legs froze him, made his teeth clench together. He ignored the agony, because after bitching about how long things had taken, now *he* was the roadblock.

"I need some help," he said.

Fuentes was there. "We got you. Yadav, take his feet."

Angus felt Khatari's hands on his ankles—gentle hands, but they hurt nonetheless—and Fuentes's hands under his armpits. They set Angus on the ground, then Khatari dragged him into the darkness of the tunnel mouth.

Hands on his feet…

…pulling him into the dark…

…stone grinding against his back…

…granite only inches from his face, so close he could smell it…

…*the darkness*, the smell of stone, the same as it had been after *she* broke his fingers, after she left him there to die…

"Boss! *Jesus*, take it easy!"

Angus shook his head, felt like he was trapped in that space between a real-as-life dream and consciously realizing he'd been asleep. Whose voice had that been? O'Doyle's? No, O'Doyle's was deeper, full of death and pain. The voice…the guy with the turban…Khatari.

The world came rushing back. Angus was in a cave, yes, but he wasn't at Funeral Mountain. Ample light in here, cast by a couple of compact, portable lanterns on the stone floor.

Angus slid his tongue across his teeth. A strange taste in his mouth.

A hand on his left shoulder. Fuentes, and past him, two BaDonkeyDonks standing motionless, blue and black plastic equipment cases strapped atop their narrow frames.

"You're safe," Fuentes said. "We got you. Calm down."

Fuentes had swapped out his ballcap for one of the tan combat helmets.

"What happened?"

"You lost your shit," Fuentes said.

Fuentes's voice…calming, soothing…*understanding*.

Angus saw movement to his right. Khatari, wincing, his right hand squeezing down on his left—blood trickling from between clenched fingers splattered on the stone floor.

"He's hurt." Angus glanced around, looking for one of the knife-wielding silverbugs.

"Yeah, I'm hurt," Khatari said, snarling and grinning at the same time. "Because you *bit* me, bro. When you flip out, boss, you *really* flip out."

That taste in his mouth…Angus realized it was the taste of blood.

"I…I bit you? I'm so sorry."

Khatari laughed. He *laughed*.

"I've had worse." He held his hand up, looked at it. Lantern light reflected off spots of blood gleaming from a very visible bite mark. "A Bangkok whore once bit me so bad it makes this look like a little scratch. It's nothing, don't worry about it."

Khatari was still wearing his turban.

"Why aren't you wearing a helmet?"

"Let's call it *personal preference*," Khatari said. "We're mercs. Dress code is pretty lenient."

Angus heard a voice in his headset—Donnie.

"Fuentes! What in the devil's dick is the hold-up back there?"

Fuentes pushed a button on a thin black box threaded into his webbing.

"Ah, Doctor Kool seems to have suffered some kind of flashback," he said. "A PTSD thing, maybe."

Donnie: "Company, full stop. Fuentes, see if the good Doctor Kool can continue or if he wants to turn back."

Turn back? No, no way. But the tunnels…the darkness…

"Give me five minutes," Fuentes said. He released the button, glanced at Khatari. "Need a medic?"

Khatari sneered. "What, for *this*? Naw, I got it."

Angus felt a sudden, crushing wave of shame. The whole operation, ground to a halt…because he was afraid of the dark?

"I don't know what happened," he said. "I was fine, then—" he looked at the rough walls, the curved ceiling "—I don't know what happened."

Fuentes glanced up at the low ceiling, at the chipped-out walls. "You have a bad experience in a cave or something?"

A *bad experience*. One that had left him crippled in more ways than one.

"You could say that."

Fuentes smiled, nodded. "Did I tell you that when there's a thunderstorm, sometimes I piss the bed?"

Such a strange thing to say.

"Uh, no. You did not tell me that."

"It's about a fifty-fifty bet," Fuentes said. "I was with Blackwater. We were doing some work in Najaf. Long story short, we were in this building, one of the locals ratted on us, and then we got lit up with mortar fire. The fucking ragheads…oh, uh, sorry, Yadav. No offense."

Khatari didn't bother looking up from the bandage he was wrapping around his hand.

"Not the same kind of rag," he said. "Fuck those guys."

Fuentes grinned. "Yeah, cool. Anyway, Costco must have had a sale on mortar shells nearby, because we got hammered for hours. Technically, we weren't supposed to be there, so it took a bit for us to get help. We…"

He trailed off. He was trying to control his emotions, rein in what was obviously a hard memory. In that instant, Angus didn't feel better as much as he felt a common bond.

"It's okay," Angus said. "You don't have to finish the story."

Fuentes forced a smile. "No, it's better to get it out. Anyway, the attack knocked out power in the area. We were surrounded. When there wasn't a fire we had to put out so we didn't burn to death, it was pitch black. Eight of us to start with. Four died. One of them, Bob Swanson, he lost a foot. Screamed like you can't believe until he bled out. So now, when I'm asleep, if there's a thunderstorm, it's like the sound of those mortar shells blowing up. Makes me think I'm back there. And just like I did then, I piss myself."

Fuentes looked Angus dead in the eyes.

"That's what happened to me. If you want to tell us what happened to you, go ahead."

Khatari finished wrapping his bandage. "We're listening, boss."

They weren't being patronizing. They both meant it. Who *were* these guys?

Angus shook his head. "I don't… talking doesn't fix anything."

Fuentes put a hand on Angus's shoulder, gave an understanding squeeze.

"There's a quote I like, Doc. From Spider Robinson, a writer. He said, *shared pain is lessened, shared joy, increased.* Combat vets get the idea. I just told you—a guy that I barely know—the reason I sometimes wake up in a puddle of piss. If you want to talk about what happened to you, it might help. We're going to be in tight spaces for the next few days, right?"

Khatari held up his bandaged hand. "And getting bit isn't exactly my favorite thing. Except for when I'm in Bangkok, of course."

Could he tell them about the rocktopi? About the horrors of Utah? No, not yet. If Donnie didn't think they needed to know, then they didn't need to know.

"I'm good," Angus said. "It won't happen again. I promise."

Fuentes smiled. "Cool. Then you still need to decide if you're continuing on or you want out. What's it gonna be?"

He could leave. They'd call a helicopter or something. He could sit this one out.

Or, he could man up and deal with his shit.

Angus looked at the pair of BaDonkeyDonks, at the equipment cases strapped to their backs. Two of those cases had big Xs done in blue tape.

The *special* cargo.

"Get the ones marked with blue tape," he said. "Open them up."

Khatari and Fuentes did so, releasing the straps. The two cases were heavy enough it took both of them to lower first one, then the other.

If Khatari's bitten hand hurt him, he showed no sign of it.

"These have keypad locks," he said. "What's the combo?"

A crackle on the headset, then Donnie's voice again: "What the unholy hell is the clusterfuck going on back there?"

Fuentes pushed his *talk* button: "Cap, I asked for five minutes."

Donnie: "That was seven minutes ago."

Angus had a push-to-talk button, too. He pressed it.

"Donnie, this is Angus. Put a sock in it. Have the men put on their KoolSuits. We'll catch up in a few minutes. Angus, out."

He released the button. *Angus, out.* Saying that had felt so cool.

Donnie: "Fifteen minutes, Doctor Kool, and we're moving out with or without you."

It might take a bit longer than that, but not that much longer.

"The combination," Angus said, "is zero, three, one, nine, six, three."

Khatari dutifully entered the numbers. The keypad beeped, then came the sound of internal locks opening up. He lifted the lid.

Fuentes looked in the box, then back at Angus, and smiled.

"Is this for real?"

Angus nodded. "Oh, it's for real. Help me put it on."

30

1,388 feet below the surface

"HOLD ON," OTTO said. "Just stop for a second, will you?"

"No time," Patrick said. "If we're talking, we're walking."

The tunnel here was a bit wider. Patrick and Otto walked shoulder to shoulder, Sonny just behind them, Jabour and Klimas in the back.

Patrick had given Otto, Klimas and Jabour the fast data dump: what had really happened in Utah; the platinum here was probably a ship just like the one they'd found there; the violence of the rocktopi and what they were; the shapeless, amoeba-like form of the creatures and how their skin flashed in mad, glowing colors; how the platinum knives found by Veronica tied the Utah and Argentina sites together; who Angus Kool was, how he'd used ground-penetrating radar to find the Utah ship, how he'd designed the next-generation mining gear that let EarthCore go after the mother lode.

"Aliens," Jabour said. "That's ridiculous, I can't believe that."

"I can," Otto said. "With the things I've seen? Yeah, I can."

Patrick glanced at him. "What kind of things?"

"Chicago kinds," Otto said. "In the height of the Pandemic."

Patrick stopped walking. "You were in Chicago?"

Otto nodded.

"So was I," Klimas said. "Trust me, it's not that hard to believe in ancient aliens."

Then the men *had* seen some shit. If that helped Otto believe what was going on beneath Mount Fitz Roy, all the better.

"So it really *is* aliens," Jabour said. "Four years of work and it turns out we weren't even studying a human culture? Un-fucking-believable. I can't even get my head around how big this is."

Why she hadn't believed Patrick but found validity in the story because Otto and Klimas did, Patrick didn't know. Years of her life spent believing one thing, only to find out she'd missed the boat completely. If there had been more time, Patrick might have felt bad for the woman. Veronica had reacted in a similar way.

"Let's keep moving," he said.

Otto's fighting experience helped the situation, but not as much as Klimas's did. Klimas clearly knew his business. Carrying Hatchet's carbine, wearing his helmet and backpack, Klimas could have been mistaken for just another member of the NoSeeUms, save for his clothes.

Otto kept Hatchet's Glock 21 in his waistband, preferring to have both hands out—he'd already stumbled twice on loose rocks and silt.

Bertha's voice in the headset: "Patrick, this is point team."

She was whispering.

Patrick held up a fist. Otto and Klimas stopped instantly—Sonny bumped into his back. He'd have to talk to the man about basic hand signals.

Patrick pushed his *talk* button. "Go ahead, Bertha."

"There's cracks in the walls. Big enough for silverbugs. No movement, but it worries me. You want us to wait?"

He didn't like the idea of his lead team getting cut off. At the same time, he didn't want everyone bunched up. Bertha's team was only four or five switchbacks ahead, maybe six hundred meters at the farthest.

"Worm, did you check the suits?"

Tommy's voice came back instantly: "Yeah, there's nothing. No trackers in the suits themselves."

Patrick breathed in slowly, out slowly, trying to control his fury. He'd assumed Angus Kool was dead. Patrick had thought only he, Sonny and Bertha knew about the platinum beneath Mount Fitz Roy. Angus had played him and come out swinging. Because Patrick hadn't even thought to check the gear he'd bought, Hatchet was dead.

"Point team, continue on," he said. "But stay quiet."

Bertha: "Roger. Out."

Patrick looked at the others, each in turn, making sure they understood how serious he was.

"We've got holes in the walls up ahead. Tread lightly. Could be silverbugs in there. Let's go."

They continued on. Otto made it all of ten steps before he started in again.

"You better keep talking, O'Doyle."

"I laid it all out," Patrick said. "What questions are left?"

Otto's eyes widened. "You're telling us you not only had contact with an extraterrestrial species, but you've also been inside a starship, and you're asking *what questions are left*? I've got nothing *but* questions."

Patrick let his carbine hang from its harness. He took off his combat helmet. The KoolSuit headband didn't sit well underneath it and was rubbing his forehead raw.

"It's not just aliens and the ship that I need to know more about," Otto said. "From what you're telling me, this Angus Kool is some kind of real-life evil genius? He's behind the force on our tail?"

The man ran a finger under his own headband, wiping sweat from his brow. It was already getting hot, but Patrick didn't want anyone turning on the KoolSuits until doing so was absolutely necessary. The V2 suit supposedly provided up to six days continued operation, but they could be down here even longer than that.

Preserve resources — every extra minute counted.

"Angus designed these suits." Patrick pulled at the side of his KoolSuit hood, stretching it out before letting it snap back into place. "And a lot of other mind-blowing stuff as well. I thought he died in Utah." Translation: *I should have killed him in Utah.* "And he probably designed that robot we saw. He's an evil little shit. He'll kill us all to get the platinum here. He must have gone to another mining company, got a big bankroll to fund this run."

They turned another switchback.

Patrick pushed his *talk* button: "Worm, you seeing anything?"

Worm's voice in his headset: "Nothing but rock and those cool cave drawings. I'll holler when we get near the target."

No news was good news. According to Jabour, they would soon reach the place where Ramiro had fallen.

"Someone tried to donate a million dollars to my university," Jabour said. "The anonymous donor wanted the location of the tunnel entrance. We didn't give it. Could that have been this Angus guy?"

"Probably was," Patrick said. "He knew about Veronica's work, knew the caves she discovered were in this general area. I bet he tried any way he could to find the exact location. Jabour, you've been here for weeks—were there a lot of big planes flying around here? Or anyone using machines to thump the ground?"

"No, if someone was using ground-penetrating radar around here, the locals would have known something weird was going on and they would have come right to me and asked if I knew what was up. And stop calling me by my last name. I go by *Sam*."

Jabour—*Sam*—had turned down big money to keep this place secret. She had integrity, while Patrick's desire to be rich had led Angus Kool here.

Bertha had tried to warn him—Patrick hadn't listened.

Millions of dollars, billions … was it worth Hatchet's life? The lives of the rest of his old team? The life of his wife?

No. But there was nothing to be done for it now.

"We know how Kool found us," Ender said. "How about you, Otto? How did you and Klimas track us down?"

Otto stared straight ahead. "That's classified."

Patrick stopped walking. Sam bumped into him.

"Fuck that," Patrick said. "Super Happy Sharing Time works both ways. You guys flew right to the plateau, so how did you know to go there?"

Otto glanced at Klimas, who shrugged.

"You're the ranking agent," Klimas said. "Tell him if you want to tell him. But let's move—if we're talking we're walking, right?"

Patrick again started down the steep tunnel, as did the others.

"We sat on Yakely pretty hard, threatened her with action from a lot of departments," Otto said. "She gave up Dillinger. He's in temporary detention, just to keep him from alerting you we were coming. He gave up your lodge location. We just missed you there, believe it or not. We let ourselves in, saw the maps and the search grid you'd laid out. The mountain was the center point, so we started there. You were still on the surface. We got lucky. Sort of."

Sonny's maps. When the old man had gotten the call from Jabour, he hadn't thought to button things up. To be fair, neither had Patrick.

Klimas leaned forward, made sure Patrick saw his look.

"We rented the helicopter, obviously," he said. "The pilot's name was Thiago. He didn't do anything to anybody. When you get payback for your friend, I'm going to get payback for him."

Patrick recognized that expression. He'd worn it himself too many times to count, was probably wearing it now. In that moment, he knew he could count on Paulius Klimas to do whatever needed to be done.

Worm's voice: "Ender, this is point."

Patrick pushed the *talk* button: "Go ahead, point."

"We have visual on the hole, through Hornet A. Nothing in the hole. No silverbugs, no Ramiro. No sign of movement in the tunnel. Do you want us to go forward?"

Patrick glanced back at Sam. Her eyes, wide with fear, with the knowledge that too much time had passed. Even if Ramiro had survived the silverbugs, the heat had probably taken him out by now. Yes, every second mattered, but one NoSeeUm lost was already one too many—he wouldn't send a partial force forward.

"Stay where you are," Patrick said. "Keep hornet eyes on the hole. Skylark, do you copy?"

He waited. No answer. A crackle of static.

"Skylark, do you copy?"

Skylark: "I read—" another burst of static cut off the rest of her sentence.

She'd gotten too far away, most likely. Patrick waited. He'd wanted her at the far range of radio hearing, which wasn't all that far with all the switchbacks.

Skylark: "Ender, do you copy?"

"I copy. Status?"

Skylark: "We're fine."

"Don't get so far behind," he said. "We're moving up double-time. Do the same, but keep your eyes open on the rear. And make sure you stay quiet, especially when you see fist-sized cracks in the wall."

Skylark: "Roger that."

Patrick didn't know Samira Jabour. Didn't know how she thought, how she felt, but he knew one thing—in a few minutes, her life was going to change.

He felt bad for her.

"Let's move," he said, and the party continued on down the steep tunnel.

31

1,618 feet up the mountain

ANGUS HAD TRIED to engineer a completely silent system, but with the time he'd had available, that had been impossible. Still, the exosuit was damn quiet.

He stood, heard and felt servos whir as he did. Most of the rig utilized the silverbug-inspired artificial muscle, but as heavy as the suit was there was still a need for hydraulics, motors, and gears, and those things made noise.

He no longer had to hold up his own weight. That reduced the pain in his legs, arms and back, turned the eight out of ten pain into five out of ten. He still hurt like fuck, but comparatively, it was so much better he almost laughed.

"I'll tell you what," Fuentes said. "That there is some impressive shit."

Khatari nodded.

Angus was taller than both of them now. How cool.

He twisted to the right, then the left, getting the feel for the exosuit's motion. Sensors on his thighs, calves and feet translated his movements into commands that drove the suit's motors and artificial muscle. Sensors on his arms served a similar function. Fifth-generation gloves gave him all the dexterity of a man who had *not* had his knuckles pulverized with a pair of rusty pliers. Additional control came from the HUD built into the suit's thick visor.

"I've seen prototypes for hyper-enabled operator suits," Khatari said. "Like that old TALOS project. That where you got this from?"

Khatari still had his turban—he'd put it on over his KoolSuit hood.

"Hardly," Angus said. "I designed this myself."

Which wasn't entirely true. He'd researched all he could on the *Tactical Assault Light Operator Suit*, a combat exoskeleton developed by the United States Special Operations Command. The TALOS suit was intended to help soldiers carry more weight, march farther and faster, endure more hardships in the field. Angus thought the project was destined for failure—too many difficulties with integrating the various systems.

Theirs would never work. His already did.

"You're a walking suit of armor." Fuentes said. "It looks badass. Does it *feel* badass?"

Angus took a step, then another. Steady steps, *sure* steps. And no more pain than he felt while lying in bed. He bent, reached for a big rock. The suit reacted perfectly, letting him wrap his armored fingers around it, motors humming as he picked it up and stood straight. The upper-right corner of the HUD screen read: *156 LB.*

"Yeah," Angus said. "It feels badass."

He felt *strong*. Not just in his body, in his soul as well. If he'd had this suit in Utah? Things would have turned out quite differently.

Angus dropped the rock. It bounced once, rolled to a stop.

Fuentes stepped closer, looking the black suit up and down.

"Is that a goddamn AA-12 on your right arm?"

Angus raised his right arm, marveling at the *effortlessness* of every little motion. Mounted atop the armor of his right forearm was the boxy body of a black Atchisson 12-gauge shotgun. Without the stock and the handle, the weapon ran from his elbow to his wrist.

"That's exactly what it is," Angus said.

Fuentes smiled. "Awesome. No magazine, though?"

"Internal," Angus said, turning his arm over to let them see a tube that ran along the armor on the underside of his forearm. "Holds five rounds at a time. Reloads from a drum of fifty in my backpack."

Khatari shook his head in amazement. "Let's hope there's no need for you to blast through fifty fucking rounds. I don't see a trigger. How do you fire it?"

Angus looked at the icons at the edges of his HUD. He checked to make sure the safety was on.

"I just do this," he said, sticking his right arm out straight. "I make a fist and relax it right away, it fires one round. I hold the fist, it keeps firing. I bend my arm—" he did so, holding his hand closer to his chest "—it automatically reloads the five-round magazine."

He didn't really make a fist, exactly—he couldn't, thanks to what that woman had done to him—but he could curl his ruined fingers together, so he'd designed his trigger mechanism around that.

"This is crazy," Fuentes said. "You look like Iron Man. But meaner. And spray-painted black."

Spray paint? Hardly. A half-inch of graphene over Level IV ceramic plate, with Level III ballistic soft suit beneath. On top of that, his personal KoolSuit was thicker and tougher than those the G4S mercs wore.

"This is wild shit," Khatari said. "Got other weapons in there?"

Only one, an experimental net he would use on the rocktopi, if there were any down here. Angus wasn't ready to talk about that yet. Somehow, these two seasoned soldiers, these tough-ass *mercenaries*, hadn't laughed at his nerd-suit. Sure, he could easily kill them both if they did, but they hadn't—he didn't want to push his luck.

For reasons he couldn't explain, he didn't want Fuentes and Khatari to think badly of him.

"This is really impressive," Khatari said, "but I got to call out the elephant in the room. You flipped the fuck out earlier, boss. You flip out while wearing this, and it could be a whole lot worse than a bite on my hand. You think maybe someone else should wear the suit?"

And there it was. Dismissal. Doubt. Khatari didn't think he could handle it.

But was that fair? Angus didn't even remember what had happened. If he blanked out again, what might he do with an armored body that could crush a man's skull, and a 12-gauge shotgun firing three rounds per second?

"I'll be all right," Angus said. "Honest. It was a one-time thing."

Khatari stared through the suit visor, looked Angus right in the eyes.

He nodded. "I believe you. But if we're both wrong, shoot Fuentes first so I have time to get away."

"Ah, go fuck yourself," Fuentes said. "We gotta get moving. You pay the bills, Angus, but if we keep Old Man Graham waiting any longer he's going to fire my ass."

Time to put the suit to use. Angus wondered if he'd be lucky enough to use it against rocktopi, or against O'Doyle.

Wait till they get a load of me.

"Then let's move," he said.

Khatari gestured to a case. "That one is labeled *SwarmStorm*. What's that?"

"And these," Fuentes said. "*BlackBugs. Alcatraz.* You planning on putting people in jail or something?"

People. That was almost funny.

"Don't worry about it," Angus said.

Fuentes moved to a long plastic tube strapped to the BaDonkey-Donk's side. "The *ButterKnife.* Look at the girth." He stood behind it, mimed that it was his dick. "Thick as a pie plate, which is what the ladies tell me."

Khatari laughed. "Your dick is that big, you'd have to go to Sea World to get dates, bro."

"Fuentes, you have a filthy mind," Angus said.

Fuentes smiled. He reached back to the second BaDonkeyDonk, patted yet another equipment case.

"*I* have a dirty mind? You labeled this one *Dirty Randy's Money Shot.*"

Angus thought, nodded. "Fair point."

"Come on," Fuentes said. "At least give me a hint? What is the ButterKnife?"

Was he going to ask the same question about every piece of gear?

"Hopefully we won't find out," Angus said. "If there's a cave-in, that thing could save our lives. Now stop asking me questions. Let's get the haulers moving and catch up with Donnie."

Angus started down the tunnel, feeling the power of the suit, reveling in it with each step.

This time, it would be different.

When he finished with Mount Fitz Roy, Utah would be nothing but a distant memory.

32

1,906 feet below the surface

BERTHA MADE HERSELF as small as she could. She leaned against the tunnel wall, staying a few feet from the switchback edge. Sleepy and Curveball were with her, alert and watching. The way they interacted with each other, so instinctive, so effortless. Worm was a few feet further back, looking at the screen hanging on his chest, one hand working the controller. He used it to maneuver the drone, which was one or two switchbacks ahead, at the hole where Ramiro Chus had probably died.

Not counting Utah, not counting the plateau up above, she'd been in combat twice. Both while she'd been in Afghanistan, both ambushes of US convoys. The first time, she'd been as brave as she could, returning fire and supporting the soldiers in her unit. Had she hit anyone? She didn't know. People around her had died. She'd watched men skilled in combat first defend against the assault, then turn the tables, taking the fight to the enemy. The two-hour encounter left sixteen people dead: one American, one Afghanistan translator, fourteen Mujahideen. Bonkers shit, with bullets flying everywhere, the blood and the screams, but it had been nothing compared to her second encounter.

The second time, the fighting was much worse. An IED had taken out her convoy's lead vehicle. The fighting lasted hours. She'd watched dozens of her fellow soldiers die. For reasons she still didn't understand, the attackers had rushed her position. At the end, it had been a battle of attrition—the last few surviving attackers faced the last few surviving US soldiers. Bertha had shot one in the head. Out of ammo, she'd used a knife on the second. She'd been face-to-face with him as he died, close enough to kiss him.

That moment had changed her. Forever. Two months later, two months of not *refusing* orders as much as being in a deep depression where she didn't really hear them, two months of nightmares, two months of her fellow soldiers trying to talk her through it because they'd been through the same trauma, her CO had—quite kindly—gotten her an honorable discharge.

So she'd seen combat. She'd seen hardcore people fight against difficult odds. The NoSeeUms were on another level. They were all like Patrick: cold and efficient.

Anders Keeley—*Curveball*—was a mess. Moving like the seasoned soldier he was, yet he seemed to be operating on autopilot. At least he wasn't sitting on his ass staring at the ground anymore. He had Hatchet's tactical axe clipped to his backpack.

Sleepy, a.k.a. *Reverend Rapson*, still had that dead-eyed gaze. The slight sheen of his clear visor made that stare even more plastic, more distant. Hard to believe this was the same man who had worn custom suits and colorful shirts that matched his socks. That man was a charade, a fancy white tablecloth thrown over a wooden table chipped and scratched and battered with age. This guy, the icicle in the shape of a man, this was the *real* Doug Rapson.

He scared the hell out of her.

Sleepy wasn't the only one who frightened her; Angus Kool had survived. She wasn't scared of Angus in a physical way—she could snap him over her knee with barely a thought—it was his brain that made her fear for her future, for Patrick's. In Utah, Bertha had seen firsthand the amazing things Angus could build. Now he had that robotic dog—what else did the little prick have up his sleeves?

On top of his smarts, Angus had motive to target her, target Patrick. In Utah, in the blistering heat, they'd taken his KoolSuit to save her. They'd left him naked. She didn't know how he'd made it out alive, but to do so he had to be far tougher than she'd given him credit for.

Bertha heard the buzz of the returning hornet. The miniature helicopter came around the switchback corner, past Sleepy and Curveball, past where Bertha stood. It flew to Worm, landed on his upturned palm, as if it was a magical pet returned to its master.

Worm opened the top compartment of his drone pack, the one above the monitor, snapped "Hornet A" into the empty slot, closed the compartment. He then opened the bottom compartment, the one below the monitor, and removed "Hornet B."

He saw her looking, came closer to her.

"Hornet A has to recharge," he said, as if she'd asked him what he was doing. "A full charge lasts about thirty minutes."

Out of all of the NoSeeUm's, Worm seemed the most…normal. Bertha reminded herself he was not only a seasoned killer, a former government assassin, he was also an ex-con that had done seven years in Allenwood prison for manslaughter.

Worm tossed Hornet B into the air. The tiny machine zipped down the tunnel, around the switchback corner, out of sight.

Patrick's voice in her headset: "We're approaching your position."

Bertha jogged to the upper end of the switchback. Carbine aimed down, she peeked around the corner—there was Patrick, approaching with Otto, Sonny, Klimas and Samira. They all had their masks down, sealing them up against the tunnel's temperature.

Patrick saw her. He smiled. It lasted only a half-second, but she saw it. Despite the dangerous situation, despite all the responsibility heaped on his shoulders, when he saw her, *he smiled*.

If she wasn't already hopelessly in love with him, that would have done the trick all by itself.

Whatever it took, she had to protect him, keep him alive.

Samira started to move past Patrick, to run past him, but he gently grabbed her arm.

"Hold on," he said. "Worm, come here."

Samira leaned away from Patrick, trying to break free—he was too strong for that.

"What are you doing?" Sam asked. "The hole's right around the next switchback."

Worm stepped closer.

"Show her," Patrick said.

Worm turned his body so that he was shoulder to shoulder with Samira.

Bertha was close enough to see the monitor's display of Hornet B's ghostly-green night-vision sight. Past the hole, a nook carved into the tunnel wall, three double-crescent knives in there, as if on display.

The image changed as the hornet descended into the shaft. It dropped to the bottom, then turned slowly—dark cracks in the uneven wall, a carpet of jagged, broken rock, a bulky backpack.

But no Ramiro Chus.

Sam stared at the screen. She looked up at Patrick—the woman had been expecting to see a body, the corpse of her friend, but there was nothing.

"Where is he? Could he have climbed out?"

"If he climbed out, he would have gone up," Patrick said. "We would have seen him. And don't forget the heat here. These KoolSuits work so well it's easy to forget. Look at the temperate readout in your visor."

Bertha's eyes reactively flicked up and to the right, where the small readout showed temperature and depth—the temperature read *138°F*.

She hadn't even thought about the high temperature. Neither had Samira, apparently, until now.

Samira again looked at the monitor. Bertha saw the confusion on her face.

"That backpack," Samira said, "that's what we used for a cooling system. Why would he have taken it off? Where *is* he?"

She wasn't getting the obvious. Patrick walked her through it.

"Something like this happened when I was in Utah," he said. "A miner fell into a pit. Hurt himself, couldn't get out. His partner went for help, so he was alone for hours. I was the first one into the pit. I didn't tell you this before, because I was hopeful, but now you need to hear it."

Samira shook her head, a wordless plea: *I don't want to know.*

"All I found was his thumb," Patrick said. "His thumb, and a bit of blood. You told me when you last saw Ramiro, he was covered in silverbugs. He yelled out that they were cutting him. Ramiro isn't in that hole because the silverbugs killed him and either worked together to carry his body out, or they chopped him up and carried him out in pieces. Your friend is dead. I'm sorry."

Samira shook her head, disbelieving, yet also accepting the horrible reality of what was going on. She was crying. Her mask prevented her from wiping the tears away.

"What am I going to tell his parents? What am I going to tell them?"

"Worry about that later," Patrick said. "After we finish our work here, after we deal with Angus."

Patrick stepped forward, leaving a stunned Samira standing there. He pushed his *talk* button.

"Skylark, status check."

Skylark's voice: "Hornet still showing nothing behind us."

"Stay where you are," Patrick said. "Stay sharp, we're going to need a few minutes."

Skylark: "On it."

"Worm," Patrick said, "get a drone down the tunnel as far as you can. Sleepy, Curveball, you're with me. Let's check out that hole. The rest of you, stay here and rest up, we'll be moving out shortly."

Patrick strode off down the tunnel. Sleepy and Curveball went around the switchback corner ahead of him, then all three were out of sight.

"His mom's crazy about him," Samira muttered. She looked at Bertha, eyes wet with tears. "What am I going to tell her?"

Bertha didn't have an answer.

33

ANGUS HAD DECIDED the rear of the column wasn't for him anymore. He wasn't about to take point, though, not with rocktopi and silverbugs roaming around. He wanted at least twenty guns between him and whatever came first. O'Doyle and his goons had already laid one trap—if someone was going to get blown the fuck up, that someone would not be Angus Kool.

So he found himself in the middle of the column, Yadav Khatari just in front of him, William Fuentes just behind. The two BaDonkey-Donks were there as well, never more than ten meters back.

The steady footfalls of the mercenaries hid the hum of his exo-skeleton. Some of the mercenaries had looked at him in his suit and snickered or rolled their eyes. Most, though, had just stared. Why not? Angus had transformed from a five-foot-six crutch-walking cripple into a six-foot-two mechanized murder machine. The smart mercs? They gave him one of those soldier-dude all-knowing nods, communicating respect without making a sound.

A guy could get used to that.

They'd passed through Samira Jabour's basecamp. Tidy little setup, or at least it had been before O'Doyle's thugs hauled in equipment bags and crates. It had been disappointing to see all the KoolSuit tubes—no more tracking O'Doyle and his people, unfortunately.

He was close enough to the front that he could get the live night vision video feed from Snoopy. It played on the exosuit visor's HUD. He'd made that image ghostly, transparent, so he could watch it and still see the tunnel floor in front of him. With the blink of an eye command, he could bring Snoopy's video full to brightness and resolution. For now, he needed to be able to see where he was going, to plan each careful step in the steep passage.

Angus reveled in the exosuit's power. He felt strong, he felt *free*. His thoughts were already spinning with ideas for reducing the size, miniaturizing some parts, replacing others. Once he got out of here, he'd focus on making the suit so thin it could easily be worn under clothes. He'd have so much money from the platinum that he could produce the frames himself.

How many crippled people were there in the world?

Future versions of this suit could help them.

Such a strange thought… he'd never really spent time considering ways to help others.

Come to think of it, a far better idea was developing the suit for military use. Armies across the globe would buy these suckers by the truckload. Infantry soldiers able to march for *days*, to carry hundreds of pounds without breaking a sweat. Those benefits alone made the suit immensely valuable, and that was before considering the ammo and weapons load the suit would handle.

If Angus was successful here, would he even *need* to sell suits? Would he need to sell *anything*? No. He'd have enough money to assemble his own little army, put *his* soldiers in these suits. Nobody would ever fuck with him again.

He realized he was daydreaming. His head felt a bit fuzzy. The pain started calling to him—minor discomfort now, but soon to be full-on agony. He would hold out as long as he could before dosing again.

A red light pulsed in his HUD.

Angus blinked his left eye twice, activating the private channel he'd set up between himself and Donnie.

"Donnie, Snoopy detected movement."

Donnie: "Is it O'Doyle?"

Angus's eyes flicked, working the HUD interface that was already becoming second nature. The screen brightened, showing Angus exactly what Snoopy saw—nothing but tunnel, rock and silt.

The Wolf's motion detectors used a combination of microwave and ultrasonic emitters. Something had moved, but whatever it was had dropped back out of sight.

"Don't know," he said. "Give me a minute."

The red light flashed again. There were big cracks in the tunnel wall. In them, something was moving … wiggling.

One thin, split-footed platinum leg stretched out.

A silverbug. It crawled out of the wall, walked along the tunnel floor. More came out after it, pouring out of the crack.

Not good.

Donnie: "Doc, talk to me."

"The silverbugs I told you about. A bunch of them."

Donnie: "Let me see."

Angus blinked through commands, sent Snoopy's feed to Donnie's KoolSuit HUD.

Donnie: "Well, look at that. You said you could handle these things, right?"

"Get your recon team back, ASAP," Angus said. "Then hold where you are."

Donnie ordered the column to halt, ordered the recon team to get out of there. Angus blinked commands, telling Snoopy to stay with recon—the machine didn't have to turn around; it could move backward as fast as it could move forward.

"Fuentes, Khatari," Angus said, "get the case marked *SwarmStorm* and bring it to me. Fast."

The two men did as they were told, quickly unbuckling the straps that held the case in place. They grunted as they lifted the case, struggling with the weight. Angus took it from them.

Thanks to the exosuit, holding the case felt like holding almost nothing at all. The HUD read *218.4 LB*.

"We have to get up front," Angus said. "As fast as we can."

Khatari nodded, faced forward and spoke in a voice that was somehow quiet and yet a commanding shout at the same time.

"*Clear the way.*"

The mercenaries ahead all pressed up against the right side of the tunnel wall, opening space. The bulky exosuit made for a tight fit, but there was enough room to move quickly, a fast walk if not an outright jog.

All these men, these trained, hard-ass soldiers, watching him walk past, getting out of *his* way—Angus had never felt so important.

He went around a switchback, saw another platoon of ten men, also against the wall, also staring.

Donnie: "Recon team is back."

As he moved down the tunnel, Angus kept an eye on the HUD, watching the retreating Snoopy's front view. The Wolf was steadily pulling away from the advancing, squirming horde of metal.

Angus ran around another switchback corner, saw Donnie waiting with the ten mercs of the first platoon and the three men from the recon team.

"Well butter my butt and call me a biscuit," Donnie said. He quickly looked Angus up and down. "Your magic suit works."

Angus set the heavy case on the tunnel floor.

"Fuentes," he said, "open it up."

Fuentes flipped the latches and lifted the lid. Inside, a black honeycomb pattern, each little hex no more than a half-inch across. In each hex, a round spot of red metal.

"You should all stand back," Angus said.

Everyone did, giving Angus room. He eye-tracked through the HUD interface, blinking like mad. He called up a menu, activated the machines stacked in the honeycombs. He was about to finish the launch sequence, switched to voice commands—it would be way more impressive that way.

"SwarmStorm, *activate*."

The honeycombed surface erupted, spurting forth a dense cloud of tiny, red, vibrating machines. They hummed audibly, like a swarm of bees. No surprise, since Angus had modeled the little robots after the insects.

"SwarmStorm, descend down this passage," he said. "Find silverbug collective. Seek and destroy."

The cloud shot down the tunnel. More streamed out of the honeycomb behind it, a long fog filling up the tunnel. In seconds, they were gone.

"I hope this works," Donnie said. "There's got to be five hundred of those things coming, at least."

Angus dimmed his own HUD, moved Snoopy's view to over his right eye only. He waited until he saw the SwarmStorm pass above Snoopy, then commanded the quadruped machine to gallop along with the swarm of tiny flying robots.

Snoopy's low-light enhanced view was serviceable enough, but Angus wanted to see this in living color. He worked the HUD menu.

The Wolf's front floodlights lit up, illuminating the tunnel's chipped gray granite, reflecting off the crawling silverbug horde that scurried across floor, walls and ceiling. There wasn't time to analyze what kind of silverbugs these were—the first kind Angus had seen, the modified "soldier" kind with the savage knife, or something else altogether new—because the SwarmStorm obeyed its command: *seek and destroy*.

The red swarm of flying robots filled the tunnel around the crawling silverbugs. The swarmbots communicated amongst themselves, a flying neural network that traded information at the speed of light. It would have been impossible for a human to count the mass of silverbugs, but the SwarmStorm worked as a unit, visually tagging each platinum sphere. In the upper left of Angus's HUD, a red counter flared to life, showing the number *51*. Then *72*, then *128*, then *251*.

The swarm counted, measured distances, speed, the air temperature and humidity in the tunnel, anything that could prove to be part of the killing equation.

310…312…

The counter stopped at *341*.

The way his swarm acted like a single organism…Angus found it poetic justice that he'd modeled his robotic neural net after the very silverbugs that were about to be destroyed.

In unison, tiny radio transmitters on each tiny swarmbot emitted a particular frequency of static, the same frequency Angus had used to jam the silverbugs back in the Wah Wah Mountains.

In his HUD screen, through the haze of the swarm, he saw the silverbugs stop moving. Those on the ceiling and walls fell away, a brief heavy rain of platinum balls and twitching legs that smashed down on top of each other, a crazy moment of bouncing, hollow metal balls that rolled and settled into a lumpy platinum carpet.

His red swarm hung in the air, victorious, above the metallic enemy.

Randy, old pal, I wish you could see this.

The static stunned the silverbugs, but only temporarily. They would never get the chance to recover. The SwarmStorm hive-mind calculated the killing blow. The red cloud thinned slightly as the tiny bots dropped down—four per silverbug—to land on the platinum shells.

Through Snoopy's front camera, Angus couldn't see the fine details, but he'd designed the SwarmStorm bots, built them, tested them, and knew what came next.

Each bot's abdomen ended in a tiny micro-motor drill encrusted with a coating of wurtzite boron nitride. The drills rotated at 10,000 RPMs—it took only seconds to punch a tiny hole in a silverbug shell. Angus's heart hammered. He felt a surge of something primitive in his chest, swimming through his head. Was this what it felt like to beat someone up? To destroy an opponent. To *kill?*

No wonder psychopaths became addicted to it.

Once the drill penetrated the shell, the bots forced a fine nano-tube—slightly larger than a human hair—through the end of the drill bit. Thorough the nanotube, the swarmbots delivered a thin stream of superheated sodium hydroxide. Four bots per silverbug, delivering a total of one ounce of the caustic fluid.

In Utah, Angus had dissected a silverbug, seen the glassine material that he deduced served as the machine's "brain." Bullets and other blunt force damage could break that glass, turning the silverbug from an advanced machine into a lump of metal and artificial muscle.

He was sure that dumping sodium hydroxide into a silverbug's innards would kill it.

Pretty sure, anyway.

Angus could barely breathe. If this didn't work, he'd have to keep the radio jamming and have Donnie's G4S mercs shoot the silverbugs one at a time.

He waited, letting the chemical do its work.

After a long minute, he eye-tracked through his commands, had the SwarmStorm shut off their static jamming.

The silverbugs didn't move.

Through Snoopy, Angus watched. Angus waited.

Another minute ticked by—still no movement from the silverbugs.

"They're dead," he said. "They're dead!"

Donnie nodded once. "Well done."

"SwarmStorm, return," Angus said.

He read data on the HUD as the swarm flew back. He'd lost 1,364 in their suicide killing missions. That should have left him with 8,636, but the swarm readout showed 8,152—he'd lost 484 to mechanical failures. Not great, but still enough to deal with another silverbug horde if need be. There was sufficient charge left in the case's battery array to power another two flights, possibly three, depending on how many swarmbots were lost in the next two hypothetical flights.

The SwarmStorm returned. Like a genie returning to the bottle, the red cloud flew into their honeycombed storage array, a buzzing cloud one moment, gone the next.

"Close it up," Angus said. "Strap it back on the hauler."

Fuentes and Khatari did as he asked.

Angus looked at Donnie—looked *down* at Donnie, just a bit, which felt amazing.

"I think *need to know* time has arrived," Angus said.

Donnie thought for a moment. "I suppose so. You want to tell them, or should I?"

"I will," Angus said. "I have an idea that will make them eager to hear more. We're moving up to the silverbugs. Bring everyone in."

As Donnie called for the platoons to close up ranks, Angus kept an eye on Snoopy's view—no movement of any kind.

Angus turned a switchback corner to see something that filled his heart with joy, with a deep sense of satisfaction. Silverbugs, everywhere, dead as fuck. Piles of them, three-, even four-deep in places. Metal insects with curled-up legs that he had willed to die.

"Quite a sight," Donnie said from behind him. "Men, pack it in here, Doctor Kool has something to say."

Back in the R&D lab, Angus had told Donnie all about the silverbugs, the rocktopi and the ship. To Donnie's credit, he'd believed Angus, immediately started preparing for the threats Angus described. Now that the men would see the silverbugs, it was their turn to get the whole story.

Or at least enough of it to prep them for what might come next.

Angus strode forward, picked up a silverbug by its thin, limp leg. The four spent SwarmStorm bots that had killed it fell away like dried up red ticks.

He turned to see fifty or sixty men packed into the tunnel, many of them kneeling so they could all see. There were so many men they didn't all fit in the tunnel segment; at least two platoons were behind the far switchback corner.

Angus checked his HUD's weight readout, activated the open comm channel, then held the silverbug up for the men to see.

"This is called a silverbug," he said. "Here's the funny part about that name. It's not actually made of silver. Or steel. This sucker is made of platinum."

Platinum-iridium, of course, but he didn't think these grunts could appreciate the finer points. He didn't have time to explain it. Best to keep it simple.

"This drone weighs nineteen pounds, four ounces," Angus said, turning his hand slightly to make the dead silverbug swing like a pendulum. "Approximately eighty-five percent of that weight is platinum. The current value of the metal alone is about nine hundred and fifty dollars an ounce. That means the little guy I'm holding here is worth a smidge under a quarter million dollars."

Behind their clear KoolSuit visors, he saw their eyes widen with that oh-so-delightful emotion: greed.

He tossed the silverbug behind him, where it gonged off the piles of its brethren, rolled to a stop against the wall, limp legs skewed in different directions.

"This pile of silverbugs alone is worth eighty-four *million* bucks," he said. "There will be hundreds more of these machines, if not thousands. And these machines aren't even why I am here. I'm after something far bigger than this. Which means—" he spread his arms dramatically, accidentally clanging his right fist against the tunnel wall "—oh, sorry about that. Where was I. Oh yes, which means, my wonderful mercs, that you all can divide the silverbugs up as you see fit. We are going to see some freaky shit down here, but if you do what I tell you, if you do your jobs, every single one of you will leave Mount Fitz Roy as millionaires."

Glimmering eyes, grins, smiles, nods … these men wanted what he was offering. They all looked excited, hungry for adventure that would make them wealthy.

"Now that you've seen the surprise bonus plan," Donnie said, "there's more. Doctor Kool has some unbelievable shit to tell you, but I believe he's telling the truth. Listen to what he says, and by the time we're done you're all going to be very, *very* rich men. Doctor Kool? You have the floor. Make it fast."

"Hold onto your balls, boys," Angus said. "I need to tell you a story about what happened to me in Utah."

34

SAM TRIED TO watch the others get ready. She tried to look at anything but the hole where Ramiro had died a horrible death.

Or at the knives he'd been reaching for when he fell.

She stood in the middle of the tunnel. Near the upper switchback corner, Worm was on one knee, his right hand working the drone controller, his left hand under the monitor hanging from his chest. Skylark was next to him, also with a controller and a monitor. Worm's drone was down the tunnel, past the hole, seeing what came next, while Skylark's was up the tunnel, watching for the men with guns and their crazy robot. Past Skylark and Tommy, Mullet stood at the switchback corner, rifle in hand, adding his human eyes to the efforts of Marie's drone.

In the other direction, downslope, Sonny was helping Sleepy fasten on rappelling gear. Curveball, the heartbroken one, was hammering a carabiner into a crack in the wall. O'Doyle stood at the hole's edge, trying to put as little weight as possible on his front foot as he looked down and in. Klimas stood at his side, ready with his rifle in case any silverbugs came pouring up the walls.

A few meters back from the hole, Lybrand knelt by the left-hand wall, holding her rifle. Otto was kneeling by the right wall, a pistol in his right hand. They were on guard against anything coming up the tunnel.

Silverbugs. Or, actual *alien beings*.

Aliens. Monsters.

How bad was Sam at her job that she'd spent *years* thinking she was studying a human culture? So many obvious clues to the contrary. The temperature, for starters. She, Veronica and Ramiro had always assumed the Chaltélians had created some kind of ventilation system to cool the tunnels, make them suitable for human habitation. It seemed logical to the three oh-so-learnéd colleagues that, at some point in the past, the ventilation system had collapsed.

But in truth, that system had never existed at all.

The tunnels had *always* been hot.

Obvious, yet she'd missed it. Ramiro had missed it. Even Veronica had missed it.

And because of that, Ramiro was dead. Chopped to pieces, apparently, those pieces carried out. Or maybe his chopped bits had been small enough to take out the same holes in the shaft walls that the silverbugs had poured through.

Jesus … he couldn't be gone. He *couldn't*.

His mother. Jess. This was going to devastate her.

Ramiro, gone.

Sam wondered if she would be next.

She didn't think she'd ever been this scared. It wasn't just the silverbugs, the men, and the machine that might be coming down the tunnel at that very moment, it was these people. O'Doyle. Lybrand. The others. All armed. All here for money. Did people like that give a damn about someone else? Maybe they wanted to help Sam. Or, maybe they were keeping her around because of her experience — maybe when they didn't need her anymore, they'd kill her.

Everyone was so quiet. When they spoke, it was in low voices, sometimes even whispers. The silverbugs reacted to sound, apparently. Was that why they'd poured into the shaft? Because Ramiro had been in pain, calling out for help?

He hadn't wanted to come. She'd made him.

"Samira, right?"

Worm was standing next to her. He was the least creepy of the bunch. Which wasn't saying much.

"Yeah," Sam said. "That's me. Shouldn't you be flying your little helicopter?"

He tapped the screen hanging from his chest. "I'm keeping an eye on it. It's resting on the tunnel floor, saving battery power. I'll see if anything comes."

"Do you … do you believe there's really aliens?"

Tommy raised his eyebrows, shrugged. "If Ender says he saw aliens, he saw aliens. Do I believe? To paraphrase an old TV show, I really fucking *want* to believe."

Ender. Before meeting O'Doyle, she'd never heard someone called that, only read the name.

"He like the movie or something?"

Worm tilted his head. "Movie?"

"*Ender,*" Sam said. "He watch *Ender's Game* a bunch?"

"Oh, no, not the movie," Worm said. "It's from the book."

Sam sniffed. "That big ox read a book?"

"Probably not," Worm said. "I'm the reader of the bunch. I read that book seventeen times so far. You read it?"

Sam had. Twice. "Yeah. So you gave him that nickname?"

Worm nodded.

"Why?"

Worm glanced off. "You'd have to see him operate. Fight, I mean."

Sam decided she didn't want to know more about that.

Patrick "Ender" O'Doyle held a rope as Sleepy descended into the shaft. Otto moved to the edge, held his pistol at the ready.

"What is he going down there for?"

"He's looking to see if one of the holes was big enough for Ramiro to crawl into," Worm said.

"There aren't holes that big."

"Ender just wants to make sure," Worm said. "Sleepy will also see if any of those holes leads to another passage. The shaft wall might abut another tunnel."

She hadn't thought about that. She wasn't really thinking at all anymore, she was receiving shock after shock, going along with whatever these people told her to do. And why not? She'd tried being the leader, the decision-maker, and look what had happened.

"If he doesn't find a tunnel, what then?"

"He'll put a rope bridge across," Worm said. "We'll make sure it's safe, get everyone across."

That was smart. No telling if the thin bit of tunnel floor on either side of the hole would support anyone's weight. It certainly hadn't supported Ramiro's.

She couldn't stop thinking about him, his death. She didn't want to think about him, didn't want to feel the guilt anymore.

"You read one book seventeen times," she said. "Must be your favorite."

"Hardly. *Stranger in a Strange Land* is my fave. Have you read it?"

Sam nodded. "Yeah, but I like *The Moon is a Harsh Mistress* better."

Worm smiled, slightly. "I didn't take you for a sci-fi reader. No offense."

She glanced at the holstered pistol on his right thigh, the combat knife on his left.

"And I didn't take you for someone who would read at all," she said. "No offense."

Worm actually laughed. "Judgmental much?"

Well, yes. Sam often caught herself judging people unfairly. One of her many personality flaws.

Sleepy came out of the shaft. Sam had a brief burst of hope that the hornet drone had malfunctioned, that O'Doyle and Klimas had been blind, that Ramiro had been down there after all, hidden under loose rock.

But Sleepy didn't ask anyone to help him pull the poor man up. He moved along the wall, crossing past the hole, then started hammering a piton into a crack in the wall, just past the three knives.

He was making the rope bridge. Because there was nothing in the shaft. Because Ramiro was gone.

Sam tore her eyes from Sleepy, instead focused on the man who, for some unknown reason, was trying to be nice to her, trying to console her in his own awkward way.

"Worm," she said. "*Book*worm, I assume?"

He nodded. "My team isn't the most original in the world when it comes to call signs. To be fair, I do read a lot."

She wondered if any of the others did. Highly doubtful.

"What's your real name?"

"Tommy," he said. "Call me whatever you like."

What an interesting guy. She'd assumed these people were typical gun-loving idiots, but he was more than that. He…

What was she doing? Having a *conversation*? Ramiro was dead. Because of her.

"Look, Tommy, I—"

He walked away from her, his attention focused on the monitor hanging from his chest, his hand working the drone controller.

"Ender," he said, "we've got company. Lights down the tunnel, many colors."

Many colors? The aliens?

"Sleepy, come back," O'Doyle said.

Sam saw the man start back over the two-rope bridge he'd made— his feet on one, his hands on the other. The ropes were close to the cave wall. If someone crossing the bridge started to lose their balance, they could just lean backward, brace against the wall, recover, then continue.

"Suppressors on," O'Doyle said. "Otto, fall back with Skylar and Mullet, maintain position there and watch our rear. We can't get caught flat-footed if the mercs catch up. Lybrand, Klimas, Curveball, Worm, Sleepy, get ready to defend against a frontal attack. Listen for the sound of blowing leaves—that means they're getting close. They make a horrible noise when you put them down, so be ready for that. When you fire, three-shot bursts. Everyone kill your lights. Don't go to night vision unless they stop glowing."

Hands shot to helmets, mining lights switched off.

Sam stared, her own light sweeping over the armed killers who were waiting for aliens to arrive.

"*Sam*," Tommy hissed. "Your light."

She reached up, fumbled with her helmet light, couldn't find the switch. Panicking, she tore the helmet off, flashed the light beam into her own eyes.

"Shit, dammit…"

"Worm," O'Doyle said, "button her up."

Sam found the switch, turned off the light. Bright ghost spots danced in her vision. How many times had she turned off that light without looking at it? A hundred? A thousand?

The barest footfall, then Tommy's voice.

"Take a deep breath," he whispered. "Let it out slow."

Only when he said that did she realize she was breathing hard, nearly hyperventilating. She tried to take a breath … it locked up halfway. It was like when she tried snorkeling; at first her lungs refused to draw in a breath, even though her brain knew the snorkel was above water, that it was safe.

"Calm down," Tommy said softly. "We need you on point for this, Sam. Concentrate."

She closed her eyes, which didn't matter because the tunnel was pitch black. What the hell was happening? She was a mile below ground and there were *fucking aliens* coming, aliens that had chopped Ramiro into pieces, and—

A hand on her back, pressing in lightly, firmly.

"Just breathe," Tommy said. "Relax."

Her lungs finally unlocked. The breath came in.

"Let it out slow."

She did so, nodded, felt stupid doing so because she couldn't see anything. She thought she'd been afraid before? That had been nothing compared to this. In the dark, with actual, honest-to-god *monsters* coming her way.

"Good," Tommy whispered. "Now, hug the wall and get low. There's about to be a firefight."

He was so calm, like he was reading off a grocery list.

Her eyes adjusted. There was still a little bit of light, coming from Tommy's chest monitor. He'd darkened the screen, yet she could see flashes of color on it.

Sam moved to the left-hand wall, slowly got down to her hands and knees, then her belly. Shooting … there was going to be *shooting*. Bullets bouncing off of stone walls. She breathed out, willed her body to lie flatter.

She didn't realize Tommy had moved away from her until she heard his whisper, soft and low, a good five feet to her right.

"Lights are getting brighter," he said. "I think they're about to turn a switchback corner, two segments from us. I'll have visual in seconds."

How could she hear him so well? She hadn't realized that so many people moving made a certain amount of ambient noise. Now that everyone was still, the utter silence of the tunnel reasserted its dominance. No wind, not even a breeze. No sound at all—she could hear her own heartbeat, hear the slightest movement of people a dozen feet away.

"Bring the hornet back," O'Doyle whispered. "I don't want them to see it before we see them."

"Bringing it back," Tommy said.

In the darkness, Sam heard the drone's soft, whining buzz as the machine returned. The buzz lessened, then stopped; the little robot had landed and shut off.

The instant of silence that followed let Sam hear not only her heartbeat, but also her shallowest of breaths. So *loud*.

Then, a new sound.

Coming up the tunnel, a sliding sound, a scraping…the sound of dry leaves blowing across pavement.

The monsters. They were coming.

Despite herself, Sam closed her eyes.

Barely audible over the sound of leaves, she heard Tommy's whisper.

"Good gravy. Look at that."

Sam lifted her head, looked down the tunnel.

Past the hole, past the three platinum knives, there was some-thing…*glowing*. The tunnel itself? No, faint lights playing off the stone walls. Reds, blues, greens, a shimmering cascade gradually growing brighter. It was coming from beyond the nearest switchback, which bent off to the left.

Sam's fear deepened, clutched her tight. That hissing sound grew louder. The colorful lights brightened, the colors reaching farther along the right-hand wall.

Around the bend came things her mind couldn't quite process—glowing, formless creatures, soft bags blazing in mad, electric colors. Rolling forward on soft legs, a fluid kaleidoscope that *flowed* more than walked. No, not *legs*…as the things moved up the tunnel, they *extruded* limbs or tentacles or boneless extensions, slow-motion chameleon tongues stretching out to plant on ground or grip rocks jutting out of the wall, press into cracks, pull the bag-body forward.

Three of them.

Strobe lights setting the tunnel wall alive with color, bodies pulsing and flashing in soft blues and greens.

She was looking at alien life.

Alien life.

A hand on her forearm: Tommy, squeezing lightly, silently telling her to stay quiet and still, reassuring her that she wasn't alone.

She had never been so grateful for the touch of another human being.

The creatures came closer.

They were the size of an over-stuffed jumbo garbage bag, a comparison her brain instantly rejected because a bag was a shapeless, *dead* thing while these magnificent horrors could not possibly look more alive.

Even if she'd wanted to stand and run, she could not—every muscle seemed frozen, as hard as the granite that surrounded her.

Tommy's hand squeezed again, as if he could read her mind, as if he could *feel* her fear, as if he knew that she needed someone—*anyone*—to keep the terror from subsuming her, stop her from screaming and running.

Locked in that infinite moment, Sam held her breath and stared.

On they came.

Boneless.

Graceful…a molten ballet of iridescence.

Jellyfish with no fixed form.

Nothing in life moved like that.

Mad patterns of colored light coursing across their skin.

Closer still. She saw black spots on that shimmering skin, *thousands* of onyx spots of various sizes, some as small as peas, some as big as marbles.

Monsters.

They were almost to the shaft mouth …

All three creatures stopped. The colors shifted from indigo, emerald green and soft yellows to rich reds, blazing oranges and ambers. Even in an alien species, Sam recognized the colors of alarm.

O'Doyle's voice, barely a whisper: "Fire."

A flurry of clacking sounds surprised Sam, made her frozen body twitch. Bursts of dark-purple light flashed across the creatures' skin.

Screeching sounds like tires squealing on asphalt, and the first two creatures sagged, one thumping against the tunnel floor, the other slapping against the left-hand wall like a glob of goo flung against a dumpster.

Tommy's hand on her arm, squeezing.

The third creature fled down the tunnel, long red/orange tongue-legs both pushing it away and reaching forward to grab anything it could and pull itself forward.

Three clacks, three bursts of purple light, three pings of breaking rock, all happening in the same millisecond.

The third creature's tentacles went limp in mid-reach. It fell, rolled over itself…

…and *faded*. Its colors dimmed, lowered, turned to the faint, barely perceptible are-you-sure-it's-still-working yellow-green iridescence of a glow-in-the-dark toy just before the light stops.

Its light went out.

Darkness reclaimed the tunnel.

"Night vision on," O'Doyle said. "Worm, get your drone back down the tunnel. Lybrand, Mullet, cover me."

Sam reached to her KoolSuit headband, pressed the detent at her right temple. A ghostly green version of the tunnel filled her vision, the face shield's tech erasing the darkness. She watched the huge O'Doyle, his rifle hanging on his chest, sidestep his way across the two-rope bridge.

When he'd crossed over the hole that had taken Ramiro, O'Doyle drew his knife, a frightening thing that Sam knew she would see in future nightmares.

Sam realized the alien that had hit the wall wasn't quite dark; in the night vision, it glowed brighter than the other two. It glowed… *black*. That seemed impossible, yet there it was.

O'Doyle started with that one.

He stepped to it, drove his knife into the soft body once, twice, a third time, then angled his wrist and dragged the blade out, slicing a long line of skin as he pulled it free. The creature pulsed, briefly, a cascade of purple shades, then went dark.

"That's hardcore," Tommy said quietly.

An alien, yes, a monster, maybe—Sam had just watched Patrick O'Doyle execute the thing.

"Why a knife? Why didn't he just shoot it?"

"Ammo," Tommy said. "Every bullet matters." He stared at his video screen. "Ender, forward passage is clear, three switchbacks up."

"Night vision off," O'Doyle said. "Back to lights."

Sam again pressed the detent at her left temple. The green version of the tunnel blinked out.

Helmet lights flicked on, filling the tunnel with moving circles of white.

"Everyone across the bridge," O'Doyle said. "We're moving forward. Skylark, Mullet, you're last across."

The tunnel came alive with a flurry of activity. Who *were* these people? They'd just gunned down glowing aliens, and now they moved with purpose as if this was nothing out of the ordinary.

Sonny walked to her, wide-eyed, shaking, his eyes flicking all over.

"This is batshit crazy," he said. "Fucking batshit."

His voice trembled. Sam was surprised to find solace that she wasn't the only one completely freaked out.

Tommy came closer, waving one hand toward the ropes.

"You two, across," he said. "It's only ten feet. Move carefully, deliberately, and you'll be fine."

Sonny went first, crossing with no difficulty. At the end, O'Doyle guided him down to the ground, making sure the old man didn't fall.

Sam went next, the ropes shuddering in her hands and beneath her feet. She forced herself to not look down into the place where Ramiro had died.

O'Doyle's hand on her waist, guiding her off the ropes and back down to solid ground.

Sam had a moment to look at the dead creatures. Deflated bodies. No flashing colors now, only grayish skin smeared with wet yellow where the bullets had ripped through them.

Then, Tommy's voice, calm but intense, saying words that brought back Sam's hammering fear.

"Movement, three switchbacks up," Tommy said. "I see colors. We've got company again."

35

1,918 feet below the surface

PATRICK STOOD BEHIND the switchback corner, waiting. Mullet waited with him.

Bertha was on one knee, cautiously looking around the edge. He heard her whisper in his headset.

Bertha: "I see color, from around the next switchback. Looks like it's coming closer. Numbers unknown."

They'd bagged three. The next batch could be one more, three more, a hundred more. Patrick vacillated on using the hornet to know for sure. Doing so might give him clear intel but also might alert the enemy to his presence. Just because the first three hadn't seen the drone didn't mean he'd have the same luck with the next bunch.

He felt confident that he, Mullet and Bertha could handle what came next, quietly take out the approaching rocktopi. If not, he was ready to fall back to the previous switchback. There, in front of the shaft, waited Sleepy, Worm, Curveball and Otto. Skylark was at the far end with Klimas, watching out for Angus's men.

When he'd killed rocktopi in Utah, their rotting-fruit/dogshit stench had filled the tunnels. Patrick had expected to smell that here, but the only thing he could smell was himself. The V2 KoolSuit was completely airtight—no odor got through.

God, but his lower back was killing him. Walking down the steep decline put pressure on it. The slope was also wreaking havoc on his right knee. And his left hip; that one was new.

His hip, of all things. Something he'd unknowingly damaged in Utah, or was he just plain *old*?

It didn't matter—he'd been through far worse pain than this. Better hurt than dead.

Dead like Hatchet.

Patrick hadn't seen or even talked to Carson Wampler in twenty years. A few days after reaching out to him, the man was gone.

Patrick's fault?

He closed his eyes, breathed deep.

It felt good to kill those three rocktopi, felt good to finish the last one off. Payback for Connell.

And not even close to being worth the cost.

If Patrick hadn't organized this mission, Hatchet would still be alive. Baking cakes, maybe. Curveball wouldn't be heartbroken.

No, that was bullshit. Adults make choices. Carson and Anders had made theirs. High-risk, high-reward.

Right?

A shoulder nudge from Mullet. "You with us, man?"

"Yeah," Patrick said. "I'm good."

Mullet shook his head. "No, you're not. Hatchet?"

Patrick prided himself on being steel, as emotionless as a statue. Had he lost that ability over the years? Or, more likely, this man he hadn't seen in over a decade still knew him better than he knew himself, better than his wife knew him.

"Sucks he went down," Mullet whispered. "He was a good man."

Mullet almost always had something insulting to say. Not this time. The look on his face alone told the story; Carson's loss *mattered*. All the bullshit the man had survived, only to buy it here.

Bertha's whisper in the headset: "Lights getting brighter. They're about to turn the corner at the next bend."

That put them fifteen meters away or so.

Mullet made a fist, thumped Patrick's shoulder. A silent message to get focused, get ready for action. Get their game faces on. Patrick *always* had his game face on.

"Lights aren't as bright as before," Bertha whispered. "Maybe there's only one or two this time."

Patrick again thought of calling for the drone, just to be sure, but it was probably too late for that. No point in making unnecessary noise. Better to let them come close and gun them down.

Filtering up the tunnel, the sound of dry leaves blowing across pavement.

Bertha reached a hand back, held up two fingers.

Patrick pressed his *talk* button: "We have two incoming. Everyone get ready."

Mullet lightly slapped Patrick's shoulder, pointed to himself, held up two fingers. He wanted to do the killing. No surprise there—Mullet *always* wanted to do the killing.

Patrick nodded, felt that rush that always came before combat. His skin prickled.

The time for death had come once again.

Mullet stepped away from the wall, faced the corner, prepared to lean out and gun down the enemy. Patrick did the same. He'd kneel down and lean out low while Mullet leaned out high. Maybe Mullet could get them all; if not, Patrick would help him finish the job.

"Wait," Bertha whispered. "Hold your fire."

What was she talking about? Kevin looked at him, the face behind the KoolSuit mask annoyed at the indecision, at the interruption.

Patrick knelt, leaned out slowly, his carbine aimed over his wife's shoulder, down the tunnel.

He saw them: two rocktopi, glowing in pinks and dark blues. Softer hues than the first three they'd seen back at the shaft.

Their color didn't matter—they were killers. Murderers. *Monsters.* He would put them down, just as he'd put down so many hundreds of killers and murderers and monsters when his government had ordered him to do so.

Halfway down the tunnel now, not even twenty feet away.

Mullet's whisper in the headset: "What are we waiting for?"

Patrick didn't know. He saw their colors play off the tunnel walls and ceiling. Why was Bertha holding off?

Something different about these two. The colors? No, they were *smaller*.

Patrick raised his barrel slightly, taking it off-target, his body reacting by instinct.

The rocktopi stopped moving. They stood there in the middle of the tunnel, tentacles stretching out, then shrinking back, vanishing. They clustered together.

They were smaller than the first three. *Much* smaller.

A burst of memory, of the first time he'd seen a rocktopi, in the Utah tunnels: a little one, about the same size as these two; Sanji Haak trying to communicate with it; then a larger, brighter arm extruding through a crack in the wall, grabbing the small rocktopi, pulling it away, into the crack.

Pulling the little one to safety, because the little one was a baby.

Mullet: "I'm taking the shot."

Patrick held up a fist, a silent command for Mullet to stand pat.

The pair of young rocktopi pulsed and glowed, their colors shifting from pinks and blues to yellows and crimson stripes. They went back down the tunnel, two chest-sized balls of brightly-colored goo rolling along on long arms like living jacks.

They reached the switchback corner, vanished behind it.

Patrick leaned back behind the switchback, wondering at what he'd just seen.

Kevin stared at him, carbine pointed down.

"What the *fuck* was that, Ender?"

Bertha leaned back behind the switchback, stood.

"They were children," she whispered.

Kevin's face twisted up with disgust. "So what? They were the goddamn bad guys."

"They were *children*," Bertha said. "You want to kill children?"

Kevin leaned close to her, his face a snarl.

"They … were … *creatures*. As in, *not human*. What if they saw us, you idiot? They'll send the alarm. They could be midgets, for fuck's sake, you don't even know if they were children or not!"

"Little people," Patrick said.

Kevin's snarl turned his way. "What?"

Patrick shook his head to clear his thoughts. *Little people?* Why had he said that? He was going to correct people's language now?

"Never mind," he said.

Kevin tilted his head toward Bertha.

"You know, Ender, if your bitch is the actual commander of this chickenshit outfit, you could have let us know."

Patrick grabbed Kevin's vest, yanked him close.

"Watch your mouth, Mullet."

Kevin stared back, eyes burning with intensity, excitement. Then, he raised both hands, letting his carbine drop down on its harness.

"My bad, big man."

He smiled.

Patrick let him go. "Sorry. I shouldn't have done that."

Kevin's smile widened. He shrugged. "Heat of the moment, bro. But seriously, folks—" he glanced at Bertha "—who *is* in charge of this op?"

"Patrick is," she said. "I mean, *Ender* is."

She spoke the nickname like it was a curse. Maybe it was. A week ago, when he'd heard it for the first time in years, he'd hated it. Hadn't he grown beyond that time in his life? But after hearing it from the mouths of people he'd fought and bled with, it was as comforting as putting on a favorite old shirt.

Was he *Ender* anymore? Was he *Patrick*? Had he *ever* been *Patrick* at all?

"Let's get back to business," he said. "We need to take out that robot dog before it reaches us. Its movement will be limited when it reaches the chasm where Ramiro fell. Mullet, can you see if you can rig something?"

Kevin stood straight, clicked his heels together and snapped off a salute.

"Jawohl, Herr Kommandant!"

He goose-stepped back up the tunnel.

Bertha and Patrick watched him go around the switchback.

"He's a real piece of work," she said quietly.

Patrick nodded. "Always has been."

"Just how well do you know him?"

"I'm *alive* because of him," Patrick said. "And he's alive because of me. A dozen times over for both. You don't know him."

Bertha sneered. "And you do? It's been, what, *twenty years* since you saw him?"

Patrick felt a rush of anger. She thought she could talk about Kevin? About the NoSeeUms? She thought she knew what they'd all been through together?

"We should have killed those rocktopi," he said. "Don't disobey my orders again."

"This isn't the military, *Ender*. You're my husband, not my goddamn CO. We're not child killers."

Child killers.

Bandah Village.

The screams. The fires. The blood. The *iron*.

"Patrick?"

Jesus Christ, had he blanked out again? What was happening to him? He couldn't allow himself to lose focus, not even for an instant. That was how more of his people would die.

"They're not human," he said. "Get that through your thick skull."

She shook her head. "I'm not killing children."

"We don't even know if they *were* children."

"Now you sound like your boy Mullet. What do *you* think they were, Patrick?"

There was no point in arguing with her—they both knew she was right.

"If you don't think children can kill you, you're wrong," Patrick said. "If the smaller rocktopi—whatever they are—attack us, you better be ready to put them down."

She nodded. "I will."

Worm's voice: "Ender, you there?"

Patrick pushed his *talk* button. "This is Ender, go ahead."

Worm: "You better get back here. Mullet is setting up a claymore. McGuiness is losing his shit."

Patrick jogged up the tunnel, realizing anew that while a steep decline caused problems, a steep *incline* would be no fun at all.

He heard Sonny yelling before he came around the switchback.

"You stupid fucking cracker! You'll bury us!"

Patrick came around the switchback to see Otto with his arms around Sonny, trying to stop the older man from lunging at Mullet, who was on one knee in front of the nook with the three double-crescent knives, a green claymore resting on the cave floor by his foot.

"I'll kill you myself, you sonofabitch," Sonny screamed.

Patrick took three steps forward, grabbed the back of Sonny's neck, and squeezed. The man stiffened instantly, stopped moving.

"Be *quiet*," Patrick said. "We have enemies in front and behind. If they hear us, that's bad. Do you understand?"

Sonny twitched his head. Maybe he was trying to nod. Maybe he couldn't because Patrick was close to breaking his spine.

Otto stepped closer. "Take it easy, O'Doyle."

Patrick let Sonny go. The older man rubbed at his neck as he scurried behind Otto.

"Mullet," Ender said, "I told you to rig a trap, I didn't tell you to use a claymore."

Mullet kept working. "By the same token, you didn't tell me *not* to use one."

"Then let me make it clear," Patrick said. "*Do not use mines.*"

Not yet, anyway.

Mullet sighed. He picked up the claymore and stuffed it in his pack.

Patrick glanced around. "He used *his* back at the main entrance, so which one of you idiots gave him the goddamn claymore?"

"I did," Skylark said. "He's always been better with those than the rest of us."

She had a point. At the same time, Skylark could be counted on to think before she acted—Mullet, not so much. The guy did so love to see things go *boom*.

"You're making a mistake," Mullet said. He pointed up the tunnel. "They have a fucking *robot dog* armed with a fucking *machine gun*. I don't want that coming down the tunnel after me. It's a claymore, not ten pounds of TNT. We set it in the nook, hidden by the fancy knives. If the robot jumps the hole, boom, it gets a face full of steel. If it stops and waits for Angus's men, then when *they* cross over, the mine will splatter them all over the place."

The tunnel did make for a confined killing zone. Mullet was right, one claymore would probably kill anyone in the tunnel segment. But if the detonation caused a cave-in, that was all she wrote.

"You're all being stupid," Samira said. "It's obvious how we take that thing out."

Everyone looked at her. She had her arm around Sonny's shoulders. He was shaking. Patrick had never seen the man look so frail, so ancient.

"College girl speaks," Kevin said. "Go ahead, libtard—tell us *dumb soldiers* how to neutralize the threat."

She did.

And she was right—it *was* obvious.

"Well I'll be," Kevin said, admiration in his voice. "Chalk one up for the Left Coast. You're smarter than I am, Cookie, but then again, that ain't saying much."

Patrick turned to Bertha. "Do we still have those ruined KoolSuits?"

She nodded.

"Get them out," he said. "Then you, Worm and Klimas go forward three switchbacks and wait. Worm, get a hornet down the tunnel, watch out for more rocktopi. Skylark, go back three switchbacks and launch your hornet to watch out for the mercs. Sleepy, go with her. Curve, Mullet, Bertha, help me set the trap."

His people scrambled to comply.

"I can do something," Samira said. "Let me help."

She still had her arm around Sonny, who twisted his silver bracelet and stared at the wall.

"You are. For now, you and Otto take Sonny down the tunnel, one switchback. Keep him calm and quiet. And if any other bright ideas pop into your head, please don't keep them to yourself."

36

SONNY FELT USELESS.

He could barely think. He'd heard that old claustrophobia cliché, *it feels like the walls are closing in*, more times than he could count, and yet, down here, that was exactly what it felt like.

How many millions of tons of granite over his head?

He was going to die down here. Die ugly.

"Sonny, try to relax," Otto said. "We have a few minutes. Sit down."

The man spoke to Sonny like Sonny was a dog? Not that it made any difference. Sonny might as well be a dog—an *actual* dog, not that walking death machine everyone seemed so worried about.

He sat, leaned his back against the tunnel wall. Gently, of course, so as not to risk a puncture of the KoolSuit. Maybe he wouldn't die in a cave-in. Or get shot by a robot dog. Or slashed up by those glowing monsters. Maybe his suit would get damaged and he'd cook to death instead.

So much to look forward to.

Samira sat down next to him.

"Here we go," Sonny said. "You're about to give me a pep talk, right? Don't bother."

She reached out, took his trembling hand. She held it tight. The human contact—even through the gloves—felt nice, slightly comforting.

"These tunnels have been here at least twelve thousand years," Samira said. "Longer than all of human history, and they're still standing. This place is stable."

Sonny huffed. "Then explain that big fucking hole in the floor that Ramiro fell through. Don't look too stable to me."

Her eyes widened. He instantly felt bad—maybe she'd forgotten, for a moment, that her friend was gone, that she'd lied to him about the platinum for years, and Sonny had gone and reminded her anew.

She squeezed his hand again. "That's one of the few structural integrity issues I've seen."

"You've never been down this far," he said. "Don't patronize me."

Sonny pulled his hand free.

He wanted her to go away. He wanted her to stay by his side. He wanted to get the hell out of there. He should never have gotten mixed up with O'Doyle in the first place.

Hard to breathe. His chest hurt. Ah, *there* was a good way out—not bullets or blades or aliens or falling rock or impossible heat, but a good old-fashioned coronary. Hell, he was sixty-seven—a heart attack was bound to get him sooner or later.

He gripped his bracelet on his right hand. He'd put it on over his KoolSuit. Even separated from his skin by the high-tech material, it still made him feel connected to something bigger, made him feel connected to the surface.

A place he would never see again.

Otto squatted down in front of him.

"Hang tough, old-timer. We're going to make it."

Sonny stared at the younger man. Otto looked to be in his forties. At least twenty years younger than Sonny, sure, but any American man in his forties was also counting the minutes until his heart told him to go fuck himself.

"What the fuck do you know, kid?" Sonny tilted his head toward Samira. "At least she's got the credibility to make her line of bullshit believable."

Otto smiled. "We've all got our areas of expertise."

The man didn't look happy, exactly, but he didn't look that upset, either.

"I don't get you," Sonny said to him. "We got aliens and killer robots after us, and you're as chill as ice water."

Otto reached out a fingertip, drew random curves in the cave silt.

"You might say I've seen a few things in my day. What matters is we face our fears and keep going forward."

Sonny pushed his foot forward in the silt, erasing Otto's lines.

"I'm not going anywhere. I'm staying right here. I'm done with all of this."

Sonny knew he sounded like a baby, like a weakling, but he couldn't help himself. What new horrors might the next switchback bring?

"If you don't walk with us, I'll carry you," Otto said. "I'm not leaving you here, no matter what you say."

For some reason, that made Sonny feel a little better. The walls didn't recede, but they stopped trying to smash him into pulp.

"I appreciate the sentiment," he said. "Us brothers gotta stick together, young blood. Right?"

Otto's eyes crinkled and his cheeks rose—he was amused, but not smiling outright.

"If you think I give a damn what color anyone's skin is, you're not paying attention to the situation we're in."

Oh, now he was going to drop some wisdom?

"Anyone ever tell you you talk like a college professor?"

Otto's eyebrows rose. "I do?"

"Yeah," Sonny said. "One with a corncob up his ass."

Otto stood, offered Sonny his hand. Sonny took it. Otto pulled him to his feet.

"Get your head around the reality," Otto said. "This is going to get worse before it gets better."

Sonny glanced at Samira. She'd lost her friend. The only way it could get worse for her was if she died herself.

"I hear you," Sonny said. "Thank you. Both of you."

Otto nodded. "Anytime. While we're here, you want to tell me why a black man is wearing a bracelet with a swastika on it?"

Sam stood. "I'm a bit curious about that myself."

Should he tell them, or let them wonder? Hell, he might never leave this place, so why not?

"It's funny you should ask," Sonny said. "Little do most people know, that the swastika didn't start with the Germans. The symbol—"

O'Doyle came around the higher switchback with Mullet, Klimas, and the others close behind.

"We're moving out," O'Doyle said. "McGuiness, you need to keep up. Ready?"

Sonny glanced at Otto, who nodded almost imperceptibly.

"I'm ready," Sonny said. "Lead the way."

37

1,906 feet below the surface

ANGUS, FUENTES AND Khatari were closer to the front of the column now, just a dozen meters behind Donnie Dimwit, who himself was a few meters behind his lead platoon. Counting the firepower of Snoopy, that put plenty of cannon fodder between Angus and any surprise attacks. Angus was *near* the front, but not *in* front—no sense in being silly about it.

The exosuit had initially eased the strain on his body, which made his pain more tolerable. After five hours in the thing, trudging down the tunnels, his pain had returned to almost normal levels.

But like so many other elements of this outing, Angus had prepared for it.

Angus eye-blinked through his HUD, called up his maintenance menu. Maintenance for the suit, and for him. He called up a dose of the cocktail that would keep him in good shape while in the suit: 15 milligrams of liquid oxy, mixed with 10 milligrams of ground Adderall.

His food tube swung out from inside his helmet, tapped against his mouth. He sucked the contents down. He'd added a little lemon flavor to his drug mix. Not exactly *tasty*, but it wasn't as awful as the food gruel stored in the suit.

He hurt so bad. Even the parts of him that weren't broken felt broken. The meds would kick in soon, and he'd be able to cope better.

When all of this was done, he'd have all the money in the world to hire the best doctors, the best reconstructive surgeons. Shit, he could open up his own clinic. The *Doctor Angus Kool Clinic for Reconstructive Surgery and Also Penis Enlargement (for Those Who Need It Most)*. He could pay the greatest surgeons more than they'd ever make anywhere else. And if they couldn't fix him, well, he'd find a way to fix himself. Metal, plastic, or flesh, parts were parts—it was simply a matter of finding out how all the parts integrated, how they worked together.

He could fix himself.

He *would* heal.

He *would* be as good as he'd been before.

The oxy started to take hold, dropping his every-minute pain from an eight to a six. Such a difference it made.

After telling the grunts about the silverbugs, Angus had told them about the rocktopi. Yes, gentlemen, actual aliens that you can shoot in the face. Not that the rocktopi had faces. Or was the entire rocktopi body a face? It didn't matter—with the promises of riches he'd dumped on the mercs, they would have been happy to pop some caps in Santa Claus, then kill their favorite sports stars, then put two rounds in the head of Jesus Christ himself.

An icon blinked in his HUD—Donnie, asking for his attention.

Angus blinked on the comm. "Go for Kool."

Donnie: "Any sign from Snoopy?"

A blinking red light in the exosuit HUD drew his attention.

"Perfect timing," Angus said. "Snoopy detected an anomaly, something in the tunnel wall."

A single beep in Angus's helmet let him know Donnie had switched to the main channel.

Donnie: "Company, hold. Be on alert."

In his rear camera sight, Angus saw mercenaries drop to one knee. Fuentes and Khatari did as well. Angus stayed standing—truth be told, he hadn't really designed the suit for "sitting." A minor oversight.

A double beep—Donnie was on their private channel.

"Talk to me, Kool. What's it see?"

Angus directed Snoopy to slowly move closer. In seconds, he recognized what it was, blinked for the Wolf to stop.

"Knives," he said. "Three of them. In a wall nook."

"The curved knives you told me about?"

"Them's the ones," Angus said.

"What are they doing there?"

A good question.

"I don't know," Angus said. "Looks almost like a display of some kind."

He thought of Utah, how the rocktopi used the Linus Highway to go to the top of the mountain and search the stars for the enemy that had nearly hunted them into extinction. The Fitz Roy rocktopi likely used this very tunnel for an identical purpose. Perhaps they wanted to make sure they never went up to the surface unarmed.

"Or like a mini armory," Angus said. "The aliens' version of a gun rack, maybe."

"Send Snoopy in."

"What if O'Doyle booby-trapped it? What if it's another mine, or a bomb or something? Send a man up to check."

Donnie sighed. "We don't want to lose any more men. You know, one of the *human beings* that work for you?"

Angus's teeth clenched together. Donnie had said that louder than before—loud enough for the men near him to hear? Maybe he wanted to make it look like Angus didn't give a crap about the men. Angus didn't, of course, but that wasn't the point—Donnie was trying to become their favorite again.

"I just thought that maybe you had a bomb specialist on the team or something."

"Know what bomb specialists use to check out a possible bomb, Doctor Kool?"

God damn, but this guy was good with the rhetorical questions.

"They use robots," Angus said.

"And so will you. Send your robot dog in. We're wasting time. First Platoon will be one switchback behind it."

All of that had been loud, too. The men knew Angus was bringing the dollars, but he'd probably just lost face. Donnie knew his business.

Angus eye-tracked commands, moved Snoopy forward. He'd use the scorpion clamp to grab the knives. Even if there was another claymore, it was possible for Snoopy to survive the explosion.

Past the nook with the knives, Angus saw what looked like trash bags lying on the tunnel floor. He felt a rush of adrenaline. It was happening. It was really happening. Angus Kool was leading an army into war.

"I see three dead rocktopi," he said. "O'Doyle's crew must have run into them."

"Are you sure they're dead?"

"When you see them, you'll think that's a funny question."

"I'm a regular laugh riot," Donnie said. "How about those knives?"

"Snoopy is closing in. Getting ready to use the scorpion neck to —"

The white-and-green HUD flashed. Angus felt a quick flash of vertigo as images of a rock wall shot by, then Snoopy's vision went blank.

MAYBE SNOOPY COULD have survived a Claymore. Angus couldn't know for sure. What he did know, now, was that Snoopy could *not* survive an unexpected twenty-foot fall.

"A pit trap," Fuentes said.

"And not a very good one at that," Dimwit Donnie said.

Angus stood at the edge of the shaft, Fuentes on his right, Donnie on his left. Khatari a few feet behind them. Past the jagged shaft mouth, red-bearded Henderson and the two remaining members of his recon team were gathering up the ropes they'd used as safety lines while free-climbing along the wall. Mercs were placing small lanterns along the walls, giving the tunnel fairly decent illumination.

Twenty feet down the shaft itself, also lit up by lights that had been lowered down, a twisted and broken Snoopy lay on its right side, half obscured by the tarp of stitched-together KoolSuits that had been its doom. The machine was motionless save for the spasmodically twitching scorpion neck and the rear left leg, which kept moving in a walking motion as if the machine were still on all fours, still prowling the tunnels. The bent foot scraping against the clear tarp in a rhythmic *skreet skreet skreet.*

Khatari stepped forward, peered over the edge.

"Looks like Snoopy got fucked," he said.

Fuentes nodded. "Yeah, and not in the good way."

Angus worked to control his anger. He could see at a glance that there would be no fixing Snoopy. Broken central column, optics shattered, front right foreleg hyper extended, the shoulder joint torn beyond any repair.

"Thought your machines were supposed to be smart," Donnie said. "Any grunt would have seen that pitfall trap."

There it was again—the Dimwit mocking his intelligence. And yet Angus could say nothing.

This wasn't his fault. Anyone could have missed it. Fucking O'Doyle's people had covered the hole with the tarp, put rocks at the edges to keep it in place, then thrown cave silt on top. Through night vision it had looked normal, had been all but invisible.

"Henderson," Donnie said, "head down the tunnel about a hundred fifty meters. You see anything move, radio it in and then haul ass back here."

Henderson nodded. He hefted his M4, then, followed by his two men, moved down the tunnel slope and vanished around the next switchback.

Donnie pressed his transmit button. "Third Platoon, bring up the portable foot bridge and get it assembled, ASAP." He let go of the button. "Without that bridge, Doctor Kool, your robots are about as useless as a nun's cunt. We're not moving the column forward without their firepower."

The shaft hole was much too wide for Oberon or the BaDonkeyDonks to jump over. Too wide for Angus, too—his exosuit could do a lot of things, but ten-foot leaps weren't among them.

"Have your men haul Snoopy out of the shaft," Angus said. "I'll move his SAW to one of the BaDonkeyDonks. And we need to recover Snoopy's batteries."

Dimwit shook his head. "The bridge will be ready in a few minutes. Hauling the whole machine up could take a half hour or more, and we need to move." He clicked his transmitter. "Second Platoon, rappel into the shaft, recover ammo and batteries from the robot."

Angus stared into the hole. "But Snoopy cost almost a million bucks to make."

Dimwit hawked a loogie, spat it down on the still-kicking machine.

"Welcome to war, son. Million-dollar machines get ruined all the time. Helluva thing, ain't it? I'm keeping Oberon in reserve, so break out your BlackBug drones. I want something out in front of recon."

"It's too soon to use the BlackBugs," Angus said. "We're still in a single tunnel. When the tunnels branch off—and trust me, they will—we'll need the BlackBugs to search a larger area and map the system for us."

There was another reason he didn't want to deploy them yet: their ability to dig. In a cave-in situation, especially one where the Butter-Knife wasn't available, the BlackBugs provided a last-ditch capacity to free whomever might be trapped—namely, one Dr. Angus Kool.

"You have fifty of the things," Donnie said. "Get ten of them deployed, immediately. While you do that, I'm going to go check on the men. That's what a leader does."

He turned and strode away, leaving Fuentes and Angus standing there.

"They could masturbate," Fuentes said.

Angus looked at him. "What are you talking about? *Who* could masturbate?"

"Nuns," Fuentes said. "I know they're supposed to be celibate and all, but their cunts aren't useless if they can still masturbate."

Khatari shook his head. "Bro, that's not how it works."

Donnie wanted to give orders? Two could play at that game.

"Khatari, run a systems check on Oberon," Angus said. "Fuentes, get to the BaDonkeyDonks and bring me the cases labeled *BlackBugs*."

Fuentes smiled. "Sweet, I finally get to see what's inside."

He jogged up the tunnel.

Angus accessed his HUD menu, started diagnostics on his suit. Everything had to be in perfect working order.

O'Doyle had fooled him once. The man would not do so again.

38

TOMMY STOOD WITH Skylark. They watched Samira and Ender. Samira leaned so close to the wall that her helmet blocked out most of the symbol, which she referred to as a *glyph*. Ender said nothing; he waited for the expert to do her thing.

They had reached the proverbial fork in the road. The tunnel split into two branches. Tommy and Skylark stood together, keeping one eye on their chest monitors. He had flown his Hornet A down the left side, the narrower side, to its maximum safe range, then lowered it to the tunnel floor. She had done the same with Hornet C, but down the larger right-hand tunnel.

Without any reason to pick one branch over the other, everyone was waiting for Samira to read the glyphs—maybe she could figure out if they said something about the two tunnels, help Ender pick the right way.

Which brought up the big question: Should Ender be picking at all? Should he still be giving the orders?

Tommy wasn't sure anymore.

Skylark leaned in close, spoke quietly, her eyes never leaving Ender.

"This is a total clusterfuck of a mission," she said. "You know that, right?"

He nodded. No point in arguing facts. Hatchet dead. Civilians along for the ride. Government agents as well. Tommy had killed a man. Maybe. He knew if he wanted to survive, to see the surface again, he might have to kill more people. And it seemed certain he would have to kill more aliens, creatures who had never threatened him, never attacked him. Creatures that had been minding their own business until Ender brought the NoSeeUms down here.

Skylark glanced at Curve. "I don't think he's going to make it."

Curve was sitting on his ass again, elbows on knees, staring down. Maybe he needed a little bit of time to get his head around what he'd lost, and where his life would go from here — *if* he got out. Tommy would do everything he could to help him, but at the same time, if Curve wasn't sharp, if he slipped up, he might get someone else killed.

"I wish I hadn't come," Skylark said. "All I want to do is get home to my daughters. I don't even care about the money anymore. I shouldn't have come."

"Me neither," Tommy said, but he knew that was a lie.

Despite the loss of Hatchet, despite all the problems, he'd seen actual *aliens*. Those aliens were dead, but not by his hand — he'd aimed high. A chickenshit thing to do, shooting along with the others so that they thought he was a team player, but he was making all kinds of in-the-moment choices he couldn't fully explain.

"Mullet worries me, too," Skylark said.

"When has he not worried us?"

"The last twenty years when we haven't had to be near him," she said.

A fair point. "He hasn't changed, I guess. But then again, neither has Sleepy."

They both glanced in Sleepy's direction. He was on his side, fast asleep, his carbine in his hands.

"I've always been jealous of that," Skylark said. "That bastard can sleep anywhere, anytime. You'd think with fucking aliens he couldn't, but … well, look at him."

Reverend Rapson. Out of everyone, Sleepy impressed Tommy the most. The man hadn't gained weight. Aside from some crinkles around his eyes—and that horrid bleach-blond dye job—he looked exactly as he had back in the day.

Skylark nodded toward Samira. "That bitch actually know anything about this cave scribbling?"

"No idea," Tommy said. "Not like I had a chance to read her research before we came here. She seems all right."

"Huh. That your Glock she's carrying?"

Tommy had given Samira his holster.

"Yep."

"Let's hope you don't wind up needing it," Skylark said.

Truer words had never been spoken.

Ender threw up his hands.

"Uh-oh," Skylark said. "Fearless leader is losing it. Again."

"I'll see if I can help."

Tommy walked toward Ender and Samira.

"You've been staring at those carvings for five minutes," Ender said. "Come on, do they say something or not?"

Samira shook her head in frustration. "I don't know. I haven't seen glyphs quite like these before."

"Figure it out," Ender said. "*Fast.*"

She glared at him.

Tommy stepped in, put his hand on Ender's shoulder.

"Give her a minute," Tommy said. "This is alien writing, after all. It can't be easy."

Ender looked at him, the snarl on his lip enough to make Tommy's insides churn, then the bigger man took a step back, a silent message for Tommy to take over.

Samira hugged her shoulders, stared off down the right-hand tunnel.

"Sam, everyone is strung out," Tommy said. "Do your best, but we need to decide quickly, okay? You're the expert here, so the call is yours."

She blinked, seemed to come back to herself, went back to studying the glyph. Her gloved hand hovered over the image, fingers moving as if they were interacting with imaginary lines.

"Wait…I thought this was all new to me, but now I see commonalities with some of the glyphs closer to the surface. I think…I think the right-hand tunnel continues the main passage we were on, leading to a specific place."

"Specific place," Tommy said. "What specific place?"

"I have no idea, but I think it's culturally important." She pointed down the left-hand tunnel. "I think that means this one didn't have as much traffic—sorry, *doesn't* have as much traffic—I'm still forgetting this place isn't abandoned."

"Two roads diverged in a tunnel," Tommy said.

Samira glanced at him. "And I took the one less traveled."

Ender stepped closer. "So you think we should take the left-hand tunnel?"

"I'm not thinking anything," Sam said. "I'm just paraphrasing Robert Frost."

Ender's eyes narrowed with confusion, then he got it.

"Oh, the poet guy," he said. "Right?"

Samira nodded.

"Both tunnels go *down*," Ender said. "That means either way, we're probably still heading toward the ship. We've got enemies in front and behind—let's go with Frost's take and go where there's less traffic."

Tommy wasn't going to argue; it was a crapshoot either way.

"*Movement*," Skylark said. She held her monitor in both hands, the controller dangling from its cord. "Coming up the right-hand tunnel. Colors flashing on the walls. *Lots* of color. And…oh, fuck me, there's a ton of rocktopi coming our way. I'm bringing the hornet back before they see it."

She grabbed her controller.

Ender stepped to the left-hand tunnel.

"This way, people, fast," he said. "Someone wake up Sleepy, he's up front with Lybrand and Worm. Worm, keep that hornet out in front of us. Samira, Sonny, Otto, Curve, with me. Skylark, Mullet, Klimas, bring up the rear. Skylark, use the drone. Mullet and Curve, cover our tracks as best you can."

NoSeeUms, civilians and government agents alike obeyed. In seconds, they'd left the fork behind.

Lybrand took point. Monitor in one hand, controller in the other, Tommy stayed two steps behind her.

From behind him, he heard a sound filtering down the tunnel. Hard to detect at first, but it quickly grew louder, so loud it could not be missed—the sound of dried leaves blowing across pavement.

He could only hope the enemy would pass behind them and continue up the main tunnel.

39

1,906 Feet Below the Surface

FRUSTRATION GROWING, ANGUS stared down as Fuentes worked carefully to assemble the first BlackBug.

"Come on," Angus said. "It's not that complicated."

Fuentes sat in front of an open crate. Stiff black foam inside, with nine baseball-sized black spheres and one empty baseball-sized hole.

"Not complicated for you, maybe, jet-age genius," Fuentes said. "Why didn't you put printed directions in here?"

Each BlackBug had only ten parts.

"They're *color-coded*," Angus said. "All you have to do is connect the parts that have the same color tags."

Fuentes squinted. "Oh, I get it."

"Just hurry up."

Fuentes held a three-segmented black leg up to the black sphere.

"On it like a comet, Boss." He clicked the leg home, smiled, then picked up a piece the size of a squat screwdriver, held it up for Angus to see. "What's this do?"

"It's a pneumatic driver. It breaks rock."

Fuentes spun it into the air, let it drop back into his hand.

"It's got a maroon tag," he said. "Where does it go again?"

How could someone be this stupid and still remember how to breathe? His idiocy made Angus twitchy.

Or maybe that was the Adderall.

"The maroon tag goes into the maroon slot, Fuentes. Do you know what *color-coded* means?"

Fuentes *mmm-hmmed* and clicked the driver component into place. He picked up another piece—a matte-black, curved blade the length of his hand.

"And this," Fuentes said. "Looks like a friggin' karambit."

"It's a foot. Just put the pieces together."

Angus took in the flurry of activity. He and Fuentes were tight to the tunnel wall. Close by, Khatari was running checks on Oberon's systems. A man stood at the edge of the shaft, pulling up a rope tied to M249 ammo belts removed from Snoopy. A group of four mercs were in the center of the tunnel, busily unpacking a crate containing thin composite panels and beams, assembling those parts into the ultralight, twenty-foot-long walkway bridge that would be slid across the shaft hole.

The tunnel was crowded, to say the least.

Other than Henderson's recon team, the rest of the men were back up the passage, waiting, resting, staying out of the way.

Donnie came around the switchback corner. He saw the open shipping case, saw Fuentes puzzling at how two more black parts went together.

Behind his clear visor, Donnie's face turned instantly red.

"Kool, god dammit, I told you to get those things assembled!"

"Almost done," Fuentes said, although Donnie hadn't been asking him.

"Almost done," Angus repeated.

"I gave you an *order*." Donnie's whispered words were rusty barbed wire, full of unforgiving, sharp points. "Next time I give you an order, you find a way to get the order done. The longer we're down here, the more you seem to be under some kind of illusion that you can call the shots."

Angus had known this would come to a head sooner or later. Might as well put this man in his place right now.

"There's no illusion," he said. "I'm paying for this, remember?"

Donnie took a half-step closer—his visor shield clacked against Angus's.

"You wrote a check, Kool. You brought fancy toys. That's your contribution to this. My men have *died*. I am in charge. If you don't like it, then get the hell out of here and we'll finish this mission without you."

Angus fought back a wave of anger. Finish the mission without him? Without him, there was no mission.

He glanced at Oberon. One phrase—*all but me*—and the donkey's SAW would shred every merc in this tunnel. Maybe Angus needed to add some code so he could have Oberon target a specific person.

The squawk of someone opening up the general comm channel.

"This is Hender...econ." Voice low but urgent, syllables chopped off by bursts of static. "We hear...ing weird, com...urther down the tunnel."

The words drove straight through Angus, rooted him to the spot. *We hear something weird, coming from further down the tunnel.* His memories played back a sound from Utah, *that* sound, the one that promised terror and blood and death...

"Recon, this is Captain Graham," Donnie said. "Be more specific. What do you hear?"

The hissing. The scraping. Like paper sliding across gravel. Noises like screeching tires.

Henderson: "Kind of a scr...ound, sir," Henderson said.

A scratching sound.

Angus blinked on his transmitter. "Henderson, this is Angus. Get back here, fast."

Donnie's eyes narrowed. "Didn't I just tell you that you don't give orders?"

"Then *you* give them," Angus said. "It's the rocktopi, the aliens. They're coming."

Donnie's glare lasted an instant more, then he backed Angus's play.

"Recon, this is Graham, fall back to the shaft, immediately. I repeat, fall back to the shaft."

A pause. Both men waited to hear if their message had been received.

Henderson: "Falling back." His voice was clearer, louder. "We see flashing colors past the nearest downslope switchback. They're right behind us."

Donnie barked out commands.

"First Platoon, prone firing line on this side of the shaft mouth. Second Platoon, out of the shaft, kneeling positions behind first. Third Platoon, get that bridge across the hole, *now*, then fall back to the donkeys. Fourth Platoon, standing position behind Third. Fifth Platoon, stay one switchback behind as our ready reserve. Everyone, *check your targets*—our people are going to be coming up that tunnel. Six and Seven, set up a second firing line in the next switchback segment, be ready to cover us if we retreat. Eighth, stay back and guard our rear."

Men who had been napping only moments before scurried to obey the orders. They threw themselves to the ground, aimed down the tunnel. Mercs climbed out of the shaft. Bits of bridge clanked together. Angus stood there, not knowing what to do, amazed that Donnie's words could instill this fury of action.

"Bridge complete," someone called out.

Angus watched as four of the bridge-building men worked together to slide the simple, gray, three-foot-wide, twenty-foot-long assembled plank over the open shaft mouth, saw the far end of it skid across cave silt on the other side.

"Boss," Khatari yelled, "Oberon is ready."

Oberon. The Wolf.

It couldn't be trusted on autopilot, not with so many bodies around. Angus eye-tracked through the menu, took control—Oberon's front-view camera popped up in the HUD. Angus saw himself standing there, in the black exosuit.

"Fuentes, Khatari," Donnie said, "get Doctor Kool back up the tunnel, to safety."

Back up the tunnel. Away from the fighting. That was the smart thing to do. The rocktopi had those *knives*. They were savage animals, hell-bent on slaughter.

"I'm staying," he said.

Donnie spun on a heel, jabbed a finger against Angus's visor.

"Get your ass *out of here!* These men are trained warriors. Don't get in their way."

The deep part of Angus, the reptile brain that cared only about food and fucking and survival, wanted to grasp ahold of those words as if they were the reins of a racehorse that would carry him away to safety. That selfish part that only gave a shit about Angus Kool … that part had been in the driver's seat his whole life.

"I said, *I'm staying.*"

Donnie's eyes widened. His face flushed red.

"You little—"

The sound of gunfire cut him off. It echoed through the tunnel, sounded like it was two switchbacks away at most, probably only one.

Henderson in the comms: "Recon team, incoming! Enemy is behind us, closing in."

Donnie strode up the tunnel, past the men lying prone, past those kneeling. Angus was facing the business ends of twenty M4 barrels. He followed Donnie, careful not to step on the mercs that seemed to carpet the tunnel. Khatari rushed to join him, as did Fuentes, who dropped the half-assembled BlackBug into its case.

Once behind the standing mercs, Donnie turned and raised his own rifle. Khatari and Fuentes did the same. Angus stared down the tunnel in two ways: with his own vision, and with that of Oberon.

He eye-tracked, had Oberon map the position of all the men to eliminate them from the targeting algorithm. He set up the firing command as a left-eye-only double-blink. The ammo counter appeared in the HUD's upper right: *200/200/200.* Each drum held 200 rounds. When the first ran dry, the second would load automatically in under four seconds.

From down the tunnel, past the closest switchback corner, came a stuttering sound, like someone *bap-bap-bapping* an aluminum chair with a steel hammer. A man screamed. Shouts of alarm, followed instantly by gunfire.

Henderson's voice: "They're shooting at us! Williams is down! We're almost there!"

Shooting at them? But rocktopi didn't have guns …

"Hold your fire until my command," Donnie said. "Check your targets. Repeat, check your targets."

So calm…how could he be so calm?

Two mercs sprinted around the switchback corner, running so fast they almost lost their balance.

Right behind them came a sweeping wall of glowing, stretching pseudopodia, blazing-bright bodies rolling along like wet tumbleweed, eyespots as black as space itself.

Donnie's voice: "Recon, hit the deck!"

The two sprinting men threw themselves to the tunnel floor.

Donnie started calling out the order to shoot. He managed the "F" sound, and perhaps part of the "I," before Angus blinked his left eye twice.

Oberon's M249 opened up on full auto, filling the tight stone tunnel with a deafening roar. The first rocktopi bloomed in wet yellow blossoms as seven 5.56x47-millimeter rounds landed in a half-second, punching into the soft body, sending pond-ripple ringlets of blue light racing up the skin. Before the first second of fire ended, Oberon had already changed targets, putting seven rounds dead-center into the next squishy beast.

A cloud of lemon-colored mist filled the air.

Some of the rocktopi lived long enough to let out horrifying screeches, the sound of industrial saws slashing across super-sized chalkboards.

In four seconds, it was over.

Angus blinked his left eye twice; Oberon stopped firing.

Six rocktopi lay there twitching, spurting yellow blood all across the silt, the walls, themselves, and on the two recon men who had thrown themselves to the ground.

Angus glanced at the ammo count: *148/200/200.*

Oberon had fired fifty-two rounds in four seconds, every round delivered on-target.

"Cease fire, cease fire," Donnie said. "Recon, across the bridge and behind the firing line, *move!*"

Henderson and the other man scrambled to their feet, crawling out from beneath the bags of flesh that had fallen on them. Once up, they were track stars coming out of the blocks, pounding steps rattling the composite bridge as they crossed over the shaft mouth, ran past the prone mercs, then the kneeling ones, then to Donnie and Angus and Khatari and Fuentes, where they turned, chests heaving, and aimed back down the tunnel at the obliterated enemy.

A strange quiet gripped the tunnel, a quiet broken only by a last, high-pitched cry from one of the monsters that quickly faded into a pathetic, leaking-balloon squeak that wheezed into silence.

Color faded from the beasts. Four were already still. Two twitched, quivered like maggots surprised at the touch of a sharp stick. Those motions didn't last long.

"Henderson," Donnie said, "where's Williams?"

"Dead," Henderson said.

"Doctor Kool," Donnie said, "send Oberon. Secure Williams's body."

Angus wasn't sure what *secure the body* meant, but he sent Oberon sprinting ahead anyway. The machine skittered across the composite bridge with no more noise than a dog running across a kitchen floor.

In the HUD, Angus watched as Oberon reached the next tunnel segment. No light. Angus activated Oberon's night vision. In the green glow, sprawled on the tunnel silt, lay a man with a double-crescent knife buried in the back of his neck.

"I see the body," Angus said.

"Send Oberon past it, three switchback segments," Donnie said. "Kill any enemy you see."

Angus obeyed, directing Oberon ahead one segment at a time. Angus *trembled*. He hadn't known what he was doing, he'd just done it. Now that the initial burst of action was over, he felt like this was all happening to someone else.

"Oberon is three segments ahead," he said. "I see nothing in the fourth segment. Looks clear."

"Hold Oberon there," Donnie said. "First Platoon, over the bridge, finish off the wounded then secure the switchback. Second Platoon, advance to support Oberon's position."

Angus reduced Oberon's view to a thumbnail in the HUD. Once again, Angus again saw what was directly in front of him, which felt a bit surreal; it would be easy to get lost in the Wolf's sight, like the best video game ever.

The bridge thumped as twenty men rushed across it. First Platoon cautiously checked the dead and dying alien bodies, then set up at the switchback. Second Platoon moved past them to join Oberon.

Six rocktopi—Angus had gunned them down. Well, his invention had gunned them down, but hell, it was *his* invention, and he'd given the command.

"Third Platoon," Donnie said, "get ready to bring the donkeys and get them across the bridge. Company, get ready to shake those tail feathers, we're moving out. Stow all lanterns. We're going black."

Mercs grabbed the compact lanterns off the floor, shut them off, clipped them to their webbing. In moments, the tunnel fell dark.

Angus activated his night vision; the world became shades of green and white. He was about to enlarge Oberon's screen when he heard a sound that made his skin prickle. An ambient sound, soft; hard to make out over the noise of the men moving around and the whining servos from the approaching BaDonkeyDonks.

He held up an armored hand. "Everyone, quiet. Stay still!"

Donnie looked at him, perhaps ready to start into another lecture about who gave orders, then he cocked his head—he heard it, too.

"Company, *halt*," Donnie said.

The tunnel fell quiet again.

And in that quiet, a hiss.

The hiss of dry leaves blowing over pavement. Initially faint, but the sound grew as if someone was slowly turning a volume knob. It got *loud*, louder than Angus had ever heard in Utah. Angus looked down the tunnel, eye-blinked through infrared, enhanced vision, motion tracking—he saw nothing other than the ten men of First Platoon and the deflated bags that had been the rocktopi.

Louder.

Louder.

Henderson rushed to Donnie's side.

"That's what we heard before they came at us," Henderson said. "But it wasn't as loud as this."

The sound *filled* the tunnel.

Fuentes pointed to the rough ceiling above the shaft, shouted to be heard over the growing din.

"Sounds like it's coming from there!"

Angus glanced up. It did seem like the sound was coming from that spot, but unless there was a hidden speaker of some kind there, it ... no, the sound wasn't coming *from* the ceiling, it was *reflecting* off of it.

A burst of freezing fear locked him solid for an instant, then he shouted a warning.

"They're coming up the shaft! They're—"

A boiling crest of reaching greenish-gray flesh stretched over the shaft's ragged edges.

Rocktopi—but they weren't glowing?

As if in answer, before a shot could be fired, the creatures seemed to *ignite*, their skin suddenly blazing with pulsing light.

Angus's HUD filled with static, his suit's night vision instantly overwhelmed by the aliens' powerful bioluminescence. He stood there, numb, frozen.

Donnie: *"Go white."*

Headlamps and rifle lights switched on. That hammer-on-aluminum sound again. Men screaming. Gunfire. Hissing leaves. Tones mashing together in a deafening assault.

Angus blinked off his night vision, revealing a tunnel raging with madness.

Rocktopi flowed like wiggling, stretching globs of neon fat, attacking the mercs, overrunning them. Double-crescent knives flashed, splattering arcs of blood across the rock walls and fine silt. Men fired M4s at close range, the rounds ripping through alien bodies. Stray bullets sparked shards of stone from the tunnel walls.

On both sides of the shaft mouth, the melee became an indiscernible mass of luminous flesh and human uniforms, of blinking black spots and wide eyes, of human cries of pain and rage mixing with the ear-piercing screech of squealing tires. The impossible colors of the rocktopi danced across stone. Lights attached to M4 barrels whipped wildly, their beams almost solid in the already thick gun smoke.

In a tunnel barely wider than his outstretched arms, Angus saw dozens of living beings fighting for survival; trench warfare where the only options were to kill or die.

A rocktopi raised what looked like an over/under double-barreled weapon: a hammer-hitting-aluminum sound, and a merc fell back, something metallic sticking out of his chest.

Fuentes and Khatari were shouting. Angus couldn't make out their words.

A rocktopi broke from the twisted mass of fighting, stretched toward Angus, a pair of crescent blades arcing forward at the end of two pseudopods that pulsed in alternating stripes of mint-green and charcoal-gray. Khatari stepped in front of Angus, M4 stuttering away on full auto—splashes of radiating color and squirts of yellow blood as bullets punched through the knife-wielding attacker.

A blade flashed.

An arc of rich red as a crescent edge sliced through armor and flesh alike.

Bleeding, Khatari stumbled back, fell at Angus's feet.

The rocktopi that had cut him—its ochre blood spurting from a half-dozen bullet holes—kept coming, glowing in jagged waves of hateful orange and electric pink.

The two curved blades came up, rose so high the tips sparked off the stone ceiling, started to whip down to finish Khatari off.

A part of Angus that he didn't know existed suddenly seized control. His right arm came up fast, made a fist.

The modified Atchisson barked five times, each round hurling eight-ounce lead balls at thirteen hundred feet per second. The clouds of metal ripped fist-sized holes into the gleaming skin, sent out a spray of yellow mist. One round punched *all the way* through, giving Angus a there-then-gone look at the fighting taking place behind the monster.

The rocktopi dropped. One tentacle arm fell limp across Khatari's red-smeared chest armor. The double-crescent knives—still beaded with the man's blood—dropped onto the tunnel silt.

Carnage. Men and aliens fighting for their lives. Blades flashed. Pistols roared.

Angus brought his right hand to his chest, felt vibrations as his suit re-loaded his shotgun magazine.

The ten men of Fifth Platoon rushed into the fray, pistols and combat knives in hand, screaming the guttural, primitive language of war.

One of the rocktopi ran from this new onslaught, rushed toward the shaft.

Angus raised his left arm, made a fist—from a chamber below his forearm casing, a steel net shot forth, instantly spun out to its eight-foot radius. He'd designed it to capture just one target, but the teeming mass of combatants were packed so closely together that the spiderweb cable covered a half-dozen bodies, living and dead alike.

He flipped his left hand up sharply—50,000 volts poured through the cable. Below the net, the fighting stopped instantly. Men stiffened and twitched. Rocktopi jiggled like vibrating Jell-O. The moment seemed to go on and on.

Angus flipped his hand down, shutting off the power.

And just like that, the battle was over. Only humans remained standing.

They had won.

Mercs, sucking air, some pressing hands against wounds, moved toward the pile of stunned men trapped below the net. Some dragged their fellow soldiers free. Others stepped to the rocktopi, raised knives…

"*Don't kill them,*" Angus shouted.

They paused, stared at him in confusion.

Angus activated his comms. "Fuentes! You there?"

Off to Angus's right, he saw a man wave. "Right here!"

In the madness, he hadn't realized Fuentes was only a few feet away.

"On BaDonkeyDonk Two," Angus said. "The crate marked *Alcatraz.* Get it, fast."

Fuentes actually saluted him. "On it!"

A merc stepped toward Angus.

"No prisoners," the merc said. "These things killed my friends."

It was Henderson. He'd lost two men to a claymore mine high up the mountain, now another to the rocktopi. In his right hand, a yellow-smeared KA-BAR knife. He reached down with his left, grabbed a handful of rocktopi, and lifted—the alien's skin stretched out like a giant plug of moonlight-hued taffy.

Angus raised his right arm, pointed it at Henderson's face. Henderson stared down the big-bore barrel—his expression changed, instantly.

"Let it go," Angus said.

Henderson hesitated.

Next to Henderson, a merc got to his feet, his hand clutching his shoulder, blood and coolant fluid coursing down.

It was Donnie Graham.

"Henderson, release it," Donnie said. "Right now. Sixth Platoon, up here and watch this hole. Seventh, advance and treat the wounded. All cuts have to be stitched quickly, then use patch kits to seal the suits. Second Platoon, maintain position, we're coming to you. And someone get me a goddamn patch kit, I'm already getting hot. Haul ass!"

The mercs moved like cockroaches scattering from a light, grabbing at their comrades, checking to see who was still alive, going to work on cuts and other wounds. The tunnel that had been a war zone became an instant triage center.

Angus suddenly felt so tired. He hadn't felt this drained since the hospital. But he wasn't wounded—he hadn't been hit at all.

A BaDonkeyDonk walked out from behind the uphill switchback. The machine gingerly stepped around fallen mercs and rocktopi alike. Fuentes was behind it, already lugging free the bulky case labeled *Alcatraz*. He found an open space in the tunnel floor, set it down flat. He opened the case, revealing two packed bundles of thin, bronze-colored tubes.

"Looks like one of those trade show things," he said. "Them pop-up booths."

That was exactly where Angus had gotten the idea.

"Get some men to help you take them out and unfold them," he said. "Directions are inside the case lid. Be careful assembling the self-propelled platform, and be *especially* careful connecting the batteries—the rigs are useless without those."

Angus felt dizzy. He walked away from the men, trying to get some space to himself, even a little. A roaring sound, but this one was coming from inside his own head, as if his blood was a raging torrent. His throat burned. The smell of gunpowder hung in his nose, too thick to be fully eliminated by the KoolSuit's air filters.

Combat. Angus had thought that actual, gun-toting combat would be kind of awesome. It wasn't. Men had died. Other men were breathing their last. He'd killed that rocktopi. Not with Oberon this time, not from a distance—he'd pulled the trigger himself.

He heard a new sound, a disturbing sound—the rubbery crinkle of body bags being unfolded.

"Kool, we need to talk."

Donnie. Angus didn't want to talk—he wanted to sleep.

Bloody tan fatigue jacket over one shoulder, naked from the waist up beneath his KoolSuit, the grizzled commander stepped over his own fallen mercs. A man walked with him, wrapping KoolSuit repair sheeting over the top of bloody, white gauze on Donnie's upper arm. The sheeting would adhere to the existing KoolSuit material, automatically integrate with the microtubule structure, making the repaired area almost as good as new.

"You fought well," Donnie said. "I'd be lying if I said I wasn't shocked by that. You might have saved some lives. At the same time, we *lost* men because you didn't tell me the rocktopi use guns."

Angus tried to focus. His thoughts seemed to slip from his grasp, to weave in and out of his control.

"They don't," he said. "I mean … they didn't. Before."

Donnie looked to his right, curled his fingers inward. Someone handed him something—the weapon Angus had seen a rocktopi fire. An oval-shaped cluster made of curved hexagonal metal plates. Two parallel pipes stuck out from one end, each with a line of small points, like metallic rose thorns, running down its length.

Angus glanced at the merc he'd seen die—he was on his back, a finger-thick rod of metal sticking out of his chest. A heart-shot, or close to it.

"These weapons are thin, flexible," Donnie said. He held the weapon sideways—it looked like a flattened football; the oval-shaped cluster wasn't even an inch thick. He grabbed the pair of meter-long parallel pipes and bent—they curved like fishing poles. When he let go, the pipes snapped back into place, straight as can be. "An ideal weapon for creatures that flow through cracks in the walls. You're sure you didn't see these in Utah?"

Angus wanted to disassemble the thing, see how it worked.

"No," he said. "We didn't encounter anything like that."

Donnie stared. "You told me they used knives and rocks. You told me they attacked like brainless zombies, but they use tactics."

"Tactics? How do you figure they used *tactics*?"

"Their frontal assault was a diversion," Donnie said, wincing as the merc finished sealing his KoolSuit. "Six of them drew our focus while *eighteen* of them came up the shaft. The ones that came up the shaft weren't flashing colors—they were *dark*. It was a stealth attack, meant to catch us unawares in the middle of our column."

There was no arguing that. Angus had seen it himself.

"They didn't act like that in Utah. I swear it."

Donnie put his blood-stained fatigue jacket back on.

"I trusted your intel," he said. "Now I have seven more dead men, and five others wounded to the point where they can't go on. I'm sending three men to escort the wounded back to the surface, so they can be evaced to a hospital friendly to G4S. That means I've lost a total of fifteen soldiers. If we continue the mission, I'm down to a force of seventy-two."

If. The single word rekindled Angus's focus, chased away the battle fatigue.

"We *are* continuing the mission," Angus said. "I didn't hire mercenaries to take a nice walk in the park and pick fucking flowers. When we find that ship, your men are millionaires, and *you* might be a *billionaire.* On top of that, we have captive alien specimens, which are worth a fortune unto themselves, and—" he pointed at the strange weapon in Donnie's hands "—we have *that*, which you can bet will start an impressive bidding war between America, China, Russia and India, at the very least. Your men died? Then maybe they should have thought about that before signing on as *fucking hired guns.* Shit happens. Now, are you going to sit here giving me the stink-eye and flapping your gums, or are we going to get this show on the road?"

Donnie's glare hardened. His fingers twitched on the alien weapon, as if he was debating the potential benefit of shoving it down Angus's throat.

"Maybe we should cut our losses," Donnie said. "Maybe my men and I will take what BHP paid us and we'll call it a day."

"That will look good on your resume. I can't wait to leave a Yelp review."

Donnie smiled. "You make a lot of threats for someone who might not make it out of here alive."

Angus held Donnie's stare for a moment, became aware that most of the mercs were watching the exchange.

How long would it take Oberon to run back here? Not long. One silent command to call the Wolf back, then all Angus had to do was say the words *all but me*—Donnie Graham and his flower-picking flunkies would be dead in seconds.

Which would leave Angus alone.

Alone against O'Doyle, the silverbugs, and who knew how many rocktopi.

Angus didn't want that. He had to fix this, and fast.

"Instead of cutting your losses, how about we increase your profits?" He blinked on his comms, making sure every mercenary could hear him. "Any of you can leave now and keep what you were paid. Pick up a silverbug or two on the way, I don't care. But every man that stays with me will get *five million dollars*. That's on top of whatever silverbugs you can carry out of here when we're done."

He was making up numbers, he knew, but five million sounded like a nice, round sum. Not the kind of money these guys could ever hope to get for a few days of dangerous work.

The mercs looked at each other. Angus saw shrugs and nods. They knew, too, that they wouldn't see money like that anytime soon. Most of these men — probably *all* of them — had risked their lives for far, far less.

Donnie glanced around, saw the reactions of his men. The look on his face said it all. He sighed.

"Doctor Kool, are you sure there isn't anything else I need to be aware of?"

So it was *Doctor* again, was it? Angus had won.

"You know all I know about the rocktopi, their guns, the silverbugs, the ship, and O'Doyle and his goons," Angus said. "I don't like surprises any more than you do, but as a brilliant man once said, *it's a long way to the top if you wanna rock'n'roll*."

Donnie offered the strange rifle. "Can you figure out how it works?"

Angus took it. The football-shaped cluster had several small dots in it. He looked closer at one of them, saw the dot was a hole that went deeper into the weapon. The poles were solid. Between them, in the body, a hole the same diameter as the rod sticking up out of the dead merc's chest.

"Probably some kind of railgun," Angus said. "I'd bet the poles accelerate metal rods to a very high speed. The dot must be the trigger. Rocktopi can form little pseudopods that would fit in there."

Donnie took the weapon back. "We've got six of these. Bring them with?"

"No, leave them," Angus said. "As far as we know, they'll explode if we handle them incorrectly. If we come back up this way when we're done, then we can decide if we should take them with."

Donnie handed the weapon to the merc standing next to him. "Stash the enemy rifles behind a switchback, away from the wounded."

"Yessir," the merc said. He took the weapon and scurried away like a good little soldier.

Fuentes rushed over. "All set up, boss."

Angus and Donnie walked to the cages—two rigs of thin bronze bars lined with fine mesh, each big enough to hold a kneeling man. Each cage rested on a platform with four small, rugged wheels. On the front of each platform, a handheld controller connected to the cages by a thick wire.

"Get the rocktopi from under the net," Angus said. "Put one each in the cages. Hurry, I don't know how long they'll stay knocked out."

Several mercs worked together, dragging a rocktopi to each cage, stuffing them inside like wet laundry.

"Someone needs to stay with the cages at all times," Angus said. "If rocktopi start moving, hit the button."

Fuentes nodded. "Got it."

Hopefully the captured creatures weren't already dying. Angus had had no idea how much voltage to apply, so he'd dialed in enough to knock out a man.

"You make such interesting toys," Donnie said. "I'll send the critters up with the wounded. Our men up top can watch them until we're finished down here."

That would get the specimens out of harm's way, but at the same time, these rocktopi had used advanced weapons, tactics—they weren't the mindless killers he'd faced in Utah.

"They live in this high heat," Angus said. "I'm pretty sure they can survive the cold up top, but I don't know for how long. We could be down here for days. A dead rocktopi is worth a lot to us—a living one is worth a whole lot more. Besides, if they're smart enough to know tactics, maybe any of their buddies we face will understand the value of hostages."

Donnie nodded in agreement. He clicked his *talk* button.

"This is Captain Graham. Listen up. We had a hard go of it just now. We lost some friends. Doctor Kool has kindly offered us a compelling bonus plan. If you want out, volunteer to go up with the wounded, but if you volunteer for that, you don't get the bonus. We continue the mission in five minutes."

Donnie strode off, growling orders, encouraging his troops to get ready to move. All up and down the tunnel, men prepared to march.

Fuentes slapped Angus's armored shoulder.

"You did good, Boss. You fought like hell."

Fuentes was … *proud* of him? Angus felt almost overwhelmed. For all his accomplishments, for all his genius, who had ever been *proud* of him?

Randy Wright. Only Dirty Randy.

"Thank you," Angus said.

Fuentes glanced to the side; his face broke into the widest smile Angus had seen yet.

"Well, look who's already up and at 'em!"

It shocked Angus to see Khatari, rifle in hand, walking toward them on wobbly legs. Blood, already dry, stained the slash through his jacket. Angus could see the damaged body armor beneath, also stained with blood.

"You're wounded," Angus said. "You need to go back up."

Yadav Khatari forced a grin. " 'Tis but a scratch."

Angus didn't want to see this man get hurt worse, didn't want to see him die.

What was happening? First he'd felt the warm fuzzies at Fuentes being proud of him, now he was being a sap about Khatari? Angus didn't give a shit about the mercs, about Donnie—why was it different with these two?

"It's more than a scratch," Angus said. "How many stitches did you just get?"

Khatari winced, a lash of pain from the fresh wound, then he stared at Angus with a stone face.

"You saved my life," Khatari said. "If you hadn't shot that thing, it would have sliced me from balls to brains. You didn't run—neither will I."

You didn't run.

Angus had stayed. He'd fought. Why this time? He'd let Randy die, so why this time? Was it the exosuit? Yes, but that was only part of it.

He couldn't explain exactly why he'd done what he'd done.

Did Khatari really want to go on out of loyalty? The man seemed sincere, but Angus couldn't believe someone would be that loyal to *him*. Khatari was staying because of the money. Of course he was.

But what if Khatari—and Fuentes as well—honestly, actually, really-really-*really* gave a flying fuck about Angus?

"I'm going to give you guys a private comm channel," Angus said, eye-tracking through his HUD menu to select a frequency. "If you hear three fast beeps, then my voice, that means I'm talking to you and only you. Got it?"

Fuentes and Khatari looked at each other. Fuentes smiled.

Khatari shrugged. "Sounds good, Boss."

Angus programmed the channel. He activated it.

"Testing. You hear the beeps?"

The men both nodded.

"Good," Angus said. "We need to talk soon about both of you getting a bigger share."

Fuentes smiled wider. Khatari smiled, too.

Angus's comm chimed twice: Donnie's direct line.

"Doctor Kool, if you'd be so kind, can you get the BlackBugs assembled before we move out? I want those machines out in front of Oberon in case O'Doyle's people get crafty again."

"Is that an order, Donnie?"

"Yes it's a fucking order. Make it happen."

The line chimed twice as Donnie clicked off the channel.

Angus sighed. The man had no sense of humor. None at all.

Time to get to work.

"Khatari, my old pal, I hope you understand what *color-coded* means."

40

"ENDER, COME BACK."

Patrick pressed his *talk* button. "Go ahead, Worm."

"Another tunnel branch. Got some glyphs I haven't seen yet. You better bring up Sam."

"Affirmative," Patrick said. "Skylark, anything behind us?"

Marie's voice came back scratchy, tinny—the column was getting too stretched out.

"Nothing. No mercs, no glowing monsters. All's clear behind."

That was good news, anyway.

"Column, hold," Patrick said. "Rearguard, close up another twenty meters before you stop, your signal- is starting to break up. Sam, follow me."

Otto and Sonny immediately sat down. The constant downslope

was taking its toll on them, just like it was on Patrick. His knees and lower back screamed.

He continued down the tunnel, Sam a step behind.

Since that first branch, they'd hit four more. Sometimes Sam had an idea which way to go, sometimes, they just eyeballed which tunnel was smaller and chose that route.

The lead group—Worm, Lybrand and Sleepy—stayed three to four switchbacks ahead. The rearguard, three to four switchbacks behind. Mullet and Klimas were doing their best to cover everyone's tracks in the cave silt, which slowed them down.

Patrick and Sam came around a switchback to find Tommy standing there, eyes on his chest monitor. Past him, the tunnel banked to the right, the same width and height as the one in which they now stood, and a slightly narrower branch led off to the left. Between the two branches, a cluster of circle-and-squiggle glyphs.

Samira's tiny bit of knowledge about the glyphs was far more than anyone else possessed. While she studied the new marks, Ender stood next to Tommy.

"How far ahead are Sleepy and Bertha?"

"Two switchbacks," Tommy said, his eyes again focused on the small monitor hanging from his chest. "Your wife is sharp. Knows her shit."

Patrick was worried sick about her being up front, but this wasn't the time to play favorites. She had experience fighting the rocktopi. She knew what to look for, could use that knowledge to make fast decisions that might save lives.

"I have something," Sam said.

Patrick stepped closer to her.

She pointed to the glyphs. "We've been taking the smaller tunnels, but I think this mark says the smaller tunnel will go *up* soon."

"By how much? How big of an angle? Will it go down again?"

"I don't know. I know the left-hand path is smaller, but the one we're on now might lead to a chamber of some kind. I think the squiggles on the top part indicate that *groups* of rocktopi use it. Maybe it's a meeting room, or a temple or something like that."

"Are you sure?"

She huffed. "Dude, I don't know anything for sure. I'm giving you my best guess."

Patrick's jaw clenched. He was blind down here.

"Any idea how far away it is?"

Samira started to shake her head, stopped, looked closer at the glyph. "I couldn't say."

If she was right, it could be anything. It could be like the farming cavern he'd seen in Utah. It could be the cavern that held the ship, although if this place was like the Utah complex, the ship was another eight thousand feet down.

Rocktopi were down here, though. Somewhere. If Sam was right, and there was a chamber full of the beasts, that would be bad news. But if that place was empty, it might be ideal. The NoSeeUms & Friends had been going nonstop for hours, and that was after a firefight where they'd lost a man. Everyone was exhausted. Maybe the room would be a defensible place to rest for a bit.

"We'll stay on this path." He pressed his *talk* button. "Up and at 'em, people, we're moving out."

41

"LOOK AT ALL of them," Dimwit Donnie said. "It's a goddamn village."

Donnie's HUD showed the same thing as Angus's — the view from Oberon's font camera, which showed a cavern about fifty meters in diameter. A single, blazing light at the apex of the rock dome lit up everything as bright as day. In the center of the cavern floor, a cluster of about twenty small buildings surrounded by thick, head-high purple plants. The single-story buildings appeared to be made of sheets of smooth granite milled from the mountain itself, as did the paving stones that wound between them. Gleaming silverbugs dotted the view, crawling on buildings, walking along paving stones, even clinging to the purple plants.

And, all over the place, rocktopi. They moved quickly, darting in and out of buildings. They seemed agitated. Their colors irritated Angus—bright teals and deep greens, pulsing spots of burnt orange, cascading stripes of blazing red. They looked like clown jizz.

"How many rocktopi are there?" Donnie asked.

The number of targets was listed in the HUD's upper left-hand corner, but Angus answered anyway.

"Between fifty-one and sixty-four," Angus said. "Their colors change too fast for any kind of definitive individual identification. Oberon's algorithm is estimating the count based on location and movement tracking."

Angus, Donnie, Fuentes, Khatari and others were one switchback away from the cavern entrance. Behind them, the mercenaries lined the tunnel wall, guns in hand, ready to attack on Donnie's command.

Donnie had scrapped Eighth Platoon, used those soldiers to fill in the casualties suffered by First and Third Platoons, and to give Henderson two more men for the recon squad.

"Show me the map again," Donnie said.

At the first tunnel branch, Angus had sent the now-assembled BlackBugs out to silently collect data and make an ever-expanding map. Modeled after the silverbugs, his four-legged, carbon-fiber bots could cling to walls and ceilings, could even crawl into some of the larger cracks. They operated as a single distributed intelligence, relaying and sharing data via ultra low frequency radio transmission. They sensed vibrations in the ground around them, letting them function as walking seismographs. By triangulating their locations with each other, they could even potentially give an approximate epicenter of quakes or tremors. They had decent cameras, although they used LiDAR for their primary sensing and mapping functions.

The farther the BlackBugs ranged, the bigger the map became.

The machines were also programmed to detect environmental anomalies, including temperature fluctuations above or below the steady gradient that increased with depth, the multi-band radio transmissions the silverbugs used, sound variances, and—of course—movement.

When the BlackBugs logged a sound that was suspiciously similar to the rustling of dry leaves, Donnie had headed the mercs in that direction. That had brought them here.

Angus eye-tracked through his display, called up the map, shared it with Donnie's HUD. The numerous, neat descending switchbacks made it look more organized than the seemingly random twists and turns of the Utah cave system. On the map, a flashing green spot marked Angus's position. A steady orange dot showed Oberon's location, just inside the tunnel that opened up into the village cavern.

"We have to clear them out," Donnie said. "I don't want to leave a force behind us."

Only four of the rocktopi carried those strange railguns. Those individuals moved in a loose circle around the buildings, like sentries on patrol.

"Doesn't look like much of a *force*," Angus said.

"Armed enemy combatants are the very definition of the word, Doctor Kool. You don't leave enemy combatants in your rearview. What do you think they're doing?"

"I have no idea," Angus said. "It looks like they're taking items out of the buildings. Maybe they're evacuating?"

That thought bothered him. Maybe those weren't *buildings* as much as they were *homes*.

"Khatari," Donnie said, "get the SwarmStorm case."

The man rushed off to do as he was ordered.

Angus had already lost almost fourteen percent of the red machines. How many might he lose here? Certainly he'd need them when the column got closer to the ship, where the silverbugs were likely more concentrated.

"I told you we don't have an endless supply of swarmbots," he said. "Maybe we should hold onto them in the event we run into a larger—"

"On my command, you'll launch them. I don't want those machines raising a warning. Oberon goes in after them. Have it take out the visibly armed rocktopi first. Then we'll advance and eliminate the rest. Try to conserve SAW ammo as much as possible."

Eliminate the rest.

"You want to kill them," Angus said. "All of them. Wipe out the village."

Donnie looked at him. "Not only is that tactically sound, it's what you wanted. Isn't it?"

It was. At least, that was what he'd wanted before.

"Maybe this is too much," Fuentes said. "I mean…I know we're here to kill and all, but the ones that attacked us earlier, those were *soldiers*."

Donnie whirled on him. "Is it time to cue the *mercenary with a heart of gold* part of this story? Aside from Doctor Kool's captured specimens, our job is to kill anything that moves."

Kill anything that moves. Donnie echoing what Angus had said back in the Utah office, what seemed like a lifetime ago.

Wasn't that the smart call? The Fitz Roy rocktopi had weapons, used tactics—who knew what they might next bring to bear. Or was that the wrong way to think about it? If they were smarter than their Utah cousins, could Angus exploit that somehow? No, not unless he could buy rocktopi loyalty as easily as he could buy the human variety.

If that happened, there was no chance of controlling the platinum.

"But it's a *village*," Fuentes said. "What if there's little ones? Babies?"

Angus hadn't thought of that.

Calmly, smoothly, Donnie drew his sidearm. The motion was so matter of fact, so devoid of emotion, that no one thought to react before the barrel was pointed at Fuentes's face.

Fuentes froze. So did Angus. So did everyone else.

"You had a chance to go back," Donnie said to Fuentes. "You stayed because you want to be a millionaire. Now that it's time for you to actually *do your job*, you think you can second-guess the command structure?"

Fuentes glanced at Angus, then back to the pistol.

Did he want Angus to help him? Did he want Angus to raise his arm and shoot Donnie?

Angus fought down an urge to do exactly that. Fuentes was an employee, an employee who was getting in the way of *trillions* of dollars.

Or was he more than that? Was he an actual *friend*?

"I asked you a question," Donnie said.

Fuentes slowly shook his head. "No, Captain, I don't think I can second-guess you. I ... I was just ... you know, wondering what the right thing is." He forced a smile. "That's all."

Donnie holstered his pistol.

"The second those things attacked us, this became a war and they became our enemy," he said. "I am in command. Don't question my orders again."

Fuentes nodded.

"SwarmStorm case open," Khatari said. "They're ready to fly."

Donnie pressed his transmitter. "All forces, prepare to move into the cavern. Deploy left to right. Kill everything that isn't us. Seventh Platoon, hold at this entrance and make sure none of them get by us. Doctor Kool, send the SwarmStorm, then Oberon."

Send Oberon in to kill everything. Armed and unarmed alike.

This was the way it had to be—one didn't become the richest man in history by worrying about the wrong things.

"SwarmStorm, activate," Angus said.

The cloud of tiny red robots rose up.

"Enter the target area. Find silverbugs. Seek and destroy."

The red fog streamed away from the case and vanished around the switchback.

Now for the messy part.

"Oberon, target any armed opposition," Angus said. "Advance and eliminate."

In an instant, the Wolf went from standing still to sprinting like a cheetah.

Armed would include any rocktopi holding anything—knife, gun, even a garden hoe. Not that such particulars mattered, though, not when Donnie was going to murder them all anyway.

Angus watched the HUD screen as Oberon entered the cavern and rushed toward a rocktopi holding a railgun.

The rocktopi saw the machine coming—how could it *not* see with all those eyes?—and raised its weapon.

Oberon's ammo counter went from 148/200/200 to 137/200/200.

The rocktopi *splattered,* soft body torn apart by SAW rounds traveling at 915 meters per second. The spray of blood hadn't even begun to arc down before the sprinting machine angled left and fired again. This time the rounds tore into an unarmed rocktopi running away, two smaller rocktopi at its side—all three burst like water balloons filled with mucus.

They hadn't been armed: Oberon's targeting algorithm wasn't accurate enough.

The robot kept sprinting, kept firing. Rocktopi after rocktopi went down. In the first ten seconds, a dozen moving, living rocktopi became hole-filled bags of flesh, their blood turned into misty yellow clouds that slowly settled down to the paving stones.

Angus felt queasy.

"The silverbugs are still moving," Donnie said. "I thought the SwarmStorm paralyzed them?"

Angus had been too focused on Oberon's kills to pay attention to the wider view. A few glances at the areas around the robot's field of fire showed Donnie was right—the silverbugs were scurrying everywhere, running free until the red dust of the SwarmStorm settled on them.

"The silverbugs must have adapted to the jamming," Angus said. "I'm not surprised. They did the same in Utah."

"Can you counter that?"

"Maybe. I'd need time to figure out what changed."

"We'll worry about that after the battle," Donnie said. "Doctor Kool, stay close to me. Company, advance. Kill anything that moves."

42

10,330 Feet below the surface

SAM HADN'T FORGOTTEN about Ramiro, not by a long shot, but even the brutal death of her ex-husband and best friend couldn't block out the sheer *awe* of what she saw.

Her take on the glyphs had proven correct. The tunnel had led to the biggest cave she'd seen yet. The other caves, including Base Camp, were akin to studio apartments—this open space felt more like the gallery of a small-town church.

Up above, a fist-sized glowing ball, too bright to look at directly. Its diffuse light illuminated bas-relief carvings that covered every inch of the curved walls, and the domed ceiling as well, representations of surface animals: pumas, guanacos, Andean cats, maras, rheas, huemel, foxes, deer, vizcacha and more. The artwork was stunning in its realism.

Even the floor was part of the overwhelming display. Hexagonal tiles, maybe three feet wide from parallel side to parallel side, each with an engraved glyph. Some of them matched glyphs she'd seen scrawled on the walls in the switchback tunnels, but most were new to her eyes.

"It's like a clubhouse for boogeymen," Mullet said, his voice echoing slightly. "Pretty messed up."

Worm glanced around the room.

"Only one entrance," he said. "I don't like it."

O'Doyle shrugged off his backpack, tossed it to the floor against the wall.

"We'll take our chances," he said. "We need a break. Worm, get a hornet out ahead of us. Skylark, send yours to watch our rear."

"Mine needs a recharge," Skylark said.

Tommy walked to the entrance. "I'll run mine out front and eyeball the way we came. Get a rest, Marie."

Skylark blew him a weak kiss. "I fucking love you, Tommy."

"Everyone take twenty," O'Doyle said. "Drink, clean out waste bags. Skylark, relieve Tommy in ten, get your hornet charged."

The rustle of backpacks sliding off, the rattle of helmets and rifles being set onto the ground. Sam took hers off as well, tossed it against a wall. Her back rejoiced in the sudden lack of weight.

"I'll take the entrance," Klimas said. "Worm, show me how to use the hornet, then take a break."

Tommy's shoulders sagged with relief. He flashed Skylark a perfunctory grin.

"You'll still love me if I take a seat, Marie?"

"Tommy, I will always love you," she said. "Let the young buck show us how tough he is—you come and sit down with momma."

O'Doyle leaned against the wall as he sat. Sam saw him wince, saw him sit slowly, gingerly. Was the constant downhill walking getting to him? Hell, it was getting to her, and she was probably half his age.

Lybrand sat next to him. A stoic woman, she showed little expression, but even she couldn't fully hide her pain. Everyone was hurting. How much farther did they have to go?

"Sam," O'Doyle said, "get some sit-down time. Please. You're going to need it."

She nodded, absently, as she turned, staring at the marvelous carvings. "I will. In a minute."

Sam moved to the center of the room, noticed that the three tiles there were missing, a triangle-ish space some six feet across, filled with silt marked with hand-drawn glyphs. Maybe they hadn't finished the floor, or maybe these tiles had been removed for repair.

All the carvings had symbols beneath them. Identifiers? Names? Despite her exhaustion, Sam felt a charge of excitement—could this room help her better understand the Chaltélian written language?

The rest of the team had taken O'Doyle's advice—or was it an order?—to sit down. Tommy was on one knee, just inside the entrance, changing out hornet drones. Mullet sat shoulder to shoulder with Skylark, her small size more apparent when she was right next to him. Sleepy lay on his back, his head on his pack, already out like a light. Otto was sitting as well, but he'd already disassembled his pistol and was examining the parts. Sonny sat next to him, watching Otto's every move, probably more as a way to focus on something other than his claustrophobia than to actually learn anything.

Curveball sat on the opposite side of the room, as far away from everyone else as he could get. Elbows on knees, head hanging down, that nasty looking axe on the ground between his feet.

He'd lost the love of his life. Sam could empathize—so had she. She walked up to him, wanting to talk to him but not knowing what to say.

"Leave me be," he said without looking up.

"I…I wanted to say I'm sorry," Sam said. "About Hatchet, I mean."

"His name was Carson. Carson Wampler. Hatchet was in the past. Should have stayed in the past. Now they're both gone."

His grief felt palpable, and calmly violent, like a still picture of a boxer gathering for a knockout punch. She was afraid of this man, and yet she was drawn to him, to his pain.

"I'm sorry Carson died," she said. "Was he your husband?"

Curveball finally looked up. All the cold of the universe in that gaze.

"He was. Why the fuck do you care?"

"Ramiro was my husband." She felt instantly stupid for having said it. "We were divorced, but I…" she shook her head. "Sorry, I know it's not the same, but I never stopped loving him, and now he's gone."

She felt the tears coming yet again, reached up to wipe them away; her hand hit her visor, yet again. A wave of frustration crashed over her.

She felt a hand on her lower leg; Curveball, touching her, looked up at her.

"It's not the same, but it's not that different," he said. "I'm sorry you lost him."

He patted her leg once, then lowered his head, rested his hands on his knees.

She knew that was the extent of their conversation. A connection, made through pain, brief and small, but real.

Sam turned away from him, blinking fast to clear the tears that her hands could not reach. Only a few words, shared with a stranger, and yet she couldn't deny she felt the smallest bit better.

Her legs and feet throbbed. Her back hurt. The suit was starting to chafe. She needed rest, no doubt, but let the carved imagery take her attention away from the hurt that lodged in her chest and belly.

This room had been carved out of the mountain. Carved out for a specific purpose … but what was that purpose? Was this a historical document? Maybe, because some of the animal species pictured were endangered and rare. Maybe even extinct. The fauna carvings were like a snapshot of a time gone by.

"A drawing pit."

Sam twitched; Tommy had crept up on her right.

"Oh, sorry," he said. "I forget that you're new. The others can hear me coming. Most of the time, anyway."

You're new. Not *you have no idea what you're doing,* or *you're a huge burden that's going to get us killed.* Just *you're new.*

He pointed to the sand. "A drawing pit, right?"

She glanced at it. "I thought it was just missing tiles."

"No, look at the edges." He knelt, ran his gloved hand along the edge of a tile. "See how the flat part facing the sand has designs on it? Aliens might be different, but I doubt anyone puts a decorative edge on something that's going to be covered up."

The edges did have a decorative edge. She'd missed that. She was so tired, she'd probably missed a lot.

"I thought you were going to sit with *momma.*"

Tommy smiled that easy smile of his. "She knows the only time I sit still is when I'm asleep or reading. I don't have a book handy, and how can anyone sleep when they're in the midst of all of this?"

She couldn't argue about that.

His excitement brought some of her energy back. She looked at the images drawn in the sand.

"That center one is a counting symbol," she said. "It looks like the number thirteen, but it's not finished. It needs another curl, and—"

"And a dot."

She looked up at him. "How in the hell could you know that?"

He pointed to one of the tiles surrounding the sand pit.

"Base twelve, right?" he said. "Looks like that tile covers one through twelve. The one next to it covers thirteen through twenty-six."

Sam looked at the tiles. Tommy was right—they depicted the symbols for the Chaltélian counting system.

"For fuck's sake," she said. "It took Veronica Reeves and me an entire season to figure out they used base twelve. You knew that from one look?"

He shrugged. "When it comes to numbers, I'm smarter than the average bear."

She looked at him. "What does that mean?"

He leaned back. "*Smarter than the average bear?* You don't know what that means?"

Sam shook her head.

"Yogi," Tommy said. "Boo-Boo? Ranger?"

"I have no idea what you're talking about."

"For fuck's sake," Tommy said. "How old are you?"

A strange question at a time like this. "Twenty-eight."

"Born in nineteen eighty-nine," he said.

"Why does that matter?"

He shook his head. "It doesn't. Like I said, I'm good with numbers, but I figured it out because it's written on these tiles like a primer. It's not a big deal."

He was wrong about that. Base twelve wasn't an easy concept to get, even with a handy, millennia-old cheat sheet.

And how many people did she know who even knew what the word *primer* meant in that context?

Tommy glanced around the room. "A lot of primers in here, looks like."

His comment reinforced her earlier observation. The simple carvings matched with symbols broke down at least some of this language to bare elements. Broke it down to *fundamentals.*

"It's a classroom," Sam said.

Tommy glanced around, nodded. "To teach the little ones, like the ones Lybrand stopped Mullet from killing."

He wasn't smiling anymore. He glanced at O'Doyle, doubt in his eyes.

"What is it?" Sam asked, quietly.

O'Doyle looked up, suddenly, as if he knew he was being watched. Tommy looked away almost as fast, his face reddening with … what, with *guilt?*

"Tommy," Sam said, "what did he tell you about this place?"

He shook his head, put on a smile that was as blatantly false as his earlier had been unabashedly genuine.

"Doesn't matter," he said. "We're in it up to our eyeballs, right?"

Sam had known these people a handful of hours, yet she already felt she understood Tommy. His understanding of things was changing, and not in a good way.

"If it's a classroom, looks like school got out early," he said. "One of those counting symbols in the sand is unfinished. Like they were in a rush, or they knew we were coming and got out quick."

Sam shrugged. "Maybe, maybe not. No wind down here. No rain. A simple drawing in this sand could last for ten thousand years. School might have let out five millennia ago."

Tommy glanced around the room, his eyes lingering on the entrance.

"I suppose," he said. "But sure doesn't *feel* like this was made thousands of years ago. Does it?"

"Science isn't about *feelings.*"

"Maybe not. But surviving usually is."

She didn't know what to say to that. She had no experience. She'd have to stick to what she knew, let these people handle what *they* knew.

And yet, staring at the half-finished glyph, she couldn't help but agree with Tommy—the glyph didn't *feel* old.

This whole room, in fact … it felt like it had been abandoned only hours earlier. Maybe even *minutes* earlier.

"Samira," O'Doyle called out, "come here, please."

He hadn't moved from his spot with Lybrand.

"He got you into this," Sam said quietly. "Didn't he."

Tommy paused a moment before answering. "He did. And he'll get us out of it, too."

Sam could tell Tommy wanted to believe that, wanted it desperately, but the words rang hollow.

"Go see what he wants," Tommy said. "I'll learn what I can here."

If she had been any place other than this, perhaps, she would probably have been offended. As if this person who'd known nothing about the Chaltélians until today could tell her something she hadn't learned after studying the culture for three years. But she had a feeling Tommy could do exactly that.

In that way, he reminded her of Veronica.

And there was the fact that Sam didn't really know one fucking thing about the Chaltélians. She hadn't even figured out that they weren't human. A curious third grader could probably deduce more than she could.

Fuck it. None of it mattered.

Sam walked to O'Doyle and Lybrand. They were both sipping from the straws on the inside-right of their helmets. Staying hydrated, just as Ramiro had told Sam to do what seemed like an eternity ago.

O'Doyle pointed to the cave walls, gesturing to the hundreds of carvings.

"We saw a room like this in Utah," he said. "But it wasn't clean like this. It was covered in graffiti."

Sam had a brief vision of teenage thrill seekers finding some hidden tunnel entrance, descending on a dare, spray-painting a priceless cultural treasure in the blind, wisdom-less existence of the angry youth.

"Graffiti?"

Lybrand nodded. "Yeah, really insane stuff. In all kinds of colors, covering carvings that looked a lot like these." She glanced at Sam. "So why isn't there graffiti here?"

Sam almost laughed. Lybrand wanted the opinion of an "expert," perhaps? Good luck with that, lady. Good fucking luck.

"I couldn't tell you," Sam said. "It's all new to me."

O'Doyle put a hand on the file floor, adjusted his position, wincing sharply when he did.

"No matter how little you think you know, it's more than I know," he said. "More than any of us know. If you're not going to sit down, then learn what you can, as fast as you can. Our lives will depend on it."

What if he was right? What if her knowledge of the symbols was the deciding factor in some critical situation? Sam could wallow in her pity party when they got out of here. Until then, she could do what she could to contribute.

"I'm on it," she said.

She walked back toward Tommy.

"Jee-sus *Christ*," Mullet called out. "And I thought MREs were bad. What is this slop?"

He sipped from his helmet straw. Sam saw the pale tan muck sliding through the clear tube.

"You've had worse things in your mouth," Skylark said. "I've seen the girls you've somehow talked into sleeping with you."

"Algeria," Tommy said. "Remember the *Prom Queen*, Mullet?"

Mullet spit out the tube. A little glob of brown goo fell on his chin.

"Fuck you guys," he said. "That was a bunch of bullshit. You should have been looking out for me."

Skylark laughed. "Oh, *she's the most beautifullest ever*. Remember saying that shit, Mullet?"

"*She's prettier than plum pudding*," Sleepy said. "I still don't really know that that means."

Sleepy hadn't moved an inch; either he'd woken up, or he'd never actually been asleep at all.

"You guys are total assholes." Mullet craned his head, tried to look at the glob on his chin. "God dammit. How am I supposed to get that off my face."

Skylark laughed again. "That's what Prom Queen said, right after she finished plucking those rope-length hairs from that bizarre forehead mole."

"Oh, please," Mullet said. "What about that time in Afghanistan where you banged the guy with two teeth, Marie? What about that?"

Sam tuned them out. Two miles underground, one ripped suit away from cooking to death, armed mercenaries on their tail, and these people were ripping on each other? Maybe it was their way of coping with the stress. Or maybe they were simple-minded idiots. Probably the latter—except for Tommy.

That man had some mental horsepower hidden under the hood, that much was for sure.

Sam studied the carvings, the glyphs beneath them. Almost immediately, a new pattern emerged. She saw a squiggle unique to all the glyphs accompanying images of animals. The same squiggle in glyphs accompanying landscapes, or images of plants. Did that mean *surface*? Or maybe it meant *Earth*.

Up near the ceiling, lines of glyphs in a row, with no images. That squiggle was in some of them.

And there, near the ceiling, larger than the rest ... was that the same symbol that had been on the tunnel wall near that hole in the floor?

Danger. That glyph meant *danger*.

"Sam," Tommy said. "Come look at this."

She drifted toward him, taking in information as she did. Three years of work weren't actually *wasted*, they'd just been waiting for a moment like this.

"Look here," Tommy said. He was next to the wall, running his hands over a set of carvings. "These are rocktopi killing animals and people."

The carvings were more stylized than the life-like animals on the other side of the cavern, but there was no mistaking a rocktopi using double-crescent knives to slash through the belly of a woman, a woman with an upturned arm, screaming in fear.

Glyphs below the scene, a row of them. The *danger* glyph second from the end. Sam saw one she recognized, both from the tunnels near the surface and from the walls in this cavern. She looked around, saw it, pointed.

"That means *people*," she said. "Or *human*, if there's a difference." She put her hand under an identical glyph below the woman being butchered.

Tommy looked to the glyph Sam had pointed to, then the scene of murder.

"You're right," he said, glancing around. He pointed to another glyph below the carving. "And I think this one means *kill*. It's in all the carvings showing a rocktopi killing something."

A rocktopi cutting up a deer. There was the *kill* glyph. the same for an image of a rocktopi killing a fox. And in an image of a tribesman driving a spear into a rocktopi.

Danger. Human. Kill.

"Holy shit," Sam said. "I think I finally understand their sentence structure. All of these are a descriptor, like *danger*, then a noun—*human*—then an action—*kill*."

Tommy's gaze flicked along the wall. His head twitched fast, like a bird trying to lock down the source of a sound.

"I think you're right," he said. "I can see what you're saying. It's consistent, even though I have no idea what most of these glyphs mean. Do you know what they mean?"

Sam shook her head. She had no idea what most of them meant, but that paled in comparison to what she'd just figured out. If they had the sentence structure right, given enough known references they could probably puzzle out the meaning of many glyphs via context, and—far more importantly—take a stab at the meaning of glyph chains.

"I need you to write down as many of these as you can," Sam said. "Prioritizing the verbs will help us figure out the rest. Let me get you some paper from my pack."

"I've got my own. I never leave home without it."

Tommy jogged to his backpack. Sam did the same, marveling at how her legs didn't feel quite as tired anymore.

She pulled her art pad and a pencil from her pack, started drawing as many glyphs as she could. She knew she didn't have much time.

A glance across the cavern at Tommy: He had a stubby pencil in one hand, a paperback novel in the other. *The Call of the Wild*, by Jack London.

She loved that book.

Sam focused on drawing glyphs, trying to discern their meaning from the context of the handful of symbols she now knew. As she drew, the magnitude of what she was doing blossomed inside her. Despite her grief, despite the nightmarish situation, she couldn't deny the explosive sensation of pure discovery.

The last three years of her life had not been wasted.

Without the body of knowledge she'd built up, she would never have made the connections she'd just made.

Yes, she'd missed the forest for the trees, missed the now-obvious fact that this was a non-human culture, but in that mental whiff had been the foundations for breakthrough.

A breakthrough *she* had made.

Not Veronica.

I'm going to get out of here, Ramiro. I'm going to make it. I'm going to bring all of this to light, and your name will be with mine on every paper, on the cover of every book. Through this, your name will live forever. I swear it.

The NoSeeUms got to their feet, started putting on their gear and grabbing their weapons. Sam looked at them, not understanding what was happening.

This time when Tommy appeared at her right, she didn't flinch.

"Pack up, fast," he said, *The Call of the Wild* still in his hand. "Klimas's hornet spotted silverbugs, six switchbacks back the way we came, headed in this direction."

He ran to the entrance, took the hornet vest that Klimas offered.

They were leaving. Sam glanced around the room, suffering a pang of loss not much different from what she'd felt at losing Ramiro. She'd always hoped to discover the Chaltélian Rosetta Stone—now that she'd found it, she had to leave it behind.

"Samira," O'Doyle called out in a quiet-yet-demanding tone. "Move your ass."

She ran to her backpack, wondering if she would ever see this place again.

"Changing up the order," O'Doyle said. "Mullet, Lybrand, Tommy and Curve up front. Klimas, Skylark, Sleepy in the rear. The rest with me. Move."

43

7,411 feet below the surface

THE PAINKILLER COCKTAIL made Angus feel sort of steady-state queasy. Not that bad, but it was always there, a little reminder that he wasn't well, that he was channeling better living through chemistry.

Now, though, it was all he could do to keep his churning stomach in check—and that wasn't because of the drugs.

When he'd designed the Wolves, he'd reveled in the thought of making the most advanced robot the world had ever seen. Better armored, stronger and more resilient than any machine, anywhere, made by any government or company, period. Slap a machine gun on that bitch. Lock and load. Give it autonomous target-determination ability.

He'd succeeded, fulfilled all the specs he'd envisioned, even greatly exceeded his initial targets for speed, agility, and independent decision-making ability.

Except he hadn't created a *robot*—he'd created a *war machine*.

Deflated rocktopi bodies littered the stone tiles. Puddles of yellow blood oozed out, spreading like animated Rorschach blots that eventually met and merged.

And what do you see in this picture?

I see death. Death, death, and more death.

The stone walls of the village's small structures had been smooth as glass. Now, many of them were pock-marked with bullet holes, splattered with sprays of yellow already drying to a pale orange.

Even the armed rocktopi had had no chance to defend themselves against Oberon. And only a few had been armed. Most rocktopi had run. Or tried to. Some of them weren't very fast—because they were smaller.

Children.

There was a word for what had happened here.

That word: *Massacre*.

Angus hadn't pulled the trigger. That didn't absolve him of responsibility, though, because he'd *designed* the trigger, he'd *built* the trigger, and he'd given permission for the trigger to pull itself.

As for his own weapon, Angus hadn't fired a shot. He'd hung back with Donnie, Fuentes and Khatari. The rest of the hired killers had done what they'd been hired to do—kill.

"Doctor," Donnie said, "what's the updated count on the Swarm-Storm?"

There had been 102 silverbugs in the village—far less than in that first encounter in the tunnel. That was the good news. The bad news was the swarmbot mechanical failure rate had jumped from 4.8 percent to 6.9 percent and would likely increase the hotter it got and the longer this campaign went on.

"We have just under seventy-two hundred bots left," Angus said.

Donnie nodded. "Better to use an asset too early than to die with it unused. Too bad a few of the aliens got away. I would have liked to prevent that."

Some of the rocktopi had run for the cavern walls, slid into cracks so narrow the mercs couldn't follow. Others had fled into a larger tunnel, the obvious main entrance to this place. At Donnie's command, Angus had sent Oberon after them.

A few of the aliens tried hiding in the stone structures. Donnie had ordered his men into those structures. *Houses*. That's what they were: Houses. The mercenaries had killed everything. Many had opted for knives instead of bullets—as Donnie said, *you never need to reload a knife*.

Angus heard men complaining that they hadn't been able to bring cell phones or cameras. Idiots. Gear like that probably wouldn't work in these temperatures. The men wanted visual proof of their kills. Donnie told them they'd just have to be satisfied with being able to buy any camera they could dream of with the money they would make when it was all said and done.

"Boss," Fuentes said, "you don't look so good."

"He's fine," Donnie said, before Angus could answer. "Helluva thing you built, Doctor Kool. If I'd had a machine like Oberon back in the day, I coulda won a war single-handedly. Shit, *two* wars."

Angus didn't know what wars Donnie was talking about. Angus didn't want to know.

He wondered if he should go into one of the houses. He knew he should. Seeing things that no human had ever seen; wasn't that his mantra? His ethos? His very fucking reason for existence?

Wasn't that why he'd come here in the first place?

Partially. Mostly. The money? Sure, being the richest person in history steered the vehicle, but adventure was the motor that turned the wheels.

Should he go in the houses? Should he see what was in there?

For the first time in his life, the answer was *no*, because he knew at least one thing that would be inside those buildings.

Bodies.

Massacred bodies.

A bit of movement caught his eye—a rivulet of yellow, flowing toward him, following the seams of the paving stones.

"Helluva thing," Donnie said. "This will make one amazing story, Doctor."

The man was grinning. *Smiling*.

"You're enjoying this," Angus said.

Donnie nodded. "I suppose I am. It's rare to get an op with such clean-cut rules of engagement. No ifs, ands, or buts about the rules here—if it isn't human, kill it." He glanced at Angus. "Specimens exempted, of course. I'm guessing eventually the story will get out to the general public. With this many people involved, you can't keep a thing a secret forever. If it does, think about the significance. A historic military accomplishment on par with Hannibal crossing the alps. Or Waterloo. Or Yorktown."

Angus couldn't believe the shit pouring out of this man's mouth.

"Or My Lai," Angus said. "Or maybe No Gun Ri or Bandah."

Donnie's smile faded. "A student of military history, are we?"

Angus shrugged. Somewhere in his past, he'd read a random list of war crimes. Like most bits of information, he'd internalized it without a second thought. A powerful memory often went hand-in-hand with genius.

The rivulet of yellow slowly drew closer, now only a few feet away.

"I'm going to make sure this encampment is cleared out," Donnie said. "Put the next five minutes to use and figure out where we're going next. If you want to take that time to paint a peace sign on your armor, go right ahead, but once you're done, forget those liberal candy-ass concepts of yours. Top off Oberon's ammo. We need to secure this entire complex, which means we eliminate any and all enemy combatants."

Donnie walked toward the houses.

"*Enemy combatants*," Angus said quietly. "Hardly."

He'd been so worried about Donnie working behind his back that he hadn't bothered to consider what kind of a man Donnie was all on his own. Him working with June July was a danger—him being utterly unbalanced was possibly just as bad.

"I've been part of some tough stuff in my day," Fuentes said. "Nothing like this."

Khatari gave him a curious look. "You never killed civilians before?"

Fuentes looked down. "I didn't say that. Shit happens. Just—" he gestured to the village "—not like this."

"It is what it is," Khatari said. "Like Donnie told us, we could have gone back. We didn't. Now, we finish the job."

The man coughed, leaned a hand on Angus's exosuit. The man was hurting. Join the club.

"My stuff is on the hauler," Angus said. "Got some fentanyl lozenges in my backpack, front outer pocket. Help yourself."

Khatari nodded, stood on his own. "That'll be just the thing."

He headed for the hauler BaDonkeyDonks.

Angus looked down. The yellow rivulet reached the tile upon which he stood. The fluid didn't follow the seam, it flowed up over the tile's edge, slowly spread in an expanding arc. Angus took a half step to the right—the fluid oozed across the space where his exosuited foot had just been.

His HUD beeped and flashed, drawing his attention away from the carnage.

Info from the leading edge of the still-expanding, still-mapping BlackBugs. Sound anomaly. Angus played the recording. The clicking of silverbugs, but rhythmic, regular.

He'd heard that pattern before.

Angus opened up his direct channel.

"Donnie, this is Angus. I think the silverbugs are tracking O'Doyle's team."

44

11,012 feet below the surface

A THICK SOUND. Constant. Unwavering.

Bertha knew what it was. The memory of that sound chilled her, made it hard to speak. She held up a fist, telling the men behind her to stop.

"Power plant, maybe," Mullet said. "For lights, like we saw in that cavern. An *alien fucking power plant*. If you'd have told me a month ago that I'd not only say that, but been totally serious about it, I'd have asked how much crack you were smoking."

The familiar roar, distant yet echoing, a sound like she was standing near a metal culvert back home in New Jersey as spring rains made streams swell and churn and rush.

She turned to face Mullet. Behind him, Curveball, and further back, Worm.

"It's a river," she said.

Mullet's face wrinkled. He looked at her like she had a dick growing out of her forehead.

"A *river*? Underground?"

Even now this guy was being an ass. He'd probably come out of the womb that way.

"Of course there are underground rivers, Mullet," Worm said. "But I didn't expect to see one this far below ground."

Did Worm know something about geology? The guy seemed to know something about everything.

"We saw one in Utah," Bertha said. "Trust me."

Mullet snorted. "Don't even know you, lady. And I'm a damn far sight from trusting you."

Bertha keyed her *talk* button. "Patrick, come in."

Mullet rolled his eyes. "Can't you just call him *Ender* like everyone else?"

She still wasn't sure what that nickname meant. She wasn't sure she *wanted* to know.

Patrick's voice, crackling from distance: "This is Ender, go ahead."

He was even calling himself by that name. Slipping back into old ways, maybe?

"I hear a river," Bertha said.

"Any way around it?"

"Unknown at this time."

Patrick: "Keep moving forward. The silverbugs at our rear don't seem to have detected us, but they're in random wandering mode. If we don't keep moving they'll see us in minutes."

"Affirmative, moving out," Bertha said.

THE CLOSER THEY came, the more recognizable the sound became.

"That's a river, all right," Mullet said. "Sounds like a rager at that."

Bertha reached the next switchback, looked back to Worm. He nodded; the way was clear.

She hadn't seen a rocktopi since they'd hit that last big tunnel branch. Luck? Patrick had made the final decision which way to go, but he'd based that choice on Sam and Worm's input. Mullet was an ass, Curveball was damn near a waste of space, but Worm seemed solid.

The hornets were a huge asset, but Bertha wasn't betting her life on them; she slowly, carefully looked around the switchback corner. Nothing but a night-vision view of rock and silt in that segment of tunnel. More often than not, that's all there was to see—nothing.

She moved around the corner, Mullet right behind her.

"So, you and Ender," he said. "How did *that* happen?"

The emphasis on *that*—maybe he didn't have the balls to say it, but Bertha knew what he meant.

She stopped, turned.

"You mean how did someone as ugly as me wind up with Patrick?"

Mullet flashed his already-too-familiar expression of indignation.

"Now hold on there, sister, it was an honest question. I know we're dealing with aliens and shit, but these tunnels are a tad boring, you know? Just making conversation."

"I'm not concerned with *conversation*. My love life isn't important. Shut up and do your job."

She turned away from him, continued on. She hadn't taken ten steps before she again heard Mullet's whisper.

"So, you and Ender—how did *that* happen?"

She wanted to kick him in the balls.

"Are you just going to keep asking me until I answer you?"

"Inquiring minds want to know."

Bertha sighed. "We met in Utah. We hit it off. Everyone else died. We survived. That good enough?"

Mullet's only response was a *hmmmmm* sound, as if Bertha's answer was, indeed, *not* good enough. This guy hadn't seen or even spoken to Patrick in how many years, and he thought his take on things mattered?

A rustle of fabric and equipment; Worm slid past Mullet.

"Two switchbacks up is a longer tunnel, about a hundred meters," he said. "Then we have this."

He knelt, held up his chest monitor.

On the screen, Bertha saw the end of the longer tunnel segment ended in a vertical crack, maybe fifteen meters high. Beyond it, a lighted space, obviously larger than the tunnel.

"From the sound of things, that crack leads to the river," Worm said.

"Can't tell how big that space is," Mullet said. "Send the drone in further."

Bertha shook her head. "Bad idea. In Utah, where there was light, there were rocktopi."

"Such a dumb name," Mullet said. "Anyone else think *rocktopi* is the dumbest name ever?"

Worm guided the hornet a bit closer to the crack.

"Let's not debate nomenclature right now," he said. He looked at Bertha. "Mullet's right, though—we need to see what's in there. The rest of the column is right behind us, and Ender won't want to turn back."

He could have just flown the drone forward. Instead, he was deferring to her, because Patrick had put her in charge of the advance team.

Mullet aimed his patented wrinkle-face expression on Worm.

"We're letting Ender's girlfriend make the call? Seriously."

"She was right about the river," Worm said. "She's fought this enemy before. We haven't."

Mullet considered, then shrugged. Both men looked at her; they were waiting for her to decide what to do next. Curveball was a few feet back in the tunnel, but he didn't seem to care what happened next.

The hornet had shown no silverbugs. Bertha could have Worm fly the drone out the crack, but with that much light, anything on the other side—silverbug or rocktopi—might see it. The movement alone could draw attention, and she had a feeling there *was* something past that crack.

"Put the hornet on the deck," she said.

Worm worked the controller. "It's down. Camera still on."

"We're moving closer," Bertha said. "Run silent from here on out."

She continued down the tunnel, not waiting for Mullet's response. A fast glance back; he was following along, a few steps behind her. Then Worm, then Curveball. Other than the *scritch-scratch* of their boots grinding on small rocks and sand, the four of them moved in almost total silence.

Bertha knew she should have been more scared than she was, but she had a job to do and she was going to do it.

She carefully turned the corner of the second switchback. Enough light coming through the crack to see without the KoolSuit's night vision, so she turned it off. The crack was a hundred meters away.

Bertha waited, watched. No movement. Other than the river's roar, there was no sound.

She moved forward at a crouch, making sure she had firm footing for each step. She didn't have to look back anymore—she knew Mullet was a few feet behind her. Maybe he was an asshole, but he was a pro.

The hornet sat on the tunnel silt, ten meters from the crack. Bertha waved Worm forward. He picked it up, put it in his chest case to recharge. When he had his second hornet in hand, ready to be deployed, he nodded.

Bertha moved to the opening. She put her back against the right side of the tunnel wall. The cavern ceiling was at least fifty feet above. Slowly, so slowly, she inched toward the edge of the crack. The river's roar told her the churning water was somewhere to the right. In front of her, to the tunnel's left, she saw a sprawling, open space. Were those … trees? Yes, trees, with thick, yellow leaves and round spots of blue.

Fruit.

Crops, maybe … but no movement.

Bertha knelt, looked back at Mullet. He had his carbine to his shoulder, suppressor-tipped barrel angled down and away from her. He nodded.

She leaned out just enough to look right.

Rocktopi, two of them. Twenty meters away. Colors flashing, but muted, not as bright as the ones she'd seen earlier or those she'd fought in Utah. Other than a slight waving of extended pseudopods, the two rocktopi weren't moving. Just past them, a big object, long and pointed, obviously metal, but burnished with scratches and scrapes. Maybe twenty feet long, with steep sides almost as tall as the rocktopi.

A canoe.

Were the two rocktopi guarding it?

Just past the canoe, the river. Mullet had been right: it was a "rager."

She couldn't see much of it, as the river was a sluice cut into the stone and sand of the uneven cavern floor. In places, she saw white water spraying up from submerged rocks. A strong current. A *dangerous* current. The river was at least forty feet wide. On the far shore, more trees. Plenty of space to hide, but she saw no movement there, either. The river flowed to the cavern wall, where it vanished into a wide, dark space.

There had been a river in the Utah tunnels, too, but far different than this. That one had been nothing more than a slash through stone, a miniature Grand Canyon with a rock roof. This seemed more … pastoral, like a small farm on the outskirts of a large town.

Bertha leaned back into the tunnel. She held up two fingers. A pair of enemies, but how to communicate what they were without making any noise? She held up her hand, wiggled all her fingers at once. A poor impression of a rocktopi's tentacles, but she felt a bit of relief when Mullet and Worm looked at each other and mimicked the gesture. They smiled at her, understanding—*two rocktopi*. Curveball nodded once. Worm put the hornet in his chest case, freeing both of his hands for his carbine.

Patrick's voice in her headset, clipped and intense but also clearer—he was closer.

"Bertha, this is Ender, we've been spotted by the silverbugs. They're forming a line. We're coming your way, fast."

In the background, she could hear the distant *click-click-click* of the little machines.

The silverbugs had formed lines in Utah, twitching in unison, a sickening dance that meant a wave of killer rocktopi were on the way.

Two of the bastards in front, Lord knew how many behind.

A simple choice.

She pressed her *talk* button.

"We're at the river," she whispered. "Two rocktopi. We'll take them out."

There might be more than two. She'd find out soon enough.

Bertha gave her carbine's suppressor a nervous twist, making sure it was tight, then tucked the stock to her shoulder. She glanced at Mullet, Worm and Curveball. All three nodded—they were ready to follow her out.

She took a deep breath, let it out slow. A hand on her left shoulder: Mullet, letting her know exactly where he was and what area he would cover. She raised the barrel of her carbine, then stepped around the corner.

She sighted the rocktopi on the left as she took five quick steps—she wanted to make sure her squad mates had clear fields of fire before she shot.

The two rocktopi moved away from each other, seemed to explode with color: blazing magenta, intense purple, neon green. Tentacles waved in unmistakable alarm. They each held something, something with long, parallel metal pipes—guns of some kind, coming up, coming to bear on her and her squad.

Without altering her pace, Bertha fired a three-shot burst, her suppressor dropping the gun's roar to a sharp *whock* sound. The first rocktopi shivered as bullets sent red rings spreading across its soft surface. She kept walking, steadily closing the distance as she fired another three-shot burst. To her left, she heard the *whock-whock-whock* of Mullet's carbine, but her focus never wavered from her target.

Her target staggered back on boneless limbs. The strange weapon slipped from its grasp.

Bertha fired a third burst. Yellow blood spurted. The creature sagged. Tentacle legs shortened, then reabsorbed into the body in a way she could only think was the rocktopi equivalent to a man's knees giving out on him.

She found herself a few feet from the enemy, as if she'd floated there. The creature's bright colors were already fading. Black spots seemed to focus on her—impossible, as the eyes were a solid black with no pupils of any kind, yet there was no mistaking the sensation.

And in that thousand-eyed gaze, she felt the creature's pain. Its panic. Its terror.

It budded a trembling pseudopod, extended it toward her.

She kicked the strange weapon aside, pulled her carbine's stock tight to her shoulder, aimed down, and fired another three-shot burst.

Next to her, Mullet did the same.

The creature stopped moving. Almost instantly, its color faded to a dirty white.

Her target was down.

A glance left: Mullet had taken out his target as well.

Sighting down the barrel, Bertha swept her weapon in a shallow angle in front of her—no movement.

"Clear in front," she said.

"Clear left," Mullet said.

"Clear right," Curveball said.

"Clear behind," Worm said.

Bertha lowered her barrel. Two dead rocktopi, deflated, leaking yellow fluid.

She quickly ejected her magazine, stashed it in her webbing, loaded a fresh one. With the enemy neutralized, she was able to get a better look at the cavern. Perhaps half the size of a football field. High above, in the arched, rocky ceiling, a light so bright she couldn't look directly at it.

The water flowed from her right to her left. Over the course of centuries, perhaps millennia, the grit-filled water had sliced downward through the rock like a bandsaw through wood. Some parts of the shore were nearly vertical, showing sedimentary lines, stacked pages of ages gone by. In other places, those walls had collapsed and crumbled, creating steep slopes of broken rock and dark sand.

Another orchard on the river's far bank. The trees there were different: no leaves she could see, but rather greenish-blue clusters that looked like colored cauliflower.

"Those trees on the other shore are fucked up," Mullet said. "Like broccoli from Frankenstein's lab or something."

Bertha examined the canoe. Long and wide, with high thick walls and a mostly flat bottom. Inside, four oars. The shafts were curved, with strange handholds carved into them, but there was no mistaking their purpose.

Worm stood next to her. "Can't row against that current." He pointed to the left, to where the river slid into the cavern wall, into darkness. "Chains mounted there. The creatures must use those to pull the boat upstream."

She saw the chains—probably platinum, of course, crusted and coated with a yellowish mold, mounted to the cavern wall by metal rings.

Bertha pressed her *talk* button: "Patrick, we've secured the cavern at the river, proceed through the crack at the end of the long tunnel segment."

Patrick: "Roger that."

"Ender," Mullet said, "you see any man-eating trees in Utah? We got some frankenbroccoli here and I don't like the looks of it."

"Mullet, shut up," Worm said. "Focus on the situation at hand. Let's check out their weapons."

He gingerly picked up one of the alien rifles, if that's what they were. Two parallel poles—each pole lined with thick points, like big rose thorns—leading into an oval-shaped base made of gleaming hexagonal tiles.

"A shotgun of some kind, maybe," Bertha said. "Double-barreled."

Tommy shook his head. "The poles are solid. There's a small opening between them in the … forestock, or lower receiver, maybe you'd call it. Could be for a beam of some kind, but it's more likely the opening is for metal slugs and the poles are conductive. I think this is a railgun."

"Railguns, alien blasters, whatever," Mullet said. "Good thing they were so slow on the draw. If these two were soldiers, their soldiering skills sucked balls."

He had his carbine to his shoulder, was slowly sweeping the barrel across the left side of the cavern. Curveball was doing the same to the right.

Worm lifted the alien weapon once, twice, as if to gauge the weight.

"You and Ender told us they didn't have guns."

An edge to his voice.

"They didn't," Bertha said. "Just the knives. And rocks. We didn't see anything like this."

Worm tried pulling the oval end to his shoulder, but there was no stock, no flat surface.

He frowned. "I don't see a trigger or a button or anything."

"Put it down," Curveball said, still scanning his area. "Before it blows up on us."

Worm set the weapon carefully on the cavern floor, next to the deflated bag of off-white skin that had been a living being only minutes before.

"*Movement,*" Mullet said. "In the trees behind us."

Bertha shouldered her carbine and spun, sighted down the barrel toward the orchard. In the strange trees, the light from above reflected off moving bits of metal.

"Silverbugs," she said. "Shit."

They crawled out, moving one moment, then as still as an inanimate statue. A sinking feeling of déjà vu … Bertha knew what would come next.

The silverbugs started jerking up and down in unison.

Patrick in her headset: "We're coming out, silverbugs in pursuit. Figure out where we're going."

"I don't like this," Mullet said. "There's at least fifty of those things. Should we start taking them out?"

Bertha had a feeling it was already too late for that. The silverbugs likely spread far back through the orchard, probably leading to an opening hidden by the orderly rows of trees. They could shoot the silverbugs they saw, wasting ammo as they did, and still not take out enough to stop the mass of them from signaling.

"The canoe," Worm said.

She looked back at him. "We don't know where the river goes."

"It goes away from here," Worm said.

She glanced at the canoe, then at the roiling river sliding into the darkness. Two choices—stand and fight against an enemy of unknown strength, or take a big canoe down a river that could lead to rapids, waterfalls, or, possibly, another enemy force, also of unknown strength.

Damned if she did. Damned if she didn't.

"Curve," she said, "help Tommy drop the canoe in the water. Tie it off first."

She turned toward the orchard, kept her carbine aimed at the silverbugs as Worm and Curveball worked the canoe. She heard Curveball grunting, the sound of metal grinding against dirt and rock.

"Fucker's heavy," Curveball said. "Worm, hurry up with the rope."

Bertha saw Sonny, Sam, Otto and Sleepy come running out of the tunnel opening. They sprinted toward her.

Bertha's guts locked up. Her muscles froze. *Where was Patrick?*

Then he, Klimas and Skylark came out together, Skylark running awkwardly as she kept looking down at her chest monitor, her drone controller in one hand. Patrick and Klimas stopped, turned, fired back into the tunnel, the sound of their suppressed weapons drowned out by the river.

Sleepy and Otto stopped, turned back to face the tunnel, waited.

Patrick and Klimas sprinted away from the opening.

Behind her, Bertha heard the heavy canoe splash into the water.

A wave of silverbugs poured out of the tunnel, scurried and scrambled after Patrick and Klimas. Their combined *click-click* was so loud she heard it over the river's roar.

Bertha sighted in as Sleepy and Otto opened up, trying to provide cover, but there was no point—there were *hundreds* of the things, legs flashing, spreading out like a metal flood.

She angled her barrel down.

"Mullet, Worm, get in the canoe," she said. "Get everyone aboard or we're screwed!"

Sonny and Sam ran past her.

The orchard *erupted* with silverbugs. They poured forth, a clattering, glimmering, moving carpet that swelled and joined with the thick stream pouring out of the tunnel.

Bertha stepped to the river's edge. The canoe was below the ground level, a rope tied to the prow held taut by Curveball, who strained and leaned back against the current's invisible pull. Sonny and Sam were already in. No benches, just a flat metal deck. Worm was in there as well, reaching up to help Skylark step down off the shore's edge.

Only ten feet from the shore, Patrick skidded to a stop, turned and fired at the oncoming mass of platinum. Bertha switched to single fire, stood at his shoulder as Otto and Klimas ran past them toward the canoe.

Bertha fired twice, each shot kicking up a puff of black smoke from a silverbug that tumbled and rolled. Her kills vanished instantly beneath the twitching, rushing wave.

Mullet: "Ender, Lybrand, *let's go!*"

As one, they turned and ran the short distance to the canoe. Patrick stepped off the edge, lurched suddenly, grabbing at his back, his carbine swinging from its harness. Bertha reached for him, but he was already falling into the canoe—off-balance, she tumbled off the edge—her helmet *cracked* against the gunwale.

She splashed into the water.

In an instant, she felt the river's impossible power, instantly pulling at her, sweeping her away, its strength undeniable...

...a hand grabbed her vest, yanked her back. She looked up, saw Sleepy and Otto reaching out. They hauled her up and in.

"We got you."

Her head screamed, filled with dull thunder. She felt at her chest for her carbine, found it. She pushed the hands off her, straightened her helmet, and sat up.

The canoe was moving down the river—*fast.*

Patrick was in the middle of the vessel, on one knee, his teeth gritted, his face a mask of agony.

The *whocks* of suppressed gunfire.

The sound of the river's deep churn.

A screaming cacophony of silverbug clicks.

"Oh, fuck me," she heard Sonny say.

She looked to the riverbank—what she saw didn't seem possible.

Like a wave of platinum ants, the silverbugs had poured over the shore's edge and spread out onto the water. Anchored by the mass clinging to the riverbank, the machines locked legs, stretched across the river's undulating surface, a floating mat that resisted the current. Hundreds more silverbugs crawled across their backs, dropping into the water to become the leading edge of the swarm, a metallic tongue stretching toward the canoe, stretching *faster* than the canoe moved.

Bertha lifted her carbine, switched to auto, and fired at the oncoming floating mass. Bullets hammered the machines, making some of them twitch and fall away to splash into the water.

Klimas, on her right, did the same.

Mullet, on her left.

The concentrated fire slowed the stretching tongue. The canoe started to pull away.

Then it slammed into a rock, throwing Bertha backward. She tumbled into Sam, fell in a tangle at Curveball's feet. He tried to maintain his balance even as he fought with the curved oar. The canoe rocked and heaved beneath her.

Bertha heard Sonny scream. She pushed herself up, saw him at the back of the canoe, two silverbugs crawling on him. Otto grabbed at one, threw it aside, even as more poured over the gunwale.

"*Hold on,*" Worm shouted, then the boat crashed into another rock, sending Bertha flying sideways into someone.

She pushed herself to one elbow in time to see Samira Jabour fall, hit hard against the canoe's edge, then tumble over the side.

In the next breath, Worm dove in after her.

"*Man overboard,*" Mullet shouted, but it was already too late—the current had the canoe, and there was no stopping it.

Bertha got to her knees as a silverbug crawled in front of her. She grabbed a leg and threw the machine over the side. She saw one on Sonny's back, grabbed it and tossed it overboard as well.

She heard men shouting and screaming, then all went dark as the canoe slipped into the chasm.

45

9,149 FEET BELOW THE SURFACE

A DOUBLE-DOSE OF Adderall did wonders for one's mood.

"Doctor Kool, the loss of scrambling worries me," Donnie said. "I really, *really* do not like knowing automated mobile units could be waiting for us, or even watching us now."

The man was wearing on Angus. What did Dimwit think, that Angus could just snap his fingers and shit out an invention or two?

"I told you before the mission, they adapt," Angus said.

He held little hope of figuring out the silverbugs' new communication technique. During Donnie's marching breaks—which were few and far between—Angus had tried modifying the SwarmStorm's scramble tech to cover all radio frequencies, but doing so weakened the unified signal. Even if the tiny machines were hitting the right frequency, they might not have enough power to overwhelm it.

What he needed was a captured silverbug or two, and time to experiment. He had neither.

It was disappointing to lose the ability to mess with the silverbugs' communication system, but he wasn't surprised. They'd figured out how to beat the scrambling in Utah; it made sense that they would figure it out here as well. That was part of the reason for designing the Swarm-Storm in the first place—they could hunt based on movement alone. Scrambling was a *nice-to-have*, but not a *need-to-have*.

An alert flashed in his HUD—a message from the BlackBugs.

"Hold up," Angus said. "I think I've got something."

Donnie raised a fist. The merc column stopped.

Angus felt itchy all over. No way to scratch. He'd figure out how to address that in the V-3 KoolSuit. For now, there was nothing he could do but suffer.

He listened to the sounds sent back by the BlackBugs.

The incessant *click-click-click* of silverbugs, jerking in unison, but also something else. Distant, hard to hear with the echo effect and all the silverbug noise.

His heart thumped. Was he hearing that right?

He eye-tracked through the menu, rewinding the sound, playing it again.

Yes, he'd heard it right—gunfire.

"I've got O'Doyle's location," Angus said. "He's on the move, but he's close."

"How close?" Donnie asked.

Angus switched to Oberon's view: Stone tunnel walls, silt-covered rocky floor. No movement. The BlackBug-generated map showed there were no branches between Oberon and the location of the gunfire.

"I don't know," Angus said. "Within two thousand. We've got to get him before he gets away."

The chance to kill Patrick O'Doyle … it was almost overpowering. It wasn't like murdering baby rocktopi—O'Doyle was a trained killer, one who had left Angus to die.

"Fourth Platoon, prepare to advance in the lead," Donnie said. "All teams, we're moving forward double-time, hostiles ahead."

Double-time? What was that, a fucking brisk walk?

"We need to *run*," Angus said. "If the tunnels branch again, O'Doyle could get away."

Like he'd done up on the plateau. Angus wanted that man *dead*.

"We will move forward under control," Donnie said. "We're not going to split our forces."

Another sound file came back from the BlackBugs. Gunfire, again, but not as loud—O'Doyle was pulling away.

No. Not this time, you big, dumb, one-eared fuck. This time you're going down.

"Fuck it," Angus said. "Catch up when you can. I'm sending my Wolf after him."

"What?" Donnie grabbed Angus's armored hand. "Kool, we don't want to—"

Angus ran forward, leaving Donnie behind. As he moved past the Recon Team, who pressed to the walls to get out of his way, he switched to verbal commands.

"Oberon—*sic 'em.*"

46

11,407 feet below the surface

SONNY LAY ON his side in the middle of the canoe, hugging his knees tight to his chest. All around him in the absolute darkness, sounds that he wanted to *go away*—the roar of a river, magnified by a stone ceiling close above; the shouts of people fighting for their lives, calling out to each other for help; the *plunk* of silverbugs splashing into the water; the incessant noise of little feet scratching on metal.

click-click … click-click-click

The boat shifted and tilted, pitched and lurched unpredictably as it raced through rapids, thumping against rocks. Sonny was tossed this way and that. Boots kicked against his back, his ribs, the top of his head, as people tried to fight by feel alone.

"*Get them overboard!*" Otto's voice, deeper than everyone's except O'Doyle's.

Someone kicked his forehead. Sonny tucked tighter, pressing his eyes into his knees.

A foot thumped into his back, and he felt someone fall over him, heard that someone land hard.

"Get this fucking thing off of me!"

That was Curveball—he hadn't said much since that other one, Hatchet, had died.

More *plunks*, fewer *clicks*.

Then, weight on him, pressing down, weight and *heat*. Sharp jabs of little hooks punching through his clothes and his KoolSuit, into his skin. So hot he felt it through his suit, felt it *burning*.

He tried to call for help, but his mouth wouldn't open. Not even breath would come.

Hands, feeling across his shoulder.

The weight lifting off of him, the little hooks ripping skin and fabric alike before they were finally torn free.

One final *plunk*, then a moment of tense stillness.

The river sounded like a stereo tuned to static and cranked up to max volume.

"Prow is clear," Otto said.

"Stern is clear," Klimas said.

"Amidships clear," someone said, a slower, more resonant tone. Was that the preacher? *Sleepy*, they called him.

A *boom* as the boat smacked into another rock, skidded off and kept going.

"Sound off." O'Doyle sounded even gruffer than normal, sounded like he was in pain.

Sonny heard them calling out: *Skylark, Mullet, Sleepy, Otto, Klimas, Curveball, Lybrand*. He was surprised that he already recognized most of their voices. The madness of this place, making some bit of his brain lock in details about people who would mean the difference between him living or dying.

"Bookworm, Jabour, McGuiness," O'Doyle said. "Sound off."

"Jabour fell overboard," Lybrand said. "Worm dove in after her, before we got into this tunnel."

"Search for them," Mullet said. "They've got to be near us. Skylark, get that hornet in the air."

"Hornet's gone," Skylark said. "Never made it out of that tunnel. I'm out of drones."

Sonny tried to speak, could not. His ears worked fine; his mouth had other ideas.

A headlamp flicked on, then another. Sonny sensed the brightness through his closed eyes.

Sonny felt a hand on his hip.

"McGuiness is here," Otto said. "Seems okay."

Tense stillness.

The roar of the river.

Another jostling lurch as the canoe careened off another rock. Bodies thumped against the canoe bottom. People grunted and cursed.

"Anyone see them?" O'Doyle asked.

A chorus of *negative*.

Sonny couldn't help them look. And why bother? In these waters, if those two had gone overboard they were dead. The boat surged upward, then dropped down like a broken elevator only to slam hard a split-second later.

"Curveball, Sleepy, get on those oars," O'Doyle said, his words tight, forced. "Klimas, take the prow, call out directions. The rest of you, keep looking for our people, they had to be swept in here along with us."

The ceiling was only a few feet above the canoe. Sonny could sense it, sense that it might be close enough to stretch his arm up and touch. He didn't dare reach out to confirm. With his eyes closed, he could at least pretend he was still in the wide-open spaces.

The darkness, the *closeness*, crushing him, compressing him.

A hand on his shoulder, firm, strong.

"You okay?"

Sonny blinked his eyes open, squinted at the multiple headlamps flicking across the boat—Otto was kneeling over him.

"I am the fucking opposite of *okay*," Sonny said.

"Sit up. You might have suit tears. Anywhere feel hot?"

"Shoulders and arms, where that thing was on me," Sonny said. "And on my back. Feels like it's burning."

Otto scooted behind him. Sonny felt the man's hands slide under his shirt.

"A couple of small tears in your KoolSuit," Otto said. "We have to patch them. And this—" he pressed his palms lightly against Sonny's back.

Sonny winced, arched his back away. "Sorry," Otto said. "You got a big hole there."

"Feels like I been branded or something."

"Suit's not torn there," Otto said. "Not sure what happened."

"The little fuckers heated up like crazy," Mullet said. "That's what happened. My gloves melted, I had to use my spares."

"Same with me," Lybrand said. "And the silverbug I pulled off Curveball tore my forearms all to hell. The silverbug temps exceeded the suit's tolerances. Everyone, check your suit integrity. Patch up, fast."

Otto slid Sonny's shirt off. Sonny let the man do it, as if he was a child, unable to take care of himself. He might as well be a child—he could barely move.

Sonny closed his eyes, whispered a silent prayer to be back on the surface again.

"Anyone not patching, keep searching," O'Doyle said.

Sonny felt a body sliding past him, opened his eyes long enough to see it was Lybrand, closed them again.

"You're hurt," she said. "Is it your—"

"Keep searching," O'Doyle said, his words clipped and angry. "They're out there."

Talking to his woman in that tone of voice? Wasn't going to end well for him. Sonny tried to think of his own past lovers to take his mind off the close air that seemed to crush him, felt Otto's hands moving him this way and that, decided to think about something *other* than lovers.

Talk. He needed to talk, to say something, anything.

"I can't take this shit anymore," he said.

His words wavered, trembled. He didn't sound like himself. Tough-as-nails Sonny. Adventurous Sonny. That guy was nowhere to be found. That guy was the ghost of a man who walked *on* mountains, not *under* them.

"You can take it," Otto said quietly. "You can, and you will. You don't have any other choice."

The man's hands worked the boiling spot on Sonny's back. Even when the suit was patched, that one was going to hurt something awful.

"You don't understand," Sonny said. "I can't handle these tight spaces. I *can't.*"

How had this happened? Glowing aliens. Clawing robots. *Miles* below ground. And Angus's killers, probably down here somewhere, looking to kill everyone that wasn't on their little team.

Sonny knew he was going to die down here. Die horribly. It was only a matter of time.

Had it been worth it? O'Doyle's pet project promised big money. Game-changing money. Enough for Sonny to live the rest of his days like a king. Enough to set up huge endowments for the charities he'd donated to most of his life. His money would send poor kids to college, help provide paralyzed war veterans with medical care and rehab, give new resources to the universities he'd partnered with for his various explorations.

"Old man, get your head right," Otto whispered. "You don't have any choice. I will not leave you behind, so if you don't sack up and be strong, you'll get *me* killed. Now, sit up and check your suit for tears. Check all over."

Otto moved off. Sonny did as he was told; he sat up, started feeling himself all over, looking for any tears that Otto might have missed.

Sonny reached to the top of his visor, flicked on his headlamp. He glanced around. The ceiling wasn't even five feet above, the uneven rock whipping past. Nine people in a benchless canoe that would have held ten comfortably. Headlamp beams searching the water all around. People tending to each other, dressing small wounds and patching small tears in KoolSuits.

People were calling out for *Worm*, for *Tommy*, for *Sam*. The roiling water had no answer.

"What do you mean *they had guns?*" O'Doyle said. "What kind of guns?"

Sonny looked O'Doyle's way. His face was scrunched up with pain. Lybrand was behind him, her hand on the small of his back, pushing hard.

"We don't know," Lybrand said. "We killed them before they could shoot at us. Worm looked at the weapons. He didn't see a way to fire them."

"So we don't even know if they *were* guns," O'Doyle said.

"Give me fucking break, Ender," Mullet said. "The things were long and pointy, and the walking bags of day-glow barf tried to aim them at us. They were *weapons.* Tommy thought they were railguns, maybe."

O'Doyle let out a small grunt of pain, one he choked off almost instantly, as if he didn't want to let the tough soldiers know he wasn't made of iron. Sonny had been like that once, when he'd been younger. Younger and tougher. Although Young Sonny had never been trapped two miles underground. Sonny wondered how Young Sonny would have handled it.

O'Doyle moved away from Lybrand.

"If they were weapons," he said, "you should have grabbed one."

"We were a little *busy,*" Mullet said.

"Quit arguing," Klimas said. "There's rapids ahead."

Klimas was in the front of the canoe. A half-dozen headlamps swung to light up his back and the river beyond.

"*Rapids?*" Mullet moved toward the prow. "What the hell do you think we're in now?"

Sonny risked a look out front, instantly wished he hadn't. Up ahead, rushing towards them, a boiling cauldron of white froth. And just at the edge of his sight, a drop-off into blackness.

Sonofabitch.

Sonny closed his eyes and returned to his fetal position.

"That's a waterfall," Curveball said. "Everyone get ropes, tie off to each other!"

The canoe came alive with activity. Sonny didn't move. He couldn't. He felt someone wrapping a rope around his waist, assumed it was Otto. The rope cinched tight.

"Ten seconds," Klimas called out. "Curve, Sleepy, straighten us out. Pull those oars in before we go over."

"Lights off," O'Doyle barked. "Switch to night vision. We don't know what's at the bottom. Switch to open channel, leave it on. If we go under, sound off when you're on the surface."

The boat thudded against another unseen object, skewed to the right.

"*Oars in,*" Klimas said. "Hold on tight!"

Someone lay down on top of Sonny, someone heavy.

"I got you, old timer," Otto said.

Before Sonny could say anything in response, he felt the canoe tip forward, and then he was falling.

47

11,012 Feet below the Surface

TOMMY STRYMON GRIPPED the chain with one hand, held tight to an unconscious Samira Jabour with the other. He stayed as low as he could, river pulling at his body, wet stone at his back, eyes behind his face shield barely above the churning surface. His head and left shoulder rang with dull pain. In the darkness, he'd misjudged where the chain was, and the powerful current had slammed him against the stone wall. The impact had rung his bell something fierce, but he'd gripped the chain and held on, and hadn't lost his grip on Sam.

He wrapped his elbow inside the chain, freeing his hand to push his *talk* button.

"Ender, this is Worm," Tommy whispered. "Come in."

No response.

"Ender, come in."

Still no response. Not even a crackle of static.

The others were too far downstream.

He and Sam were alone.

Tommy released the button, unsure if the machines could detect the radio signal or not. He stayed very still. He observed.

A thick mat of silverbugs floated on the river's surface, thin legs interlinked, the mat anchored by hundreds of the small machines that remained on dry ground. Fire ants used a similar strategy to avoid drowning during floods. The silverbugs' round bodies were apparently watertight.

Had the machines spotted him?

Tommy had watched them swarm into the canoe, seen Sam try to avoid one only to step on another—her ankle had rolled under her. She'd fallen hard, smacking her helmet against the canoe rail, then she'd rolled overboard, unconscious.

She'd sunk instantly, dragged down by the weight of her backpack. He dove in after her. His backpack was far heavier than hers, but if he gave up the ammo inside he might as well drown anyway, so he'd kept it on. His KoolSuit started delivering him stored air. He saw Sam's limp body scraping along the river bottom. He'd swum with the current, feeling the river's raw power, caught her and held her tight.

Pulling her along, Tommy kicked his way up, breaking the surface only to see silverbugs scrambling into the canoe as it vanished into the tunnel's darkness.

Tommy hadn't thought, he'd reacted, swimming hard, pulling the limp Sam away from the silverbug mat. The current carried them into the tunnel as well—darkness had swallowed them up. He kept swimming until the current rudely introduced Tommy and Sam to the chain and wall. Head spinning, he'd managed to grab the chain and hold tight.

By the time he recovered from the impact, the canoe was long gone, swept far downstream. He didn't dare go after it. There was no telling how long the river would flow through the dark passage, or if the rapids would get even worse. Surviving them on his own would be hard enough—hauling Sam, one or both of them would likely grind hard against jagged rocks and tear their KoolSuits, and then the heat would get at them.

His HUD showed the surrounding temperature: *188°F.*

A little cooler in the water than it had been in the cavern, but that didn't matter. If his suit ripped, he couldn't repair with the rapids tossing him all over the place. The water was plenty hot enough to kill him in short order.

Tommy's combat helmet was still on. That was something, at least. Score one for the apple-polisher who always made sure the chin strap stayed fastened. His carbine had stayed on as well, his sling holding it in place.

He didn't dare go downstream.

He couldn't stay here.

There was only one direction left.

He thought of taking Sam's backpack off her, letting it go, but her KoolSuit repair kit was in there at the very least. He wasn't sure what else she might have packed away. For now, they were on their own—Tommy couldn't afford to give up *any* supplies.

Tommy twisted his body, got Sam's back between his legs, hooked his ankles around her belly. Hand over hand, he pulled himself along the chain. Why didn't he see the cavern's light? The river must have pulled him around a bend. A current this strong could have drawn him hundreds of meters downstream in the time it took him to grab Sam and swim to the far side.

He kept pulling. Left hand grip, right hand reach, right hand grip, left hand reach. The current dragged at her, at him, at their clothes, at their packs. In minutes, his arms were already tired. Minutes more, and his legs and core joined in the complaint.

Finally, Tommy reached the bend he knew would be there, pulled them both past it, and saw the light at the end of the tunnel. Literally. It was enough to push him past his fatigue, enough to keep him going. He should have done fewer dishes, more lat pulls. In his younger days, he probably wouldn't even be breathing hard, but his younger days were long gone.

What the hell was he doing in this place, anyway? Oh, that's right—he'd come for money.

By the time he'd pulled them both to the edge of the light filtering down from above, his arms were screaming, his legs threatened to abandon Sam to the current, and his chest was heaving. He laced his left arm through the chain, wrapped his right around Sam, and looked to the shore where he and the others had boarded the canoe.

Silverbugs *covered* the riverbank. How many of them were there? Thousands. Either the floating mat had retreated to dry ground, or it had broken off and been swept away. The river itself was once again clear of the machines.

Even if the silverbugs had been gone altogether, he couldn't reach that side of the river without again being rocketed downstream. He could feel Sam's heart beating, strong and steady, but he had to get her out of the water and evaluate the extent of her injuries.

The chain led to the tunnel mouth. There, maybe, he could get Sam to shore, but if he tried it the silverbugs might spot him.

Damned if he did, damned if he didn't.

Those weird fruit trees. Wide yellow leaves, thick trunks—cover. He had to get Sam in there.

Tommy tightened his legs around her. Hand over hand, ignoring his screaming muscles, he moved as smoothly as he could to the chain's end. There, he got his arm around her chest, stretched his feet down but felt nothing below him. Gathering his last bit of strength, he fought the current, used the stone wall's craggy surface to pull himself and Sam around the tunnel edge. The current ebbed slightly. His boots found the river's silty bottom.

Quietly, slowly, Tommy dragged Samira out of the water and onto the sandy bank. The silverbugs would see him any second now. They'd make another mat, cross the river—if there weren't already a bunch of the shiny bastards on this side of the water.

He stayed low, crawling on his belly, up the steep, rocky bank, hauling Sam behind him. Inch by agonizing inch, he dragged Sam into the trees. Soil here, thick with brittle bunches of the fallen broccoli-looking stuff, which apparently turned a burnt orange when it dried. He found a high stack of brown branches that had been cut—*pruned*, his subconscious reminded him, pruned by aliens that were supposed to be mindless savages—and slowly pulled Sam behind it.

Tommy peeked over the top. He was a good fifteen feet inside the tree line. Unless the silverbugs could see through these branches, he and Sam were out of sight. He ducked back down, pressed his fingers to Sam's neck. Her pulse was fast, but strong and steady.

She'd live.

The exhaustion caught up with him, overwhelmed him. Tommy Strymon rolled to his back, let his helmeted head rest on the leaf-strewn ground.

He needed a minute. Just one damn minute.

48

14,520 feet below the surface

"HAUL HIM IN," Mullet said. "Come on, pull."

Bertha leaned her head against the canoe rail, tried to get her breathing under control. Curveball lay next to her, gasping, his carbine still clutched to his chest. A foot of water sloshed inside the canoe.

They were still in a dark tunnel. Bigger than before, much wider, but the same rough stone walls to the sides, the same rough stone ceiling above.

Mullet and Klimas pulled on a rope, dragged Sleepy out of the river and into the canoe.

"Sound off," Patrick said, forcing out the words.

Everyone did, groaning out their names. Everyone except Sam and Worm.

"Mullet, grab that oar," Otto said. "Help me keep us in the middle."

Bertha sat up. Her clothes were soaked, heavy. How far had the canoe dropped? Maybe fifty feet. She really had no idea, knew only that hitting the water below had felt like driving a truck into a brick wall. The KoolSuit masks had kept anyone from drowning, had done nothing to protect against the raw impact. Every part of her hurt.

The canoe floated along in silence. Even the sound of the river had died down to a light gurgle.

Bertha could say one nice thing about the rocktopi—the glowing bastards really knew how to build a boat.

She knelt next to Curveball, who was still on his back, water all around him.

"You okay?"

In answer, he lifted his head, then held up his right hand. The pinkie stuck out at an odd, sickening angle.

"Hold the end of it," he said. "Hold it tight."

"What? It's broken, can't you see that?"

Curveball let his head drop back into the sloshing water. "It's probably just dislocated. Hold the fucking thing."

She pinched down hard on the end of his pinkie. Curveball didn't wince, but one eye twitched slightly.

"Tighter," he said.

Bertha complied, pinching harder.

Curveball yanked his hand back. Just before the pinkie slipped from her grasp, she felt a *snap* as something inside fell back into place.

"Get your med kit," he said. "Splint it up for me."

Bertha slid her backpack off. She opened it up. Damp inside in places, but it had mostly kept out the water. She opened her med kit, found a metal finger splint, carefully put it on Curveball's pinkie. If it hurt him, he didn't show it.

Patrick in the comm: "Worm, come in. Sam, answer me."

Bertha heard no response.

"Everyone keep an eye out for them," Patrick said. "If they made it to the waterfall, they should be nearby."

Bertha wrapped tape around the splint. Curveball said nothing, just stared off into the darkness. His aura of loss, of depression … it made her wonder, not for the first time, what it would be like to lose Patrick.

"Sorry about your man," she said.

Curveball looked at her. "Thank you. He was…he was the best person I've ever known."

The KoolSuit's green-tinged night vision made it odd to talk to someone this close, face to face. It hadn't struck her before, but now, in the calm, the quiet, she found it weird. As if anything down here *wasn't* weird.

Bertha ripped the tape, smoothed the last of it down on the splint.

"He pretended to like the bakery," Curveball said. "I knew he hated it. Hated every minute of it. I liked civilian life. Him? Not so much. He loved our time in the NoSeeUms. Loved it. In a way, I guess he died doing something that made him happy."

It was the most he'd said since Hatchet died.

She closed up the kit, put it back in her pack, tried to think of something to say.

"I don't know you at all," she said, "but it sounds like you're coming to grips with his death. That's good. We need you sharp if we're going to make it out alive."

He turned his head, gave her a quizzical look.

"Coming to grips? Honey, just because I can string a sentence together doesn't change a thing. I hope you make it out of here alive. I really do. I won't. Anders and I will share our final resting place. And I'll take as many of those motherfuckers with me as I can."

Cold. Calculating. Assured. And a little bit terrifying—would Patrick fight to keep Curveball alive when the man wanted to die?

Just one more threat to her, to her man.

"Worm, Sam, come in," Patrick said.

Again, no response.

"Everyone reload," Patrick said, his voice heavy. "River might be as calm as it's going to get. There's light up ahead, probably another cavern. Looks like ten or fifteen minutes until we get there. Let's get ready."

He'd done something to his back. He was trying to hide his pain. Maybe he could hide it from the others, but not from her.

Hatchet, Worm and Samira, gone.

Patrick, hurt.

Curveball, possibly suicidal.

No idea where they were, or what they might face next.

And Bertha couldn't control any of it.

49

10,906 feet below the surface

ANGUS WATCHED OBERON'S view as the machine sprinted through the tunnels.

The BlackBugs had sent back more sounds of gunfire, and sounds of something else as well: a river.

If it was like the river in Utah, O'Doyle's team might be trapped there—Oberon could gun them all down.

Angus was five or six switchbacks behind his killer robot, far slower than the machine but still marveling at his exosuit-powered speed, at the length of his strides. Glorious technology, turning him into New Angus, something far more than Old Angus had ever been.

"Kool, god dammit, *slow down!*"

Donnie, screaming on the private channel. He could keep screaming. Patrick O'Doyle was about to die, and Angus hoped to see it happen.

Angus slowed slightly, his metal feet skidding across the cave floor as he turned a switchback corner. He came around too fast, crashed into the far wall, bounced off as bits of broken rock tumbled down behind him.

"Kool! You're too far ahead!"

Too far ahead.

Too far ahead of Donnie, Fuentes and Khatari, and all the men with all the guns.

Turned out the cautious, calculating Old Angus was still in there after all.

He slowed to a jog, then a walk, then a full stop. He blinked through the commands to minimize Oberon's view. Angus looked around. He was alone.

Maybe the suit was all that and a bag of chips, but he hadn't paid all those men someone else's money so that *he* could be the first to face bullets.

"Kool, come in!"

"I'm here," Angus said. "I stopped. I mean, I'm waiting. For you to catch up. Hurry, we're close." He expanded Oberon's view back to full-size in the HUD. "Oberon is in a long segment. There's an opening at the end, a big crack that leads into a lit cavern, looks like. I'm sending him in."

"Negative, Kool, bring that thing to heel. We need backup to support that asset!"

Support the asset? What the hell did Dimwit think was going to happen? Oberon's SAW would shred O'Doyle and his bunch of assholes. This was a *real* fight, not a slaughter of unarmed whatever-the-fuck the rocktopi were.

But the pit-trap … Snoopy's spine broken …

Donnie was right.

"Oberon," Angus said, "halt and return."

The machine started to slow, but the long tunnel segment had let it build up speed—it couldn't stop on a dime. Momentum carried Oberon through the crack and into the cavern beyond.

In the HUD, Angus saw what his invention saw: glimpses of strange alien plants; an expansive, illuminated cavern; the rocky ground *covered* in a massive, undulating field of silverbugs.

"Oberon, return to me!"

In the HUD, Angus saw Oberon turn and start toward the tunnel's dark mouth, then the view twitched suddenly, accompanied by a *clank* of metal. A second jittering clank. Then another. And another.

From either side of the tunnel entrance, silverbugs raced in, cutting Oberon off from the tunnel mouth. Angus saw a silverbug leap forward, heard another *clank* as the view blurred, blocked by the too-close curve of a round platinum body.

"Oberon, self-defense!"

The HUD's blurry view shook and twitched. Angus heard the SAW's staccato bark, saw the first three digits of the *200/200/200* counter blur as the numbers counted down.

More *clanks*, coming almost as fast as the machine gun fire.

In the HUD, a new number appeared, in red — a temperature readout.

In that instant, Angus understood what was happening.

AUTOMATIC FIRE JERKED Tommy out of his daze. He rolled to his knees, keeping his head below the top of the pile of branches. He absently realized his clothes were already dry.

Tommy rose slowly, looked over the top of the pile toward the sound of the gunfire.

Across the river, close to the tunnel mouth, he saw it — a robot just like the one that had tripped the booby trap on Hatchet's body. A dozen silverbugs clinging to it, more swarming toward it like a horde of silver termites rushing toward some threat to the hive. The silverbugs leapt, landed, clung.

The robot dog kept firing, but there were too many bogeys to shoot. More and more clung to the machine, obscuring its shape. The robot slowed, its movements sluggish.

The silverbugs coating it seemed to waver, to shimmer.

Shimmer from *heat*.

In that shimmer, the silverbugs began to glow orange …

The robot dog stumbled, sagged. It fired another burst from the SAW — two silverbugs spun away like kicked soccer balls — then the dog fell beneath an ever-growing pile of crawling platinum.

The gunfire ceased.

The fifteen or twenty silverbugs that had seemed on the verge of melting gradually cooled, their platinum shells fading from orange back to their normal metallic sheen—they didn't move.

They'd destroyed themselves to take out the dog.

But there were thousands more of the things, crawling around.

For a moment, Tommy heard nothing but the river's roar.

Then he heard a noise, coming from somewhere on *this* side of the river.

click-click, click

Time had run out.

He knelt next to Sam, shook her gently. Blow to the head or not, they had to move.

"Wake up," he whispered. "Get your pack on and stay quiet—we're in trouble."

ANGUS STARED AT the temperature readout: *403°F.*

It was ticking down—*400°F, 307°F, 304°F*—but it was too late. Oberon was dead. Angus mentally calculated which parts had burned or melted from that level of heat—far too many for the machine to ever work again.

It was an inanimate object. Oberon had no emotions, could show no loyalty, could demonstrate no love, and yet Angus couldn't fight the fury that welled up inside of him.

"You motherfuckers," he said. "You smart fucking assholes."

In Utah, the silverbugs had adapted by adding knife blades—an ideal weapon for slicing up soft-bodied people. But a knife wouldn't work against a Wolf. Somehow, the distributed intelligence of the silverbugs had figured that out and devised an offensive strategy that *would* work against a machine.

"*Kool!*" Dimwit Donnie, chirping in the comm like a goddamn salt-and-pepper-mustached Chihuahua. "What's your status? We're closing in on your location. Are you all right?"

"I'm fine," Angus said. "They killed my dog."

"What? Oh, Oberon? God *dammit*, Kool, I told you to—"

Angus switched off the channel.

The worthless shit-sippers had killed his incredible machine.

How many silverbugs had he seen before Oberon shut down? Hundreds.

Thousands.

Angus eye-tracked in his HUD, opened up the private channel he'd created not that long before.

"Fuentes, Khatari, come in."

SAM WAITED UNTIL the last possible second.

She gripped the base of her face shield, pushed it up to make it retract into the headband, felt the instant, scorching heat on her face, then threw up for the fourth time. She pressed the center of her headband—the face shield extended, sealed itself to her hood.

Her skin stung slightly from the three-second exposure to the hot air.

"Be *quiet*," Tommy whispered.

It was strange to hear him with her ears only. He was afraid "the enemy" might pick up the signals, so he'd shut off their radios.

Her head hurt so bad she couldn't even open her eyes. Weak, shivering, her knees on the dirt and rocks and dried leaves of this alien place, she waited for her stomach to betray her for a fifth time.

"I can't help it," she said.

He told her to be quiet again, but this time without words—he grabbed her shoulder, squeezed hard enough that she couldn't miss the point.

"They're close," he whispered.

She whispered back: "Rocktopi?"

"Silverbugs."

The dull, endless pain in her head blossomed wider. Sam gagged, but this time she managed to hold it back. She blinked away tears, willed her eyes to open. Tommy was next to her, on one knee, one hand on her shoulder, the other on his rifle. They were behind a stack of cut branches that blocked the view of the river. She glanced around, saw that the branches hiding her were the same as the branches on the tall trees that surrounded her.

Pruning—the "rocktopi" were farmers. Amazing.

"The trees here are so weird," she whispered. "I wonder if the rocktopi eat the blue-green … whatever the hell you'd call those clumps."

"Mullet called them *frankenbroccoli*. A good enough name as any."

Sam winced as another blast of pain flooded her head. She rocked to the side, would have fallen if Tommy's clutching hand hadn't steadied her. She wasn't sure what was worse—the nova blast inside her skull, or his iron talons digging into her flesh.

"Control that if you want to live," Tommy said. "Do you know how to shoot?"

Any other time in her life, she would have felt repulsed at the thought of a gun. Not now—not when she faced a real life-or-death situation.

"Show me," she said.

Tommy removed his pistol holster, quickly fastened the hard plastic and canvas rig to Sam's belt, wrapped the straps around her leg. The holster was at mid-thigh.

"When you grab the grip to draw, make sure you feel it firm in the webbing of your thumb," Tommy said. "Do that, and your fingers will be in the right place. Give it a good tug to draw it. Try it."

Sam did as she was told, grabbing the weapon's grip. She pulled—at first it resisted, stayed put, until she pulled again and felt the holster let go.

"Right hand around the grip," Tommy said, as calm as could be, like this was a shooting range and she was his student. "Your finger should always rest along the *outside* of the trigger guard, until you're ready to shoot." With one hand, he flattened her right finger, placed it along the side of the pistol. "Left hand wraps around your right. Don't lace your fingers. You press your *palms* together, that's where your strength comes from. Keep a firm grip, but don't *clutch* at it. Got it?"

She pressed her palms together, felt the solidity of the pistol grip between them. The weight of the weapon … she wasn't helpless. She might be fucked nine ways to Sunday, but with this weapon she might have a chance at surviving—the gun *centered* her.

"Is there a safety or something?"

"Trigger safety," Tommy said. He angled the pistol so she could see the trigger. "Slide your finger across the trigger, but don't *pull*—you'll feel a little tab in the center."

She used her fingertip, touched lightly.

"I feel it," she said.

"If that isn't depressed, the gun won't fire. You pull the trigger firmly, it will depress as part of the pull. Got it?"

"Yeah, I think so."

"Don't shoot unless I tell you to." His head turned sharply to the side. "Hear that?"

Another wave of nausea. Sam fought it down, tried to focus through the pain. She heard it, a distant scratching sound.

click-click, click-click

Tiny metal feet on stone, or scurrying across dirt, or maybe on the frankenbroccoli surrounding them. The same noise she'd heard when Ramiro had been attacked, when those crawling machines had chased her, O'Doyle and the others.

click-click-click…

Coming from the left.

Tommy leaned in so close that, had she not been wearing the suit, she would have felt his breath in her ear.

"We have to run for the river," he said. "We have a better chance at surviving the rapids than we do those machines."

She could barely stay on her knees without falling over, and he wanted her to *run?*

"Three-count," Tommy whispered. "When I say *now*, you run to the river and dive in. If I fall behind you, or they take me down, you *do not stop.* Understand?"

He wasn't sure if he'd make it. He was a trained soldier—if he couldn't make it, what chance did she have? Sam felt cold inside. Her guts churned anew, this time from fear instead of pain.

Tommy got both feet under him, rose up slightly. His clutching hand forced her to do the same.

"Three…"

A fist in her throat; she felt bile rising up again.

"Wait," she whispered, "I—"

"Two…"

Her eyes squeezed shut. Her stomach clenched. She slapped at her visor, pushing up her face shield just before vomit surged out like a geyser—first the rancid smell of her own bile, then that *heat.*

Tommy let go of her shoulder.

"*Hold it down,*" he whispered. "We have to run!"

She closed her shield, her skin again stinging from the brief exposure. She couldn't run, she *couldn't*, she needed a minute, just a few seconds.

A rattle, a rustle, so close…

Sam opened her eyes. A silverbug leapt over the stacked branches. Tommy leaned back and swung his weapon all in the same motion. The rifle butt slapped the silverbug like a baseball bat hitting a volleyball, a *tonk* of plastic on metal that sent the round machine sailing through the air.

Another silverbug scrambled over the branches, scrambled toward *her*.

ANGUS WALKED DOWN the long segment of tunnel, exosuit feet firm against the loose silt. Only a few silverbugs remained in the crack that led to the cavern. Past them, he saw his invention, his Oberon, as still and dead as a box of rocks.

He raised his right arm and sprinted forward.

SAM DUCKED. The leaping silverbug—four long, thin arms stretched wide—flew past her, hit Tommy in the chest and knocked him to his back. The machine thunked to the ground near his feet. Spindly legs instantly adjusted, and it scurried up his legs toward his head. He grabbed the rifle strapped to his chest, one hand on the barrel and one on the stock, used it to push the machine away from his body. Platinum spider limbs grabbed and curled, locking onto his arms and the rifle itself.

Sam reached to help him, but something slammed into her backpack, sending her crashing to the ground. She rolled to one side and grabbed at her pack's shoulder straps, sliding them free.

THE SILVERBUG LAUNCHED itself through the air.

Angus squeezed his mangled right hand—the Atchisson fired once.

Lead shot punched through the platinum-iridium shell, making a sound strangely similar to an aluminum can being smashed underfoot. Angus knew the machine was destroyed even before it clanged against his chest armor, bounced off, and thudded to the tunnel floor.

He kept running forward. Another silverbug sprang toward him. He aimed, he squeezed …

SAM'S THOUGHTS FLASHED to golf, of all things. She held the silverbug's split foot in both hands, raised the machine high, then twisted her hips and swung it down to smash against the shimmering orb on Tommy's chest, one gleaming wrecking ball cracking into another with a sound like a soda can crushed underfoot. The impact sent Tommy's hot-and-getting-hotter attacker rolling across the ground, scattering sticks and orange clumps of dried vegetation.

Even gripping it by its leg, Sam felt heat pouring off the silverbug's round body, so intense it was like holding her hands too close to a campfire.

She turned, twisted, had thoughts of another sport randomly flash in her head—an Olympic hammer-throw—and let go. The machine sailed through the air, thunked against a tree trunk.

Both silverbugs righted themselves and came scurrying toward her.

Tommy, at her side, the squat rifle in his hands, stock tight to his shoulder. He fired six times fast—the loud shots startled her, making her wince in time with each pull of the trigger.

The two machines twitched for a moment, the air near their round shells shimmering slightly, then they fell still. Three holes in each of them, so close together they were almost one misshapen spot. Curls of black smoke rose up from somewhere inside.

Long tears in the sleeves of his fatigues. Blood dripped down.

"Draw your weapon," he said.

The pistol—she'd completely forgotten she had it.

Sam pulled it from her thigh holster.

Tommy turned, stood back-to-back with her.

She pressed both palms against the pistol grip, the way he had shown her.

"I don't see any more of them," she said. "Are they gone?"

Tommy didn't answer. He didn't have to. From deep in the trees, from every direction, a cacophony of little clicking feet told her that a scorching death was moments away.

ANGUS STEPPED INTO the light of the cavern, feeling the internal whir of his shotgun reloading. A wave of silverbugs flowed across the ground, intent on cooking him alive.

Time for payback.

"Suck a bag of dicks, you motherfuckers," he said.

From behind him, the SwarmStorm poured out of the tunnel mouth, billowing into the air.

TOMMY STOOD THERE, his back pressed against Sam's, trying to understand what had just happened.

"Those red things," she said. "How did you do that?"

Tommy shook his head. "I didn't do anything."

Scattered all around them, dead silverbugs, some still twitching, most motionless, legs either limp or curled in like those of dried-up insects.

Tommy couldn't believe he was still alive. He turned in a circle, the number-crazy part of his brain automatically counting the metal spheres—twenty-seven dead silverbugs, all with little red spots on their shells.

They had started to come at him and Sam together, a unified wave, when a red cloud swept in, tiny flying machines that clustered on the silverbugs in a way not that dissimilar from how the silverbugs had clustered on the dog-robot. There had been a whining sound, so high-pitched Tommy wasn't sure if he'd heard it or just imagined it, then the silverbugs had collapsed.

That same red swarm had then flown off—noticeably thinner than it had been when it first arrived.

"The silverbugs cut me," Sam said. "My leg's bleeding. Your arms are cut."

As if her words were a key that opened his awareness, he registered the pain that his combat-trained mind had kept at bay. His hands felt like they'd been dipped in boiling oil. He looked at palms—the KoolSuit material had melted away. His skin was an angry red, pinpricks of blood oozing up from a dozen spots.

He remembered slapping at the silverbug, trying to get it off his chest, his rifle.

Tommy's vision blurred. For a moment his hands looked like ghosts, spectral floating things out of a horror movie, then the world swam before him.

Sam grabbed him around the chest.

"Sit down," she said. "You almost fell."

Tommy did as he was told, needed her help to do even that.

"Stay still," Sam said. "I'll get your spare gloves."

As she tugged at his pack, he became aware of the heat. Not just in his hands, but everywhere, all over his body.

The world turned fuzzy.

He felt someone pulling at his left hand, first taking something off, then pulling something on. His skin? That was strange. You weren't supposed to be able to pull off your skin. It *hurt*. And so hot in here.

Was he dying?

Cooking like that machine had cooked?

Tommy saw himself shimmering, a heat-blur about to burst into flames.

He closed his eyes, felt something tugging at his right hand.

Then he felt a chill, starting at his hands before tingling all through his body.

His head hurt. His hands felt like they were on fire, but he'd been burned before and knew the feeling—he would live. For a little while, at least.

"Tommy?"

He opened his eyes. His vision cleared. Sam was right in front of him.

"Tommy? Talk to me."

"I'm okay," he said. "That was … rough."

She gently grabbed his wrists, looked at his hands. Beneath the clear KoolSuit material, his skin glowed red. Smears of blood trapped between his real skin and the fake one that covered him from head to toe.

"First-degree burns, at least," Sam said. "What the hell were those things doing?"

"Trying to cook us alive. Swarming strategy, combining their internal heat. Honeybees do something similar to giant Japanese hornets."

Sam stared at him. "Giant Japanese hornets. Let me guess. You read about that in a book."

"YouTube, actually," Tommy said. "I'm just glad they weren't the kind of silverbugs that had knife-faces."

Her expression wrinkled with confusion. "Knife-faces?"

"I'll tell you later."

He focused on the pain, tried to encapsulate it, push it to the back of his mind. As bad as he hurt now, he'd hurt far worse before and kept on fighting.

The twenty-seven-year-old you did that, old man—can the forty-seven-year-old handle it?

As if there was room for such doubts. He would handle it because he had no other choice.

"Let's get back to cover and out of sight," he said.

Sam helped him to his feet. They walked back to the pile of branches, crouched behind it.

Tommy looked through the trees and across the river. There, he saw hundreds of gleaming platinum spheres, as still as the ones nearby.

And, standing just outside the tunnel exit, a man, alone—a man in a suit of armor?

"What the hell," Sam said. "Is that…powered armor? Like from *Starship Troopers?*"

She was referring to the book, not the movie. There hadn't been powered armor in the movie.

Tommy started to say that E.E. Smith's *Lensman* series was the first book to use powered armor, but he chased the thought away—it wasn't the time to be a pedantic nerd.

The armor looked fairly bulky. Without it, the man inside had to be small. The exosuit didn't look fully enclosed, which meant the man was facing the same temperatures that he and Sam were, yet he showed no ill effect.

Because he, like Sam and Tommy, was wearing a KoolSuit.

"I think that's Angus Kool."

"That guy O'Doyle talked about?"

"I'm guessing, but yeah."

"Agent Otto asked if Kool was an evil genius," Sam said.

The KoolSuits, the SAW-armed robot dog, the little red flying silverbug killers, and now what looked like full-on powered armor.

"He's responsible for Hatchet's death," Tommy said. "He'll kill us if he sees us."

Sam lowered her head, her eyes squinted shut. She was in pain. She had a concussion, for sure. That she was fighting through the pain, it said something about her.

"If he'll kill us," she said, "do we have to kill him first?"

Tommy again stared across the river. Kool was just over a hundred meters away. No wind down here; Tommy could make that shot in his sleep. The suit had a visor. Bulletproof? Maybe. Only one way to find out.

You won't have to kill people, Ender had said.

A lie. How could Tommy have not realized that was a lie?

Because he wasn't as smart as everyone seemed to think. Because he was a middle-aged man who washed dishes for a living. Because he was an ex-con. Because, deep down, Tommy Strymon was dumber than a pile of cat shit.

"Yeah," Tommy said. "We kill him first."

He pulled his carbine stock tight to his shoulder. Sam said nothing as he sighted in on the man in the exosuit.

One round to the face. For Tommy, an easy shot, even with the stubby carbine.

Sam's arm on his shoulder. "Hold on."

Tommy looked up. Armed men were pouring out of the tunnel mouth. A squad of ten, wearing KoolSuits underneath the same tan uniforms as the men he'd seen on the plateau, through the hornet's camera. Another squad of ten. Then another. They spread out, one squad moving to the river, the next setting up a perimeter at the edge of the orchard.

"Uh-oh," Sam said. "I think Iron Man over there sees those dead rocktopi."

ANGUS STARED DOWN at the two deflated corpses, sticky with already drying yellow blood.

O'Doyle's people had killed them.

Angus felt a chill wash through him. He looked across the river, left and right, scanning for movement. Nothing but weird trees. A *lot* of trees. Trees he couldn't see into. Too many places to hide.

Was O'Doyle over there? Did he have a sniper rifle? Was he getting ready to take a shot?

HE'S LOOKING FOR us," Sam said. She heard the hard edge of fear in her own voice. "What if he sees us?"

"Don't move," Tommy said. "Speak only in whispers."

She watched the man in the strange black armor. Angus Kool's steps were tentative, hesitating. The man looked left, then right, then left, searching.

"He can't see us through the branches," Tommy said. "Not from that distance. Even if he's got a parabolic mic, he can't hear us over the river noise, not if we stay quiet."

"What about infrared or something? Body heat?"

"Look at the temp."

Sam glanced at her HUD: *195°F.*

"Air's hotter than we are," Tommy said. "He can't see us with infrared, not with this cover in front of us."

Kool started backing away from the river, one mechanized step at a time. The commander, if that's what he was, strode toward him, working his way around the piles of still-twitching silverbugs. The mercenaries spread along the far shore—they, too, were scanning the other side of the river, looking through rifle scopes, using binoculars.

Most of the mercenaries wore helmets like Tommy's, but more than a few wore tan ballcaps. One wore a turban. Some had scarves, some had fatigue jackets on, some wore T-shirts under their gear. Much more variation in their outfits than those of the NoSeeUms.

"They're going to come over here," Sam whispered. "They'll find us."

She felt Tommy's hand on her shoulder.

"Sam, stay calm. The river is wide, with the rapids and a strong current. It's a risk for them to send men over here, which means they'll only send a few. This orchard is about ten acres. That's a lot of space to search. Unless soldiers have changed dramatically since I served, anyone they send over here probably won't be that motivated to look in every last nook and cranny. They will be looking for obvious shit. We find a good place to hide, stay there, they might pass us by."

Tommy didn't sound the least bit upset. Just another walk in the alien park for him, maybe.

"*Might* pass us by," Sam said. "What if they don't?"

"Depends on how many there are. We'll have to put them down and fight until we can't fight anymore."

Sam looked to the river, wished they were closer to it.

"We could make a run for the water."

Tommy shook his head. "We're twenty-five meters away. They have too many guns, we wouldn't make it. They'll search this side of the river. That's what I'd do if I were them. If we stay out of sight, they'll move on after Ender and the others. We can survive this."

She had to trust him. What other choice was there?

"All right," she said. "So what do we do now?"

"Find every shell casing, fast. We can't leave any sign we were here. Then we need to hide."

KOOL, YOU ARE an ignorant squirt of whale piss," Donnie said. "You don't go *anywhere* alone. Those silverbugs could have taken you out, and you were standing out here in the open like a goddamn thick-headed walking target!"

That's exactly what Angus was—a walking target. Except, no one had shot at him. He'd gotten lucky.

"O'Doyle's team was here," he said. "Look."

He pointed to the two dead rocktopi; a pair of G4s mercs were already there, removing the strange alien weapons.

"They were here, all right," Donnie said. "What do you think those chains are for?"

Angus saw where Dimwit was looking. Across the river, on the wall leading into the tunnel, he saw the chains, coated with what looked like mold.

"They must have boats," he said. "Current's strong. The rocktopi probably use the chains to pull the boats back up the river."

Donnie studied the chains, then looked at the trees on the far shore.

"You're probably right," he said. "No boats left for us, unfortunately. Let's move you further back, away from the river."

This time, Angus decided to listen. He walked with Donnie toward the alien orchard, still waiting for a shot to ring out, for an Old West gunfire echo, to feel a bullet hit him in the back. The sooner he was out of sight, the better.

Dead silverbugs, everywhere. Angus stepped over them or around them, mostly, but they were thick enough in places he simply kicked them aside.

"Your SwarmStorm really did a number," Donnie said. "How many did we waste on this bit of folly?"

Angus realized he hadn't done a tally. He blinked through his HUD menu, dreading the numbers he would see.

The SwarmStorm had taken out 1,284 silverbugs. And the failure rate had increased to a shocking eleven percent.

"We have twelve hundred left."

"God dammit," Donnie said. "How many silverbugs will that account for?"

Angus thought of padding the numbers, but what was the point? He'd fucked up. If he wanted to get out of here alive—and rich—Donnie needed the facts.

"Assuming the failure rate increases again, to, say, fifteen percent, assume we can take out two hundred and sixty silverbugs. Tops."

"Let's hope your tactical decision doesn't wind up costing us the farm."

They walked by the crumpled form of Oberon.

"Can you repair that thing?" Donnie asked.

Angus glanced at the machine as he walked by. "All the processors and most of the servos are fucked. Maybe the SAW still works. We're lucky the rounds didn't cook off."

"You are an idiot," Donnie said. "You wasted another mechanized unit. I have no Wolves left. Aren't you supposed to be smart?"

They reached the first row of trees. "I am smart. See all these fucking silverbugs I killed? How about some credit for that, huh?"

"You could have taken them out *and* kept Oberon functioning. Now I need you to check that SAW. If it's working, put it in one of the haulers. I know we'll have to leave some cargo here to make the hauler faster. Put that big brain to work and do whatever modifications you have to do to give me a replacement Wolf. I need firepower and *speed*."

There wasn't much Angus *could* do, other than lighten a hauler's load by removing cargo. He'd set those robots up to *carry*, not to *sprint*.

They walked through the second row of trees, then the third. Angus saw mercs out ahead of him, making sure there were no threats. Under cover, protected by these men, he finally relaxed a little.

"I'll figure something out," he said. "I can convert one of the haulers, but it will take a while. How much time do we have here?"

Donnie shook his head, let out a breath that was more sigh than growl.

"Well, we've been going nonstop since we entered the tunnel," he said. "The men need a rest."

Angus couldn't argue. Suit or no suit, he was exhausted. How long had he been awake now? He checked his HUD—thirty-two hours, fifteen minutes, twelve seconds.

"A rest sounds good to me."

Donnie glared at him. "I wasn't asking for your permission." He triggered his comm. "Henderson, get your recon team across that river and search the other side. Second Platoon, provide cover from the near shore. Third and Fourth, set up a perimeter on this side of the river, thirty meters back from the cavern wall, make sure we don't get surprised by another wave of silverbugs. The rest of you, set up camp in this orchard, and get our prisoners in here."

50

11,012 feet below the surface

TOMMY MOVED ONLY his eyes.

Three scout mercs carrying M4s crept through the frankenbroccoli trees. They probably thought they were as stealthy as little well-armed mice, but they weren't. Clearly experienced operators, sure, but they weren't in the NoSeeUms' league.

The best place to cross the river was obviously at the upstream tunnel mouth, as it gave swimmers the most time to reach the far shore before being swept into the downstream tunnel. He'd suspected anyone who crossed to this side would want to get back with the rest of their troops as fast as possible, which meant they might carefully check the first few piles of branches, maybe the last couple at the cavern wall, then they'd want to rush back and give the "all clear."

Tommy had picked the middle of the frankenbroccoli orchard as his hiding spot. He'd all but buried Sam, carefully moving a pile of branches enough to dig a shallow trench for her to lie in, covering her with dirt save for her mask and one air vent, then finished her concealment by stacking pruned branches on top of her.

He'd set up shop inside the next pile of branches over, close enough to gun down anyone who might uncover Sam. Tommy wasn't as well-hidden as she was, but if the shit hit the fan, he needed the ability to move fast.

A scout merc crept closer to him. Red beard. Focused eyes, *angry* eyes.

Ten feet away. Tommy could raise his carbine and kill the man all in less than a second. The man's two comrades were nearby—Tommy could *probably* take them out as well, but it would be a close thing.

The merc moved toward Sam's pile of branches.

Still Tommy did not move. He trusted his hiding place, trusted that he'd hidden Sam well—to panic would get them both killed.

The merc with the red beard stopped in front of Sam's pile.

Tommy breathed slow and steady.

The merc raised a foot, kicked at the yellow branches once, twice, a third time. The top of the pile spilled over. The merc glanced at the branches, then continued on.

Luck of the draw. If Redbeard had kicked Tommy's pile, Tommy would have had no choice but to kill the man. If Redbeard had been thorough, carefully checking every pile, he'd have found Sam, and Tommy would have had no choice but to kill him. A half-assed effort had saved not only Tommy and Sam's lives, but Redbeard's as well.

Tommy breathed slow. He waited. Soon, Redbeard came back, two other men near him. They were more relaxed now—they thought they'd cleared the orchard. And, as Tommy had guessed, they were in a hurry to get back to the other side, to the relative safety of more guns.

TOMMY AND SAM crouched behind yet another pile of branches, looking across the river at Angus and the mercs. He brushed at her shirt, shaking free dirt, bits of yellow sticks and dried blue leaves.

"I was so scared," Sam whispered.

Tommy nodded, picked a bit of bark away from her collar.

"Scared is smart," he said. "When you stop being scared, that's when you do dumb things. How's your noggin?"

"It's bad. Not the first concussion I've had. When you climb mountains, things tend to happen. I'll live."

Men were still coming out of the tunnel. Many had gone into the far orchard and were out of sight. Tommy estimated the enemy force at between eighty and a hundred.

The recon mercs were gone, but he and Sam were still in serious danger.

Two robot dogs came out of the tunnel, both heavier than the one that had been cooked by the silverbugs. Both machines had cases strapped to their backs. Looked like the things could haul several hundred pounds of equipment.

Behind them came … rolling carts of some kind. Metal frames on them, with … rocktopi inside?

"Cages," Sam said. "The mercs took prisoners. Why?"

Thin bars made up the cages' metal frames. Fine metal mesh ran along the inside of the bars.

"Local intel, maybe," Tommy said. "The rocktopi do live down here. Maybe Angus wants to use them for directions through the tunnels. You think there's any way he can talk to them?"

Sam thought for a moment, shook her head. "I don't think so. I don't want to die here, Tommy."

He glanced at her, was submerged in an instant and all-powerful flashback of the girl he'd killed twenty years earlier. Sam was older than that girl. If Tommy hadn't killed that girl, would she have become a woman as beautiful as Sam?

Tommy closed his eyes, shook his head to chase away the thoughts, because those thoughts were bullshit—if he hadn't killed that girl, she would have killed him. It was that simple. All the moral posturing in the world couldn't change the simple fact of Darwin's Law—the strong survived. The weak perished.

That day, Tommy had been strong.

So why had it changed his life? Why had it ruined him?

A question he'd asked himself a dozen times a day for twenty years, and he was no closer to an answer then he'd been the day he'd pulled that trigger.

"There's no way out of here," Sam said. "Just that one tunnel on the other side of the river, none on this side. We'll have to swim for it."

She been unconscious before she fell out of the boat. She didn't know the river's powerful pull.

"River is a last resort," he said.

"Then what do we do?"

He wanted to tell her the truth, tell her *I have no fucking idea what we do*, but those words wouldn't come. Samira Jabour was relying on him, *only* on him, and that stirred up something he hadn't felt for a long, long time—the need to *protect*, to make someone else feel safe.

"We wait," Tommy said. "We watch, we think, we hope an opportunity presents itself."

She paused, then nodded.

He had to admit, that had sounded pretty good, even to himself.

"While we're waiting, we eat and drink," Tommy said. "Can an old soldier buy a girl dinner and a drink?"

He half expected Sam to be annoyed, but she surprised him by actually laughing a little.

"If you're telling me you've got some Scotch and a chicken piccata for me, you have a date."

"If by *Scotch* you mean water and by *chicken piccata* you mean sandpaper-flavored gruel, then yes."

"You certainly know how to charm a girl."

"This is the soldier's way," Tommy said. "You get a break, you drink, you eat, no matter how bad it tastes."

She nodded, worked her helmet tubes so she could do both.

Tommy did the same.

Together, they watched the enemy.

He estimated their forces at around eighty soldiers. Most of them were out of sight, in that other orchard. Probably sleeping, resting up for whatever came next.

He had no idea how he could get past them. For that matter, he wasn't sure where they could go, either. Sam was right—there was no way out of this cavern, especially not for that many men. Unless they had some boats stored in those crates, there was no way they could take the river.

They would have to go back out the same tunnel they'd used to come in.

If he and Sam could just stay out of sight until then, Tommy could figure out what to do. One problem at a time. Wait these bastards out, then find a way to track down Ender and the others.

If Ender and the others were still alive.

"I got Ramiro killed," Sam said.

She said it in a quiet voice, a voice that made Tommy's heart break for her.

"He was your ex-husband?"

Sam looked at the ground. "Yeah. We had a couple of good years together. At least they were good for me. Him, turns out not so much."

"And you guys were divorced, or you were *getting* divorced?"

"We signed the papers two years ago." She glanced at him. "Why?"

Why? Good question. Why was he asking her personal questions now? Maybe because that's what the NoSeeUms had always done when they were in the dead times of a mission. Maybe because he'd never met anyone like Sam. Maybe because he was an idiot who couldn't focus on the all-important task of staying alive.

"Most exes hate each other," he said. "At least that's what I've heard. Never been married myself."

And what a shocker that is—middle-aged dishwashers are at the top of every quality woman's shopping list.

"He could have hated me," Sam said. "Hell, he *should* have hated me. He could have left me in the dust and done his own thing. Instead, he backed my play when he didn't have to. And that got him killed. I got him killed."

Survivor's guilt. Tommy didn't know the details of her life with Ram, but he knew what Sam was feeling.

"Was Ramiro stupid?"

Her eyes snapped toward him. "No. He was brilliant. Why would you ask a question like that?"

Tommy shrugged. "If he was smart, like you say, then he was capable of making his own decisions. I don't know anything about the man, but if he followed you, Sam, it was because he felt helping you was important. He followed you because he was your friend."

She didn't move, save for the tears tracing down her cheek.

"Adults make choices," Tommy said. "Ramiro made his."

Sam sniffed. "You made a choice, too. I fell overboard. You came in after me. Why?"

Tommy looked back out at the enemy, let his mind relax by counting soldiers and guns.

"You're part of the team," he said. "Team members look out for each other."

Sam cleared her throat. "I hope this doesn't seem judgmental, but... you seem too... too *smart* to be a soldier."

Tommy smiled. "Maybe that's a smidgen judgmental, yeah."

"How did you wind up with O'Doyle and the others? Did you always want to be a soldier?"

Such a strange thing to talk about now. Was she really making small talk? But no, it wasn't small talk, it felt like something beyond that. She wanted to know more about him.

"What I wanted to be was an astronaut," Tommy said. "Ever since I was a little kid, ever since I started reading, I wanted to go to outer space."

Had he forgotten about those dreams until that very moment? Until Sam asked him? Yes, he had, because failed dreams were poison.

"So why didn't you?"

Tommy chuckled. "Multiple reasons, I guess. Northwood, Iowa wasn't the kind of place that produced big thinkers. That was part of it, I suppose. My dad died when I was little. I never knew my mom. I lived with my grandfather, who didn't really give a crap about me. We were poor—I couldn't afford college and my grades weren't worthy of any scholarships. Yeah, I know, I'm smart, but high school classes bored me to tears and I rarely paid attention. I wanted out of that town. I enlisted in the Army at seventeen. I guess I figured I'd put in four years, then go to college after that. Turned out I was good at... being a soldier. Very good. I'd never been good at anything before."

He'd started to say *good at killing people*. Sam, somehow, seemed to understand that, seemed to get that Tommy hated what he'd done with his life.

So she changed the subject.

"So what are the mercenaries doing over there, anyway?"

"They're making camp," Tommy said.

"For how long?"

The million-dollar question. "Not long, I think. There's shell casings all over the shore, plus the two dead rocktopi. They know we were there. That robot dog came in first, probably to kill all of us, but it was a little too late. Angus and his cronies will know we used the river. They'll want to pursue. At the same time, this cavern looks pretty defensible—like you pointed out, there's only one way in or out, not counting the river. Thirty to sixty minutes in a protected area will allow most of them to get some shut-eye."

Sam sighed. "I'd like to get some sleep. I'm so tired."

He could see the fatigue on her, both physical and emotional. She'd been in combat for the first time, she'd lost a close friend, and she'd seen things that would make anyone's world spin. Add in a concussion, she had a lot on her plate.

"Go ahead," Tommy said. "I'll take first watch."

She nodded, started to lay down, then sat up straight.

"Wait a minute...you asked if Angus could talk to them."

A statement, not a question. "Yeah. He can't. So?"

She looked at him, eyes showing both her sudden excitement and her battle against grinding fatigue.

"He can't," she said. "But we can."

She slipped off her backpack. Tommy didn't notice the temperature, thanks to the KoolSuit, but the constant heat had already completely dried the canvas bag.

"I'm afraid if you go shouting your head off, the bad guys might hear you."

From her pack, she pulled out her sketch pad. The paper had wrinkled from the soaking, but it, too, was dry. She opened the book, fast at first, then carefully when the stuck-together pages started to rip.

"We don't need to shout," she said.

Sam showed him a page—one of the symbols she'd drawn in the classroom cave.

He looked at the drawing. Then he rose up slightly, looked across the river. Maybe fifty meters to the two caged rocktopi. If Sam made her drawings big enough, they might be able to see them. A thrill shot through him—he might be able to communicate with actual aliens— but reality instantly snuffed the flare of excitement.

"We can't risk drawing the attention of the mercs," he said. "This isn't the time for experiments. We sit tight, wait for them to leave, then we find the others."

"What if they're already dead? Shouldn't we get our own asses out of here?"

She was scared. He didn't blame her.

"I will not leave this place without my people," Tommy said. "I'll die here if it comes to that. I'm going to find them."

She gestured to the cavern walls, the ceiling.

"Find them *how*, Tommy? We don't know anything about this place. We don't have a map."

He opened the drone pack on his chest. When he did, a splash of water spilled out of it.

Sam leaned in. "Does it still work?"

Tommy pulled out the hornet. It wouldn't turn on. He tried to activate the monitor screen. It, too, was dead.

"Shit out of luck," he said. "Dunking it in water didn't help matters. How about that little computer on your forearm?"

Sam looked at it. She tapped a few buttons.

"Dead," she said. "Tommy, how are we going to find the others?"

He had no idea.

"We'll figure something out."

"By *figure something out* you mean we will *take a wild fucking guess*," Sam said. "We can't contact O'Doyle and the others. We have no idea where we are. We don't know these tunnels—the rocktopi do."

Local intel. Tommy stared at her, blown away by the audacity of her idea. He wanted to believe she could do it, but it just seemed so … so *unbelievable.*

"We've killed their kind," he said. "Shit, there's two of their dead right across the river. Their machines attacked us, tried to *cook* us. What, you think they're going to *help* us after all that?"

"If someone got you out of a cage, wouldn't you feel grateful?"

What she wanted hit home. Her idea wasn't *audacious*, it was *suicidal.*

He again looked across the river. He stared at the two cages, each with a rocktopi inside, each rocktopi pulsating with violent colors and angry, clashing patterns. Caged. Like prisoners of war … or like animals?

"You want me to rescue them," he said. "You're fucking nuts, lady."

Firm words, but they lacked the intensity he'd intended. They lacked conviction, because, despite the idiocy of what she wanted, *he* wanted it, too.

When they'd faced the aliens earlier, he'd fired high, unable to bring himself to shoot the most important discovery in human history. And now here were two of those aliens, being held against their will.

Tommy imagined himself taken captive, put into a cage, carried around with an invading force that spoke an unknown tongue. If it was him in those cages, with the rocktopi as his captors, what would he be thinking? Would he be waiting to be tortured? Wondering when the end might come, and how they would kill him?

Yes. That's exactly what he'd be thinking.

And if another group of rocktopi came and let him out, how would he feel?

Sam was right—*grateful*. Maybe not for long, but as the saying went, *the enemy of my enemy is my friend.*

"Do you know what to say to them?"

She started drawing. "No. Not really. But we can try. Get out your novel, the one you drew on."

Tommy did as she asked. *The Call of the Wild* was just as wrinkled as her pad. She took it from him, studied what he'd drawn.

"I'm assuming their distance vision is comparable to ours," she said. "We'll stay back in the trees and hold the signs still. You said the mercs are resting, sleeping. Maybe they won't be looking around as much as people who are looking for a way to escape."

"*People*? Sam, rocktopi aren't *people*."

She stopped drawing, looked up at him.

"What does being a *person* mean to you? I researched their culture for years. Until a few hours ago, it never occurred to me they weren't human. Maybe that's because there wasn't enough difference between us and them to make me think otherwise. We saw a *classroom*. The rocktopi teach their children reading, writing and math, just like we do. The reason you think the word *people* only applies to humans is because we've never met another sentient species. Now, are you going to sit on your ass, or are you going to help me?"

She was a civilian, yes, but her idea had merit. He could make Sam sit here and wait, do nothing, lay low and hope the mercs moved on, or they could try to connect with the captive rocktopi.

Fortune favors the bold.

"Right now we're off the mercs' radar," he said. "If we do this, there's a good chance the mercs will see, and if they do, we're fucking toast. Are you comfortable with that?"

She thought for a moment, considering his words.

"Your friends shot first, asked questions later," Sam said. "I don't think you liked that. I didn't like it, either. Am I comfortable with the risk? Adults make choices, Tommy. I'm making mine."

This woman … he wanted to know more about her, so much more. Sam didn't hide her emotions, she *owned* them. Powerful and fragile at the same time.

And she was right—Tommy didn't like what Ender and the others had done.

"All right," he said. "What symbol are you starting out with?"

"The same one that would have kept Ramiro alive if I'd known what it meant."

She drew. He recognized it.

"That's the one near the hole where Ramiro fell in," Tommy said. "You think flashing them a *danger* sign is the right move?"

"It's the only sign I'm one-hundred percent sure of the meaning. Besides, if being kept in a cage doesn't qualify as *danger*, what does?"

"Good point. Follow me, I'll find us a good angle."

He got on his belly, crawled out from behind the pile of branches. He moved a little bit at a time, glancing up frequently to see if he had a good line of sight to the prisoners. He knew he couldn't block Sam from all of the guards, but the fewer who had a chance to see her, the better.

Tommy found a spot one row from the orchard's edge, next to a larger frankenbroccoli trunk. He pointed where Sam should go; she took the left side, he took the right. From this spot, they could both see the rocktopi cages, the two guards standing by those cages, and no one else.

The guards' attention seemed focused on the rocktopi—not the rest of the cavern, and not across the river.

"Here goes nothing," Sam whispered.

Slowly, so slowly, Sam moved her art pad in front of the tree, leaned it back against the trunk.

Tommy waited.

And waited.

And waited.

The rocktopi on the right seemed to explode with blazing light, a burst of more colors than Tommy could process.

"Oh my god," Sam said. "It's so beautiful. It's like a … living disco ball."

Tommy stared at the living light show, at colors he recognized and others he couldn't begin to describe.

The guard kicked the base of the cart; the lights instantly faded back to normal levels. The rocktopi seemed to shrink in on itself, to tighten, to contract.

"That fucker," Sam said. "He kicked Disco."

Tommy glanced at her. "You named it? It's not a puppy."

Her eyes remained fixed on the scene across the river.

"Stop telling me what they are *not*, and look at what they *are*," she said. "Those are sentient beings, Tommy. Just like we are."

He opened his mouth to argue with her, but no words came. She was right. The rocktopi weren't human, but they weren't animals, either. Even from this distance, as strange as they were, there was something … *intangible* about them. Something far beyond the intelligence one could see in the eyes of a chimp.

"I named one," Sam said. "You name the other."

"This isn't a game."

"Do I sound like I'm playing?"

Sharpness in her voice. The situation and the stress? Or was it because he was correcting her too much. It didn't matter.

"Naming them is dumb," he said.

Sam didn't seem to hear him. She pointed to the one on the right.

"*Look*. It's signaling."

Tommy saw it. A flat, white spot on the rocktopi's body, and on that spot, in thin black lines, the same symbol Sam had drawn.

"I'll be damned," Tommy said.

"I don't know if I have the symbol right, but the rocktopi is mimicking it."

He could barely breathe. The alien had seen them, was trying to communicate with them. It wasn't making noise, wasn't banging at the electrified cage bars like an angry gorilla.

"It's staying quiet," Tommy said. "It's being … *subtle*. This is mind-blowing, Sam."

She slowly, quietly pulled the pad back, started drawing on a new page. Tommy watched the two guards. One of them sat on his butt, worked his water tube. The one who'd kicked Disco's cart still stood there, staring at the other rocktopi. Neither guard reacted to the symbol. And why would they? If Tommy hadn't been with Samira, he could have been looking right at the rocktopi and completely missed that symbol—it was just another pattern in an endless chain of colors.

Tommy again looked at the alien, and felt a strange, undeniable sensation—eye contact.

"It sees us."

"Yeah, I felt that, too," Sam said.

As Tommy watched the alien, the symbol changed.

"New symbol," he said. "What does it mean?"

She looked around the tree trunk. "Don't know. Give me a minute."

He heard her flipping through his copy of *The Call of the Wild*. Tommy felt an absurd rush of pride—Sam was going to use *his* symbols to try and communicate.

That new symbol … Tommy remembered drawing it.

"Sam, that symbol it's flashing, it was at the top of the symbols in the classroom. It was bigger than the others, what's why I wrote it down."

"Okay," Sam said. "Maybe that prominence means it's significant."

"Uh, Sam? That new symbol is flashing orange now. Is that important?"

"Jesus Christ, Tommy, give me a second, will you?"

He waited, watched, listened to pages flip.

"Holy shit," Sam said. "I think the symbol means *the language*. That's the symbol for their written word. He's asking if we speak the language."

"*Habla Español*, so to speak?"

"*Un poco*," Sam said. "How do I communicate that to him?"

Tommy couldn't help her. He tried to be patient as he heard her drawing something new.

The standing guard turned, seemed to look out at the river. Tommy slowly lifted his carbine, sighted in. The optics made the man's face snap into detail. The guard looked stressed, tired, but showed no sign of awareness of Sam's actions, nor that his captive was communicating with would-be rescuers.

Sam slowly put the pad in front of the tree.

"This is the symbol for *outside*," Sam said. "It's in the tunnel leading to the plateau and was with the animal carvings we saw in the classroom."

"So it could also mean *surface*. Or *mountain*. Or—"

"Tommy, shut up," Sam said. "Give it a minute."

The rocktopi didn't seem to react. Colors coursed up and down its extending and retracting pseudopods. Then, it let out a piercing screech, a sound that made the standing guard jump, made the other rocktopi pulse in fear or anxiety or sympathy.

The guard turned, grabbed something sitting on the front of the cage cart. A controller of some kind? The guard pressed a button. Arcs of electricity lanced through the rocktopi, sparked off the thin cage bars. The captive rocktopi twitched and jerked, let out a horrid sound that could have peeled paint off the walls.

Alien or not, there was no mistaking that for anything but a cry of pain.

The guard released the button.

The rocktopi seemed to recover, then turned a deep sapphire blue. It screeched again, this time an obvious sound of rage and promised violence. A pseudopod shot toward the guard—when it hit the cage's fine mesh, another audible *crack* of electricity.

The alien shuddered. It stayed in the very center of the cage, small bumps coursing across its black-dotted, madly swirling skin.

Tommy watched through his scope. The guard yelled something at the rocktopi, held up the controller as if to say, *make trouble and you get* this *again*.

When the alien made no noise, no movement, the guard put the controller back on the front of the cart. He looked around, perhaps to see if anyone was watching, then sat down himself.

"It was so *loud*," Sam said. "It wanted to tear that guard apart."

Loud, violent...

A fragment of a sci-fi book popped into Tommy's thoughts: *Hell Divers*, a post-apocalyptic tale full of screeching, mutated predators.

"Not *it*," he said. "Call him *Siren*."

"I thought naming them was dumb."

Maybe it had been, but Tommy saw the anger in the creature, the bloodlust to lash out at someone who'd hurt it. Tommy had given in to his own savage instincts more times than he could count. In that instant, he felt a strange yet powerful sense of kinship with the alien.

The rocktopi were sentient beings, with a written language. And a *starship*. What had Ender been thinking with his storm-the-castle strategy? Had the rocktopi in Utah *really* been savages?

Or had the "savage" actually been Ender?

"Siren is signaling," Sam said. "It sees us. It's flashing the same *outside* symbol, and several others. I don't know what the other symbols means."

Context was everything, and even though Tommy didn't understand the symbols, the context of the situation made the alien's message clear.

"It's asking us to help it," he said.

A pause. "I think you're right. Holy shit."

Tommy felt his heart hammering in his chest. Against trained killers with guns, he felt almost nothing at all, but this…this was different. This was overwhelming.

He and Sam were *communicating* with alien beings.

"Tommy, how do we help them?"

He forced himself to calm down. The thrill of discovery needed to take a back seat to the realities of life and death. The people across that river wanted him dead. Him and Sam both, no doubt.

"Can you ask them if there's a way out other than the tunnel they came in?"

"That's complex, but I'll try," Sam said. "Give me a minute."

Tommy studied the enemy's position. Absolutely zero chance of succeeding with any kind of direct attack, especially with the fast river between him and the rocktopi. He still had two grenades—that wouldn't do much against a force that size.

Sam put the pad in front of the tree again. Both Disco and Siren started flashing new symbols.

Wait…the rocktopi and their guards had been the last ones into this cavern. They'd been at the rear of the column.

Which meant they would be the last ones *out*.

"I used the symbols for *tunnels* and the one that I interpreted to be *choice*, or *alternative*, that I saw at the forks we hit," Sam said. "I think they understand what I'm asking. And I think … I *think* they're saying there is another way out. I'm not sure. That's the best I can do, Tommy—if they're giving us specific directions, I have no idea how to interpret it."

Tommy twisted his water tube toward his mouth, took a sip of water, then twisted it back into its housing.

He mentally tried to talk himself out of the only possible strategy. He failed—he couldn't think only of his own safety. This was bigger than that. Far bigger.

"Tommy, what do we do?"

He would do what had to be done. Would Sam?

"We're separated from our unit," he said. "We can't afford to turn on the comms and call out, as the signals might get detected, and our people are probably already out of range. We're heavily outnumbered. We don't know where we are, don't know the layout of this place. If we try to rescue Disco and Siren, we could die in the effort. Even if we succeed in getting them out, they might kill us the first chance they get. With that in mind, what do *you* think we should do, Sam?"

He wasn't going to make this decision on his own.

"I say we try to save them," she said. "This is an intelligent race. I feel in my gut that we can communicate with them. Just basics, probably, but we can. They'll know the layout, maybe know how to find O'Doyle and the others. It's our best chance, maybe our *only* chance, to get a guide who knows these tunnels."

She waited for him to respond.

"We're gambling on so many levels," Tommy said. "If we do save them, where do we go?"

"That's what we'll have to get them to tell us."

Calling it a *gamble* was an understatement. He would be risking his life and Sam's on an assumption that the rocktopi could understand what he was asking of them.

"If we can't communicate with them quickly enough, or they go through a passage too thin for us to fit through, we're dead," Tommy said. "You willing to put your life on the line?"

Now he waited for her. His friends had gunned down those rocktopi, both in the tunnel and on the riverbank. The aliens hadn't stood a chance. O'Doyle talked of how the rocktopi slaughtered people, but was it somehow better if people slaughtered rocktopi? If Tommy could do something to stop the killing, to protect this sentient species, to try and make real contact, didn't he have to try?

And yet, he knew going after them was stupid. He was outgunned, and the only support he'd have was an archaeologist with no weapons or combat training. Part of him wanted Sam to object, to give him a reason not to do this.

She didn't give him that reason.

"I think they're our only real chance," she said. "You won't leave without your friends. I know I have no chance of surviving without you. So if we're staying, going after O'Doyle, we need Disco and Siren to help us." She shrugged. "Otherwise, we wander around until the silverbugs get us, Angus gets us, or we run into rocktopi that assume we're their enemy."

They'd barely survived the handful of silverbugs they'd faced. They'd have no chance against a larger number. Limited food, limited ammo, in hostile territory… if he didn't gamble, Sam was right—they were dead anyway.

"You need to understand what this means," he said. "To rescue them, we are going to have to kill people. Have you ever killed anyone?"

Sam shook her head.

"It's bad," Tommy said. "I'll try to keep you from it, but I need you ready to use that pistol. Both of our lives will depend on it. If you're not up to fighting, to killing, you can try to make it out on your own. Is that what you want?"

Sam thought about it, but only for a moment.

"No," she said, shaking her head. "I'm staying with you. Ram was on his own, and now he's dead."

Tommy tried to read her face. She knew the realities of what they faced. But there was a difference between *knowing* what had to be done and *doing* it.

"We'll have to use my claymore," Tommy said.

"I told you, that could cause a cave-in."

Tommy nodded. "That's what I'm counting on. A cave-in might be the only way we survive this. When they break camp, we'll make our move. Until then, we need sleep just as much as they do. I'll take first watch."

51

14,978 feet below the surface

PATRICK O'DOYLE CROUCHED in the prow, his body hidden by the canoe save for his eyes, the top of his head, and his weapon. Behind him, the others stayed low, peering over the rails.

He'd fucked up something in his back. How bad, he didn't know. Of all the wounds he'd suffered over the years, his *back*? An old man's injury.

That's what he was—an old man.

An old man who should have never come here.

Up ahead, the river tunnel led to the light of a new cavern.

"McGuiness, take the oar from Sleepy," Patrick said. "If the shit hits the fan, get down and stay down. Otto, take the other oar."

Sonny moved up from the back of the canoe, wobbling slightly as his weight shifted the balance. Sleepy handed his oar to the old man, then immediately re-checked his weapon.

"I can fight," Otto said. "Sure you don't want me with a weapon in my hands?"

Patrick could see the man wasn't trying to be difficult; he wanted to survive, was more than willing to do his part.

"I know what my people can do," Patrick said, glancing back at him. "I don't really know what *you* can do yet."

Otto nodded toward Klimas. "You don't know him, and you aren't asking him to row."

"Come on," Patrick said. "You going to tell me that you're a better soldier than a SEAL who's half your age?"

Otto glanced at Klimas, then shook his head and moved to take the oar from Mullet.

"Skylark on my left, Sleepy on my right," Patrick said. "Mullet port side, Klimas starboard. Bertha, Curve, in the stern. Curve, how's that hand?"

"I can shoot straight."

Yes, but was his *head* straight? Probably not, and it didn't matter — when the killing started, Curve had always done his job.

"Stay in the stern," Patrick said. "Be ready to come up and support where needed."

"On it," Curveball said.

The man was talking again, responding to orders well enough, it seemed, but the loss of Hatchet hung heavy on the man's soul. If Bertha died, would Patrick feel any different?

He hoped he wouldn't find out.

The tunnel opening drew closer. Maybe two hundred meters to go. The river burbled, a strangely happy sound amidst what could turn out to be a deadly situation.

A canoe floating down an unknown river, heading into a cavern of unknown size, with a possible enemy of unknown number. The NoSeeUms would be ready. So would Bertha, Klimas and Otto.

A hundred and fifty meters.

The light from the cavern ahead played off the river's rippling surface.

The closer the canoe got to the opening, the more Patrick could see of the chamber. Another cavern, a big one, maybe as big as the Kidney-Shaped Cavern in Utah had been. Far up ahead, Patrick could see that the river bent to the left. On the right-hand shore, clusters of yellow and blue. Looked like the same trees he'd seen when they'd taken the canoe, when the silverbugs had stretched out across the river, caused the loss of Jabour and Worm.

Worm. *Tommy*. Was he dead? Had Patrick's folly resulted in the loss of another NoSeeUm?

Who would die next?

The canoe floated on.

Patrick pressed his *talk* button, whispered: "Fifty meters until we enter that cavern ahead. Stay sharp. Go to the open channel."

The closer the canoe came to the entrance, the more Patrick could see. Rocky shorelines on both sides. On the left bank, he saw structures … small grayish buildings of some kind. A lot of them made of stone slabs. Houses? Storage? Was it a village of some kind?

The canoe slipped into the light. Carbine stock tight to his shoulder, Patrick slowly twisted in place from left to right, taking it all in. A cavern, *huge*, gray granite walls arching up to a ceiling at least two hundred meters above, with a miniature sun blazing so bright he couldn't look at it.

Mullet: "This is fucking bonkers. You could fit a domed stadium in here with plenty of room all around it."

Otto: "Center of the cavern, is that an obelisk?"

"Quiet," Patrick said, but he flashed a quick look that way.

A black tower. From that far away, it was hard to gauge the obelisk's height. Maybe twenty meters tall?

What *was* this place?

Far ahead, the river's bend seemed to angle toward that obelisk. Stone buildings packed on the riverbank up there. Too many of those buildings to call this a village. This was a full-fledged *town*, if not a small *city*.

Curveball: "That frankenbroccoli orchard on the right bank is dense, a lot of cover. Stay sharp."

Sleepy: "Some trees on the left bank, before the houses start. Watch for movement."

But there was no movement. No rocktopi, no silverbugs, no sign of Angus's mercenaries.

Klimas: "Could this cavern be abandoned?"

Skylark: "Orchards on both sides look neat and tidy. That doesn't happen on its own."

That didn't mean much—in Utah, Patrick had seen silverbugs tending to crops. Still, the place didn't *feel* abandoned. The nagging Spidey-sense that had kept Patrick alive during missions all over the globe told him he was being watched.

"Stay sharp," he said. "We're not alone in here."

The canoe floated past a single stone building on the right bank, a building surrounded by frankenbroccoli trees.

No sound save for the river's steady gurgle.

Something about that house … Patrick kept his carbine trained on it. Movement, behind the house …

… something *big* …

It rose up on four gleaming legs.

"Contact," Patrick said, "three o'clock!"

A silverbug, a *huge* one, the size of a small tank, rose up on four sewer-pipe-sized metal legs. It stormed around the house, split feet carrying it over a crop of knee-high purple plants. It was like watching a gleaming, living water tower race toward them.

"*Sonofabitch*," Sonny shouted.

Patrick and Sleepy fired three-shot bursts. The machine didn't slow. They fired again, Klimas joining in. Patrick heard suppressed gunfire as the rest of the squad did the same. Bullets sparked off the platinum shell, but the concentrated barrage didn't slow the machine—long legs plunged into the river. The round metal body kicked up a wave of water.

On the silverbug came, far faster than the current that carried the canoe. Knee joints jutted up from the surface before disappearing beneath again, feet somewhere on the riverbed below. What looked like rounded rungs ran up the curved side.

Patrick started to order everyone to bail out, but before he could say the words, a long platinum arm reached out—the silverbug mech was on them. The arm ended in three long metal fingers that grabbed the canoe prow and *lifted*. The boat angled sharply upward. Patrick switched his carbine to his left hand, grabbed the canoe rail with his right, used it to keep himself from falling backward. He heard yells, heavy splashes as someone tumbled in.

The end of his suppressor only an inch from the giant silverbug, Patrick fired, saw bullets punch holes through the metal.

Something inside the big sphere sparked—the machine rang like a gong. It dropped the canoe, which slammed down against the water, throwing Patrick forward into the prow. His faceplate smashed against the sloping metal, cranking his head back. He fell flat, scrambled to his knees, hands grabbing at the carbine suspended from its harness.

He shouldered the weapon and aimed—the huge machine was lurching away through the river, staggering on three thick legs while the last leg waved spasmodically.

A new sound rang out—dozens of hammers smashing into dozens of aluminum benches. Dents as long as a finger appeared in the canoe hull, as if someone was stabbing the outside of it with invisible spears.

Patrick ducked down, as did the rest of his team.

Klimas: "Five, maybe six hostiles on the starboard bank, armed with railguns."

"Everyone return fire," Patrick said. "In three, two, one!"

He popped up, stock to his shoulder, eyes hunting the starboard bank. Four glowing, shimmering rocktopi, higher up on the stone bluff. He fired a three-shot burst, switched his aim to the next hostile, and fired again. The four rocktopi dropped down, screeching—Patrick didn't know if they'd been hit, but at least they weren't shooting anymore.

"Klimas, Sleepy, keep them pinned down!"

Mullet: "Hostiles, two o'clock."

Skylark: "Five of 'em!"

Patrick pivoted left, fought down a cry of pain as his lower back froze him up in mid-turn. He grunted, finished the turn, saw rocktopi on the bank, their two-barreled weapons aimed at the canoe.

He heard that hammer-on-aluminum sound even as he opened up with his own weapon.

Rocktopi rounds kicked up huge splashes from the river, punched into the canoe hull. NoSeeUm bullets answered back—one of the rocktopi dropped. A second rocktopi fell, then a third. The fourth turned and ran, but the fifth held its position—it aimed and fired.

An invisible fist slammed into Patrick's chest, knocking him to his back. A dull, disoriented moment, then the pain announced itself with a vengeance. He groaned, felt at his chest—a hole in the fabric, a dent in his body armor.

Skylark: "Ender's hit!"

She knelt by him, her hands searching his chest.

"It didn't go through," she said. "You—"

Red blood sprayed onto Patrick, across the inside of the canoe. Skylark fell to her side, eyes wide with surprise, blood spurting from the stub of a half-inch-thick metal bar sticking out of her neck.

Mullet: "*Skylark's hit!*"

Patrick grabbed her, pulled her down flat, threw his body over her.

Mullet at the rail, firing at the rocktopi, covering Patrick and Skylark.

Patrick laced his fingers around the bar in her neck, pressed down hard against Skylark's wound. Blood seeped out, as did her suit's oily coolant, the two fluids mixing together.

She blinked, weak and confused.

"Marie," Patrick said, "stay alert, stay with me!"

Sleepy: "*I'm hit!*"

The sounds of suppressors, of hammers on aluminum, of torn metal.

Water soaked into Marie's fatigues, rose up around her shoulders, Patrick's knees.

He couldn't stop the bleeding.

Marie tensed, grabbed at his wrist, then her grip relaxed. She lay still, half-lidded eyes staring out.

She was gone.

Bertha: "That big fucker's coming back!"

Patrick rolled off Skylark. Water sloshed in the canoe bottom. He gripped his carbine, crawled toward the stern, pushing past McGuiness, who was curled into a ball, and Otto, who'd given up on the oar and was firing his pistol over the starboard side. Past Sleepy, who lay on his back in the bloody water, his right hand clutched to his left shoulder. Where was Curveball? Where was Klimas?

Patrick saw Bertha at the back of the canoe, crouched down and firing. And past her, the huge silverbug, pounding through the river. Patrick leaned on the rail next to his wife. He managed a single burst before the silverbug reached out and grabbed the end of the canoe. He switched his aim to one of the split feet, then the giant machine yanked the prow high, so hard that Patrick flew backward through the air.

He soared over the water, arms waving madly, turning as he flew, saw the stone bank rushing up at him.

He hit hard. For a brief moment, he found the strength to roll onto his back. He squinted against the artificial suns high above, felt water lapping against him, then everything faded to gray.

52

HIDING BEHIND THE same tree they'd used to communicate with the rocktopi, Sam watched the last mercenaries enter the tunnel on the far side of the river. Four men in the rear guard. One of those limped—he was wounded. In front of them, the two rocktopi cages, each with their own driver/handler.

Six men, *at least*, that Tommy had to kill to rescue Siren and Disco.

Jesus … using the rocktopi "names" seemed so logical, so normal. Part of that intangibility of knowing they were sentient beings, maybe.

"Hold tight," Tommy said. "We'll wait to see if they run drones out to watch their back."

"How long are we going to wait? Won't they get away?"

"They have too many men. And prisoners. They can't move as fast as we can. We'll catch them."

And then … what? Was Sam actually going to be in a fucking *gunfight*? A gunfight against mercenaries with a leader in powered armor, to rescue imprisoned aliens.

"That's long enough," Tommy said. "Game on. You do what I say, when I say, understand?"

Sam tried to ignore the butterflies in her belly. "I got it."

"Show me your weapon."

She stood, drew the pistol from her thigh holster.

"Show me your stance," Tommy said.

Sam complied, spread her feet past shoulder width, bending her knees slightly, holding the pistol in both hands, palms pressing in on the handle. She kept her finger off the trigger.

"Excellent," Tommy said. "Remember, if you have to shoot, you're shooting to kill. Center-mass, aim for the chest. Got it?"

This was madness. What was she doing?

"I got it."

"Good. Holster it, and let's go."

She holstered the pistol, felt it click into place. The holster would hold it there while she and Tommy crossed the river. She hoped, at least.

He stepped back from the tree, wound his way through the trees, heading for the upstream cavern wall. Sam followed.

"The river is a bitch," Tommy said. "You a good swimmer?"

Sam had spent her childhood summers at her parent's lake cabin. She'd been swimming as far back as she could remember. She looked through the trees to the raging river.

"I am, but I don't think swimming in a calm lake compares to this."

"You'll manage," Tommy said.

He didn't sound confident.

They reached the cavern wall. The river slid out of it, angry water frothing up against boulders.

"You've got from here—" Tommy pointed to the far end of the cavern "—to there to make it across. Remember that if you get dragged under, you've got at least five minutes of air left. The suit will handle that automatically. No matter what, you have to get across before you're swept into the downstream tunnel. Got it?"

She nodded. More and more, that was all she could do—she seemed at a loss for words.

"All right," Tommy said. "Sooner started, sooner done. Go in as quiet as you can, stay below the surface as much as you can. I'll be right behind you."

Sam again looked to the water. How had it come to this?

Before she could change her mind, she came out from behind the tree, moving as quietly as she could. She stepped carefully through the rocks at the water's edge, felt the current even before she was in up to her knees. Sam lowered herself into the water. The river roiled up around her.

She slid beneath the surface, trusting the KoolSuit to feed her air. The weight of her gear and pack instantly dragged her to the bottom. She pushed off, breast-stroked and kicked as the river rocketed her downstream.

Simple math: make it across, or be carried into the darkness.

The current slammed her ribs against an unseen rock. The pain seemed a distant thing as she kept swimming, kept moving forward.

Seconds later, she hit the bottom again, but this time because it was so shallow. She'd made it. On hands and knees, she crawled out of the river. A glance to her right—the cavern wall, only ten feet away. She'd almost been sucked into the tunnel and left on her own.

A hand on her back. "You okay?"

Tommy, whispering, right next to her.

"I hit my ribs," Sam said.

"Broken?"

Sam thought for a moment, winced at the throbbing pain. It wasn't as bad as the ache in her head. "No, I don't think so."

"Then get up," Tommy said. "We need to move."

She wasn't quite half his age, but wasn't all that far from it. How did he have the energy to keep going?

Tommy jogged across ground still littered with dead silverbugs. He ran with his rifle at his shoulder, aiming into the dark crack. At the edge of the tunnel, he moved to the side, knelt down.

"I have to test the detonator, see if the water fouled it," he said. "Aim your pistol at the entrance. If anything comes out, start shooting and don't stop until you run out of bullets."

The tension in her chest, the fear tingling at the small of her back. There were trained killers in that tunnel. If they came out, *she* had to shoot them?

Sam drew her pistol.

Tommy slid off his backpack. He pulled out the claymore, set the green plastic rectangle aside. He took out what looked like a dull green clicker. He attached something to it, clicked the handle—a small light on the attachment flashed orange.

He looked up, angry.

"Don't watch me, watch the opening!"

Sam twitched, felt a rush of anxiety as if she was a child and her parents had caught her doing something wrong.

She aimed the pistol at the crack in the wall.

They were about to go in there, pursuing people that would gun her down as soon as look at her. But she had to do it—she'd *communicated* with the rocktopi, one sentient race acknowledging the existence and value of another. To think that an alien race had lived here for twelve thousand years, predating every human civilization, only to be discovered and wiped out because of greed? Even if it cost her her life, she had to try and stop it.

Tommy stood, pulled his backpack on. He'd put the claymore inside it.

"I want you to repeat a phrase in your head as we're walking," he said. "*Fast is fine, but accuracy is final*. If you have to shoot someone, aim at their chest and fire. Don't think about it, just do it."

Fast is fine, accurate is final. Fast is fine, accurate is—

"Turn on your night vision," Tommy said.

Sam pressed the detent at her temple. Her visor flared to life with the green-tinged view.

They moved into the long tunnel. She'd been here before, with a wave of silverbugs behind her, running as O'Doyle and the others fired down the tunnel. How long ago had that been? A handful of hours, at most.

Ahead of her, Tommy moved like a ghost. His feet seemed to land in the right places, avoiding loose rocks. Sam had far more experience in the Fitz Roy tunnels than he did, yet he moved like a seasoned pro while she felt like a rank amateur. She tried to match his footsteps.

Tommy reached the first switchback. He stopped, leaned around it very slowly, then waved her on.

He did the same at a second switchback.

At the third, he stayed in place.

He slid his backpack off, took out the claymore. He opened up thin legs on the mine's bottom, pushed the legs into the tunnel silt. The face marked FRONT TOWARD ENEMY now pointed down the tunnel segment. Sam saw that Tommy—or she—would be able to stay behind the switchback corner and detonate the mine, which would likely shred everything down the tunnel segment.

Tommy pulled a small coil of wire from his backpack.

"Is that a trip wire?"

"It's electrical," he said. "We'll detonate this by hand, no trip wire. Keep an eye out."

Sam moved to the edge and slowly peered around it. Nothing in the tunnel segment, but she knew that Kool's men might be around the next switchback corner. Her hands shook—if she had to fire, could she even shoot straight?

Tommy tapped her on the shoulder. She leaned back behind the edge. He held up the clicker. A wire ran from it to the mine.

"If they take me out, you get behind the switchback wall, grab this detonator, push this clip out of the way, then squeeze it hard and fast. It will make a helluva boom. Then you *run*. Take your chances in the river. Got it?"

Her whole body began to shake.

"Sam, are you still willing to do this with me?"

She breathed in sharply, focused on making her body obey. The shaking stopped.

"I'm ready," she said.

"Good. Don't fire unless I do. We'll keep radios off until we get separated. You remember how to turn it on?"

She felt at the waistband of her KoolSuit, found the detent there that turned the radio on and off. She nodded.

"Good," Tommy said. "Let's go."

He silently moved around the switchback corner, careful not to step on the mine. Sam drew the pistol and did the same—the shaking started again.

Fast is fine, accurate is final. Fast is fine, accurate is final.

They moved down two more switchbacks, Tommy carefully checking first, then waving Sam on.

At the third corner, he leaned out, then back. He put his facemask against hers.

"They're right there," he whispered, his words barely audible. "They're undisciplined, getting careless. I'll take out the first four, then the cage guards. You come behind me, figure out how to get the cages open."

She had her orders, Tommy expected her to follow them. Both of their lives hung in the balance.

Tommy stepped back from the switchback corner. He held his rifle butt to his shoulder. He didn't do a big spinning swing, like they did in the movies. Instead, with his rifle already leveled, he took a half-step to the side, which moved him slightly past the protecting stone wall.

The harsh *clack* of his weapon. Tommy barely moved his shoulders as he switched aim. Eight shots, maybe nine, all in two seconds.

"Let's go," he said, and he ran down the tunnel.

Sam stayed close behind him, the pistol heavy in her hands.

Four mercenaries on the ground, two still moving. As he jogged past them, Tommy shot each man in the head. Sam saw a sheet of red explode against the inside of one man's visor.

Tommy—*Bookworm*—was methodical. Efficient. No hesitation.

She'd known he was a killer, but knowing it in the abstract was different than seeing it up close.

It horrified her.

Tommy reached the next switchback, repeated his moves, sliding to the side again, firing again, running again.

Sam was so scared she could barely see. Fear gripped her, held her, told her that she could go no further, but she pushed past it—Tommy was ahead of her, he needed her.

She moved past the switchback corner. The rocktopi cages, their captives blazing in glorious, fit-inducing colors that played off the tunnel walls and ceiling. Two men on the ground—the two men she'd seen with the cages back by the river. Both men were facedown, still moving, trying to rise. Tommy drew his knife. He slid the blade into the back of first one man's skull, then the other.

The men stopped moving.

Six human beings, dead. Just like that. Were their lives less important than those of the two rocktopi? Sam pushed the thought away.

Tommy stood. He switched out his magazine, tilted his head to the cages.

"Turn on your radio," he said. "I'll buy time, you get them out."

She'd barely switched her radio on before he vanished behind the next switchback corner.

ANGUS HEARD DONNIE'S voice on the comm: "Rearguard, come in."

Khatari raised a fist. Angus and Fuentes stopped. So, too, did the BaDonkeyDonks walking behind them.

No one answered.

Donnie: "Rearguard, come in."

Fuentes and Khatari exchanged a look. Their hands flexed on their rifles.

The rearguard wasn't answering. Were they in trouble? Were the rocktopi attacking? Seventh Platoon was the only thing between Angus and the rearguard.

Donnie: "Seventh, move to the back, quiet and fast, assume hostiles hit the rearguard. Fuentes, Khatari, Kool, back them up."

SAM STOOD ALONE at the cages, staring at two alien creatures. Glowing patterns across them, shifting and pulsating. Their pseudopods did the same, stretching out to just before the electrified metal grate, then shrinking back, vanishing into the boneless bodies.

Like looking at a confusing image that suddenly snaps into clarity, she realized the patterns of both rocktopi had repetitive elements. The colors changed in wild shifts, yet the alternating moving angles and spinning curves stayed mostly consistent. From just her brief time seeing them across the river, she *recognized* them, knew which one was Disco and which one was Siren.

Sam saw the controller laying on the tunnel silt, connected by a cable to the underside of the rolling cage. She holstered her pistol, picked up the controller. The buttons seemed simple, like a video game: arrows pointing left and right, a plus/minus toggle that had to be for speed. A red button for stop, green for go … and a switch protected by a clear plastic cover.

Tommy's urgent, whispering voice in her headset: "White lights moving down the tunnel toward me. Hurry, Sam, they're coming! I'll try to slow them down with grenades."

She felt a slight tremble in the ground beneath her. The explosion seemed quieter than she'd expected—not like in the movies at all. The sound echoed through the tunnel. Small rocks plinked off her helmet, dropped down around her.

Sam popped open up the controller's clear plastic cover and flicked the switch.

Tommy: "Grenade two, out."

Sam ducked down, covered her head. A second explosion, more rocks falling, *bigger* rocks. Was this it? Was the whole thing going to collapse on her?

THE GROUND TREMBLED slightly for a brief second, then hard enough to make Khatari and Fuentes put a hand to the wall to steady themselves. The shaking stopped almost as quickly as it had begun.

"Come on," Khatari said.

He ran forward, Fuentes right behind. Angus rushed to keep up, his powersuit's feet thudding on cave silt.

A voice Angus didn't recognize on the comm: "This is seventh. Fuckers threw grenades at us. No casualties in our platoon, but the tunnel caved in—we're cut off from the rearguard."

Angus came around the next switchback corner, saw the men of Seventh Platoon pulling at fallen rock that filled the tunnel. Khatari and Fuentes rushed to join them.

All that rock … it would take them forever.

But Angus had prepared for this.

"Everyone get back," he said. "BaDonkeyDonk Three, to me!"

THE ROCKS STOPPED dropping.

Sam looked up—Siren was out of the cage, only inches in front of her, long pseudopods waving, blazing bright in swirling crimson and deep, iridescent blue.

She couldn't move. She couldn't think.

She'd thought she would die from bullets, from a cave-in … in that instant, she knew it would be the rocktopi that would kill her.

Siren didn't *turn* from her, it *flowed* away, rolled to the other cage. It scooped up that cage's controller.

Tommy: "There's a cave-in. We're safe for now, but hurry up."

The rocktopi popped open the plastic cover and flicked the switch, exactly as Sam had done.

Disco's cage didn't open; a faint hum vanished, a hum she hadn't even realized was there.

Pulsating with shades of orange and cascading black stripes, Disco's pseudopods gripped the metal mesh and ripped a chunk of it free. Fasteners popped and scattered across the silt. The creature flowed through the opening and onto the tunnel floor—just like that, it was free.

Sam dared not move.

"They're *out*," she whispered.

Tommy: "Are you in danger?"

Sam stood there, only a few feet from two alien creatures that had—up until seconds ago—been imprisoned and were probably pissed as hell. The two creatures didn't come closer, but they didn't leave, either. They were looking at her, she could *feel* their stare.

"I don't know," Sam said. "I sure don't feel safe. Where the hell are you?"

Tommy, whispering: "Four switchbacks up. I can hear men on the other side, I don't know what they're doing."

"WHAT CAN WE do to help?" Fuentes said.

"Get everyone back behind the switchback." Angus unlatched the end of the tube strapped to the donkey's side. "You, too. It's going to get hot in here."

He opened a small compartment on his powersuit's waist, drew a retractable cable, and plugged it into a port on the back of the tube.

Angus had a moment to realize he stood alone in the tunnel. Khatari, Fuentes and Seventh Platoon had moved down the tunnel.

Time to see if the ButterKnife worked outside of the lab.

A new menu appeared in his HUD. With a blink, he turned the ButterKnife on.

"JUST GET OVER here," Sam said, her eyes fixed on the glowing creatures.

Tommy: "I'm coming…hold on. Something is happening. Temperature is spiking here."

Sam's teeth ground together. Something was happening where he was? No shit, something was happening where *she* was.

The aliens glowed in multi-shaded hues. Patterns of color coursed across their soft bodies.

"I'm not sure you heard me," Sam said. "They are *out* of their cages and—"

Tommy: "What the…they're melting through the cave-in! Get to the river, *go-go-go!*"

She turned and ran, sure that Siren would drag her down from behind, that they would strangle her with their flashing pseudopods. She made it one switchback before she noticed the ambient temperature spike up, as if a heatwave had just rolled in.

SO POWERFUL.

Angus couldn't help but laugh as he controlled the ButterKnife, making the green laser move in a slowly expanding circle that melted a growing hole through the fallen rock. Granite glowed white-hot around the edges, spread across the silt in molten globs.

He'd used a similar device to drill a hole two miles deep—punching through a few feet of fallen rock was child's play by comparison.

He blinked off the laser. The white faded to red, which itself slowly lost color.

No one on the other side.

Donnie: "Doctor Kool, I'm my way to your position. Status report?"

"We punched through the cave-in. Send more troops. We should go after the assholes that attacked us."

By *we*, of course, Angus meant the mercs. He wasn't about to lead the charge this time, not after what happened the last time he went rogue.

Donnie: "The enemy has grenades and claymores—I'm not sending my men down the barrel of a shotgun. Kool, send one of your machines through first. Seventh Platoon, follow it and find our rearguard. If you have a shot, take it, but move with caution, as rearguard is probably already dead."

FROM THE TUNNEL behind her, Sam heard echoing gunfire.

Tommy: "Faster!"

Sam sprinted as fast as she could, so fast she almost lost her balance coming around the switchback corners. She saw the claymore, pointed at it while skirting wide of it, hoping the rocktopi would follow suit and not knock the thing over.

Tommy: "Get them to the river. I'll do the claymore."

Her legs burned. Her stomach roiled.

More gunfire from behind.

The rocktopi flowed past her, long pseudopods stretching out like Silly Putty, some even reaching forward and up to the tunnel walls and ceiling, maybe for balance, she wasn't sure.

Sam cried out when she heard an explosion behind her, felt a concussive wind slap against her back. A rumbling beneath her feet.

She came around the last switchback corner, sprinted down the long tunnel toward the opening that led to the big cavern. Ahead of her, Disco and Siren flowed and stretched, their speed surprising, the grace undeniable.

Her exhaustion vanished. Sam sprinted faster than she ever had in high school track, and she was out of the tunnel, into the light.

The two rocktopi were at the riverbank, their tentacles waving. Were they beckoning to her?

Tommy: "Get them to show us a way out of here! Fast!"

He'd done his part, now she had to do hers.

Sam ran toward the river, careful to avoid the hundreds of dead silverbugs.

Her sketch pad ... she needed her sketch pad.

She started to shrug it off as she closed in on the two rocktopi. She slid it free, but it fell, skidding across the ground to thump against Disco, flashing red-orange and turquoise. She knelt to grab the pack—a brief glimpse of a pseudopod moving in front of her, moving *toward* her, then she was wrapped up, yanked forward.

In an instant, she was *engulfed*.

Skin glowing in a dozen shifting colors pressed against her visor, blocked out everything else.

Sam found her breath—and she screamed.

BOOK FOUR
CAPTIVES

53

14,978 feet below the surface

BERTHA LYBRAND CRAWLED onto the shore. Gravel and rocks ground against her knees and hands. Her right shoulder felt numb—the canoe gunwale had slammed against it when the silverbug mech tipped the thing over.

She had to get away from the water, get to some of those crops and find a place to take cover, figure out where everyone else was, then find Patrick.

Her comm, still on the open channel …

"This is Lybrand," she said as she crawled, tried to stand. "I—"

Something grabbed her ankles, yanked her. She fell to her stomach, visor smearing with wet dirt and tiny rocks.

She kicked, felt the strength of what she was fighting against, knew she would not break free. It dragged her backward. A tug on her carbine harness; she heard metal slicing against canvas and the weapon was gone.

The world lurched—she was thrown hard against the riverbank stone.

Bertha couldn't see. She drew her Glock, wiped at the mud on her visor, saw a shimmering cascade of mad colors right in front of her. She angled the weapon up to fire—something slammed into her head.

Black spots formed, gray swirled.

She rolled right, away from the blow, got to her hands and knees before something smashed into her lower back. Her arms gave out; she fell on her chest, a bomb of agony radiating up her spine.

Pistol still in her hand. She tried to rise again, tried to fight through the pain to find a target. Kill them, now, or they'd slice her to pieces, crack open her skull and stir the brains inside.

A rope wrapping around her wrist—not a rope, she knew what it was—and the Glock was yanked from her hand.

Bertha got her feet under her, rose on wobbly legs. She would not die on her knees.

Her knife. She still had the knife.

She turned to face her killers, drawing the knife as she did.

A half dozen rocktopi in front of her, all with their double-barreled railguns leveled at her face.

One held her Glock. Another, her carbine.

That moment—her last moment—stretched out forever and ever.

She would die not knowing if Patrick was safe, or if he was just as dead as she was about to be.

The moment ended, because the rocktopi didn't fire.

She should be dead. Why were they waiting?

One lowered its railgun. A pseudopod—teal with cascading black and gray stripes—pointed at her. No, it pointed at her knife.

The pseudopod then pointed to the ground.

It wanted her to drop the knife.

"Fuck you, you nasty glob of snot," she said. "Come and get it."

The creature let out a short, sharp screech.

The other five rocktopi did something that required no translation. Their railguns still aimed at her face, the creatures moved a bit closer to her, gave their weapons a single, intimidating shake: *drop it, or else.*

"This is Lybrand, does anyone copy?"

No answer. Were they all dead, or was her comm messed up?

The river on her left. A stone bluff to her right. No sign of the canoe. No sign of Patrick or the others.

She was screwed.

The sound of a hammer hitting metal—one of the railguns fired, scattering the sand by her left foot. Six inches of finger-width metal rod stuck up from the spot.

A warning shot.

If she fought now, she would die. If she surrendered, maybe she'd live long enough to see Patrick again.

With five alien weapons aimed at her face, Bertha Lybrand dropped the knife.

The rocktopi surged forward.

54

9,205 feet below the surface

ANGUS DIDN'T KNOW if he should say something or keep his trap shut. Khatari and Fuentes were practically standing at attention, staring straight ahead. Were they afraid of what Donnie might do next? If a pair of killer mercs were intimidated, maybe staying quiet was the right thing to do.

Donnie stared at the hole melted through the fallen rocks. He reached out toward the glassy surface, hesitated.

"It's cooled off," Angus said.

Donnie nodded, ran his fingertips across the smooth, rippled material.

"Went through granite like soft wax," he said. He leaned back, looked up at the broken ceiling. "You sure it's safe to be here?"

Just when Angus had started to think of the man as something other than *Dimwit*, ol' Donnie had to go and say something incredibly stupid.

"We're in a cave-in area," Angus said. "Of course it's not *safe*. The melted rock has fused together, though, and fully cooled, so it's solid and weight-bearing. That said, I'd rather not be here any longer than we need to be."

Dimwit tapped a boot toe against a glob of granite that had cooled into a misshapen puddle on the floor.

"Amazing," he said. "Didn't help Seventh Platoon, though, did it? Six of them dead. I'll use the four that are left to fill up Third. Third's still depleted from that ambush at the shaft."

Donnie stared at Angus. Angus said nothing. Was he supposed to respond to personnel transfers or something?

"We lost men," Donnie said. "We lost prisoners, we lost equipment. O'Doyle and his bastards are beginning to make me angry. You know the man—what do you think he'll try next?"

Angus thought of answering with a simple shrug, but the burning look in Donnie's eyes told him that was a bad idea.

"We worked for the same company, Donnie. It's not like we used to whisper sweet nothings over a nice glass of merlot. I know fuck-all about the guy."

Fuck-all, other than that he showed up in Angus's nightmares, snarling and scary, carrying that big knife…

"This isn't the time for jokes," Donnie said.

"I'm not joking. I'm more of a chardonnay man, to be honest."

Fuentes snorted a single, sharp laugh. He stood there, eyes bulging, trying to simultaneously hold back more and keep his eyes anywhere but on Donnie, who glared daggers at the man.

"Six more of my men are dead," Dimwit said to Fuentes. "You think that's funny?"

Fuentes swallowed, shook his head.

"And you, Doctor," Donnie said. "Do you think body bags are hysterical?"

Well…no. Angus did not. Men were, indeed, dead. The mercs had, indeed, lost the two rocktopi prisoners. Angus didn't even know what had compelled him to make a shitty joke. Something about the way the exosuit made him feel, maybe, as if he was immune to Donnie's anger.

The men in those body bags could have been Angus.

Or Yadav Khatari.

Or William Fuentes.

No, it most certainly was *not* a laughing matter.

"Gallows humor," Angus said. "Sorry, Donnie, I'm not all that experienced with this kind of thing, you know?"

Dimwit regarded him for a moment, perhaps searching for the next joke, or to see if Angus was full of bullshit. For once, Angus was not—he genuinely felt *bad* about making light of the situation.

"Sir, recon supposedly cleared the cavern," Khatari said. "They did a shit job."

Donnie nodded. "You're right about that. I'll have some words with Henderson. Doctor Kool, I need you to focus—what do you think O'Doyle might try next?"

"If I had any idea, you'd be the first to know," Angus said. "Trust me, that dude scares the fuzz off my sack."

Donnie's mustache twitched once to the left, returned to center.

"Very well, Doctor. I need you to make my requested modifications to one of the donkeys. How long will that take?"

"An hour or so," Angus said. "And we can't be on the move while I do it."

The mustache twitched again. "I need it done in forty-five minutes, Doctor. Can you get that done?"

What was this, some kind of rah-rah coaching tactic? Maybe Donnie was destined for a life as a motivational speaker or something.

Still, it wasn't *that* unreasonable of a request. If Angus got help from Khatari and Fuentes…

"Yeah, I think I can get it done."

Donnie nodded. "Make it happen. We're not taking one more step in this hellhole until I have proper firepower in front and behind."

14,971 feet below the surface

WAKE UP…

A distant voice, an invisible call from a dream of nothingness. The words seemed almost tangible, things he could reach out and touch.

The voice of a woman.

The woman he loved.

A pulsing pain in Patrick's head sparked, expanded, pushed away everything else.

Pain, and *heat*.

"Pat, wake up."

Bertha's voice. Not a dream.

"Baby, come on," she said. "*Please* come back to me. We're in trouble."

Her words hit home, brought with them memories of the river, the boat, the giant silverbug.

Memories of Skylark.

Patrick opened his eyes.

His head was in Bertha's lap, her arms around him, cradling him. The heat hit him anew.

He glanced at his HUD:

BODY TEMP: 102.1°F

DEPTH: 14,971 FT

"My suit … is it leaking?"

"Your right thigh," Bertha said.

He looked, realized his leg had been hurting all along. His fatigues, ripped and stained by blood and coolant fluid. A shallow, three-inch gash in his thigh, probably from when he'd hit the shore and slid, his leg scraping against a sharp rock.

"The wound isn't bad," Bertha said. "Torn skin. It's already stopped bleeding. They took our packs and everything in our pockets, so we don't have bandages, repair kits, or replacement coolant. We tried pressing the sides of the suit together, but it wouldn't seal."

He heard the fear in her voice. If he didn't fix his suit, he didn't know how long he'd survive.

Patrick tried to sit up—his lower back fired off a warning shot that locked him up tight. His chest felt like someone had driven a crowbar into it. A wave of dizziness swept over him. He closed his eyes, fighting back nausea.

"Mullet, help me," Bertha said.

Another set of hands on him. Patrick was lifted to a sitting position, held there. He wanted to look out but could not; the pain in his back kept his eyes scrunched tight.

He felt someone fumbling at the side of his helmet.

"Drink," Bertha said.

The helmet straw touched his lips. He took it into his mouth. The first splash of water surprised him—how could something so simple taste *so good*—then he drank greedily.

"Easy, big guy," Mullet said. "You might spew, and I'm pretty sure barfing in these helmets is bad news. A little bit at a time, okay?"

Patrick nodded, took one more big suck before he let Bertha retract the tube.

The water didn't wash away his pain, but his dizziness started to fade.

"How long was I out?"

"Two hours or so," Bertha said. He heard the relief in her voice. "Your chest is bruised, but I don't think anything is broken."

He slowly rolled his left arm, then his right. Hurt like hell, but he'd broken his ribs and his sternum before—this pain wasn't in the same ballpark.

His back, though … had to do something about that. Memories of a colonel he'd served under, a man who had fucked up his body by jumping out of perfectly good airplanes. The colonel was always throwing out his back.

"Help me to my belly," he said.

Bertha and Mullet did that. Patrick hurt so much he could barely open his eyes. He kept his hips against the flat, hard ground, did a prone pushup, held it. His back didn't snap back into place, but he felt the pain ebb slightly.

"How bad is it?" Bertha asked.

"Bad," Patrick said. "But I won't let it stop me."

A wonderful platitude, but was it true? As tough as he was, as much as he prided himself on enduring through pain and fatigue, from here on out he'd have to move carefully—in a combat situation, that kind of muscle-locking pain would get him killed.

Him, and others.

Just like Hatchet. Just like Worm. Just like Skylark.

Patrick rolled to his butt.

He and the others were in a bowl of some kind. A *pit*, made of red stone. At the center of the bowl, what looked like a shower drain. The pit was maybe fifteen meters in diameter, not quite three meters deep at the center.

McGuiness sat cross-legged, rubbing at his silver bracelet, staring off into the distance.

Both Otto and Klimas were looking around, quietly taking in everything they saw.

Curveball was on his butt, elbows on his knees, staring down as he had so often since losing Hatchet.

Sleepy lay on his back, eyes closed. His left sleeve had been roughly cut away, bloody gauze wrapped around his upper arm and shoulder. Over the gauze, sheets of KoolSuit repair material that had fused with the rest of his suit.

"Curve patched Sleepy up on the riverbank," Bertha said. "Before the rocktopi captured them and took away their packs."

Curveball spoke without looking up.

"The bolt, or rod, or whatever it is, grazed him," he said. "Ripped off a chunk of skin. Another inch to the right, it would have gone through the bone, taken his arm right off. He'll be all right. Can you believe he's actually asleep? The man has talent."

Patrick quickly looked everyone over, hoping he'd missed something. He hadn't. No packs. No carbines. Empty sidearm holsters. Empty knife sheathes.

"Bookworm and Jabour," he said. "Any sign of them?"

Bertha shook her head.

"Skylark's missing," Mullet said. "We haven't seen her."

Marie's neck, the spraying blood …

"She's dead," Patrick said.

Mullet's face hardened. "You're sure?"

The firefight … Mullet had had his hands full. Even in the close confines of the canoe, he hadn't seen what Patrick had seen.

Patrick nodded. "I'm sure."

Mullet's face hardened.

"They fished some of us out of the river," he said, his voice cold. "I wonder if they found her body."

If they had, what would Patrick and the others do with it? Haul it up to the surface when this was over? Considering that "over" might come at any moment, Marie's corpse—like Hatchet's—would be one of many that never left this place.

"They probably hacked her to pieces," Bertha said. "Then buried the parts. That's what these bastards do."

Curveball finally looked up, stared at Bertha with haunted eyes.

"Not sure I buy that *mindless killer* thing anymore," he said. "If these things were as brutal as you and Ender keep claiming, why aren't *we* in little pieces?"

Bertha didn't have an answer. Neither did Patrick. Based on what he'd seen in Utah, everyone should already be dead.

So why weren't they?

"They'll torture us," Mullet said. "They'll put those silly knives of theirs to work, find out what we know."

Sonny huffed. "How they gonna do that when we can't speak to them and they can't speak to us?"

Mullet thought, shrugged.

Patrick slowly stood. The bowl had a lip—also made of red stone—and just past that lip, all the way around the rim, stood a dozen glowing, flashing rocktopi armed with those double-poled weapons.

Mullet said Worm guessed those were railguns.

Worm. Tommy, *gone.*

Patrick felt the aliens' stares, black eyespots locked on him.

They were watching. Guarding.

Beyond the rocktopi, Patrick could barely make out the tops of stone buildings, like the ones he'd seen from the canoe. From somewhere beyond the pit, he heard distant screeches and cries. The way those sounds echoed... this cavern had to be huge.

He turned in a circle, taking it all in. From the pit, he couldn't see much of the city. The obelisk looked to be about two hundred meters to the northwest. The towering black needle reached up toward the cavern's arched ceiling. He couldn't see its base.

"I need details on this place," Patrick said. "Who saw what?"

"We didn't see shit," Mullet said. "They captured us, put us in bags, dumped us out here. They got me, Otto and Klimas while we were still in the water. Sonny, too, I think. They snagged Curve and Sleepy while Curve was patching him up."

Patrick's vision blurred... the heat again, coursing through him. His thigh wound felt like it was burning in the sun, like it was starting to *cook*—the leaking, smeared coolant wasn't enough to fully stave off the scorching air temperature.

"We have to get the repair kits. I'm burning up."

"We tried talking to them," Bertha said. "We tried pantomiming, everything we can think of. Either they don't understand what we want, or they don't care if we die."

Patrick's legs felt like rubber. He took one step up the bowl's slope—instantly, the two closest rocktopi leveled their weapons at him.

He took a step back. The weapons lowered.

What was happening? He'd acted, they'd threatened him, he'd backed off, they seemed to accept that.

Communication. *Clear* communication. Not with words, but with insinuation.

What the hell was going on?

"If we're prisoners," he said, "why aren't we chained, or in a cage or something?"

Otto stood, limped closer, favoring his left leg a bit. He gestured to the rocktopi guarding the pit rim.

"Think you could chain those things? Tie them up? Maybe the concept of *restraints* is alien to them. If you'll pardon the pun."

Mullet started laughing, fake and loud. He put one hand to his forehead, the other on his stomach.

"*Alien to them.*" His eyes scrunched tight. "Oh my … *god* … it's *alien* to them. Otto, you are a regular comedian!"

"O'Doyle," Otto said, "anyone ever tell you that your friend is a real dick?"

"Yeah, I've heard that once or twice."

A new rocktopi moved into view on the bowl rim. It, too, held a railgun. The creature shrieked, a sound so high-pitched that Patrick couldn't help but wince.

The other rocktopi came closer to the edge, pointed their weapons down into the pit. Two of the aliens descended into the pit, pudding-soft extrusions carrying them down the stone slope.

"Told you," Mullet said. "Torture time."

The two rocktopi pointed their railguns at Patrick, then past him, then at him, then past him. They were using the weapons to gesture in a particular direction—just like a man holding a rifle might do.

Patrick glanced to the other side of the bowl, saw that the rocktopi there had moved aside.

"They want us to move," he said.

Mullet flipped them off. "I say we take these bitches. Who's with me?"

"No one is," Patrick said. "Everyone get up, nice and slow. Somebody wake up Sleepy. For now, we go where the monsters want us to go."

Twelve armed guards around the rim, possibly more just out of sight, armed with weapons Patrick and the others didn't know how to use. He had no idea why he was still alive, but he wasn't about to put his wife—and everyone else—needlessly at risk.

He limped up the pit's stone slope, toward the space the rocktopi had cleared out. He focused on his balance; the world swam around him. So *hot*.

The others fell in behind him.

As he climbed up the bowl, he had to wonder at his own words—*go where the monsters want us to go.*

But *were* they monsters?

Yes, they were. They'd killed Skylark. Their silverbugs had attacked, causing the probable death of Worm and Samira.

And yet, a nagging feeling wriggled in Patrick's chest. Had he made a mistake, completely misjudging and underestimating the enemy? Had that mistake gotten his friends killed?

He grunted as he crested the bowl's edge. Armed rocktopi were waiting, a line of them on either side of what Patrick assumed was a street, or at least a wide path made of large colorful tiles that gleamed like enamel. One-story buildings on either side. The building walls looked to be made from solid slabs of cut stone.

"Mullet, with me," Patrick said. "The rest of you fall in behind. Don't try anything."

Mullet lined up on his left. Patrick needed to keep a close eye on the man, make sure he didn't do something stupid that would get more people killed.

Bertha lined up behind Patrick, Klimas on her right. Otto and McGuiness were next. Sleepy and Curveball brought up the rear.

Patrick had entered the mountain with twelve people. Only eight remained.

Armed rocktopi formed up like an honor guard, six on each side of Patrick and the others. The rocktopi that had given the screeching order to move came to the front. It pulsed a burnt orange and emerald green, then flowed down the street, pseudopods extending.

"Let's go," Patrick said.

The rocktopi marched them toward the obelisk.

Patrick tried to take in his surroundings, but it required almost all of his focus just to put one foot in front of the other. He checked his temperature: *102.5°F.*

He was losing coolant fluid.

How much longer could he keep going?

A quiet voice in the comms—Klimas: "Poor tactics. They're not accounting for fields of fire."

Patrick glanced at their guards—they were directly across from each other, not staggered at all. If they had to fire on the NoSeeUms, and they missed, they might hit their own comrades. Even if rounds found their intended targets, the railguns were so powerful the projectile could go right through a human and still hit a rocktopi on the other side.

Military tactics 101: set up overlapping fields of fire. Never be in a position where friendly fire can damage your own forces.

How could the rocktopi soldiers not know that?

"Amateurs," Mullet said. He smiled, spoke to the rocktopi on his right. "You smegma globs are a bunch of fucking amateurs. You know that, right?"

The guard screeched, aimed his railgun at Mullet. Mullet ducked his head and lifted his hands up, a gesture of compliance. Hopefully the rocktopi understood it.

The NoSeeUms & Company kept walking.

Patrick glanced back to check on Bertha. She gave him a single nod. She looked pissed as hell, ready to cut something.

Mullet slowly lowered his hands.

Klimas: "I don't know much about aliens, but our escorts seem freaked out."

Patrick glanced at the rocktopi on his immediate left. It marched along, weapon in hand, tentacle legs forming, reaching, retracting.

He slowly moved his hand to his talk button, pressed it.

"What makes you say that?"

Klimas: "Their rifles."

Patrick looked again. This time, he saw it. Some of the rocktopi's railguns were shaking.

Not much, and not all of them. Three on the left, two on the right…the tips of their double-piped weapons trembled slightly. No matter how different humans and rocktopi might be, if one wanted to shoot straight, one had to be able to hold one's weapon steady.

How could he have missed that? The heat, getting to him.

Mullet: "I'm telling you, these things have no idea what they're doing. They aren't proper soldiers. We can *take* them."

Klimas: "Think carefully about that. If you make a move, I'm with you, but they have the guns and we don't. If we can take them, it won't be without casualties. We—"

The rocktopi escort closest to Klimas screeched, sprinted in. Boneless extrusions raised the weapon, brought the twin rails down like a club. Klimas raised an arm just as the blow struck, making him stumble.

Bertha caught him before he fell.

As fast as the rocktopi was, Mullet was faster—he reached out and snatched the railgun right out of the rocktopi's grip. Mullet pinned the thin, oval-shaped body between his torso and his right elbow, cupped a hand under the lower meter-long rail.

He aimed the weapon at the rocktopi he'd just taken it from.

Screeching from all around, louder than any that had come before, like a dozen tanker trucks locking up the breaks on a hot summer day.

The disarmed rocktopi froze. Everyone froze.

"What the *fuck* are you doing?" McGuiness screamed, loud enough to be heard without comms. "You'll get us all killed!"

Mullet's aim didn't waver. "*This* is how you hold a firearm, you walking blob of candy store vomit."

The rocktopi who still had their weapons seemed confused. Two were steady and solid, aiming their weapons at Mullet as they moved closer to him. Others aimed *everywhere*—at Mullet, at Klimas, at Bertha, then back again, the motions of soldiers on the edge of panic.

Patrick put his hands up, shouted so he'd be heard without comms. "*Stand down, people,*" he said. "*Do not engage!*"

The lead rocktopi flowed toward Mullet, its railgun just as steady as his, aimed at Mullet's head.

This wasn't a chance to escape—it was an invitation to slaughter.

"Mullet," Patrick said, "stay cool."

The man smiled wide. "Do I look worried?"

His twin-piped weapon didn't waver a millimeter.

"Put it down," Patrick said. "Real slow."

Mullet made a *tsk-tsk-tsk* noise. "Where's the Ender I used to know? Back in the day we'd have taken our chances. Back in the day you'd have already stomped two of these motherfuckers and skinned a third to wear as a nice bathrobe on cold winter nights."

The lead rocktopi stopped a few feet from Mullet, the tip of the alien weapon only inches from Mullet's head. The man didn't flinch, didn't waver, didn't even stop smiling. The rocktopi he was still aiming at quivered visibly, skin pulsing with shades of deep purple.

"Times change," Patrick said. "And you don't even know how to fire that thing."

"It will make a helluva club," Mullet said. "Anyone else ready to rush these shit piles with me?"

No one answered.

He sighed. "Bunch of slack-jawed homosexuals. What do you all think they're going to do when we get done with this little stroll? Give us a greasedown and a shiatsu?"

"Put it *down*," Sonny said. "This ain't no Rambo movie, you dumb sonofabitch!"

Seconds dragged on, each longer than the last. Some of the rocktopi screeched, waved their guns around, shifting aim from person to person. One came up from the rear of the column, moving smoothly, weapon level and steady. It closed in on Mullet. It positioned itself at a right angle to the lead rocktopi—up a proper overlapping field of fire.

"Kevin," Patrick said, "I think you have about three seconds before they gun you down."

Mullet's eyes flicked left, then right, taking in the threats.

"Fuck a duck in a bag," he said.

He angled the barrel down, slowly bent his knees, and placed the alien weapon on the tiled roadway. Just as slowly, he stood, raised both hands.

The lead rocktopi stretched in, jabbed the ends of the double-pipe railgun into Mullet's ribs. Mullet grunted, stumbled, dropped to a knee. The rocktopi squished out a new pseudopod, snatched the weapon lying on the ground, then moved back.

It screeched and flashed with a dozen pulsing colors.

Rocktopi swarmed in from all sides. Three came at Patrick. He push-kicked the first one to reach him—it was like hitting a bean bag. He didn't have time to see if his strike had done damage before the other two were on him. One wrapped tentacles around his head and neck. He twisted sharply, a move that would have sent a human attacker flying, but the rocktopi's tentacles stretched, absorbing the energy of his throw while tightening down.

More tentacles wrapping around his chest, his hips.

One grabbed his left arm, held it as tight as a lock made of steel.

He punched with his right arm, felt his fist slap into meat, felt that meat flex and pinch down—his right hand was trapped.

Childhood thoughts flashing…a storybook…Br'er Rabbit punching the Tar Baby, getting stuck…

The tentacle around his neck, tightening, a python's strength.

Can't breathe…

He fought—the harder he fought, the more immobile he became.

Can't breathe so hot so hot can't breathe…

Blackness swarmed over him.

A desperate moment hoping, begging, *praying* that Bertha had gotten away, then all went gray.

A distant part of him felt the python around his neck relax, recoil.

His lungs heaved, drew in air. He lurched, still couldn't move. His fists and feet remained trapped in the Tar Baby.

The gray dispersed. Patrick breathed deep, forced himself to relax.

The rocktopi had him held tight.

From what little he could see, they had the others as well—Bertha beneath two large rocktopi, Klimas held by three, a tentacle around his neck, Mullet buried under a pile of four.

"You *jackass*," Sonny screamed from somewhere out of Patrick's line of sight. "You shouldn't have fucked with them!"

Patrick heard a series of screeches—loud, defined, commanding—then he was yanked to his feet. The coil of boneless muscle around his neck flexed, reminding him of what would happen if he didn't behave.

The Tar Baby released his feet. His captors yanked him forward, forcing him to walk down the colorful road. The one who had hit Mullet was again in the lead, still holding its railgun, with extra pseudopods wrapped tightly around Mullet's arms. At least one rocktopi held each person. Even Sonny. Tentacles around waists, arms, necks…the aliens weren't taking chances.

"The leader," Klimas said, his words ragged and uneven as the three rocktopi holding him yanked him this way and that. "It has a scar. See it?"

As soon as Klimas pointed it out, Patrick wondered how he'd missed it. A ragged white line on the thing's body. Sometimes a stretching pseudopod included that line, but the scar showed no color, did not illuminate no matter what colors flashed. No black dots on the scar, either.

"Yeah. I see it."

"Keep an eye on that one," Klimas said. "Most of the rocktopi seem like…well, like untrained *civilians*. That one, and the other one that closed in on Mullet, they know what they're doing."

Patrick saw what Klimas saw, yet he still didn't understand the big picture. Why were the rocktopi keeping him and his people alive?

"I see it," Mullet said. "Let's call him *Slash*."

"They're all different," Otto said. "Some have scars, but it's more than that. Their colors shift, but some of the patterns seem to repeat. Maybe the patterns are almost like a fingerprint."

As he was dragged stumbling along, Patrick looked at the rocktopi holding Mullet, then at the one holding Klimas. It took a few seconds to see the different repeating patterns of stripes, but as soon as Patrick saw them, he knew he couldn't *unsee* them.

"A fingerprint, or a name tag," Bertha said. "If they communicate with color, maybe they have a self-identifier or something. If the one holding Mullet is *Slash*, what do we call the other one that seems to be trained?"

"*Axl*," Mullet said. "If you have a *Slash*, you've got to have an Axl."

The two most-dangerous aliens were officially named. No one offered names for any of the other rocktopi. Those individuals didn't seem to stand out. Not yet, anyway.

From behind, Patrick heard an ear-splitting rocktopi screech. He started to turn sharply—the back that hadn't failed him during the brief fight now exploded in a breath-seizing burst of agony. He stayed still, waited until the pain subsided slightly, then slowly turned.

Bertha stood alone, looking at the rocktopi that had been holding her only moments before. The alien pulsed in strange colors, colors Patrick couldn't even begin to describe.

"Bertha, what happened?"

She shook her head. "I don't know. It had me wrapped up, then it released me like I was…*poisonous* or something."

Axl flowed toward her, pulsing angry light. The one that had been holding her seemed to shrink in on itself, become smaller.

Patrick was yanked forward again. He stumbled, looked down the road.

Up ahead, he saw the stone obelisk rising high above the houses. Fifteen meters tall, maybe more. At the very top, a stone sculpture of a rocktopi, curled tentacles reaching out in all directions. Up high like that, the image looked like a stylized, wavy-armed sun—exactly how the Utah tribe had depicted themselves.

The rocktopi hauled him and the others toward the obelisk's thick, round base, which was decorated with bas relief carvings. Colorful paving tiles ringed the base, making a circular plaza perhaps twenty meters in diameter. On the west side of the plaza, placid blue water—a lake that took up most of the huge cavern's southwest quadrant. The same river that had brought Patrick and the others here burbled against the northwest portion of the plaza before flowing into the lake.

The rocktopi waved their railguns, directing everyone to line up shoulder to shoulder, their backs to the obelisk base's south arc. The edge of the base was just above the back of Patrick's head.

Slash screeched ear-piercing sounds. The honor guard rocktopi formed what looked like a firing line. Patrick found himself looking down the "barrels" of a dozen alien railguns.

"You idiots," Mullet said. "I told you this would happen. They're going to gun us down. We had a chance to fight but you all pissed it away."

He refused to ease down, to accept the situation. He was going to push this conflict into a lethal finality.

"They won't shoot us." Sleepy, talking slowly, his voice deep and calm. "If they were going to kill us, they would have already. So don't give them a reason to change their minds."

Bertha slid past Mullet, stood shoulder to shoulder with Patrick.

"Look at this place," she said. "It's so different from Utah."

An understatement. This town or city looked *clean*. Worn from centuries of use, *millennia* of use, but orderly, well cared-for.

"Patrick," Bertha said, her voice tight and low, "look between the buildings."

Dozens of rocktopi, peeking out from behind building corners. Full-sized ones, like the honor guard, like Slash and Axl, like the ones he had ordered gunned down in the tunnels higher up, but also smaller versions.

Smaller versions—there was a proper word for that.

That word was *children*.

Seeing the little ones next to the adults made it impossible to ignore, impossible to delude himself into thinking he and Mullet hadn't almost gunned down *children* in the tunnels, would have done exactly that if Bertha hadn't stopped them.

Children. With them, adults—mothers and fathers?

Families.

This place, clean and orderly. The rocktopi, taking him and the NoSeeUms captive instead of chopping them into bits. Firearms. The battle on the river, the rocktopi using firing groups, flanking from both sides…using *tactics*, not rushing forward like mindless killers.

The rocktopi here were…*civilized?*

No, this had to be something else. *Had* to be. He'd never considered—not even for an instant—that these aliens could be any different from the animals he'd fought in Utah.

But weren't the rocktopi here just as savage? Veronica Reeves had documented a massacre site at the base of the mountain, where primitive people had been butchered.

"Ender, you told us they were monsters," Sleepy said. "You had us shoot them on sight. These creatures are organized. They're smart, and they seem to understand the concept of *mercy* far better than we do. I'm going to throw out a wild guess that you and your wife have absolutely no idea what you were talking about."

Patrick shook his head. "I don't understand. I just don't understand."

"Tell that to Skylark," Sleepy said. "Tell that to her daughters. Tell that to Hatchet. Tell that to Bookworm and Samira."

Mullet groaned, a sound of exhausted frustration.

"Reverend Rectum, shut your piehole," he said. "Everyone knew the risks. So the beasties are smart. So what? They any smarter than the people we've killed?"

Sleepy said something back, but Patrick didn't catch it, because Bertha leaned close.

"It's not our fault," she whispered. "We couldn't have known."

That excuse wasn't going to cut it.

"No, it's not *our* fault," Patrick said. "It's *mine*. You tried to tell me not to do this. Tommy, Carson and Marie would be alive if it wasn't for me. I just don't understand—how can *these* rocktopi be so different from the ones in Utah?"

But maybe he already knew the answer. The melted hole in the middle of the Utah ship—evidence, possibly, of a nuclear accident, one that must have ravaged their population. Mad graffiti, like crude prehistoric drawings, painted on top of exquisite carvings as detailed as anything from the Renaissance. The aliens below Funeral Mountain had acted like cavemen, like primitives, because their advanced civilization had collapsed thousands of years ago.

Without the accident, could the Utah tribe have wound up like this?

"I should have known they were smart," he said. "They came in *spaceships*. I should have known."

Bertha touched his hand. "*We* should have known. I chose to join you. I could have refused, demanded you stay home, but I didn't. I came with you. It never occurred to me that the rocktopi here might be anything more than what we saw in Utah. It didn't occur to Sonny, either."

Bertha and Sonny weren't in command of this operation. Patrick was. He should have seen this obvious possibility—no, this *probability*.

His failures, compounding.

Patrick knew he was responsible for this. Him and him alone.

Movement down the street. Four rocktopi came out of a one-story building—a *garage?*—pulling something behind them. A cart of some kind. Metal wheels, metal base, with an opaque glass bubble on top. Plastic, maybe. The shadow of something moving inside played against that material. A rocktopi? It didn't move like one…

The four aliens pulled the cart closer to the obelisk, to the captives.

"Uh-oh," Mullet said. "Torture chamber on wheels. Count on it."

"Shut the fuck up," Sleepy said.

The cart rolled closer, onto the plaza tiles. The rocktopi turned the cart. The bubble's front was opaque, but the sides were clear—the source of the shadow became clear.

A man, leaning on a makeshift crutch.

"Holy shit," the man said. He shook with excitement, slapped his hand against the inside of the clear walls. "Holy *shit*! McGuiness?"

"Sonofabitch," Sonny said, breathless. "That's Ramiro Chus."

56

14,982 feet below the surface

BERTHA STARED, STUNNED. They all did. Ramiro Chus: *alive*. He leaned his weight on a crutch, a metal pole bent at the top to tuck under his armpit. He wore jeans and a T-shirt. It was well over two hundred degrees down here, so how...

...the bubble had to be temperature controlled.

A madman's wide-eyed stare. Scabbed-over scratches on his forehead, his nose and his stubbly face, probably from silverbug feet. He moved in quick jerks, head snapping this way and that.

"They kept him alive," Sonny said. He sounded as confused as Bertha felt. "I don't get it. And why the hell are *we* alive?"

Ramiro stared out in disbelief. "McGuiness! You came to rescue me? Where's Sam? Did she bring you?"

"She called me for help," Sonny said. He gestured to the rest of the team. "Unfortunately, this is your help. As you can see, we ain't doing so good."

Ramiro again glanced across the team, head twitching this way and that, like a bird, from person to person, his expression a mix of elation and confusion.

A rope-wrapped metal splint around his left shin. Sam had said he'd broken his leg. The splint gleamed ... was that platinum? Probably, just like the crutch.

He must have set the bone himself. If so, the man was far tougher than he seemed.

"But you guys have this under control," Ramiro said. "Right? You're getting me the hell out of here? *Right?*"

Ramiro's wide smile bordered on insanity. Dark circles around his bleary, red eyes. His jittery motions and the waver in his voice betrayed his stress. He'd been trapped down here with no hope of rescue, and yet when rescue had arrived, his rescuers were telling him he was going nowhere.

Sleepy gestured to the rocktopi guards. "Hate to break it to you, buddy, but the only way we're getting out of this place is if the beasties let us. I don't think that's going to happen. Two of us died already, two more are missing, probably dead as well."

Ramiro's smile faded. "Four people? Dead?"

"That's right," Sleepy said. "And the rest of us soon to follow, I think."

Ramiro blinked, gave his head a little shake.

"But you came all this way," he said. "We *have* to get out. They keep asking me questions, or trying to, and I don't have answers. I'm ... they could kill me at any moment. We *have* to get out. And where's Sam?"

No one spoke.

Bertha glanced at Patrick. He was in charge of the operation—he should be the one doing the talking. But he didn't say anything. He just stared at Ramiro as if it wasn't possible the man existed at all.

Patrick wasn't going to answer, so Bertha answered for him.

"We were attacked by the rocktopi."

Ramiro's face wrinkled. "The *what?*"

"Your captors," Bertha said. "That's what we call them. We were on a boat in the river. They attacked us. During the attack, Samira and one of our team went missing. I'm sorry, but she's probably dead."

Bertha realized, instantly, that she'd left out the part of the NoSeeUms gunning down rocktopi in the tunnels, of almost doing the same to the rocktopi children.

Ramiro shook his head. "No. No way. Sam is *dead?*"

"Just deal with it," Mullet said. "We've lost people, too."

Bertha glared at him. "Jesus, man, do you have to be a prick about everything?"

Mullet nodded. "I'm the real-real, baby. I tell it like it is."

Ramiro looked down. He sagged, palms against the bubble walls.

More loss. More heartbreak.

Curveball limped toward the bubble. Rocktopi screeched, weapons snapped up, pointed at him. He ignored them … or perhaps he was daring them to shoot, *wanted* them to shoot.

They didn't.

He reached up, pressed his hand to the bubble opposite Ramiro's on the other side.

"I'm sorry," Curveball said. "She was strong, seemed like a good person. But like my friend said, we've lost people, too."

Ramiro lifted his head, met Curveball's gaze. Tears tracing his cheeks, Ramiro nodded once.

"Why didn't they kill you?" Sonny asked.

Ramiro wiped away tears with the backs of his hands.

"I don't know. I thought those spider-machines were going to kill me. When I saw the … the *rocktopi* … I thought I was done for. Years ago I helped Veronica dig up that massacre site. They kill people, or the spider-machines do. Like I said, I think they haven't yet because they want information."

"Information," Otto said. "What kind of information?"

Ramiro glanced off. He'd been down here, alone, in a lethal environment surrounded by alien nightmares he assumed were going to butcher him at any moment. Even if he could have gotten out of that bubble on his own, he had nowhere to run.

"They wanted to know about my gear," he said. "My coolant system, my clothes, my backpack. They keep touching the metal clips on my backpack, asking *where*. I think that's what they're asking. And my little computer, they're obsessed with it, even though it stopped working. From the heat, maybe. They touch it, make the symbols for *where*, and also, I think, *how many*."

"And what have you told them?" Otto asked. Something in his voice made Bertha think he knew something, or maybe had a hunch about something.

Ramiro shrugged. "I tried to tell them I brought everything with me, but I don't know the symbols for that. I've learned enough to stay alive—how to tell them I'm hot, cold, I need water. I haven't eaten in two days. They offered me food, but as far as I know it's poisonous."

Ramiro struggled to control his emotions, to speak without sobbing. Bertha's heart ached for the man.

"They actually saved my life," Ramiro said. "My leg was broken. I couldn't move. I was dying from the heat and dehydration. The little robots swarmed over me. I panicked. I thought they were cutting into me, but it was those hooks on their feet. I got a few cuts, but nothing that bad. Then, they came. They glowed, like angels. They got me out of the shaft. I don't remember much after that until I woke up in this thing."

Bertha traded glances with Patrick, with the others. The stress had gotten to Ramiro.

"You call them *angels*," Sleepy said. "And yet instead of taking you to the surface, they brought you down here, into the blazing furnace, where there is weeping and gnashing of teeth."

Klimas turned to him. "Really? You're going to paraphrase Matthew right now?"

"Matthew," Sonny said. "Who the hell is *Matthew*?"

"The book of Matthew," Sleepy said. "Thirteen-fifty. *So it shall be at the end of the world—the angels shall come forth, and sever the wicked from among the just, and shall throw them into the furnace of—*"

"Shut the *fuck* up," Mullet said. "If your God gave a squirt of donkey piss about any of us, we wouldn't be in this fine mess in the first place."

Behind his visor, Sleepy's lip curled—Bertha saw his hand absently grope at his empty sidearm holster. He looked down at that hand, perhaps surprised at his reaction. He crossed his arms, leaned his back against the obelisk base, said no more.

Patrick fell forward, hit the ground face-first.

"Patrick!"

Bertha knelt by him. She heard screeches of warning, ignored them. She tried to roll him over; his dead weight fought her. Hands, helping her—Mullet and Otto. They flopped Patrick onto his back. His skin, pale. Lips, whitish, visibly dry. Eyes half open, staring out blankly.

"*Patrick!* Wake up!"

She didn't realize she was shaking him until strong hands pulled her away.

"He's in heat stroke," Klimas said, "we have to—"

Bertha half-turned, drove an elbow into Klimas's ribs. His hands slipped away. She turned back, dove toward Patrick, only to be grabbed by both Otto and Sleepy.

"Calm *down*," Sleepy barked.

They pulled her away from Patrick. Mullet knelt at his side, held Patrick's wrist.

"His heart's racing," Mullet said. "His suit is out of coolant. We need our packs or he's screwed."

Bertha again tried to lurch toward her man, was again held back. Patrick wasn't moving—he was *dying*.

The sharp *thunk* of hands slapping glass.

"Get him in here!" Ramiro turned toward the rocktopi guard, pointed at Patrick, then at the floor of his cart. "Bring him in here!"

Strange rifles snapped up, aimed. Rocktopi slowly moved toward Patrick.

Bertha's mind raged against itself—getting Patrick into the bubble was the only way he could survive, but were the butchering creatures going to put him in there or were they going to finish him off?

She tried to pull free; Sleepy bent her arm up and back so sharply Bertha hissed in pain.

"Calm down or he'll die," he said. "This is Ender's only shot."

Sleepy's words cut through her anguish. She wanted to tear Patrick's helmet off, hold him, kiss him, *save* him, but none of that would keep him alive.

"Let me go," she said, her words calm and measured.

Sleepy did.

The rifle-brandishing rocktopi closed in on Patrick. Mullet stood, palms-up, backed away.

Bertha fought her instincts, fought the urge to rush the rocktopi, tear them to pieces with her hands to protect Patrick—if she didn't let them take him, he was as good as dead.

Alien weapons still leveled, the rocktopi extruded pseudopods that wrapped around Patrick's arms. They dragged him across the tiles.

He was dying … they were going to let him die … or kill him …

Bertha's hands clenched into fists. An arm around her shoulders—Curveball, trying to comfort her as best he could, to let her know she wasn't alone.

The two rocktopi dragged Patrick to the far side of the rolling bubble. Tentacles reached to unseen latches. A hatch in the clear glass swung up. Ramiro winced, gasped at the sudden rush of hot air. The rocktopi pushed Patrick inside—the hatch swung closed.

In all her life, Bertha had never felt so helpless. She'd never known true love, had given up on ever having a man, on having a family—and then she'd met Patrick. Their love hadn't been storybook, not unless it was a horror story, but they'd fallen for each other hard. In a few short months, he had come to be the center of her world. Without him, that world would collapse. She couldn't go back to the way she'd been before she met him, back to that hollow, lonely existence.

If he died …

She didn't see a rocktopi adjust any controls, but one of them obviously changed something—Ramiro first hugged himself, hands sliding up and down his arms, then began to shiver.

"It's cold," Ramiro said. When he spoke, Bertha saw his breath crystalize.

"This makes no sense," Sonny said. "They shot the hell out of us, killed one of us, and now they're *saving* O'Doyle's life?"

Bertha understood it no more than Sonny did, than the rest of them did. She didn't need to understand. All that mattered was keeping Patrick alive.

"It's *freezing* in here," Ramiro said.

Patrick moved. Slowly at first, just a slight roll to his side.

Ramiro knelt by him. He spoke softly, but even through the clear bubble, Bertha heard every word.

"Take it easy, man," Ramiro said. "You've got heat stroke, but you're going to be okay."

Bertha couldn't see Patrick's face, his eyes. She saw his helmet nod—he'd heard Ramiro, understood him.

A wave of relief roared through her.

"Thank god," she said.

Sleepy nodded. "Amen."

"Give it a fucking rest, preacher," Mullet said.

Ramiro stood. He was shivering so badly Bertha could hear his teeth chattering. With shaking hands, he picked something up off the floor—flat and thin, made of metal or some kind of plastic. He held it in one shaking arm, pointed one trembling finger and seemed to draw on it. He then held it up, showed it to the rocktopi nearest the bubble.

"Turn…the temp…b-b-back up," he said, his words making vapor clouds that drifted in the bubble. "P-p-please."

As he turned, showing the flat object to more rocktopi, she saw what he'd written—strange symbols of curves and swirls.

"You can write their language?" Sonny asked.

"Some symbols," Ramiro said. "They taught me how t-t-to write *hotter* and *c-c-colder.*"

Bertha heard a slight hum and a hiss of air.

Ramiro sagged with relief. He smiled.

"Thank you," he said to the assembled rocktopi.

He shivered for another minute or so, then his body relaxed. Such extremes of temperature.

Bertha watched Patrick. Ramiro helped him sit up. He mumbled something Bertha couldn't hear, then Ramiro fumbled with the bottom of Patrick's visor, pushed it up into the headband.

Patrick looked ashen, he looked sick. She knew how he felt—in Utah, it had been her with the ruined suit, roasting alive, confused and disoriented. Patrick had taken Angus's suit, put it on her. That had saved her life. But by doing so, Patrick had left Angus to suffer the same fate she would have.

If only he'd put a bullet in Angus instead.

Patrick had survived. A miracle? Sleepy might think so, but Bertha didn't know, didn't care. Patrick was alive—she had to get him out of this place, get him back to the surface.

Stay alive. Keep Patrick alive. Find a way out.

A new round of screeches, distant but coming closer.

"The natives are restless," Mullet said. "Wait, is that racist?"

"Jesus Christ," Sonny said. "Do you *ever* shut your fucking mouth?"

Mullet waggled a finger at him. "Now-now-now, old man, don't blaspheme. Haven't you been listening to Preacher Man all this time?"

"Kevin," Sleepy said, "for all that is holy, please be quiet. Please."

The crowd of aliens parted. Two rocktopi approached, each carrying a rifle and a double-crescent knife. They shimmered a deep red, with cascading, expanding rings of turquoise. There was something … *formal* about them, from the colors of the weapons to the way they walked.

Twenty feet from the obelisk, the two aliens stepped aside, revealing a third who had been behind them. This rocktopi glowed only one color — the shimmering white of a distant star. It moved slower than the others. Each pseudopod extension or retraction seemed to be in slow motion. The more Bertha looked, the more she realized it wasn't pure white — there were colors and patterns flowing across its skin, but they were very faint.

"It's an old bastard," Sonny said. "Just like me."

Old. That word fit.

The pale rocktopi came closer, moving at an agonizingly slow pace. Far behind it, approaching the plaza, Bertha saw more rocktopi coming. These glowed in a myriad of colors — and each carried a backpack.

"Our gear," Mullet said. "Sweet Baby Jesus — if that's our gear and our weapons, when we get out of here I'm going to your church, Sleepy. Praise the lord and pass the ammunition."

The old rocktopi drew even with Ramiro's cart.

"Let's call that one *Whitey*," Mullet said.

Mullet seemed to like being the one to name the rocktopi. No one objected.

Whitey's black dots weren't all black. Some were light gray, some were a milky white.

It let out a sound, a hiss more like the tearing of a thick pile of papers than the screeches Bertha had come to expect.

The rocktopi behind it came forward, tossed the backpacks into a pile near the obelisk base.

Bertha wasn't sure what to do, if going for the packs might somehow be a threatening act to the rocktopi, but the NoSeeUms didn't hesitate. Sleepy, Mullet and Curveball each found their own pack, started rifling through them.

"Mags gone," Mullet said. "And my backup knife."

"Same here," Sleepy said.

Curveball pulled out a KoolSuit patch kit, a med kit and one of the forearm-sized coolant canisters out of his pack, handed them all to Bertha.

"Get your husband fixed up," he said.

Bertha started toward the bubble, remembered what she carried in her own pack. She set the supplies down, opened her pack, took out the tightly rolled spare KoolSuit.

"We need to give it to Ramiro," she said, holding the roll up for the others to see. "We'll never get him out of here alive without it. Anyone object?"

A pause. A pause that felt…selfish. Selfish, but not unjustified. If they gave the suit to Ramiro, any further severe damage to *anyone's* suit probably meant a slow, agonizing death.

"Give it to him," Sonny said. "And he probably needs water, so does O'Doyle."

Ramiro let out a laugh that sounded half-insane.

"Is that a KoolSuit? I read about those! Holy shit, you guys *are* going to save me!"

Bertha looked at the white rocktopi. She used the rolled-up suit to point at the glass bubble, at the water and other gear, then at the bubble again.

Whitey extended a half-dozen pseudopods that shimmered with the palest pinks, the faintest yellows.

"That means you can approach," Ramiro said. "I think. Probably best to set them at the door, then clear away."

Bertha took a water canister from her back, gathered it, the coolant, the med kit, the repair kit and the replacement KoolSuit roll, then walked around the bubble cart. She set the items on the ground in front of the hatch door.

Looking at her through the glass, Patrick forced a smile.

"I'm okay," he said.

He wasn't. His face looked sallow. The heat had taken a huge toll on him, but it was more than that—something seemed broken in his soul.

The bubble's hatch opened again as a rocktopi quickly placed the items inside, then shut it.

Patrick yanked on the tear in his pants, widening it, making room to get at the wound. He opened the med kit, ripped open a gauze package, pressed the white fabric against his cut, against the fresh, red blisters forming on his exposed skin.

"Go back with the others," he said as he pulled a sheet of repair material from the kit and applied it over the blood-spotted gauze. He used his fingers to smooth down the sheet's edges, letting it meld with the undamaged areas of his KoolSuit thigh.

Bertha wanted to be in there with him. But he was in command, and she'd promised to treat this madness like a real mission.

She forced herself to turn away.

When she came around the cart, she found Whitey and his two guards blocking her path.

A thousand eyespots, facing every direction, yet Bertha had that strange sensation that Whitey was looking only at her.

"Ramiro," she said, "what do they want?"

"I don't know."

"Stay calm, babe." Patrick's voice, a life preserver to a drowning woman. As messed up as he was, having him near gave her hope. Hope, and a need to do whatever it took to survive.

Whitey stretched/flowed/walked toward her.

"Leave her *alone*," Patrick growled. "I will tear you apart, I—"

Bertha held up a hand toward him, cutting him off.

"Just fix your suit," she said. "I'm okay. Nobody move, let it do whatever it's going to do."

She was anything but okay. The apparent leader of these blood-thirsty creatures stretch-walked closer to her. Bertha forced herself not to move, not to flinch.

Whitey let out a long hiss.

Bertha heard a screech to her right. She looked—the one that had made the sound … that pattern of purple spirals … she *recognized* it. It was the same rocktopi that had been holding her, the one that had suddenly let her go.

Whitey budded out a new pseudopod. Bertha felt her lip curl in revulsion at the ghostly appendage, a soft-bodied snake stretching toward her.

Whitey's colors, while very faint, were beautiful, a shimmering, endless cascade of movement. She realized that—like Axl and Slash— Whitey had a specific pattern shifting in and out of his faint swirls. His "fingerprint." Unmistakable, yet indescribable, eerily identical to seeing a human face for the first time and unconsciously logging it, taking down the indefinable details, so that the next time you saw that person you instantly knew you'd seen them before. Now that she had seen Whitey's pattern, she knew she could never again mistake this rocktopi for another.

The pseudopod, only inches away from her now. She stayed rock-still, pushing back the urge to slap at it, to turn and run.

The pale, pulsating tentacle tip touched her chest.

Bertha fought down her fear, her memories of what these butchers had done in Utah.

Whitey stayed motionless for a moment.

His tentacle began to glow with a pulsing, faint yellow light.

With a start, Bertha realized that the light beat in time with her heart.

This overgrown amoeba, *touching* her. What did it want? When would the knives come out, cut her to pieces?

Whitey reached another pseudopod toward her.

Bertha felt her gorge rising. The other ones had grabbed her, roughed her up—somehow that was different from this…this *tender* touch.

The second pseudopod touched her chest, then slid downward, past her sternum to her stomach.

Bertha refused to close her eyes. It was going to punch that tentacle into her belly, drive it *through* her, because this was how the bastards killed. Whitey was going to tear her guts out and leave her screaming and…

…the second tentacle began to throb a soft yellow, much faster than the one showing her pulse.

"Ramiro," she said, "what is it doing?"

A pause. She watched the two flashing tentacles.

"I think those both represent heart rates," Ramiro said.

Heart *rates*. Plural.

The truth blossomed, pushed out anything else.

Bertha's knees felt weak.

"Holy shit," she said, her words sounding distant, as if they came from someone else. "I think I'm pregnant."

57

14,982 feet below the surface

PATRICK STARED OUT through the glass, unable to form a thought. No one spoke, not until Mullet broke the silence.

"Congrats, Ender," he said. "I guess your shriveled-up old balls still got some life in them."

Patrick heard him clearly. No comms needed. The bubble must have had some kind of sound reinforcement.

He looked out through the glass at Bertha, saw she was looking back at him.

"You're pregnant?"

Confusion on her face. And horror. And joy.

"I don't know," she said. "But I …" she glanced down at the whitish tentacle touching her belly. She put her hands on her belly, one on either side of the faintly pulsing limb. "Pat … I think that's our baby's heartbeat."

Our baby…

This couldn't be happening now. Not down here, not in this hell.

"Bertha, are you sure?"

He wanted it to be true. He wanted it to be anything *but* true.

She looked at him again. Confusion still, but the horror was gone—she was wide-eyed with joy. She laughed once, uncomfortably, the kind of sound someone makes when they have no idea how to process what is happening to them.

"I think I already knew," she said. "Somewhere, deep down, maybe I knew. But…I don't know, Pat, all I know is…I think Whitey is right."

Pregnant.

He was going to be a father.

Patrick glanced at the others. They stood still, watching him, watching Bertha. Only Klimas moved, slowly handing backpacks to their respective owners.

"They removed all weapons," Klimas said. "Claymores, grenades, mags, knives…the works. But they left our repair kits, extra water and ration charges."

Had they known what the repair kits were before they'd given the packs back? They had to. Otherwise, wouldn't they have taken them along with the weapons?

The rocktopi were smart. Smarter than he'd ever considered possible.

Bertha…pregnant.

Patrick closed his eyes, tried to focus.

He heard Otto's voice.

"The leader is fixated on Bertha. Whitey knows she's with child. Maybe he'll let her go."

Sonny laughed, a sound of darkness, of desperation.

"Youngster, I like you, but you're naive as hell. They aren't going to let her go. They won't let none of us go. Not now, not ever. You think they stayed hidden for twelve thousand years just to let us out so we can blab our heads off? We're all going to die down here."

Bertha's eyes instantly went from wide to narrow, from overwhelmed to angry.

"You don't know that," she said to Sonny. "If they wanted us dead, they would have just killed us, or let us die. They wouldn't have let us repair Patrick's suit. It doesn't make any sense."

Sonny met her gaze.

"It makes sense if you use a word that explains what they're doing," he said. "But that word don't quite make sense in these circumstances. That word is *humane*. Things that ain't human are being humane to us. We're on death row, sister—they're just making us as comfortable as possible before the end. The only reason we're still alive is so that they can figure out if more like us are coming."

Sonny's words fought to knock Patrick out of his stunned silence. Were they all doomed? He'd thought so, even accepted it, in a way, but now ... Bertha was *pregnant*. There had to be a way out of this.

Whitey let out another sandpaper sound. A rocktopi flowed/rolled to the bubble, slapped a glowing pseudopod against the bubble glass, then pointed to the obelisk.

Ramiro thought for a moment, then nodded. "I think he's asking if we want to get out of this thing. I know I do. I've been in here for days. Once I figured out why they came to our planet, all I've done is work on understanding symbols."

Patrick felt so weak, he wasn't sure he'd caught everything Ramiro said.

"You know why the rocktopi came to Earth?"

"Yeah, I can show you." Ramiro pointed to the obelisk base. "It's all right there."

Patrick wanted to know that, but the history lesson could wait. He stood, slowly—Ramiro had to help him.

"Let's get you out of here," Patrick said. "You need to get the KoolSuit on. Strip down."

Ramiro didn't hesitate. If he had any concerns about the others seeing him naked, he didn't show it. He set the crutch down, gently unwrapped the rope around his leg, then removed the metal splint, set it aside. He undressed, wincing as he slid his pants past his broken left foreleg. Horrible bruising there.

With Patrick's help, Ramiro donned the KoolSuit and pulled his clothes on over it. He finished by sliding the splint over his shin, then tying it tight with the rope.

Patrick helped him with the hood.

"Night vision is here," Patrick said, pointing to the detent in his own headband. "And the visor comes down like this."

He pressed the center of his forehead; his visor extended down. He heard the *shwoop* of it sealing to the KoolSuit hood. After a race to escape the silverbugs, a firefight on the riverbank, a plunge off a high waterfall, getting thrown about the canoe by the house-sized silverbug, then tossed through the air to land face-first on rocks, the suit still worked like a charm.

Angus Kool built amazing stuff.

Ramiro lowered his visor. Patrick walked him through the simple HUD, then Ramiro reached down and picked up his drawing tablet. He drew a symbol.

"This means *outside*," he said. "I think. If not, they'll get the hint."

He held the tablet up to the clear wall, letting the rocktopi see the symbol.

A rocktopi flowed forward, opened the bubble door. Ramiro stepped out first, still holding the tablet. Patrick started to step out, had to grab the curved door frame to keep from falling. He reached out a hand to Ramiro, who took it. Patrick stepped out, leaning heavily on the smaller man, who grunted with the effort.

Patrick's booted feet hit the tiles. He wobbled; Ramiro helped him stay upright.

Bertha ran to him.

He started to tell her to stop, to stay still, but before he could draw enough breath she was there, her arms gently wrapping around him. He held her, his soul easing at touching her again, even if their skin was separated by clothing and KoolSuits.

He was hers. She was his.

They were alive.

So was their child.

Bertha slid under Patrick's free arm, shifted his weight onto her.

"I got you, baby," she said. "I got you."

She helped Patrick toward the obelisk. Ramiro hobbled along on his crutch. Halfway there, Patrick patted her shoulder.

"I can walk on my own," he said.

Bertha didn't argue. She carefully let him go but kept her arm near his back, just in case.

His back. It hurt, but not bad enough to slow him. Whatever was wrong in there, he knew it was a landmine waiting to blow.

They reached the obelisk. Klimas handed him his backpack. Patrick slowly slid it on.

"You look like dog shit," Mullet said.

Patrick nodded. "That means I look way better than I feel."

Everyone made space for him. He rested against the obelisk base, Bertha on his right side.

The rocktopi that had been lurking behind the houses started to slowly come forward, crowding in behind the line of rifle-wielding guards. So *many* of them, like villagers coming out of hiding to see the condemned criminals.

Whitey and his two red guards moved a bit closer. Another rocktopi came out of the crowed—three protrusions held a Glock carbine. Patrick saw that the weapon held no magazine.

Whitey took the weapon, slowly held it up, parallel to the line of people. He made tearing-paper noises.

A rocktopi rolled out of the crowd, onto the open space of the plaza. Patrick watched, stunned, as the creature began to flash glyphs on its round body.

"Ramiro, what's it saying?"

"Give me a second." Ramiro looked at the rocktopi, then touched a fingertip to the pad. He drew a symbol, wiped his hand across it, erasing it, drew another, looked at it. "I think the white one—Whitey—he wants to know about the weapon."

The man's voice wavered. He wasn't sure.

"Know *what* about the weapon?" Patrick asked.

Ramiro again looked at the rocktopi in front of him, studied the glyphs.

Whitey let out more sounds, *angrier* sounds. He gave the unloaded carbine a shake.

"Hurry up," Sonny said. "It's getting pissed."

Ramiro kept drawing. "I'm trying, okay? I don't know what it's asking. I'm trying."

"Try harder," Sonny said. "And faster."

Patrick felt helpless. He had no idea what the glyphs meant. If Ramiro couldn't figure it out, no one could.

"Wait a minute," Otto said. "They've been down here for millennia. Those questions Ramiro said they were asking, about his clothes, his gear. The metal in his backpack … I don't think they've ever seen modern humans."

Ramiro looked up from his tablet. "Shit. He might be right. The massacre site we found up on the surface, Veronica Reeves carbondated that to three thousand years ago, roughly 980 BC. Centuries before most cultures started working with steel. They find me with manufactured clothes, my gear and my computer, then all of you with KoolSuits and weapons. The aliens have never been seen because they are so far down, but maybe their being so far down also meant they couldn't see *us*."

"No way," Klimas said. "If they came in a spaceship, surely they could create some kind of monitoring system, to keep an eye on the indigenous population. They had to know humans were smart enough to eventually develop industry and technology. Didn't they?"

Memories of Utah rushed back. On the surface, there had been no signs of the rocktopi. None at all save for platinum dust carried out by the river, dust that likely would never have appeared if not for the accident that probably destroyed their culture.

"You don't understand how scared they are," Ramiro said. "They have — or had — another alien race hunting them, trying to exterminate them. I'll explain that when I can, let me focus on this right now."

He drew another symbol on his tablet, stared at the signaling rocktopi, wiped the symbol clean, drew another.

"I think I understand," he said. "Whitey wants to know where we got the guns. And … he's also asking *how many*. I think."

Where they got the guns? Why would they want to know that?

"We bought them at Walmart," Mullet said. "What the fuck do they care where we got them?"

"Because they don't think we can make them ourselves," Otto said. "If that massacre was the last time they saw humans — three *thousand* years ago — all people had back then was fire and pointy sticks. As far as the rocktopi are concerned, we suddenly have firearms, computers, and environmental suits that let us survive down here. Maybe they're worried that the race hunting them wants to use humans in some kind of proxy war."

Patrick tried to imagine what it would feel like to encounter that kind of technological leap — maybe like seeing chimps in a jungle one day, only to come back a little while later and see them driving cars and talking on cell phones.

But the question of *where* wasn't the one Patrick found most intriguing.

"Whitey also asked *how many*," he said. "Is that in reference to the guns, or to something else?"

Ramiro shook his head. "I don't know."

"Well *figure it out*," Sonny said. "These sonsabitches are going to gun us down."

Ramiro's eyes were wide with fear, with doubt. He glanced around, briefly looking at each person in the group, perhaps realizing that the lives of everyone he saw—including his own—relied on his ability to communicate.

He nodded. "I'll try again."

A commotion in the crowd of aliens. Three smaller rocktopi—bigger than the ones Patrick assumed were children, smaller than the ones wielding the rifles—flowed out of the crowd and stopped near Whitey. Adolescents, perhaps? They flowed close to each other, then linked extended pseudopods, almost seemed to … to *join*.

Nausea, sudden and intense. Patrick's head felt full of hot lead. His brain seemed to push at his eyes, his ears, his nose, his throat, threatening to squeeze its way out of every hole in his skull.

The last time he'd hurt this bad, someone had been grinding on his ear with a fireplace poker so hot it lit up the otherwise dark room in a deep, reddish light.

"Look at 'em," Sonny said. "What are they doing?"

Patrick said nothing, focused on keeping his gorge down, grateful for the flat stone against his back, the only thing that allowed him to stand on his own two feet.

Three rocktopi pressed together, mashing against each other, almost like glowing balls of playdough compressing into a single lump.

"Psychedelic alien garbage-bag gangbang," Mullet said. "I bet Rule Thirty-Four doesn't cover this one."

The aliens looked like one big mass of flesh, but Patrick could still tell them apart thanks to different color patterns pulsing across their black-dotted skin. The more he saw of these "smart" rocktopi, the faster he saw differences, saw individuals.

All three of them flashed a bright orange, each pulsing the color at different tempos. The pulsing rates slowed, came into synch, until all three pulsed as one.

The mass of alien stretched out, making a flat central area the size of a hula hoop.

On that circular area, colors pulsed. More than orange now: reds, yellows, scarlets, grays…

Patrick stared, stunned and dumbfounded as the colors morphed into a moving image, splotchy yet still identifiable as one of Angus Kool's robot dogs. It was like watching a slightly out-of-focus movie projected onto a bedsheet hung in someone's backyard. The robot, in the distance, low to the ground, streaking closer, mechanical legs pumping and flexible body bending like a sprinting cheetah.

From the robot's chest, the staccato bursts of muzzle flashes.

The image shifted, twisted in the other direction. Patrick saw stone buildings, crops…a village. Rocktopi ran in multiple directions, pseudopods reaching and flailing, their malleable skin coursing in bright greens and neon yellows and ruby reds, colors that Patrick, somehow, knew were shades of fear, of terror, of panic.

One of the rocktopi burst apart as SAW rounds punched through it. Streamers of thick yellow flew, splattered on the ground. The creature dropped, a lifeless blob with bright colors rapidly giving way to grayness.

The view shifted to the left—three rocktopi, one full size, one small. Bullets traced across them in a neat line of yellow spray. Children and adult alike, they fell.

"Jesus our savior," Sleepy said.

The carnage continued: bullets tearing into buildings and rocktopi alike. Two more killed, then three more, then one more, lethal rounds shredding victim after victim.

The view Patrick was seeing…a rocktopi running for its life.

The cavern wall seemed to rush closer.

The view whirled, perhaps 180 degrees. He was looking back at the village now—and the human soldiers in it.

Angus's mercenaries.

The men spread out, finishing off the wounded, killing anything that the robot dog had missed.

A massacre.

O'Doyle closed his eyes for a moment, and in that moment he was instantly back in Bandah with the NoSeeUms, bullets coming from everywhere, from every*one*, he and his team trying to stay alive, shooting anything that moved. Some of the villagers turned out to be armed— most were not.

His skin crawling, the memory threatening to strangle him, he opened his eyes and went from one massacre to another.

"Kool's bastards are efficient," Mullet said. "I'll give them that."

No teasing tone this time; he was watching what Patrick watched, undoubtedly awash in thoughts of the same night in Bandah.

"Is this a video recording of some kind?" Otto asked. "Or … or one of their *memories*?"

No one had an answer.

As suddenly as it had started, the slaughter ended—because there was no one left to kill.

A swirl of a direction change, a blurry view of tunnel walls, then the image faded away.

"We only saw in one direction," Curveball said. "If their black spots are eyes, can't they see in all directions at once?"

"I don't know," Ramiro said. "I haven't seen anything that might be a camera, but these guys have spaceship tech, so a camera might be one of those black spots. I don't know."

The survivor deep in Patrick's reptile brain filed away that bit of intel—if that had been an actual memory, not a recording of some kind, then maybe the rocktopi could only see forward, just as he could.

Whitey again moved toward Patrick and the others, his motions slow.

Paper-ripping sounds.

Axl screeched.

Alien rifles snapped up.

"What's going on?" Sonny said. "What are they doing?"

Patrick didn't have to ask. He'd seen behavior like this before—it didn't matter if it was human or alien, the results would be the same.

"Execution," Otto said. "I think we were just put on trial, and the sentence is death."

Sleepy took a step away from the obelisk base. One rifle was already trained on him; two more joined it. He stood still, his hands up.

"That wasn't us," he said to Whitey. "We didn't do that."

"Not this time, anyway," Curveball said. "I guess this is justice. We got away with one slaughter, now we'll die for one we didn't do."

Mullet caught Patrick's eye. That look on Mullet's face—he was going to attack, and he wanted Patrick to attack with him.

"I ain't gonna die sitting back waiting to get shot," Mullet said quietly. "Let's rush these motherfuckers."

Patrick shook his head. "No, hold on, give me a minute to think."

Curveball took a half step away from the wall. "We don't have a minute."

The rocktopi screeches grew louder, more frantic—Slash and Axl pleading with Whitey to give the order to fire, or maybe they were bullying him into it.

Patrick was losing control of the situation. But why should he control anything? His decisions had brought them here. His mission. His choices.

"I don't get this," Curveball said. "Why don't they just pull the fucking triggers already?"

"Because they don't *want* to," Klimas said. "Because they've never done anything like this before. Because they aren't warriors. I think they've lived in peace for so long they forgot how to fight, if they ever really knew how to begin with."

The confused honor guard…the panicked reactions when Mullet snatched the alien weapon…

Klimas was right.

The rocktopi that Mullet called *Axl* pulsed gray and violet, screamed something, a string of harsh syllables that made Patrick wince. The creature flowed toward Whitey. One of the red ones stepped in front of it—Axl used his rifle as a club, swinging the oval-shaped butt hard to first send the red's double-crescent knife flying, then a reverse stroke to knock the boneless creature aside.

Patrick saw a new color wash across *all* the rocktopi, all save for Whitey and Axl, a brief wave of sparkling pink.

As strange as this place was, as alien as these creatures were, Patrick knew what was going on—Axl wanted Whitey to give the order to fire, but Whitey was hesitant to give it.

Another glance at Ramiro: he erased a symbol, started over. The tablet shook in his hands.

Spots of pale crimson flashed on Whitey's body. He rolled away, behind the firing line. But this time, the two red guards didn't go with him. They instead moved closer to Patrick. No … closer to *Bertha*.

Each alien reached out a single pseudopod—like someone offering their hand.

"We hit those two red ones first," Mullet said. "Let's get it on."

The way the red rocktopi were just waiting, tentacles extended. *They're being humane.*

Patrick knew what was about to happen. And he knew what he had to do.

"Bertha," he said, "they want you to go with them."

"Like hell I will," she said. "I'll stay with you."

He turned to her, gripped her shoulders. Through his visor and hers, they locked eyes. He had to convince her.

"They want you to go with them because they don't want to kill an unborn child," he said, his words small whispers. "Stay alive. Get our child out of here. Whatever it takes."

She stared back at him, her head shaking slightly. "No. I won't leave you."

He squeezed her shoulders harder, almost succumbed to an overpowering need to shake some sense into her.

"Just *go*."

"This is bullshit," Mullet said. "Let's dance."

Mullet pushed off the obelisk base, rushed the rocktopi. They had an instant to fire, to cut him down, but they hesitated and he was on them. He kicked out, his foot punching into the nearest one, sending it rolling backward, pseudopods slapping against the tiles like a blown-out tire.

He reached for the weapon of another, but the rocktopi hesitation vanished. Rifle butts flashed, hitting Mullet once, twice, a third time. He stumbled, dropped to one knee. Another rifle butt slammed into his head.

Sleepy ran to him, reached for an attacker's weapon, but went down under the weight of three rocktopi that surged out from the crowd. Yellow pulsed and crimson flashed.

Curveball, Otto and Klimas started forward to join the fight, but Patrick's bellowing command stopped them in their tracks.

"Everyone, *stop*! No one move!"

Rocktopi tentacles wrapped around Sleepy's wrists, ankles and waist. He tried to resist, but it was like watching someone pull against rubber that gave under strength only to snap back into place. In seconds, his chest was heaving and he'd gotten nowhere. The aliens shoved him back into line against the obelisk base. Curveball and Klimas caught him before he hit the stone. Sleepy bent at the waist, exhausted.

The rocktopi continued to hold Mullet tight, their tentacles wrapped around his ankles, his wrists. The aliens stretched him out on his back on the brightly colored paving tiles. Two more rocktopi came in, leveled rifles at the man's face, the ends of their weapons only inches from his visor. Mullet pulled, tried to kick, tried to punch, but just like Sleepy, there was no escape from their elastic strength.

Axl's piercing cry transcended language barriers. He pulsed blue. The message was clear—he wanted permission to fire.

Whitey stood there on boneless limbs, wavering slightly, like a sea anemone in the softest of currents. He hissed, a long ripping of newspaper.

Axl rolled away, toward Mullet, reaching out and grabbing the first rifle it could, snatching it away from the nearest rocktopi. Axl lowered the weapons, pressed the twin pipes against Mullet's visor.

They were going to kill him. Patrick started forward, stopped himself, torn between his loyalty to his old friend and his desperate need to get his pregnant wife clear of the carnage to come.

Mullet stopped struggling. He stared up into his own death.

"Go ahead, you fucking freak," he said, calm and measured. "Do it."

No yelling. No cursing. No threats. Mullet wanted to die. He *welcomed* it. In those last seconds, Patrick finally understood who Kevin Bliss truly was, understood the pain of a horrible secret the man had carried with him for two decades.

Axl fired.

A *clang* and a spark, but not from the end of the barrel—the weapon broke where the barrels met the oblong stock. Curls of smoke rose up.

Mullet was still alive.

The weapon … it had malfunctioned.

Axl tossed the rifle aside. It landed on the tiles, spun halfway around, skidded to a halt.

The alien stretched out a new pseudopod—one that held a gleaming, double-crescent knife. The snakelike limb whipped up, cavern lights sparkling on the razor edges, then the blade whipped down in a blur.

A screech louder than any before.

Everything stopped.

The point of Axl's blade, unmoving, a half-inch from Mullet's wide, eager eyes.

Patrick turned toward the source of that new screech. At the edge of the plaza, the river right behind them, were two rocktopi, standing side by side with Samira Jabour and Tommy Strymon.

58

14,982 feet below the surface

TOMMY TRIED TO take it all in — hundreds of glowing rocktopi, some armed, some hiding near buildings and already shrinking away from him, the towering Obelisk … and the NoSeeUms.

"Ramiro?" Sam jammed her sidearm into its holster and took off running across the plaza, either oblivious to the danger of a firing line, or not caring about it.

Tommy's hands stayed on his carbine, but he made no motion to aim the weapon. Sixteen rocktopi holding what he assumed were railguns, another nine holding double-crescent knives. Who knew how many more weapons were hidden amongst the hundreds of glowing, amorphous creatures that lined the tiled clearing? He was a fast shooter, and accurate, but there was no chance he could get them all before they returned fire.

Sam threw her arms around Ramiro. "I thought you were dead!"

"They said you went missing," Ramiro said, his one-armed hug so tight he lifted her off her feet. "I thought *you* were dead."

Tommy stood alongside Disco and Siren, the two rocktopi he'd rescued. In turn, the pair of aliens had wrapped up him and Sam, then rolled into the river. Tommy hadn't been able to see anything, hadn't been able to move at all. He hadn't been able to reach Sam, either—something in the rocktopi bodies blocked radio transmission, maybe.

Such a strange sensation it had been—not being able to see, not knowing where he was going, and yet feeling…*safe*. Physical contact with Siren. Even though the creature was an alien, of a shape and body plan unknown on Earth, even though Tommy's skin was completely covered by clothes and the KoolSuit, the sensation of touching another sentient being had changed things.

He'd sensed the movement, known he was on the water. His stomach had lurched when he'd felt a great drop, and again when that drop suddenly stopped. A waterfall, possibly. Bound up like a piece of gear held by form-fitting Styrofoam, he'd been able to do nothing but breathe and wait. When Siren and Disco had finally let them go, he and Sam found themselves at the edge of this plaza.

Tommy looked around the plaza. So many rocktopi. *Aliens*. An entire town's worth of them. All sizes, from as small as a beach ball up to a big one that must have had more mass than Ender and Sleepy combined. Tommy glanced at the one that had rescued him; slightly shorter than most of those holding railguns. If the armed rocktopi were fully grown, the one that floated him down the river had to be an adolescent.

Ender's quiet voice in his headset: "Good to see you, Worm."

The man stood at the base of the black obelisk, along with the rest of the team. They looked like ass in a can: Sleepy, the sleeve of his fatigues ripped off, a bloody bandage beneath a layer of KoolSuit repair; Curveball, metal splint on his finger; Otto and Klimas, clothes tattered and torn, but not much worse for wear; McGuiness, hiding behind Otto and Klimas; Mullet, on his back, three rocktopi holding him as if he was about to be drawn and quartered.

"Nice timing, nerd," Mullet said, his tone conversational. "Now would you please shoot these pricks?"

The rocktopi didn't lower their weapons, but they also didn't shoot.

Tommy looked for Lybrand and Skylark, realized that O'Doyle was standing in front of Lybrand, shielding her with his body. Before now, he'd treated her like any other member of his team. Was she hurt?

Lybrand was there … but Tommy didn't see Marie.

"Skylark," he said. "Where is she?"

The silence answered his question, a wordless finality that required no further explanation. The weight of life, of exhausting existence, pulled at him, hooked his soul down to a new low. He'd gone twenty years without seeing her, without even talking to her, yet the loss gutted him, even more than Hatchet's death had.

The cost. High risk, high reward.

Three daughters, now without a mother.

Was any reward worth this? No.

Tommy looked at the gathered rocktopi, in all their colorful splendor, at the two glowing a deep, bright red, at the one that looked white, at the others holding rifles and knives. Had any of these been the ones that killed Marie?

He'd heard the phrase *itchy trigger finger* a thousand times. He finally understood what it meant, how it felt. He could kill at least ten of these bastards before they cut him down.

So easy, so satisfying — just start shooting, just start *killing*.

Ender: "Breathe, Worm. Keep your head."

A twenty-year absence from that man, too, yet Ender could see at a glance when *Bad Tommy* was ready to come out and play.

Tommy's rage vanished, pushed out by the hard fist of grief.

"Marie's children," he said. "What about her daughters?"

Sleepy: "We'll take care of her girls. If we get out of here alive. So chill, Tommy. Now isn't the time for you to lose it."

A rocktopi rolled out of the pack, stretched out pseudopods that pressed down on the colored tiles of the open space. The creature flowed toward Tommy.

Ender, quiet and calm: "We call that one *Slash*. It's one of the leaders. The big one on Mullet — we call it Axl — it just tried to kill Mullet but its weapon malfunctioned. Be careful."

Tommy had arrived a moment too late. A blessing in disguise? If he'd seen the rocktopi about to shoot Mullet, he would have put the thing down without a moment's hesitation.

This *Slash* moved slowly toward Tommy. Colors coursed in definite patterns over its black-spotted body. Something oddly familiar about those patterns. Tommy saw a long, ragged white line in the middle of its round body—a scar, maybe?

"Talk to me," Tommy said quietly. "What's the play?"

He expected Ender to answer instantly. Ender did not. In the brief pause, Slash came closer. The voice that finally answered wasn't Ender's, wasn't even all that familiar.

Otto: "The white one is in charge. We think. Slash is highly ranked, but that's all we know right now."

The scarred alien being slowly closed the distance. The other rocktopi stayed where they were, more like they didn't know what to do rather than they'd been ordered to remain in position.

Mullet: "Shoot that motherfucker."

He was still held down by aliens, and still talking shit.

Ender: "Mullet, shut up. Worm, I don't know what those two rocktopi you came here with are all about, but aim your weapon at one. Show what will happen if Slash keeps coming."

First Ender didn't have an answer, and now his best plan was for Tommy to take a hostage?

Closer Slash came, only ten meters away now, the double-crescent knife held in a thick pseudopod gleamed.

Tommy's eyes flicked across the railguns aimed his way. If he tried to aim his weapon at the rocktopi that had saved his life, would any of those weapons fire?

Slash closed to five meters, colors and patterns coursing across its skin, tentacles and extrusions moving like coiled cobras waiting for just the right moment to strike.

Its blade…why hadn't it grabbed a railgun from one of the others? Why hadn't it ordered the others to shoot? Because Tommy was standing too close to the rocktopi that had rescued him and Sam? Or because fighting with the knife carried meaning of some kind?

Tommy opened his hands, let his carbine hang from its harness. He drew his KA-BAR and dropped into a fighting stance, point in front of him, directed at the alien.

Three meters away, Slash stopped.

Mullet: "Yeah, Tommy, cut that bitch."

Ender: "Kevin, shut your damn mouth!"

Tommy heard them, but kept his eyes fixed on the scarred alien, felt the scarred alien staring at him. The creature's colors shifted, swirled, undoubtedly signifying some emotional change, but Tommy had no idea what that might be. Fear? Rage? Maybe it was a brawler, maybe it *wanted* a close-up fight.

Slash, Ender had called it.

The alien crept another meter closer.

Trapped far underground, in the midst of an impossible sci-fi setting, and he was going to have a knife fight with a glowing alien.

Maybe he and the others had trespassed. Maybe in one light or another, he was the bad guy here. The aggressor. The invader. Did that matter? These things had killed Skylark. So, no … it didn't matter.

"Come and get it," Tommy said.

A piercing screech, so close, from right behind him—from Siren. Tommy jumped, hating himself for having turned his back on something he knew nothing about, but Siren flowed past him, pulsing colors and patterns, extruded tentacles waving wildly.

Slash stopped—the smaller rocktopi blocked its path.

Sonny: "Holy shit. They *match*."

The instant Sonny said those words, Tommy saw, understood. The smaller rocktopi pulsed with a bright amber with repeating curves of emerald green, while Slash pulsed a yellow-orange with curves of violet—the *colors* were different, but the *patterns* were identical.

Tommy quickly glanced at the other rocktopi gathered around the plaza; a hammering headache of more colors than his mind could name, yet none seemed to have that same pattern. All the patterns were different. No, not *all*—where beachball-sized aliens stood side-by-side with fully grown ones, those patterns seemed to match.

Were the patterns *inherited*?

Slash shifted to Tommy's left, trying to get around Siren, but Siren moved as well, a dollop of glowing pudding on thick tentacles that blocked Slash's path.

The two creatures flashed an insane strobe of colors and patterns, both screeching in rapid-fire, piercing tones that reminded Tommy of two baboons fighting for dominance.

Then, in an instant, Slash stopped making noise. Its wild colors faded to more subdued tones, and its rapidly shifting color pattern slowed.

Siren and Disco rolled into the open space of the plaza. Tommy felt instantly exposed without them; now there was nothing to stop the aimed railguns from firing. Except the railguns weren't aimed at him anymore. The points had dipped, were aimed this way and that, as if the massed rocktopi had become distracted. He couldn't tell where the black spot-eyes were looking, but he felt they were no longer focused on him.

Siren and Disco seemed to smush together, like cell division running in reverse.

Ender: "Some of them did this a few minutes ago. They can play back their memories, or something like that. They want to show us something."

The new lump of dual-rocktopi pulsed orange, each one flashing at different rates that quickly came into sync. As Tommy watched, a portion of them flattened, and in that flat area, images appeared—not crystal-clear, but detailed enough to make out what they were.

Images of a chaotic firefight in a tunnel, of brutal hand-to-hand combat between mercenaries and flashing rocktopi.

At the sight of the mercs, the hundreds of watching rocktopi pulsed with splotches of green and tan—splotches that matched, almost perfectly, the camo pattern on the mercenaries' jackets.

There was something disturbing about the uniform behavior, something ominous.

"It's like they recognize the uniforms," Tommy said.

Otto: "They do. The mercs slaughtered a bunch of them in another cavern. Survivors showed us the … the *footage*, I guess you'd call it."

On the melded rocktopi, scattered, fuzzy images continued to flash.

Images of the cages, from the inside, the ever-present tunnel walls and ceiling. Two mercs standing outside of the cages.

Tommy made out a flutter of movement, coming down the tunnel.

The two mercs dropped.

Seconds later, Tommy saw a fuzzy version of himself run past, and vanish … *off-screen*, for lack of a better word. Sam appeared, blurry but recognizable, running down the tunnel toward the cage.

Sam, lifting the controller.

Disco, tearing the metal mesh, sliding out of the cage. This was

Siren's view. A mad sprint around the switchbacks. The images shook suddenly, slightly, and Tommy knew the claymore had just been detonated. Out of the long tunnel, rushing toward the river, scattered silverbugs everywhere. A disorienting, shifting spin of view—Sam, running, trying to take off her backpack, dropping it. The view shifted again—Tommy, sprinting out of the tunnel, racing over and around silverbugs, becoming larger as he came closer to the "camera." Behind him, at the tunnel mouth, mercenaries fanning out, firing.

Then, a blur of tentacles reaching out, swallowing Tommy up, a paramecium engulfed by an amoeba. He saw the shock and horror on his own face, only for a moment, then the view shifted again—floating on the river. Bullets splashing up tiny geysers, then into the darkness of the river tunnel.

The image faded. Siren and Disco separated like two lumps of flashing gum pulling apart.

The white rocktopi let out a sound like that of a newspaper tearing in half.

All around the plaza, railgun tips lowered toward the ground, double-crescent knives vanished inside soft bodies.

Sonny: "Holy shit, I think they understand that we're not with Angus."

Was he right? Tommy wanted his carbine in his hands, but the rocktopi had lowered their weapons … they'd made the first move of good faith. Slowly, he sheathed his knife, let his hands rest at his sides.

"Sam," he said, "put your pistol on the deck."

Still standing next to Ramiro, Tommy saw her frown.

"The deck?"

"On the ground," Tommy said. "And do it real slow."

Sam nodded. She drew her Glock—*Tommy's* Glock—knelt, set the weapon on the tiles at her feet.

The rocktopi didn't take it. Nor did they try to take Tommy's. Slash stayed close by, his pattern still moving slowly, his earlier apparent fury completely gone.

Ender: "You rescued those rocktopi. You went after the mercs, you …"

Tommy heard the guilt in his voice. A lot of guilt. And no matter how bad Ender felt, it wasn't bad enough.

"I killed them," Tommy said.

Ender held his gaze for a moment, then the big man looked down. Nothing else needed to be said.

The cost. High risk, high reward.

Here, with the tension reduced, at least for the moment, Tommy's actions finally hit home. He'd sworn he'd never kill again. Empty words then, empty words now. He'd let himself believe he wouldn't have to do the only thing he'd ever been good at. Was that Ender's fault? Partially. But most of the blame lay on Tommy's shoulders. He should have known better. Deep down, he *had* known better, yet he'd chosen to ignore it.

Sleepy: "They tried to kill Mullet, Tommy. I think they would have killed more of us after. You saved us. You and Sam both."

Did that matter? Did that give Tommy a free pass? Did it balance things?

No. He'd killed six people. At *least* six. Tommy couldn't be sure how many the claymore had taken out. Or the grenades. Or the cave-in.

Six more to his lifelong total: confirmed kills number twenty-five through thirty-one. For some things, there was no balance to be had.

And yet…he'd saved the lives of two sentient beings. He'd made physical contact with an alien race. He'd *communicated* with them. Those same aliens could have left him and Sam to die. They hadn't— they'd saved him and Sam both. And here, when Tommy had been hopelessly outnumbered, Siren had defended him. Defended him against Siren's father, or mother, or at least a family member of some stripe. And then, Siren had shown the rocktopi what Tommy had done, which, perhaps, saved the NoSeeUms, Otto, Klimas and Sonny.

Maybe there was some balance to be had after all, but Tommy'd be damned if he knew how those scales worked.

Tommy again looked around the plaza. At his friends. At dumbshit Ender, who'd underestimated *everything*, who had caused this tragedy to happen. At Slash, at Siren. At the gathered rocktopi, at their boneless, graceful bodies, all glowing, beaming with light that swirled in a million colors.

They were beautiful.

He was ugly. Blackened and twisted on the inside, whatever might pass for his soul forever destroyed by the things he'd done, but the rocktopi—they were *beautiful*.

Klimas: "Since we're all pals and shit, can someone get these puffy Pillsbury pricks off of me?"

Ender took another slow step forward. He pointed one finger at Mullet, the other at the mostly white rocktopi. There was a pause, then the white rocktopi made that tearing newspaper sound.

The aliens restraining Mullet let him go, scooted away from him fast. Mullet stood, made a show of brushing himself off.

"Pussies. I was just about to whip whatever you snot-blobs use for an ass." Mullet looked at Ender. "What now, fearless *leader*?"

The way he said that last word made it clear he wasn't sure if Ender *was* the leader anymore.

Tommy wasn't sure, either.

Two NoSeeUms dead—who would be next?

"Ramiro, Sam," Ender said. "Help me talk to them. We have to figure out where we all go from here."

"Before you do that, you have to understand what brought them here," Ramiro said. "Let me show you."

59

14,982 feet below the surface

THE CAVERN'S IMMENSE size helped ease his claustrophobia. Constant tension burrowed through Sonny, from the tips of his toes to the top of his head, but it wasn't nearly as bad as it had been in the mind-choking tunnels.

He rubbed at his bracelet. The fucking monsters still ringed the plaza, some of them holding those weird weapons that had killed Skylark. Who was next? Sonny had a bad feeling it would be him.

Three fucking *miles* underground?

His chest hurt. He felt like he was riding the razor's edge of a heart attack, every minute, every second.

As if that wasn't bad enough, the mercenaries were hours away, and Angus Kool was walking around in a suit of armor straight out of a sci-fi movie. At any other time, Sonny might have doubted Tommy's story, but not now.

You got to relax, you sonofabitch, or you're going to die before you even have a chance to get out.

Otto came closer, a concerned expression on his face.

"Sonny, you okay?"

"You keep asking dumb questions," Sonny said. "Figures that you work for the government."

Otto huffed, smiled. "Ramiro's going to tell us what's up. Focus on that, all right? It might help."

Sonny thought of telling Otto to go fuck himself, but the man was so damn earnest. "Yeah, sure," Sonny said. "Focus. I'll give it a whirl."

Ramiro finished his slow, hobbling lap around the obelisk base. The kid had asked for a couple of minutes to review what he'd seen, make sure he had it straight before sharing it with everyone.

The stupid little fuck. If Sam and Ramiro had just used common sense and taken a big fat check, Sonny would still be up on the surface.

Ramiro turned from the base, awkward with his crutch, and faced Sonny, Sam and the others. A history lesson while killer aliens stood watch? Sure. Why the fuck not?

"This is their story," Ramiro said, gesturing to the obelisk base.

Sonny had seen the carvings on the base, of course, but he'd had more important things on his mind than some stupid fucking alien art. He didn't even like *human* art.

"It's done in squares," Ramiro said. "Starting here."

He pointed to a square that was about eight feet tall, as tall as the base itself. In the square, a detailed carving, a cylinder with two tapered points. It made Sonny think of a double-ended vibrator.

"That's what the Utah ship looked like," O'Doyle said. "Or it probably looked like that before it got all fucked up."

Ramiro limped to the next square, the next carving. A long, segmented shape, with thin thorns or barbs jutting from it all down its length.

Worm, the smart one, stepped closer. Sonny could feel the excitement coming off the man. A nerd with guns and grenades. Wonderful.

"It's almost…insectile," Worm said. "Like a fat stick bug. Or maybe a wasp."

A *wasp*. It clearly wasn't that—Sonny had no idea what in shit's name it was—but the length, the thinness, the spikes…something about the shape felt…*threatening*.

"It's a ship," Ramiro said. "From another race, I think."

He shuffled to the next square. In it, the wasp-thing and a trio of double-ended vibrators. Lines emanated from the wasp-thing, slicing into one of the vibrators, which looked to be breaking into pieces.

"Oh, cool, space battle," Mullet said. "Awesome. They should make a video game."

There was something *off* with that boy.

"I think the rocktopi were refugees of sorts," Ramiro said. "They came to Earth because that other race destroyed their home world."

He pointed to the next square in the series. Smaller wasp-ships, hundreds of them, surrounding a planet. In the center of the planet, the stylized sun symbol that the rocktopi used to depict themselves.

Lines ran from the ships to the planet. And like the vibrator-ship in the square before, the planet was cracking, emitting flames or magma—as if it was about to explode into a thousand pieces.

"Lord above," Sleepy said. He shook his head. "I…can you imagine being on a starship and seeing the Earth destroyed?"

A silence fell over the plaza.

Ramiro tapped an image etched into the carving.

"This glyph represents the wasp-ships," he said. "Or maybe the race that flew them, I'm not entirely sure."

Sonny didn't know one rocktopi symbol from the next, but even he could see this symbol was different. Rectangular, not round, with angry, barbed points jutting out from it.

Ramiro walked a few feet to the next square. It showed three of the tapered cylinders, trailed by dozens of wasp ships.

"Genocide," Otto said. "It wasn't enough to destroy the rocktopi's home planet. The wasps wanted to exterminate them."

Was Sonny supposed to feel bad for the rocktopi? Maybe they'd started the shit. He didn't know. He didn't want to know.

Ramiro pointed to another square at the base's far curve. On it, a single tapered cylinder, hovering beneath a strangely familiar shape. It looked familiar, but Sonny couldn't quite make the connection.

"My God," Sam said. "That's the peak above us. That's Mount Fitz Roy."

Sonny thought back to the helicopter ride to the plateau. Pictures or video of Mount Fitz Roy's distinctive outline didn't convey the mountain's sheer mass. Only when seeing it from the air had Sonny truly understood its immensity. And there, on that carving, a rectangular piece of the mountain hovered in the air above a sprawling landscape—the ship was directly below it.

"Fuck that bullshit," Mullet said. "The squidleys couldn't lift up an entire goddamn mountain. Could they?"

O'Doyle and Bertha nodded.

"That's what they did in Utah," O'Doyle said. "They picked the whole thing up, carved out the cavern, set the ship inside, put the mountain back like putting a cork back in a bottle."

"More like a gravestone on a tomb," Sonny said.

Billions of tons of rock. *Trillions*, maybe.

Sonny glanced at the glowing squidleys—he found he liked the word—that surrounded the plaza. How advanced did they have to be to do something like move a mountain? And if they were so advanced, why were they down here, hiding away from the world?

"The rest of the carvings appear to be local history," Ramiro said. "Realistic representations of rocktopi, one after another. Maybe they're former leaders or heroes. I don't know."

Sonny glanced up, at the rocktopi sculpture atop the obelisk's peak. A famous leader? The ship's captain? A religious figure? No way of knowing.

"They stayed hidden all these years," Worm said. "No trace of them on the surface. No friendly contact with humanity. Because they're hiding. They're *afraid*. After all this time, they're afraid of the wasps, afraid of doing anything that might reveal their presence to the race that destroyed their planet."

Mullet laughed, a dismissive, insulting sound.

"No wonder they're such utter pussies." He shook his head. "Twelve thousand years of hiding like cowards? No fucking honor, man."

Honor. A stupid term for stupid people, a concept that sent people to jail or put them in a coffin.

A sharp screech made Sonny jump.

At the plaza's edge, that angry-looking squidley, the one everyone called *Slash*. It surprised Sonny that he recognized it on sight, but he did.

The alien stretched out a thick limb, the end of which split into longer, thicker bits, like the snake-hair of a movie medusa.

The snake ends pointed at people: O'Doyle, Sam, Ramiro, Worm, Lybrand, Otto—and one at Sonny.

"Go fuck yourself," Sonny said.

But he didn't say it very loud.

"I saw this before," Ramiro said. "Whitey wants to talk to us."

60

14,982 Feet below the surface

THE IMAGE faded out.

Sam watched the two aliens separate from each other. One had two globs of some kind of stretchy, white material on its skin, globs stained at the edges with yellow blood—the rocktopi equivalent of a bandage, most likely. The wounded alien was the only survivor of the battle the merged aliens had just shown.

"Good thing there weren't survivors of the bunch we gunned down," Tommy said. "Would be bad news if Whitey had that footage."

"Shut up," Lybrand said, softly. "We can't take a chance that they might understand what we're saying. Let's hope they chalk those kills up to the mercs."

Sam didn't like hiding the info from Whitey, but what choice did she have? Kool's mercs had slaughtered hundreds of rocktopi—would fessing up to the three they had *not* killed do any good?

The two rocktopi flowed out of the square room, a room that seemed just as alien as the aliens themselves. On the walls, engraved images painted in wild colors—rocktopi, obviously, but also strange landscapes with unknown plants and what could only be bizarre animals of some kind. Thick lines near the ceiling glowed with constantly shifting colors that cast the room in strange hues. Odd devices, the use of which Sam could only guess at, were on the floor or hung from the walls. Some of the devices had lights, some did not.

Sam and Ramiro sat on the stone floor, he with the white tablet the rocktopi had given him, she with her water-warped sketch pad and Tommy's water-warped copy of *The Call of the Wild*. Behind her and Ramiro stood Tommy, Otto, O'Doyle, Sonny and Lybrand. They all faced Siren and the two rocktopi O'Doyle's people had named *Whitey* and *Slash*.

Sam thought she and Ramiro had been included in this meeting because they understood at least a little of the rocktopi language. O'Doyle because he was clearly the leader. Tommy, probably, because Siren had seen him in action, seen him take out six of the same people who had slaughtered hundreds of rocktopi. As for Otto, McGuiness and Lybrand, Sam didn't know why they'd been chosen.

Gray symbols flashed across Whitey's skin. Sam didn't recognize any of them.

"Those are symbols for time," Ramiro said. "I learned some of them when I was trying to figure out how long I'd been down here. Give me a second."

Sam watched him draw shapes on the tablet.

"That artificial sun in the City Cavern ceiling is always on," he said as he worked. "They don't have a day and night cycle. They used an hourglass to show me their units of time. The time period he's showing now is in the ballpark of ... I think about twelve hours."

An hourglass. A simple but efficient concept. She wondered if it was filled with platinum dust.

"Twelve hours," O'Doyle said. "He just showed us Angus and his men. Does he know where they are? If so, how? Ramiro, ask him that."

Yet another question. Sam and Ramiro were getting hammered by them, from both sides.

O'Doyle wanted tactical info: How many rocktopi were there, total? How many silverbugs, both the normal-sized and the larger variety?

How many railguns? Did the rocktopi have other weapons? Was there another way out of the mountain? And the answer he wanted more than any other—was there a map of the tunnels?

Whitey had questions, too, questions Sam was trying hard to understand. She now understood the symbol for *difference*—Whitey demanded to know the *difference* between O'Doyle's group and the group that had slaughtered the village. The old alien also flashed a combination of symbols she believed meant *intent*, which Ramiro interpreted as Whitey asking:

Why had the mercs slaughtered the village?

"Hurry up," O'Doyle said. "We need to know if that's what Whitey meant."

His words came slow, ragged. He was in a lot of pain.

Ramiro puzzled over what to draw on his tablet. After a pause, he left his time symbols and drew a question mark next to them. He showed the tablet to Whitey.

"A question mark," Tommy said. "They know what that is?"

"I learned some of their symbols, they learned some of mine," Ramiro said.

A patch of Whitey's skin flattened. On it, a new small, gray shape appeared: two legs, two arms, a head. A human, but it looked blocky, heavy.

Sam recognized the shape's outline—she'd seen it across the river.

"Kool's powersuit," she said.

She looked at Tommy. He squinted, then nodded.

Another image appeared next to the first: a simple circle and lines that could only be one thing.

"That's the symbol for silverbugs," Ramiro said. "Whitey must have some of the machines watching Angus."

"That's helpful," Tommy said. "We need to assume Whitey's intel is accurate—we have around twelve hours until Angus gets here."

Otto shook his head. "I don't understand how we can be that far ahead of Angus."

"The river," Sonny said, instantly. "Water follows the path of least resistance and all that. Angus has to get all those people and gear through switchbacks. Makes sense to me. And this is their turf. They knew how to find Angus to attack him. They must have some rocktopi acting as scouts or something. If he says it's twelve hours for that sonofabitch to get here, we should believe it."

O'Doyle thought a moment.

"We can't count on that number," he said. "Whatever we decide, we'll be ready in six hours. Sam, Ramiro, ask them my questions. How many soldiers do they have? Does he know *exactly* where Angus is, and if so, how? Is there another way out of here? Hurry up, we need to know this stuff."

Sam heard the man, knew she needed to act, but it was hard to take her eyes off Ramiro. She'd come to grips with his death, gone through the emotional wringer of losing her best friend, losing the most important person in her life, only to find him alive. Alive for now, anyway.

Would they all die down here?

Like Hatchet?

Like Skylark?

On the short walk to this building, Ram had filled her in on his experience. He'd spent two days with the rocktopi. They'd tried to communicate with him. In the process of his desperate language immersion, he'd learned their sentence structure and the meanings of hundreds of their symbols. She and Ram were still functionally illiterate in the rocktopi language, but by working together they were quickly decreasing the time it took to understand the aliens.

"Whitey is asking a question," Ramiro said. "Two symbols. One is that non-person symbol. I don't know what the other one is."

One symbol Ramiro had learned stood out: the symbol for *humans*. It was the same symbol the rocktopi used to identify themselves as people, but with an extra curl that signified the concept of "negative." In short, the rocktopi symbol for humans meant "non-people."

Sam tried not to assign any specific interpretation to that, tried to keep reminding herself that this race had an entirely different set of meanings, morals and values. But to be thought of as a *non-person* by a group that could kill her at any moment? That was a trifle disturbing.

She studied the other symbol flashing in dark gray across the alien's whitish skin. She'd seen it in the classroom cavern.

"I think that means *unknown*," she said, "but maybe in relation to numbers?"

Tommy squatted down behind her. "Like an X in an equation? A variable?"

Sam again read the symbols on Whitey's skin—now the question made sense.

"He wants to know how many humans there are," she said. "He can see how many of us there are, so he either means how many in Angus's group, or how many total, us and Angus's group combined."

Whitey's earlier question, about the difference between the two groups. She still couldn't explain that, but maybe she could further establish that there were, indeed, two *separate* groups. She had to show them that all humans weren't the same.

Sam took the tablet from Ramiro, looked at it.

"Just draw with your fingertip," he said. "Basically, it's an Etch A Sketch."

She huffed a laugh. Here she was, trying to communicate to an alien race that once had the technology to cross the stars, and the equivalent of a child's toy was the tool she'd use to do it.

Sam started to draw out the numbers symbols she'd seen in the classroom cavern, couldn't remember them. She reached for her sketch pad.

"Inside cover of my book," Tommy said. "I wrote down their integer symbols."

She flipped open *The Call of the Wild*. There, below a list of seventeen dates, were the symbols for the rocktopi numbers. The list of dates distracted her for an instant—had he really read the book *seventeen* times?—then she began drawing on the alien Etch A Sketch.

The first number was easy: the single rocktopi symbol for *eleven*.

The second was harder.

"O'Doyle, how many men does Angus have?"

He thought for a moment. "Let's say … ninety-five."

"Then make it eighty-nine," Tommy said. "Since we know six of them are gone."

Sam heard the chill in his words, wondered if he was staring at O'Doyle when he said them. She pushed the thought away, focused on the numbers. She drew the rocktopi number for *seven*, then for *five*.

With normal numbers, using base-10, the 7 would mean seven

groups of 10, with five ones: (7 x 10) + 5 = 75. In base-12, however, the 7 represented seven groups of *12*, with five ones: (7 x 12) + 5 = 89.

She held the board up for Whitey to see, felt the alien's stare leave her and focus on the numbers.

"We need to speed this up," O'Doyle said. "Angus's men are coming. We either need a way out, or we need to see if Whitey has additional resources for us to fight them."

Whitey again flattened part of his formless body, again flashed symbols—fourteen of them this time.

"The one in the middle is *danger*," Ram said. "And I see *rocktopi*, and *non-person*. I don't get the rest."

Sam shook her head. "Neither do I."

Whitey hissed his ripped paper hiss. Slash's color patterns became brighter, angrier.

Ramiro leaned closer to Sam. "He's getting impatient."

"That makes two of us," O'Doyle said. "You two don't seem to understand that we have a *company* of well-armed mercs on the way, that—"

"She understands *just fine*," Tommy said. "How about you shut the fuck up, Ender? You don't know a damn thing about communicating, all you know how to do is kill. Kill and get *us* killed. Be quiet and let Sam do her work."

Sam turned, looked up, saw the two men staring hard at each other, saw the anger on both of their faces. Lybrand, Otto and Sonny watched as well—none of them knew what to say.

O'Doyle broke the staredown, looked at Sam.

"Yeah, all right," he said. "Just try to hurry. The clock is ticking."

Sam faced forward, still feeling the tension between the two men, still feeling the pressure on her. If she didn't come through, Ram might die. Tommy might die. *She* might die.

Whitey let out another hiss, short and loud and angry. Slash screeched, so sharp and piecing that Sam twitched. The sound transcended language—it was a threat.

The rocktopi had knives. They had those weird guns. There were hundreds of rocktopi just outside of this house. And O'Doyle was right— Kool and his killers were out there, somewhere. Sam had to figure out how to talk to the rocktopi, but it was so hard to focus, and she just didn't have enough knowledge.

The symbols on Whitey's black-spotted skin pulsed, almost as if he was repeating the same sentence but with more volume.

Siren, the smallest of the three rocktopi, stretched out a pseudopod and moved closer.

Sam heard O'Doyle bristle behind her, saw Siren stop suddenly.

"Leave him alone," Tommy said. "Siren won't hurt Sam."

Sonny grunted. "*Siren?* You soldier types seem to like giving these things names."

A nervous stillness, then the alien came closer. He stretched out, picked up two objects off the floor—just colored lumps of glass as far as Sam could tell, one a deep red, the other sapphire blue. Siren set the red lump on the floor in front of Sam.

She looked at it, then at Siren, at the alien's flowing body, the swirling patterns of color.

"I don't understand," she said.

She found herself wishing Veronica Reeves was still alive, was here to handle this.

Siren slowly stretched an extrusion to the tablet Sam held. The glowing tip of the tentacle drew a glyph—a glyph that was part of the complicated sentence Whitey still had displayed on his body. Siren then set the blue glass in front of Sam, picked up the red glass, then moved back to stand by Slash and Whitey.

Sam's body started to shake. She didn't get it. She just didn't get it.

"A trade," Tommy said. "The symbol means *trade.*"

Rocktopi … danger … non-person … trade.

Sam leaned back, shocked that she understood, or at least *thought* that she understood.

"They want our *help.* They want to trade for it."

"Trade," Patrick said. "Trade what?"

Sam recognized another symbol, one she'd seen in the classroom cavern alongside any image of a dead animal or person. But the symbol wasn't quite the same … it had that same curl that meant *negative.* Negative death?

No, she had it backward—the symbol meant *living,* or maybe *not die.*

"Our lives," Sam said in a rush. "I think they want us to help them in exchange for our lives."

"But help with what?" Sonny said.

"With Angus Kool," Otto said. "They want us to fight him and his men."

Silence hung in the air. Otto was right. It now seemed obvious. The rocktopi had attacked Angus and been ripped to shreds. Just Tommy, alone, had taken out six of Angus's men.

"How about them apples," Tommy said. "They want us to kill for them."

A darkness in his words, a darkness Sam hadn't heard before.

"That can't be right," Sonny said. "If it is, it's bullshit. They've been hidden down here for twelve thousand years, protecting their secret, murdering anyone that came *close* to finding out they were here. Say you guys kill Angus and his men, you save the day and protect the village like the fucking Seven Samurai. You think they're going to let us go after that? Let us blab about what we've found down here?"

Years ago, with Veronica, Sam had seen the ancient village that the rocktopi had destroyed. She'd seen the broken, butchered bones of the villagers. Angus had massacred a rocktopi village, yes, but the rocktopi had done the same to humans.

"Sonny has a point," she said. "We are the first people down here. Their entire culture seems to revolve around remaining undiscovered. That they'll let us go … it doesn't make sense."

A puzzle with missing pieces, pieces that might better explain the rocktopi's behavior.

"They haven't been *invaded* in those twelve thousand years," Otto said. "Maybe this is a new situation. They attacked Angus and got torn up—they think they can't win this fight without more firepower. Maybe they're willing to trade the devil they know for the one they don't."

O'Doyle put his arm around Lybrand's shoulders.

"Maybe it depends on the deal we make," he said softly.

The two rocktopi continued to flash colors at each other, one bright, the other faint. They let out squeaks and piercing cries. Sam wondered if they could talk completely with light, or if there were some concepts that could only be conveyed with "words."

Siren stretched out a tentacle, gently took the sketch pad from Sam. With the older two aliens still discussing, or perhaps arguing, Siren drew a picture. The creature turned it around so all the humans could see: the same symbols Sam had used to write *eighty-four,* the presumed number of Angus's men, and a crude picture of … a mushroom?

"Oh no," O'Doyle said.

Whitey and Slash stopped arguing.

"Someone please tell me this isn't happening," Otto said. "Please."

"It explains a lot," Tommy said.

Sam turned to him. "I don't get it—it's a mushroom. Are they saying they grow mushrooms down here?"

"Not a *mushroom*," Tommy said. "A mushroom *cloud*. They think Angus brought a nuke with him."

61

ANGUS, FUENTES AND Khatari were again in the middle of the column, along with the two haulers that carried supplies and Angus's special gear. The middle was safer. It also kept Angus away from Donnie, which was good. The man was still incensed at the loss of his men, at the loss of his prisoners.

The column had halted while Angus made further modifications to the haulers he'd converted into SAW-carrying combat units, filling the role that Snoopy and Oberon had once held. The modified donkeys—which Angus had dubbed "Goofy" and "Cujo"—did not have the speed of their predecessors, but with their cargo removed they had good speed, were hard to stop, and were capable of doing significant damage.

Donnie had moved Fifth and Sixth Platoons to the back of the column, trailed by Cujo. Recon, along with Second Platoon remained up front, following behind Goofy. Third and Fourth were in the middle with Angus, so they could quickly respond to attacks either from the front or the rear.

Everyone was on high alert. No one was going to sneak up on the mercs again, that much was for certain.

Six men lost in the attack. Combined with the other deaths and injuries, the merc company was down to sixty-eight men.

It would be enough. All they had to do was get to the ship, deposit the bomb, then march back up and let physics do the work.

Angus glanced at the donkey carrying the man-sized case that contained Dirty Randy's Money Shot. Angus hadn't really believed that Donnie's G4S contacts could get their hands on a nuke, but they had. In Bulgaria, all things are for sale—including "lost" nukes from the former Soviet Union.

Donnie had had so many questions. If Angus had wanted to detonate the bomb on the surface, the sale probably wouldn't have happened. G4S didn't want that kind of heat. Neither did the person who'd sold the bomb, most likely. The nations of the world would not let something like that rest—they'd track down those responsible.

But a bomb detonated three miles below ground? It would barely be noticed. A brief blip on seismographs, which most would explain away as a shift between the Nazca and South American tectonic plates. Some detective-minded geologist might try to dig further, but what was there to find? There would be no repetition, no pattern, just the one-time anomaly.

Angus had shown Donnie the science, explained to him that, in effect, no one would know. If they placed the bomb and took the mercs back to the surface before detonating, the mercs themselves wouldn't even know a nuke had gone off. A victimless crime, so to speak.

Angus had also explained to Donnie what had happened in Utah, how the rocktopi had likely lowered their doomsday orb deep into the mantle. The subsequent detonation of what *had* to be a massive bomb, nuclear or something else, had torn Funeral Mountain apart and destroyed trillions of dollars' worth of platinum. Angus assumed there was a similar doomsday device hiding in the Fitz Roy ship, and that if he didn't kill all the rocktopi in one fell swoop, they might use it. Bye-bye billions.

The information had been enough for Donnie to take to his superiors, enough for G4S to kick in the money needed to buy the bomb. It hadn't been cheap. Donnie was still getting his three percent of Angus's future wealth, but G4S had negotiated their own deal—seven percent.

All in all, one hell of a deal. For seven percent of future revenue, G4S had given Donnie and Angus a genuine RDS-46 nuclear warhead. The RDS-46 was made to be part of a Russian MIRV, or *Multiple Independent Reentry Vehicle*. One missile carried several warheads, each capable of hitting a separate target.

As far as nukes went, the five-megaton RDS-46 wasn't "big," but the bomb's effects on the surface were far different from their effects in a tunnel system. The nuke would devastate the rocktopi in three ways.

First, the tunnels would concentrate the overpressure wave, creating a death wind traveling at speeds approaching 1,000 miles an hour, hitting anything in its path at somewhere around 200 pounds per square inch. That kind of force shattered buildings—it would turn a human being into bone-flecked porridge, splatter rocktopi like bugs against a windshield.

Second, the heat. The squishy bastards liked things hot, but there was a big difference between the current air temperature of 200 degrees Fahrenheit and the 10,000 degrees Fahrenheit generated by the blast. The tunnels would channel that heat, creating an instant blast furnace that would incinerate every bit of biomass up to somewhere around a thousand feet below the surface.

Third, the radiation. Anything not killed by the blast wave and the heat would, without a doubt, be horribly irradiated. Even if the rocktopi hid in their old ship, it wouldn't make much difference—neutron radiation would tear through the entire thing.

Not that the radiation would even matter, most likely. He planned on finding the ship, setting off the nuke inside it, or at least right next to it. The explosion would likely melt much of the ship. He'd seen similar results in Utah, where some ancient explosion had melted a huge hole in the hull.

The blast would kill all of the rocktopi. Every last one. Smart business, sure, but also a delicious touch of revenge for Dirty Randy.

And if it failed, or wasn't useable for any reason, he had his last-ditch solution: the ButterKnife. The fact that it could melt through rock had been a bonus, not the weapon's original intent. He'd designed it, specifically, to melt through the platinum-iridium alloy he'd discovered in Utah. The ButterKnife could cut into the ship to gain access, and if need be, it would allow him to take out the orb on sight.

He hoped he didn't have to use it, though. To paraphrase one of his favorite movies, he'd much rather plant the bomb, leave, then nuke the entire ship—just to be sure.

Angus's private channel beeped twice. He eye-tracked, opened the channel.

"What's up, Donnie?"

"Soon I'll halt the column to give the men time to rest and eat. When I do, I'm coming back there to talk to you. You're going to go over that map with me again and show me any new intel."

Donnie broke the connection without waiting for a response.

"Well, fuck you, too, Dimwit."

62

14,982 feet below the surface

"A NUKE," SONNY said. "That little shit is smart enough to build his own nuke?"

"It's possible he could have bought one," Otto said. "Myths about old Soviet nukes available on the black market have been around for decades."

Tommy knew full well there were places in the world you could buy just about anything: ancient artifacts, weapons, men and women, even boys and girls. The world was diseased. Once upon a time he'd thought he was part of the cure.

"The squidleys got to be lying," Sonny said. "Angus wouldn't bring a damn *nuke* with him. That doesn't make any sense."

But it did make sense. A *lot* of sense.

"A low-yield nuke would kill everything in these tunnels," Tommy said. "The overpressure wave alone would be lethal. Then there's the heat. The tunnels would become an oven, thousands of degrees hot. Angus could plant the bomb, set a timer, then go up to the surface, or at least to a depth where he and his men would be safe from the blast effects. He would wipe out the rocktopi in one shot, clearing the area, then do the actual mining at a time of his choosing."

Sonny's eyes narrowed. "*Overpressure?* I thought you were just a grunt. You seem to know a lot about nukes."

"He reads," Ender said. "Let's say Angus actually has one. How could Whitey know about that?"

"The silverbugs, maybe," Otto said. "Whitey said he had some watching Angus. Maybe the machines can detect low-level radiation?"

There was no telling what tech the once-spacefaring race might have.

Lybrand shook her head. "But wouldn't even a small nuke collapse the entire tunnel system?"

"And then there's the radiation," Sonny said. "I don't know dick about nukes, but the sonofabitch Kool would have to dig through contaminated ground."

"No, he wouldn't," Otto said. "Look at what happened to Detroit and Chicago after the Pandemic. Petra Prawatt does work for us at the Department of Special Threats. She cleaned up both cities, and others as well. *Bioremediation* it's called. Long-term radiation isn't the threat it used to be."

Petra Prawatt. *The Atomic Angel*, the media had dubbed her. After World War II, it had taken two years to clean up Hiroshima. With Petra's work, the cleanup of Detroit and Chicago had taken two *months*.

"Lybrand is right," Otto said. "A nuke would collapse all the tunnels. Angus would have to dig down here to get the platinum. We're over two miles below the surface. Can he dig that far?"

"He already has," Ender said. "The Utah shaft he engineered was like two and a quarter miles deep. Angus set it up so it would connect to the tunnels that were already there, which went the rest of the way down to the ship. He wants to kill the rocktopi, okay, but wouldn't he want to keep the tunnels intact here as well?"

Maybe Angus could do both.

"It depends on where he puts it," Tommy said. "Ender, you said the cavern that holds the ship will be even bigger than the one we're in now?"

Ender nodded. "If the ship here is the same as the one in Utah, the cavern that holds it should be four miles long and a half-mile wide."

Even if it was half that size, that was still a large area.

"If Angus wants to keep the tunnel system intact, he could detonate a small nuke in the ship cavern," Tommy said. "The pressure wave and the heat would still roll through the tunnels, but the tunnels themselves wouldn't bear the main force of the explosion. Maybe that's what he has in mind."

Sam stared at the drawing of the mushroom cloud. "So we're screwed? After all we've been through, we're going to die anyway?"

"Their ship," Ramiro said. "If it's that big and it's made of platinum, could we hide in it and survive the initial blast?"

Ender shook his head. "There was some kind of accident at the Utah ship. Angus thought it was a nuclear blast. Melted a big hole in the ship. The rocktopi were taught not to go near the entire ship, maybe because of radiation."

Tommy wished he'd seen the Utah ship. And despite the guilt of breaking his promise and killing again, despite the tragedy of losing Hatchet and Skylark, he hoped he would see the ancient Fitz Roy ship before he died down here. To come this far, get this close, and *not* see it? Tommy didn't believe in hell, but that was as close to a real hell as he could come.

Sam stood up. "This is ridiculous. This guy isn't going to set off a nuke and kill an alien race."

Tommy heard the fear in her words.

"You don't know Angus Kool," Ender said. "He doesn't give a shit about anything but himself. He's the smartest human being I've ever met. Trust me, if he wants to wipe out everything down here so nothing stops him from claiming the platinum, he'll figure out a way to do that. He…"

Ender's words trailed off. He stared, his eyes blank.

Lybrand put a hand on his arm. "Patrick? You okay?"

Ender blinked, swallowed.

"Yeah, I'm okay. I just realized something. The nuke isn't just for the rocktopi. The Utah ship had this orb, a big bomb that caused the volcano. The orb's blast was so powerful it made the platinum unrecoverable. If Angus thinks there could be one like that here, that's why he wants to use the nuke—to make sure it can't be detonated."

"A volcano-bomb?" Sonny shook his head. "This just gets better and better. Do they have one here?"

"We need to find out, but it doesn't really matter if they do or they don't," Ender said. "If Angus *thinks* there could be one, that it could detonate, then *poof*—there goes his fortune. He's definitely going to try and set it off near the ship, to make sure no one—silverbugs, rocktopi, *us*—can detonate the orb and stop him from getting rich."

A heavy silence followed.

The concept sounded insane to Tommy. And yet here he was, with aliens, in a place older than human civilization. Did a man wanting to nuke an ancient interstellar shipwreck *really* sound that crazy? No. It did not.

"We need that map," Ender said. "Sam, we need to get an idea of how long we have until the mercs get here. Tell Whitey we need that map."

Tommy's anger toward Ender faded. Yes, the man had made bad decisions. He wasn't the leader he used to be. But the situation had changed. If Angus Kool had a nuke, everything had changed.

"The mercs are higher up the tunnel," Lybrand said. "We can cause cave-ins, stop him from getting down here."

Ramiro huffed. "Which means we can't get out? No thanks, genius."

Lybrand started to say something—Tommy held up a hand, cutting her off.

"The mercs have a device that lets them burn through rock," he said. "I caused a cave-in when I rescued Siren. That barely slowed them down."

He hoped they wouldn't ask him what the device was, because he didn't know himself.

"I'm not surprised," Ender said. "The laser-drill Angus invented for Utah vaporized rock. He must have miniaturized that tech."

"Then we have to run," Lybrand said. Her hand went to her belly. "We have to get out of here."

Sonny threw up his hands. "How? Unless there's another way to the surface, Kool and his men are between us and the outside. Sam, ask these things if there's another way out?"

"We can't just *leave*," Sam said. "I mean, I don't want to die, but this is bigger than us. This is *sentient life*. It's the biggest discovery in the history of mankind. We have to stay and protect them."

Tommy felt a surge of connection, of understanding. Sam got it. Out of everyone, at least Sam understood how important this was.

"If they can lie, so can we," Sonny said. "Tell them we'll help them so we get our guns back. Get the guns, walk out, and maybe find a side tunnel that will let us duck Angus. You all said the rocktopi don't have soldiers left. Hopefully they won't try to stop us, but if they do, we take them out."

"*We*," Otto said. "You going to tote a gun and kill aliens, old-timer? Aliens that could have killed all of us but didn't, because apparently they value life more than we do?"

"Goddamn right I'll kill them," Sonny said. "I'll do whatever it takes to stay alive."

"I won't," Tommy said. "I'm staying."

All eyes turned to him.

"You all do what you must," he said. "I'll help them fight."

"So will I," Otto said.

That surprised Tommy. Was Otto saying that because he thought it was the right thing to do, or because it was his job with the Department of Special Threats to protect the alien race? Maybe it was both things.

Sonny shook his head. "You're both fucking nuts. It's pointless."

"I'm also staying," Sam said.

She met Tommy's eyes. He saw the fear there, but she would stay despite it.

"Sam, no," Ramiro said. "These guys are pros. If they want to fight, that's for them, but we're not soldiers, we're—"

"We're the only ones that can communicate with them, Ram," Sam said. "Tommy needs our help. I won't stand by as someone wipes out the most important find in human history."

Utter conviction in her words. Tommy had known her only a few scant hours, but already he knew—at a deep level—that she would not be talked out of it. Tommy found himself wishing he'd met her somewhere else, under difference circumstances, because if she stayed, she would die.

Just like he would.

"If there's a way out, I'm taking it," Ramiro said. "I … I've had enough."

If Sam was surprised, if she was disappointed, she didn't show it. She patted Ramiro's hand, a silent gesture of understanding.

"I think we run," Lybrand said. "Tommy, I don't know you, but Sonny's got the right idea here. We get our weapons, we get out. There are enough tunnel branches that maybe we can evade Angus."

Tommy hadn't known her long, but he knew she was no coward. She'd just found out she was a mother-to-be—maybe that impacted her decision.

"Do what you have to do," Tommy said. "I told you, I'm staying."

"But *why?*" Bertha shook her head. "We're outmanned and out-gunned. That little motherfucker might have a *nuke*. If there's no chance to win, why would you throw your life away for people—I mean, for *creatures*—that are doomed?"

He started to say *because it's important to humanity*, or something like that, but a flash of memory cut through him, made him realize that wasn't the real reason he would fight.

Tommy closed his eyes, but that didn't stop the cascade of images. The bodies. The crying. The screams. A moment of shame that he had carried for twenty years. A moment of shame that had changed him forever. That had ruined him.

Yes, he would probably die.

And that was all right—if he had done the right thing two decades ago, if he had acted like the honorable warrior he'd thought himself to be, he would have died then.

Once, he'd stood by and let people be slaughtered.

He would not do that again.

Tommy opened his eyes. "Your husband knows why."

Ender tried to hold Tommy's gaze but could not. He looked down at the ground.

"Bandah," O'Doyle said.

That word. Just the sound of it brought goosebumps, brought chills that no amount of heat could ever mitigate.

"*Bandah*," Otto said. "Wait a minute … O'Doyle, that was you guys?"

Otto, Tommy and O'Doyle knew what that word meant. Sam, Ramiro and Sonny exchanged glances, shrugs.

Ender opened his mouth to speak, but nothing came out. Tommy knew why. Twenty years of a guillotine hanging over your neck had a way of shoving words and thoughts down into a place where they would never escape—not if you wanted to survive.

"Yeah," he said, finally. "That was us."

Bertha turned to him.

"*Bandah.*" Ice in her voice. "What is that?"

He stared at her. He hung his head—he couldn't answer her.

"It's a bad place," Tommy said. "A bad place where we did bad things. Ender, I need to do this. Maybe you should go, I get that, but Mullet, Sleepy and Curveball get to make their own choice."

The tension in the air, thickened by the ghosts of the past.

Bertha grabbed Ender's hand, held it tight.

"Patrick, if we get a chance to get out of here, we have to take it. You know that, right?"

He kept his gaze fixed on the ground.

"*You* have to take it," he said. "For our baby. I…Tommy's right. I have to stay. I have to help them."

Bertha was silent for a moment. Tommy was aware of the ticking clock, of a company of mercenaries on the way—they all were—but this discussion was about life itself. Life for a person who had not even come into existence yet.

"They traveled through fucking *space,*" Bertha said. "They have more troops, more guns than us. Let them fight their own goddamn battle."

Desperation in her voice, and a barely controlled fury. Sam wasn't sure why Bertha had joined this mission, but now all she wanted was *out.*

Ender finally raised his head, met his wife's stare.

"When we came out of the river tunnel, the rocktopi had us dead to rights," he said. "Mid-range shots that any enlisted man could hit eight times out of ten. When we returned fire at a group of five at-tackers, *three* of them ran. I don't think these people have ever faced enemy fire. They spared our lives when they captured us, sure, but during that battle they were trying to kill us. They had the high ground, a target that couldn't maneuver, numerical superiority, and they only managed to get one of us. It's not just that they're bad shots and have old weapons—I don't think they've fought *anything* for a very, very long time. Sam, can you ask them the last time they fired their weapons against an enemy?"

Sam turned her attention to the white tablet. She pressed a finger, lifted it, held it like a knife hovering just over an enemy's throat. She was looking for a way to communicate Ender's question.

She sketched out symbols, then held the tablet up to Whitey and Slash.

The aliens' normal, at-rest patterns continued for a few moments. Slash started to pulse a series of magenta and aquamarine. Whitey's pattern of light-gray shifted, took on a more rapid swirling. Were they talking to each other with light? Or was this the rocktopi version of confusion, of deep thought?

Slash squealed a string of sounds. Whitey paused, even his swirling, gray-on-white patterns freezing in place. He gave an answering string of noise.

Slash stretched out a stubby, flat pseudopod. Glyphs formed, their symbols for numbers. Sam studied them, trying to make sense of them.

"What's he saying?" Sonny asked.

Sam held up one finger to him: *Let me concentrate.*

Even with Base-12, Tommy knew the numbers instantly.

"One thousand, six hundred years. He's probably estimating."

"Sixteen hundred years," Ender said. "Who would they have fought? What was their enemy's level of tech? Could they have been an organized military, like the Incas?"

"Early Mapuche tribes, maybe," Sam said. "Or some other tribe lost to history. Tech-wise, you'd be looking at bows and arrows. Boleadoras. Spears, slings and clubs. The Mapuche didn't even have metal weapons."

Otto nodded slowly. "That's why the rocktopi need us. They can't fight because they've never had a *need* to fight. I bet Slash and Axl are the last of a dying part of their culture, individuals that have actually trained for combat. The rocktopi already fought Angus's men and got destroyed. The few soldiers that are left … I don't think they stand a chance."

"This is ridiculous," Sonny said. "They are fucking *Star Trek* creatures. They aren't the bloodthirsty killers we saw in Utah, I get that, but if these things are smart enough to communicate with us and they came in a spaceship, they have to have better weapons, don't they? Phasers or lasers or some shit like that?"

His question made perfect sense. The technology to reach Earth at all staggered anything humans had yet developed. Could this alien race really only be armed with knives and poorly maintained railguns?

And yet, Occam's Razor indicated one obvious conclusion.

"If they had better weapons, they would have used them already," Tommy said. "The rocktopi haven't had to fight. Not for decades, not for centuries, but for *millennia*. And the army they had was prepared to go against primitive man. That's why they need us. Their only chance to stop trained human killers is to send other trained human killers against them. And that's what we are."

Lybrand grabbed Ender's hand.

"Baby, listen to me," she said. "You don't owe these murdering creatures anything! They killed Connell, remember? They killed everyone. They killed Skylark. We are *not* throwing our lives away for them!"

He smiled at her, a smile as dark as Tommy's soul.

"Consider it a means to an end," Ender said. His smile faded.

He pulled his hand away from her, stepped closer to Whitey. Ender pointed at Sonny, at Ramiro, at Bertha, at Bertha's belly, then straight up. He pointed at himself, Tommy, Otto, then pantomimed shooting a carbine.

"Patrick, don't," Bertha said. "Please. *Please.*"

He didn't answer her, didn't turn to look at her, just stared at Whitey.

The moment stretched out. Did Whitey understand Ender's offer? Tommy couldn't say why, but he had a feeling the alien got the gist.

Whitey gave a short squeal, extended a pseudopod. The snake-like limb hung there—on it, the rocktopi symbol for the number four. Tommy realized Whitey was pointing in the direction of the obelisk.

The alien *did* understand.

"He's asking if the others will fight," Tommy said. "Curve, Mullet, Sleepy and Klimas."

Sam looked from Tommy to Ender and back again, perhaps surprised that they were communicating by gestures alone.

"Good," Ender said. "He's negotiating. If he's doing that, then maybe there is a way out after all. Sam, any idea how to tell Whitey I have to ask the others if they will fight?"

She glanced at her tablet, then up just as fast.

"No," she said. "I don't know how to ask that."

Ender nodded. "Then stay here and figure out how to ask my other questions. How many railguns, how many silverbugs, how can we get a map. See if you can tell him that we won't do *anything* to help until we get our guns, and until we know there is a safe way out. And find out if they have an orb like the one in Utah. Otto, Bertha, you help Sam, ask anything else that might help us."

Lybrand stared at him, her expression a mixture of anger, of betrayal, of fear.

"Where are you going?" she asked.

"To see who wants to fight Angus," Ender said. "Tommy? Will you come with me?"

He wanted the NoSeeUms together for this. The ones that were still alive, anyway.

"Yeah," Tommy said.

Ender walked to the door of the stone hut.

Bertha followed him. "I'm coming with you. If you're fighting, I'm fighting."

O'Doyle spun sharply, winced as pain caught him off guard. His face scrunched tight, his hand went to his back.

"Baby," Bertha said. "Let me help you."

She reached for him—he slapped her hand away.

"I'm fine," he said. "You stay here. I have to talk to my team. *Alone.* Tommy, let's go."

Lybrand didn't say a word, but anyone could see it was all she could do to keep from screaming.

Ender walked out.

Tommy started to follow him, stopped. He pointed at Siren, then waved his hand inward: *Come with me.*

Siren pulsed a myriad of colors, then flowed toward Tommy.

Human and alien walked out together.

63

14,982 feet below the surface

PATRICK WAITED QUIETLY as Bookworm finished laying out the tactical situation. The less he had to talk, the better. If he didn't move too quickly, his back was tolerable. His chest hurt so bad it was difficult to breathe. He could only imagine the size of the bruise. Worse than both things, though, was the pounding in his head—the effects of heat stroke didn't just go away, they hung around for a while, tried to make themselves at home.

"That's what we're facing," Worm said. "The rocktopi will give us our weapons back. Ender wants us ready to repel Angus's force in five hours."

A pause. They stood in a circle near the obelisk base: Patrick, Worm, Klimas, Mullet, Sleepy and Curveball. Thirty minutes earlier, Patrick and the others had faced death at the hands of a rocktopi firing line.

Now he was asking his squad mates to risk their lives again, this time to help those same aliens—aliens that had killed Skylark.

Slash stood nearby, his ever-present, unique pattern pulsing in alternating bands of crimson and light gray.

"So there could be eighty to ninety mercs," Sleepy said. "With supplies. And ammo. And killer robots. And, possibly, a nuke that will kill anything in these tunnels if it goes off. On top of all that, the aliens we were fighting *against*, that we are now fighting *for*, have shitty weapons and no combat training. Do I have all that right?"

Patrick thought, briefly, about putting a more positive spin on things, but what was the point? He'd made mistakes. His people had died. Perhaps it was best for everyone to make their decision based on the reality of the situation.

"Pretty much," he said. "Some of them know how to fire their weapons, but if they were well-trained, we all would have died in that canoe. Aside from Axl and Slash, any real soldiers they had died attacking Angus."

Patrick wasn't sure how many rocktopi would help in the fight. Some were too young, some were too old. He had no idea what cultural aspects might keep some of the others from fighting. He'd take as many as he could get.

"I don't get it," Mullet said. "The aliens want to *hire* us to do this mission?"

Patrick considered, shrugged. "In a way. We help them, and in exchange they agree to get some of us out of here before the fighting begins. That's the deal."

"*Us*," Sleepy said. He crossed his arms over his chest. "Who, exactly, are the *some of us* that get to leave?"

The million-dollar question.

"If we can make this deal with the rocktopi, Bertha, Sonny and Ramiro are leaving," Patrick said. "If any of you want to go, I believe you'll be able to leave with them."

He didn't know if that was true. If he had been in Whitey's place, he wouldn't have let trained soldiers leave. Bertha was the exception. Even that was hard to understand—in the past the rocktopi had butchered men, women and children alike, but now they seemed to be deferential toward an unborn baby?

Maybe it was a trick. Patrick didn't have any other options. He would pursue any chance to get his wife and child away from this place.

Sleepy spread his hands, gestured to Mullet, Klimas and Curveball.

"What about us, Ender? You going to make us fight and die so your wife can run to safety?"

Patrick didn't have an answer, because that was exactly what he was asking. The odds were too great. He had no illusions that he and Worm would make it out of this alive. Anyone who stayed would most likely die as well.

Patrick had known about his unborn child for perhaps an hour, and already it had changed him. Before hearing that news, he would never have asked the NoSeeUms to throw their lives away.

"Hold on," Curveball said. "Angus is with the mercenaries?"

Worm nodded. "Yeah. I saw him by the river. He was wearing an exosuit, looked like really advanced stuff."

"I don't give a shit if he's in a tank," Curveball said. He looked at Patrick. "Angus is the one that hired the gunships that killed Hatchet? You're sure of that?"

The look in Curve's eyes—he wanted blood.

"Pretty sure," Patrick said. "He's behind it at the very least. Without his involvement, there wouldn't have been gunships in the first place."

Curve stepped to the obelisk. He sat, leaned back against the base.

"I'll fight," he said. "Try and save that bastard for me. I want to spend a little quality time with him."

As messed up as Curve seemed to be, he was still one of the best operators Patrick had ever worked with. Having him on board meant Patrick could kill more of Angus's troops.

Mullet raised a hand.

"Jesus Christ, Kevin," Patrick said. "Just say what you've got to say."

The man nodded toward Slash. "Are we *really* standing here, with a fucking snot-bubble *alien*, talking about fighting an un-winnable battle against mercenaries to try and save the lives of *more* fucking snot-bubble aliens—the same snot-bubble aliens who just so happened to kill Skylark?"

He had such a way with words.

"That's right," Patrick said.

Mullet lowered his hand. "I'm out. You dumb fucks wanna tussle with gung-ho mercenaries? Have at it. I'm getting the hell out of Dodge."

Sleepy crossed his arms. "You told us we were fighting monsters—not human beings. I've got a congregation that needs me alive. I'm leaving."

Patrick wasn't surprised. Maybe it was too much to ask a man of god to commit mortal sin.

Worm stepped into the middle of the circle, faced Sleepy.

"Doug, we need you," he said. "And you, too, Kevin. We can't just let these people be slaughtered."

Mullet shook his head, exasperated. "They aren't *people*, man! They're *nightmares*. The alien bugaboos ain't our problem. They already killed one of us."

"And we killed several of them," Patrick said. "We can't change the past. The surviving rocktopi don't stand a snowball's chance in hell unless we help them. Do you want to just stand aside and leave them to die?"

Mullet nodded. "Goddamn right we do."

"We stood aside once," Worm said, his voice low and raspy. "Twenty years ago."

Sleepy's face furrowed with anger. "This isn't Bandah, Tommy."

"Woah-woah-*woah*," Mullet said. He tilted his head toward Klimas. "Ixnay on the Andah-Bay while we have a *government official* standing right next to us, capisce?"

"This *isn't* Bandah," Sleepy said again, louder this time. He stared daggers at Worm. "Fuck you for bringing it up, Tommy. Fuck you."

Worm stared back at Sleepy.

"It's no different," Worm said. "We *stood* there, Doug. We stood there and didn't do a goddamn thing."

Sleepy's eyes softened. He looked away.

"We had orders," Mullet said. No sarcasm. No smirk on his mouth. "We were *grunts*, man. We didn't question orders."

"We should have," Worm said. "And you know it."

Mullet stared off into the distance. "We're not supposed to talk about it."

Not supposed to talk about it. Under the threat of death. Only now did Patrick realized he'd used that threat as a shield, as a way not to think about Bandah, as a way to excuse what he'd seen, what he'd done.

Or, rather, what he *had not* done.

"Kool's men are coming," Klimas said. "We don't have time for all this chitchat. I've read about the Bandah Massacre. Fifty-six civilians died. If you guys had something to do with that, tell me right now."

Patrick heard the judging tone in Klimas's voice. So far he'd been a solid ally, but clearly there was a limit to what he'd forgive.

"We can't talk about it," Mullet said. "We can't."

Worm rolled his eyes. "Give me a break, man. I'll tell him."

Sleepy and Mullet both shook their heads, but they didn't argue.

Patrick closed his eyes. Images of the past burst into life, as if it happened yesterday, as if it happened five minutes ago, as if it was happening *now*.

"We were a black ops unit," Worm said. "It was during Operation Infinite Reach. We were deployed to—"

"Worm, *stop it*." Mullet, his eyes pleading. "We gave an oath to never tell."

Kevin Bliss, badass killer. He didn't sound so badass now. He sounded like what he was—a middle-aged used car salesman who didn't want an assassin to show up in the middle of the night and put a bullet in the back of his head.

"He'll keep this to himself," Worm said. "Won't you, Klimas?"

A threat, not a request.

"He works *for the government*," Sleepy said. "You tell him and you're signing our death warrants."

Klimas held up a hand. "Fuck that. If you want me to stay here and fight by your side, I need to know what kind of soldiers you are. You have my word—whatever you tell me stays with me."

If he did stay and fight, it would stay with him to the grave. Or at least whatever might pass for a grave down here.

"We were tasked with taking out a Taliban leader named Abdeen al-Malak," Worm said. "Someone high up got intel that he was holed up in an Afghani village—Bandah. We HALOed in twenty klicks northwest, where we met up with a local warlord, Amail Gilani."

"Gilani," Klimas said. "The Butcher of Mapan?"

Patrick nodded. "That's the guy. He provided the intel as to al-Malak's location. A CIA agent was embedded with him. We never did learn the agent's name."

Maybe that was a good thing. Maybe the only reason Patrick had never tried to track the bastard down was that he still didn't know who the man was.

"Call him *Douchebag*," Mullet said quietly.

At another time, that might have made Patrick laugh. Not now. Nothing could make him laugh now.

"Douchebag gave us the intel that Gilani had provided," Worm said. "Al-Malak and thirty of his troops controlled Bandah, which was in Gilani's territory. Gilani had a beef with al-Malak that went back to Soviet occupation. We never knew the details of that. He wanted al-Malak dead, but he didn't want to use his own men."

"So he contacted the CIA," Klimas said.

The way he said that, the expression on his face—Klimas had his own experiences with the CIA, and they weren't positive.

"Probably," Patrick said. "We weren't privy to that intel. We drew the mission for two reasons. First, the intel wasn't hard enough to send a cruise missile, and second, because we excelled at getting in and out of places with no one knowing we were there. But this mission went tits up. Al-Malak had taken hostages, hidden them away. We didn't know that until after. He used the hostages as leverage with their family members. He … he …"

The spiked words lodged in Patrick's throat.

"He made the family members fight," Sleepy said. "Some with guns. Some with knives. Some with bombs. He told parents he'd kill their children. He told children he'd kill their parents. Brothers, sisters, mothers, fathers, grandparents … he told people what he wanted done, and if they refused, he killed the ones they loved."

Sleepy sounded like a soulless man, the opposite of his on-stage preacher persona. Two decades on and the memories of Bandah were salt poured into wounds that would never heal.

Mullet picked up the thread, surprising Patrick.

"We knew al-Malak was in the village but didn't know where." His words—dry, distant, as if speaking them too loud might rouse vengeful spirits. "We had to go house to house. Like Ender said, we were real good at that. We took out half of al-Malak's men in their sleep. I don't think we woke up a single villager when we did. But one of al-Malak's men heard me coming. Before I got to him, he sounded the alarm."

"Firefight started," Worm said. "We called for Skylark to come in for air support, but she was a good twenty minutes out. That was how we worked. We took out more of al-Malak's men, but they weren't amateurs. They fought. Our buddy Swampy took a round in the eye. He was the first to go."

Patrick remembered how Swampy had fallen backward, landed on his side, instantly still and quiet as if he was just taking a nap.

"How many were in your unit?" Klimas asked.

"Ten," Patrick said. "Two teams of five, plus Skylark. We had al-Malak pinned down. We were taking out his men. We *had* him. Then the villagers started coming out of the woodwork."

Saying it out loud was torture. It was also cathartic. Patrick hadn't spoken a word about Bandah for two decades—not since the post-mission brief, where his own countrymen promised certain death if he talked about it to anyone, ever.

"There was this little girl," Sleepy said. "I remember her because she had blue eyes. She reminded me of that famous *National Geographic* cover. Landslide, Tommy and I were working the village's left flank. This crying little girl ran toward our position. I guess we all thought she was running away from the bad guys, you know? Looking for cover. Looking for help."

Patrick had been with Mullet and El Gato. He'd seen the girl running toward Sleepy. In the heat of the moment, he hadn't given her a second glance.

"Landslide waved her in," Sleepy said. "He pulled her down, covering her with his own body. I watched as this little girl—couldn't have been more than ten, I think—pulled a butcher knife out of her robes. She stabbed him in the neck. I knew he was dead the second I saw the blade go in. I was stunned. I don't know how long I froze. Tommy got her. Put a blade in her belly."

Patrick glanced at Worm. Worm stared off.

"I remember thinking, *if she wants to use a knife, let's use a knife,*" Worm said. "I was so angry. I'd known Landslide for two years. He'd saved my life. He was my brother. I...I cut that girl. I didn't rush it.

Only later did I find out that the girl did it because her little sister was being held hostage. I … I …"

Tommy "Worm" Strymon started to sob. He sat down where he was.

Curveball got up, walked to Worm, sat down next to him, put his arm around the man's shoulders.

"I put out the call to watch for civvies," Sleepy said. "But I was too late."

Mullet sighed, shook his head. "This old couple got Knuckles. The old man was strapped with a bomb. I remember the woman crying, holding onto his arm, like she wasn't going to let him die alone. He didn't. He blew the fuck out of all three of them. If Knuckles had just shot them instead of trying to help …"

He shrugged.

"So you guys killed the whole village," Klimas said. "You lost your shit and shot everyone. Men, women, and children."

Patrick heard the darkness in the man's voice, felt instant fury that Klimas would dare to pass judgment, but just as quickly that fury drowned in the guilt Patrick had carried for two decades.

"We had four casualties in less than a minute," Patrick said. "We still had to locate al-Malak, and we had civilians coming at us from all directions. I gave the order to shoot anyone who approached us, anyone who could be a conceivable threat."

The village became a kill zone. Patrick had shot two people, killing them both. One was a man armed with a pistol. The other was a woman in her forties. Only after it was over did Patrick learn she hadn't been armed at all, that she'd been a decoy, ordered to rush toward the Americans or her granddaughter would be shot in the head.

"We killed thirteen civilians," he said.

"Bullshit," Sleepy said. "Those weren't civilians. They were enemy combatants. *They* came at *us*."

No one contradicted him. What he said was partially true, at least.

"All told, we killed thirteen villagers," Patrick said.

"I told you I read about it," Klimas said. "It wasn't *thirteen* civilians, it was *fifty-six*."

As if talking about the shooting, the killing, and losing squad mates hadn't been enough, now came the worst part of the story. Patrick glanced at Worm, who continued to sob. Then, at Slash, the rocktopi who made no noise, who seemed to be patiently watching and listening, crimson light coursing up and down his pseudopods.

Patrick wondered what the alien was thinking.

"We got the rest of al-Malak's men," Mullet said.

He didn't mention that five of those men surrendered. He didn't mention what Worm, Sleepy and Hatchet did to those prisoners. He didn't mention that Patrick could have ordered his people to stop but instead gave in to the rage, the loss and the frustration. He didn't mention that Patrick let it happen.

War crimes? Maybe. It depended on how you looked at it, really.

"What about al-Malak?" Klimas asked.

"We captured him," Mullet said. "Before Skylark got there to evac us out, Gilani rode in on horseback, along with about a hundred armed tribesmen. Even Douchebag was on a horse."

Patrick would never forget that moment. Armed men on horseback, storming into the village like something out of a bizarro western. Douchebag, with his thick black beard, dressed like the rest of Gilani's men, an AK-47 slung across his back.

"Douchebag took al-Malak," Patrick said. "But the people in the village … Gilani felt they had betrayed them for helping al-Malak."

"*Helping.*" Mullet huffed. "Fucking unreal, man. Like they had a choice."

Klimas's eyes softened. His expression shifted, from judgmental to sympathetic, a soldier understanding what his fellow warriors had faced.

"The other forty-three civilians," he said. "Gilani?"

Patrick nodded, hoping—not for the first time—that he could forget that night, knowing he never would, knowing it would be the last thing he thought of when the reaper came for him.

"Gilani's men dragged people out of their houses," said Curveball, his arm still around Worm. "At first we thought they were going to be questioned, but Gilani didn't have any questions. He lined them up. Some of the villagers were the hostages al-Malak's men had held at gunpoint."

Patrick closed his eyes. He could still hear the villagers crying, wailing, some even cursing. They had all known before he had what was coming next.

"We tried to stop it." Patrick remembered the terrified faces of the villagers, their tears, their begging and pleading. "I aimed at Gilani, told him to tell his men to stand down. I had … I don't know … maybe twenty AK-47s aimed at me, the rest of Gilani's men aiming at my squad, my squad aiming at Gilani's men. We were one trigger pull away from a bloodbath."

"We would have been okay with that," Sleepy said. "As long as Gilani died, I would have been okay dying that night."

Longing in Sleepy's voice, the same wish Patrick felt, that they all felt, wishing they'd died doing the right thing that night.

"Douchebag stepped in front of my weapon," Patrick said. "If I ever see that guy again, I'll kill him, but he had balls of steel, I'll give him that much. He said Gilani was our *vital ally* in the area, that we had to have his intel. I'm still not entirely sure why I lowered my weapon. Douchebag … he *was* in command. Maybe that was part of it. Maybe part of it was I didn't want to die. I don't know."

Curveball stood. "I know why you did it. We all do. You stood down because you didn't want *us* to die."

Mullet nodded. So did Sleepy.

"He's right," Worm said. He looked up. Behind his visor, his cheeks glistened with tears. "We all wanted to fight. We were all ready to die. You stood down so that we would live. We all knew why, Ender. We've always known."

Telling the story for the first time in twenty years had opened the floodgates of memory, of emotion. He'd lost four people. He wasn't going to lose more. That night, he'd made a *choice*. A horrible choice, one that no human being—even a stone-cold killer—should have to make.

He'd preserved the lives of his comrades, but at what cost? They'd all joined the NoSeeUms knowing the risks. He'd saved their lives, but in the process, he'd taken away the one thing a true warrior treasured above everything else: Honor.

Patrick had ordered his team to stand by while Gilani executed unarmed civilians.

"I should have killed Gilani," he said. "I know it. I fucked up."

Curveball walked up to Patrick, put his hand on Patrick's shoulder.

"It's not your fault," Curve said.

Patrick closed his eyes, shook his head. "You going to tell me it's okay because I was just following orders?"

The tears finally came, and he couldn't stop them.

"If you followed orders, so did we," Curve said. "It was war. You made a call, Ender. An impossible call. And because of that call, I got twenty years with Hatchet. I'll be honest—if I had to choose between the lives of those villagers and my twenty years with him, I'd do the same thing all over again. Life sucks. People die in tragic ways. Do you understand that if you *had* killed Gilani, the villagers would have died anyway? His men would have executed them as soon as they finished with us."

Sometimes, when Patrick couldn't sleep, when the terrified faces of those helpless people stared out at him from the infinite darkness, he tried to tell himself the same thing.

"That doesn't make it right," he said.

"No, it doesn't," Curveball said. He let go of Patrick's shoulder, looked at Klimas. "After Skylark got us back to base, command separated us. Our unit was disbanded. They told us if we ever talked about it, we were as good as dead. You heard enough yet?"

Klimas nodded. "I'm sorry you all had to go through that."

Patrick wondered, briefly, if Klimas had ever gone through something similar. If the man had, Patrick decided he didn't want to know about it.

Worm got to his feet. "I stood by and watched innocents get gunned down. I won't make the same mistake again."

"The Bandah villagers are gone, man," Mullet said. "You dying here won't bring them back."

Sleepy spread his hands. "We *can't win*."

"I don't care," Worm said. "I've spent twenty years regretting that day. I should have died then. We all should have. This won't make up for it, I know that, but it will sure as hell make me feel a little better. It will make me feel like the warrior I should have been instead of the coward that I was."

Coward.

Patrick nodded to himself. *Coward.* That hit the nail right on the head.

Sleepy stared down, shook his head. "You have a knack with numbers, Worm, but you also have a way with words. Thank you for what you just said. It helps me see things clearly, for the first time in a long, long while. I'll stay. I'll fight."

"You'll *die*," Mullet said. "Your flock will be without its shepherd. You know that, right?"

Sleepy looked up, nodded. "I know. I can't tell you how many times in the last twenty years I've thought about Bandah and wanted to kill myself. The only reason I didn't is because it would damn my soul for all eternity. I thought the Lord had guided me to the money that would help my church, but now I understand His wisdom and truth—He kept me alive this long, stayed my hand from suicide, so that he could put me here in this moment, so I finally do what's *right*."

Patrick waited for Kevin's inevitable insults, but this time none came.

"Ah, fuck it," Mullet said. "Selling used cars is a fate worse than death anyway. I'd rather go down swinging than spend my days telling people why a Toyota with a hundred thousand miles on it is the bargain of the century. And to be honest, the NoSeeUms are the only friends I've ever had. Better to die with you."

Patrick's body flushed with a deep feeling of satisfaction. He wasn't ordering his team to do this, they were volunteering. Not for money, this time, but out of a sense of duty. *Personal* duty. This was their choice—if they fell, *when* they fell, he knew he'd suffer no guilt.

Because a warrior is made to fight.

Patrick turned to Klimas. "And you? If you want to leave and escort my wife safely out of here, I'll be forever in your debt. Not that *forever* will be all that long for me, I'm afraid."

"You're out of luck," Klimas said. "If Otto is staying, so am I. Besides, you old farts need some youth to help you out."

Seven men. Maybe they couldn't stop Angus, but they could make that little piece of shit pay one hell of a high price.

"I can't see any of us making it out of this," Mullet said. "Who will see to it that Skylark's children have at least some kind of financial support?"

With the insanity swirling around this place, it was easy to forget about those three now-motherless girls. But not everyone would stay, not everyone would fight.

"I'll make sure Sonny talks to the people at EarthCore," Patrick said. "The company will make sure Marie's daughters are taken care of."

He had no way of knowing if that was true or not. He was sure that Sonny would embrace that mission and do his best. How much help the girls got would come down to what Barbara Yakely was willing to give, and what Harvey Dillinger could set up.

Patrick faced Slash. He gestured to himself, to the others, then pantomimed shooting a rifle.

The rocktopi stood there for a moment, colors coursing, then pointed to each man in turn, to himself, then extruded two pseudopods and—like Patrick had—made an unmistakable pantomime of firing a weapon.

"Holy shit," Mullet said. "Is he saying he's going to join us or something?"

Patrick felt Slash looking at him and knew that was exactly what the alien was saying.

A crackle of static in his headset.

Bertha: "Patrick, you there?"

"I read you."

"Get back here. Sam got Whitey to understand about the map. They have one they can show us—it's inside their ship."

64

"YOUR BLACKBUGS HAVE yet to find those big caverns you said would be down here," Donnie said. "I need you to make an educated guess on when we will reach them, and the ship."

Angus stood alone with the mercenary commander, sharing information across their HUDs. No Khatari, no Fuentes, no one else at all, because the rest of the men didn't know about the portable nuke. Donnie wanted to keep it that way.

In Utah, the rocktopi shipwreck had been about 16,000 feet below the surface. Just a hair over three miles. The aliens' ancestors had lifted up a rectangular chunk of Funeral Mountain, put the ship inside, then lowered the chunk—weighing *billions* of tons—on top of the ship.

While the Fitz Roy geology wasn't quite the same as that of Funeral Mountain, Angus had to assume there was some relevance to that depth, and, therefore, it was reasonable to assume the ship here would be at about the same depth.

"We have about a mile to go, vertically," Angus said. "Could be more, could be less."

"With the switchbacks, how long of a march?"

Again, he had to make an assumption. The switchbacks had been fairly consistent during the first mile's descent, but their lengths had varied since. The angles had varied as well. He had no constant by which to estimate.

"Two or three miles," Angus said. "But odds are we'll encounter areas where we have to break out the climbing gear. That will slow us down."

"So you can't effectively tell me how much longer it will take?"

Angus found himself wishing he'd come up with a way to get the mercs on the river. That would have kept them close on O'Doyle's tail. There was no telling how far ahead he was.

"Could be a few hours," Angus said. "Could also be a day or more."

Donnie fell quiet, thinking.

"We have enough supplies for three more days," Angus said, the silence making him anxious. "We'll be done here by then, I'm sure of it."

The map had grown quite a bit. Many branches, snaking this way and that; it reminded Angus of the roots of a tree, splitting and multiplying and spreading out. If not for the map, he and the mercs would have hit several dead ends.

There were more tunnels here than Angus had seen in Utah. Quite a few more, and that was making things difficult. The BlackBugs had already started to reach their range limit. Even when working as a distributed intelligence, they still relied largely on line-of-sight for their chain communication. The endless switchbacks hindered that.

"All these tunnels," Donnie said, "it's almost like the rocktopi want us to get lost. Maybe to set up an ambush."

"I told you before, the silverbugs probably dug the tunnels, and thousands of years ago at that."

Donnie's eyes narrowed. "A trap set up a thousand years ago might still work just fine today. Remember that. How many silverbugs do you think they have left?"

Angus shrugged, which felt odd in the exosuit. "We haven't seen any of them since the orchard."

"Could we have destroyed them all?"

Angus loved how Donnie used *we* when something positive had been done. As if he had anything to do with the SwarmStorm.

"I doubt it," Angus said. "I killed a lot of them, but there's no way of knowing how many they have left."

Donnie glanced off again.

"O'Doyle's people freed those rocktopi for a reason," he said. "The aliens attacked us once. Some of them escaped that village we conquered. They have to know we're coming to wipe them all out. That tells me they're going to attack us again. Keep expanding the map, but make sure a few of your BlackBugs remain ahead of our lead element. Let's see if we can spot the next ambush point before the ambush happens."

65

14,982 Feet below the surface

THE NOSEEUMS SAT on the obelisk plaza, cleaning their weapons. Otto and Klimas did the same. Bertha cleaned hers as well, tried to concentrate on clearing sand and grit from the slide, but she knew what was coming and it was hard to pay attention to anything other than Patrick's voice.

"The rocktopi don't have an orb," Patrick said. "Sam was able to get them to understand what we were asking. As far as she can tell, they've never heard of such a thing. I don't know why Utah had one and they don't here, but right now it's not an issue."

Mullet chuckled. "Yeah, now all we have to worry about is a nuke, right? Fantastic."

Bertha wished that idiot would keep his mouth shut.

"Tommy, Sam and I are going to the rocktopi ship to see this tunnel map they say they have," Patrick said. "They have a rough idea how far away Angus is, but they don't know exactly, at least as far as we can tell. Once we understand the tunnel layout, we might find a place to take Angus on before his units get into the main cavern."

Bertha breathed slow, tried to contain her anger, her fear, her frustration. She should be the one going with Patrick, not Tommy.

The rocktopi had returned all of the gear: sidearms, carbines, knives, backpacks and everything in them. The Glocks were designed to take a beating and keep delivering; a little sand and water wasn't going to hurt anything, once they were cleaned. Mullet had lost his carbine in the river. The rocktopi or maybe one of the giant silverbugs — which Tommy had dubbed *silvermechs* — had gone to the bottom and retrieved it.

"Curve, Sleepy," Patrick said, "I need you to work with Slash and give the rocktopi a combat crash course."

Sleepy looked up from his disassembled carbine. "How long do I have?"

"Three hours," Patrick said. "You know what we're facing. Train them up the best you can accordingly. Get creative. Ramiro will help you translate until it's time for him to go. Copy?"

Sleepy glanced at Curveball, who seemed too focused on sharpening his dead husband's hatchet to notice anything else.

"Yeah," Sleepy said. "We got it."

"Klimas," Patrick said, "I need you to scout this area and identify key locations for defensive emplacements. Whitey seems certain that Angus will be coming through that big tunnel entrance in the northwest wall."

Bertha felt worthless. The NoSeeUms were one thing, but Patrick was trusting a total stranger to do that important task? As if she couldn't help with that?

Klimas stood, looked around the cavern.

"That will take me about an hour," he said. "I count three entrances into this space. You want me to focus solely on that northwest one, or should I account for all of them?"

"All of them," Patrick said. "We have to be as ready as we can. If the map is real and it changes the intel, we'll adjust. But since the northwest entrance is the most likely point of ingress, Mullet, I want you to booby trap the hell out of the tunnel approach to it and the area outside of it.

When Angus attacked the little village, it looked like the mercs fanned out in platoons. Account for that."

Mullet finished assembling his cleaned carbine, clipped it to his harness.

"You're afraid of cave-ins," he said. "So I supposed you want me to use thumbtacks and bubble gum to MacGyver up some shit?"

Patrick shook his head. "At this point, tunnel cave-ins are the least of our concerns. Use the claymores."

Mullet leaned back in mock surprise. "Really? Why, Ender, I do declare—I take back half the bad things I've said about you. What about C4? Can I use that?"

"Not just yet," Patrick said. "But I'm not ruling it out. Everyone, give your C4 and your claymores to Mullet."

All around, the soldiers paused the cleaning, dug through their packs, and handed their mines and plastic explosives to Mullet. Bertha didn't mind giving hers up—carrying explosives on her person had always creeped her out.

Mullet set the mines at his feet, including his own. Six claymores side by side.

He smiled wide. "Best. Christmas. Ever."

"Otto," Patrick said, "you'll work with Axl and some of the rocktopi. We need to test-fire every railgun, make sure we know which weapons are reliable."

Otto finished assembling his Glock. He stood. When he did, Bertha heard an audible *crack* as the man's knee popped. Otto winced slightly but seemed fine.

"I'll get it done," he said.

An old man with popping joints. Even *he* had a role to play, while she didn't?

"And Bertha," Patrick said, finally mustering the balls to look her in the eyes. "We can't spare weapons for Ramiro and Sonny, so you're their protection when the three of you head up."

She slid her sidearm into its holster.

"I'm not going," she said.

She stared at him.

He stared back, but not with the *do what I say* attitude that was his norm.

"I need a word," he said. "In private."

He didn't wait for her response. He walked around the obelisk's wide base to the other side, out of sight.

"Don't be an idiot, sugar," Mullet said to her. "You don't want to stay here. It's going to get nasty."

The last thing she needed was advice from his dumb ass.

"Fuck off," Bertha said.

She walked around the obelisk base, found Patrick waiting for her.

"Bertha, you have to—"

"The answer is *no*. I'm a soldier, just like you, just like your so-called friends you haven't seen in twenty years. I am *staying with you*."

She was nearly shouting. She couldn't help it. Even with the comms off, the others probably heard her. She didn't care. Patrick was hers and she was his. They belonged together, full stop.

He reached out, took her hands. Even through the KoolSuit gloves, his touch broke her anger, brought forth the fear of being without him.

"You have to go," he said, his voice as soft and loving as hers had been loud and harsh. "Take Sonny and Ramiro and get clear of this place before it's too late."

Sonny had wanted to run away from the very beginning. Bertha couldn't blame Ramiro for opting out, but she wasn't like either of those men. She could fight. She *would* fight.

"I'm not leaving," she said. "I waited my whole life to find you."

He squeezed her hands. "You have to go."

She fought against tears, fought against them because they would make her look weaker in his eyes.

"I'm just as good as your NoSeeUms," she said, hearing the pleading tone in her voice yet unable to stop it. "I don't need you to protect me."

He leaned back. "I'm not protecting *you*. I'm protecting the baby."

The baby.

Was it even possible she'd forgotten that she was pregnant?

Maybe because it still didn't seem real. Maybe because of this insane situation. Maybe because she knew Patrick was trying to send her away and she would rather die than be without him.

The baby. *Their* baby.

Before she'd joined the Army, she'd thought about having a child. Finding the right man, getting a house, starting a family … all that shit that gets force-fed to small-town girls. Then she'd enlisted. Then she'd seen what the world really had to offer.

Then she'd killed a man.

After that, any thoughts of a family were distant things, wistful remembrances of what a stupid little girl had thought life was supposed to be.

Fairy tales.

Disney.

At first, she'd thought finding Patrick had been a fluke. Later, she'd realized it was fate. That same fate now had their child growing inside of her. A human life—half her, half him.

"We can win," she said. "We can fight them. Together. We can win and stay alive."

He gripped her shoulders. He smiled at her, the same tender smile she saw at night, or early in the morning.

She desperately wanted to kiss him. She couldn't, because of these fucking suits, these fucking visors, this fucking *place*.

If only they'd never come down here.

"You know as well as I do what we're up against," Patrick said. "I'll fight to win. I'll do whatever it takes to get back to you. If it was just you and me, we'd tear them apart, but honey, it isn't just you and me. We can decide for ourselves how we want to live—our kid can't."

Her anger flared again, but it was an echo of its former intensity, a sputtering match compared to a burning forest. He was right. The baby couldn't make decisions. She needed to get out.

"Then come with me," she said. "Tommy will fight. That's what Whitey wanted, someone to fight. We're going to be a *family*, Patrick. Fuck everyone else."

She already knew what his answer would be.

"I can't do that," he said. "If I fight, they'll take you out of here. If I don't fight, they won't."

"Then watch where I go and follow me. *Please.*"

He smiled a sad smiled, pulled her in, held her close.

"They're smarter than that," he said. "Once I go to see the map, they're going to take you, Ramiro and Sonny away from the others, then lead you up. None of us will know the way out. That doesn't matter, though—I gave my word. You and our child get to live."

Honor. Loyalty. Loyalty to fucking alien creatures that might still kill him after he lived up to his promise. He was going to die for that? For his *word*? It was ridiculous. It was *stupid*.

Bertha closed her eyes, put her head against her man's chest. The tears came. She hated herself for crying.

"The nuke," she said. "What are you going to do if it's real?"

He held her, rubbed her back. She felt the strength in his arms.

"You don't need to know that," he said. "I've got a plan."

"A plan where you act like a real commander and send someone else, not go yourself?"

His silence was answer enough.

Ender they called him. Now he was going to end himself.

This couldn't be happening.

"I can't even kiss you goodbye," she said. "I love you."

He held her at arm's length. "I love you, too. I have from the moment I saw you. Even if I die, my love for you will never end."

Bertha stared at his face, trying to lock in every pore, every hair, every scar. If she did survive, she wanted to tell their child everything she could about his or her father.

"They could be lying," she said. "What if they kill me once I'm clear of the others? What if you fight and win, and then they murder you anyway?"

"It's a chance we have to take. And if they were going to do that, I doubt they would have returned your weapons. Whitey indicated he was bringing you some kind of cart to get you to the surface faster, and that there would only be two rocktopi escorting you up. Keep your eye on them. If they pull anything, do what you have to do. If you see more than two, you'll know it's a trap. This isn't a sure thing, but it's the best chance we have to get you and the baby out of here. Promise me you'll go. I'm begging you."

Patrick O'Doyle. Begging. Had she thought her heart couldn't break any more than it already had? If so, she'd been wrong.

This wasn't about her. It wasn't about him. Not really. It was about the baby.

Bertha couldn't deny it anymore. She had to do this.

"I promise," she said.

She threw her arms around him, squeezed him tight.

He again rubbed slow circles on her back.

"I have to get going," he said. "Sam thinks it will take us twenty to thirty minutes to get to the ship, and she wasn't able to get them to say how far inside the ship the map room is."

He started to pull away. She held him tighter, refused to let him go. He was still hurt, wasn't himself. He was leaving most of the NoSeeUms in the City Cavern—he'd have only Tommy to protect him. If there was trouble in the ship, she had to be there to keep Patrick safe.

"Not yet," she said. "I can't go yet. Let me go to the ship with you, then I'll leave. Please."

He had begged her, now she was begging him. Their pride, cast away, because pride didn't matter—love did.

She felt him nod.

"All right," he said. "We'll do that together. Then you go."

66

15,861 feet below the surface

DESPITE THE COMING fight, despite the clinging sense of loss at the deaths of Hatchet and Skylark, despite the guilt he felt killing six more human beings, Tommy couldn't help but feel one driving, dominant emotion—he was *excited*.

Siren led the way down the narrow tunnel—no switchbacks in this one, it was a straight shot, maybe twenty-five degrees steep. Tommy followed Siren, Sam followed Tommy, Ender and Lybrand brought up the rear. Dots of light in the ceiling illuminated the mad collage of colors, patterns and carved symbols splashed across the walls.

The low ceiling meant Tommy had to keep his head bent slightly. Sam had no problem, as she was two or three inches shorter than Tommy, but Ender had to walk either at a slight crouch or with his helmeted head tilted to the side. The man was trying hard to hide his pain. Trying, and failing.

Ender was a tough motherfucker. He could endure.

Bringing Lybrand was a mistake. Not that she couldn't handle herself in a fight, but if Ender was doing this to buy her safety, she should already be on her way up, even if that meant walking all the way instead of waiting for whatever vehicle the rocktopi were preparing.

Yet again, Ender was letting personal feelings get in the way of making the right decision.

Tommy flexed his fingers on the carbine. It felt good in his hands, gave him a small sense of peace. Was he going to die soon? Probably. Would he be able to defend himself, stay alive as long as possible, and go down swinging? Thanks to his weapons, yes.

The carbine. His knife. Without them, he'd felt naked. Now the emperor had real clothes. Perhaps it spoke to the rocktopi's desperation that they'd returned the gear. Were Tommy in Whitey's position, he wasn't sure he'd do the same.

It was hard to stay focused. Impossibly so. He was about to see something he'd never believed could happen in his lifetime, something just as improbable and amazing as the glowing alien being leading the way.

"Hey, Ender," Tommy said. "How big did you say the Utah ship was again?"

"Four miles long. A half-mile wide."

Four *miles*. Twenty-one aircraft carriers laid end-to-end. Impossible to even imagine.

"You think this one will be the same?" Tommy asked.

"How the hell would I know? It's a fucking shipwreck buried in a mountain-sized tomb. You're going to see it in a few minutes. Just keep moving."

Ender's harsh tone brought reality crashing back. After this he was—supposedly—going to send his pregnant wife to the surface. Odds were he'd never see her again.

Siren let out a chirp. Tommy knew it was a fantasy concocted somewhere in his head, but he felt he understood the noise—Siren was saying *hurry up*. While the language barrier between the two was all but insurmountable, Tommy sensed an undeniable connection with the alien. He had saved Siren's life; Siren saved his.

Some bonds didn't require words.

Up ahead, Tommy saw a patch of darkness.

"I think we're coming to the entrance to the cavern," he said. "I can't believe we're going to see an actual starship."

The stuff of books. The stuff of movies. The stuff of dreams.

"Tommy," Sam said quietly, "you sound … I guess the best word is *giddy*. With Angus coming, knowing the rocktopi might try to kill us anyway, aren't you afraid?"

The question caught him off guard. *Was* he afraid? No, he wasn't. Odd.

Or maybe it wasn't odd at all. He'd left his soul in Bandah. In a way, he'd *wanted* to die, every day since then, right up until the moment Ender had told him he would see aliens. Thoughts of suicide had vanished. Tommy wanted to defend this irreplaceable culture, protect it as much as he could until his final curtain closed.

For the first time in twenty years, when he was almost assuredly going to die, he truly wanted to *live*.

Irony can be a real asshat.

"No, I'm not afraid," he said. "I've been ready for death for a long time. I guess I didn't expect to squeeze so much life in at the end—it's an unexpected delight."

"An *unexpected delight*," Sam echoed. "For a killer, you have a way with words."

Maybe she meant that as a compliment, somehow, but her reminder of what he truly was stole some of his excitement.

They reached the dark opening. Siren kept moving forward, glowing a soft plum with pulsing spots of navy blue. The creature was a tiny spot of color moving through a sea of pitch black.

Three headlamps probed the vast darkness. From somewhere in the unseen distance came a rich, faint roar, a rumble, so dispersed it took Tommy a few moments to place it: the sound of falling water.

Another sound, too—or rather, a *lack* of sound. In the tunnels, every step brought an imperceptible audio reflection from the surrounding stone. But not here. Here, there was no echo, each footstep hit and was gone.

They walked on. Their headlamp beams played off something maybe eighty meters ahead, something that appeared dull-gray. Something … *huge*, a towering wall that rose up and up and up.

The ship.

"Mother of God," Tommy said.

They drew closer. Parts of the surface *gleamed*, as if from some internal radiance that lit up only when a headlamp beam touched it. Ender had been right; the ship did look like a half-buried cartridge with bullets on either end. At least Tommy assumed both ends were pointed—to his right, perhaps a quarter mile away, he saw one end, but to his left the monstrous ship was lost in the darkness.

To the left … parts of the hull looked torn, even melted.

"It's damaged," Tommy said.

Ender and Lybrand's headlamp beam joined his, lit up great gashes in the hull. The *size* of the ship—some of those holes had to be two hundred meters long, maybe more.

"Maybe it got torn up coming in," Sam said. "When they put it in the mountain?"

Ender shook his head. "Maybe, but I don't think so. Scraping rock wouldn't melt spots. My guess is battle damage."

The wasps. Could that damage have come from the rocktopi's genocidal enemy?

"The holes are *big*," Sam said. "If it took that damage in space, how could it keep going?"

Lybrand's beam flicked right, then back to the damage.

"It's part of the design, supposedly," she said. "We were inside the one in Utah. All the rooms were like bubbles. The people we were with seemed to think the ship was made out of a giant dollop of molten metal, that they injected air into or something like that."

A four-mile long, half-mile wide *dollop* of molten platinum-iridium? The tech boggled the imagination.

Siren picked up speed. Tommy almost had to jog to keep up.

In all his life, Tommy had never felt so small. So insignificant. He tore his gaze from the rising wall of platinum to look at the floor beneath him. Brightly enameled, hexagonal tiles, each the size of a small car, each with a scene on it—alien landscapes, rocktopi with hundreds of different colors and patterns, plants, strange animals.

"The Utah ship cavern was lit up," Lybrand said. "I wonder why it's dark in here."

Sam's headlamp angled toward the ceiling high above.

"The cavern is at least twelve thousand years old," she said. "Maybe the lights just burned out."

Tommy looked up as well. The headlamp beams dimly illuminated the rocky ceiling, which he guessed was a quarter-mile above. Seeing a ceiling that high above gave him a brief instance of vertigo—he had to take a step to keep his balance.

"There," Sam said. "That might be one of their artificial suns."

Her beam played off a grayish, curved shape embedded in the stone. It looked small, but Tommy had to remind himself the object and ceiling alike were well over a thousand feet above. That "sun" was probably the size of a house.

An impatient squeal made Tommy jump. Siren waved tentacles, pulsed with spots of turquoise.

"Keep moving," Ender said. "We have a job to do."

They continued on toward the ship.

Tommy realized he was only seeing half of it. It rested in the floor as if a trench—a *huge* trench—had been carved out for a perfect fit. Ender had said the Utah ship was a half-mile wide. It this ship was the same size, that meant about 1,300 feet were visible—a height taller than the Empire State Building—and *another* 1,300 feet were hidden beneath.

"Jesus," Sam said as she jogged. "I mean … *Jesus*. This thing has to be bigger than the Great Pyramid."

Numbers flashed in Tommy's thoughts. *Four* Great Pyramids touching at the tips, angled sides pressed against each other to make a square, would easily fit inside the hull's diameter. And how many of those pyramids-turned-squares could fit within the ship's length? At least forty.

"This ship could hold a hundred and sixty pyramids," Tommy said.

That he had lived long enough to see this miracle …

All those times in his apartment, the barrel of the Raven MP-25 pistol in his hand, the cold feel of the barrel against his temple—172 moments where he'd been a finger-twitch from death. He thought of Sleepy's words, how Sleepy thought God had kept him alive this long so that he could finally do the right thing.

Tommy didn't believe in god. That didn't stop him from whispering a silent *thank you*. He had no illusions about heaven or an afterlife, but if he was wrong, if there was a higher power that—for whatever reason—had kept him from pulling that trigger so that he could be here, now, so that he could see *this*? Tommy felt a need to express his immeasurable gratitude.

An ancient, alien race, an ancient culture, and it fell on *him* to defend them.

Him … a middle-aged, suicidal dishwasher.

"This is so amazing," Sam said. "It's been down here for thousands of years, since before recorded human history even began. Before we invented the wheel. Before we domesticated herd animals. Before Mesopotamia. Before Göbekli Tepe. Before the goddamn *Holocene*. It's just … *all this time*."

Finally, they reached the hull. Tommy squinted against headlamp beams reflecting off the brighter spots of the battered surface. He saw himself, his fatigues tattered and worn, far more than they should have been for just a few days of use. Scratches on his visor, small dents in his helmet. Two day's scruff on his face.

He again looked left, down the length of the ship—nothing but smooth metal that faded off into the distance.

"I don't see a door," Sam said. "There's not a seam of any kind."

As if in answer, Siren extruded tentacles that blazed a luminescent gold, laid them against the hull. The metal seemed to stretch back like a snapping rubber band, creating an oval opening.

Siren flowed in, his bioluminescence reflecting off of curved, gleaming platinum. Ender followed, then Sam. Tommy couldn't move. Sam stopped, turned.

"Tommy, you ready?"

A chill washed over him. His heart fluttered. His stomach tingled. Yes, he had *seen* an alien ship, but it had overwhelmed him to the point where he'd forgotten the real payoff of this trip—to go *inside* of one.

"Yeah," he said, nodding. "I'm ready."

67

12,532 feet below the surface

"YOU'RE RIGHT," DONNIE said. "Those fissures look like bad news. They might try to hit us there. Outstanding work, Doctor Kool."

Angus couldn't fight a flush of pride at Donnie's words. "Thank you, s—" he caught himself almost saying *sir*. "Thanks."

The two men stood there, once again slightly apart from the rest of the mercenaries. Angus fed data to Donnie's HUD, showing the wall fissures that were of concern.

"Good spot for an ambush," Donnie said. "How far ahead are they?"

"They're thirteen hundred feet below us. We'll reach that spot in four hours, maybe five. The fissures line three consecutive switchback segments."

"Not good. That's a lot of space. Are the fissures wide enough for rocktopi to come through?"

Angus thought of rocktopi sliding through cracks in the walls, those curved knives flashing. It wasn't a pleasant thought.

"They're wide enough, but I don't know how deep the fissures go," he said. "The BlackBugs marked them and moved further down the tunnel. There are enough fissures that it would slow down map exploration to have BlackBugs explore them all. The fissures might go back ten, fifteen feet, they might go back a lot farther. Maybe they connect to other passages, maybe they're just holes in the wall."

Donnie thought for a moment.

"Having a big map won't help us if we get ambushed," he said. "When we get closer, bring enough BlackBugs back to explore, say, the first hundred feet or so of each fissure. If we can spot the enemy, that will determine our course of action."

"There's something else you need to see."

Angus eye-tracked through the display, focusing in on a zigzag switchback line that seemed to float above the web that made up the BlackBug tunnel map.

"Based on the angle of this line, I think it might lead to the kind of big caverns we expect to see down deep, or maybe even the ship cavern itself. That tunnel could also lead up to the surface."

"A *second* path to the surface? But you told me that the Utah tunnel system had only one way in."

"This isn't Utah," Angus said.

Donnie fell quiet. Angus waited, watched the man's eyes flick left, right, up, down, taking in the map.

"That tunnel looks far from where we are now. Could we use it? Is it a better way down than the path we're on now?"

Angus had considered that option as soon as he'd seen the path, but the numbers didn't add up.

"To get there, the BlackBugs moved through some areas that are too narrow for us to traverse. We can't get to it from where we are now, not without descending to whatever cavern it connects to."

"Where O'Doyle might already be," Donnie said. "Could he use that to escape?"

Angus nodded. "If he finds it, and if it does lead to the surface, then yes, absolutely."

The thought of O'Doyle making it out alive chased away Angus's sense of pride.

"We can't risk that," Donnie said. "I need a way to plug that tunnel. Your BlackBugs can dig. Can they dig enough to cause a cave-in?"

Like so many other parts of the BlackBugs, Angus had modeled their pneumatic drivers after the rock-smashing head-wedges of the silverbugs. The drivers would let them widen a narrow space, or even, in a pinch, chip out a path from scratch. He had designed the BlackBugs to *clear* a passage, not *block* one, but rock was rock.

"It would take a little reprogramming," Angus said. "I can have them drill through the tunnel ceiling at an angle until the weight of the stone causes a collapse."

"How many would it take to make that happen?"

Angus closed his eyes, calculated the amount of rock that would need to be loosened in order to cause a cave-in.

"Five ought to do it. And maybe...four or five hours to get the job done."

"How many BlackBugs are operational?"

They'd lost a few to mechanical problems, but the failure rate was nowhere near that of the SwarmStorm.

"Ninety-four."

"Then send the five," Donnie said. "Have them climb high in that tunnel, to maybe a mile below the surface. Every minute O'Doyle's people spend ascending before they see the path is blocked means an additional minute *descending*, which compounds the time they're not preparing for us. Can your BlackBugs kill?"

Angus smiled. "Is a frog's ass watertight?"

"Doctor Kool, perhaps I was misguided in my initial dislike of you." Donnie pressed his talk button, opening up the main comm channel. "This is Graham. Get your asses up, people, we're heading out and moving double-time. Recon, in the lead with Goofy. First Platoon, back them up. Sixth, take rearguard with Cujo. We've got a dangerous spot coming up, we should be there in three or four hours. Get your heads in the game—it's almost time to fight."

He released the button.

"Rousing speech," Angus said.

"I do what I can with what little I've got, Doctor Kool. Would it be too much of me to ask for you to stay in the middle of the column with Khatari and Fuentes, between Third and Fourth Platoons? I would like to make sure we properly protect that brain of yours."

The sense of pride returned, even more powerful than before.

"Sure, Donnie," Angus said. "I can do that."

68

16,000 feet below the surface

SAM HAD no words.

Words had no function in this place. Words were archaic. Useless. Because words were insufficient to describe such things.

Tommy was just as quiet as she was, just as wide-eyed, just as awestruck. Even O'Doyle and Lybrand—who had seen a marvel like this before—seemed blown away by the ancient relic.

The houses in the City Cavern were square, with flat walls and flat ceilings. Sam hadn't thought much about that design, because that was what she'd seen all her life. Now, however, she guessed that the rocktopi's flat walls, flat floors and right angles existed because stone didn't lend itself to curves.

Metal did.

Inside the ancient shipwreck, there wasn't a right angle to be seen.

Anywhere. There wasn't anything *flat*, either. Corridors curved and sloped, dipped and climbed. Smooth, oblong rungs ran along the ceiling of every passage, their purpose made obvious by Siren swinging from them like an orangutan swinging from branch to branch. Even the floor was curved.

Their helmet spotlights flicked here and there, punching holes in the dark areas that weren't faintly illuminated by Siren's soft glow.

The alien led them through the corridors. Metal tunnels curved off at all angles, down and up and left and right and everything in-between. The ship's passages felt like an endless haunted house, a curving M.C. Escher painting stretched out into three dimensions.

Some corridors were barely big enough for O'Doyle to walk through. Others were so large they could have easily accommodated four lanes of highway traffic.

At every intersection, smooth walls and no edges, as if the passages had been bored out of solid metal by some bizarre species of worm. The inside of the ship was a mad molehill of metal, the inorganic made organic, the inanimate brought to life.

Siren led them past many rooms, all with oblong doorways that had smooth, rounded edges. Some of the rooms were as small as a closet, some as big as a warehouse. In all of them, Sam's headlamp beam played off of curved walls with no corners, no edges. Strange objects lay inside those rooms. Furniture? Computers? Religious artifacts?

The ship made her feel small. Not from a size perspective, although it definitely did that, but from an intelligence perspective. An alien ship, a *massive* one at that, and she, Ramiro, Veronica and others had spent years believing the glyphs and knives—and yes, even the massacre site— had been the product of an ancient human culture.

How could she have been so utterly wrong?

They passed tunnel after tunnel, snaking and curving away. They passed room after room, each one gleaming and empty. Many rooms had what looked like bits of colored ceramic on the curved walls, some embedded in metal bulges.

"Ender," Tommy said, "is this what the inside of the Utah ship looked like?"

O'Doyle stopped walking. Tommy, Lybrand and Sam stopped,

waited. O'Doyle glanced around, perhaps seeing the hallways in a new light.

"There had been an accident of some kind," O'Doyle said. "A nuclear reactor melted down, maybe. And there was a river that must have changed course at some point. It eroded a path right through the ship. We used that river to get from one side to the other, so we could take a tunnel up to the surface. I was in bad shape at the time. So was Bertha."

She nodded, held up the hand that was missing two fingers.

"I'd just lost these," she said. "The silverbugs there had blades."

The woman said it so matter-of-factly, as if the missing fingers were as insignificant as a stubbed toe. Sam wondered if she could ever be as tough as that woman.

"We were more focused on staying alive than checking the place out," O'Doyle said. "I assume most of it looked like what we see here, but we didn't have time to walk around inside it. The rocktopi there … well, they weren't the ones here. We were fighting for our lives."

They continued on through the labyrinthine sprawl of curving platinum tubes.

Siren stopped above an opening. The alien waved a tendril, gesturing down the corridor in a manner exactly like that of a person sweeping an arm to say, *this way, please, this way.*

O'Doyle pulled his rifle butt to his shoulder, but kept the barrel pointed down.

"Easy," Tommy said. "Doubtful this is some elaborate trap."

O'Doyle glanced back at Tommy, gave a slight nod. He lowered his rifle slightly.

Siren let out a short screech, waved his tendril faster.

"He wants us to move it," Tommy said. "Seems like he's in a hurry."

O'Doyle started down the corridor again. He looked into the opening as he passed by, paused, then continued on.

Tommy followed him. Sam passed by the opening, looked in, stopped.

Inside, the light of two rocktopi pushed back the darkness. They appeared to be working on one of the wall bulges, which had been removed and rested on the floor like half a beachball of metal.

Lybrand looked in.

"I don't like this," she said.

They seemed harmless enough to Sam. "Why? What's wrong?"

"In Utah, the rocktopi wouldn't go near their ship," Lybrand said. "It was like … against their religion or something. When they finally did come into the ship, they came to kill us."

Sam felt the two rocktopi looking at her.

Siren let out an impatient screech—the alien, O'Doyle and Tommy had moved further down the curved corridor.

"Move it," Lybrand said.

Sam jogged to catch up.

SIREN SWUNG FROM rung to rung, his light gleaming off the polished metal. Or was *he* a *she*? Or maybe something else altogether. Sam didn't know, and at that moment, she wasn't all that concerned with proper pronouns.

Siren swung into a room; the four humans followed.

The room was round, but not circular. The curved walls, domed ceiling and slightly concave floor made Sam feel like she was on the inside of a slightly misshapen metal egg. Eight bulge-panels dotted the walls, each with a cluster of ceramic protrusions: red, pale yellow, forest green.

"This doesn't help," O'Doyle said. "We need a fucking map, and we need it *now*. Sam, tell Siren to stop screwing around and show us what we came to see."

Sam shrugged off her backpack. She pulled out the tablet, started to think about what symbols she could use, but before she could draw anything Siren reached out eight pseudopods—multicolored taffy stretching near the breaking point—and touched each tip to one of the round panels. The tentacles snapped back into his body, sending little ripples of flesh and color across his skin.

The room came to life.

Beams of colored light flashed out of the panels. The center of the room glowed, became a blazing hologram that looked like the myriad branches of a circulatory system.

"There's your map," Sam said.

Tommy stepped closer to the room-sized, three-dimensional image. O'Doyle did as well.

So many tunnels, *thousands* of them, connecting, branching, intertwining. It really did look like a circulatory system, a complex network of veins and arteries leading to a "heart" that was the City Cavern. Sam saw the straight passage that angled down to the map's largest element—the Ship Cavern in which they now stood.

The map's tunnels were portrayed in thousands of colors. A labeling system, perhaps.

"Sam," O'Doyle said, "give your pad to Bertha. Bertha, can you draw this map?"

Lybrand looked at the tangle of holographic tunnels, tilted her head this way and that.

"I can try," she said.

Sam handed her the warped sketch pad and a charcoal pencil. Lybrand sat cross-legged on the floor, began to draw.

"That's the main passage," Tommy said, pointing to a zigzag line that rose far higher than any other. "Up at the top—that's the entrance. Even with all the tunnel splits we followed, I'll lay odds that the mercs are still on that main path."

"I need to know where Angus is on the map," O'Doyle said. "Sam, ask Siren."

Sam moved her fingertip to trace the blocky outline of Angus's armor, the one Whitey had signed, on the tablet. Next to it, she drew a question mark. She showed the tablet to Siren.

The alien pulsed with expanding rings of orange and caramel-brown, then extended a pseudopod into the map and pointed to a streak of crimson on the main passage, about halfway between the top and the City Cavern.

"Not very exact," Tommy said, peering into the map. "That line covers thirty-four switchbacks, way too much space for the merc column."

O'Doyle stared, nodded. "Must be an estimated location. Maybe the silverbugs watching them are staying too far away. I'm sure Angus has ways to take the things out. But by the looks of this, we have a little bit of time before they get here."

Would that *little bit of time* be enough? Sam had no idea. O'Doyle had assigned his friends to train the aliens—how long would it take to turn the "civilian" rocktopi into fighters?

"Bertha," O'Doyle said, "it looks like there's several entrances into the City Cavern from various tunnels. Make sure you get those, okay?"

She nodded. "I will."

"There's the river cavern." Tommy pointed to a new area. "And that vertical line must be that big waterfall. Sonny was right, that's how we got so far ahead of the mercenaries."

The visual helped Sam put that in perspective. The river went steadily down. It bent and twisted, yes, but compared to the switchback-laden path of the tunnels, the river was practically a straight shot to the City Cavern.

O'Doyle stepped closer. The map's light played across his body, his helmet, his visor. His head flicked left, right, up and down as he searched for something.

"The main switchback tunnel is the only way out on this map," he said. "Where's the passage that they'll use to get Bertha to safety?"

Lybrand's hand paused in mid-sketch. She started to look up, stopped herself, went back to drawing.

"Sam, ask Siren," O'Doyle said. "Ask him where the fucking path is that gets Bertha out of here."

Not just Bertha—Sonny and Ramiro as well. Sam desperately wanted Ram to escape, to survive.

Sam tried to think of what symbols to draw to communicate O'Doyle's question. It was complex, and her vocabulary was so limited.

"I'm not sure how to ask that," she said.

Tommy turned to face Siren. "Let me try. He and I seem to connect. Or *she*. Or *it*."

A giggle escaped Sam—delight that she and Tommy were so much alike—but even to her it sounded like the laugh of an insane person. Maybe she *was* insane. Enough shit had gone down that it wouldn't surprise her, not one bit.

Tommy pointed to Bertha, to the map, then up, then to the map again.

A silent pause, then Siren flattened out a spot on his body and showed a symbol in red—the same blocky armor outline Whitey had used to represent Angus Kool.

"That's not a goddamn answer." O'Doyle's voice was thick with anger. "Sam, figure out how to ask him so he understands the fucking question."

"Siren understands just fine," Tommy said. "Think about it. If you were in their shoes, would you show us another way out *before* we fight? Before we live up to our deal?"

O'Doyle's eyes widened. Sam took a step away. He was so big, so *frightening*.

"If Whitey backs out on the deal, I'll *kill him*," O'Doyle said. He walked toward Siren. "You hear me? If he—"

Tommy slid between O'Doyle and the alien, put a hand on O'Doyle's chest.

"Easy, Ender," Tommy said, his tone smooth, almost passive. "Cool down. The deal is they get Bertha, Sonny and Ramiro out before we fight. If they don't live up to their end of the bargain, neither will we. Give them a chance."

O'Doyle's nostrils flared. His furious eyes flicked from Siren to Tommy. Tommy did not move.

"Yeah, okay," O'Doyle said, visibly forcing down his anger. "You're right. We gave our word. We'll honor our deal."

Bertha had stopped drawing. She just stared at the sketch pad.

"We need to plan," Tommy said softly. "Let's get back to that, all right?"

O'Doyle nodded. He turned back to the map.

Bertha started drawing again.

"We stick with the assumption that Angus needs to get his nuke down here," O'Doyle said. "It looks like the tunnel we took to get here is the only way to reach the ship. That gives us a chokepoint. That's good. Worm, how do you think he'll get the nuke down here?"

Sam hated that Tommy's friends called him that. The others had nicknames, too, and that was fine, but Tommy was smarter than all of them combined. To her, *Worm* seemed somewhat disrespectful.

"If I was Angus, I'd use one of those dogs," Tommy said. "They're fast, they're tough. The ship cavern is massive. If he can get the dog through the chokepoint and down here, it's game over—the dog can run around in all this open space and avoid conflict long enough for Angus and the mercs to get back to the surface before the nuke blows."

"But we saw the silverbugs kill that dog," Sam said. "Couldn't we put silverbugs in the tunnel, where the dog can't avoid them?"

Tommy shook his head. "We can't let it get that close. Angus has those swarmbots. He won't let the dog move without them again, I'm sure of that. We can't count on silverbugs to stop the thing."

"Catch it in the city," Bertha said without looking up. "Lots of buildings, streets, cover. Get the rocktopi down here, out of the way."

O'Doyle and Tommy exchanged a glance.

"Sounds smart," Tommy said.

Ender grunted in agreement. "She's right. If we don't have to worry about the rocktopi, we can use guerrilla tactics all day. Booby trap whatever we can find, shoot and move, confuse the hell out of the mercs. That will neutralize their superior numbers, at least to some degree. We make them pay for every inch they take."

"Make it *too* costly," Sam said. "Will that be enough to make them turn back?"

O'Doyle and Tommy considered her question.

"Maybe," O'Doyle said. "But with a fortune waiting for them if they win, I doubt it."

Siren let out a sharp screech. Sam wished with all she was that she could understand their spoken language.

The alien came closer to Tommy, then stretched out an extrusion, pointed to a spot on the map. The spot wasn't far above the City Cavern, and was close to the main passage.

Tommy peered at the map. "Yeah, I see it. What about it?"

He talked as if Siren understood what he said. Sam wondered if Siren's chirps and squeals were the same kind of thing, a sentient being thinking out loud to someone who didn't know the language.

Siren flattened a spot, again formed the icon that represented Angus. Then, the icon of a mushroom cloud. The alien's tendril pointed at Tommy, then at itself, then at the spot on the map—pointing to communicate, just as Tommy had done earlier.

Tommy stared at the map. "Yeah. Yeah, you're right."

"Worm," O'Doyle said, "don't try and tell me you're so smart you learned how to speak rocktopi."

"I didn't understand a sound Siren made," Tommy said. "I didn't have to. It's all in the context. Siren is going to attack the mercs, try to take out the nuke before it gets here. He wants me to go with him."

Tommy stepped *into* the map. Colored light played all over his body, making him look—at least a little—like a rocktopi.

He put a fingertip on the same line Siren had indicated.

"Look at this side tunnel," Tommy said. "Maybe thirty feet of rock separate it from the main passage, but check this out—" he moved his fingertip down the line "—looks like the main passage has some cracks or fissures in the walls, here, here and here. Now, look down here, at this bend in the river. A vertical shaft leads up from that bend to the side tunnel. I think what Siren is showing is that he can go upstream, then we climb that vertical shaft, get into the side tunnel, then use the fissures to ambush the mercs in the main passage."

Sam couldn't believe what she was hearing. And yet, what he said made sense, seemed to jibe with Siren's pointing. Sam felt a burst of shame that—in this critical time when pride should not matter—she felt *jealous* that Tommy seemed to be able to communicate with the aliens far better than her. Tommy, who had never even seen a glyph from this culture until he entered the mountain, where Sam had been studying them for four years.

"That does look like a good spot for an ambush," O'Doyle said. "But it's also an *obvious* spot. The mercs will see it coming. They'll be ready."

Tommy stepped out of the map. "I've got an idea that will make it less obvious. I have to try it, Ender. Look at the map—those fissures are the last spot where we can attack the merc column without tackling it head-on and facing one of their armored, machine gun-wielding dogs. If we don't get the nuke at that spot, the nuke *will* make it to the City Cavern."

O'Doyle stared at the map.

"You're right," he said. "You and I will join Siren's attack."

Lybrand stood up fast; the sketch pad fell off her lap, the charcoal pencil rolling across the curved floor.

"Like hell you will," she said. "I didn't agree to leave just so you could throw your life away the first chance you got. Let someone else go!"

They saw something Sam did not. Throw his life away? Was that what *Tommy* was doing?

"I have to go," O'Doyle said. "It's my call, I'm—"

"*In command*," Tommy said, cutting him off. "Commanders stay back and call the shots, they don't do runs like this. You know that's true. It will be rough going—your back won't handle it. And besides, you're too big. To make this work, we'll have to dig new tunnels—smaller men mean smaller tunnels, smaller tunnels mean less digging, less digging means we get there faster. Curve and I are the smallest. We'll go."

O'Doyle sneered, his eyes narrowed.

"You're volunteering Curve? What makes you think he'll go?"

Tommy pointed to Siren, to a spot on Siren's skin—the spot showing the icon that represented Angus Kool.

O'Doyle's sneer faded.

"Curve will go," Tommy said. "We'll try to hit the middle of the column, where the nuke—and Angus—would likely be. If Curve has a shot at killing him, not only will he volunteer, if you try to stop him, he'd probably use that axe on *you*."

Sam didn't know what to say, what to think. They were making life-and-death decisions. Whichever way they went with this, people were going to die.

"You're right," O'Doyle said, softly. "You and Curve. But I have to keep most of the rocktopi back here, Tommy. If you fail ..."

Tommy nodded. "If I fail, you still have to stop them in the City Cavern. I get it. Let me take Siren, Curve, and nine rocktopi."

O'Doyle took a deep breath, moved as if to rub his face, then looked at his hands, as though remembering the visor made that impossible.

He let his hands drop.

"Fine. You and Curve take your weapons, obviously. How many railguns do you think you need?"

"None," Tommy said. "If we don't get the job done, you guys will need all the firepower you can get down here. Sam? Help me. Tell Siren we need to leave the railguns here, that he and the others can only take knives."

Finally, she could be of use again. She considered which symbols to draw. Thinking of how Siren and Tommy had communicated, she set her tablet on the ground.

She looked at Siren, pantomimed firing a rifle, then opened her hands as if she'd dropped the rifle to the ground. She made a "C" out of each hand, stacked the left hand on top of the right—together, they made a double crescent.

"Wow," Tommy said. "You're smart as fuck, you know that?"

She pointed at Siren, made the double crescent again. She gave both hands a sharp shake, hoping that emphasized the point. Siren was silent a moment, the alien's amorphous body undulating softly. Then, it let out a squeal. It seemed to reach a tendril *inside* its body—when it came out, it held a double-crescent knife.

"That's freaky," Bertha said. "How do they not cut themselves?"

Siren put the knife back in his body. Bertha was right—that *was* freaky.

"Siren gets it," he said. "They're just as smart as we are. Maybe smarter."

Sam heard a sound—strange at first, because ringing echoes thickened it, fattened it, but within seconds, she knew it was the same sound she'd heard before running for her life.

click-click, click-click

"Silverbugs," O'Doyle said.

Lybrand shot to her feet.

O'Doyle moved to the room's opening, leaned out.

"There's a shit-ton of them coming this way," he said, then stepped back from the opening, aiming his rifle. "Worm, Bertha, spread out, keep them from angling in along the walls."

Siren squealed so loud that everyone winced.

"I hate it when he does that," Sam said, wishing she could wiggle a finger in her ear.

The icons representing *Angus* and *Nuke* faded from the flat spot on Siren's glowing skin. In their place, a glyph that Sam recognized.

The message was clear.

"It's the symbol for *cart*," she said. "The silverbugs are going to lead her to the cart. The rocktopi are ready to take her up."

Lybrand and O'Doyle looked at each other. Love in their eyes, love and *hurt*.

"We've got enough info," he said. "We'll go out with you."

Lybrand shook her head. "No. You stay here. If you walk out with me, I…I don't think I can do it."

O'Doyle stared at her for a moment, then he nodded. He stepped to her. He held the bottom of his visor, compressed it up with a single, sudden lift.

Lybrand did the same. The two soldiers kissed, fast but intense, the way Ramiro used to kiss Sam before everything fell apart.

O'Doyle and Lybrand separated, sealed their visors—their faces were already red, after only a few seconds of exposure.

"I love you," O'Doyle said.

Lybrand nodded. "And I love you. Whatever it takes, Patrick, *survive*. I won't accept anything less."

She turned away from him and quickly walked through the opening, out of sight.

The silverbugs in the room scurried out after her.

O'Doyle stood there, staring after her, blinking rapidly, his eyes watering—maybe from the heat, maybe from saying goodbye. Probably both.

Sam's heart broke for him.

Tommy picked up Sam's sketch pad and pencil. He held them out to her.

"I've got to go, too," he said. He tilted his head to O'Doyle. "Make sure he gets out of here okay, all right?"

She took the pad and pencil. "How about you, Tommy Strymon? Are you going survive?"

He smiled. "I'll try."

With that, he walked to O'Doyle, offered his hand.

O'Doyle looked at the hand as if Bertha's leaving had been a straight jab and Tommy's leaving was the knock-out punch.

They shook.

"I'm sorry I brought you here, Tommy," he said. "I'm sorry for a lot of things."

There had been tension between the two, but now that tension was gone. They hugged, each giving the other two light thumps on the back.

"Water under the bridge," Tommy said. He gestured to the room around them, to the map. "When it's all said and done, you made my dreams come true. I'll do my best to get that nuke. If I fail …"

Sam fought back tears. If he failed, well, the rest didn't need to be said.

"If you fail, we'll finish the job," O'Doyle said.

Tommy faced Siren. "You ready, my strange little friend?"

Siren squeaked, flashed an alternating pattern of red and orange.

"What does that mean?" Sam asked.

Tommy laughed. His laugh, Sam noted, didn't sound crazy at all.

"I have no idea what it means," he said.

Human and rocktopi left the map room together.

Sam watched the open doorway for a few moments, then turned to O'Doyle.

"Looks like it's just you and me. What's next?"

Patrick O'Doyle took a moment to gather himself.

"Next, we look at the map drawing and see if Bertha missed any-thing," he said. "Then we head up and get ready to fight."

69

SONNY, LYBRAND AND Ramiro followed a pair of adult rocktopi through the orchard west of town. The two aliens flowed and stretched down a narrow, multicolored tile path that wound through the strange trees.

—or maybe it was a sidewalk, Sonny didn't know—heading toward a cluster of stone buildings at the base of the City Cavern wall.

The tall trees were thicker than he'd thought. He could see only ten or twenty yards in any direction. The rocktopi town was already out of sight, blocked by trunks and the odd foliage. He couldn't even see the obelisk.

"This is taking too long," Ramiro said. "Is this the way out? Are they taking us out of this hellhole or not?"

Sonny glanced at Lybrand, saw the woman grimace.

"For the tenth fucking time, I don't know," she said.

Sonny couldn't blame her for being irritated—Ramiro was getting on his last nerve as well. They were so close to getting out. Sonny believed, he *had* to believe, that he was going to see the sky again. Ramiro needed to calm the fuck down, or he was going to mess everything up.

Ramiro's crutch clinked against the tiles, reminding Sonny of the sound of silverbug feet clicking on rock.

"Maybe they lied," Ramiro said. "Maybe they're going to kill us here. Where's the damn tunnel out of here?"

Lybrand grabbed Ramiro's arm and yanked it, stopping him. Her other hand clenched the pistol grip of her rifle, which hung from her chest. For a moment, Sonny was sure she was going to shoot him.

"We made a *deal*," she said. "Patrick fights, we get to leave. So we're following these two and that's that. If you ask me where the tunnel is one more time, I'll shove this rifle barrel right up your ass. Got it?"

Ramiro glared at her. He was bigger than she was. Not by much, though. Sonny had no doubt which of them would win in a fight. Neither did Ramiro.

She let him go, walking quickly to catch up to the rocktopi who hadn't bothered to slow down for the drama. Sonny and Ramiro hurried after.

It was obvious that Lybrand felt guilty about leaving. Too bad for her. Sonny wasn't going to feel bad for an instant. O'Doyle was staying to buy the life of his woman and, supposedly, his child. The others were staying because of some evil shit they'd done way back when, apparently. When they were twenty-somethings.

What the fuck did twenty-somethings know? Next to goddamn nothing, that's what. If they were staying to make up for something they were probably *ordered* to do, that was their choice. The wrong choice, but theirs to make. If Sonny held himself accountable for all the bad shit he'd done in his twenties and thirties—*forty fucking years ago*—well, there wasn't enough paper in all the world to keep those receipts.

Sonny lived for *today*. Not for things done in a different time, by a man who was, for all intents and purposes, an altogether different person.

Otto and Klimas were staying as well. Something about this being their job. What a load of garbage—what job description involved saving ancient aliens buried three miles underground from a hundred killer mercenaries? And yet, they seemed committed, in a way that Sonny really couldn't understand. They'd given him, Ramiro and Lybrand clear instructions on who to contact, how to contact them, and what message to deliver. Otto seemed to think the US government could make an instant deal with the Argentinians, then airlift troops in from Ushuaia, wherever the fuck that was.

Ancient aliens. Sonny shook his head. He'd seen that dipshit show on cable, a bunch of idiots who thought aliens had built the pyramids. Or at least he'd *thought* those people were idiots. If he made it to the surface, he'd never look at that show the same way again.

Soon, hopefully, he'd be out of here. In this big cavern, his claustrophobia wasn't bad. In the narrow tunnels and tight switchbacks that were soon to come, it would be so much worse. He'd have to endure it—Charlotte McGuiness's baby boy was not about to get shot, stabbed or sliced. Or nuked, for that matter.

Sonny studied the pair of rocktopi walking in front of him. He would never get used to the way they moved, like gelatinous starfish that could sprout as many limbs as they liked and reabsorb those limbs just as quickly.

He glanced at Lybrand. "You think these two will go up with us?"

She nodded. "As far as I understand."

"Then we'll be spending a bit of time with them," Sonny said. "We need to give them names. Your buddy Mullet seemed good at that."

She shook her head. "Mullet ain't my buddy."

Her voice was tight and level. She kept both hands on her rifle, as if she was ready to use it at a moment's notice.

"I'll name them, then," Sonny said. "How about… Slappy and Crappy?"

Ramiro pointed to the one on the left. "Is that one Slappy?"

Sonny shrugged. He'd picked two funny names, hadn't given a thought as to how to tell the aliens apart.

Lybrand tilted the barrel of her gun toward the alien on the left.

"That one has a diamond-shaped pattern. Make that one Slappy. The other's pattern is softer curves. That's Crappy."

As they walked, Sonny stared at the rocktopi on the left. He saw what Lybrand was talking about. When colors—bright yellows, soft green, pale pinks—coursed across the alien's skin, their shades shifted slightly when they passed over areas that were roughly diamond-shaped.

"I see it," Ramiro said. "More like a parallelogram, but I see it."

Lybrand said nothing.

The path curved, and just like that they were out of the orchard. In front of them, three square stone buildings built right up against the cavern wall. A gravel path, perhaps ten feet wide, ran along the wall and in front of the buildings.

Slappy and Crappy moved to the buildings, then stopped.

"What are they waiting for?" Sonny asked.

Lybrand sighed. "Don't ask me."

Ramiro started pacing. He absently waved his hands, as if shaking off a bee sting.

"We've got to get out of here, *now*," he said. "Those mercs are coming. Sonny, tell them to get us out of here."

The man was falling apart.

"Take a breath," Sonny said. "We're going to be okay."

Sonny heard a hum, and a sound so familiar it seemed out of place down here; to his right, the soft crunch of tires rolling across gravel.

From around the corner of another building came a thin, four-wheeled vehicle that seemed to be made of gleaming metal bars. It rode across the multicolored tiles on wide, gray tires. In the front of the vehicle, a glowing rocktopi.

The vehicle slowed, came to a stop a few feet away.

"Hell yes," Ramiro said. "We don't have to walk up? *Hell yes*."

The small vehicle seemed more low-slung go-kart than car. The bottom of the frame was only a few inches above the tiles. The top of the cart didn't reach Sonny's waist. No seats, just a slightly curved bed. The thing was made to carry perhaps four rocktopi, maybe five or even six if they mashed together and packed in tight. There wasn't a hard edge to be seen—it was all curves, a cross between a seatless dune buggy and a sculpture made of silvered glass, as organic as the rocktopi themselves. Sonny realized the tires were actually metal mesh; he could see right through them.

If he hadn't seen it rolling toward him, he might not have known it was a vehicle at all. For something that had four wheels and served a rather obvious, familiar function, he couldn't imagine anything looking as alien as this.

"Look at it," Ramiro said, as excited as if he was in a dealer's showroom, looking at the new Lambo he'd just bought roll into view for the first time. "What is that in the back? A trunk?"

The rear of the vehicle had a curved section, about the size of a toy chest. On its smooth surface, a handful of alien symbols glowed yellow.

The *trunk*, if that's what it was, gleamed, just like the bars of the frame…

"Christ on a crutch," Sonny said. "The *whole thing* is made of platinum. It's worth a fortune."

"Forget it," Lybrand said.

Sonny looked at her. "Forget what?"

"Forget thinking we can keep this thing," she said. "We will not do *anything* that might jeopardize Patrick's position with the rocktopi."

Sonny hadn't been thinking any such thing. Well, that was a lie. Maybe he could change her mind on the way up. Even if those curved bars were hollow tubes, there had to be at least two hundred pounds of pure platinum in the thing—it was worth three or four million for the metal alone.

The driver (it felt strange to think of a rocktopi as a "driver") flowed out of the buggy. It shied away from Sonny, Ramiro and Lybrand, moving slowly, cautiously. It must have decided it had enough distance, because it turned and sprint-flowed back the way it had come, a tumbling ball of light and legs.

Slappy and Crappy flowed into the vehicle, taking up the relative positions of driver and front passenger, although Sonny didn't see anything that resembled a steering wheel.

Bertha lightly kicked a curved bar that ran from the front to the back.

"Looks like this sucker has seen some use," she said.

Most of the vehicle had that soft, almost luminescent gleam that Sonny had come to expect on all of the rocktopi's platinum creations. The lower bars—bumpers, perhaps?—were duller, as if the bright sheen had been sanded away. Scratches and gouges lined the surface.

"Maybe it's a rough ride up," Sonny said. "That might explain the switchbacks, which we didn't see in Utah. The rocktopi here engineered a shallower angle for vehicles, maybe."

Ramiro ran a gloved hand along the frame. He looked at his hand—Sonny saw the dust on his fingers and palms.

"An alien ATV," Ramiro said. "One that's been sitting in whatever passes for a garage down here for…what…a thousand years? Looks like it runs, though. Thank god we don't have to walk—that incline would be murder."

"Reminds me of one of those moon landing carts," Sonny said.

Ramiro nodded. "Maybe going to the surface is like going to the moon for them. I wonder if going up there is as dangerous to them as coming down here is to us."

Slappy—no, it was Crappy—let out an impatient squeak.

Ramiro grabbed a bar, gave the dune buggy an experimental shake.

"Seems solid enough," he said. "They didn't have these things in Utah? Why not?"

Lybrand shrugged. "Don't know. We never will."

"As long as it gets us out of here, I don't really care," Ramiro said. He climbed in and knelt down in the back, holding tight to one of the bars that curved over the top.

Ramiro's eyes gleamed with selfish hunger. Sonny wondered if the man was thinking about Sam at all. She'd risked her life to save him, brought him help, rescued him from a nightmare and certain death, *then* decided to stay and help people she barely knew, and this guy seemed to have already forgotten her.

Sonny shook his head. The rocktopi weren't *people*. The idiotic sentiments of Otto and the others were wearing off on him. The sooner he got the hell out of there, the better.

He stepped onto the lower bar, then climbed in and squatted next to Ramiro.

Lybrand stood there, staring back toward the town, toward the obelisk that towered above it.

"Get in," Ramiro said. "Come on, Lybrand, let's go."

She ignored him.

Sonny felt bad for her. She and O'Doyle might have both been kissed by an ugly stick, but they'd found each other and were as tight as tight gets. No pretense, no artifice. They had a deep *I will kill anyone who looks cross-eyed at you* love, a kind Sonny hadn't known with any woman.

People make choices. O'Doyle had made his. Sonny couldn't

do anything about that, nor could he do anything about Lybrand's heartbreak.

"Unless you want O'Doyle's sacrifice to be wasted," Sonny said, "get your big ass in here."

She turned sharply, glared at him.

A flash of movement from the driver's seat—Slappy lived up to his name, slapping a yellow and green tentacle against the curve bar, *whap-whap-whap*. The message was clear—*time to go*. The gesture was so similar to what an impatient person would do it was spooky.

Lybrand stood there for a moment more, her anguish almost palpable, then she stepped toward the vehicle and climbed in. Sonny felt the frame sag slightly under her weight.

Slappy let out a low, long noise, more of a *hoot* than a *screech*.

The front wall of the middle stone house angled up, revealing a dark space inside. It wasn't a house at all, just a shell covering a tunnel that led *up*.

"Thank god," Ramiro said.

The vehicle drove into the tunnel, leaving the cavern, the rocktopi city, O'Doyle and the others behind.

70

THE CLIMB BACK up the tunnel to the City Cavern had drained the last of Patrick's strength. Going down had been one thing—coming up, another entirely. His chest hurt. The gash in his leg, as well as the blisters lining either side of it, burned, a constant reminder that he couldn't get at them through his suit.

And, of course, there was his back.

It felt like he had a billy club embedded in his spine just above his pelvis. He needed rest, but there wasn't time—one hour left in his preparation deadline. He had to make sure his people were ready to fight by then. If they got more time, they'd take advantage of it.

Patrick pressed his *talk* button. "Everyone report to the plaza, ASAP."

While Patrick was dragging from the climb up, Sam seemed barely winded. She was young and in great shape. That had been him, once, an eternity ago.

The woman had grown on him. He'd initially dismissed her as a coddled academic, but she was much more than that. Strong. Smart. Sam stood up for what she believed in, even though doing so would likely cost her her life.

That had been him once as well. An eternity ago.

They stepped onto the plaza's colorful tiles. No one there yet. Patrick got on his belly—maybe he could mitigate the back pain.

"You're in rough shape," Sam said.

"No shit. I'll be fine in a minute."

Which was bullshit. The only way he'd be "fine" was if he got off his feet and rested for a week or so.

Patrick kept his hips on the ground, pushed up with his arms, locked his elbows. He arched his back as far as he could. The pain ebbed, but only slightly.

Footsteps on the tiles.

He got to one knee. He almost managed to stand without a hiss of pain.

Almost.

"We shoulda brought a wheelchair," Mullet said. "I'd give you some of my Geritol, old man, but they're suppositories and I don't think you'd like those secondhand."

The rest of the team gathered. Mullet, Otto, Klimas, Sleepy. Three or four dozen rocktopi stood at the plaza's edge, most holding double-crescent knives, a few holding railguns.

"Tommy and Curve said their goodbyes," Mullet said. "I hope they get the little bastard."

"And the nuke," Otto said.

"Yeah, and the nuke." Mullet grinned. "Good hunting to them. They always were tunnel rats. I bet Curve puts that axe right in Angus's head."

Sleepy didn't seem quite as pleased. "You think there's any chance they'll make it back?"

Patrick answered by not answering at all.

"Yeah," Sleepy said, disgusted. "That's what I figured."

This wasn't the time to debate the man. What was done was done.

"Wait a minute," Klimas said. "Where's Lybrand?"

Patrick felt a fresh stab of loss, realized that part of him had hoped she had broken her promise and decided to stay here—stay with *him*.

But she, apparently, was like him, and was as good as her word.

"Bertha, Sonny and Ramiro are on their way to the surface, as Whitey promised," Patrick said. "I need updates. Otto, what's the count on working railguns?"

"Thirteen," Otto said. "It's a logical weapon considering their circumstances. No propellant charge that might break down over time, or accidentally go off. The railguns have almost no moving parts. Simple, effective, low-maintenance. There were eight more that might be repairable. Whitey had some rocktopi take them away. They must have repair facilities or a machine shop somewhere."

Hopefully some of them could be fixed. Every weapon mattered.

"Klimas," Patrick said, "what did you find?"

The younger man walked to the base of the obelisk. He knelt next to a small diorama of sand, rocks and dried branches. Patrick had been in so much pain he hadn't even noticed it.

"Gather around," Klimas said.

Everyone did.

Pebbles marked the cavern's roughly circular walls, gaps in it showing various tunnel entrances. Fine gray silt represented the city streets. Small rocks marked the many single-story houses. In the diorama's center, a tall, thin rock represented the obelisk. Crumpled, dried blue leaves marked the river—which entered from the northwest—and the lake that took up most of the cavern's southwest quadrant. Small bits of broken sticks signified the farmland that ran along the west side of the river, and the orchards at the cavern's east side.

"It's funny when you think about it," Sam said.

Patrick looked at her. "What is?"

"We just went from a holographic, 3-D map to literal sticks and fucking stones."

Mullet bent at the waist, looked down at the diorama.

"Good god, Klimas," he said. "And I thought Worm was a nerd. I bet you loved art class. Were you the teacher's pet?"

Klimas nodded. "If you ever saw my art teacher, you'd know why. There are a total of seven entrances into this cavern." He touched a fingertip to the pebble ring's widest gap. "This is the main entrance tunnel, due north of us." He pointed to the second-largest gap, at the bottom. "That's the tunnel to the ship cavern. The other five mark smaller tunnels."

Where he'd marked the tunnels matched what Patrick had seen on the holographic map, and what Bertha had drawn on the pad.

"I put two claymores up the main tunnel," Mullet said. "Some of my best work, to be honest. When we hear those bad mamma-jammas go *kaplooey*, we've got about fifteen minutes until the bad guys get here. Whoever or whatever those bitches send first is going to get fucked up right proper."

Sleepy knelt next to the diorama. "Those claymores only help if the mercs actually take the main tunnel. Could they use any of the other entrances?"

"Let's see," Sam said. She took her warped sketchpad out of her pack, set it down next to the diorama. The tangle of thick black lines stood out in sharp contrast to the warped white paper.

Bertha had drawn that. Looking at the pad sent a fresh pang of loss through Patrick's heart.

She tapped a heavy dark spot in the center of the paper. "This is the City Cavern, where we are now." She tapped a black circle. "This is where the mercs are — or were, about thirty minutes ago. The silverbugs are tracking the merc column. So far, they've stuck to the main passage. There *are* other routes they could take to get here, but they're narrower, tighter, and they'd take longer, to the tune of three hours, minimum."

Patrick's back felt a little better. Not much, but that tiny respite helped clear the fog in his head.

"I'm still certain that Angus wants to irradiate the shipwreck and the cavern it's in," he said. "Tommy thinks he'll put the nuke on a robot dog. We have to stop it."

Mullet laughed. "Stop a killer armored robot strapped with a SAW, while we're also fighting mercs that outnumber us maybe ten to one? Good times, man. Good times."

"There's a lot of open space in the City Cavern," Klimas said. "If the mercs engage us enough for it to slip in, I don't like our chances of being able to take it out before it finds the tunnel to the ship."

"We won't let it get in free," Patrick said. "I'm going to have Whitey move all the rocktopi to the ship. The city will be a free-fire zone for us.

We can do anything we need to do. The mercs either have to come in and take us out, or, like Sleepy said, engage us and try to slip the dog through. Suggestions?"

Klimas picked up two thin sticks.

"We could set up defensive walls here—" he laid one stick on the east side, halfway between the obelisk and the tunnel entrance, with the long side of the stick angled toward the opening "—and here." He put the other sick on the west side, a mirror-image of the one to the east.

"That's good," Sleepy said. "Overlapping fields of fire for anything coming out of the tunnel. If the mercs focus on one wall, we're pouring rounds into their flank from the other. We can put a sniper position at the base of that disconnected V, near the obelisk. But I doubt they'll be dumb enough to come straight in. They'll try to hug the cavern wall, maybe tie us up while they send the dog sprinting around our flanks."

Patrick reached for a longer stick—his back told him that was a bad idea.

"Klimas, hand me that stick."

The man did as asked.

Patrick used it to tap sand that represented the river and the lake.

"Unless the dog can swim, they won't send it west," he said. "The river cuts off one side of the cavern. The lake abuts the east edge of the city, which means if Angus wanted to send the dog sprinting down the riverbank, it could be under fire the entire way. Not to mention the dog would be potentially pinned in by silverbugs, something we know he wants to avoid."

A lot of assumptions, but they made sense. Unless Angus had brought in *multiple* warheads, he would try to send the nuke-dog along the safest route possible.

"So that cuts off the east side," Sleepy said. "How do we cut off the west?"

Patrick didn't have an answer. Neither did anyone else, apparently.

"Well, fuck," Mullet said. "You guys wanna play cards?"

Sam held her hand out toward him, palm-up—she wanted the stick. Patrick gave it to her.

"We use a similar tactic as the west-side plan." She tapped the stick against the east-side orchard. "We use the threat of the silverbugs."

"But you said he has those swarmbots," Patrick said. "Can't he use those to carve a path through any silverbugs we throw at him? And do we even know many silverbugs are left?"

"We do," Otto said. "Ramiro got that number from Whitey. Apparently, there was a big kill-off higher up in the tunnels. Whitey reports there are about a hundred silverbugs left. It was strange, though. Ramiro drew a symbol for the silverbugs, then the symbol that he thought meant *how many?* Every time he asked, Whitey responded by flashing the *human* and *how many?* symbols. Ramiro got frustrated, Whitey looked frustrated, but finally Whitey gave him the info."

At this point, Patrick could give a shit about the alien leader's odd, repetitive question.

"It might be enough," Sam said. "The swarmbots destroy themselves when they attack. Angus has to have a limited supply—there's only so much stuff those haulers can carry. When Tommy and I first saw the bots, they were in this thick cloud. After they killed the silverbugs and flew back to Angus, the cloud was *much* thinner. If we put the silverbugs in the orchard, have them move around fast, in and out of cover, maybe Angus will think there are too many for his swarmbots to take out. He might keep the bots back to protect the nuke-dog."

Patrick looked at Sam in a new light—her idea was excellent.

"Impressive," Sleepy said. "Use cover as an illusionary force multiplier. Ender, maybe you should put her in charge."

Sam smiled, pleased at the compliment. It was nice to see her smile. Maybe in the real world she did that a lot. Patrick hoped she would survive the ordeal to come.

"We'll put *half* the silverbugs in the orchard," he said. "We'll use the other half to do exactly what Sam suggested—we'll have them rush the dog as soon as we see it. Maybe that will get Angus to exhaust his red bots early. Anyone got a better idea?"

No one did.

"Then we go with that," Patrick said. "We're counting on Angus and the merc commander to be somewhat predictable. Let's say they do come straight up the middle. We have to defeat them head-on, but we also *have* to make sure we take out any robot dogs we see. They're fast, armored, and tough. We might not have the firepower to stop them. Otto, could the railguns damage the dogs?"

Otto held up a metal rod, about the thickness of his thumb and as long as his hand.

"This is what the railguns shoot," he said. "I believe it's platinum-iridium, same as the ship and most other metal around here. Very hard, very dense. You saw what the rounds did to the canoe hull. Without knowing what kind of armor the robot dogs have, though, I can't say for sure if these rounds will have any effect."

Patrick stared at it. A rod just like it had killed Skylark. And one had hit him — if he hadn't been wearing body armor, it would have punched through his chest and killed him as well.

Maybe the railgun couldn't take out the dogs, but those rods would make one helluva dent.

"Sleepy," Patrick said, "make any progress getting the rocktopi ready to fight?"

Sleepy shrugged. "Some. They don't function well as individuals. We need to use them in teams. We can't spare ammo, so I haven't tested their resolve with live-fire exercises. You saw how most of them fled when we returned fire from the canoe. Not that I blame them for running — their bodies are bags of liquid, and it's not like they can wear body armor, not the way they move."

Body armor. The way they move. A thought teased at the edges of Patrick's mind, but he couldn't lock it down.

"We'll figure something out," he said. "What else?"

"*Nothing* else," Otto said. "There's three of the big silverbugs, but that's it. No weapons on them. Turns out they're used for farming and construction. Basically, they're tractors with legs."

Mullet rolled his eyes. "The squidleys come from fucking *outer space.* No death rays? No teleporters? No *nothing?*"

Otto shook his head. "Ramiro pressed on that question, which Whitey seemed to understand just fine. No other weapons."

Not good. Patrick needed to find a way to leverage what was available.

"Sam, I need you to talk to Whitey," Patrick said. "Find out if the rocktopi can build new silverbugs. I doubt there's time to make one of the big bastards. If they can make more of the standard-sized ones, though, find out if they can give them weapons. And find out if they can make weapons to retrofit the existing silverbugs.

And … those swarmbots you and Tommy saw, how did they kill the silverbugs?"

Sam pursed her lips, shrugged. "I'm not sure. The bots land on the shells, seconds later the silverbugs stop moving, the bots fall off. If I had to guess, I think they drill through the shells, squirt something inside."

"Then ask Whitey if new silverbugs can have thicker shells," Patrick said. "Maybe we can get some that are swarmbot-proof. Can you do that?"

The look on Sam's face made it clear she didn't have the first idea how to communicate those things.

"I'll try," she said.

If anyone here could figure it out, it was Samira Jabour.

"You'll find a way," Patrick said. "I know you will."

Thicker shells … that concept tugged at a memory, but he couldn't place it. He glanced at the timer in his HUD — thirty-three minutes until his self-imposed deadline.

He stared at the diorama. The silvermechs were construction machines? That meant they could likely double as *demolition* machines.

"Klimas, start mapping out the defensive walls," Patrick said. "But farther back than you indicated. We're going to knock down buildings, create a longer, wider killing zone the mercs have to travel through. Otto, Mullet, you help him. Sleepy, keep training the rocktopi. Anything you can do to get them ready could make the difference."

Sleepy nodded. "What about you? You look like you'll topple over if a stiff breeze hits you. You going to sit your country ass down before you *fall* down?"

Patrick wished it was that easy. He felt so tired. Even a tiny bit of sleep could help with his back, help get him ready to fight, but every minute he slept was a minute the mercs came closer, the *nuke* came closer.

Thicker shells …

Body armor …

The way they move …

The parts came together in a memory of Utah, of fighting in the caves.

"Sam," Patrick said, "in the next hour, do you think you can teach the rocktopi to understand a few words of English?"

She thought, shrugged. "Maybe they can't make the same sounds we do, but they can hear just fine. You saw how Siren and Tommy communicated. If we keep things simple enough, I can try."

It wouldn't take much. If, that was, these "civilized" rocktopi could reproduce what their savage cousins had done.

"I'm going with you to talk to Whitey," Patrick said. "I need to ask him for something else."

ENLIGHTENMENT

71

14,311 feet below the surface

CURVE: "I OWE you, Worm. I mean it."

Tommy could only hear the words in his headset, even though the man was just a few feet behind. The constant din of fifty tiny jackhammers slamming against granite drowned out any other ambient noise.

"I know, Curve," Tommy said. "You told me twice already."

Curve: "And I'll probably tell you a dozen more times."

Tommy crawled on his belly, moving forward at a snail's pace. He had to be careful of the sharp stone shards beneath his chest, stomach and legs, and also the sharp stone jabbing into his back and his right side where he pressed up against the wall of the newly made tunnel.

The word "tunnel" wasn't quite right. This was little more than a horizontal fissure, perhaps a foot and a half high, so narrow Tommy and

Curveball had to drag their packs behind them and push their carbines ahead of them as they crawled.

Up ahead, reflecting the light of Tommy's headlamp, a gleaming mass of silverbugs mashed into the tunnel's dead end, a wiggling cork plugging a stone bottleneck. The silverbugs' angular heads pounded into the stone face, chipping off fist-sized chunks of granite. Needles of broken stone flew in all directions. The little long-legged machines squirmed over each other, on each other, around each other, all trying to find a clear spot of granite where they could hammer away another piece. The packed silverbugs reminded Tommy of baby spiders clinging to the abdomen of their mother.

On Tommy's left, the machines scurried past, some crawling forward to join the drilling, some moving back down the fissure, pieces of granite held to their wedge-shaped heads by curls of prehensile wire. The machines were moving the excavated rock, stashing it into various cracks in the strata or dumping it somewhere far behind.

Curveball: "I'm going to kill that motherfucker."

He'd said *that* six times so far. Tommy wasn't about to tell him to stop. He'd never loved anyone the way Curve had loved Hatchet. Tommy couldn't imagine what it was like to lose that.

"I know you want revenge, but I need to know you'll stay focused," Tommy said. "This isn't just about Hatchet, you get me?"

Curve didn't answer at first. Tommy kept crawling, a few inches at a time. The silverbugs coated the fissure's end. Granite dust covered their round shells and long legs, dulling their finish.

"Curve? You get me?"

Curve: "I get you."

"Good."

Curve: "You promise me that if you reach him first, he's still alive by the time I get there. He's mine. Promise me."

Tommy knew he'd have to find a way to control Curve. The odds of surviving this run were already low enough without the man doing something stupid in his quest for revenge.

"I can't promise you that and you know it," Tommy said. "We've got one shot at this. I need you sharp. Making this personal will cloud your judgment."

Curve: "*Fuck* my judgment. You know what, Worm? I'm going to kill that motherfucker."

Seven times.

A chunk of granite clinked off Tommy's visor, making him flinch. He stared at his HUD, waiting to see if his suit's integrity had been breached. It had not. If his KoolSuit tore here, he knew he probably couldn't move enough to repair it—the space was so tight that he couldn't turn over.

Curve: "Company coming. Oh, for fuck's sake, this thing is crawling right on top of me."

The *thing* was either Axl or Siren. The two seemed to be in command of the other eight rocktopi that had joined the mission. Would any of them make it out of here alive? Would Tommy? Would Curve?

Tommy doubted it.

But if they got the nuke, it would be worth it.

"Curve, Axl was the one that took you upstream, then carried you up that vertical shaft. You two should be cuddle buddies by now."

Curve: "Him wrapping me up on the river was disgusting. Him carrying me up the shaft was disgusting. Him crawling over me here is disgusting. I'm not in the mood for jokes, Worm, you get me?"

"Yeah, I get you," Tommy said.

Axl and Siren kept moving to the front of the new tunnel, checking the progress, then moving off to the other spots involved in the ambush. Maybe they were maintaining discipline in the troops, maybe they were checking hiding places in the fissures. Tommy wasn't sure, and it wasn't like he could ask them what they were doing.

Even over the incessant noise of the tiny platinum jackhammers, Tommy heard the hiss of dry leaves sliding across concrete. Seconds later, he saw hints of shifting colors playing against the fissure walls around him, reflecting off the curved silverbugs ahead. Then, Tommy felt the alien sliding on him, over him, solid yet giving, a creature of firm muscle with no bones.

Axl slipped past, tentacles gripping rock edges to propel him forward. The alien looked like he was swimming through air, a jellyfish moving effortlessly through a tube of water.

Axl seemed to check on the silverbugs, then, just as quickly as he'd come, he turned around and flowed past and over Tommy.

"He's on his way back," Tommy said.

Curve: "I wish that freaky fuck would make up his mind. How much farther until the end?"

Tommy wasn't sure. He had no map. He was relying on Axl and Siren to guide the silverbugs to the right spot. As far as Tommy knew, he was crawling toward nothing at all.

"We'll be there soon," Tommy said. "Just keep moving."

Keep moving toward the fight, hopefully.

Could they engage the mercs, take out the nuke, *and* make it out alive? Maybe. Probably not. Tommy felt the same jittery nerves he'd always felt before a battle, but this time there was something more to it.

If he died here, it would give some meaning to his otherwise meaningless existence. Nothing he'd done had made a difference. Not really. Dictators and warlords still ruled the places where he'd fought. The criminals he and the NoSeeUms had killed had been replaced by other criminals. The government he'd fought for had broken promises to allies, abandoning those allies to the enemies Tommy had once helped fight.

Nothing he had ever done had made a difference—this would.

And that would make his sacrifice worth it.

Silverbugs crawled past him, carrying away chunks of broken rock even as others scrambled forward to take their place.

Tommy Strymon crawled on.

72

THE CART'S SINGLE headlamp lit up the tunnel wall as the vehicle came around yet another switchback and swung wide. Sonny winced against the pending impact—the side rail ground into the wall, metal scraping against stone.

"God *dammit*," Lybrand said. "Can't you bastards drive?"

Maybe a flash of color or a pulsing pattern was an answer, but Slappy and Crappy made no sound. The cart once again accelerated up the tunnel, whisper-quiet motor driving mesh wheels over silt and rock.

"You'd think they would get better as they go," Ramiro said. "The longer we drive, the worse they get. Maybe they're getting tired."

Sonny didn't care, as long as they kept going. This tunnel was wider than the ones they'd used to descend from the plateau, but try telling that to the clutching feeling in his chest, try telling that to his pounding pulse and shortness of breath.

He knew—logically—that the tunnel wasn't going to suddenly cave in on him, that the sides wouldn't slam together and turn him into jelly. *Knowing* and *feeling* were two different things.

To make matters worse, the cart was not built for people. With Lybrand pressing up against his left side and Ramiro against his right, Sonny felt doubly confined. No room, anywhere.

He tried to keep his mind off of it by focusing on how Slappy drove the cart. There was a dashboard of sorts: a horizontal row of four glowing symbols. Two of the symbols changed as they climbed. Three simple joysticks sticking out of the center of the control strip maneuvered the cart. Push the left one forward to accelerate, bring it back to vertical to let off the gas, pull it backward to move the cart in reverse. The center one appeared to be a brake: pull it back gently to slowly decelerate, yank it backward for a sharper, harsher stop. The right-side lever was steering at its simplest—push right to turn right, left to turn left.

The cart accelerated up the tunnel segment. The mesh wheels absorbed most of the impact on rocks and divots, but not all. The rough ride was beginning to wear on him, one jolt after another making his old body ache.

Sonny tensed up as the cart approached the next switchback corner, preparing for another rough turn, but before it got there, Slappy pulled back on the brake. The cart slowed, then stopped.

"What the hell," Ramiro said. "Why are we stopping?"

Slappy and Crappy flowed out of the cart, their light playing off the tunnel walls.

"Get them back in here," Ramiro said. "We have to go."

Sonny and Lybrand shared a glance—he was just as annoyed with Ramiro's whining as she was.

"Get out and stretch while we can," she said.

She stepped off the cart, grimacing at pain somewhere in her body. Sonny did the same. Ramiro stayed in the cart, glaring daggers at Slappy and Crappy.

Sonny stood straight for the first time in an hour, his fingers digging into the small of his back, bringing a small bit of relief to muscles tight from hours of being crammed into the small cart.

He bent backward at the waist and made the horrible mistake of looking up.

The jagged ceiling … so *close*.

He was going to die here. He would never see the sun again. He was going to die in this tomb, this goddamn massive grave, he—

A hand on his shoulder made him jump.

"Sorry," Lybrand said. "Are you okay?"

Sonny could feel his racing heartbeat in his temples, in his eyes.

"Yeah, lady, I'm fine. I'll be fine."

She smiled at him, a sad smile of understanding.

"You will be," she said. "Very soon. We're halfway there. Just hang on."

Her words made him feel a little better, pushed some of the panic back down, where he could control it. They weren't friends, exactly, but they'd been through plenty together. Lybrand was as solid as solid gets.

"I know you didn't want to leave," he said, "but I won't lie—I'm glad you're here with me."

Her smile faded. She looked back down the tunnel.

"Do you think Patrick will make it? Him and the others?"

She was asking *him*? He didn't know the first thing about soldiering. Angus invented all kinds of shit. The guy was a genius. He was apparently wearing a suit of fucking Iron Man armor.

O'Doyle didn't stand a chance.

"Yeah," Sonny said. "I think he'll make it."

Ramiro slapped at the cart's platinum bars, yelled at the two rocktopi.

"Get back in, you assholes! Come on!"

The two aliens didn't get back in. Slappy extended a pseudopod toward the icons on the control strip. Just like with the suits, when he tapped them, light faded from the icons.

"What the fuck," Ramiro said. "What is he … is he *turning off the cart*?"

When the motor's soft whisper faded to nothing, Sonny realized that was exactly what Slappy was doing.

"We're only halfway up," Lybrand said. "Why would he turn it off here? Why not take us the rest of the way?"

Both Slappy and Crappy started flowing up the slope.

Ramiro awkwardly climbed out of the cart, rested heavily on his crutch.

"You alien idiots!" He pointed to the cart. "Get back in there and turn it on!"

Slappy and Crappy kept moving away.

Sonny's heart sank—he *was* going to have to walk the rest of the way. A mile and a half up that steep incline? With the walls closing in around him? He didn't know if he could do it.

Bertha put a hand on the cart's top rail.

"Why would they turn it off? It doesn't make any sense."

She stared at the thing, a puzzled expression on her face.

Ramiro quickly hobbled after Slappy and Crappy.

"Get back in the goddamn cart!"

He lifted the crutch, brought it down on Slappy—the metal pole squished a dent in the alien's body.

Sonny rushed to Ramiro, yanked the crutch away from him.

"Stop it, kid," Sonny said. "They drove us this far, we'll have to hoof it the rest of the way. Don't piss them off, not when we're so close."

Ramiro turned. His head tilted to the left. The younger man's eyes blinked rapidly—he seemed angry, confused and terrified all at the same time.

"Yeah," he said. "We are close. I can make it. We're almost there. I can make it."

He started up the tunnel's steep slope. Slappy and Crappy waddled after, Slappy apparently indifferent to the blow the crutch had just delivered.

Sonny followed them for a few yards before realizing that Lybrand was still at the cart, still staring at it.

"Hey," Sonny said. "What are you doing? Let's get out of Dodge, okay?"

She looked at him, that quizzical expression still on her face. She looked up—Sonny knew, instantly, that she wasn't looking at the tunnel ceiling; she was thinking about the surface.

"They shut it off so it won't be detected," she said.

Sonny looked at the cart, over his shoulder at Ramiro and the rocktopi, then back at Lybrand.

"Who gives a shit," he said. "Come on, let's go."

She looked at him, looked past him.

"They didn't want to drive any further up the tunnel," she said. "The lights in the ship cavern, those were off. And there were few lights on inside the ship."

Was she going to stay here and jabber all day and night? "Earth to Bertha," Sonny said. "There's this short little madman with a Napoleon complex in the form of a nuke. Your husband stayed to fight him so you could get out, because *you are pregnant*. Don't just stand there. Come on."

He didn't like the hard look that settled in her eyes.

"They are terrified of the race that was hunting them," she said. "That's why they turned off the cart and their suit lights. They won't take any chance that this close to the surface, even the smallest bit of tech might give off a signal that could be detected."

Sonny glanced over his shoulder again—Ramiro, Slappy and Crappy were almost to the next switchback. Sonny didn't like the idea of losing sight of them, not in this horribly tight space.

"Lady, let's go," he said. "Don't make me leave you here. Are you coming or not?"

She shook her head. "No. I'm not." She pressed her comm button. "Ramiro, get back here, on the double."

Sonny heard Ramiro in his headset: "Fuck that."

Lybrand pressed her button again: "Come back here now, or I will shoot you."

Sonny felt a wash of cold course through him. She wasn't playing, he could hear it in her voice, see it in her eyes.

She and Patrick both had told them about Veronica going nuts in Utah. Was Lybrand going crazy, too?

If so, she was the only one carrying guns.

"Take it easy," Sonny said. "Just take it easy."

Ramiro crutch-walked back down the tunnel. "Unless you fixed the cart and can take me up, we're wasting time."

"We're not going up," Lybrand said. "We're going back down."

Ramiro stared at her, dumbfounded. "What do you mean, *we?* Why would we go back down there?"

"Because I think I just figured something out," Lybrand said, her volume and intensity building. "All along, this place has been so different from what I saw before. They're smart here, they didn't suffer whatever plague hit the ones in Utah. The ship here didn't have a giant hole melted in it or a river slicing through it. Parts of it are functional, like the map room. The Utah rocktopi wouldn't go near their ship. It was forbidden by their religion or something—here, they have no problem going inside. All of that was bugging me, but I couldn't figure out why. Not until they turned off the cart. They don't want anything that might let some kind of detectable signal reach the surface. That's why the ship cavern lights were off, that's why everything there was dark. To stay as hidden as possible, they keep almost everything completely shut down!"

She was yelling. Sonny glanced at the gun hanging from her chest, the pistol at her side.

"So what?" Ramiro held up his hands in annoyance. "What does that have to do with anything? Why would you want to go back?"

She looked at Ramiro, then at Sonny.

"Because the ship here isn't like the one in Utah," she said. "It's not a wreck, it's just *turned off*—I think the one here might still be able to fly."

73

13,572 feet below the surface

DIMWIT KEPT THE company moving, and the fast pace was starting to take its toll—even on Angus, despite his suit doing most of the work. The men around him stumbled occasionally, showed other signs of fatigue. When they finally faced O'Doyle or the rocktopi, would they be ready for the fight?

A tough call: push hard and arrive hopefully before the enemy could dig in, or go slower and be better rested when the fight began. For once Angus didn't second-guess Donnie's decision; Angus had no experience leading men into battle.

Fuentes walked in front of Angus. Khatari was just behind, struggling to keep pace. Maybe his wounds were adding to his problems. Fuentes showed few signs of tiring.

Angus's HUD flashed a yellow alert—new information from the

BlackBugs. He blinked through to the new screen. Faint seismic vibrations. *Very* faint, but still there, still measurable.

He switched his comm to his private channel with Dimwit.

"Angus to Graham."

Donnie: "Graham here, go ahead."

"I'm picking up some vibrations, but I don't know what they are."

Donnie: "Vibrations. From us? Or from the BlackBugs, maybe?"

As if the physical fatigue wasn't enough, Dimwit had to live up to his nickname and tire Angus mentally as well.

"No, Captain my Captain, it's not us. I filtered out our vibrations hours ago. Nor is it from the BlackBugs—if every single one of them stomped at the same time, it wouldn't register at all. The vibration are coming from somewhere ahead of us, but I can't get a lock on the location."

Donnie: "How are you picking it up?"

"Through the BlackBugs' feet."

Angus briefly wished he believed in Jesus so he could ask Jesus why this man was so dumb.

Donnie: "What do you think is causing it?"

Angus thought back to Utah, to that shocking moment when he realized how hundreds of miles of passages had been created.

"It's got to be silverbugs," he said. "I saw them digging tunnels in Utah."

A pause, the kind of pause Angus had come to dread. Had he said something wrong again?

Donnie: "Doctor Kool, am I to understand that the silverbugs can dig *new* tunnels, and that you never informed me of this rather important bit of information?"

That sinking feeling—hadn't he told Donnie that? Well, maybe not, but wasn't it obvious?

"How, exactly, did you think the tunnels were built?"

Donnie: "I don't know. You said they were *ancient*. I thought it was some lost engineering project, like the Pyramids. You didn't tell me the machines could build new ones *while we were in here*."

Angus wanted to respect Donnie. He really did, but the man made it so, *so* hard.

"The silverbugs can make new tunnels," Angus said. "Let's move on."

Donnie: "How fast can they dig? How many feet per hour?"

"I don't know."

Another long pause. Angus kept walking, as did Fuentes ahead and Khatari behind. Angus wondered if they'd heard him talking, if they knew about his latest screw-up.

Donnie: "They're digging now. This means the silverbugs could potentially hit us at any time. Correct?"

"I guess so."

Donnie: "You *guess so*. And you can't tell me where these vibrations are coming from? How close they are?"

"No, I already told you that," Angus said. "I'll keep monitoring. I might be able to triangulate them soon, the further we go."

Donnie: "You do that, Doctor Kool. And please, if I may ask ever-so-kindly, how about you rack that big brain of yours for any other tiny details that might help us not get killed. I don't want any further confusion. Can you do that for me?"

The disrespect in his voice. The arrogance. To think that Angus had started to like this asshole.

"Yes, Donnie, I can do that."

Donnie: "Outstanding. Out-*fucking*-standing. Things are going to heat up very soon. Doctor, I need you and your men to stay with the payload, protect it at all costs. Understood?"

Angus fought back a sudden giggle.

"Sorry, Donnie, protect the *what*?"

A pause. "You know what I'm talking about, you little shit."

"Hey, no need for insults," Angus said. "I want to make sure there's no *further confusion* as to what I should and shouldn't do. I need to protect *what*, exactly?"

The helmet speakers made the older man's sigh sound thin, tinny.

Donnie: "Protect Dirty Randy's Money Shot. Can you handle that, Doctor?"

Angus smiled. Maybe annoying Dimwit wasn't the smartest thing to do, but Angus couldn't help it. Besides—it was fun as hell.

"Yes, sir," Angus said. "I can handle that."

The line beeped as Donnie switched to the main channel.

Donnie: "This is Captain Graham. Keep up the pace. Next rest is in one hour. Shake those tail feathers and let's move."

74

8,482 feet below the surface

BERTHA DIDN'T UNDERSTAND what was happening. If there was a possibility to save everyone, why wouldn't Sonny and Ramiro jump on it?

"We don't have time to debate this," she said.

Ramiro shook his head. "There is no debate."

It was all Bertha could do to not punch him right in the mouth. She waved at Slappy and Crappy.

"You two, get over here and turn this thing around," she said. "We're going back."

The two aliens swayed slightly, but they didn't return to the cart.

"The *fuck* we're going back," Ramiro said. "Are you crazy?"

Sonny shook his head. "Don't be an idiot, Bertha. O'Doyle gave his life for yours. Don't throw that away."

He wasn't coming, either? Maybe she'd expected more from him. If so, that was her mistake—the man visibly *shook* from his claustrophobia. Sonny could barely keep up a conversation, let alone fight. What was he, eighty?

But maybe she could still make him understand his best way out might not be to keep going *up*, but to go back *down*.

"Listen, both of you. I'm telling you their ship *works*, we can—"

"You already told us," Ramiro said. "Twice. We didn't agree with you the first time, or the second, so don't try a third."

What a shitbag. What had Sam ever seen in this guy?

"You don't understand," she said.

"Sonny and I understand just fine. You told us the ship was all shot to hell, remember? How can it work if it's all shot to hell?"

"It's no different than a modern naval warship," Bertha said. "Sure, it's damaged, but they can obviously seal off the damaged sections and keep going. The damage wasn't as bad as the Utah ship, I'm sure of it."

"I don't care," Ramiro said. "Sonny, do you care?"

Sonny looked down; he didn't want to be part of the conversation.

The coward.

She focused on Ramiro. "You don't care about saving Sam? You don't care about saving the rocktopi?"

"Sam made her choice," Ramiro said. "And the only real way to save this culture is to do what Otto and Klimas told us to do. If we do that, they said US forces will be here in hours. That's a helluva lot more help than Sam can get from us going back down there and getting killed."

Bertha opened her mouth to argue with him, but she closed it just as fast. Ramiro was right—going to the surface and contacting Otto's people was one way to help the rocktopi. But that help might not come in time, not if Patrick couldn't stop Angus.

If he couldn't, he would die down there.

She could get him out. She *knew* she could.

"Fine," she said. "You go up. You, too, Sonny. I'll go back by myself."

Ramiro held out a hand. "Give me a gun. We don't know if Angus found a way to this tunnel. Without you, we need to defend ourselves. You're supposed to be the badass that protects us long enough to get to the surface, remember? Weren't those your *orders*?"

He was right again. Patrick had wanted her to take these two men out, to take *herself* out. She had promised him.

Her insides felt like broken glass grinding against raw flesh. She'd always been a foot soldier, a grunt. It had always seemed better to let other people tell her what to do, where to go, how to act.

But if she wanted Patrick to live, she had to make her own call.

Bertha removed her sidearm holster. She offered it—Glock still inside—to Sonny.

"Give it to *me*," Ramiro said.

She shook her head. "He's more stable than you are."

"Are you shitting me?" Ramiro pointed at Sonny. "He's *shaking*, and you want to put a gun in his hand? No offense, Sonny."

The older man came closer, took the pistol from her.

"Thanks," he said. He looked at Ramiro. "It's better if I hold onto it. You're kind of a selfish little bitch. No offense."

Ramiro sneered at Sonny, then turned and hobbled up the tunnel, the bottom of his makeshift crutch kicking up little splashes of silt.

Sonny put his hand on Bertha's shoulder.

"Going back is the wrong call," he said quietly. "You know that, right?"

His eyes begged her to come with, but she saw that he knew her mind was made up.

"I know," Bertha said.

Sonny sighed. "Good luck, lady. Good luck to all of you."

He walked up the tunnel.

Bertha looked at the cart controls. It didn't look that complicated; she would figure it out as she went. Which dial had they used to shut it off? She spotted it, reached in, and turned it—the cart's quiet engine hummed to life.

Screeches from Slappy and Crappy made Bertha jump.

She turned, saw the aliens flowing down the tunnel toward her, pseudopods glowing orange and yellow, carrying them toward her. Slappy reached inside himself in that strange way the rocktopi had—the tentacle came out holding a double-crescent knife.

Bertha shuffled away from the cart, brought up her carbine.

"*Back off,*" she shouted, still moving away. "*What are you doing?*"

Slappy and Crappy both reached the cart, and there they stopped.

Bertha kept her weapon fixed on them, but she didn't need to shoot—their intention was clear.

"Looks like they don't want to walk back," Sonny said.

Bertha lowered the carbine. She wanted that cart. Did she want it enough that she'd shoot the two rocktopi?

No. She wasn't going to shoot them, they'd done her no harm.

Would that cost Patrick's life? Her own life?

Maybe—but that was her decision to make.

"Keep it," she said. She looked to Sonny. "Good luck, old man."

He nodded. "Good luck, lady."

Bertha adjusted her gear, then started jogging down the tunnel.

75

"WE DON'T HAVE ammo to spare," Otto said. "You sure we need to do this?"

The skirmish at the City Cavern river showed Patrick that the Rocktopi had never been shot at before. When faced with enemy fire, most had run.

If that happened against Angus's forces, it was game over.

"A bullet used for training isn't lost if that bullet keeps a soldier in the fight," Patrick said. "If we don't train them, they don't stand a chance."

He, Otto, Sam and Slash stood at the obelisk base, surveying the humans and rocktopi who had gathered for what would likely be the last exercise before all units moved to their assigned combat positions. Patrick had to make sure the rocktopi would do three things: follow orders, stand firm, and—no matter what—continue to fight until the order was given to retreat.

The Utah rocktopi had been less civilized, but they'd been far braver, charging into the face of murderous fire. Patrick found it ironic that he had taken a tactic from those aliens to use here, to teach the Fitz Roy rocktopi how to fight for their home and their kind.

A tactic almost as old as war itself.

Patrick remembered the shield walls moving up the tunnels, inch-thick metal blocking the fire from his Mark 14 EBR.

"We saw it in Utah," he said. "Silverbugs cut the shields and gave them to the rocktopi. It worked against us. Maybe it will work against the mercs."

"I suppose so. Just checking, though, that you *really* need *me* to get shot at to prove your point?"

Patrick nodded; a stab of pain in his back made him regret it immediately.

"Quit your bitching, Otto. Get with your troops."

"A goddamned shield wall." Otto sighed. "If this kills me, I'll never forgive you."

Otto jogged to the edge of the plaza, where a line of eight rocktopi hid behind eight rectangular sheets of platinum. The shields had been provided only minutes earlier. The fronts of the shields were flat and smooth, while the edges were rough, gleaming with the shine of freshly cut metal.

He watched as Otto gently took a shield from the rocktopi in the center of the line.

"He's brave," Sam said.

A statement of fact, yet her words made Patrick cringe inside. Otto was ready to lead from the front, while Patrick had no choice but to stay to the side lest he jack his back up even more. It was feeling better, but he didn't dare risk aggravating it—he needed as much recovery time as he could get before the coming fight.

"This is crazy," Sam said. "You're really going to have them shoot at each other?"

Patrick started to nod, caught himself.

"I am," he said. "This is necessary."

"I suppose so. *Ut est rerum omnium magister usus*, and all that."

He glanced at her. "What?"

"It's Caesar," she said. "*Experience is the teacher of all things.*"

"Where'd you learn that?"

"I don't know," she said. "I read it somewhere."

"Now you sound like Tommy."

She looked down. She knew as well as he did that Tommy and Curveball weren't coming back.

Two more deaths on my conscience. And they won't be the last.

"The whole scene just looks kind of Roman," Sam said. "You know?"

She was right. With the obelisk towering above, and rectangular shields resting on colorful plaza tiles, it did look like something out of a gladiator movie. Except for the squishy aliens holding the shields, of course. Patrick looked to the other side of the plaza, where a second line of eight rocktopi stood, holding similar shields. Behind and to the left of that line, Sleepy and Klimas crouched low behind a new berm of dirt and sand.

Three of the railguns had been repaired, bringing the total to sixteen functioning weapons. Patrick had divided them into two squads of eight. He planned to position the squads in the tighter confines of the city, between houses. If he could draw the mercs in, the platinum shields could keep the rocktopi protected in front while the stone houses protected their sides. The inexperienced rocktopi wouldn't last long in a fight against experienced operators, but with that kind of mobile cover they might be able to take out some of the mercs, reducing Angus's numerical advantage.

Unless, of course, those hauler robots carried heavier weaponry. A single recoilless rifle would shred a shield wall. A risk, for sure, but Patrick's instincts told him the rocktopi would only fight in groups—as individuals, they would be impossible to command. Most would run.

Would the rocktopi in the shield wall stay together, or would they run as well?

Time to find out.

"Tell Slash to get ready," Patrick said.

Sam pointed at the alien, then at a platinum shield lying on the tiles by the obelisk base. Slash picked it up, put it edge-down, the front facing the space between the two lines of combatants.

"Sam, you can stay behind the obelisk base if you like," Patrick said. "No chance a stray bullet can hit you there."

She shook her head. "You need me here, so I'll stay with you. The rocktopi need to learn how to operate in battle, and so do I."

The woman would have made a fine soldier. She was right—he did need her.

Even if human mouths were capable of making rocktopi noises, there was no time to even attempt learning to speak that language. Sam had succeeded in teaching the rocktopi a few key words of English. The rocktopi could speak those words no more than Patrick could speak rocktopi, but if the aliens knew what those words meant, that was what mattered.

Patrick, Klimas, Otto and the NoSeeUms had spent an hour giving the rocktopi a crash course on operating as a unit—how to fire and move; advancing; retreating; how to enter a building; how to move behind cover. Fast lessons. Patrick hoped it would at least be enough to keep the rocktopi from getting killed right off the bat.

"Slash," he said in his best drill sergeant voice, "prepare to fire!"

The alien let out squeaks and squeals.

The shields of both walls shifted slightly, long edges pressed together with an almost musical ringing sound. In Utah, the shields had probably been cut from the ship itself. Patrick didn't know where Whitey had ordered these cut from. The ship here? Some building or machine Patrick had not yet seen?

It didn't really matter.

Patrick stepped behind Slash. Sam was crouched down, totally protected by the shield, but Patrick kept his eyes above the top edge. He needed to see how the troops reacted.

Ammo was precious; they would only get one chance at this live-fire exercise. He hoped these rocktopi volunteers would do well.

He called out his command: "Fire!"

Slash let out a blood-curdling scream.

Thin tentacles rose up from behind Otto's shield wall—alien eyes acquiring targets. An instant later, railguns rose up. The weapons fired, their hammer-on-aluminum sound followed instantly by the clang of thumb-sized platinum rounds slamming into the platinum shields of the group across the plaza, or cracking against the colored tiles in puffs of broken masonry. A shield in that line fell forward, slapped down with a puff of dust as its holder fled, stretching out long extrusions and moving fast.

The stupid creature didn't realize that by dropping the shield it was in far more danger than if it had stood pat.

"Otto, *advance*," Patrick said, his voice booming across the plaza.

Awkwardly, Otto's rocktopi line moved forward, shields in front of them, most of their bodies hidden behind an inch of alloy. Flowing, glowing limbs took them forward five meters, then ten—in the center, Otto fought against the shield's weight to keep up.

"*Hold*," Patrick shouted.

Slash called out another command; the rocktopi stopped, their shields clanging against the clearing's tiles, railguns pulled down behind the protective arc of platinum.

Patrick looked to Sleepy and Klimas. He nodded.

The two men pulled their carbine stocks tight to their shoulders. With the efficiency of lethal machines, they fired single shots at Otto's line—a round smacked into the center of each shield, plinking off the curved platinum.

Two of the rocktopi dropped their shields and ran.

Sleepy and Klimas hunkered down, waited.

Now came the real test. The rocktopi left on the field of battle had taken fire while hidden behind their shields—could they press an attack?

Patrick pressed his *talk* button. "Otto, advance and take the objective."

Through his visor, he heard Otto roar one of the few words the aliens had learned.

"*Attack!*"

Otto and the five rocktopi still holding their shields raised them slightly off the ground, rushed at Sleepy's position. Tentacles lifted railguns high; the rocktopi fired as they moved forward. Railgun rounds slammed into the berm, kicking up sand and dirt. Sleepy and Klimas dropped behind the berm.

The rocktopi closed the distance. Klimas popped up again, this time on the berm's far right, and fired two shots—bullets pinged off shields. Railguns quickly aimed at him; he dropped down out of sight just before rods kicked up sprays of sand.

Otto and the aliens reached the berm. Patrick flashed a hand signal at Slash, who screeched a command. Otto and the rocktopi quickly formed a curved line, giving them some protection on the flanks. The railguns dropped down behind the shields, but a few thin tentacles stayed up, letting the rocktopi stay aware of their surroundings and any potential counterattacks.

The aliens had successfully understood and implemented commands from both a human and from one of their own kind. While there were only a handful of commands, Patrick needed to know orders could be given no matter who fell.

Sleepy: "I couldn't get off a shot. I was pinned down."

Klimas: "They reacted fast to my movement. I could only get off those two shots."

Sam tugged on Patrick's pants leg.

"Can I stand? Is it safe?"

He nodded.

She stood next to him. "They did good. Right?"

Patrick shook his head. "Three of them ran. A goddamn *drill*, and they ran."

They were out of time. With another day, even another four or five hours, he knew he could teach the volunteer rocktopi to be better fighters, or at least weed out the ones that would be more liability than asset. The lack of prep time frustrated him—with everything on the line, every little bit could make the difference between victory and defeat.

"I don't know," Sam said. "Didn't you say these people have never fought before? You see three that ran. I see thirteen that didn't, including the five that moved straight toward people shooting at them. I mean, I couldn't have done that, you know?"

Three days ago, Patrick would have dismissed Sam's comments without a thought. She was a civilian, after all. Untrained and untested. After spending time with her, though, after seeing the difference between her and Ramiro, Patrick found he took her words to heart. Maybe Sam was the tiniest bit Pollyanna, sure, but she was also right—some of the rocktopi were willing to fight for their survival.

"Don't underestimate yourself," Patrick said. "You could have left with Ramiro. You didn't." He put his hand on her shoulder. "You have my respect, Samira. Hey, where's Slash?"

Samira pointed down the street that led to the plaza. Slash blazed in oranges and yellows. He was screeching up a storm, slapping tentacles against a pair of rocktopi that quivered, flashed colors Patrick had come to associate with utter terror—those two had fled when the bullets flew.

"You should stop him," she said. "He's abusing that person."

Patrick had had men run before: what he'd done to them was far worse than what Slash was doing.

"Their culture, their rules," he said.

He glanced at his HUD. Time was up—they needed to deploy and do their final preparations before the fight began.

76

13,884 feet below the surface

THEN SHE PUT a figure-four leglock on my head," Fuentes said. "I swear to god, there we were, buck naked in a Phuket alley, covered in goat cheese and corn flakes, with, like, twenty dudes cheering us on in Thai, and she made me tap out."

Khatari grunted in amusement. "Would have been something to see. Except the part about you being naked, I mean. I got no interest in seeing whatever tiny thing passes for your junk."

"Shit, you *wish* you could see it," Fuentes said. "You're lucky you didn't die back there when we got attacked—I was going to send you off to the afterlife with a tea bagging. You know, two for the road."

Khatari laughed quietly. So did Angus. Khatari and Fuentes had been trading stories to kill the time spent in switchback after switchback after switchback.

In their life as soldiers and mercenaries, they'd collected many tales. Angus wasn't sure if the stories were true, or just bullshit, and he didn't care. Even for him, the tunnels had become *boring*.

Stories or no stories, he knew things wouldn't stay boring for long.

Angus was beginning to worry about his battery charge. The two remaining BaDonkeyDonks carried several spares, but with the extra weight they were now carrying, their own batteries were draining faster than expected.

He expected that, once they reached the ship cavern, he'd have to cannibalize the batteries and leave the BaDonkeyDonks, as well as any cargo they had left that the mercs couldn't easily carry.

When it was all said and done, all that mattered was keeping two things as charged as possible: Angus's suit, and whichever donkey carried Dirty Randy's Money Shot.

As a man of science, Angus didn't believe in ghosts. He wished, though, that they were real, that Randy still existed on some supernatural plane, and that the man could see the royal fucking Angus was going to give the rocktopi.

An update icon flashed in his HUD—BlackBugs had added to the map. He called it up, studied the new information.

"Guys, can it for a minute," Angus said.

Fuentes and Khatari fell quiet.

Angus keyed the private channel to Dimwit.

"Donnie, I've got more info on those fissures that are coming up. No sign of rocktopi in them, but some of them go back much further than a hundred feet. Considering how fast the rocktopi can move, even if they're way back in those fissures they can still rush forward and hit us as we pass."

Donnie: "How far ahead are the fissures?"

Angus eye-tracked through the map, spinning it this way and that.

"At our current pace, Goofy should reach them in about twenty minutes."

Donnie: "What about silverbugs? Could they come through those fissures?"

"Probably."

Donnie: "Should we send the SwarmStorm into them? We know the little bastard machines are trying to track us."

Sending the bots in wasn't a bad idea, exactly, but what purpose would it serve? The SwarmStorm's failure rate was a major issue—sending them into the fissures, even if they didn't find any silverbugs, meant a risk of losing five to ten percent of the bots for *nothing*.

"I think we should keep it in reserve," Angus said. "I'm sure there will be more silverbugs in the bigger caverns. We'll need the Swarm-Storm then, for sure."

Donnie: "Very well, Doctor. We'll be on guard. Those fissures are an ideal spot for an ambush. The rocktopi can't hide forever—sooner or later, the troops they have left have to come out and fight."

A map update alert flashed in Angus's visor. He eye-tracked, opened it.

"Stop your grinnin' and drop your linen, Donnie—found 'em. Get back here, you need to see this."

FUENTES AND KHATARI leaned against the BaDonkeyDonks, watching Angus and Donnie. Somehow, in the midst of this craziness, the two men managed to look *bored*.

"Well done, Doctor Kool," Dimwit Donnie said. "We have our next objective. Outstanding."

Angus had shared his map data with Donnie's HUD. Both men were looking at a color-coded LiDAR map of a big rocktopi cavern. Angus felt relieved to have finally found the thing.

"Buildings, streets, a goddamned obelisk, for crying out loud," Donnie said. "It's like a small city. Is the ship in there?"

Donnie clearly didn't understand how *big* the ship was.

"The ship is probably bigger than the entire city cavern," Angus said. "My guess is a tunnel leads from this cavern to the ship, which is probably another thousand or so feet below the city."

"Have you located that tunnel?"

"Not yet," Angus said. "Only one BlackBug so far that reached the city cavern. It's at the northernmost part, near the entrance that the path we're on leads to. The unit identified two other entrances so far—a river mouth, which we can't use, and one on the northeast side. That one we can't reach unless we go *way* out of our way, and we obviously can't take the river, so I think we're still limited to the main entrance."

"Is that the entrance to the tunnel those five BlackBugs caved in?"

"No," Angus said. "That one leads to somewhere on the west side of the city cavern, but I haven't seen that opening yet. I'll find the tunnel that leads to the ship, Donnie. Trust me. It will take some time, though—I have that BlackBug advancing very slowly, very carefully, so as not to be seen. If it senses *any* movement at all, it goes still. I'd bet my balls the rocktopi, silverbugs and O'Doyle's people haven't noticed it yet."

Donnie snorted. "I'd be careful when it comes to gambling with your nuts. With what you can see so far, is there any chance their doomsday device could be in the city, not the ship?"

Angus still wasn't sure there *was* a doomsday device. The rocktopi here seemed far more civilized than the ones in Utah had been. The Utah rocktopi had been dumb as fuck. So dumb that the silverbugs had actually seemed to be in charge. Maybe the machines had made the orb, or at least activated it.

Maybe, but that wasn't something he could risk. He had to assume there was a doomsday orb here. He had to knock it out of commission before the rocktopi—or the silverbugs, for that matter—could activate it.

"It's possible," he said. "But I still think it will be on the ship."

Donnie nodded. "Then nothing has changed. We have to get your bomb to that ship ASAP. How long until we reach the city?"

"At our current pace, about nine hours."

"We'll move faster," Donnie said. "We can make it in seven. Any signal from the five you sent up to block that alternate tunnel to the surface?"

"No. I'm certain they caused the cave-in. Collapses are hard to control even under the best conditions, though, so it's possible they were crushed by falling rock."

"Or it's possible they were destroyed. By O'Doyle's people, or the rocktopi."

"Yeah," Angus said. "I'm afraid that's very possible."

Donnie's mustache twitched left, then back to center.

"If they made it out, they made it out," he said. "That doesn't change our current mission. We move forward. As for the city cavern, I want you to pull your BlackBug out of there."

"What? Why? We've been looking for the big cavern for hours."

"And you found it," Donnie said. "I'm not taking any chance that O'Doyle's people will learn about that particular advantage of ours. That could affect how they plan to fight us. Keep expanding the map in other areas, but pull the BlackBug out of that cavern, real slow. When we get closer, we'll send in a whole mess of them so we get real-time intel on O'Doyle's positions before we go in. We'll find the entrance to the ship cavern then—it's not like the thing is going anywhere."

"But—"

"Just do it, Doctor."

Angus blinked tired eyes, wished he could rub them. "Yeah, okay."

"Outstanding," Donnie said. "Right now we need to be focused on those fissures. I'll be up front, you stay in the middle with the payload, and *don't* correct me on that name."

With that, Donnie strode down the tunnel.

"Boss," Khatari said, "what's going on? We got action coming up?"

Angus felt another sensation pumping through him—*excitement*. If the rocktopi attacked at the fissures, could he prove himself again?

"Yeah," he said. "I think we have a fight coming soon."

77

14,409 feet below the surface

CURVE: "MY SPOT'S almost ready."

His signal crackled, cutting out slightly due to distance.

"Copy that," Tommy said. "Mine as well."

Curve: "These murdering assholes are in for a surprise."

How many people had Curve "murdered" over the years? Seemed like he hadn't kept track. None of the other NoSeeUms had, either. The burden of maintaining a death-count seemed to be Tommy's, and Tommy's alone.

The silverbugs had finished their freshly dug passage with a conical indent into the stone, the point of which was a small hole that opened into the main tunnel.

Curve had a similar position further up the tunnel, although his didn't have an opening. When he finished there, he would join Tommy. Together, they would wait.

Tommy crawled backward, away from the cone-shaped indent, unspooling wire as he went. He worked his way around a thick bulwark of stone, into another tiny crawlspace.

"Breach charges placed," he said. "Running wire now."

Curve: "Same here. You think this will work?"

Tommy wasn't sure. There was no guarantee the mercs were still coming down the main passage. If they'd taken another route, this was a wasted effort. And if they did take this path, the timing had to be just right.

"There's a lot of variables," Tommy said.

Curve: "No shit, Sherlock. Just remember, Worm—when we breach, I get Angus. Got it?"

An undisguised threat in Curve's voice. He wanted blood.

"Worry about the mission objective," Tommy said. "Bomb first, then Kool. There's a lot riding on this."

Curve didn't respond.

Tommy stopped crawling. His weight on his belly and elbows, the spool of detonator wire still in his hands. Rough rock beneath him, against his sides, digging into his back.

"Curve, talk to me. We hit the bomb first. Cool?"

Curve: "Maybe you don't worry about your old pal Curveball. Maybe you worry about the glow-in-the-dark slugs doing their job."

Tommy was worried about both things. While he didn't know exactly what Curve would do once the fight began, he knew the man wouldn't run. The rocktopi, on the other hand, were a wild card. Would they stand and fight? Or would they scatter, leaving Tommy and Curve to do the dirty work?

"We'll hope for the best," Tommy said. "Get back over here. Be careful with the wire."

Curve: "I will. I'm going to kill that motherfucker."

Two men and ten rocktopi against a company of mercenaries and a guy in an honest-to-God sci-fi suit of powered armor.

Would it work?

If the mercs stuck to the main tunnel, they'd find out soon enough.

78

2,462 feet below the surface

A STONE THROAT, swallowing him down.

That's what the tunnels felt like. Sonny's headlamp lit up an ever-moving circle that sliced through the dimness. Up ahead, Slappy and Crappy continued on.

Just a few hundred steps up the steep angle and Sonny was already exhausted. If it hadn't been for the crazy go-kart that had taken them most of the way, he would have had to rest frequently during the ascent. It would have taken days to get out.

Another twenty-five hundred feet of ascent.

Sonny glanced at his HUD: *102°F.*

Did he need the stupid KoolSuit anymore?

He didn't, but it had become a second skin to him, had kept him alive when he would have otherwise died a horrible death. It had become a talisman unto itself, as powerful as that silver bracelet that he *never* took off. Maybe he'd leave the suit on even after he got to the surface.

Ramiro's voice in his headset: "I can't wait to get the hell out of here. I'm never going underground again."

Sonny could get behind that.

The crutch and the broken leg didn't seem to slow Ramiro at all. He'd gone up ahead, not waiting for the stumbling rocktopi or a claustrophobic old man. A dick move, but what did it matter? They'd be out soon, and Sonny would never have to see him again.

He'd never see O'Doyle, Lybrand or Otto, either.

Such was life.

"I'm putting up my visor," Ramiro said. "Oh my God, that's so much better. I'm keeping this suit, though—thing is worth a fortune. I might as well get something out of it."

He was worried about money? Pretty callous, considering. But then again, if the suits *were* worth a chunk of change, why not cash in on that? Despite O'Doyle's promises of riches, Sonny knew he wasn't going to see a dime from this operation.

Being sad for the loss of a friend didn't mean one had to take a vow of poverty or anything. *Not* selling the suit wasn't going to keep O'Doyle, Lybrand and Otto alive, now was it?

A man's scream—Sonny heard it in his headset and echoing off the tunnel walls.

"Kid? What's going on?"

The fading echo of the scream clarified in Sonny's thoughts—it was a scream of frustration rather than terror.

"There's a fucking cave-in here!"

Sonny couldn't see it, but Ramiro's words were enough to drain the last of his hope. A cave-in? Not now, *not now.*

"How bad is it? Can we crawl through?"

A pause.

"The entire passage is blocked," Ramiro said. "I don't know how much rock is here, but it's a lot of goddamn rock. Hey—" his tone changed, his volume dropped "—I think something's moving up here."

Ahead of Sonny, Slappy and Crappy continued up the slope, heading for the next switchback. Ramiro couldn't be more than two or three switchbacks ahead, otherwise the radio wouldn't work—and the radio worked well enough that Sonny heard a thin sound.

clack-clack, clack…

"It's probably a silverbug," Sonny said. "Maybe it's here to get at the cave-in."

"I never need to see another one of those fucking things again."

Ramiro sounded as scared of the machines as Sonny was of the tunnels.

"Just take a breath," Sonny said. "You're panicking."

Sound advice—too bad Sonny couldn't follow it himself. He wished he could talk to Slappy and Crappy. He also wished the pair would move faster.

"I see it," Ramiro said. "Wait a minute… it's not… it's not *sil*—"

A grunt of alarm cut off his words, followed instantly by another scream.

This time, a scream of pain.

Another.

And another.

Sonny drew his pistol. Up ahead, Crappy pulled a double-crescent out of his body.

"Kid, what's happening? Talk to me!"

Ahead of Slappy and Crappy, Ramiro came tearing around the switchback corner, hopping on one leg, his wide-eyed face splattered with blood that blazed wet-red in Sonny's headlamp beam.

Ramiro stumbled, fell hard, face-first in the tunnel silt.

There was something on his back.

Something *black*. Spindly like an insect. Twitching like a ravenous spider.

Four legs that seemed too thin to support the black baseball-sized body, legs that ended in a long, curved, single claw. The machine thing looked like a silverbug, only a little smaller. Smaller, but *meaner*.

From behind Ramiro, another black bug scurried across the silt, and two more moved along the wall, a blur of legs, fist-sized spiders coming fast.

Slappy stretched back down the tunnel, away from the danger, but slowly, hesitantly, as if unsure what to do.

Crappy stayed put, colors shifting to deep greens and dark blues.

The two black bugs pounced. Black legs folded back like those of a praying mantis, then snapped forward and drove down as the machines landed on the alien. Sharp points plunged through pliable skin—yellow fluid gushed out in streams. Crappy reacted, finally, did so with blinding speed, sweeping the double-crescent knife down—the blade cut through one of the black machines, sending up a cloud of purple sparks. The bug fell away.

The surviving black machine drew its forelegs back. They dripped with yellow syrup. The claws drove down again, drove *deep*, the fangs of a rattlesnake vanishing in flesh. Crappy collapsed to the tunnel floor, his soft body quivering, pulsing blue and black.

The bug drove its sharp legs in again and again and again.

Crappy lurched, drove his knife through the thing.

Knife and rocktopi alike fell still.

From behind the dying alien, in the headlamp beam, a flash of movement. Ramiro, crawling, crying, the black bug on him driving a long claw into his back over and over again, red blood and yellow coolant splattering the walls each time it came back up.

Ramiro reach out a hand for help.

The claw drove straight through the top of Ramiro's head, jutted out the bottom of his chin. In his open mouth, Sonny saw a gleam of red-coated black.

Sonny was sprinting away before he knew what he was doing. A distant part of him felt the shock in his knees of each hammering downhill step, felt the pounding in his feet. He came around a switchback corner too fast, caught his shoulder on the stone. He spun, thought he was falling, some deep part of him took over, kept his balance, straightened him, kept him moving.

Even over his thudding footsteps, Sonny heard the distant sound of death.

clack-clack-clack-clackclackclack

Distant, but growing louder.

Sonny realized the pistol was in his hand, put there by that same primitive survival instinct that kept him on his feet.

He sprinted around another switchback, glanced back, saw Slappy close behind, double-crescent knife in one glowing tentacle. And past

Slappy, three black spiders scurrying toward him, one on the floor, two on the walls.

Sonny fired three times, the muzzle flash casting instantaneous shadows on the rough stone walls, then he was around the corner.

The cart. There it was, facing up the tunnel as they'd left it.

Sonny holstered the pistol as he ran, jumped into the vehicle. He turned the dial he'd seen Lybrand turn—he felt the engine's slight vibration beneath his feet.

"*Sonofabitch,*" he screamed as he knelt down, grabbed at the levers. He looked up the tunnel toward Slappy. "Come on, you big—"

Two black spiders hung on the rocktopi, sharp legs driving through pliable skin. Slappy slowed, skidded, let out an inhuman screech that burned into Sonny's brain. The alien's stubby arm swung the double-crescent knife—a blade point punched into the black sphere, sending out a short stream of purple sparks.

The third black spider scuttled across the wall, sprang off it, landed on Slappy.

Black knife-claws punched into Slappy, over and over, again and again.

Sonny cranked the accelerator lever all the way back.

The cart shot backward, see-through metal mesh wheels crunching against the cave floor. Sonny had to look over his shoulder as he gripped the steering lever—the cart barreled backwards toward the next switchback corner.

Sonny cranked the steering lever to the left. The cart turned, slid. Platinum runner bars gonged as the cart slammed into the tunnel wall, throwing Sonny hard against the stone.

Spots of black. The cart seemed to lurch and buck under him.

The cart wasn't moving. Why wasn't it moving?

The impact had thrown him, made him lose his grip on the levers.

He looked up the tunnel—his headlamp lit up two black spiders sprinting across the silt, coming straight for him.

It took everything he had to look away from them.

Sonny grabbed the accelerator lever and cranked it backward again. The cart's rail ground against the wall, metal squealing as tires spun, sending up rooster tails of silt. Steer—he had to *steer*. He pushed the steering lever away from the wall. The cart cooperated, grinding free from the wall. The rooster tails dropped off—the cart began to pick up speed.

A dull thud, something hard but nonmetallic slamming into something made of metal. A squiggling spider tumbled into the cart, just to Sonny's left. It righted itself—Sonny gripped the steering lever too tightly, making the bumper rail grind hard against the wall. Momentum sent the spider flying to the rear of the cart, where it hit the trunk and spun over it.

Looking over his shoulder, Sonny angled the cart toward it. The spider rose up just as the cart ran it over. Sonny flashed a glance forward, saw the broken, twisted spider roll to a limp stop in the silt, then he awkwardly looked backward again, tried to time the next switchback corner.

He cranked the steering lever. The cart fishtailed around the corner, came up on two wheels. Sonny straightened the steering lever and the cart dropped back town to four tires, hitting hard enough to bobble his head like a child's toy.

Movement from above made him flinch away.

A black claw sliced a gouge across his right thigh.

Sonny threw himself out of the cart. He hit hard on the silt, tumbled. The cart slowed, ground against the wall, metal screeching.

He rolled to his butt, his old body screaming in complaint. His headlamp pointed down the tunnel, toward the cart.

Long black legs rose up over the dash.

The spider scrambled toward him.

An instant of utter calm surprised Sonny, almost made him hesitate.

Still on his butt, the spider's silt-speckled, red- and yellow-smeared legs a blur as it closed the distance, Sonny drew Lybrand's pistol.

The spider sprang though the air, front legs arcing back before switchblade claw-tips drove forward.

Sonny fired, his finger curling in fast-fast-faster, the muzzle flash a pulsating strobe light.

A burst of purple sparks blinded him.

The spider thudded against his chest.

Sonny scurried backward, one hand reaching behind him, the other holding the pistol, his feet kicking at the silt. He heard a sound, a cross between a whine and a scream.

It took him a moment to realize the spider wasn't moving.

Sonny stopped crawling. He raised the pistol—his hand shook so bad the weapon's barrel seemed to flop around, a life-and-death version of the rubber pencil trick. He fired anyway.

He missed.

The slide locked open.

He was out of bullets.

His ears rang.

The whining scream—he realized that had been his.

The spider didn't move. Not even a jittering twitch from one of the legs.

It was dead.

"Sonofabitch," Sonny said.

His chest heaved. Was he having a heart attack? His thigh burned. He looked at it. His pants, slashed. Blood staining the sliced fabric. Yellow fluid, too. For a moment he thought it was Slappy's blood somehow, but Sonny realized it wasn't rocktopi blood—it was coolant.

"Son of a goddamn bitch," Sonny said.

He tried to get up—his legs wouldn't cooperate. He tried again. The world spun, and he found himself on his back, breathing hard, a useless pistol still in his hand.

His light played off the tunnel ceiling.

The ceiling...so *close*.

The walls, so narrow.

His breath came faster, shallower.

His chest *hurt*.

He would never get out of there, he was going to die here, buried in a mountain tomb.

All he'd wanted to do was see the sun again.

Just one more time...

79

14,409 feet below the surface

SO CRAMPED. KNEES to his chest, crammed into the tiny crawl-space with Curveball and Siren, Tommy's joints kindly informed him he wasn't getting any younger. He wasn't as bad off as Ender, but still, his middle-aged body wasn't suited for a space that a child could barely fit in. Curve wore Hatchet's axe on his hip—the holder's hard plastic dug into Tommy's thigh.

In his time with the NoSeeUms, Tommy had participated in seven ambushes. Each came with different challenges, different terrain, different objectives. This one was no different, except that it provided the best defensive position he'd ever enjoyed—a good three feet of solid rock sat between him and his intended targets. He'd be protected from any initial retaliation.

So would Siren. Most of him, anyway.

The rocktopi's gray skin showed no light of any kind. If not for subtle movements, what seemed to be nervous reactions making tiny tentacles bud out and sink back in, Tommy would have thought the creature dead.

One fleshy extrusion stretched out from the crawlspace, around the thick stone bulwark, and jammed into the marble-sized hole that opened into the main tunnel. The hole was just big enough for one of Siren's little black eyes to peek out.

Close to Tommy's face, a small, dinner plate-sized flat spot on Siren's skin. On that flat spot, gray lines showed a blurry but decent fisheye-view approximation of the tunnel beyond the wall.

It was like looking at a child's pencil drawing—just enough detail to make out the shapes, to understand what the dark gray lines represented. A single rocktopi seemed to have lower picture definition, if that was the way to describe it, than two or three of them together.

Tommy marveled at the race's strange biology. What he wouldn't give for a book that explained it in detail. But there was no book. And if one was ever written, Tommy wouldn't be around to read it.

This was, more than likely, the end of the line.

He hoped his sacrifice would make a difference. He hoped Siren would fight well, maybe even survive.

The plan had several moving parts. Tommy, Curve and Siren were three switchbacks up from where the fissures started. Axl and eight rocktopi waited in the deepest fissures—Axl would lead that attack. Three silverbugs were slightly past the fissures. Those silverbugs were still digging, not to make an opening but rather just to make noise.

The goal was to stay quiet, let the mercs move into the fissures. Hopefully they'd focus on the sounds of the silverbugs chipping away at rock. When Tommy detonated the breach charges, everyone would attack.

No way of knowing if it would work. So much hinged on how the mercs moved through the switchbacks, on their order of march.

Tommy hoped to catch Angus completely off guard. Maybe Angus had a map, maybe he didn't, but the crawlspace Tommy and Siren were in hadn't existed an hour earlier. No matter what map Angus had, their hiding spot wouldn't be on it.

Hopefully.

"I can't see," Curve whispered. "Move so I can see."

They'd shut off comms altogether. They wouldn't turn them on again unless they were separated in the coming fight.

"Tommy, *move*. I'm crammed in here like a sardine."

The man was jammed up against Tommy's side, but Tommy maneuvered enough to give him a quick elbow—a silent way of saying *shut the fuck up*. They had no way of knowing what the mercs could or could not hear.

"They'll be here soon," Curve said. "I can feel it."

Just a whisper, but Tommy heard the bloodlust in his words.

Curve hadn't taken the hint. He needed to stay quiet. Tommy started to turn, to see if he could silence with a stare, when he saw movement on Siren's flat spot.

Tommy raised his detonator so that Curve could see it. He felt Curve pat him twice on the back—Curve was ready with his own detonator.

It was hard to make out the images showing on Siren's skin. The sketch view of the tunnel hadn't changed, but there was some kind of blur. Not *lines*, exactly, more like *dots*. Like … snow, maybe? That didn't make any sense. Was Siren panicking at the last second?

The dots cleared. Tommy saw more movement. Lines, this time, something coming around the switchback corner some thirty meters up the tunnel segment. One of the killer robot dogs? It took Tommy a moment to puzzle out the shapes the moving lines were supposed to represent.

No, not the dog—men.

A tingle flickered across Tommy's scalp.

Once again, it was time to break his promise to himself.

Once again, it was time to kill.

Two men. No, three. They moved quickly but cautiously. Why men, though? Where was the dog? So far, Angus had always led with the SAW-equipped, armor-plated killing machines.

The men stopped halfway down the tunnel segment, a motion that looked practiced, almost casual.

Back up the tunnel, the moving child's sketch showed a SAW-dog come around the switchback corner. Two more men behind it. The dog didn't seem as sleek as the one Tommy had seen get cooked at the river. A hauler, but it carried no cargo.

Now it made sense. The merc commander had mixed his units,

embedding the SAW-dog with a recon fire team. They didn't want their machine falling into a pit or being surprised by a silverbug swarm.

Smart. Very smart.

Now came the waiting game. Would the mercs see the tiny bit of black that was Siren's eye? Tommy doubted they would. The men had been walking in relatively uniform tunnels for *days*. Even the best-trained soldiers eventually suffered from optical fatigue.

Siren didn't need to go unnoticed for long. Only for a few more minutes.

Just long enough for the head of the column to move past.

One of the other haulers would be carrying the nuke. Tommy could only hope the remaining haulers were together, in the middle of the column.

That's where he would have put them.

He watched the lead men come closer.

He waited.

80

ANGUS FELT THE tension among the men. Very soon, the column would reach the fissures. Dimwit expected a fight. Everyone was on edge. With nothing going on, these tunnels were as boring as a post-lunch PowerPoint presentation. With danger pending, though, the caves here felt just like the ones in Utah had.

Terrifying.

Angus was glad to be in the middle of the column. If the rocktopi came sliding out of those fissures, they'd have to go through the three platoons of mercs to reach him.

He was starting to think that Donnie *wanted* rocktopi to attack there. Maybe that was a good strategy—kill as many rocktopi as possible before getting to the City Cavern. Or maybe Donnie was a dumbass and his strategy ideas were idiotic.

Angus preferred to believe the former, as the latter was too stressful to consider.

He'd sent a few BlackBugs deeper into the fissures; they'd found nothing. That didn't mean much. Aside from mapping functions, the bots focused, primarily, on movement. The rocktopi could be deep in those fissures waiting for the right moment to attack, staying very still, their soft bodies hidden under rocks.

Hiding with those railguns.

Hiding with *knives*.

Ready to rush out, to slice and dice.

Angus shook off the fear. Had he not faced a rocktopi assault head-on? Him and Fuentes and Khatari, fighting together, kicking ass and taking names.

Fuentes was two steps ahead of Angus. Khatari, two steps behind. A couple of badasses.

No, Angus most certainly did *not* need to be scared anymore. Wary? Yes. Cautious? Of course. Smart? Absolutely. But *scared*?

Fuck no.

Not in this suit he didn't.

Goofy was up with the recon guys. Angus had the Wolf's camera view in the HUD, one-quarter size and up to the right. A subroutine scanned all channels for activity, letting Angus listen in on the soft-spoken conversations between the mercs: Henderson calling out procedure for going around switchback corners; rearguard periodically reporting in; the various mercs reporting in to Donnie.

The machine learning algorithm had already made Goofy adept at integrating with the recon team, and Cujo with the rearguard. Machines and men moved together in almost total silence, as if they'd trained together for months, not hours.

Angus could sell that algorithm for a tidy sum.

If he made it out of this place, that was.

What was he doing here, anyway? The machine learning algorithm, his powersuit, the Wolves, the BaDonkeyDonks, the BlackBugs, the SwarmStorm, the ButterKnife … the things he'd invented for this endeavor alone would easily make him more money than any rational person could spend in a lifetime. In *ten* lifetimes.

Even if he didn't get the platinum, he could dominate the military sector. There was big money in weapons. *Hey, y'all, I gots me a powersuit that'll sell hundreds of thousands of units to militaries all over the world, take a peek at my sweet-ass prototype.*

Checkbooks would open so fast the wind would blow his hair back.

Would selling his goodies to armies galore make him as much as if he succeeded in killing all the rocktopi and claiming the ship? No, but he had to admit something to himself—this wasn't just about the money.

The firefight, killing the rocktopi, saving Khatari's life, the verbal sparring with Dimwit Donnie, shredding silverbugs, getting revenge for Dirty Randy, being a part of this mission…all of it combined to make Angus understand something about himself, something deeper than he'd thought himself capable of.

This wasn't just about money. Not really.

Three miles below ground, with monsters trying to kill him, Angus realized that his drive to acquire the ship had the same roots as his drive to invent things that others thought were impossible to make.

He wanted to do this because he was the *only one* capable of it, the only person in human history who could make it happen.

This was putting-a-man-on-the-moon shit. Building-the-Great-Wall-of-China shit.

Angus heard the beep of Dimwit's private channel.

Donnie: "Doctor Kool, how far is our lead element from the fissures?"

Angus kept walking, eye-tracked through his map. The icon that marked Goofy pulsed a soft green.

"Three minutes," Angus said. "Maybe four."

Donnie: "I'll send Goofy and recon through, followed by First and Second Platoons. Third will hold just outside the fissures. You stay right behind them. Keep Goofy in the rear with the Fifth and the Sixth unless I call for him. When we have the fissures secure, you'll escort the package through the area."

"I'm sorry, Donnie, escort the *what*?"

A pause.

Donnie: "Kool, we might be about to face an ambush. Men could get hurt. Men could die. If you want to find out what that does to my sense of humor, then you keep making jokes at my expense. Understand?"

A shiver ran up Angus's spine. No, this wasn't the time to make Donnie say *Dirty Randy's Money Shot*.

"I understand. Sorry. Sir."

The last word had slipped out, but this time, Angus didn't feel bad about it.

Donnie: "Give me an update on the vibrations. Have you locked in an epicenter yet?"

The BlackBugs were still picking up the subtle vibrations, which were coming faster now.

"I think so. At least the main source. It's about fifty meters past the fissures."

Angus heard the beep of Donnie switching to the main channel.

Donnie: "Recon, advance. Everyone else, move forward as planned."

Angus imagined what it would be like to be attacked at the fissures … blobs of mottled gray skin sliding out of those cracks, wicked knives flashing in the glow of headlamps. It would be worse than the fight at the shaft.

A thump on his shoulder: Fuentes, hard-eyed, nodding.

"We got you, bro," he said. He lifted his gun slightly. "They come at you, they get a taste of this."

Bravado, silly and cheesy, yet it made Angus feel better.

"Lead on, MacDuff," Angus said.

Fuentes moved down the tunnel. Angus followed, Khatari right behind them.

And, after Khatari, the BaDonkeyDonk that carried Dirty Randy's Money Shot.

81

14,409 Feet below the surface

THE MERCS MOVED in ten-man platoons, each platoon about forty meters behind the one in front of it. Give or take. Enough room so that a tunnel segment had only one group of ten men at a time. Smart.

Two platoons had already followed the recon squad down the tunnel. On Siren's skin, Tommy was watching a third—four of the men in that platoon had already passed by his position. Six more, and he would see what came next.

Angus?

The haulers?

Tommy's heart kicked. The tingle of an adrenaline surge. He felt ashamed; promises to himself or no, hunting armed men brought forth a rush like no other.

The fifth man stepped past. Tommy saw his face in profile, ballcap tight over KoolSuit hood and mask.

The men in this platoon should have had more space between them. They were bunching up. Getting sloppy. Experienced guys, sure, but a far cry from the best of the best.

The sixth merc passed by—four more to go.

Up the tunnel, at the switchback corner, more movement. One merc, then, *Angus Kool.*

Siren's child-sketch version of Angus, anyway, but there was no mistaking the blocky, dark armor. He was thirty meters behind the platoon still passing by in front of Tommy's position. A merc came around the corner right behind Angus, this one wearing a tan turban instead of a combat helmet or ballcap. Behind that merc came two haulers, their backs and sides stacked with slim plastic crates.

The nuke… it had to be in one of those cases. Tommy was going to get Angus *and* the bomb.

Come on, assholes, just a little closer…

The seventh merc passed by. Three more in that platoon, then Angus would close in.

Almost there…

The eighth merc passed by, then stopped, turned. Tommy didn't see this face in profile—he saw *both* of the man's eyes. The lines sharpened slightly, as if the man was looking directly into a camera.

Even in the sketch-like image, the man was close enough that Tommy saw his lips, saw him mouthing words: *What is that thing?*

Tommy yanked on Siren. The alien's extrusion shot around the bulwark, back into the fleshy gray body.

Tommy triggered his detonator.

THE RIGHT-SIDE WALL exploded outward in a shower of flame and broken stone. Angus had a split-second image of the men of Third Platoon being slammed against the left wall, then they vanished in a cloud of smoke and dust that filled the tunnel, billowed toward Angus like a raging tornado.

"*Get down,*" Fuentes screamed.

Angus thought he saw Fuentes diving to the silty tunnel floor, but the swirling haze instantly blocked all sight.

Angus stood there, frozen, for what could have been one second, what could have been one hour.

The roar of another explosion, but from behind rather than in front. This one was more muted, the sound dampened by the switchback corner. An instant later, the echoing, heavy *clinks* and *tonks* of rock falling, bouncing, rolling.

The dust and smoke thickened. Looking out his visor was like looking out a car window in a white-out blizzard.

A palm slapped his armored shoulder.

"Boss," Khatari said, "*get the fuck down.*"

Khatari knelt, hunched down small, his rifle in his hands. Angus knelt, too, not knowing what else to do.

What was happening? Did the rocktopi have explosives? Or was it O'Doyle's men? There shouldn't have been an attack here, *couldn't* have been—there were hundreds of feet of solid rock all around.

Questions and answers and orders flew across the comm lines. Angus couldn't process any of it; the words were gibberish drowned out by screams of agony and calls for help.

Fuentes was in front of him, also on one knee. Only a few feet away, yet Angus could barely see him through the dust and smoke.

"Captain, this is Fuentes, we're under attack. Unknown forces breached the walls, ahead of us and possibly behind. Casualties in Third Platoon."

Donnie: "Second platoon is under attack at the fissures. Recon, First Platoon, fall back to help them. Fifth move forward with Cujo and protect the payload. Sixth, guard our rear."

The *payload*? Angus needed them to come up and protect *him*.

A new voice: "This is Wheeler, rearguard. A bomb collapsed part of the tunnel. We're trying to clear space for Cujo now."

A chill washed over Angus—a cave-in behind, enemies possibly in front. He was trapped here. He needed Cujo's firepower.

Donnie: "Fuentes, Kool, Khatari, protect the payload at all costs."

"Khatari, Angus, get ready to fight."

Fight? But with who? The rocktopi? Silverbugs? O'Doyle? Too much was happening at once. Angus couldn't get his head straight.

The ButterKnife…Angus could use that to clear the cave-in back up the tunnel. But what if there were more bombs? What if the tunnel ceiling caved in on top of him? He could be buried here, the ButterKnife buried along with him. If that happened, he'd need the BlackBugs and their pneumatic drivers to cut him free.

No smoke inside his helmet—he could see his HUD readout just fine. He blinked in rapid-fire movements, switched to voice commands.

"All BlackBugs, converge on Cujo, help clear the cave-in. Cujo as soon as you're clear, come to me."

Angus switched to night vision, but the thick dust made it useless. He switched it off.

O'Doyle had trapped him here, cut him off from support. O'Doyle was coming, that giant man with his hateful eyes, his scarred face…

…and his knife.

"Fuentes," Angus said, "we need to get the ButterKnife out and cut a hole so Cujo can get free and—"

"Not yet," Fuentes said, his voice sharp, dominant. "They breached the wall in front of us. They're coming and we won't show them our backs. Protect the payload, that's our job."

Noise and smoke. The cries of the wounded. The confusion. All of it slipped to a lower tier in Angus's thoughts. Fuentes made it so simple: *that's our job.* Angus wasn't helpless. He wasn't a liability—he was part of this unit.

Fuentes dropped to his belly, aimed his rifled down the smoke-filled tunnel. Angus glanced back up the tunnel. Khatari, a few feet away, and just past him, the two BaDonkeyDonks, standing perfectly still, like statues in a smoke-strangled battlefield.

Angus's body shook. He focused, made himself relax. With a deep, ragged breath, he dropped to one knee and stared past Fuentes into the dust and smoke.

TOMMY DROPPED HIS knee onto the wounded man's chest. Smoke and dust everywhere, so thick, but when Tommy slid his knife into the merc's throat, he saw the man's eyes widen in surprise.

The merc blinked once, twice, then stared up. Tommy saw his life fade away.

Kill number thirty-two.

The breach blast killed four of the mercenaries. They lay there, bodies broken, shards of granite sticking out of them like they were pincushions.

Tommy heard a rocktopi squeal, then a wet gurgle as Siren killed another of the wounded.

Through the smoke, Curveball came closer, a bloody knife in his hand. He holstered it, gripped his carbine, knelt next to Tommy.

They'd had to detonate early, but it wasn't a disaster. Curve's charge had been planted one switchback up, in the tunnel ceiling, meant to cause at least some degree of cave-in. If it had worked, it would block the next platoon back from coming to Angus's aid. If it hadn't caused a collapse, hopefully the debris would slow those mercs down long enough for Tommy and Curve to get the haulers.

Long enough to take out the nuke.

Decision time. No wind, no breeze to take away the haze of swirling dust. Mercs somewhere higher up the tunnel, and somewhere further down—Tommy, Curve and Siren were between significant enemy forces.

The hole they had just made was the only way out of here.

Curve reached out, tapped the V40 grenade hanging from Tommy's webbing, tilted his head up the tunnel. They could throw a grenade into the smoke, hope to take out Angus and the two men marching with him, but Tommy couldn't see them—if he threw a grenade and the trio had already moved back, that grenade would be wasted.

If only Angus and the dogs had been closer. The blast would have taken them all out. Wishful thinking. The enemy and their nuke were somewhere further up the tunnel, hidden by the smoke.

Siren slid out of the haze, waited just behind Tommy and Curve. Maybe the rocktopi wasn't a seasoned warrior, but he was *here*. He hadn't run.

Tommy tapped Curve's carbine, pointed upslope, toward where Angus and the haulers had to be.

Curve nodded.

Tommy shouldered his carbine, fired a three-shot burst up the tunnel. As he did, Curve ran at a crouch, following the left-hand wall. Curve took a knee and raised his own carbine. Tommy was already moving along the right-hand wall when Curve fired his first three-shot burst.

TREMBLING INSIDE HIS suit, Angus hunched low, pushed himself against the wall to his right as if he might melt into the stone and disappear. The dust was thinning, but he still couldn't see shit.

Gunfire from down the tunnel. He winced as a bullet struck the stone wall just in front of him—a granite chip cracked off his visor.

"They're leapfrogging," Khatari said. "Coming right at us."

Fuentes: "Anyone forward of Doctor Kool, hit the deck. We're firing your way in three, two, one…"

TOMMY SLID TO a stop, dropped to one knee, fired three rounds.

Was that a shape in the smoke ahead?

He aimed at it.

The bark of automatic fire, flashes lighting up the haze like lighting bursts in a storm cloud. He ducked, tried to make himself smaller.

A *crack*, the loudest sound Tommy had ever heard, a searing pain across his cheek, another in his left arm. His ears rang. He felt himself wobbling, couldn't stop himself. The tunnel floor shifted beneath him.

Powerful snakes wrapped around his chest, yanked him backward.

Bullets ripped across the stone where his head had just been.

Disoriented. The tunnel, spinning, or was that the smoke? Spiderweb cracks in his visor. No icons, no lights. Was his HUD dead? What was wrapped around him?

Siren. The rocktopi had pulled him down, saving his life.

Familiar-sounding gunfire, in short bursts—Curveball, nearby, protecting him, firing away.

Tommy grabbed his carbine, rolled to his stomach, spun in place, fired bursts up the tunnel. The enemy continued to fire back.

A blind firefight in a narrow stone tunnel. It was no good—they couldn't advance.

"I'm hit," Tommy said. "We've got to fall back! I'll cover you, get to the breach!"

Tommy glanced left, saw Curveball on his belly.

The two men locked eyes. Tommy knew, instantly, that Curve would not run. He was going to kill Angus Kool, here and now, or he would die trying.

The smallest of smiles.

Curve shrugged off his carbine. He got to one knee, even as bullets kissed the walls, ceiling and silt around him. Staying low, he yanked the axe out of its holster and drew his sidearm.

"Don't want to live without Carson," he said. "Whether I get Angus and the bomb or not, I ain't coming back. I love you, my brother. Make 'em duck for me, then get to the breach and get back to the others."

Even if there had been time to try and stop him, Tommy knew there was no point. For Curve, it would end here, now, one way or another.

Curve hopped up, rushed forward at a crouch.

Tommy fired three short bursts, then three more, then three more as the dust and smoke swallowed Anders "Curveball" Keeley.

An instant. An eternity. Tommy's face felt hot. A hole, somewhere, in his visor, in his arm, maybe both. The heat, forcing its way in. He had to get out of there, patch the holes, or he'd die.

He glanced back at Siren. The rocktopi remained gray, a blood-smeared double-crescent knife in one thick pseudopod. Tommy felt Siren looking back at him, and in that frozen moment, felt something even deeper, a silent understanding between warriors that superseded culture, concept, or even species.

Siren was ready.

Less than two seconds after Curve vanished into the smoke, Tommy rose and rushed forward.

BULLETS WHIZZED UP the tunnel, bounced off stone, seemed to be everywhere all at once. Angus felt stone shards clatter against his helmet.

Khatari fired on auto, short bursts angled left, then right, then down.

From the smoke, answering flashes—closer than they'd been before.

Some insane fucker was *charging*?

Angus lifted his arm, tilted his hand down, felt the Atchisson's kick all the way through his shoulder. He fired again, and again, a fourth time, not sure if he was even aiming.

Something hit his chest, hammer-hard, the blow reverberating through his back and shoulder.

Pain. Numbness.

Had he been shot?

A *crack* as loud as God, *inside* his helmet, so sudden and deafening his ears rang—but not so much he didn't hear the instant alarm: a hole in his KoolSuit.

Jesus Fucking Christ… he'd been shot *twice?*

His brain wouldn't work. He couldn't process any of it. What had he been thinking? He was a tinkerer, an inventor, not a goddamn *soldier.*

Dead. He was dead.

Another flash from the smoke, even closer than before.

Fuentes grunted. "I'm hit!"

Well, shit, he was shot, too.

And **YOU** *get a bullet and* **YOU** *get a bullet and* **YOU** *get a bullet, and everyone gets a bullet!*

"We're being overrun," Khatari said. "Angus, order the payload to retreat! Fuentes, go with them!"

Angus couldn't form a thought of his own, so like a puppet responding to yanked strings, he seized on Khatari's order.

"BaDonkeyDonks Three and Four, retreat up the tunnel. Get to the rearguard."

Did his inventions know the term *rearguard?* He wasn't sure.

Both donkeys took off, though, galloping up the smoky tunnel. Fuentes scrambled to his feet, sprinted after them, clutching at his shoulder. In seconds, human and machines alike vanished behind a switchback corner.

Wait a minute… Angus should be going with them, away from the bullets. What the—

Something thudded into his back. He'd been shot *again?*

He was going to die down here; he had to shoot back, kill the people trying to kill him, he had to *fight—he had to fight…*

Angus turned, raised his right arm.

In the thinning smoke, a man, sprinting forward, firing a pistol.

In his other hand, an axe.

Oh fuck this shit fuck all of it I want out of here I want out of here…

Through a visor Angus had invented, he saw the man's sweaty black skin, saw his gray beard, saw eyes that blazed with *hate,* with pure, murderous evil.

Angus tried to raise his arm. It moved in slow motion, as if he was an ancient machine with centuries of rust coating his joints.

The man fired at Angus, muzzle flash bright in the haze.

Angus felt another *thud*, this time in his stomach.

Time froze.

He had to shoot to live but his arm was so slow, why was it *so slow?* The man was aiming for Angus's face — *his face* — Angus wasn't fast enough …

More gunfire, but from behind — Khatari stepped forward, rifle tight to his shoulder, firing.

The two men shot at each other, fifteen feet apart and closing.

Khatari flinched, stumbled, kept firing.

The attacker twitched twice, as if stung by bees. He dropped his gun, turned his shoulders as he ran, twisted and *threw* — something long whizzed though the air, end over end.

The axe blade *thonked* into Yadav Khatari's head, slicing through turban, visor, KoolSuit, skin and skull alike. He fell, a limp thing, dead before he slammed against the silt and skidded to a stop.

And YOU get an axe in the head!

Angus almost laughed at the crazy thoughts flashing in his head, but he couldn't laugh. He couldn't move at all. Fear locked him in place, drilled his feet into the tunnel floor, froze every circuit in his suit.

The alarm blared in his ears, yet it sounded distant, like a TV playing in another room.

The man ran toward him.

He looked into Angus's eyes.

The man smiled the smile of the devil.

Angus found out that one part of him, at least, still worked.

His bladder let go.

TOMMY FELT HOT air in his lungs, draining his strength.

He felt weak, sapped of all energy.

Tommy willed his body to move faster — his body refused to comply. His feet slid through the silt, each step a dragging chore.

Up ahead, through the smoke, Tommy saw Curve stop, put his foot on a body, then reach down and yank.

He came up with the axe in his hand.

Right in front of him, Angus Kool.

The haulers, the mission objective, the *nuke*—gone.

Tommy had failed.

He tried to raise his carbine. It felt so heavy, an anvil of solid iron.

His foot caught on a hidden bit of rock. He stumbled, started to fall.

Siren caught him.

ANGUS FELT PARALYZED, as if he was spun up and bound in a spider silk nightmare.

The man held the axe in his right hand. Khatari's blood—and maybe a little of his brains?—dripped from the blade.

"Fuck you," the man said.

One hand on the end of the axe handle, the other halfway up, he swung the bloody blade at Angus's head. The blade—like Angus's arm had done—seemed to move in a slow-motion blur of death.

Angus's eyes slammed shut before the blow struck home.

His head rocked back and to the side. The gong-like impact snapped his eyes open. He saw the axe bouncing up, a rebound that smacked it against the tunnel ceiling.

The man's lip curled into a twisted sneer.

He seemed to understand that Angus could not move. He seemed to know that terror had driven into Angus as deep as the poison of a rattlesnake.

"I guess you really are bulletproof," the man said. His hands twisted, turning the axe. "Let's see if the spike works."

Maybe the blade hadn't penetrated, but Angus knew that the heavy, thick spike on the back of the axe head would.

What a horrible way to die.

"Bye-bye, motherfucker," the man said.

From behind him, Angus heard the whine of servos.

The man turned his shoulders, reared back with the axe, then stepped forward to swing like a homerun hitter teeing off on a fastball.

Frozen by fear, Angus still twitched when Cujo's SAW roared.

Bullets tore the man's chest, puffs of dust kicking up out of his camo jacket as each one struck home. Ten? Twenty? The man shook, seemed to try to take a step away—he turned to his left and fell, the axe slipping from his grip.

*   *   *

TOMMY STRYMON knew death.

When he heard the SAW open up, when he saw puffs of blood erupt from Curveball's back, when he saw the man hit the tunnel floor, he knew his friend was gone. Curve's right hand stuck up, the arm stiff, his fingers curled as if they thought they were still holding the hatchet.

Analysis and decisions made in a fraction of a second:

Angus, in a suit of armor.

Just past him, the four-legged killing machine.

No cargo on that robot—no sign of the nuke.

Curveball, dead.

Tommy grabbed one of the two V40 grenades hanging from his webbing.

He pulled the pin as he turned and ran, tossing the grenade over his shoulder, hoping that Siren could also make split-second decisions, that the alien would be smart enough to follow Tommy and get the fuck out of there.

ANGUS INHALED SHARPLY, managed a half-breath before his lungs locked up again. New dust in the air, and in it, a slight reddish mist.

Through the mist, he saw a man and a rocktopi, running away down the tunnel.

"Cujo, attack the two targets in fro—"

A sharp *bang* that would have been deafening if not for his helmet, and in that same instant, sharp *clinks* of something hit his armor, as though someone had thrown a handful of gravel at him.

A grenade?

He waited for the pain, waited for his body to tell him about the holes in his skin, his muscle.

But…nothing.

He raised his right arm, looked for a target, but a new cloud of smoke and dust obscured everything down the tunnel.

Angus eye-tracked through his HUD, took control of Cujo.

"Sic 'em, boy."

The machine took off, long legs propelling the thin body down the tunnel and into the cloud of dust.

TOMMY THREW HIMSELF into the hole. Jagged rock ground at his fatigues, at the KoolSuit gloves. The breach charge had opened up a big hole, but that hole rapidly narrowed to the coffin-sized tunnel the silverbugs had chiseled out of the rock.

He had no chance against that machine.

The sound of dry leaves scraping across concrete—Siren, sliding in behind him.

A part of Tommy's mind registered the growing heat, told him he was in trouble even if he did get away, but that part was a tiny voice against instincts shouting, *screaming,* to crawl, to move.

He reached out with hands and arms. His body ground against the rough stone floor, against loose granite chips.

Behind him, he heard another sound, the same one he'd heard just before Curveball got ripped into hamburger—the whine of mechanical motors.

The SAW-dog was close to the breach point.

Tommy crawled faster, gritting his teeth against the hail of bullets that would tear into his feet, his legs, his ass.

ANGUS WATCHED HIS HUD, saw Cujo move toward the hole in the wall. Loose rock and bodies all over the place—what was left of fourth platoon. Smears of yellow coolant. Bits of intestine. A severed arm. A man with no legs, his bloody torso on the ground, his back against the wall, head down as if was taking a nice little siesta.

So much *blood.* On the bodies, gleaming red on the few spots of silt not covered by jagged rock, on the rocks themselves.

Angus eye-tracked, guided Cujo to the hole.

TOMMY CRAWLED, FASTER and faster, pushing his carbine in front of him. He felt rock shards cutting into his arms, but he didn't slow. The tunnel was so narrow he couldn't turn and aim the carbine behind him, so narrow he couldn't even draw his sidearm, let alone shoot it.

A weight on him, spreading across his body, pressing him down. Python-like strength as tendrils grabbed at him, ran under him, pulled at his webbing.

"Siren, *what the fuck are you doing?*"

Tommy couldn't crawl with the alien on top of him.

He felt a tentacle slide under his chest, felt it quickly search, pause, then yank free.

The whine of motors, louder, more magnified—it was coming in.

Then, another sound—the familiar *ting* of a thin piece of metal clattering against rock.

ANGUS ZOOMED IN. Was that movement? Yes, down that tiny tunnel, the shapeless gray of a rocktopi, flowing over the soles of a pair of boots.

Dead to rights.

Angus blinked twice.

TOMMY HEARD THE roar of the SAW, but only for an instant before a far louder noise ripped through the confined space—a V40 grenade detonating.

The weight lifted off of him.

A flicker of light, yellow and pink.

Tommy crawled, even faster than before, the sound of scraping dry leaves close by.

THE HUD SCREEN blurred, vibrated with bursts of static.

Angus quickly called up menus, checked this status, then that. Cujo was fully functional save for one thing—the blast had jacked up its camera. Hopefully that could be repaired.

How many grenades did that motherfucker have?

"Cujo, retrace your steps back to me."

Best to get the machine away from that tunnel, get him back where Angus would be protected.

He eye-tracked through his menus. He shut off the alarm. The hole in his helmet was already closing, built-in foam beads expanding to plug the leak.

That done, he knelt next to Khatari.

"Oh, man," Angus said, his words small, soft. "Oh … oh, man."

His skull, split open. Blood and coolant on the silt below him, staining the rumpled tan turban. Blood and brains, maybe. It didn't seem possible. This man had been alive only minutes before. Now he was nothing but meat and bone.

Angus heard pounding footsteps coming down the tunnel, approaching the switchback corner.

Without standing, he aimed his right arm to the corner.

In his comm, Fuentes: "Khatari, Angus, we're approaching your position, are you under fire?"

Angus didn't lower his arm so much as it dropped.

"I don't think so," he said.

Fuentes said something else—just sounds, random syllables that didn't register.

Angus stared down at the body of the man that Cujo had killed, then, again, at Khatari.

"Oh, man," Angus said. "Oh, man."

HEAT COOKING HIM, Tommy crawled through the darkness.

He had to get clear, get away from the main passage before he stopped to dress his wounds, to try and patch his suit.

If the mercs came after him, he knew he was dead—all they had to do was follow the trail of blood.

Blood that wasn't all his.

Siren flowed along behind him, carrying both Tommy's carbine and the one Curveball had dropped before his ill-fated charge. The alien occasionally slid across Tommy's back, moving forward to check the tunnel for danger, maybe. When Siren did that, or when he came back, Tommy saw the streaks of yellow.

The alien was wounded. Maybe by the grenade. Maybe by that oh-thank-god-short burst from the SAW-dog. Maybe both.

No night vision. Like the HUD, it was broken. Tommy didn't know where his mining helmet was. Even if he still had it, using a light would be a big neon sign flashing to his pursuers: *Here's your target, take him out!* Even Siren remained dark.

Tommy hadn't shown the alien how to throw a grenade. He hadn't even shown Siren the grenade at all. The rocktopi had seen Tommy throw the first one, and that, apparently, was enough.

The thin tunnel slowed Tommy down, but it didn't bother Siren in the least. The rocktopi could have fled down the passage, left Tommy to fend for himself—instead, Siren had covered Tommy's body with his own.

Twice, now—first at the river and now here—Siren had saved Tommy's life.

Now, Tommy and Siren struggled to reach the end of this sewer-pipe-sized hole in the mountain, trying to reach the passage that would let them get back to O'Doyle, back to Disco and Whitey, back to Mullet and Sleepy, back to Otto and Klimas.

Back to Sam.

No, he wasn't going to think of her, think of seeing her again. Tommy had failed. The mercs still had the nuke. The entire rocktopi race was in danger. And Curve was dead.

The loss sat like a weight on Tommy's chest.

Maybe there was an afterlife. Valhalla, maybe. That sounded nice, a perfect fit for Hatchet and Curve. They could be together, forever. Maybe some of the soldiers they'd killed would be there as well—Hatchet and Curve and their former enemies telling stories of the battles they'd all fought.

Or, maybe not Valhalla. Maybe an actual place of peace. Maybe heaven. Maybe somewhere the two warriors could leave their violent past behind forever—somewhere where they were just *Carson* and *Anders*.

It took Tommy a moment to realize he'd stopped crawling.

So fucking *hot*.

His left arm still worked, although it felt mostly numb. The pain had faded. Not good.

It wasn't the first time he'd been shot. He'd seen enough bullet wounds in his day to know he was in trouble if he didn't dress his soon.

He had to keep going. He had to warn Whitey and the others.

The tunnel suddenly rolled to the side. Tommy pressed his palms flat—a dizzy spell.

His HUD flickered on every now and then but didn't stay on long enough to give a readout. Tommy had already stopped sweating—he could only guess at the temperature.

Keep moving. He had to keep moving.

Arm over arm. Body sliding over rough rock, across loose shards of chipped granite.

He was still able to drink from the helmet tube; that kept him from complete dehydration. His heart beat far too fast. He felt dizzy.

Had Slash and the other rocktopi attacking from the fissures survived? Tommy doubted it.

In a strange way, the loss of Siren hurt worse than the loss of Curveball.

He kept crawling. How much further to the tunnel that led back to the City Cavern? No matter how far, it was *too* far. He wasn't going to make it.

He'd known this was a one-way mission. His suit was failing.

Tommy Strymon was cooking to death.

He still had his sidearm, and it was a helluva lot more powerful than the .25 he had back in his apartment. One pull of the trigger, and the heat would no longer be a problem.

Die from heatstroke, or from a bullet?

Seemed like an easy choice.

But not quite yet.

He could still crawl.

For a little while longer, at least.

82

14,409 feet below the surface

"WE'RE GOING TO get those bastards," Donnie said. "Every last one of them."

He stood there with Angus and Fuentes. All three of them looked down at the body bag that held Yadav Khatari. Cujo stood close by, an unmoving metal statue.

Fuentes touched the body bag. "He was a good guy."

For once, Fuentes wasn't smiling.

"Doctor Kool," Donnie said, "are you sure you're not wounded?"

Angus looked at him; the question didn't seem to make sense.

Donnie put his fingertip in a dent—a dent right in front of Angus's heart.

"This round should've killed you, Doc." Donnie reached up, ran his hands across Angus's helmet. "This some kind of self-hardening foam?"

Donnie's words seemed to open a floodgate—pain that Angus had somehow tuned out suddenly came roaring back. How many times had he been hit? His chest hurt, his left arm hurt, his stomach hurt…and oh lord, his *head*.

He thought of explaining the self-sealing mechanism's mechanics, but at that moment he wasn't really sure how it worked. A much smarter Angus had designed that system.

"Yeah," Angus said. "It's foam."

"You get shot in the head?"

Angus felt synapses firing, firing and missing.

"No, not shot—" he pointed to the axe "—he hit me with that."

Donnie looked at the weapon, still next to the man who'd tried to kill Angus with it.

"You were shot at point-blank range, and got hit in the head with a tomahawk," Donnie said. "Whatever you made this suit out of, Doctor Kool, it certainly did the trick."

Angus wished Khatari had been wearing one.

Donnie reached out a toe, poked at the dead man Cujo had gunned down. No body bag for him. He could rot for all Angus cared.

"This guy and his friend who got away took out Third Platoon," Donnie said. "Eight men, gone. Add in Khatari and the three we lost at the fissures, that's twelve casualties. We're down to fifty-four. Would have been worse if the rocktopi knew better than to bring a knife to a gunfight."

"They didn't have railguns?"

"Not a one," Donnie said. "The critters fought hard, I'll give them that. A few of them slipped back into the fissures and got away. This was a coordinated, multi-pronged attack. No question anymore—O'Doyle's people have integrated with the rocktopi."

Through the mental fog, Angus thought of the man he'd shot at, the man who'd run. He'd been side-by-side with a rocktopi.

If Donnie was right…

"There's no telling how many rocktopi there are down here," Angus said. "If O'Doyle is working with them, we'll be way outnumbered. Maybe we should go."

Donnie raised an eyebrow. "Come again?"

"There's all those silverbugs we took out," Angus said. "The platinum in those shells is worth millions. It's not the ship, but at least we'd be alive to spend our money."

Donnie's mustache twitched to the left, then back. "Fuentes, give us a minute."

Fuentes stood, looked at Khatari's body bag.

"Sorry, bro," he said, then he walked down the tunnel.

Donnie looked like he was struggling to control his words.

"Doctor Kool, for the sake of our budding relationship, I'll pretend you didn't say you'd take *millions* instead of *billions*. We've been hired to do a job. We will do that job."

"But we only have fifty-four men," Angus said. "And someone has to take the wounded up to the plateau. I mean … *I* could take them up, right?"

And if I do that, I won't end up like Khatari …

"I'm afraid you've proven yourself to be a valuable combat asset," Donnie said. "You're not going anywhere. Get your head straight. We're going to take an hour or so here for the men to eat, bandage up their wounds, and recover a little. Then we're moving out. I'll keep the payload up front with me, so I can keep an eye on it." He paused. His eyes narrowed. "Come to think of it, you'll stay up front with me, too. For the same fucking reason."

Angus glanced at Cujo. The machine stood close by, motionless.

How easy it would be to blink a command, to have the machine do to Donnie what it had done to the man lying dead on the tunnel floor.

Donnie sighed. "Look, Doctor, I'm coming across like a hard-ass, because I am a hard-ass. Back in Utah, you and I hatched a plan. A plan where you would become the richest man in history. Do you remember that plan?"

Richest man in history? The fog started to clear.

"Yeah," Angus said. "I remember that."

Donnie nodded. "Good. So do I. If you don't become the richest man in history, I don't get three percent of that wealth. And the men still with us? You promised them a payoff. Words matter, Doctor Kool. Promises matter. Especially to men like them. Especially to men like *me*. Understand?"

Finally, after all the time planning and prepping, after all the time in these tunnels, Angus *did* understand. Donnie wasn't in this to help

June July, wasn't in this to help BHP Billiton—Donnie was in this for *Donnie*.

BHP Billiton may have offered him a juicy side deal, but what they *didn't* offer was three percent of a fortune never before seen.

Donnie didn't get filthy stinking rich unless Angus got filthy stinking rich first.

Angus had been thinking about this all wrong, all along.

"You really are on my side," Angus said. "In your own selfish way, I mean."

Donnie nodded. "That's right. Now, if you don't mind, can we get back to business?"

They were below 14,000 feet. The BlackBugs had to find the bigger caverns soon. The ship might be just 2,000 more feet down.

To turn back now wouldn't just be wasteful, it would be *stupid*.

Angus was a lot of things, he knew, but stupid was not one of them.

"Yeah," he said. "Let's get down there and butter that muffin."

83

BERTHA BARELY SLOWED as she came around the switchback, one hand sliding on the rock to help her swing around the corner.

She felt like she'd been running forever, and she still had miles of tunnel to go. Her feet and knees cried out with each footfall: the incessant downhill pounding had punished the joints. Her back wasn't much better. Her legs burned with fatigue.

She'd fallen. Twice. A downslope sprint didn't give her much reaction time or balance when she stepped on an unseen rock or into an unexpectedly soft patch of silt. She'd banged her left shoulder pretty hard. Her left forearm was worse, though, because she'd fallen onto a sharp bit of granite and sliced open KoolSuit and flesh alike. She'd scrambled up, kept running, sliding off her backpack to get the patch material, repairing the suit as best she could while still moving down the tunnels, toward the City Cavern, toward Patrick.

There wasn't time to stop. Not even for a few seconds.

If she was right, there might be a way to save everyone.

If she was wrong...

Well, then she would die alongside Patrick.

And so will the baby...

Waves of guilt threatened to drag her under. Her reckless decision—based on nothing more than a hunch and a desperate need to keep Patrick alive—was more than likely going to get her killed. Her and her baby. She'd made a choice...the life growing inside of her had not.

How had she ever doubted Patrick's heart? He had a past. So did everyone else. He'd slept with Skylark, what, *twenty* years ago? Maybe more? As if that mattered—the man was willing to fight and die so Bertha and the baby could get to safety.

More than that, Patrick was willing to ask *others* to fight and die. Nothing could spell out who he prioritized more than that. Nothing.

Bertha slowed slightly, trying to time her steps. She spotted a good chunk of stone to use as a handhold that would let her slingshot her weight around the switchback corner, letting her make the 180-degree turn as fast as possible. She reached out, grabbed the rock, started to swing around...

The rock came loose.

Her momentum sent her stumbling into the tunnel wall. Shoulder and helmet smashed against rough stone. She fell—for the third time—face-first in the silt and skidded to a halt.

A moment of nothingness, that dreaded instant before the pain hits when you wonder if the pain will hit at all...

Hit it did, a blossoming ache that made her wish she'd kept ascending toward the surface. Her helmet had saved her from having her head bashed in by a stubby bit of rock, but the helmet couldn't do anything to stop her brain from bouncing off the inside of her skull.

Get up, you stupid, ugly woman...you're wasting time...

Bertha slowly pushed herself to her feet, pain radiating through her left arm and shoulder, a gray cloud swirling inside her head.

She wanted to stop, to rest, to recover.

But she would not.

Bertha took one step, then another … then she heard a noise.

A crunching sound, behind her.

Something was coming.

She gripped her carbine and moved to the switchback corner, used it for cover as she aimed back up the tunnel segment toward the next switchback.

The crunching grew louder.

She saw light—whatever it was was about to come around the corner.

Bertha turned off her headlamp.

The coming light grew brighter, playing off the tunnel wall, then the source came around the corner.

The go-kart. And in it, Sonny McGuiness.

Bertha stepped out into view.

Sonny slowed the vehicle to a stop.

The back end of the cart was crumpled, the trunk warped and distorted as if the thing had been rear-ended. The left-side guard rail hung at a funny angle, almost touching the ground. Dents and gouge marks along its length that hadn't been there before.

He held onto the frame, leaned out slightly.

"Hey, Momma," Sonny said. "Wanna go for a ride?"

A blood-soaked slice on his thigh. Through the cut fabric, she saw a KoolSuit patch, and through it, a blood-soaked bandage.

"You changed your mind?"

Sonny slowly shook his head. "Nothing quite that heroic. The tunnel out is completely blocked. The only way I live is if you're right about the ship. So here I am."

Bertha glanced up the tunnel again, waiting for the others to come, but she saw no movement.

"Ramiro?"

"A new kind of robot bug got him. Slappy and Crappy as well." He picked up something off the cart floor, held it up by one long, thin leg. "Say hello to my little friend."

A silverbug, only it was black. Three legs, one jagged joint where another had come off. The top of the round shell was cracked, deeply dented.

"Bastard almost killed me," Sonny said.

"Get rid of it. Angus might be able to track it or something."

Sonny looked at the battered black thing.

He tossed it up the tunnel. It hit the silt, limp legs flopping about until it came to a stop.

"Common sense, I suppose," Sonny said. "My brain ain't working right. Maybe when we get back to the booger city, you could take a look at my leg? The thing cut me pretty bad."

"How long ago?"

Sonny thought. "Thirty minutes, maybe?"

"Then it didn't hit an artery," Bertha said. "If it had, you'd be dead. Want me to drive?"

"I'm hurt, not stupid. You know how women drivers are."

An empty joke. He was talking just for the sake of it, maybe to stop from crying—she saw the pain in his eyes, both physical and emotional.

Bertha crawled into the cart. She held the frame as she sat down next to Sonny. The space wasn't made for humans, was uncomfortable as hell, yet her body sighed almost audibly with pure relief.

"Hold on tight," he said. "I'm getting pretty good at power sliding around these corners, but I ain't perfected the skill just yet. Might be a few bumps."

Sonny pushed a lever forward. The mesh tires crunched on gravel as the cart rolled down the tunnel.

84

BOILING, TO HOT, to warm, to cool.

A strange, tinny sound, like a distant giant slowly exhaling.

Tommy blinked slowly awake to total darkness, then reached out in panic—he was falling.

His hands bashed against hard rock and soft alien.

A stern chirp made him stop, a chirp that echoed in a strange way.

Tommy stilled himself. Rocktopi tentacles around his waist, under his arms. Nothing under his feet.

"Where am I?"

In answer, living flesh illuminated all around him, lighting up the walls of a rough, narrow shaft in shimmering, soft colors and patterns. Tommy looked up—high above, he saw nothing but blackness. Far below, the same.

They were in the vertical shaft again, heading back to the river, and then to the City Cavern.

It should have been a terrifying scene, a living nightmare of monsters taking him down and down and down to who-knew-what kind of fate, but he wasn't scared at all. Siren was one of the rocktopi holding him—the other was Axl.

Tommy put his gloved hand on the adolescent alien's body.

"Thank you," Tommy said, feeling immense, inexplicable relief.

Siren chirped.

The group of rocktopi started down again, extrusions gripping the rock face, stretching out long as they lowered their soft bodies. Three more rocktopi climbing down the rock as well, super-sized slime molds clinging to the rough surface.

"Where are we going?"

The aliens didn't answer, of course.

He hurt so bad. He'd lost a lot of blood. His mouth, so dry. He reached up with his right arm, worked the helmet tube so he could drink. The water was hotter than the air inside his suit.

Wait…holes had been torn in the suit. And in his visor—a hole now plugged by some kind of fibrous white glob.

Tommy looked at Axl's body, the alien's extrusions. The same material dotted him, a small spot here, a small spot there, a line there. The material stretched with the alien's movement, although not as much as its skin.

Siren had similar plugs dotting his skin, as did the other three rocktopi.

Tommy looked at his left forearm. Red and yellow stained the sleeve of his fatigues, although the colors looked odd in the rocktopi light. Tommy slid up the sleeve—clumsily wrapped, blood-stained bandages, and over them, clumsily wrapped KoolSuit patch material.

Clumsy, yes, but the battlefield repair had done the job.

"You patched me up," Tommy said.

Siren gave out a little screech in reply.

The alien had seen Tommy throw a grenade, and by watching, had learned to do the same. The rocktopi must have also seen Tommy and the others taking the patch material out of their backpacks, using it to repair their suits. As for the hole in his visor, they'd used the same material they used on their own wounds.

So smart.

Tommy's HUD seemed dead. If he made it back to the City Cavern, maybe he could repair it, but for the moment he didn't know the outside temperature or his internal temperature. He'd felt cool, but maybe only because he'd been so hot earlier. His suit was functioning enough to keep him alive, but he knew he'd lost coolant—how long before what little he had ran out?

Three wounded rocktopi above. He recognized their patterns, although he didn't have names assigned to them. It was becoming second nature to see a rocktopi pattern and remember it—no different than the uniqueness of every human face, really. One of them carried both carbines.

"Where are the others?" Tommy asked before remembering Axl and Siren couldn't actually understand what he was saying.

Tommy tapped the extrusion Siren had circled around his chest. When Tommy felt that sensation of being stared at, he held up ten fingers. He pointed to Siren, to Axl, then to the three rocktopi above, then closed one hand, leaving five fingers extended.

Simple enough for Siren to understand?

Axl responded, budding out a pseudopod the size of a baseball bat, which itself split ten thin, glowing tentacles. The light on five of the tentacles blinked out.

Tommy got it. At the fissures, nine rocktopi had attacked the mercs. Five aliens had died, their light extinguished forever.

He again became aware of that strange sound, that echo of a giant's breath. The long shaft they were in distorted it, made it echo, but he finally made sense of it.

It was the sound of the river.

They were close.

85

14,053 feet below the surface

THE FISSURE-SLASHED tunnel looked like a living Rorschach painting done in red and yellow.

Blood everywhere. Blood and bodies.

Dead rocktopi, formless white blobs half-deflated on the silt. Mixed in with them, dead men in formless black body bags. Maybe it was poetic, somehow, that in death, the two species didn't look all that different.

Fuck poetry—Angus had never understood it. Words were shit. *Real* poetry? Real poetry was how Cujo moved, how the machine followed Angus around. Real poetry was the *200/200/200* showing Cujo's ammo. Angus would not let that machine out of his sight again.

Donnie lightly kicked a dead rocktopi.

"We got five of them," he said.

It must have been a horrific fight. Nasty-ass rocktopi sliding out of the thin fissures, wielding their knives, right on top of the men who were passing through. A close-quarters battle in a tunnel that wasn't even four feet across.

Three of the platinum, double-crescent knives lay on the ground, near the dead rocktopi. Each knife was worth hundreds of thousands of dollars, yet no one had bothered to pick them up. Maybe the time for souvenirs had passed.

"We need to end this," Donnie said. "We can't afford to lose more men before the final battle begins. How much further do we have to go?"

Angus eye-tracked to his map. "Depends on how hard you want to push the men after this fight. At the rate we were going, three hours."

Donnie stared at the body bags, his mustache twitching left, then back.

"We have to press, go faster," he said. "We can't give them time to set up another ambush. Any map updates?"

"No. I recalled all the BlackBugs when the cave-in blocked Cujo. Should I send them out again?"

Donnie thought for a moment.

"Yes, but not to map," he said. "Can they shift gears and hunt silverbugs?"

Angus nodded.

"Good," Donnie said "We want all the BlackBugs near our position, scouting and attacking. That's more important than mapping, at least for now. Any damage to the two hauler donkeys?"

"None. The payload is fine."

"When we're thirty minutes from that cavern with the city, we'll break out all the heavy weaponry," Donnie said. "At that point, we'll strip all cargo from one of the haulers and send it far up front to trip any booby traps."

Donnie's plan made sense. BaDonkeyDonk Four could withstand far more damage than the mercs. Hopefully, BaDonkeyDonk Three would remain in pristine condition—when this was over, the machine could drag out a few hundred dead silverbugs.

Money. Always his thoughts came back to money. Angus had come here for it, for great steamy gobs of it, but was that the most important thing anymore?

"I watched Khatari die," he said, not knowing why he'd said it.

Donnie grunted. "That happens in this business. You had to know we'd lose some of our men when you hired us to come down here."

Our men. Donnie still didn't think of them as *mercenaries.*

"Yeah, I guess," Angus said. "But … I didn't know it would be like this. Khatari was … he was my friend."

My friend. That was illogical. He'd known the man for little more than two days. So why did the man's death hurt so much? Why did it hurt even more than Randy's had? Randy had been Angus's best friend, but "best friend" was just a phrase. He'd been Angus's best friend because he'd been Angus's *only* friend.

"We're at war," Donnie said. "In war, you lose soldiers. Khatari was your comrade. I was wrong about you, Doctor. I thought you were a pussy. Turns out you're a fighting man. Just like me. Just like Fuentes. Just like Khatari. He was your brother in arms, and that's a deeper bond than civilians will ever understand."

That was a stretch.

In the last two days, he'd faced death not once, not twice, but three times. He'd fought. He'd killed. But if he was such a great *fighting man,* why was Khatari dead?

"I froze up," Angus said. "When that guy came at me with the axe, I … I couldn't move. I was so scared. If I hadn't frozen up, maybe Khatari would still be alive."

Maybe that was why his death hurt so much — because Angus knew he could have stopped it. He'd fought side-by-side with the man. *He was your brother in arms.* It sounded utterly corny and trite, but it was real.

"Maybe he would have survived, maybe not," Donnie said. "What matters now is the people responsible for Khatari's death are somewhere below us. We can get payback. You can be a part of that. Understand?"

Angus did.

"Yes, sir," he said.

Empathy in Donnie's eyes. Empathy, and purpose.

"You are a part of this unit, Doctor. Let's get ready to kick some ass."

86

14,982 feet below the surface

IT WAS ALMOST enough to make him forget about Bertha, about their child.

Almost.

Patrick "Ender" O'Doyle sat atop a fifteen-foot-tall silvermech, exactly like the one that had attacked the canoe when Marie died. Sam sat at his right. He'd tied ropes through smooth rungs built into the machine's hull. He and Sam held tight to those ropes as the silverbug moved through the streets. If that wasn't stunning enough by itself, the leader of an alien race was at Patrick's left.

"Pretty smooth ride," Sam said. "For a giant robot, I mean. I would have thought it would be bumpier."

Four long legs moved the machine along at maybe ten miles an hour. Not that fast, but a helluva lot faster than walking or jogging.

Patrick was using the machine to move quickly between defensive positions, as well as to survey weak areas that might be shored up. Whitey had insisted on coming along—if Whitey came, Sam had to come, too.

Patrick stood, holding the ropes tighter to make sure his boot soles pressed down hard against the silvermech's smooth hull. He looked west, across the town. The streets were full of rocktopi, coursing along like a slow, multicolored river toward the tunnels that led down to the ship.

"So many," Sam said. "Will they get down there in time?"

Patrick wasn't sure. No Tommy, no Curve, no Axl, no Siren. The attack could have succeeded and the nuke was gone, or it could have failed—impossible to tell.

Patrick could do nothing but prepare and wait.

Whitey had agreed to send his non-combatants to the ship. The final battle against the mercs would take place in an empty underground city. If the NoSeeUms and Slash's forces lost, those refugees would die soon after.

"I hope the mercs don't split up when they get closer," Sam said. "You're putting everything into stopping them at the main tunnel entrance. Isn't that kind of putting all your eggs in one basket?"

A question Patrick had been asking himself for the last few hours.

"Yes, but frankly, we only have one basket, so that's where the eggs go," he said. "We got another update from the map room about an hour ago—the mercs are still in the main passage. I highly doubt they'll split their force. Massed firepower is massed strength. They will want to hit as fast as they can, as hard as they can."

If he'd been in the merc commander's shoes, he knew it would have been a tough call. In the end, though, Angus knew the rocktopi had the tech to level the mountain—the merc's best strategy, overall, was to force the conflict, not give the enemy ample time to realize there was no chance to win. Blitzkrieg, Shock and Awe, Human Wave, whatever one wanted to call it—hitting hard and fast with superior firepower was a time-tested strategy.

"Are you counting on the silverbug scouts to know when the mercs are almost here?"

"Not reliable enough," Patrick said. "We're using that, but I don't want to be dependent on getting information from the map room. Mullet has set up multiple booby traps in the main tunnel. When we hear his claymores go off, we know we have fifteen, maybe twenty minutes before Angus arrives. Think of it like an air-raid siren."

Sam took a quick look around the city, from the western hard point to the eastern one.

"I suppose that's enough time to get everyone in position."

"That's enough questions for now," Patrick said. "We're coming up on the east-side hard point."

Another silvermech there, its two long arms moving chunks of rock to close off the street. Rocktopi were around it, helping it. At least that's what they were supposed to be doing—the street was only half-blocked.

"Sam, ask Whitey if he can make his people work faster."

His *people*. It grew easier and easier to think of the rocktopi as people, not as *things* or *animals* or even *aliens*.

Even as he prepared for battle, even as he tried to push away his desperate worry for Bertha and the baby, Patrick couldn't quite tear his thoughts away from the three rocktopi he and his squad had gunned down at the shaft. The rocktopi had been unarmed. They'd probably had no idea of the threat that awaited them, no concept that there could be true danger in a home that hadn't faced a threat in thousands of years.

If the rocktopi were truly equal to humans, then those three hadn't been *killed in combat*, they weren't *collateral damage*—they had been *murdered*.

Murdered at Patrick's order.

It wasn't the first time his actions had gotten civilians killed. If he could get a break in the fight to come, though, maybe just one tiny bit of luck, it would be the last.

"I asked him if his people could work faster," Sam said. "I'm pretty sure I got it right."

"His answer?"

"I think he said he'll send Slash to deal with them," she said.

Patrick had seen how Slash dealt with those who had run from the live-fire drill. Whatever it took to get that bulwark built faster, Patrick supposed.

"Shit," Sam said, "he's asking that same question again—*how many people?*"

Over and over again. Patrick was getting tired of it.

"Can't you get it through his thick hide that we don't know how many mercs there are?"

"I tried," Sam said. "I'm sure he understands that the mercs are another group, separate from us, and that we don't know their numbers. I don't think that's what he's asking."

"Then what *is* he asking, Sam?"

She glared up at him. "I don't know, okay?"

"Maybe you don't understand the question."

"If you want me to drive while *you* play interpreter, I'm all for it."

Patrick wouldn't know where to begin. The language barrier infuriated him. The information Whitey kept asking for, could it be critical to the coming fight? Could it be the key to keeping everyone alive?

"Tommy's not back yet," Sam said. "He's not coming back. Is he."

A statement, not a question, and one that dredged up a torrent of shame. Patrick had stayed behind while he'd sent two men on a mission that would undoubtedly get them killed.

"Worm has lived through worse," he said. "Have faith."

She might only have a few hours left to live. No point in taking away what little hope she had left.

Did Sam have feelings for Tommy? Maybe. In another time, another place, the two might have made a good couple.

They reached the eastern position. The silvermech already there was moving large stone slabs into place to make an irregular wall that blocked the street. Two dozen rocktopi were moving smaller rocks into place, creating a lower secondary wall behind the first, one with multiple gaps along its length.

The end result would be a kind of narrow trench, solid in front and slightly porous in back. Defenders would be spread out along that trench, able to fire over the front wall at the enemy. After each shot, those defenders could duck down, out of sight, and crawl along the base of the wall to find a new position before popping up again—Patrick had no doubt that the mercs could quickly take out any rocktopi that kept firing from the same position. The rear wall would help protect from grenades or mortars lobbed behind the position, while the open spaces would let the defenders retreat without exposing themselves to enemy fire.

There were three large silvermechs in total—the third and final of their number was to the west, swinging a platinum ball the size of a large motorcycle to smash the one-story buildings, clearing a field of fire between the wall and the opening of the main tunnel leading into the city.

If the mercs came through that opening, they'd have to pay one helluva price to advance toward the wall and clear the rocktopi out.

As long as the rocktopi didn't run at the first salvo of enemy fire, that was.

Patrick studied the work in progress, looked for ways to make things go faster, for little modifications that would make the position stronger.

A tug on his pants leg.

"Uh, O'Doyle?"

He looked down at Sam, but she wasn't looking at him. She was staring back into the city. She pointed.

Patrick looked—far off, a wheeled vehicle, coming down the street.

It was the only thing with wheels he'd seen yet, and as such, he knew exactly what it was. In it, two people. He couldn't see their faces but knew them instantly from their shapes.

Sonny McGuiness … and Bertha.

Joy and anger, frustration and relief. She was still alive. But she wasn't supposed to be here. She was supposed to be out. She was supposed to be *safe*.

"You drive," he said.

He handed Sam the rope, or tossed it to her, he wasn't sure which, wasn't sure if she caught it. Moving as fast as he could without aggravating his back again, he crawled down the platinum rungs.

Sam must have had some control, because the silvermech bent its four long legs, lowering its big body toward the ground. When Patrick reached the bottom rung, he was able to lightly step off, onto the tiled street.

The silent buggy was rolling to a stop. The thing looked like it had been in a demolition derby.

Bertha got out and ran toward him.

Patrick's anger waned, a tide briefly going out before the power of the moon and the ocean inevitably drove it back again. She threw herself into his arms. He caught her, held her, hugged her.

"Thank god," she said. "You're still alive."

He had fallen for Bertha Lybrand because of her steel soul, because she was diamond-hard truth in a world filled with softness and lies. That Bertha, though, bore little resemblance to this one—she melted into him, as if her existence was incomplete without him. He loved this version of her, the fragile version, just as much as he loved the warrior that she was. Both halves together made a whole far greater than either part could ever be on its own.

His woman.

The love of his life.

He pulled her tight, held her, his very essence finding a moment of peace at her touch, a moment of forever perfection.

Then the tide rolled in.

He gripped her shoulders, held her at arms' length.

"What the fuck are you doing here? We agreed that you needed to go. We made a deal."

She stared at him as if she didn't dare let herself believe he was real.

Sonny slowly stepped out of the cart, moving like the old man that he was.

"Relax, hombre," he said. "There ain't no way out. Angus made some kind of black silverbug that caved in the tunnels."

Samira came down the rungs, stood next to Patrick. She looked from Bertha, to Sonny, to the cart, then back to Sonny.

"Ramiro," she said. "Where is he? Is he coming back, too?"

Sonny came closer, stood in front of her.

"I'm sorry, girl," he said softly. "Ramiro's dead."

Patrick felt a strange stab of relief—if the gods of war had to take someone, a sacrifice, at least it wasn't Bertha. Or Sonny.

"No," Sam said. She shook her head. "You all thought he was dead before and he wasn't. He's not dead now. He's *not.*"

Patrick's heart broke for her. She had been through so much. It wasn't fair.

Sonny reached out gently, took Sam's hands.

"I saw him die," he said. "Him and our two squidley escorts. He's gone, Sam. He's gone."

Sam stared at him. Her lip curled into a snarl. She yanked her hands free, turned and walked away.

Sonny started after her.

"Let her be," Bertha said.

Sonny stopped, leaned toward Sam as if he thought he should go after her anyway, then he walked back to the cart.

Bertha took Patrick's hands. She smiled. Her eyes blazed with hope.

"Sonny told me the cave-in sealed the tunnel," she said. "But that's not why I came back. I came back because I think I figured something out that might save all of us."

14,982 feet below the surface

RAMIRO WAS DEAD.

Sam sat cross-legged in the middle of the tiled street, in the shadow of the huge silverbug. She fought against thudding grief. He'd survived so much, only to die on the way out? It wasn't fair.

She'd denied it at first, but she believed Sonny. If the way out hadn't been blocked, Sonny wouldn't have come back.

And it wasn't just Ramiro—still no word from Tommy and Curveball.

"Sam," O'Doyle said, "I need you to focus."

She came back to the moment. Under the silvermech's curved shell stood O'Doyle, Otto, Sonny, Bertha and Whitey.

Bertha had told O'Doyle that the ancient ship might work. Ridiculous. And yet when she said that, O'Doyle had stopped everything. He'd called for Otto, who rushed over.

Everyone else was still prepping defenses and trying to get the rocktopi riflemen ready. Mullet oversaw the western hard point, Klimas the east. Sleepy and Slash were training additional rocktopi volunteers—brave souls that would fight with only knives unless more railguns were repaired before the mercenaries arrived.

Sam had communicated to Whitey the death of the two rocktopi that had gone with Sonny, Bertha and Ramiro. That was about all she'd managed to get across to the alien leader—her head felt thick as the rock that surrounded this place.

"Ask him again," O'Doyle said, his voice tight, as if he was struggling to control his temper. "Ask Whitey if the ship works or not."

Sam had tried asking that. Twice. Whitey didn't seem to understand the question. She couldn't get Ramiro out of her thoughts; so hard to focus on finding the right symbols. Ramiro could have helped her. Tommy could have, too.

They were gone.

It all fell to her.

Bertha had left Sonny and Ramiro to return here, to share her idiotic theory. She was a soldier—if she hadn't left them, would Ramiro still be alive?

Sam hated her for that.

"*Sam!*"

She jumped at the harshness in O'Doyle's voice.

He stared down at her. She expected him to yell at her, to scream at her to get her shit together. Instead, O'Doyle squatted down, grunting slightly as he did.

"I know you're hurting," he said. "You lost someone you loved. So did I. No matter how this began, we're at war. In war, people die. People we love. But unless you want to see more people die, you need to get your head in the game. Ramiro's dead, but that doesn't mean you're alone—you're part of a unit now. You're a NoSeeUm. You can do a job that none of us can do, and we need you to do that now. And if you want to survive yourself, you need to put your grief on the shelf and deal with it later. Understand?"

She stared into his eyes, ready to unleash her hurt upon him if his empathy was a false front.

It wasn't.

He'd lost Skylark. He'd lost Hatchet. Probably Tommy and Curveball as well. Did he feel those losses as deeply as she felt the loss of Ramiro?

No, not just hurt in his eyes—there was also *guilt*. Those people had come here because O'Doyle had asked them to come.

Just like she'd asked Ramiro.

For all of O'Doyle's brusque manner, for all of his violence, Sam realized the man knew *exactly* how she felt.

And in that understanding, she found strength. She wasn't alone. She was a shit-heel that had gotten her best friend killed—but she wasn't the *only* shit-heel here.

"We need you, Sam," O'Doyle said. "We need you right now."

She glanced at Otto. He nodded, solemn and understanding—he'd lost people, too.

She looked at Bertha, the woman who'd caused Ramiro's death. Bertha didn't smile, she didn't nod, but her eyes spoke volumes of empathy, of understanding.

She looked at Sonny.

"Get on with it already," he said. "Before my little ass gets nuked."

Sam stood. With all that she had left in the tank—and that wasn't much—she pushed her grief down, promising herself that she would wallow in it later. If she made it out alive, she would honor Ramiro Chus for all the good things that he had been.

"All right," she said, repositioning the white tablet. "Let me try again."

Sam drew the rocktopi symbol for the ship. That much, at least, Whitey understood. What could she draw for *does it fly?* She'd started with the simple question mark, then tried everything she could think of.

Maybe … she drew the symbol for *outside* next to the ship symbol, then the question mark, then held it up for Whitey to see.

The alien made no noise, showed no symbols. She felt his stare on her.

How could he not understand that?

"Try again," O'Doyle said. "Think, Sam. *Think.*"

Sonny stepped closer. "Jesus fucking Christ on a pogo-stick made of mirrored dildos. Give me that."

He reached down and yanked the board out of her hand.

"Hey!" Sam grabbed for it but Sonny turned away, shaking the board to clear her symbols.

"Sonny, let her work," O'Doyle said.

"In a goddamn minute," Sonny said. "If this sonofabitch wants to pretend he's a dummy, then let's treat him like a dummy."

He started drawing.

Sam reached for the board again, but stopped herself. Tommy and Siren had had a knack for communicating with each other; maybe an old man and an old alien could do the same.

Sonny held the board up so she could see it.

"This is how it's done," he said. "You can mail me my honorary archaeology language degree later."

On the tablet, a child's drawing, one she understood instantly. A single, jagged line—a passable outline of Mount Fitz Roy, roughly the same symbol for it that the rocktopi used. At the base of the jagged line, a simple double-tapered shape—the ship.

Sonny turned the tablet toward Whitey. Sonny pressed a finger to the center of the ship, then dragged it up, making a new line that crossed the top of the mountain and went beyond it. Sonny then tapped the ship and drew a question mark.

"Couldn't be any simpler, you squishy alien fuck," the old man said, harsh words he delivered with syrupy sweetness. "Now put that amoeba brain to work."

Whitey reached out a tentacle tip; black spots hovered near Sonny's drawing. The alien took the tablet from Sonny. Whitey drew. His picture was almost the same as Sonny's, except for two differences: Whitey's line showed the top of the mountain lifting up, complete with little waves lines indicating motion.

"He gets it," Sonny said. "Holy shit, Bertha might be right. That ship might work."

Sam felt his excitement. Maybe she felt it, too. Everyone did. They exchanged glances, were all instantly caught up in a burst of hope that they might make it out alive.

"It can't be," Otto said. "I mean … this ship has been *here* for twelve thousand years. We have no idea how long it took to get here, how old it is. And O'Doyle, didn't you say it was all shot up?"

O'Doyle nodded. "It is, pretty bad, but maybe it's compartmentalized.

Think how big it is—a half-mile thick. Even the gouges we saw would be nothing more than superficial damage."

"And there were rocktopi inside," Bertha said. "That's the big difference between here and Utah—I think the rocktopi here were working on the ship. Maintaining it. Maybe just fundamental systems, I don't know, but they're maintaining it. They can fire it up and we can fly away. Simple, right?"

Sam heard the eagerness in Bertha's voice, bordering on hysteria, as if she *wanted* to believe far more than she actually did.

"We don't know that," Otto said. "I don't think moving a ship this big—or the mountain, for that matter—is a simple thing."

"Of course it is," Bertha said. "They lifted up the mountain and put the ship *in*, didn't they? If they can do that, then they can lift up the mountain and fly the ship *out*."

O'Doyle held up his hands for silence.

"We can save everyone," he said. "Most of the rocktopi are already in the ship. If we can fly out of here, we all live." He stepped closer to Whitey. "How long to get it flying?" He seemed to remember anew that the alien couldn't understand him. "Sam, ask him."

A mountain lifting up, a miles-long alien ship rising into the Argentinian sky—who knew how people would react. But that didn't matter right now. Not when there was a chance.

Sam stepped closer to Whitey. She didn't take the tablet from him; she drew on it while he held it. A shapeless alien, different from not just humans, but from any Earth lifeforms outside of single-celled organisms. So different, and yet standing there with him felt almost normal.

Again, the intelligence, the *sentience*, it seemed to mean more than body type or even language.

Sam felt her confidence growing. She drew symbols that represented time, tapped the ship Whitey had drawn, then looked at him. When he did nothing, she repeated the symbols. She wasn't going to make this more complicated than it needed to be, because it couldn't get any simpler—*ship, fly, time*. Still he didn't respond, so she drew it a third time.

A faint flicker of iridescent purple coursed over Whitey, then he extended a tentacle tip and drew. As Sam watched, the image quickly took shape.

A glyph.

A *square* glyph—one with many barb-shapes pointing both up and in.

Whitey drew it above Sonny's uplifted mountain. The alien then circled the square glyph once, twice, then again, each line getting heavier, angrier.

Sam understood; any trace of hope faded.

"Whitey says he won't leave," she said. "He seems to think flying the ship out of here might draw the attention of the wasps."

O'Doyle shook his head. "Bullshit. That's not what he said, it doesn't make any sense. Ask him again."

Sam whirled on him, the loss of Ramiro and the futility of it all seizing her. "Doesn't make any sense?" She spread her arms, a gesture that took in the City Cavern. "They've been down here twelve millennia, hiding from a race that *destroyed their planet*, that almost wiped them out of existence. You don't think they'd be just a wee bit concerned about that? Huh?"

O'Doyle pushed her aside, grabbed the tablet away from Whitey. The man used his flattened hand to wipe away the drawings, then drew a symbol of his own.

He held it up to Whitey—a simple drawing of a mushroom cloud.

"*Fuck* whatever *might* be chasing you," O'Doyle said. He shook the tablet. "This is *here*. This is *now*. If we don't get the ship going, you're going to die here, and so are all your people."

Whitey's extrusions reached out, snatched the tablet away from O'Doyle. A flash of malleable white; Whitey again drew the bold, heavy lines of the wasp symbol. The alien leader held it up, fast, only an inch from O'Doyle's face, then let out an ear-splitting screech.

"Sam," O'Doyle said, his hands forming fists, "tell this motherfucker that I'm going to tear him apart if he doesn't do what I say."

Otto stepped closer. "Calm down. Don't do something that ruins any chance of us working together before Angus even gets here."

O'Doyle's face twisted into a mask of rage. He pointed at Whitey.

"Your kind will be wiped out," he said. "Gone forever, and us along with you. My *child*, along with you." He pointed upward. "You're getting my wife out of here, understand?"

A pause. No one spoke. No movement at all save for the soft undulations of Whitey's body.

Then, Whitey pulled the tablet closer to his shifting body, sketched out a symbol. Just as he turned it for O'Doyle to see, Sam had a sinking feeling—and when she saw the drawing, she knew why.

Once again, the symbols for *how many?*

O'Doyle grabbed the tablet, threw it to the tiles. He stomped on it once, twice, three times. He started to stomp a fourth time when his body went rigid and his hand flew to the small of his back. Bertha moved to him fast, reaching out awkwardly to help him—not knowing what to do, she stood next to him, her hands near him but not on him.

"This is fucking batshit crazy," Sonny said. "They wanted these gunslingers to fight for them so they don't get nuked, but they've had the power to fly away all along? It doesn't make any sense."

"We're missing something," Otto said. "Something fundamental. They told us about the nuke, not the other way around. They asked us to fight for them. They're so afraid of the wasps they'd rather gamble that we can help stop Angus than just flying away. What could knowing how many people there are have to do with them reconsidering that decision? What's the context of the question?"

Sonny said something to Otto, and the two began speaking rapidly, a debate bordering on an argument, yet Sam didn't really hear them.

How many people?

Whitey had asked it over and over, but—as Otto pointed out— what was the context? Whitey felt caught between a nuke and possibly revealing the Mount Fitz Roy location to the wasps, so what could a question about how many people were in the tunnels have to do with …

No. It couldn't be that simple. Could it?

And yet, if Whitey responded to potential danger, potential threats to his people, what was something he would *definitely* need to understand.

"I know what he's asking," Sam said.

She said it in little more than a whisper, yet Sonny and Otto stopped talking, looked at her. Bertha looked her way, too. Even O'Doyle, his hand still on his back, stared her way, waiting.

"He's not asking how many mercenaries there are," Sam said. "He's not asking how many people are in the tunnels—he wants to know how many people there are *in the world.*"

Otto's face went blank. O'Doyle and Bertha exchanged a glance, neither sure if they understood.

Sonny's face wrinkled with derision. "Why the *fuck* would the old sonofabitch want to know that? What's that got to do with anything?"

"Because the answer tells him if the rocktopi's time here is up," Otto said. "Until us, they've killed all the humans who got close to them. Not because they're monsters, not because they're evil, but because they think *staying hidden* is the key to their survival as a people. As a species. Right now he's working with us to stay alive, but he knows they've been discovered. Even if he believes in his deal with us, he's not stupid—if the human population is too big, he knows it's only a matter of time before someone else finds him here. Their entire existence is fleeing genocide from one race, so he must default to thinking any other race—us included—might also try to wipe them out."

O'Doyle frowned, as if on the edge of understanding but not quite there. "The number of people matters? There were plenty of humans around when they landed, weren't there? That's why they picked this isolated area, in the middle of a big-ass mountain range. No fertile land, nothing but rock … they had to be smart enough to know no one would end up here."

"But people *did* end up here," Sam said. "Thirty years ago, El Chaltén had less than fifty permanent residents. Twenty years ago it had grown to sixteen hundred people, and now it's at almost three thousand. This place isn't that remote anymore. Hikers are all over the mountain during the season."

What would it be like in another ten years? Another twenty? Even if everyone here—everyone who survived, that was, if *anyone* survived—managed to keep the secret, even if EarthCore and whatever company that bankrolled Angus decided not to pursue a potential billion-dollar find, it was still only a matter of time before someone else stumbled onto this place.

Hiding from primitive tribesmen was one thing. Staying hidden from modern man, with all the tools available, was another thing entirely.

"They were surprised by our gear, our clothes, our weapons," Otto said. "Because they've been buried down here, they haven't seen the growth of technology, of industry. For the same reason, they haven't seen population growth. When they landed there were a few scattered tribes using wood and stone. Sam, any idea of the Earth's population then?"

Twelve thousand years ago. The Holocene, before the dawn of civilization. Before *farming*. Humans survived as hunter-gatherers.

"Most estimates put the population between two and ten million," she said. "That's not South America, that's *global*."

Bertha squinted, as if she wasn't sure she could believe Sam's numbers.

"New York City alone has like eight million," she said. "There were, max, ten million people on the entire planet?"

Sam nodded. She knew Otto was right.

The landing rocktopi must have assumed an intelligent native species would multiply, but how easy might it have been to underestimate humanity's penchant for breeding?

"They were surprised we had *metal*," Otto said. "Humanity went from stone tools to space stations, all while the rocktopi hid three miles below ground. Just like they didn't think we'd have advanced tech, you can bet your ass they didn't expect our population to be almost seven billion—*seven hundred times* larger than when they landed. Whitey wants to know *how many people*, but I don't know if he's ready for the answer."

Everyone fell silent.

When Whitey got his answer, what would happen? Maybe use an as-yet-unseen weapon to try and keep their existence hidden? No—if the rocktopi *could* have killed Sam and O'Doyle and the mercs, they probably would have done so already.

"I don't know what to do," Sam said. "What do you want me to tell them?"

"The truth," O'Doyle said. "We have to convince them their only hope for survival is to *leave*. Maybe if he gets the answer to his question, he'll realize his people will *never* have peace here. That time is over for them. And if their ship doesn't take off, we're all dead anyway—the only question is how we die. Answer his question."

Sam again looked at the broken tablet. "Thanks for breaking that."

"Use paper," O'Doyle said. "Get it done. We're out of time."

Sam shrugged off her backpack and pulled out her warped sketch pad.

She translated seven billion into rocktopi numbers. Base-12 had become second nature to her. She added the rocktopi symbol for *humans*. For good measure, she did a quick drawing of the Earth, sketching out the continents of North and South America.

"Here we go," Sam said, then held the pad up for Whitey to see.

She felt the rocktopi leader's attention leave her, settle on the drawing.

Whitey fell still. Not even the slightest undulation on his pale body. Sam hadn't realized the rocktopi were in constant motion—tentacles waving, colors coursing, new pseudopods slowly forming—until that very moment, until she saw him as frozen as ice.

"Damn," Bertha said. "Did he just have an alien heart attack or something?"

Sam waited.

Still no movement.

"Maybe he's gotta take a shit," Sonny said.

Sam glanced at her drawing—had she made a mistake with the rocktopi numbers? No, as far as she could tell she'd gotten it right.

A ripple coursed through Whitey's body. He looked older than ever.

The rocktopi leader pointed to Sam, then O'Doyle, then each of the others. Whitey pointed to himself, then in the direction of the rocktopi funneling into the tunnel that led to the ship.

Then, he pointed upward—just as O'Doyle had done.

A breath slid out of Sam, one of both astonishment and relief.

"Whitey will launch the ship," she said.

O'Doyle looked at her. "Are you sure? We can't waste time with mixed messages."

Sam closed her eyes, realized how important her next words were. If she was wrong…

But she wasn't. She *knew*.

"I'm sure."

"It's a starship," Otto said. "It's been mothballed for millennia. How long will it take them to prep the ship for liftoff? It might take days. Weeks, even."

Sam tried to turn the sketch pad to the next page, but it was too warped—she tore the page free, tossed it aside. She started drawing on the newly exposed paper. She'd barely begun before Whitey reached out extrusions, a half-dozen white snakes that took the pad and her charcoal pencil away from her.

He drew. Why he sometimes chose to flash symbols on his skin and sometimes to use the tablet or paper, she didn't know. Some cultural thing, perhaps.

Whitey turned the pad for the humans to see.

"I don't know any of that," O'Doyle said. "What does it say?"

Breath halting, heart hammering, Sam studied the symbols Whitey had drawn, mentally processed the information into human time.

"Two hours and fifteen ... no, two hours and *ten* minutes." She looked at O'Doyle. "Will that be enough? Will Angus get here before that?"

He didn't answer for a moment. He stared at the pad as if he understood what Whitey had drawn.

"I don't know," he said, finally. "Sam, tell Whitey to get the ship activated as fast as he can. If Angus gets here before the ship is ready to fly, then we'll have to fight to hold him off until it is."

So that was that. One way out. An *impossible* way out. Just because Whitey thought the ship worked didn't mean it did, didn't mean the technology that would lift up an entire mountain still functioned correctly.

They had a chance. A slim chance, maybe, but still a chance. Ramiro was gone. She would miss him, always, but she still had a chance to live.

She began to draw.

88

15,892 feet below the surface

SONNY FOLLOWED THE alien exodus through the narrow tunnels, the faint sound of a distant river playing off the walls. He'd somehow gotten separated from Lybrand. She was up ahead somewhere, out of sight past the line of glowing rocktopi.

Right in front of him, one of the creatures carried a tiny blob pulsing pink and crimson. A baby, not even as big as Sonny's head.

Behind him, a rocktopi that dragged two smaller, squirming versions of itself. The small aliens squealed and mewled. Sounds of fear, Sonny had no doubt. A parent and two crying, frightened children, fleeing certain death.

He focused on the colors, the sounds—anything to help him ignore his surroundings.

These tunnels had some lights, strips of illumination running along the ceiling. That—and the light from the rocktopi themselves—helped him some, but it took all of his concentration not to drop into the fetal position on the silt below his feet. Lybrand had assured him that this tunnel ended at a space so large his claustrophobia would not be an issue.

Every three or four steps, he found his hand grazing the pistol strapped to his belt. O'Doyle had given him another ten rounds. One magazine of ammo—that was all Sonny had until he died, or this shitshow came to a long-overdue close. There was only so much ammo available, and most of it was needed up in the City Cavern. Sonny couldn't argue with that. If all went well, O'Doyle, Otto, Klimas and the others would burn through that ammo killing that shifty fuck Angus Kool and the mercenaries.

If all went *perfect*, Sonny wouldn't have to fire a shot.

The aliens' light flickered against the tunnel walls in a thousand clashing colors. On those walls, carvings and glyphs. A bunch of gibberish. Maybe it meant something. Maybe, but he didn't care to know what.

He had his doubts about this *escape plan*. Did the ruined ship work? Could the aliens really lift up the mountain and fly the ship out? And if they could do that, would they actually drop Sonny and the others off on the surface?

He doubted it. He doubted it very much.

But there was no other option. There were only three ways out of this place.

The first would be to walk up to the killers led by that little prick Angus Kool and ask—oh so politely—might Sonny *please* just slide on past? He wouldn't tell no one, no sir, not one single soul.

Yeah. They'd go for that.

The second way out was the secondary tunnel, which was blocked by a cave-in. Sonny realized only then that he hadn't seen said cave-in—Ramiro had reported it, right before getting a carbon-fiber spike shoved through his brain. But the kid had wanted out even worse than Sonny, so Sonny doubted Ramiro had made a mistake.

Besides, there could be more of the black bugs up there. No thanks.

The third way? No big deal, really—just take a fucking spaceship that landed here twelve fucking thousand years ago.

Great odds.

Lybrand's voice in the comm: "Heads-up, Sonny. We've reached the proverbial end of the tunnel. You holding up okay?"

He was most certainly *not* holding up. He'd gone from almost out of this mountain to far, *far* deeper beneath it.

"I'm fine," he said.

Even he heard the warble in his voice.

A hundred or so steps later, Sonny stepped out of the tunnel and into a dark cavern. His boots treaded on large colorful tiles. Walls? Ceiling? He couldn't see either. They were lost somewhere in the darkness. He heard the river more clearly. It was somewhere far away in the darkness.

Lybrand had been right—Sonny felt his stress lower, his anxiety drop down a few notches. He couldn't see the boundaries, but he didn't have to; his body seemed to understand the enormity of the space, almost as if he was standing up on the surface during a pitch-black night.

The surface. If he could make it back to that fabled place, he'd wouldn't go near another cave for the rest of his life.

He saw Lybrand walking toward him, her headlamp beam flicking left and right, up and down, her rifle held in her hands.

"There's supposed to be a ship down here," Sonny said. "So where is it?"

Lybrand turned her head, pointed in the same direction as the rocktopi line.

It took Sonny's eyes a moment to adjust; it took his brain a moment to realize what she was looking at. A wall of some kind. A *big* fucking wall. Quite a ways off. A towering, reflective surface, the base gleaming with the colors of the aliens apparently moving inside.

"I see it," Sonny said. "The ship behind that wall or something?"

Bertha looked at him, her headlamp beam aimed at his chest.

"Sonny," she said. "That *is* the ship."

A sound like a huge gong, reverberating through the immense, dark cavern. Then a crackling, a sizzling that echoed and echoed and echoed.

High above, something glowed faintly. A *row* of somethings.

"Nice," Bertha said. "I guess they're finally lighting up the place."

The sizzling sound grew louder. *Much* louder, filling the air, making Sony's hair stand on end.

High above, a huge light began to glow, like the break of dawn quickly giving way to full morning light. Far down the cavern, another light, then another—his seasoned eye for distances told him the lights were over a mile apart. Could there really be that much space down here?

O'Doyle had claimed the ship was four miles long...

The lights grew brighter; Sonny had to look away. He blinked rapidly, persistent strobes dancing in his vision. As those streaks faded away, he finally saw the cavern's walls, the impossible dimensions of the place.

"Sonofabitch," he said, almost breathless. "Son. Of. Ah. Bitch."

Sonny McGuiness had spent most of his life under the open skies, staring up at the stars, marveling at the incalculable expanse of space, at the Earth's relatively minuscule place in the cosmos. This cavern was completely enclosed, a tiny fraction of Earth, which was itself a fraction of the solar system, itself a fraction of the galaxy, and so on—and yet, in all his years, he had never felt as *small* as he did at that moment.

The ship. A metal leviathan that defied imagination. It curved up and away, the apex taller than any building ever created by man. And the *length* of it. The ship faded off into the distance like a drawing of infinite perspective Sonny had made as a boy in art class.

Massive, yes but the light revealed more than the size—it revealed *damage*. Gaping holes, as if someone had pressed a curling iron into a candle. Great tears in the hull, with ragged, gleaming edges.

"I might not be an expert on interstellar travel," he said, "but that thing looks more beat-up than a truck stop hooker's cooze."

"The one in Utah looked even worse."

Sonny glanced at her. "Did anyone claim that one could still fly?"

"Nope," she said.

Things had already gone from *bad* to *worse*. Looking at that hulking wreck, Sonny felt like they'd gone from *worse* to *fuck it, let's just lay down and die.*

He slowly turned in place. The ship was only half of the majesty. The walls ... towering, curving slowly upward toward the artificial suns blazing above. Up to maybe five hundred feet high, there wasn't an inch of untouched stone to be seen. All across the endless expanse of wall, engraved symbols painted in bright colors. Smooth pillars that dwarfed any skyscraper. Battleship-sized statues of rocktopi. Alcoves as big as city blocks. The floor, made of brightly colored hexagonal tiles, each the size of a tank.

It was like being in the grandest church ever imagined, a medieval place of deep worship, the focal point of a religion at its absolute zenith of power and influence.

"This is unreal," Sonny said. "Was the Utah cavern like this?"

"There were carvings," Bertha said. "And statues. Big ones. But everything in the cavern was cracked and chipped and broken. Parts of it had caved in. There was loose stone all over. It was like an ancient ruin. It was dead. Not like this place."

Sonny turned in place a second time, trying to get his head around the majesty of it all. Engineering beyond anything humans could accomplish.

"I'm going to the map room, do a last check to see if the mercs are still in the main tunnel," Bertha said. "Then I'm heading back up."

She was going to leave him alone down here? With all the creatures?

"You should stay down here," he said. "Think of the baby."

Bertha smiled a sad smile. "I am thinking of the baby. The baby needs a daddy. Patrick is my man—if he's going to fight, I fight at his side."

She was stupid. Or brave. Or both. Her courage filled him with shame.

"I just wouldn't be no good in a shoot-out," he said. "If I was younger, well…"

She looked at him. Her hard-as-nails attitude softened slightly.

"How old are you again?"

He glanced down. "Sixty-seven."

"You know who doesn't have to fight? Sixty-seven-year-olds. When we come back this way, we'll be moving fast. We need you and Sam down here to tell us what's going on."

She was trying to make him feel better about hiding down here. It wasn't working.

"That's real nice of you to say," he said, "but—"

Bertha slung her rifle and stepped forward in the same motion. She wrapped her arms around Sonny in a hug so strong he couldn't draw a breath.

"You were brave when it mattered the most," she said. "Even if I don't make it out of here, what you did in Utah, driving up to get us—it gave me more time with Patrick. I can never, *ever*, thank you enough for that. You stay down here, and when the time comes, you'll be the friendly voice guiding us in. Okay?"

She let him go, held him by his shoulders.

"Okay, Sonny?"

He looked into her eyes, saw her intensity. She was ready to fight, and God have mercy on whoever was dumb enough to get in her sights.

"Yeah," Sonny said. "Okay. Kick some ass, lady."

She thumped him once on the back, turned, and jogged toward the ship.

89

"DOCTOR KOOL, PLEASE tell me that wasn't what I think it was."

Donnie stared up at the tunnel ceiling. *Everyone* stared up at the tunnel ceiling.

The tremor had hit fast, shaken everything around them, faded away. Angus had one hand on the wall. He'd thought he was a goner. He waited—pretty patiently, considering the circumstances—for his breath to return.

"Dude," Fuentes said. "Was that an earthquake?"

Up and down the tunnel, terrified, wide-eyed men stared at the ceiling. The same men who had fought hand-to-hand against the rocktopi and who had served in countless battles now watched helplessly, knowing their skills or bravery couldn't save them if the roof came crashing down.

"*Doctor Kool*," Donnie said, "talk to me."

Angus held up one armored finger: *Just a minute.*

His diaphragm finally relaxed. He sucked in air as he eye-blinked through his HUD menus. Yes, it had *felt* like a tremor, and, yes, Mount Fitz Roy was in an active region, but there hadn't been a significant seismological event in decades.

It wasn't an earthquake. He had an overpowering, awful feeling that it was something far, far worse.

Angus called up seismograph readings from the BlackBugs. The results chilled him: a 4.1 tremor, originating from somewhere further down in the mountain. His algorithm was still processing the epicenter location.

No precursor tectonic activity since he'd entered the mountain.

No known historical precursor activity in more than two years.

And, *no aftershocks*. None. If it had been a true quake, there should have been at least some residual vibration …

"Doctor Kool, I need information. You—"

"Put a fucking sock in it, Donnie," Angus said. "Hold on one goddamn second."

Angus closed his eyes. His mind raged, processing what he knew, making connections, linking bits of data together.

No tectonic activity in the area, then a 4.1 tremor, then absolutely nothing. What could cause that? An explosion, definitely, but a blast that powerful would have assuredly driven air up the tunnels, and Angus's instruments showed zero change in air pressure. So if it wasn't an explosion, and it didn't appear to be tectonic activity, then …

Angus opened his eyes, opened them wide.

Could the rocktopi have activated their doomsday weapon, the same one that blew the living shit out of Funeral Mountain?

Maybe. But if O'Doyle was still alive, and he was working with the rocktopi, would they throw in the towel and commit mass suicide? It didn't quite add up. The doomsday bomb he'd seen in Utah had been hanging on a cable—unspooling a cable didn't cause a 4.1 tremor. And if they had lowered it, they probably hadn't detonated it, or the entire mountain would still be shaking before it collapsed and lava scorched everything to hell.

So if it wasn't an earthquake, and it wasn't the doomsday device, what else could possibly shake the ground like that?

The rocktopi … they once had the technology to literally move mountains.

Could they still have that tech?

If so, what would they use that for if … if …

Oh, *shit*.

"Donnie," Angus said, "I need a word in private. I think we're in trouble."

90

14,978 feet below the surface

TOMMY HAD FOUGHT wars on five continents.

He had gone without food for weeks, without water for days.

He'd been stabbed. Shot. Burned. Nearly blown up.

In all his days of fighting, though, he had never hurt like this.

And yet the part of him that had always been restless, that had never found a home—that part was finally at peace.

Tommy Strymon, an orphan from Iowa, a smart kid who had never had a chance and had joined the Army as the only way out he could find, that kid now rode inside of an alien as they flowed down an underground river, a river that was part of an ancient, lost culture older than the history of mankind, heading toward a final battle with a genocidal enemy.

For a boy whose only escape was science fiction novels, he was now *living in* one. More than one, actually. It was like living all of them.

If he didn't make it out alive, it was a helluva good day to die.

He'd touched alien beings. He'd communicated with them, fought side by side with them. Hell, the only thing missing from this bizarre, real-life sci-fi movie was getting to fly in their starship.

Getting to go into space itself.

A wave of nausea hit him, dragging his existence from storybook dreamworld to harsh reality. He could lift the mask if he had to, but that would let in more superheated air, and his suit was already failing. Besides—how would Siren react to being puked on?

No HUD, so Tommy didn't know his body temperature, but he didn't need a readout to tell him he was getting warmer and warmer. If he made it back to the others, he could recharge his coolant. Until then, he had to deal with the growing heat.

He'd lost blood, too. Perhaps more than he cared to admit. Axl's battlefield dressing had stemmed the bleeding but hadn't stopped it; Tommy felt the sticky wetness beneath the KoolSuit skin.

His physical pain contrasted with the wonder of his situation, which itself filled him with guilt. How could he find *any* excitement and satisfaction in this experience when he'd lost another friend, when he'd failed the mission?

He'd failed the primary objective, yes, but he and Curve had also done a significant amount of damage to the enemy. Eight dead from the breach charge and the subsequent cleanup kills. Curve had killed another when trying to take out Angus. Not counting any mercs that Siren and the rocktopi might have taken out at the fissures, that was nine enemy soldiers gone—ten percent of the enemy forces, possibly even higher than that.

Would that be enough to turn the tide in the battle to come?

Tommy didn't know. He didn't know if he'd live long enough to find out.

He hoped he could get back in time. He had to let Ender know the mercs still had the nuke. The mercs *would* enter the City Cavern. If the NoSeeUms couldn't take out the nuke when they came in, then it was bye-bye starship. Bye-bye NoSeeUms. Bye-bye alien race.

Siren unfolded. Tommy found himself in the river cavern. Around him, the forms of swimming rocktopi, like glowing sea monsters lurking mostly below the surface. Up ahead, light, where the river entered the City Cavern.

Siren, Tommy, Axl and the others flowed out of the tunnel, into the artificial sunlight. As a group, they swam toward the bank that abutted the obelisk plaza.

One of the rocktopi kept flowing down the middle of the river. It floated on, half-submerged. Pale white tentacles bobbed lifelessly. Its light had gone out. It was one of the fighters that had been wounded at the fissures.

It had succumbed to its injuries.

From species to species, it seemed, death was death.

How many more would die before it was over?

Siren brushed up against the shore. Axl reached out extrusions, helped Tommy step onto the rocky bank.

He heard the shouts of humans. Such a strange way to think about it, not *shouts* but *the shouts of humans.*

Mullet was the first to reach him. He put his arm around Tommy, helped him up the bank.

"Glad you made it back, brother," Mullet said. "Curveball?"

A one-word question, with an answer that required no words at all — Tommy shook his head.

Sleepy and Klimas helped carry Tommy to the base of the obelisk, laid him down on his back.

Tommy closed his eyes. He needed to rest, just for a little bit.

No one else asked him about Curveball. Tommy was grateful for that. They all knew. They were all shoving their grief down, hiding it away for later, just like he was.

"The nuke," Ender said. "Did you get it?"

Without opening his eyes, Tommy again shook his head.

The silence that followed carried a heavy sense of dread.

"Then we stop them here," Ender said. "Worm, take as much time as you need. Sam, can you take care of Tommy? We've got to keep training."

Maybe Tommy fell asleep for a moment. He wasn't sure. When he opened his eyes, he saw Samira Jabour looking down at him through her visor.

"You made it," she said, and she smiled. "I've got suit patches and a first aid kit. Tell me where it hurts. I'll take care of you as best I can."

91

14,305 feet below the surface

MEN PACKED TIGHT in the tunnel, shoulder to shoulder. Some were kneeling, some standing. They tried to make room, to let everyone see Angus Kool and Captain Donnie Graham.

"Men, we are faced with an unexpected challenge," Donnie said. "We are going to cover this fast, then we are going to haul ass to our objective. You all felt the tremor. Doctor Kool, tell them what you think that was."

Angus felt the eyes of killers upon him. They had accepted him to some degree, but he knew they would think it was his fault he hadn't anticipated this as a possibility.

And he couldn't blame them for that.

To think that it had never—not even once—crossed his mind that the goddamn ancient thing might still work?

Inexcusable.

"The alien ship is a platinum-iridium compound," he said. "It's four miles long, a half-mile wide. It's three miles below the surface. To get the ship there, the rocktopi had to lift up the entire mountain above us. Somehow they raised it up, carved out a big-ass hole, put the ship inside, then settled the mountain back down."

The men looked at him with narrowed eyes. Not in disbelief—they'd already fought against aliens and killer robots, alongside a man in a suit of powered armor, and they knew this wasn't Kansas anymore—but in expectation of bad news.

"The most likely explanation for that tremor we felt was they are testing, or activating, the same technology that let them do that thousands of years ago. The only reason I can think of for them to activate that tech now is … hold onto your jumblies, fellas … they're hoping to get in their ship, lift up the mountain, and escape us."

The mercs glanced at each other, realization hitting home for some. Others looked doubtful, confused.

"They are bugging out," Donnie said, simplifying things. "That's bad news for us. Doctor, explain why."

When Angus had told Donnie his hypothesis, the man had *not* been happy. No confusion on Donnie's part. While he wasn't a rocket scientist, he'd put the pieces together almost instantly. He'd risked bunching up his forces again, knowing he might have very little time to disseminate the information, knowing he had to get everybody fully onboard *right now*, not later.

"Even if their technology works flawlessly," Angus said, "movement on that scale will no doubt cause significant settling throughout the mountain. That means we have to assume that every single tunnel in this complex will collapse. And not just the tunnels—caverns, too. Everything. They'll be safe in their ship. They won't give a damn if everything else falls apart."

The looks on the faces of the men: fear, rage, exhaustion. They had been through so much, only to learn that things had just gotten far worse.

"It took us over two days to reach this depth," Donnie said. "That was all downhill. It would take us *at least* two days to exit. We have no idea how long they will have to test their system before they leave. But since this is the first tremor we've felt since we came in, and since the rocktopi seem to have a good idea of where we are at any given time, it's a reasonable bet they're activating the system so they can leave before we reach them. We're two hours from their main population center. I am operating under the assumption that they plan to take off within those two hours so they don't have to face us. If I'm right, and we try to go back instead of going forward, we won't even get *close* to the plateau before they lift up the whole damn mountain and kill us all."

He let that sink in. Every second counted, Angus knew that, yet he wasn't about to second-guess Donnie at that moment. Donnie knew the stakes, knew the best way to motivate his men. He wanted to live and be rich, just as much as Angus did.

"If we march fast and hard," Donnie said, "if we really show some guts, we can make it in *one* hour. Once we're there, we have to quickly locate our next objective—the ship itself. Men, if the rocktopi are bugging out, the only way for us to survive is to reach that ship and disable it, or kill all the bastards *before* they can bring everything down on our heads. Everyone saw the cave-in that Doctor Kool melted through?"

The mercs nodded. Once word had spread about what Angus had done, all of the men had wanted to see it for themselves.

"For that, he used a device he calls the *ButterKnife*," Donnie said. "Doctor Kool believes he can use that device to render the alien ship inoperable, or at least do enough damage that it can't take off."

There was enough power remaining in the ButterKnife for three more uses. *Maybe* four, depending on what needed to be melted through. Hopefully there would be no more cave-ins—if he could put all the ButterKnife's remaining energy into one shot, Angus was almost certain he could melt a hole in that ship so big that there was no way it could take off.

"We have to close in," Donnie said. "If, in the process, we kill all the boogers and our human opposition, then wonderful, we win. If we can't accomplish that, once the ship is disabled we follow the original plan—plant the nuke, get back to the surface, detonate it, and turn every living creature down here into radioactive bacon."

The logical part of Angus knew he and the men were screwed. But the way Donnie talked, the way he *inspired*…the emotional part of Angus responded. He felt hope blossom. Dimwit was right about one thing, at least—there was no point in running.

"We are *conquistadors*," Donnie said. "We are Hernán Cortés and his men, marching on the Aztec Empire. Cortez burned his ships so that his men could not retreat. In effect, *our* ships are burned. Men, the only way out is through. These bastards want to squash us beneath a billion tons of rock. This is kill or be killed. If any of you want to run back up the tunnel, if you want to run for *two days*, if you want to leave your fate in the hands of others, then go. You have thirty seconds to decide. The rest of us with the courage to face our enemy head-on are moving forward, we're moving *fast*, and with the intention to do grievous harm when we arrive. Get ready to shake those tail feathers. To sound like a very, very bad cliché, gentlemen—follow me if you want to live."

With that, Donnie turned and walked down the tunnel, sliding past the packed men.

Angus stood and watched. Fuentes walked up, stood at Angus's side.

"Old fuck can really give a speech," Fuentes said.

A few mercenaries mumbled to each other, voices quiet and conspiratorial. Many flashed glances at Angus, enough that Fuentes put his hands on his rifle, glared back at them.

Twenty seconds later, two men stood and started jogging back up the tunnel.

But only two.

Angus glanced at Fuentes. "What about you? There's no telling if they'll get that tech to work in the next two hours. If you leave now, you might have a chance."

Angus wanted Fuentes there for the final battle. With Khatari gone, Angus wanted that more than anything. But Angus also wanted Fuentes to live. If he ran now, maybe he could make it.

Fuentes shook his head and smiled.

"Naw, man. I'll take my chances aiming at the enemy instead of the enemy aiming at my back. How about you? You got them super legs. You don't get tired. You could probably be out of the mountain in twelve, maybe thirteen hours. You going to make a break for it?"

Yes, Angus *could* run. The bottom line was, he didn't want to.

"I came here to kick ass and chew bubblegum," Angus said. "And I'm all out of bubblegum."

Fuentes groaned and rolled his eyes. "Oh Dios mío, you are one corny nerd."

Donnie on the comm: "Time's up, men. Form into your platoons. Fuentes, Kool, I want the payload on Cujo. I need you two, Cujo and Goofy up front with me. And Kool, make sure that hauler is stripped down and ready to spring any booby traps."

The man knew far more about combat than Angus ever would. While he might be *Dimwit Donnie*, now wasn't the time to second-guess him.

Fuentes smiled at Angus. "You ready, Boss?"

Angus nodded. He strode down the tunnel, Cujo the killer machine and William Fuentes right behind him.

92

14,982 feet below the surface

SAM KNEW THIS would be the last time she saw the obelisk plaza, the cavern, this amazing, ancient city. She also knew she'd be damn lucky to see anything else, to make it out in one piece.

The silverbugs at the mouth of the main tunnel had scattered. That meant the mercs were coming—roughly thirty minutes until they arrived. There was time for one final briefing, then all would report to their assigned areas.

O'Doyle. Bertha. Mullet. Sleepy. Otto. Klimas. And Tommy Strymon, who looked like he was already on death's door. He leaned against the obelisk base, probably couldn't stay standing for long without it. Behind his cracked and patched visor were half-lidded eyes. His skin looked almost gray.

Sixteen rocktopi, each carrying a heavy platinum shield, each armed with a railgun. Sam knew four of them on-sight: Siren, Disco, Slash and Axl. Axl didn't look much better off than Tommy. The alien's light was perhaps half of its normal luminescence, especially in the areas around plugs of white pressed into its skin.

Another twenty-four rocktopi armed with nothing but double-crescent knives. They weren't trained warriors, like Slash and Axl. They weren't even auxiliaries, or reserve units, like the ones carrying the shields and railguns. O'Doyle would save these troops as long as he could, try to use them if Angus's mercs moved into the denser areas of the city, and in the nooks and crannies of the tunnel that led to the ship.

Based on O'Doyle's plan, odds were most of these alien soldiers wouldn't survive. They all knew that. They were willing to fight anyway, ready to sacrifice their lives if it meant their race's survival.

"Bertha just came up from the ship," he said. "The map still shows the mercs on the main path, although we don't have a specific location. We're going to assume they won't change course, which means we'll face them soon. Sam, give us the latest on the rocktopi."

The fight would soon start. Once her report was finished, she'd head down—she wondered if she would see any of these people again.

"Whitey is down in the ship," she said. "He's been sending messengers to keep me informed. He's overseeing the refugee boarding. We have a little over an hour until liftoff."

It was strange to think of rocktopi boarding a ship built by rocktopi as "refugees," but that's what they were. From what Sam could gather, most of the aliens had seen the ship as nothing more than a museum with some functional industrial spaces, little more than a relic containing archives of their ancient past.

She'd learned much in the past few hours. She'd learned that a hundred or so rocktopi performed constant maintenance checks on the ship. That was their reason for being, a quasi-religious existence—they were monks, the ship was the chapel. But periodic checks on systems were the bulk of their devotion, because she had also learned that rocktopi were barely necessary at all to keep the ship in working order.

The silverbugs did most of the work.

That was, apparently, the original purpose of those robots: ship maintenance and repair. They had done their job for twelve millennia, keeping the ship's vital systems in working order. And now, that work was about to pay off—*if* O'Doyle could keep Angus at bay long enough.

"Whitey reports that the ship's anti-grav device is working," Sam said. "That's what picks up the mountain, apparently. Don't ask me *how* it works, I have no idea. As near as I can translate, ship engineers are using the device to create small tremors that will let them detect new fissures and faults. Keep in mind that to them, the word *new* means anything that's appeared in the last twelve thousand years. They have to mark those faults to make sure the mountain doesn't crumble when they lift it up."

Mullet raised a hand. "How long until they lift the mountain?"

"They begin the process about an hour before takeoff," Sam said. "At that time, the entire tunnel complex will become unstable. This place is going to shake. A lot. They've told me there will be falling rock."

Sleepy glanced up at the cavern ceiling high above. "Death from above. Any rocks that fall from up there will be at terminal velocity by the time they hit. If it takes twenty minutes just to get to the ship, won't we get hammered in the tunnel that leads there?"

That question put Sam even further into the realm of the unknown. She was fairly confident she knew what Whitey's messengers had told her, but if she got it wrong, people might survive Angus and the mercs only to die on their way to the ship.

"They have some protection, as I understand it," Sam said. "The tunnel that leads to the ship should be shored up by their anti-grav tech, and also some of the ship cavern, but they said that's far too big to make completely safe."

Sam couldn't help but quickly glance around the City Cavern. This amazing place—twelve *thousand* years of history—was going to collapse. The Ship Cavern, too, and all the wonders it contained, would be gone.

O'Doyle walked to the middle of the group, where everyone could see him.

"Here's our timetable," he said. "Real-world time is eighteen hundred hours right now. Our deadline to get aboard is nineteen hundred. It's a twenty-minute hike from here to reach the ship cavern. That's walking time. We will be running, but also tired from fighting. We have to account for any wounded we might be carrying with us as well, although we're working on something for that. So, let's assume we need ten minutes, *max*, to reach the ship—that means we have to abandon our positions *no later* than eighteen-fifty. Everyone understand that?"

The humans nodded.

"Expect Angus's forces to reach this cavern at eighteen-thirty. We have to assume he has a map and knows the location of the tunnels that lead to the ship. Tommy, unopposed, how long do you think it will take the robot dog to reach the ship cavern?"

Tommy started to push away from the obelisk base, seemed to think better of it, leaned back against it.

"They're quick," he said. "Even in the tunnels. In an open space like this, they'll be fast as hell. If they know where to go, we have to assume it will take them about fifteen minutes to go from the mouth of the main tunnel all the way down to the ship cavern."

"That means we have three primary objectives," O'Doyle said. "First, bottle them up near the entrance so they can't deploy as they see fit, can't spread out. Second, identify the machine that is carrying the nuke and take it out at all costs."

Mullet raised his hand again. "Kool won't detonate it if he and the mercs are still in blast range, right? We'll be in the ship and gone long before it goes off."

"*If* the ship works," O'Doyle said. "Even if it does, we have to assume there will be problems, delays. If we take out the nuke, that buys us more time. Which brings me to our third objective—kill as many of the mercs as we can. *If* we stop the nuke, and *if* we do enough damage to them, then we might be able to hole up in the ship while Whitey and the others troubleshoot any issues that arise. If we leave the mercs mostly intact, they are more likely to figure out a way to stop the ship from leaving. If we want to live, if we want to save the rocktopi from being cooked alive in their own ship, we slow the mercs down, take out the nuke, then cripple them as a fighting force. Any questions?"

"A big one," Sleepy said. "Say there are no delays. Say the ship works fine. Say one of us is isolated and injured, or lags behind due to avoiding incoming fire. If we aren't at the ship by nineteen hundred, can the rocktopi hold it for us?"

Sam had anticipated that question, asked it of one of the messengers. She didn't like the answer. Neither would these soldiers.

"They can't hold it," she said. "Apparently, lifting up the mountaintop and raising the ship are *not* separate elements, they're part of the same process. At nineteen hundred, all entrances into the ship will automatically seal. Anyone not aboard at that time…"

She couldn't bring herself to say the rest. She imagined one of these brave soldiers — human or rocktopi, it didn't matter which — being just a few moments too late, forced to watch the ship rise up, knowing he or she would soon be buried in an eternal tomb of granite.

"I see," Otto said. "So you're telling us that punctuality is a virtue."

Mullet laughed. Tommy did, too, then coughed.

Sam couldn't understand how anyone could laugh at a time like this.

"We all know what we're fighting for here," O'Doyle said. "Not just our lives, but the lives of the rocktopi."

Slow nods from the NoSeeUms. Grim faces. *Determined* faces.

"Not just for us and the squidleys," Mullet said. "We do it for Skylark."

"And Hatchet," Sleepy said.

"And Curveball," Tommy said.

"And El Gato," O'Doyle said. "He killed himself because he couldn't deal with the memory of Bandah. If we pull this off, he gets some honor back."

Sam didn't know who *El Gato* was. She wasn't about to ask.

Klimas pointed at Tommy. "He's in no shape to fight. He should be at the ship."

"I ordered him to go there, but he refused." O'Doyle looked at Bertha, gave her an insider's grin. "Some people don't know how to follow orders."

She nodded, love and pride on her face for all to see.

Tommy forced a smile. "I don't want to miss the party, and you all know how much I love a good party."

"Final assignments," O'Doyle said. "I'm at the east wall with Sleepy, Slash, his rocktopi squad, and our little surprises. Bertha, Otto, Tommy, you're at the west wall with Siren, Axl and the other rocktopi squad."

Tommy straightened. "I'm the best shot and you know it."

"You're also beat to hell," Ender said.

Tommy twirled his trigger finger in the air.

"I feel like hot garbage, but this little guy works just fine. I can still shoot."

"But you can't *run*," O'Doyle said. "If you're at the west wall and you need to bail, the houses will provide cover while you follow the shoreline right back to the ship tunnel. Klimas will take the sniper position in the center, Mullet will be his spotter. If the shit hits the fan, they'll lose themselves in the streets and buildings. Agreed?"

Klimas and Mullet nodded.

Tommy looked like he wanted to argue but didn't have the strength.

"I suppose you're right." Tommy sounded more than tired—he sounded *defeated*. "Following the shoreline makes sense."

"Bertha, Otto, Tommy," O'Doyle said, "we'll have more strength at the east wall, and we'll show that strength, so I suspect the mercs will hit there hardest. If things get hot at the west wall, though, the three of you bail out and get to the ship. You do *not* wait for me. Got it?"

Otto nodded. Tommy shrugged. Bertha stared down at the tiles. She nodded as well.

"That's the plan," O'Doyle said. "I'm sending a countdown clock to your HUD."

Sam glanced at her HUD, didn't see anything. Then, in the upper-right, a countdown timer appeared: 56:26.

The 26 ticked down to 25, then 24, then 23.

"Fifty-six minutes and counting," O'Doyle said. "If you're not on board when it hits *zero*, you're fucked. No exceptions. Got it?"

Heads nodded.

An echo like distant thunder. Everyone looked north, to the main tunnel entrance.

"Got one," Mullet said. "Almost time to party."

O'Doyle stood in front of Sam.

"You did great work," he said. "Time for you to head down to the ship."

He offered his hand. They shook.

"Good luck," she said.

He forced a smile. "We won't need it."

The people walked off the plaza, headed toward their positions. With a few sharp screeches, Slash and Axl led their units after them.

"Hey," Tommy said. He was still leaning against the obelisk base.

Sam went to him, again wondering how he even had the strength to stay upright. He was going to die, was probably dying already.

She felt the tears coming.

"None of that," Tommy said. His smile was tired but genuine. "You and I got to live our dreams, right? You solved the mystery of the lost Chaltélian culture, I got to live a real-life science fiction story."

She blinked rapidly, unable to stop the tears. She'd cried for Ramiro. Now she cried for Tommy.

"But you didn't even get to see the ship," she said.

He took a slow breath, nodded. "Yeah. That part sucks. But, hey, all I need to do is survive the next hour, then I'll get to *ride* in the thing, right?"

She doubted he could even make the hike to the ship, let alone survive the coming battle.

"You shouldn't fight," she said. "You're a mess."

"Believe it or not, I've been in way worse shape than this and still fought."

"You're full of shit, Tommy Strymon."

He laughed, a sound once again stopped by a wet cough that scrunched his eyes tight. He bent at the waist—she stepped closer, put an arm around him, held him up.

Sam gave him a moment to recover.

He cleared his throat, stood straight.

"I'm sorry you lost Ramiro," he said.

She nodded. "It hurts. It will hurt when I lose you, too."

He regarded her for a moment, then smiled again.

"In another time, another place, you and I could have shared a lot of books. If you get out of here and I don't, I hope you don't forget me."

The tears came faster now; there was no stopping them.

"As if I could," she said.

He pushed himself off the base, leaned on her for support.

"Samira Jabour, you say the nicest things. Now, help me get to my position, then you get the hell out of here."

Her arm around his waist, feeling his solidity, his weight, she led him off the plaza tiles.

On the surface

TIM FEELY SHIVERED against the cold. He should have brought something warmer.

He stared northwest, taking in the iconic mountain and the sky that seemed to have no end.

"It's big," he said.

Lianna Wilkerson nodded once. "I've seen bigger."

No smile on her mouth. Tim couldn't see her eyes behind her dark sunglasses. Her idea of a joke? Maybe a dig on him? She always had something to say about size, height, shit like that, even though she never made it obvious she was referring directly to Tim's small stature.

He didn't mind so much. She *was* taller than him. Hell, at six-foot-three, Lianna was taller than almost everyone. Even with the bulky red jacket, she looked long, lean and lethal.

"It's not the size," Tim said, "it's …"

He remembered his most recent sexual harassment seminar, chose to not finish the sentence. He was the boss now, couldn't make the same jokes he'd once made. At least not in front of a woman.

Why the hell had he gotten out of the Land Rover? Should have stayed inside, where it was nice and warm. No end of scenery in this place, though. From the rugged lodge to the little crystal blue lake to the snow-capped mountains to the sprawling hills around them, pure beauty.

Pure beauty that wasn't supposed to include earthquakes. Even with the Land Rover driving across the poor excuse for a road that led to the lodge, he'd felt it. They all had.

People had reported tremors before Utah kicked up a brand-new volcano.

"He's been in there awhile," Lianna said. "Should we go in after him?"

Before Tim could answer, the front door of the lodge opened. P.J. Colding stepped out. The guy looked so at home in a black parka. At least to Tim, anyway. Maybe that was because of the time they'd spent together on Black Manitou Island in the dead of winter, and Colding had constantly worn a similar jacket.

Colding walked up to Tim and Lianna. The man always seemed to take his sweet time.

"No one home," he said. "This place is definitely their base of operations, though. Personal effects of O'Doyle, Lybrand and the others."

Stitches on the left side of his neck, from just behind the jaw to the left side of his Adam's apple. A parting gift from Swinestine.

"What about Otto and Klimas?" Tim asked.

Colding shook his head. "No sign of them. Sorry."

Tim wondered, and not for the first time, why he'd come at all. Colding could handle himself, and with Lianna—once a light heavyweight title contender—the two of them knew what they were doing. Tim was little more than a liability.

And yet, he'd had to come. He'd been through a lot with Clarence Otto and Paulius Klimas.

The two men had reported that they'd arrived at this place, trying to track down O'Doyle's team, and then, nothing. Nothing for three days. That wasn't like either man.

Tim couldn't rely on the local authorities to check things out. The Argentinian government would not take kindly to US operatives—of any agency—doing work on Argentinian soil without permission.

At least Tim didn't have to deal with the little mercenary base at Villa O'Higgins. The CIA was handing that. A quiet, polite conversation had gone down between the CIA and G4S: *Those armed people you have operating in Argentina without the knowledge of the Argentinian government? You got them here quietly. Make sure they leave the same way, and leave now. Otherwise, the satellite footage we took will go public, and all the people you bribed to set up that camp will be exposed. So, move it along, and here's a few million for your troubles.*

Tim had no idea whose budget that "few million" would come out of. Probably his. If so, it was worth it — the Department of Special Threats quietly focused on biological hazards, not on rousting mercs from foreign soil.

But what had the mercs in that camp seen? Would they talk? Undoubtedly, as there was nothing to be done about that, but with a little luck any claims that filtered out to the internet would find a home only on *Coast to Coast AM* and conspiracy theory YouTube channels.

Maybe it was doubling down on a bad decision to come here. Maybe. Still, Tim was the boss, and most of the time the boss got to do what the boss wanted to do, which included making bad decisions.

"Shit," Tim said. "What do we do now?"

Colding sighed, looked to the towering peak of Mount Fitz Roy.

"I honestly don't know," he said. "No sign of them, no word from them. We should be careful about going into El Chaltén and asking questions. You want to get the Argentinians involved yet?"

Tim most certainly did *not* want that. He had a cover story ready to go, his guy at the State Department ready to jump in, to do pre-emptive damage control if necessary. But even with that, Tim would be in deep shit for sending two agents here, and then—like the dumdum he was—sending two more as well as coming himself.

"Try calling them again," he said.

Wilkerson nodded. She reached into a jacket pocket, pulled out a small cell phone.

"DST Two, this is DST Three," she said. "Do you copy?"

She waited. No response.

"DST Two, this is DST Three," she said again. "Come in."

Still nothing.

She put the phone away.

"We can try the helicopter company again," Colding said.

Tim shook his head. There were shenanigans afoot there. He had a feeling someone at the company had been paid off, so as not to talk about the helicopter that Otto and Klimas had chartered. If Tim threw in the towel and called the Argentinian government, that would change things quickly.

"Not just yet," he said. "Otto and Klimas were looking for a tunnel system. Maybe they found it. None of O'Doyle's people are here. I think we have to wait a little longer, see if anything comes up."

Colding tilted his head toward the lodge. "I thought you might say that. Their kitchen is full. I put on a pot of coffee. If we're going to wait, let's wait inside, where it's warm. We'll search the place more thoroughly. Maybe we can find something."

To be in that place if O'Doyle and his killers came back? Not good. But at the same time, it would keep him, Colding and Lianna out of sight, away from the town.

No need to panic yet. About O'Doyle, the tremor, or the insane idea that a volcano might pop up like an angry jack-in-the-box.

Tim would wait, see if there was a way to help his people.

"I take mine black," he said.

BOOK SIX
WAR

94

37:51
37:50
37:49

The sound of thunder echoed across the city.

"They triggered the other claymore," Sleepy said. "They sure aren't being subtle."

Patrick stayed low behind the wall of broken stone walls and jagged boulders. He stared north, into the darkness of the tunnel mouth a hundred meters away.

His skin tingled. He felt the rush of the coming battle. The danger, the pending violence … he had to admit that he still loved it. Life and death, the ultimate game.

"It's not too late for your soul," Sleepy said.

"Fuck off."

"I'm serious, Patrick. I can baptize you right now. Give your soul to god before your body is taken from you."

At any other time, he might have punched Doug for saying shit like that. But not now. Not when the end was near.

"I'm good," Patrick said, his eyes still fixed on the tunnel mouth. "But I appreciate the offer. Really. And I'm sorry I got you into this."

A rustle of gravel under boots as Sleepy adjusted his position.

"The good lord guided me here," he said. "So there can be no *fault* to apologize for. I am where he wants me to be."

What kind of god would want his follower to be *here*?

Patrick started to ask just that when he saw something in the tunnel mouth.

He pushed his *talk* button, locked it open.

"Movement in the tunnel," he said. "Everyone, comms on."

He held his hand behind him for Slash to see, the gesture for *get ready*.

A few frightened squeaks from the rocktopi—a single sharp screech from Slash shut them up.

The tunnel mouth erupted, a wave of scurrying black bodies moving on long legs spread out across not only paving tiles, but also up the cavern walls.

"Hold your fire," Patrick whispered. "It's the black ones Sonny told us about, got to be three dozen of them. Conserve ammo—don't shoot them unless you have to."

Time for the first surprise.

Patrick flashed another signal behind him.

A sharp, answering chirp from Slash.

From cracks and crevices in the rubble wall, a dozen spotless, newly machined silverbugs raced forward to meet the enemy.

The still-unseen factories inside the ship had been hard at work producing silverbugs. These didn't have the small dents and scratches of their maintenance-oriented brethren—the new ones gleamed like scurrying, curved mirrors. Instead of a wedge-head, these machines led with a stubby, angled spike protruding from a gleaming cylinder.

Two waves of spindly machines rushed toward each other, scurrying over rubble and rock and tile, *click-click-click* streaming toward *clack-clack-clack.*

The first silverbug reached the first blackbug. The blackbug's front leg reared back like the leg of a dark praying mantis, then drove down at the oncoming silverbug—a single, pointed black claw glanced off the polished platinum shell. The silverbug's thin front legs reached out, grabbed the black ball, pulled it close. Black legs squirmed, but before the machine could scramble free, the silverbug's angled spike shot forward like a boxer's snap-jab, driving deep into the black shell.

The blackbug shivered.

The spike retracted, punched a second hole, this time with a spurt of purple sparks to mark the impact.

The black machine rolled to its back, legs sticking up and twitching like a freshly killed insect.

First blood to the silverbugs.

The waves of silver and black slammed into each other, two armies of ants eager to slay their foes, twitching legs and claws and spikes flashing across the paving stones. Silverbugs seemed to win most of the encounters, but they didn't win them all—in seconds, the tiles were littered with ruined bodies, black and silver alike.

Patrick had a moment to think ahead, to consider the best way to send the surviving silverbugs into the tunnel mouth to do what damage they could, when that very mouth erupted with a thin, reddish cloud.

The cloud swept over the machine battlefield.

EAT IT, YOU fucks," Angus said.

He watched the BlackBug video feeds as his depleted SwarmStorm tore into the shiny new silverbugs. His HUD counter blinked to life in red numbers, showing the count of enemy machines: *9,* then *12,* and stopped at *15.*

Less than 500 swarmbots left. More than enough to clear out fifteen silverbugs.

The swarmbot counter started to drop—but the silverbug counter dropped much slower than it had before, and those deaths looked to be the result of BlackBug strikes, not the SwarmStorm.

"Doctor Kool," Donnie snapped, "tell me what's happening."

Angus didn't know. So far, his SwarmStorm had shredded the silverbugs. What had changed?

He looked closer at the video feeds. These silverbugs were shiny. They had blades. A new design, but the shells looked like the same platinum-iridium as the rest, so why would they…

Thicker shells. Not just knives, but *thicker shells*.

"Doctor Kool!"

"*Hold on*," Angus said.

Someone in O'Doyle's camp was far too fucking smart.

The SwarmStorm counter continued to drop, far too fast. The bots were reacting as programmed—when the first four attacking each silverbug didn't stop the rocktopi machines from moving, more bots descended.

Angus called up his programming interface. The swarmbots' drills would only go so far in. The thicker shells rendered the weapon useless— he had to have his bots ignore the shell, look for and attack any areas that might be thinner.

The silverbug "head," the protrusion with the curved blade. Where there was a head, there was a neck…

84:25
84:24
84:23

"Ender to Worm."

Tommy: "Go ahead, Ender."

"The new silverbugs are still fighting. Are the thicker shells working?"

Tommy: "I think so. The older silverbugs would have been taken out by now. They…hold on, I'm seeing new ones drop."

Patrick saw it, too. The machines started to fall, some perfectly still, some with legs twitching. The last of the new silverbugs fell still. They'd done damage, though—only a handful of black machines remained on the tiled road.

"So much for that," Patrick said.

Tommy: "The swarm cloud is going back into the main tunnel. I can barely make it out—I don't think Angus has many left."

If he didn't have enough to send into the woods to clear out the silverbugs there, the mercs might not think they could take that route.

"Flying robot swarms that kill autonomous murder machines," Sleepy said. "At least this fight isn't boring."

The few surviving black spiders scurried to the cavern walls. Five of them, maybe six. Up they went, climbing the rough stone, spreading out along the walls, heading for the arched ceiling. If they had cameras, Angus was probably using them as an underground equivalent of eyes in the sky.

"Ender to Mullet, you two see those black machines?"

Mullet: "Yeah. I count five … no, six."

He and Mullet were in a rocktopi house with a hole knocked through the wall. It gave Klimas a perfect sniper position to fire at mercs advancing out of the tunnel mouth, but with the roof over his head he couldn't shoot *up*.

"Mullet, maintain your position," Patrick said. "Klimas, back out of there, keep buildings between you and the merc force so you're out of sight, and take out those black machines. Top priority."

Klimas: "On it."

The red cloud—now so sparse Patrick could barely see it—flowed back into the tunnel mouth.

Patrick glanced at his HUD: *34:01, 34:00, 33:59.*

The silverbugs had bought a few precious seconds.

A gunshot echoed through the cavern. Patrick saw a brief bit of motion—a blackbug falling off the wall.

Worm: "Any sign of those dogs yet?"

"Negative," Patrick said. "Worm, you in good enough shape to shoot straight?"

Worm: "The day I can't shoot straight is the day I'm in a pine box."

Tommy had always been the best marksman of the NoSeeUms. Even on death's door, he was probably a better shot than anyone else.

"If you see those black drones, Worm, take them out. Everyone else, stay cool, stay low. Be ready for whatever they send next."

FIFTY METERS FROM the tunnel mouth, Angus watched his HUD map. Six small green dots that represented BlackBugs spread out across the cavern. A seventh had just blinked out.

The remains of BaDonkeyDonk Three lay next to him. Angus had briefly toyed with the idea of trying to fix it, but the machine had tripped two claymore mines. One rear leg was completely gone. A front one worked partially but wouldn't extend all the way. The camera had been blasted to shit.

The merc column had reached the edge of the cavern without taking additional losses. Sending the hauler first had been a great idea, Angus had to admit. And it had been Dimwit's idea. Even a blind squirrel finds a nut once in a while.

"Doctor Kool," Donnie said, "I see glimmers of metal in the trees east of the city. Do you confirm?"

Angus switched through the views from the BlackBug cams. LiDAR remained their key function—mapping the as-yet undefined parts of the cavern—but the visual cameras were picking up some things the LiDAR did not.

Things like light from the artificial sun reflecting off dozens of curved metal shapes moving through the trees.

Sweet jumping Jesus … was there no end to the number of these things?

"Shit," Angus said. "They've got silverbugs in the woods."

"How many?"

"No way of knowing, not with the trees providing visual cover like that. If there's enough of them, they could take out Goofy and Cujo before they get through the woods."

"Can you send the SwarmStorm in to take the silverbugs out?"

A glance at the HUD showed the number of swarmbots that remained: 28.

That was all he had left. Over 400 had destroyed themselves trying to take out the thicker silverbugs. Such a fucking simple strategy, and yet it had crippled one of Angus's remaining weapons.

"Not enough swarmbots left," Angus said. "And their charges are almost drained. They'd be good for maybe another fifteen minutes, then they'll fall out of the sky. I can rig a recharge for them, but it won't give us much—batteries are nearly drained across the board."

That was because Angus had siphoned power from all devices, making sure his suit had plenty stored in case he needed to make a desperate run for the surface.

"The city, all those buildings," Donnie said. "They could have more silverbugs in there?"

"Obviously."

"We'd need to clear out the woods to let Goofy go around and flank," Donnie said. "O'Doyle's smart. He wants us to come right up the middle. We have no choice but to hit those walls hard, drive his forces back."

Angus heard the faint crack of a gunshot filter up the tunnel—a green dot blinked out.

"Donnie, I think they're shooting at the BlackBugs. We only have five left."

"Then make them scramble so their snipers can't draw a bead."

Angus cursed under his breath—he should have done that already. He blinked through the menus faster than ever before, activating a randomizer pattern that would make the BlackBugs alter their movement while still spreading out across the cavern to get maximum map coverage.

"There," he said. "No one in the world can hit them now."

Another faint gunshot, but this time the remaining green lights stayed on.

A MISS.

Tommy breathed out slowly, looked through his scope, tried to track the tiny spec of black crawling across the stone some two hundred meters above and away. Small, fast, moving in strange patterns … a damn near impossible shot.

"Klimas, this is Worm, I'm tracking a target on the west side."

Klimas: "Copy, Worm, I've got the east."

At least they wouldn't both miss shooting at the same target.

Tommy breathed in slow, breathed out slow. The black spec moved randomly, except *nothing* was truly random. There was always a formula.

He watched it turn left, forward second, then right, two seconds angling to the left, then right …

The part of Tommy's mind that he didn't know how to control began to count.

"DOCTOR KOOL, I need the location of that tunnel."

Even with the KoolSuit, Angus began to sweat. The cavern was too big for the nuke-laden Cujo and the mercs to just go in there and wander around, hoping they might stumble upon the right tunnel, especially with O'Doyle's trigger-happy grunts firing away. Angus had to get the location of the tunnels that led to the ship cavern.

Another faint, echoing gunshot; no green lights blinked out.

He had quite a bit of data already, but not enough. With his knowledge of the Utah complex, if he could spot additional tunnels, even a hint of their decline angle would likely tell him what he needed to know.

If this place was anything like Utah, and Angus knew that it was, at this depth any tunnel that led *down* more than likely led to the ship.

And speaking of *more than likely*, if he didn't get to the ship, he was more than likely dead.

"Doctor Kool?"

"I'm *trying*, Donnie! I need a little more time."

Another gunshot—a green light blinked out.

What the fuck?

"That's impossible," Angus said.

Donnie turned to him. "What's impossible?"

Only four left.

"Doctor," I said, "*what's im*—"

"Shut the fuck up, Dimwit! I have to fucking concentrate!"

Another gunshot—another green light blinked out.

Three left.

KLIMAS: "HOLY SHIT, O'Doyle—your boy is on a different level. I can barely get a scope on these things and he's one-shotting them left and right."

Patrick kept his eyes fixed on the tunnel mouth. He didn't need to respond. Worm had always been one of a kind, a magician's hat of hidden talents. *Everyone* knew Worm was special, except for one person—Worm himself.

But this wasn't the time to dwell on wasted potential.

Worm: "Got another one. East side clear."

Klimas: "Worm, help me, take my west side targets if you can."

Worm: "Copy that. Lybrand, spot for me. Call out the targets as you see them."

"I DON'T FUCKING *know how they're hitting us,"* Angus screamed. "I'm telling you, the bugs are on a random pattern!"

Donnie glared at him. Angus turned away from the man. He had to focus. Was there time to change the randomizer program? No, not with only two BlackBugs left, and whatever Rain Man sharpshooter was taking them out.

A creeping dread lurked at the back of Angus's thoughts. He'd written that randomizer pattern himself. It was uncrackable, yet the immediate evidence did not lie—it had been cracked, cracked fast, cracked thoroughly.

That dread…was someone in that cavern *smarter than him?*

The faint crack of a gunshot; both green dots remained.

Angus was halfway through a sigh of relief when another shot came, and this time, a light blinked out.

The last BlackBug was more than halfway across the cavern ceiling, moving toward the far end. The map expanded in real-time. Fewer buildings in the south end of the city—finally, the BlackBug started scanning the cavern's back wall.

Angus blinked through his menus, abandoning the randomizer, instructing the last BlackBug to sprint toward the cavern's end.

Just a few more seconds, and Angus would have the info he needed…

Another shot—the green light stayed on.

TOMMY POPPED IN a fresh magazine, doing it by feel alone, trying to keep his eyes on the area across the cavern where he'd seen the black speck. In an odd way, it was easier than shooting at people—people could be *truly* unpredictable.

Machines, apparently, could not.

"In," Tommy said. "You got it?"

Lybrand's carbine rested on the stone wall, as stable as the stone itself.

"I got it," she said. "It's moving straight now."

That wasn't good—that meant its owner, probably Angus, wanted it to get to a specific spot.

Tommy knelt next to her, used her barrel as a guide. In seconds, he spotted the spec. She was right, it was moving straight, its progress altering only to move around outcroppings. It was already at the downward curve of the cavern ceiling's south side.

Already close to the tunnels that led to the ship.

That was where Angus needed it to go.

"Shit," Tommy said.

He let his brain do the math of range, distance and angle …

ANGUS WATCHED THE map expanding in real time. The west and east edges began to curve together—the BlackBug was almost at the end.

That hateful crack of gunfire.

The last green light blinked out.

"Doctor Kool," Donnie said, "kindly tell me you got what we needed."

The BlackBug was gone, but the algorithm continued to calculate the data it had collected. The map lines converged, closer, closer … *a gap* … the lines continued and touched.

Angus held his breath as his software did its thing.

Then, the gap revealed itself as a tunnel mouth.

A tunnel mouth that led sharply *down*.

"Fuck you," he said. "Donnie, I got it!"

PATRICK KNEW HOW to stay calm. Even three miles below ground with a tunnel about to vomit killers, even with a nuke in play, he knew how to stay calm.

He watched. He waited.

Worm: "The drones appear to all be gone."

"Good news," Patrick said.

Worm: "I wish it were. I got a bad feeling that he was looking for the entrance to the ship cavern, and that he found it."

A wash of anger cut through the calm.

Mullet: "A *bad feeling*, Worm? Don't tell me you're getting all superstitious like our Bible-thumping buddy."

"Cut the chatter," Patrick said. "They're coming in regardless, they don't have a choice. Stay sharp."

"LISTEN UP, MEN," Donnie said. "I only have time to say this once."

Angus felt his heart hammering behind his chest armor. This was it. It had been so close, but he'd gotten the info Donnie wanted. That tunnel led to the ship, there was no doubt.

"Your HUD's maps are updating," Donnie said. "Our objective is the tunnel at the far end of the alien town. The enemy has two defensive emplacements, one a hundred meters south-southwest, one a hundred meters south-southeast. We need to eliminate all enemy personnel in those points to clear the way for our payload delivery vehicle. Platoons One and Two, deploy along the west wall. Four, Five and Six along the east wall. Recon stays in reserve with me. Men, I will remind you that time is of the essence—the longer we take to kill the enemy, the more likely our collective nuts get boiled in a big bath of molten magma. Kill anything that isn't us."

Angus turned off his comm, had to hold back a giggle.

"*Collective nuts get boiled in a big bath of molten magma?* Donnie, you have such a way with words."

"I do at that," the man said. "If you could focus on the task at hand, Doctor, make sure you keep Cujo close to you. It's time to send in Goofy."

30:25

30:24

30:23

Tommy lay on his belly at the west wall, carbine aimed between two chunks of broken rock. The thin space gave him almost full cover yet offered an uninterrupted field of view across the rubble of a hundred smashed stone houses all the way to the main tunnel entrance.

He still hurt, hurt *bad*, but he'd locked the pain away. His military career, from boot through multiple deployments, had taught him how to function and fight effectively while injured, exhausted, hungry and thirsty.

Lybrand was five meters to Tommy's right, Otto fifteen meters to his left. Both were crouched down like he was, waiting for a target, carbines resting on the wall. Between Tommy and Otto, Axl, Disco, Siren and six other rocktopi stayed low, well out of sight from the tunnel mouth. Each alien held a carved shield and a railgun. Some of them trembled—fear, at least, was one thing the two species shared equally.

Otto: "You two are so calm. I feel like I'm going to puke."

Despite his admission, his voice remained smooth.

Lybrand: "*Calm*. That's funny. Good thing the KoolSuits handle our waste, because I'm so scared I'm literally pissing myself."

Both of them admitted their fear. Good. Tommy knew soldiers. Some got through the tension with puffed-up bravado, some by pretending that a battle was just another day at the office. The ones who operated best, in his experience, were the ones who understood that their life could end in an instant. Fear—*controlled* fear—made one sharp.

"Just keep breathing, both of you," Tommy said. "Slow and easy. Once the bullets start flying, you won't have time to worry about anything else."

Otto: "Gosh, that helps me so much."

Ender: "Can the chatter. Be ready."

Tommy would rather have had his NoSeeUms with him, but he believed Otto and Lybrand would stay tight, would do their jobs until they got hit.

As for the rocktopi hunkered down and waiting, Tommy couldn't say. Axl—maybe just as injured as Tommy was—would stand and fight. Siren, too. The little alien seemed to have a bit of magic in him. He'd survived two battles against the mercs. Maybe he'd be good luck.

Two other rocktopi had survived the fight at the fissures. Both of them were with Slash over at the east wall. That was where Ender thought the worst fighting would be, so he'd loaded up on numbers, equipment, what little combat experience there was to be had, and his various "surprises."

Lybrand: "Movement, tunnel mouth."

Otto: "I see it."

NoSeeUms sounded off as Tommy looked for and spotted the movement. Everyone saw something in the shadows.

What was it? The nuke-dog? No, a man, a man with a long weapon, *two* men …

"RPG," Tommy said.

A flash, a burst of smoke—an explosion, black smoke at the east wall. Another flash. Tommy slid down. An instant later, the shuddering roar of the rocket hitting the wall's piled stones. His helmet speakers attenuated the sound instantly—he *felt* the impact more than heard it.

The attack had begun.

ON THE HUD, Angus watched Goofy's view.

The machine streaked toward the east wall at thirty miles an hour. No short tunnels, no tight switchback corners, the converted donkey hit its top speed almost immediately.

"Hit it again," Donnie said.

Two mercs holding RPGs again stepped forward toward the tunnel entrance. They stayed in the shadow. Over the still-dissipating echo of the first round of explosions, Angus heard the now-familiar reports of O'Doyle's people firing single rounds.

One man fired at the west wall, one at the east.

In the HUD, Angus saw the bright flare of the RPG as it shot past and slammed into the east wall. A flash, a concussive blast of black smoke and dust and flying stone.

Goofy was fifty meters out, closing fast.

Whatever the RPG hadn't killed, the machine would.

Twenty-five meters from the target…

Angus saw something through the cloud of smoke and dust, something rising up from behind a stone building just past the impromptu wall.

"Oh, shit," Angus said.

Goofy was ten meters from the wall when the biggest silverbug Angus had ever seen rose up on long, thin legs…

27:48
27:47
27:46

"Here it comes!"

Patrick sighted through the smoke, trying to target the robot dog's head.

God, the thing was so *fast*. Legs a hazy blur, head as still and rock steady as if it was perched on a thick pole set deep in the cavern floor.

A shadow passed overhead—the silvermech stepped over the wall.

Sleepy: "God's hand guide thee."

The robot dog slowed, almost comically so, mechanical legs chopping at the ground to bleed momentum, metal feet skidding across the rubble-strewn tiles.

O'Doyle fired.

The robot's armored head twitched; *a hit*.

He didn't know if the round did any good. Feet still pumping, skidding, the dog banked left, trying to get clear, but it had been moving too fast to make a sharp cut—one of the silvermech's long arms reached out, matched the dog's speed. The three-fingered hand grabbed, but the timing was off—the closed fist slammed against the dog's flank, sent the robot tumbling across tiles and rubble.

The dog flailed as it slid to a stop, righting itself, coming up on four feet. Jesus, the *balance* of the thing—it moved like a living creature, like a wolf or a panther.

A panther…with one lame leg. The bent metal limb didn't quite reach the ground.

The silvermech took another long step toward its now three-legged prey, again reached out a three-fingered hand. This time, the dog was ready—it opened up with the SAW. A stream of 5.56-by-45 millimeter rounds *clang-clang-clanged* off the silverbug's round hull.

Klimas: "They're throwing smoke."

Past the battling machines, Patrick saw white smoke billowing up from a half-dozen spots.

"Hold your fire," he said. "Don't waste rounds shooting into the smoke. Get ready for their main advance. After we hit them in the open, we'll send in the other two silvermechs."

000/184/200

"Kool, get your ass back here!"

Angus ignored Donnie's command.

In the HUD, Goofy's feed showed nothing but static.

000/146/200

Angus ran to the tunnel mouth, dodging around the members of First Platoon who were launching smoke grenades out of the tunnel. Canisters clattered and spun across the ruined buildings, spewing clouds of white fume. Past the expanding smoke, Angus saw the massive silverbug striding toward Goofy, saw that Goofy's rear right leg was fucked all to hell.

000/016/200

Angus didn't dare take control of Goofy—if anything went wrong with the remote link, the robot would be dead in the water and the silverbug would destroy it. Angus could do nothing but watch, hope the AI he'd programmed learned fast enough to defeat this new, unanticipated threat.

000/000/192

Goofy backed up as best it could, pouring steady fire at the giant silverbug. Bullets sparked off the big platinum ball. Did any of the rounds penetrate? Angus had no idea.

The silverbug strode forward, reached out a long limb (*arms*, the big one had actual *arms*). Goofy tried to retreat, but the hobbled machine was too slow—the three-fingered silverbug hand locked down on Goofy's front left leg. The silverbug jerked Goofy into the air, at least twenty feet high, then it whipped the robot down hard like a caveman smashing a club, cracking paving tiles and scattering ceramic shards.

Goofy—front left leg torn free—bounced and landed on its side. It tried to right itself on its two working legs but only managed to spin in a pathetic circle.

The silverbug strode closer, reached down with both arms to finish the job.

Angus glanced behind him: Cujo, SAW fully loaded, ready to be thrown into the fray. But locked to Cujo's back was Dirty Randy's Money

Shot. The ancient rocktopi ship might not be able to take off at all—if Cujo got destroyed, then there'd be no mobile delivery vehicle, no way to make sure the nuke remained in play while Angus headed up the tunnels to safety.

He couldn't use Cujo. Not yet.

The rocket-flash of an RPG—the sound of the world's biggest gong as a blossom of fire sent the giant silverbug teetering to the right. Long legs awkwardly flashed, thudding against the ground. The machine looked like it was falling, but it recovered its balance, lowered the ball body toward the ground.

Donnie: "Hit it again."

A voice Angus didn't recognize: "We've only got three rounds left."

Donnie: "Saving them doesn't do us any good, *hit it again*."

Another sizzling flash. An RPG round smacked into the big silver ball—gong and explosion alike echoed through the huge cavern.

The giant silverbug rose up on its long legs, took one step forward, then all four legs gave out. The curved bottom slammed against tile and rock. It tilted to the right, then moved no more.

Donnie: "Platoon Four, move into position, divide your fire between the two defensive positions. All other platoons prepare to advance on my command."

"*Wait*," Angus said. "What if there are more of those big motherfuckers?"

Donnie: "Kool, stay quiet until I ask for you. Platoon Four, get into position."

Men ran past Angus's position, working around Cujo and Fuentes.

Donnie was making a mistake—Angus knew it, could feel it in his bones.

He eye-tracked through menus and activated his private comm link to Fuentes and Khatari.

No—just to Fuentes. Khatari was gone.

"I don't have any more video feeds," Angus said. "You stay close to the mouth, tell me what's happening. Stay on this frequency. *Do not* let anyone make you go anywhere else, even Donnie. Got it?"

Fuentes nodded. "I got you, boss. I'll man this post."

Angus felt the fingers of fear wrapping around him. He couldn't let that happen, he couldn't be afraid, not *now*. He turned and ran back up the tunnel. As he did, he blinked through his HUD—the shit had hit the fan, and he was going to need drugs to cope with this.

A *lot* of drugs.

26:01
26:00
25:59

Patrick: "Silvermech is down."

Klimas: "I'm back in the sniper's nest, ready to rock."

Bertha tried to control her breathing. Twenty-six minutes to go? When the mercs advanced, how long could she and the others hold out? How many mercs were gearing up to attack? They had RPGs…what other weapons did they have? Were there more of those SAW-wielding robots?

Control yourself. You got this. You've done this before.

She had. She'd faced a blistering attack in Afghanistan and stood firm. She'd faced a total onslaught in Utah and stood firm. She could do the same here.

All across the killing zone, white smoke spread out in expanding clouds. There wasn't wind to shift it—it hung like a softly curling mist from a zombie movie. She alternated between looking through her scope and just her eyes, hunting for targets. There were hints of movement through the smoke, but at a hundred meters, she wasn't taking a shot unless she had them in the clear.

Tommy: "Lybrand. Ten meters west of the tunnel entrance, you see those guys?"

Bertha squinted, wishing the fog away. "Yeah, I think so."

She couldn't quite make them out. They were carrying something, or setting something up.

A burst of dread ripped through her.

"Oh fuck," she said. "Patrick, I think they've got mortars."

Patrick: "I see them. Klimas, ten meters west of the entrance, you see them? Can you take them out?"

A moment of dead air.

Klimas: "Negative, the smoke is too thick."

Patrick: "Take a few shots, give them something to think about."

Klimas: "On it."

Patrick: "When the rounds come get into the trench. Unless one lands right on your head, the double-walls should protect you. Hold your positions and listen for my orders."

Bertha heard two noises in rapid succession: the single *crack* of Klimas taking a shot, followed by the deep, echoing *fwoomp* of a mortar.

Patrick: "*Incoming!*"

Bertha slid to the bottom of the wall, tucked into a ball around her carbine, her heart pounding as the frozen moment stretched out. To her left, Tommy did the same, and past him, the rocktopi covered themselves with their shields.

How did they know to do that?

The first mortar shell landed somewhere behind her, past the trench's back wall. It was like being hit by a pair of gods—the concussion wave hammered her from above, while the ground beneath her gave her a full-body kick so strong she bounced a few inches.

The rocktopi beneath their shields began to scream. Maybe it was a war cry of some kind—how could she know?—but the piercing, high-pitched sounds reeked of fear, of borderline panic. The wails cut into her soul, made primitive parts of her want to join them, to scream and run away.

Control yourself. Hold your position.

Another round hit, somewhere in front of her main wall, delivering another one-two punch. Dirt and rock rained down all around her. The blasts were so powerful she heard them *through* her helmet, despite her sound system's instant attenuation.

A third shell landed, behind again, but closer—she felt the blast through her entire body. She tucked even tighter around her weapon.

She had no idea she was screaming until she heard Patrick's sharp rebuke.

"Bertha! Shut the fuck up, we need this line open!" His words rattled in time with another explosion. "Everyone, they're trying to keep our heads down, that means they're coming. Any second now."

Her breaths came fast and shallow. She shook, shook so hard her carbine rattled against her visor. Another explosion, so close the rock slab in front of her seemed to *slap* her, sent her flying. She hit the lower rear wall, hit it *hard*. The world spun. She found herself facedown, felt her carbine beneath her. Breath gone, ears ringing, the ache of the impact reverberating through her bones. Everything was gray, everything was tilting, shifting.

Someone screaming in her comm.

Several someones.

She couldn't make out the words.

Hands under her armpits, dragging her along the ground. Bertha tried to see who it was, couldn't turn her head that way, not with that wincing pain in her neck. She looked out into a city decorated with smoke clouds, tufts of cotton spread across an expanse of stone boxes, saw another mortar round drop—she actually *saw* the shell hit, like a high-speed camera revealing a bullet's trajectory.

The round exploded, instantly shifting time from super-slow-mo to ultra-fast-forward. A jagged chunk of stone roof flipped through the air. One building was destroyed outright—a second sagged, then collapsed like a house of cards when a drunkard bumped into the table.

Those buildings were probably there for thousands of years. Thousands of years.

Otto: "Lybrand, you're too heavy for this!"

She rolled to her hands and knees, felt the hands that had been pulling her slip away. She was past the back wall, exposed—Otto had come out of the trench to get her, had been dragging her toward a gap in the rear wall.

Not even fifty feet away, a house exploded, body-sized chunks of deadly rock spinning through the air like jagged saw blades, smashing into other houses. She and Otto ducked low as rubble rained down around them.

Tommy: "Lybrand, Otto, get into position. Skirmish line advancing toward us."

Bertha scrambled through the opening, threw herself against the inside of the front wall. She found a notch, aimed through it.

Across the rubble, coming through the smoke, she saw the ghostly forms of slowly advancing killers—a World War One vision brought forth violently into the modern age.

She sighted in on the leader, a half-fog/half-human ghost coming to murder her.

"I got one," she said, "taking a shot."

Patrick: "Negative! Hold your fire! Let it play out."

Bertha realized she was shaking so bad she didn't know if she could shoot straight at all. She kept her sights fixed on the man, saw more men moving through the smoke with him. They were advancing in groups of two, a wide line of fifteen to twenty men spaced out wide, leapfrogging their way toward the wall.

They, too, held their fire—Bertha and her team weren't the only ones conserving ammo.

Another mortar round slammed home behind her, so close it lifted her off the ground an inch or two before she fell back down, her aim spoiled. She tried to reacquire her target, but he'd moved behind a thick block of broken stone, both he and the stone mostly obscured by hanging smoke.

24:38
24:37
24:36

Patrick sighted through a notch in the rubble wall. A hundred and fifty meters away, the enemy crept through the smoke. He needed to deploy his rocktopi auxiliaries. If he did so, those brave souls would die. They'd volunteered for the duty—at least as far as he could tell—but if there was another strategy that could keep them alive, wasn't he obligated to use it?

He slid down behind the wall, flashed a hand signal to Slash.

Sleepy saw the hand signal.

"Ender, what are you doing? Keep those in reserve!"

"We need to press the enemy," Patrick said. "We'll make them use all of their RPGs."

"Don't do it," Sleepy said. "Save our armor for house-to-house fighting, like we planned!"

That was the right call, the *strategic* call. Patrick knew that. He felt a tension he'd never before felt in combat. Would this decision save lives, or would it lose the battle?

He had to try.

Patrick again flashed the hand signal to Slash.

THREE SWITCHBACKS AWAY from the tunnel mouth, Angus might have deluded himself into thinking it was over were it not for the dull, echoing *booms* of mortar rounds hitting home.

"Talk to me," Angus said. "What's going on out there?"

His hands worked with speed, precision and conviction, unhooking clamps and clasps. Even with the armor, his fingers operated with dexterity. It seemed a lifetime ago when his hand was a crippled thing—which it would be whenever he took the suit off.

But that eventuality didn't matter, not now, not in the heat of battle.

Fuentes: "Some movement behind the walls, not enough for anyone to take a shot. Shit-ton of smoke, it's just hanging there."

Angus disconnected the last clasp—the weight was more than he'd expected, and even with his augmented strength he almost dropped what he'd come to get.

Fuentes: "Wait…oh, *shit*, boss. Two more of those fucking giant silverbugs, coming out of the center of town. They're moving fast!"

"Stay there," Angus said. "I'm on my way."

22:58
22:57
22:56

Tommy focused on controlling his breathing, relaxing muscles clenched iron-tight from blast after blast after blast.

Mullet: "Ha! Look at the *size* of those bitches. Take that, you cocksuckers."

Klimas: "Movement. Merc advance units are falling back, fast."

Ender: "Mortar crews abandoning their positions, retreating to the tunnel mouth."

That meant the barrage had stopped. A breathless *thank god* escaped Tommy's lips. No atheists in foxholes, nor in trenches getting hammered by enemy artillery.

Body trembling, he scrambled up the pile of jagged rock and rubble, just enough to peek over the top. So much smoke.

The two long-legged silvermechs strode across the rubble, smoke slipping around their metallic sphere bodies, like a scene straight out of *War of the Worlds*. Retreating mercs fired at the big mechs, their bullets bouncing harmlessly off the rounded shapes.

Otto: "Lybrand, you still with us?"

Sharp breaths punctuated his words—he sounded on the edge of panic.

Lybrand: "I'm here. Worm?"

Tommy glanced in her direction, then in Otto's. They were both tucked up tight down in the bottom of the trench, covered in dirt and gravel, as were the long shields that hid the rocktopi.

"I'm still in one piece," Tommy said. "I think."

He looked out across the battlefield again, watched the towering platinum machines close in on the tunnel mouth.

A flash, a blurry streak ripping through the smoke, a burst of orange as an RPG round smacked into the round shell. The silvermech staggered, righted itself, paused a moment—then continued to advance.

Mullet: "*Ha!* You stupid fucks! I hope you all get stepped on!"

Another flash. Tommy saw the blur hiss past the second tall, round machine.

A miss.

An echoing *boom* as the round came down somewhere in the alien city.

Tommy heard Mullet's saw-toothed laugh.

There, at the tunnel mouth…men running *in*, and one form, all alone, stepping *out*. Even through the smoke, Tommy was sure he recognized the bulky shape.

"Ender this is Worm," Tommy said. "I think Angus is advancing."

Ender: "Advancing? *Angus?*"

Klimas: "I see him, too. He's carrying something. Carl Gustaf, maybe."

A recoilless rifle? What *didn't* these assholes have? Would that take the silvermechs out of commission?

The machines continued to advance. No more RPG rounds shot out. Small arms fire sparked off the huge platinum shells.

Tommy squinted, trying to make out the shape that Angus carried. If it was a recoilless, why was Angus carrying it at his hip?

22:34
22:33
22:32

The merc retreat had given Patrick a moment to hope, an instant to think that he'd not only *delayed* their advance, put possibly pushed them back altogether.

That moment evaporated when an armored Angus Kool strode forward, a four-foot-long tube held at his right hip.

A blinding beam of green light appeared in the smoke above the silvermech. The beam angled downward, slicing right through a leg—the leg split in two, globs of molten metal dripping down like orange fire.

Mullet: "*Jesus fucking Christ!*"

The silvermech stumbled to the left, long legs stutter-stepping as the machine tried to keep its balance.

Patrick sighted in. "Tommy, Klimas, take him out!"

He fired at the shadowy shape, single pull after single pull, not caring about ammo, knowing he'd made a mistake, underestimated that little bastard, knowing he was about to lose his biggest advantage unless someone landed a lucky shot…

ANGUS TWISTED SLIGHTLY, letting the green beam slice the legs out from under the staggering machine. Metal separated, molten globs raining down to the rubble below. Still-moving legs tumbled like fallen trees, while the round body dropped and hit with the sound of a car driving headlong into a brick wall.

A thud against his chest, then his thigh.

Donnie: "Kool, get back here! They're shooting you!"

The loudness of god, sudden and overwhelming, coming at the same time a crack split across his visor.

Fuentes: "Boss, on your right!"

Angus turned, faced a thick cloud that seemed to slide apart before him, mist parting for the monstrosity sliding through it, curls of smoke trailing from metal dinged with scratches and bullet scars.

Long arms reaching for him, metal fingers splayed. A faceless head rushing in to smash him flat, to tear him limb from limb.

Angus took one step back, swung the ButterKnife barrel toward the burnished beast—a double-blink triggered the weapon.

The green beam lashed out, its light so bright the gleam from the spherical shell made him squint.

The beast came closer, the hands reached in.

Angus lowered his elbow, angling the beam up, turning a smooth curve of platinum-iridium into a gash of white-hot liquid metal.

The monster fell, hit hard, kicking up shards of tile and scatters of broken rock. It skipped off the broken ground, flew right at him. Angus threw himself to the right (*can't let the molten gash hit me molten gash that's a good new dirty name for a weapon*) just as the big ball slammed into him, a massive bowling ball sending a pin flying.

An instant of stillness, of odd quiet.

He landed, tumbled wildly, helpless to stop himself.

Angus Kool slid to a sudden stop.

Donnie: "*Holy shit-balls, boys, did you see that?*"

A jumble of voices inside his helmet. Whoops and hollers and joyful curses—men shouting his name.

Donnie: "Mortar crews, another three rounds, platoons spread out and advance. Let's take it to them, men!"

20:46

20:45

20:44

Sleepy: "You dumb shit, I told you!"

Patrick vibrated with anger, anger at himself.

Stupid, stupid, stupid!

He looked out across the smoky clearing, stared at the fallen form of not one, not two, but *three* silvermechs. He'd committed them too early, and because of that they were gone.

All because he'd wanted to save some lives.

Mullet: "Robots and frickin' lasers, man. This is wacky."

So goddamn stupid. He knew better. Why had he done that?

Bertha: "They're throwing more smoke, and … oh shit, I think they're manning the mortars again!"

That snapped Patrick out of his pity party.

"Tommy, come in."

Tommy: "I'm here."

"They're coming for sure this time," Patrick said. "Get ready for the signal, we'll use the rocktopi on my command."

He could only pray it wasn't too late.

"BOSS, GET up!"

Fuentes, but not just in helmet comm, close enough that Angus heard him even through the powersuit helmet.

Angus coughed. His body seemed to vibrate from the inside. Had he taken too much Adderall? He didn't remember how much he'd dosed. *Fuck* did he hurt.

"Talk to me, man," Fuentes said. "You still with us?"

Angus's eyes fluttered open. There, right in front of him, Fuentes, dirt and dust smears across his visor. Behind that thin layer, eyes that blazed with excitement and crinkled with worry. At the man's side, a sight grander than grand could be: Cujo.

Angus started to move—his head told him that was a bad idea. "What happened?"

Fuentes smiled wide. "What happened? *You* happened, you shooting-from-the-hip motherfucking demon of war, that's what happened! Look."

He pointed. Angus looked.

There, one arm still twitching, one three-fingered metal hand clutching, opening, clutching, opening, was the giant silverbug, a fist-sized gash cut through the hull like a toaster slot. Black smoke roiled from some internal fire.

"The ButterKnife," Angus said. "Where is it?"

Fuentes pointed again.

The bazooka-sized laser lay on the ground. Scratched a bit, but no worse for wear. Angus pushed himself up. If it was broken, he was so fucked.

He slowly stood, servos stabilizing his Jell-O legs. He picked up the heavy ButterKnife, re-connected the cable from his suit, then checked his HUD—fully operational, three uses remaining.

He almost collapsed with relief.

There was still a chance to stop the ship.

Donnie: "Doctor Kool, we need you in the fight. Take the east flank, keep what's left of your SwarmStorm with you to protect against silverbugs that might come out of the woods. Mortar crews, fire three rounds. When the third round hits, I'll sound the advance—close fast before they can recover."

Fuentes slapped Angus's armored shoulder.

"You ready to kick some ass?"

Angus blinked, tried to keep his balance, remembered he didn't have to, the suit did that for him.

Fuentes, scared but eager, ready to fight.

When it came to bullets, Angus was about to move the wrong way—*toward* them.

It shocked him to find he wasn't scared. Not at all.

He was just pissed.

Somewhere behind one of those walls was Patrick O'Doyle, the man of his nightmares.

"Yeah," Angus said. "I'm ready. Help me get the ButterKnife strapped to Cujo. We can't let anything happen to it or the nuke."

Before, Cujo had been there to protect Angus, now Angus would have to protect Cujo.

19:05
19:04
19:03

Another mortar slammed down, shuddering the ground beneath Tommy.

He'd been under fire before, but this was different. Never like this, never so *close*, never so *intense*, never so *unrelenting*.

A second blast showered him with sharp rocks, a hard hail that battered his body like a dozen sharp jabs.

Tommy groaned, rolled to his side, heard the dirt and gravel raining down around him.

Otto: "They're finding their range! The next one might drop right in the trench. Do we back off?"

Ender: "*Hold your position!* It has to stop soon, they won't risk shrapnel hitting their own men."

Well, wasn't that lucky for them?

Tommy heard the distant *fwoomp* of another mortar. With a sudden burst of energy, he scrambled under a shallow angle of broken wall, tucked up tight.

The blast was farther off, the impact not as bad as the others.

He listened for more explosions, more fire.

There were none.

Klimas: "Movement in the smoke. Multiple targets."

Ender: "Tommy, get the signal ready. Everyone hold your fire."

The mercs were coming. Once again, time to kill.

Before the final bullet brought him down, Tommy wondered how many more lives he'd take, how many more souls would weigh down his conscience.

Every ounce of him aching, screaming in complaint, suffering from concussive blasts, needle shards of rock, and—still—heat stroke, Tommy slid down the wall. He crawled toward where the rocktopi had been, but they were gone.

No, not gone—just hidden by a layer of dirt kicked up by the mortar impacts.

Tommy crawled to the first shield, slapped on the long slab of metal.

A single, thick tentacle slid out from underneath, black dots staring out.

Tommy made a fist, thumped it three times against his sternum—the signal to begin.

The shield angled up like a rising drawbridge as Axl rose, black-dotted skin pulsing a deep orange. The rocktopi swelled up like a pufferfish, let out an angry squeal.

Past him, the other rocktopi slowly rose up, dirt and rock sliding off their thick metal shields.

SIXTY METERS FROM the wall, Angus, Fuentes and Cujo carefully moved through the smoke, cautious of the treacherous footing presented by slabs of rocks and broken stone walls. Fuentes moved at a crouch, something Angus couldn't do in the armor.

"They ain't shooting," Fuentes said. "Maybe the mortars took them out."

Or maybe they'd run, fled from the barrage.

The thick smoke cut natural visibility to only a few feet. His own KoolSuit technology prevented him from seeing the mercs in front of him clearly—their clothes, weapons and gear all stayed close to the ambient temperature of 200 degrees Fahrenheit.

The smoke wasn't just from the grenades. Black columns billowed up from the rocktopi city, from fires started by mortar fire, or maybe that RPG, or maybe the ButterKnife beam.

Or, maybe, started by O'Doyle's people.

The black smoke hung like a thin but growing cloud in the center of the arched ceiling, cutting into the light kicked out by the artificial sun. The cavern had been bright as day—now it seemed overcast, growing darker by the minute.

Fifty meters from the wall.

The rocks and rubble there were the same temp as everything else down here—if anything was behind that hastily constructed fortification, it remained hidden.

Hidden, but *there*. He knew it. O'Doyle and his people hadn't run. Angus *knew* it.

Forty meters out—why weren't they shooting?

A piercing screech, so *loud*, from the east wall, then an answering call from the west. Were the rocktopi about to spill over the top, come rushing in a wave like they'd done in Utah?

Donnie: "Keep moving forward, stay low. Kool, commit your remaining SwarmStorm now, we can't risk you getting flanked."

Angus blinked through his menus. The cracked HUD screen still worked, although spots of it remained, like a computer display with a cluster of dead pixels. He was able to activate the remaining swarmbots— all twenty-eight of them—and deploy them to his left.

Another sound, far fainter, so low he wasn't sure he'd heard it right.

Angus stopped moving. Cujo, keying in on him, did the same.

"Fuentes, hold up," Angus said.

The mercenaries ahead kept moving. The smoke didn't stop the sound of their booted feet crunching on broken stone.

But there was something else …

Fuentes knelt, his rifle stock to his shoulder. He aimed toward the wall, now only thirty-five meters out.

Angus heard the faintest whisper of that other sound, and a stab of fear sliced through him.

It was the sound of dry leaves scraping across concrete.

From ahead, somewhere in the smoke, came a scream, a scream choked off by a wet gurgle.

Fuentes stood, backed up. *"They're coming out of the ground!"*

Boneless shapes slid up from the rubble, oozing out from under slabs of broken stone, squeezing out of thin cracks, sluglike gray bodies only slightly darker than the white smoke drifting across the ground — except for the double-crescent knives held in snakelike tentacles that gleamed in the thinning light.

They'd been there all along, out of sight, hiding, *waiting*.

Fuentes fired at something on Angus's right.

A merc ran out of the smoke, trying to retreat to Angus's left. A rocktopi tentacle whipped out from beneath a fallen stone wall — a crescent blade sliced across the backs of the merc's legs. Blood and coolant flew in a long arc. The merc fell hard, hands clutching at the brutal wounds.

The alien flowed out from under the rock, a multi-limbed nightmare come to kill.

The rocktopi stretched toward Angus, half of its double knife smeared with red and yellow.

Angus extended his arm, made a fist, firing the shotgun. A rocktopi scream — of pain, or of rage? He fired again as the alien slid into wisping white smoke that curled behind it, hiding it from sight.

Smoke that had given the mercenaries cover now hid the killers in their midst.

Donnie: "Kill these bastards, they're slowing us down."

The comm rang with shouts, calls for help, calls to form up. With *screams*. The air filled with the roar of gunfire and the piecing cries of aliens.

"Boss, back-to-back," Fuentes said. He spun, pressing his back to Angus.

Angus matched the move. The two men stood there, watching the smoke all around them.

"Use Cujo," Fuentes said.

But Angus could not. In the mist, he saw mercenaries moving this way and that. Friendlies and enemies all around.

"Cujo can't tell people apart from rocktopi," he said. "Not in these conditions."

Angus knew that if he unleashed the robot, it would slaughter the very men Angus needed to fight O'Doyle.

His mouth dry, his eyes wide, his hands shaking, Angus felt his shotgun automatically reload the two rounds. An alarm beep from his HUD—his pulse was high. One hundred and … the dead pixels hid the last two digits. One-ten? One-twenty?

Angus watched the ground, the rubble, tried to peer through the smoke. He tuned out the screams of the mercenaries as he waited for the next attack.

18:16
18:15
18:14

Bertha sighted in, cursing the dimming light, cursing smoke that was now more closer to black than it was to white. She couldn't make out a target.

Two dozen rocktopi had risen up from their hiding places in the rubble. They were little more than civilians given a knife and taught how to slash humans. She held no illusions that the surprise tactic would win the day. They were sacrificing themselves to cut down on enemy numbers and to buy time; time for the survival of their species.

Bertha knew her unborn child's life might rely on that same sacrifice.

She fought back anxiety, frustration. In the smoke, she caught brief glimpses of the mercenaries as well, but not enough to lock in on a target and take a shot. More than anything else, she saw white, boneless limbs writhing in the smoke, here then gone, flashes from gleaming double-crescent knives leaving after-images lingering in her vision.

Otto: "I think I have a target."

Bertha had to stop herself from looking over, a natural urge to see where Otto was aiming.

Patrick: "Enemy is engaged. If you have a clear shot, take it."

She heard Otto fire. She heard Tommy fire.

Bertha waited for a merc to show himself.

FROM THE SMOKE all around, Angus heard screams, shouts, gunshots, squeals … the scraping sound of the murderous rocktopi.

Donnie: "This is Captain Graham, we're taking fire from both walls and possibly from a sniper position in the city. All units, ready grenades, prepare to charge your objectives."

Charge? Was he crazy? They couldn't *charge*, they were under fucking *attack*.

"Not good," Fuentes said. "Donnie never leaves an enemy behind. He must not have an idea how to clear them out of this area but he's going in anyway."

Angus searched the smoke in front of him. Visibility down to ten feet, tops.

"Keep your eyes open," he said. "They came after the nuke once, maybe this is a setup to do it again."

The machine stood there, unmoving, the long ButterKnife strapped to its back. Cujo had plenty of firepower, but this wasn't the time to put it in play as an offensive weapon. The nuke or the laser—one way or another, Angus was going to finish this job.

Something in the smoke … movement. The smoke itself, or something inside it …

The monster rushed forward out of the darkening haze, pale tentacles whipping and waving.

Angus aimed his arm, squeezed his fist tight once, twice, three times, felt the shotgun kick. Yellow blood splashed, electric colors coursed across the gray skin. The beast flopped down, screeching, tentacles whipping wildly.

Movement from the right. Angus turned, fired, but the rocktopi was already inside his range—the shotgun blast tore off a chunk of grayish flesh just as the creature slammed into him.

Tentacles whipping, flesh slapping hard against his visor …

Angus heard and felt a blade thunk against his thigh armor. A tentacle wrapped around his shoulder, another around his waist. The knife slashed across his chest plate—the blade couldn't penetrate his armor, but if the tip punched into a gap or a joint he was fucked.

He bent his right arm in, put his fist against the soft body, and squeezed once, twice—yellow blood splattered across his visor, but the creature didn't let go. The auto-reloader started filling the magazine, but a pair of protrusions budded off the beast, wrapped around his right wrist, pushed the arm away.

Angus grabbed with his left hand, wrapping his fingers tight around those tentacles. Servos whirred as he pulled as hard as he could—the two tentacles stretched, sharply, suddenly, thinned, then ripped free.

The rocktopi fell to the uneven ground, holes in its body spurting yellow blood. The beast started to squirm away, a beanbag-sized puddle of panicked colors flowing across the rubble.

Angus lifted an armored foot, smashed it down on the animal. It screeched, extruded new tentacles, tried to reach up for him.

He reached down fast, grabbed the soft body with both hands. His fingers sank deep into the pliant flesh. Foot still pressing it to the ground, Angus stood sharply, lifted both hands and spread them wide.

The rocktopi's body resisted momentarily, taffy pulled to the breaking point, then it ripped into three pieces, spraying clumps of stringy yellow across the rocks and stone.

Angus snarled, felt a primitive rush flood through his being.

He'd killed it. Killed it with his bare hands. His *armored* hands, okay, but still—he had *never* felt so alive.

Fuentes…

Angus turned to help his friend, saw the man on top of a flailing, screeching rocktopi, driving a KA-BAR down into the flesh again and again. With each thrust, Angus heard the blade tip *clink* against the rock beneath the dying flesh.

The alien didn't move. Yellow blood spread out across the rubble beneath it.

"It's dead," Angus said. "Get up!"

Fuentes stood, stumbled back from the dying creature. He snatched up his rifle off the ground, stared at the fresh corpse.

"Fuck," he said, breathless. "*Fuck.*"

They again stood back to back, both of them smeared in the blood of their foes.

Angus's chest heaved as he looked this way and that, trying to see everything around him all at once.

In the smoke, nothing else moved.

Donnie: "All right, this is it. All advance. Leapfrog by twos, suppressing fire on the walls. Make them keep their heads down. Grenadiers, launch a salvo on my mark. Move in!"

14:41
14:40
14:39

Bullets whined and sparked and crunched off the wall. Patrick stayed just below the peak, waiting for a break in the fire. He couldn't wait long—he had to know what was coming.

He stayed calm, breathed slowly. He'd been under fire enough times to know how to stay just out of sight.

"Mullet, Klimas, talk to me."

Mullet: "Mercs moving in, hard to see them in the smoke."

Patrick looked up. Thick black smoke turned the blinding artificial sun into a faint light that barely made him squint. Yet one more thing Patrick had fucked up—the cavern was so big he'd never thought about the effects of potential fires. The ceiling acted like a dome, capturing the smoke, forcing it down onto the battlefield and the city alike.

Mullet: "Thirty-five meters out, closing. They're leapfrogging."

Bertha: "We're kinda pinned down over here!"

The mercs' rate of fire hadn't slowed. The mercs weren't spraying and praying—they were smart enough to use single-fire—but their consistent fire didn't leave a window of opportunity.

Sleepy: "That's steady fire, Ender, these guys know what they're doing."

Sleepy didn't sound worried, but he'd never sounded worried. Not even in Bandah.

Patrick had to get eyes on the enemy.

He dug his toes in, pushed himself up along the wall's slope toward a thin gap between two rocks.

Looking through the gap, he saw the battlefield. The heat of the fires created air currents—possibly the first here in millennia—that mixed clouds of white with oily tendrils of black, slowly churning them into soupy murk. In that murk, he saw muzzle flashes, the shapes of men coming forward.

He couldn't allow them to advance unchallenged.

Patrick brought up his carbine.

"Fire at will," he said. "Pick your targets."

Maybe a few well-placed shots could drive them back again, buy more time.

He leaned back enough to aim through the gap, sighted in on a shape in the thickening smoke. Patrick fired—the shape kept coming. He fired again.

The shape dropped.

More men visible in the smoke now. Not even twenty-five meters out. How many? Thirty? Forty?

Patrick ducked down, glanced at his HUD: *14:03, 14:02 …*

He had to use his last reserves.

Looking down into the trench, he saw Slash, half-covered by the platinum shield, felt the alien's stare. Patrick made a hand signal, then pointed over the wall. Slash's soft body flashed in shades of dark orange.

Patrick rose up again, aimed through the slot—twenty meters, close enough to see faces behind the mercs' smoke- and dirt-streaked visors, close enough to make out expressions of anger, of battle-lust, of fear.

He sighted in on a man, started to pull the trigger when a bullet kicked off granite splinters just to his right. Patrick flinched away, instincts overpowering his discipline. Another round hit close to the same spot, kicking out more stone shards.

Patrick dropped below the wall line.

A fraction of an inch difference and the bullet would have hit him in the face, assuredly killing him.

Darkness blossomed in him, a cold feeling, something he'd rarely felt in battle—*fear*.

Not for himself. Fear for his child. For his wife. If he died, his child would grow up without a father, just as he had. If Bertha died, his child would too …

Slash screeched, snapping Patrick back to the moment. The rocktopi rose, shields in front of them. Tentacles holding railguns stretched up, above the wall's peak. The aliens didn't have to raise their heads up to see—the dozens of eyespots let them track the incoming mercs.

Patrick swallowed, fought back his fear, and again sighted out of the slot.

Slash screeched again—nine railguns fired simultaneously.

A cacophonous sound of hammers hitting aluminum. Railgun rounds slammed into the advancing force. In the smoke, Patrick saw two men go down, saw men hit the deck, saw some move backward.

"West wall, prepare to move to secondary position. Worm, you ready?"

Worm: "Finger on the clicker."

"Move out on your call."

Patrick started to ask about Bertha, see if she was hit, if she was still alive, but he stopped himself, focused on the job. She knew what she was doing. So did Worm. So did Mullet, who had helped ensure the west wall team could get clear when the moment came.

Patrick sighted in on a merc, fired, missed. The merc seemed to see where the shot had come from, aimed at Patrick just as Patrick fired again—the man tumbled to the ground, clutching his knee.

Sleepy: "*Grenades incoming!*"

Patrick ducked down, tucked up.

A muffled explosion in front of the wall. Another behind. A third *inside* the trench. Something thumped onto the ground to his left, something *wet*. Again his discipline failed him as he took his eyes off his zone to glance right—next to him lay a severed rocktopi tentacle, thick yellow oozing out of the ragged, torn end.

ANOTHER ALARM—internal temperature rising.

Angus blinked through menus, trying to find the fault. One in his visor. He could patch that manually. Where was the other? There, his schematic showed a crack on his lower left thigh—the rocktopi's knife had punched through after all. Only a little, but there was no margin for error. He realized, only then, that his thigh hurt in that spot.

Donnie: "Rocktopi are firing from both walls. Stay low, use the smoke to your advantage."

The visor crack should have self-sealed, the foam should have filled the hole. Why hadn't it? Angus blinked through HUD menus, looking for the system failure.

"Boss, we have to move forward," Fuentes said. "Send Cujo, clear those motherfuckers out!"

Move forward? Not while his suit was on the fritz.

"We were ordered to keep Cujo with us," he said searching for the error. "We don't know if their ship can actually—"

His HUD went blank. *Completely* blank.

"Oh, no," he said.

He blinked madly, hoping maybe the screen was the only thing out, that the eye sensors were still functioning.

Nothing happened.

The sound of explosions, gunfire, men shouting and screaming, that strange aluminum *ting* sound of the rocktopi.

"Come *on*," Fuentes shouted. "They need us!"

Without his visual interface, he couldn't control most of the suit's functions. Would the automatic loader work? What else was broken?

Angus couldn't breathe. No interface, no way to repair the faults.

He slammed his left palm against his helmet. Nothing. He hit it again.

The HUD flickered back on.

He sucked in a breath, as deep as if he'd been drowning.

Donnie: "Doctor Kool, coming up behind you."

Fuentes took a knee, shouldered his rifle. He scanned the wall some twenty meters through the smoke, searching for a target or at least trying to *look* like he was searching for a target.

Angus went through menus with a newfound sense of urgency. He had to fix the issue now, the HUD might drop out again.

Donnie slid out of the smoke, stood next to Angus. He glanced at Cujo, then nodded, satisfied the machine had not yet entered the fight.

"Doctor Kool, we're taking that wall," Donnie said. "Let's move."

It should have been over already. Angus had fought hard. He'd taken out the giant silverbugs, killed rocktopi with his own hands. He was *hurt*, for fuck's sake.

"I'm wounded," he said. "You go on without me."

Captain Donnie Graham—in the middle of a smoke-choked subterranean battle—actually laughed.

"Without you operating the ButterKnife, we die. If I'm going to die because of your cowardice, I'll at least have the satisfaction of killing you myself."

The old man pointed his pistol at Angus's face.

A cracked visor wasn't going to stop that bullet, not this close.

Angus saw the gun tremble a moment before he felt the ground rumble beneath his feet.

Donnie and Fuentes stumbled like drunks, the world shifting, gravel and pebbles bouncing and skittering. He saw rocks fall from the ceiling, punching little vertical holes in the thick layer of smoke.

The tremor stopped, instantly and totally.

"Fuck," Fuentes said. "That their ship?"

The ship was the only thing it *could* be. There wasn't time to run. If Angus didn't find a way to stop it, the cut on his thigh would be the last of his worries—the collapsing mountain would smash his suit like a beer can.

With him still in it.

Wounded or not, afraid or not, if he wanted to live, there was only one path: *forward*.

"I'm ready," he said.

Donnie slapped his armored shoulder. "That's the spirit. We're joining up with Sixth Platoon, and we're taking that wall."

13:09

13:08

13:07

Otto: "Reloading!"

Bertha fired again.

Another human being went down.

She knew there would be a price to pay for this, that—if she survived the day—the images of those men twitching and falling would never be forgotten. One she'd hit, literally, right between the eyes, killing him instantly. The way his body had gone instantly lifeless, a rag doll collapsing to the floor…

Otto: "Back in!"

Bertha saw another target; she fired the last two shots in her magazine.

"Reloading!" She slid down, moved to her right as she ejected her spent magazine.

Too many mercs, too close. When was Patrick going to call the retreat?

An explosion, so close—dirt and rocks slapped against her helmet, her suit. She froze for an instant, waiting to feel the pain of the shrapnel that surely had punched holes in her body. Or maybe she wouldn't feel the wounds at all until it was too late.

Bertha reached for another magazine. She shook so bad she couldn't grab it. Breaths came in short, shallow spurts.

She had never known fear like this.

Reds and purples caught the corner of her eye. Five feet to her left, a rocktopi, color already fading. The grenade had gone off only inches away, tearing the soft flesh apart, turning the thing inside out like a blood-drenched sweatshirt carelessly torn off and tossed on the floor. Multicolored organs, ravaged and exposed, all coated in viscous yellow. If that rocktopi hadn't been between her and the grenade, she would have been the one torn to pieces.

She…and her baby.

These men, these mercenaries, they wanted to kill *her child*.

An explosion of another kind, one of pure hatred, blossomed in her chest, driving the fear away, leaving behind nothing but rage.

Bertha slapped the fresh magazine home—only one left after this, sixty rounds before she ran dry—then moved further to her right and crawled up to the wall.

Tommy: "West wall, get ready to fall back. I'm sending Axl's unit into the city. Once Axl is clear, I blow the claymores and we move. Make sure you *stay down* until I tell you to go."

When Patrick had told Mullet to lay the last two mines on the west wall, to cover her probable retreat, Bertha had been angry. Shouldn't one claymore be used for the west, and one for the east to cover *Patrick's* retreat? Now, though, with every ounce of her ice cold, with her hands shaking, with death coming for her, she whispered a fast and silent *thank you* for his decision.

Worm: "Axl's unit is out. Firing claymores. Three, two ..."

Bertha slid down, tucked up, and started a prayer that she didn't get to finish.

Worm: " ... one. *Fire in the hole!*"

Mullet had placed the claymores ten meters out from the front wall, one at either end, angled slightly inward to shred any enemy troops at or near the long pile of rubble. The shaped charge detonated simultaneously, a deafening blast like a shotgun spraying seven hundred eighth-inch steel balls outward at four thousand feet per second in a sixty-degree arc.

With the sound of the claymores still echoing, Bertha peeked through a gap.

Not ten feet away, close enough to see in the dimming light and thick smoke, a man, torn in half, ragged legs pointed north, his torso and head angled southwest, his guts splattered in all directions.

Further through the mist, another man, crawling slowly, his helmet gone, his right thigh spurting blood.

Then came the cries. The screams. How many wounded men called out? Four? Five? She couldn't see them.

Movement in the smoke ... just shadows, but shadows moving *away*.

"This is Lybrand. The mercs are running!"

Otto: "Not on my side! I've got three coming over—"

She heard the *tink* of metal on stone, saw a grenade bounce off the top of the wall. It dropped into the trench ten meters to her right.

Bertha threw herself flat, head toward the grenade—her world vanished in a cloud of noise and smoke.

12:12

12:11

12:10

Patrick couldn't move his left arm. A piece of shrapnel in his shoulder. He had no idea how bad it was bleeding, didn't have time to look.

He was already feeling the heat.

A target through the slot, twenty meters out. With just his right arm, he rested the front handgrip on a rock, pulled the stock tight, and fired. Bullets sparked up at the man's feet. The man dove away, rolling, as behind him muzzle flashes lit up the smoke. Bullets hammered the slot, metal sparking off stone—Patrick rolled away.

Sleepy: "Reloading, last mag."

Worm's voice, scratchy, full of static: "We're almost out over here."

Patrick had half a mag loaded, his last loaded mag in his webbing.

The enemy didn't seem to be short on ammo.

Something hit the ground next to him and he knew he was dead … but it was a smoke canister, not a grenade. White billowed from the nozzle.

Fifteen meters to his right, a grenade erupted, tearing a rocktopi to pieces, sending another one tumbling down the trench.

Too many men. His position was about to be overrun.

He flashed a hand-signal to Slash. The rocktopi screeched, and instantly the others with him rushed out of the trench, through the gaps in the rear wall, their shields held behind them.

Two of them didn't move—they were already dead.

"Sleepy, give it to them on my command. Klimas, can you cover us?"

Mullet: "Middle is open, we've got eyes on your wall."

With all the smoke and the distance between the sniper's nest and the wall, Patrick knew Klimas might hit jack shit, but if it got the mercs' attention, slowed them down, that was still something.

Patrick let his carbine hang from its sling. With his right hand, he pulled his last grenade from his webbing. He wedged it under his left armpit to keep the lever pressed down, then pulled the pin.

"Worm, fall back. Sleepy, *now!*"

Patrick grabbed the grenade, twisted in place as he tossed it over the wall—but it was his back that exploded.

He cried out, fell to the trench floor. Not now, not *fucking now.*

He heard the sharp boom of his grenade detonating, heard Sleepy's detonate as well.

Sleepy: "Ender, let's boogie!"

Patrick had to move, had to get out of there or he was dead.

Fighting against the pain, he got to his feet.

"Abandoning east fortification," he said, and he crouch-ran through a gap in the rear wall. He looked to his left just as Sleepy ran through another gap—and saw a grenade arc down behind the man, hit a stone and bounce up again.

"Sleepy, *gren*—"

A flash, an instant puff of smoke and dirt.

Sleepy fell forward, limp, didn't try to break his fall.

His right shoulder, shredded: clothing, KoolSuit, and skin alike. Only a thin strip of wet, dirt-speckled muscle kept the arm attached to the body.

Sleepy's helmet … on the ground, five feet away from him, still rocking slightly. Blood spread out around him, coating the rocks, soaking into the dirt.

Even through the mixed black and white smoke, Patrick saw the man's blank eyes staring out, staring at nothing.

Douglas "Sleepy" Rapson was no more.

I hope your god welcomes you home.

Mullet: "They're coming over the east wall. *Move*, boys!"

Patrick ran, as best he could, a lurching, pain-filled stutter-step that would—he prayed—take him back to his wife.

THE SUIT BREACH alarm blared. Or was that her ears ringing?

Still alive? How?

Her training. In the Army, she'd been drilled that when a grenade landed close by, you didn't try to grab it and throw it back—there would never be time for that movie bullshit—and you didn't dive *away* from it, because feet were among the least-armored places a soldier had on her body. The *most*-armored? Her head.

She hadn't thought, she hadn't strategized. Her muscle memory had kicked in, and she'd done as her instructors had shown her to do so many years before.

How long had she lain there? Felt like hours. She glanced at her HUD: *11:30, 11:29, 11:28 …*

She'd been down for only seconds.

Seconds where a merc could have put a bullet in the back of her head.

Bertha got to her hands and knees, dropped into a squat, got her hands on her weapon. A cold burst of sickness, of horror—a chunk of shrapnel stuck out of the carbine's side. She angled it, looking closer, saw her fears confirmed: the metal shard had driven in just below the slide.

The weapon was useless.

Through the alarm and the ringing in her ears, she heard a man screaming on the comm.

Otto: "Lybrand! Tommy's hit!"

Tommy. Patrick's friend.

Life and a sudden awareness surged through her. Carbine dead. Killers about to come over the wall.

Bertha ejected her magazine, stuffed it into her webbing. She drew her knife, moved left down the smoke-filled trench. So dark now, as dark as dusk, growing blacker by the second.

"Otto, I'm coming."

Otto: "They're at the wall again! Throw your grenades and let's get the fuck out of here!"

Still moving down the trench, Bertha's left hand acted of its own accord. She pulled the V40 from her webbing, used the pointer finger of her knife hand to pull the pin. She stopped, looked up to the top of the wall—there, a merc leaning over, stock to his shoulder, barrel swinging toward her.

She was dead.

So was her baby.

Goodbye, Patrick … goodbye, my love.

The sound of an iron hammer hitting aluminum. The merc's helmeted head snapped back. He turned, and as he did Bertha saw the hole in his helmet, just above his left eye. The merc sagged backward, out of sight.

Bertha turned, caught sight of a dirt-streaked platinum shield. From behind it, tentacles held up a railgun. In that snap-glance, she recognized the orange and red patterns flashing across the black-dotted skin.

Axl.

Otto: "*Lybrand!*"

She realized she was still holding the V40, still had the lever squeezed tight. She flung the grenade over the wall, then down the trench, through the smoke. She heard the grenade go off two seconds later, had no idea if it did any damage.

She found Otto kneeling next to Tommy. Tommy lay on his back, arms weakly held against his chest. Bertha skidded to a stop next to them. Blood and KoolSuit fluid soaked Tommy's midsection.

A gut wound.

Mullet: "West wall, are you clear? Hostiles closing in, climbing the wall—get the hell out of there!"

A shadow passed over her head, then a platinum shield slammed down halfway up the wall—Axl was giving Tommy cover. She heard automatic rifle fire, heard the tinny plink of bullets hitting the shield. Axl stretched his railgun high and started firing.

"*Get him out of here,*" Otto said, then leaned right, fired toward the top of the wall at something only he and Axl could see.

The mercs were right on top of them, literally *right on top of them.*

"I'm out," Otto said, ducking back behind the shield.

Bertha's hands moved on their own again, grabbing the magazine from her webbing, handing it to Otto. He slid it home.

"Get Tommy to the ship," he said, then leaned out again.

Bertha grabbed Tommy's arm, pulled him over her shoulders in a fireman's carry. He came to, but only enough to cry in agony.

Bullets pinged off Axl's shield, each ringing report making Bertha wince. The alien fired another round with his railgun. Otto let off three quick shots.

The plinking of enemy bullets stopped.

"*Let's go,*" Bertha said. "Otto, Axl, *come on!*"

Otto shook his head. "If we all run, they'll cut us all down."

His words hit her, hit hard. No way, *no way.*

She adjusted Tommy on her shoulders, heard him cry out again, then reached to Otto, grabbed his shoulder, tried to pull him away from the wall.

He twisted his shoulder sharply—her hand slipped free.

"Think of your child," he said.

The simplest of statements. Her child. Patrick's child. She couldn't drag Otto if he chose to stay—and he was staying to protect her, protect the baby, staying *because* of her baby.

She had wondered if humans could be as self-sacrificing as the rocktopi. How utterly ignorant she'd been.

A flash of color before she felt rocktopi tentacles on her, pushing her, *shoving* her, toward the rear wall. Axl, his shield still angled toward the top of the wall, his railgun still aimed above it. Bertha felt the alien's stare upon her, felt his fear, his *anger*—he wanted her to get Tommy clear.

A human being and a rocktopi, willing to fight to the end to protect others.

She could not let that be in vain.

Bertha turned and moved toward a gap in the rear wall, struggling under Tommy's weight.

"Don't…leave them," Tommy said, grinding the words out through clenched teeth.

Bertha didn't answer him. She reached the gap, and she ran south.

Behind her, she heard Otto's carbine and Axl's railgun.

"NO FIRE COMING from the east wall," Donnie said. "Let's get in there. Fourth, move in to the left, Fifth to the right. Sixth, in the middle with me. First and Second Platoons, stop fucking around and *take the west wall*. All advance."

Stop fucking around? Men were dying. None of the platoons had their full complement. As far as Angus could tell, he'd lost at least a dozen of his mercenaries in the last five minutes alone. Donnie had not yet done a head count. Maybe he didn't want the men to know the score before they pushed forward, through the city and to the ship.

Angus could only hope Donnie knew what he was doing.

"All right," Donnie said. "Forward. Kool, lead the way."

Angus had been afraid Donnie would say that. It made sense—Angus's armor, even as damaged as it was—seemed to be enough to protect him from whatever O'Doyle's people were firing. He was like a tank, leading the way.

"Cujo," he said, "stay behind me."

Angus moved toward the wall. The machine obeyed. Donnie and two men fanned out on Angus's left, Fuentes and two men on the right.

No fire from the wall. Smoke clung to the long pile of broken rocks like bits of gaseous cotton caught on rough bark.

Donnie: "Half cover, half up and over. *Advance!*"

Angus didn't know if he was supposed to be in the *half cover* or *half up and over* group, but Donnie's guttural *advance* had him sprinting toward the wall, his powerful mechanized motor driving up the loose slope. Angus hopped off the top, landed with both feet in the smoke-lined trench.

No one there.

Cujo came down right behind him.

Nothing in the trench but three or maybe four ravaged rocktopi corpses and three dented, rectangular platinum shields. The aliens had used ones just like these in Utah. Yellow blood and multicolored guts were all over the place.

Off to the left, through a wall gap, one of O'Doyle's people, chest-down in a pool of blood.

Fuentes: "Trench is clear."

Another man repeated the message, then another.

Donnie: "Everyone close in. Move through the gaps in the rear wall. Stay low, watch for booby traps. Shake those tail feathers, let's go."

9:18

9:17

9:16

High voltage electricity flowing through a stiletto still white-hot from the smith's forge, the point lodged in his belly.

Tommy had always heard gut wounds were the worst way to go. More than once, he'd seen men screaming from such injuries, men who were not long for this Earth. He'd *seen* the pain, *heard* it, but he'd never *felt* it.

Until now.

Now, he knew why they screamed.

Shrapnel in his belly. He hadn't seen the grenade land, hadn't had a chance to roll away, to dive for cover, to react in any way. It had detonated close by, driving shards of metal under—or maybe even *through*—his body armor.

How much more could he take?

So many wounds, so much damage to his body. His eyes kept scrunching tight from the pain—he kept forcing them open.

As Lybrand ran, each step sent a lightning strike through Tommy's body. She had him in a fireman's carry. He opened his mouth to say *let me down, leave me to die,* but the words wouldn't come out. Despite the pain, despite the hopeless situation, he wanted to live.

Tommy looked back through the dark smoke, to the walls. Otto and Axl—blazing with furious colors—in the trench, human and alien side by side.

A man rolled over the wall, fired as he slid down toward the trench. Axl turned the shield toward the threat—maybe the platinum blocked the bullets; if it didn't, there was too much smoke to see.

Otto shot three times; the man dropped.

Mercs spilled over the top of the wall, four, five, six—too many to stop. They fired. Axl sagged, his shield dropping to the trench floor. Otto twitched, jerked—he fell. Otto's voice in the comm, weak, faint: "I'll see you soon, Margo…I'll see you soon."

Tommy didn't know who *Margo* was. He would never find out—a merc put a gun to Otto's head and pulled the trigger.

Lybrand turned sharply, going behind the corner of a stone house. The sudden shift sent a wave of pain through Tommy that almost made him pass out.

Ender: "Bertha, Tommy, Otto, get to the plaza, now!"

Blackness blossomed, swallowed Tommy up.

A new jolt of pain brought him back. Bertha was carrying him to the obelisk.

Ender's voice. Klimas, shouting something—he sounded angry, frustrated. Tommy couldn't see what was happening.

Mullet: "I got him."

Tommy's limp body lurched as he was passed from one person to another.

"Hold on, little buddy," Mullet said. "We're getting you out of here."

Klimas: "Ender, how far out?"

Ender: "I'm almost there. Sleepy's gone."

What little strength Tommy had seeped away. Sleepy. Otto. Axl. There was no end to it. Who would be next?

A rhetorical question—Tommy knew it was him.

The world spun. He landed on something hard, hard and flat. Whatever he was on dipped once, twice, three times. He had a strange flashback of being in a car with his friends on the high school wrestling team, him packed into the middle of the back seat, and how the car had dipped when the team's heavyweight got in.

Tommy forced his eyes open—he was at the plaza, on the south side. There, in the obelisk's shadow, was Mullet, Klimas, and the beat-up go-kart.

Tommy heard gunfire, the plink of bullets hitting stone. A finger-sized chunk of the obelisk landed in the cart, right next to his head.

Lybrand: *"Come on, Patrick!"*

Ender: *"Go-go-go!"*

More gunfire. The cart lurched forward, jostling Tommy's ruined guts. He cried out, felt a hand on his chest.

The cart dipped suddenly—the heavyweight getting in.

Ender: *"Floor it!"*

16,000 feet below the surface

6:18
6:17
6:16

Sonny McGuiness huddled just inside the oval opening. The ship and the ground beneath it shook. Rocks dropped from the ceiling, jostled free by the intermittent, angry tremors. The falling stones created a steady yet non-rhythmic pattern as they shattered paving tiles or slammed against the platinum hull.

Sam: "Sonny, any sign of them?"

She asked the same question she'd asked ever other minute. Sonny stared across the opening, through the growing rain of rock, toward the opening from the tunnel that led up to the City Cavern. He saw movement in the opening—a fast surge of hope drained away at the sight of colored lights. Two rocktopi rolled out of the tunnel, sprinted/flowed toward another ship opening. No guns, no shields—if they were fighters, they'd dropped their weapons and just ran.

He couldn't blame them.

"Still no sign," he said.

Sam: "We don't have much longer. They have to hurry. Doors shut in six minutes and the rocktopi won't wait!"

Sonny laughed at the madness of it all. Yes—O'Doyle and the others needed to hurry. He had no control over that.

A crackle on the comm: "…uny…in."

"*Mullet*," Sonny said. "That you?"

"…ing in. D…us up."

Coming in—don't blow us up.

Had they killed all the bad guys?

Sonny again looked at the detonator in his hand, had an irrational burst of panic, thought his fingers might contract on their own, press home the trigger and blow the tunnel opening, trapping Mullet and the others.

His fingers did no such thing, but that strange feeling echoed through him.

"Uh, roger that," Sonny said. "Will not detonate."

"Men…nd us. Get ready to …"

He caught enough of the words to know what they meant.

Men right behind us. Get ready to detonate.

Sonny swallowed, wished he could get at that itch in his balls. He was going to have to pull that trigger after all.

When he did, people would die.

96

14,973 feet below the surface

DONNIE: "HOLD YOUR fire until you're fired upon. Keep moving."

The thick smoke made it damn near dark as night. The doors of every stone house threatened like the maw of a man-eating monster.

Fuentes: "Keep sharp. Check those openings. They could be anywhere in here."

Angus felt no pain. None. He felt *amazing*. The drugs, sure—he'd slammed sixty milligrams of Adderall—but this elation had to be from the fighting, the *winning*, at least to some degree. He was a goddamned warrior. He could not be stopped, *would* not be stopped.

He took another step, then the ground beneath him trembled, far worse than if had before. Donnie stumbled, staggered against a stone house. The other men dropped to one knee, tried to keep their balance on the shaking ground.

Small bits of rock plunged down from the ceiling, punching through the smoke and kicking up new curls of white.

Angus ran to Donnie, grabbed the older man's shoulder.

"They're getting ready to move the mountain," Angus said. "Or they're moving it already, I don't know! We've got to haul ass, *now!*"

The shuddering stopped. In the strange silence that followed, Angus heard a patter of stones landing on the flat roofs of the stone houses, plinking off the ceramic paving tiles.

"Men, you heard Doctor Kool," Donnie said. "Time to throw caution to the wind. All units advance to the tunnel at the cavern's south end. If you want to live, get there fast."

Donnie eyes were wide with energy, with pure *joy*. He was enjoying this moment. Did he not understand he was almost assuredly going to die down here?

Dimwit indeed.

Donnie started forward, Angus at his side — they both stopped when a heat-driven current of air swirled away the smoke down the street about thirty feet away, revealing a wall of platinum.

Shields, five of them.

"Shit," Donnie said. "Anyone got any grenades left?"

No one answered.

Donnie raised his pistol and fired once. His shot *clanged* off a platinum shield. The other men followed suit.

A screech reverberated off the stone walls. Alien weapons rose up from behind the shields, then a cacophonous hammer-on-aluminum sound as they fired. A merc spun around, a metal rod sticking out of his chest.

Mercs moved to building corners, to open doors, returned fire.

"Cujo," Angus said, *"clear the way!"*

The robot sidestepped a merc to create a clear field of fire, then opened up. Sparks flew from the shields. The rocktopi seemed to waver for a moment, then a shield fell. The rocktopi who had dropped it flowed down the street, skin pulsing in greens and yellows, before Cujo's concentrated fire ripped it to shreds.

Another of those blood-curdling screeches — the four remaining shields clanged together, once again a unified wall of metal.

"Fuck this," Donnie said. "*Charge!*"

The old man sprinted forward, followed by Fuentes and the rest of the platoon, all of them screaming, shooting as they ran, straight at the rocktopi wall, who fired back.

"Cujo, *cease fire!*"

Angus ran at the wall, his suit covering huge strides.

An ear-piercing screech—the platinum wall surged forward to meet the oncoming humans.

A merc leapt up and kicked out as the lines slammed into each other, his feet pounding into the center shield, knocking shield and rocktopi both tumbling backward. The merc landed off-balance, tried to right himself—a glowing tentacle lashed out, slicing the curved blade of a platinum knife through the back of the man's thigh.

The rocktopi line broke. Donnie fired his pistol four times at point-blank range, each bullet kicking up a puff of yellow blood—his target sagged backward, dropped the platinum shield. Angus finished the rocktopi off with a blast from his Atchisson.

Knives flashed. Guns fired.

A platinum shield rushed Donnie.

Angus fired at it without thinking—his buckshot bounced harmlessly off the thick metal. The shield slammed into Donnie, knocking the man to his back. He tried to bring his pistol up, but the shield pinned him down; atop the shield, a rocktopi pulsing in wild patterns of orange and red, a long, white scar down the middle of its round body.

Angus stepped closer and fired once, twice, three times. Buckshot tore ghastly holes in the soft body, sprayed the shield and Donnie's visor with yellow blood. The creature sagged to the side.

Donnie struggled to squirm out from under the shield. Angus reached down, grabbed the hunk of metal and slid it to the side.

"Outs*tand*ing work, Doctor," Donnie said. Still on his back, he reached up a hand. "Help an old fella get—"

A flash of red fading to pink, pale yellow, and the dull gleam of sharp metal.

The tip of a double-crescent knife punched into Donnie, just below his right collarbone.

The rocktopi…Angus hadn't finished it off.

Donnie opened his mouth in a silent scream.

The faintly glowing tentacle contracted, *yanked.* The platinum blade jerked downward, slicing through clothes and KoolSuit, skin and muscle, dragging Donnie across the ground in a lurching, stop-start motion. Bones snapped as the dying alien's desperate strength pulled the thick, razor sharp metal through Donnie's ribcage, deep into his belly, and out his crotch.

Fuentes stepped in, snarling, yelling, opening up on full automatic at the dying creature. The rocktopi twitched, spasmed, then fell limp.

Its color faded.

The rocktopi did not move.

Neither did Donnie. He stared out from his mask, a look of surprise on his face. His mustache twitched once to the left, returned to center, and he moved no more.

Dimwit was gone.

"Mother*fuckers*," Fuentes said. "What the hell are we supposed to do now?"

Angus quickly took in the carnage. Donnie and two other mercs, dead or clearly dying. Five dead rocktopi.

"Boss," Fuentes said, "what do we do?"

He was staring at Angus. So were Henderson and the other surviving mercs.

They were waiting, waiting for him to give orders.

Twenty-odd men had attacked the west wall—only eight remained standing.

"We have to get to the ship," Fuentes said. "Right?"

Another tremor began.

The sound of stone rain.

This place wouldn't last much longer.

Donnie was gone. Someone had to lead.

Angus's HUD winked out for a second, stuttered back on again. Cujo's ammo counter read: *000/188/200*. The machine still carried the nuke—and the ButterKnife. This wasn't over. There was still time.

Angus blinked through his menus, made sure he was on the frequency that would let him address everyone.

"This is Doctor Kool," he said. "Captain Graham is dead. I'm taking charge. Wherever you are, whatever you have to do, get to the south tunnel entrance ASAP. If we don't get down to that ship and stop it from taking off, we're dead. Move out."

97

15,902 feet below the surface

3:59
3:58
3:57

O'Doyle's arm felt numb.

His breach alarms chimed softly. He'd lost coolant. He should have felt hot, but he felt the opposite—chilled for the first time since he'd entered these damned tunnels.

Which meant he'd lost blood.

A lot of blood.

And he was still bleeding, despite his right hand squeezing his left shoulder as tight as he could.

The cart had bought them a few precious seconds. They'd left it at the tunnel mouth—it was too big to fit into the narrow space.

The tunnel ceiling was too low for anyone to carry Tommy on their shoulders, so Mullet had Tommy's feet, Klimas his arms. Even with Tommy's weight, they moved faster than Patrick could—he'd lost sight of them.

He could barely walk. It felt like one of the rocktopi had put a railgun round in his back. Running down the tunnel, half hunched over, his head tilted to the size, Patrick grunted in pain with every step.

How much farther? However far, it was too far.

He didn't know how much more he could take.

"Don't you quit on me," Bertha said. "Don't you dare."

She was right behind him, covering his back. He should have been covering hers.

The tunnel blurred slightly. He blinked rapidly, wishing he could reach through the visor and rub the exhaustion from his eyes.

"Keep moving, baby," Bertha said. "We're almost there, I promise. Keep moving."

The tunnel shuddered so hard Patrick hit his head against the ceiling—the right wall seemed to slap him. When the shaking stopped, he found himself facedown on the silt.

"*Get up.*" Bertha pulled at him. "Get the fuck up, Patrick, I can see the tunnel exit, we're only a hundred feet away."

He could not get up. He could barely breathe, let alone rise. It was over.

"Go on," he said. "Save yourself, save the baby."

She knelt next to him. "If you stay, I stay."

A burst of anger overwhelmed him, fueled by energy he didn't know he possessed.

"Get the *fuck* out of here," he said. "We're out of time! After all this, you're going to let our child die?"

Bertha pulled at his shoulder, which sent a new wave of agony through his back.

"All of us or none of us," she said.

She wasn't screaming, wasn't yelling. She was barely louder than a dinnertime conversation, but he heard the steel in her voice—she would not listen to reason.

Mullet: "We're at the ship cavern entrance. Sonny, you there?"

Sonny: "I'm here! Hurry your asses up, this place is falling apart!"

Mullet: "Here we come, old man, just keep those fingers off the trigger."

Patrick looked at his HUD: 3:12, 3:11, 3:10…

"All of us or none of us," Bertha said.

Klimas: "O'Doyle, hurry up! The cavern lights are going out, get in here."

Patrick did not love his wife at that moment—he hated her. He hated her stubborn ass with all that he'd ever been. If she wanted to die with him, so be it, but their kid couldn't make that choice.

He pushed himself up, screaming in pain as he did. Bertha helped him, somehow managed to get under his arm despite the narrow confines.

She guided him down the tunnel.

He focused on putting one foot in front of the other, on anticipating the pain of each step and not letting it drag him down.

In seconds, they reached the tunnel exit and stepped out.

A few hours earlier, the Ship Cavern had been a thing of staggering beauty, of timeless perfection. Now, twelve millennia of engineering and art were coming apart at the seams.

Only one artificial sun above remained active, and that one flickered and sparked, a huge strobe light pulsing with an irregular pattern. The other artificial suns had gone out. Rocks rained down, some the size of his fist, others bigger than cars, hitting with the impact of small bombs. Fissures split the floor, reached up the walls like deadly fingers of negative space. Pillars cracked and sheared. Huge statues cracked, dropped away from the walls to slam into the ancient tile floor.

Far ahead of him, he saw Klimas and Mullet—they looked tiny. They were still carrying Tommy. They were almost to the ship's oval opening, and in that opening, Sonny McGuiness.

"Come on," Bertha said. "Move your ass!"

Patrick took one more step—he cried out, screaming in pain as whatever had gone partially wrong with his back finally went *all the way* wrong.

He fell. Bertha grabbed at him, tried to stop him from falling—he was too heavy, slipped from her grasp.

He hit the tile floor hard.

"Get up, goddamnit!"

Bertha pulled at him, tried to lift him. He was almost three hundred pounds—even if she could get him up, she would never make it to the ship on time.

"Patrick, *please!*"

He had no words to convince her to save herself, save the baby.

Through a haze of suffering, Patrick looked at the HUD: 2:48, 2:47, 2:46…

He wouldn't make it. He would die here. Bertha and their child would die with him.

From all sides, he heard and felt the unbelievable thunder of huge rocks smashing into the floor. Was there some kind of protection above him and Bertha? If so, it wouldn't last long.

He felt a small rock hit his leg, striking with a force somewhere between a punch and the sting of the world's biggest bee.

Bertha cried out, fell to her side, her hand clutching her shoulder.

Patrick heard another noise. Faint for a moment, fighting to register over the cannonade of granite. It grew louder, and he knew what it was.

The screech of a rocktopi.

In the stuttering strobe of the last artificial sun, he saw a new kind of light—colored light, pulsing with many hues.

Patrick lifted his head, and saw them—four rocktopi, all carrying platinum shields.

Siren, Disco and two others. Tentacles wrapped around Patrick's legs, his arms, his chest, his back. He was lifted off the ground. He looked to his left, saw a rocktopi pull Bertha to her feet, saw her start running for the ship.

Maybe she would make it after all.

Patrick looked up, was instantly enraptured by the beauty of the collapsing cavern. Rocks rained down in a strange stop-start motion as they caught the pulses from the dying artificial sun. Some left comet trails of dust behind them, some did not. Might as well look at it, because one of those rocks was going to smash into him and finish him off— there were just too many.

A platinum shield rose up on his left, and another on his right.

The metal edges touched.

Beneath them, thick snakes of colored lights, cerulean blue and kelly green and golden yellow, holding up the shields.

Falling rocks hammered into the shields, an aberrant rhythm joining the spastic light show.

And then, he found himself inside the ship.

Before he slipped under, he heard a sound he hoped would stay with him for all eternity.

The sound of his wife, crying with joy.

98

15,891 feet below the surface

ANGUS CARRIED the ButterKnife.

He followed Cujo through the straight, narrow tunnel, calculating as he went. The way the mountain shook around him: so much force.

He was a genius. There was no doubt of that. He was among the greatest minds humanity had ever produced. But *this*? Even more than the ship itself, even more than interstellar travel, this much *power*—he was a club-toting caveman in the presence of gods.

It was too late for the nuke. There was only one chance to survive this shit—get to the cavern below, slice that ship up with the Butter-Knife. If he could cause enough damage that it wouldn't fly, the aliens would have to stop this madness. There would be time for at least one long, sustained blast. There *had* to be time.

He could *survive*.

Fuentes: "Come *on*. Move faster, Angus!"

"Stay cool, man, I'll get us out of here, I promise."

The rest of these idiots could die for all Angus cared, but he and Fuentes would escape this death trap.

With his armor on, Angus was so big the mercs couldn't pass by him. Fuck 'em — it wasn't like they could stop the ship without him.

Thirteen men followed him down the tunnel — Fuentes, Henderson and the others from the east wall attack, along with the six survivors of the west wall assault. Well, the six survivors who could still *run*, anyway; if there were any wounded mercs back there, they were on their own.

He absently wondered if the men left up top to guard the tunnel entrance had stayed. Perhaps they'd taken their chances and tried to climb down while the entire mountain shook beneath them. Perhaps they were already entombed, buried beneath collapsing stone.

Angus was protected from such a fate, at least for the moment — the rocktopi had generated some kind of force field in this tunnel. He saw broken rock above him, but it hung there, did not fall. It was like looking up into a glass bowl full of rocks, pebbles and dirt. In places, though, puffs of silt slipped through, and every now and then a cluster of rocks or a handful of granite shards tumbled down; whatever this shield was, it was failing.

From up ahead, he heard a strange ringing sound, almost musical in its tone and complexity.

The tunnel's slope leveled out. He saw a dark spot ahead, a spot punctuated by flashing light.

He checked the depth in his HUD: *15,993 FT.*

"We're almost there." Angus saw the end of the tunnel. "Cujo, hold at the opening."

The machine did so. Angus stopped just behind Cujo, stared out into a biblical cataclysm.

Rocks rained down, some as small as his fist, some the size of trucks, smashing into ceramic tiles. A single light high above flickered and pulsed, magnifying the madness.

And ahead, *the ship*. Falling boulders slammed against it, making the miles-long hull ring from the deluge of stone. Far off to the left, giant gouges in the hull, as if a planet-sized monster had dragged a claw through the metal.

Even through this hellish hail, he could see that this ship was in far better condition than the one in Utah had been.

As the artificial sun above stuttered on and off, Angus saw one steady light on the endless, towering hull, light coming from an oval at ground level.

An opening, a way inside.

It didn't matter; he had to disable the ship before the mountain tore itself apart.

"Stay behind me," Angus said. "I'm going to take that thing out."

He spread his feet, braced himself against the shuddering ground.

The oval door, closing, that point of light, slowly fading … and at the same time, rising almost imperceptibly higher.

The ship was lifting into the air.

Angus didn't know where to aim, so he pointed the ButterKnife straight ahead.

He fired—the green beam burned into the platinum hull.

Rocks dropped into the beam, lighting orange-hot as they fell through, some bursting into pieces from the instant and massive amount of energy.

A boulder the size of a house slammed down, embedding in the cavern floor, blocking the beam. Stone instantly melted white-hot—it would take several seconds to burn through it.

Angus raised the beam, angling it above the rock. He felt a moment of satisfaction as the ButterKnife sliced into the massive hull, a molten-metal scar forming.

Henderson: "The tunnel's collapsing! Run!"

Angus was shoved forward, so hard that he stumbled on the debris-strewn ground, fell forward. Pebbles and rocks plunked off his armor as mercs rushed out around him.

He scrambled to his feet, looked back to the tunnel just as the force field gave way. One moment men were there, the next, they were gone, vanishing beneath tons of stone that smashed down in the blink of an eye, spilled out of the tunnel.

Fuentes: "Angus, keep firing!"

Several mercs had made it out of the tunnel: Fuentes, Henderson, seven or eight more Angus didn't recognize. They held arms above their heads, shielding themselves as they stared up, trying to dodge falling rocks.

Angus heard a metal-and-plastic *crunch* that chilled him to the bone—he scrambled to his feet, picked up the ButterKnife.

It was cracked.

A split in the middle, making the tube bend at a slight angle.

Ruined. Broken. Useless.

Anxiety and terror clawed him, scooped at him from the inside out. He looked to the ship, saw the oval light, still closing, but *slowly*, not yet shut.

Mercs sprinted toward the ship, taking their chances with the hail of death striking down from above. One merc crumpled when a bowling-ball-sized rock smashed in his head.

A chest-size boulder slammed down next to Angus, hit so hard it bounced and rolled away—that rock would have smashed him flat as a can.

Fuentes: "Angus…help…"

The man lay on the ground, his left foot a mashed pulp of muscle and bone; the boulder had hit him.

Angus dropped the ButterKnife, lifted Fuentes, held the man in his arms.

Behind the visor, Fuentes' face wrinkled into a rictus of agony.

Angus could save him—the suit's speed would get them both to the ship.

He turned to run when he felt another weight on his shoulders, making him stagger to the left.

Henderson: "*Go go go!*"

The man had leapt onto Angus's back.

Another merc wrapped his arms around Angus's left leg.

What were they doing? He couldn't make it in time with all of them hanging onto him.

Fuentes slapped his hand against Angus's chest armor.

"*Please*," the man said, his face so close that Angus heard him through the helmet. "I don't want to die. *Go!*"

Angus took one step forward, then another, felt the suit's sluggish response. His HUD flashed a new number: *541 LB*—the weight of the men hanging on him.

The oval door, now half its original size.

Angus could get to it before it closed, but only if he ran at top speed, a speed he couldn't hit with the extra load.

No time for debate, no time to ask these desperate men to do something he knew they would not do.

Angus looked into the terrified, pain-riddled face of the man he held in his arms, perhaps the truest friend he'd ever known.

There was only one way to survive.

"Cujo," Angus said, *"all but me."*

The Wolf's SAW let loose a four-shot burst.

Bullets punched into Fuentes' side, *through* him—Angus felt the rounds impact his armor. Henderson screamed something, as did the merc hanging on Angus's leg. Maybe they reached for weapons, maybe they didn't. It didn't matter. Cujo delivered four-shot bursts with surgical precision.

Henderson and the other merc dropped away.

Fuentes went limp. Angus tossed him aside and sprinted for the ship.

Behind him, even over the cacophony of the granite barrage, Angus heard the SAW firing—Cujo, taking out the remaining mercs who escaped the tunnel. In the HUD, the ammo counter blurred toward *000/000/000.*

The meticulously engineered suit delivered. Powerful legs drove Angus forward, letting him cover ten feet with each stride. He glanced up as he ran, trying to time the larger rocks, and at the ground, trying to avoid steping on any that would trip him up.

He wove his way around the deadly hazards. Ahead, three mercs still on their feet, rushing toward that shrinking point of light, that last beacon of salvation.

A blast of static in the HUD—Cujo was offline, undoubtedly smashed by a rock. Angus didn't bother looking back.

He caught up to the slowest of the three mercs, was about to pass him when a stone slab the size of a Cadillac smashed the man flat— blood sprayed out, splashing Angus in a wave of gore.

The opening, fifty feet ahead … almost closed.

He sprinted past the last two mercs; out of the corner of his eye, he saw one of them go down.

Angus glanced up again, swerved right to avoid a boulder that hit like a meteor, its impact making the ground ripple. Rocks he didn't see or couldn't avoid slammed into his armor. Stone and tile shards came at him from all directions: not just above, but from the front, the back, and the sides as falling rocks shattered upon impact.

The ship rose higher. Much of it remained below the cavern's ravaged floor, but it *was* rising.

Angus reached the ship just as the oval closed, just as that last bit of steady light winked out.

The last mercenary hit the hull next to him, bleeding arm raised in a futile effort to shield his head from the deadly downpour.

"Doctor Kool, what do we do?"

Angus aimed his right arm at the merc, made a fist. The shotgun blast shredded the man's neck and jaw—he dropped.

There had to be a way into the ship. Those huge gouges in the hull; could he reach them?

The ship continued to rise—the area between the hull and the edge of the tiled floor widened, a space of growing blackness.

Angus ran left, in the direction of the gouges.

Even with the suit's power, he saw he would not reach them in time.

Wait…*there,* a gouge that had been below ground, now exposed for the first time. Angus leaned out, got his armored fingers on the torn metal. He *felt* the ship rising now, starting to pull him up off the ground. He focused, got one arm inside the gouge, then his head…

His shoulders would not fit.

The ship rose—his feet dangled on empty air.

He would not fit.

His armor was too thick.

His armor…

Angus blinked madly through his HUD, searching for the right menu.

A rock hit his armored back so hard it sent a wave of concussive agony coursing through his body. He nearly passed out, started to slip, then his armored fingers squeezed down hard on the ship's torn metal.

Come on come on comeoncomeon…

He found the item. EMERGENCY JETTISON: BLINK THREE TIMES.

Angus blinked three times.

He heard and felt tiny *pops* as small charges in the suit's clamps detonated, breaking the mechanisms. His chest plates and leg armor dropped away beneath him. The Atchisson shotgun slipped free, tumbled down. His gloves split into a hundred pieces—his hands scrambled to hold on as the bits slid between his skin and the gouge's ragged, sharp edges.

Boots disintegrated, shoulder plates fell. The last of his gorgeous suit plummeted into the darkness below.

Exposed to the stone rain, small rocks hit him like bullets, punching hard into his flesh, hammering his head.

Desperation drove him. He flailed in the gouge, trying to pull himself up. His right hand, useless without his suit's special glove, slapped against metal. He got his left arm all the way in, fingers finding a handhold in the darkness.

Falling rock battered his exposed legs. Impact after impact. The primitive part of him took over, blocking out the pain, focusing on one thing and one thing only—*get inside or die*.

He got his torso in, kept pushing, kept wriggling, felt jagged shards of metal cutting into his KoolSuit, slicing his flesh.

Get inside or die.

Finally, he slid through into total darkness, landed hard on a curved floor, slid to a stop.

He was bleeding. Some of his bones were broken, he knew it.

The rip in the hull … he was inside, but still exposed to the air outside. He had to get out of this room, find somewhere airtight, or he'd be dead before the ship even exited the atmosphere.

Angus took one deep breath, pressed his bloody hands on the hard floor, started to push himself up.

His arms gave out almost immediately.

He was … *weak*.

No more suit. His body had been crippled even before the horrid beating he'd taken from the falling rocks. Whatever strength he'd found to get through that gouge was gone, spent completely and utterly.

Blackness swirled.

He had made it all this way, but it was not quite far enough.

He felt the ship vibrating under him, heard the symphonic crash of stone hitting metal.

So *hot* in here …

His HUD. He still had his KoolSuit on. He could find a way to repair the cuts. Stop the bleeding, fix the suit, and …

… and …

The blackness overwhelmed him, dragged him down.

99

A LARGE ROOM.

Rounded walls, not a hard edge in sight.

Bertha Lybrand sat cross-legged on the slightly curved floor, her gloved hand gently stroking Patrick's arm. He lay on a platinum shield that doubled as a decent stretcher. Blood on that shield, red and yellow alike. Dents, scratches, smoke streaks, chunks of cave silt, bits of broken rock … Bertha wondered whose it had been.

She heard distant gongs—rocks falling against the massive hull.

Her HUD showed the temperature: *123°F*. Hot as hell by normal standards, but downright air conditioned compared to the cavern they'd left behind. The rocktopi seemed to understand that most of the KoolSuits were damaged, were lowering the temp in this room to accommodate.

Klimas lay on his back, staring straight up at nothing. Tommy was a few feet away, on some kind of pedestal or platform, a smooth platinum extrusion that seemed to have grown out of the floor itself. Mullet was on Tommy's left, holding his left hand, Sam on his right, her head against Tommy's chest.

Sonny sat against the curved wall, his hands at the sides of his head. He nodded slowly, rubbed at his silver bracelet, mumbled something Bertha couldn't make out.

In the middle of the large room, a glowing hologram, showing the iconic shape of Mount Fitz Roy and its sister peaks. Lines of light seemed to divide the range into a long, rectangular section.

Beneath that section, the unmistakable form of the rocktopi ship.

It struck Bertha, out of nowhere, that this was the *second* alien ship she'd been inside of. A story she could, hopefully, one day tell her child.

Or, if she was lucky enough, her *children*.

The sounds of rock hitting metal suddenly stopped. The following silence seemed wrong, somehow more frightening than the death music of those constant impacts.

Sonny lifted his head. "It stopped? Are we out?"

"Not yet, I don't think," Bertha said. "Look at the hologram."

It showed the ship as still inside the rectangular channel left behind by the rising mountain.

"Well slap my ass and call me Sally," Mullet said. "We're *flying*, Worm. We're in a spaceship, and we're flying."

Tommy slowly turned his head, looked at his old friend.

"Are we going into space?" Tommy asked. "I always dreamed of going into space."

Mullet opened his mouth to speak, but words did not come out. All he could do was nod.

A hand on her leg. Bertha looked down to see Patrick gazing up at her, forcing a smile. The hurt in his eyes, not just from his physical pain, but from emotional wounds as well.

"Hey, hot stuff," he said. "We gotta stop meeting like this."

He was trying to lighten the mood. Even now, he was trying to be there for her. But it wasn't the time for jokes. Bertha wondered if she would ever laugh again.

She put a hand on her belly. "Otto died so I could get away."

She couldn't quite comprehend that. The man had barely known her, but he had made a clear choice—his life for hers. For her baby's.

"I know," Patrick said. "A lot of people died."

Hatchet. Skylark. Curveball. Sleepy. Otto.

And soon, Tommy. Mullet had looked at his wounds. So had Klimas. They'd both seen enough combat wounds to know he was done for. If there had been a hospital nearby, maybe, but there was not.

Tommy's remaining lifespan would be measured in minutes.

Those weren't the only deaths.

Slash.

Axl.

Dozens of mercenaries.

Hundreds of rocktopi.

All for what? For money.

In that way, their little war was no different than all the others that had been fought all through history.

Money. If you drill down far enough, it is *always* about money.

Patrick reached over, took her hand.

"We made it," he said. "We now have the rest of our lives to feel bad about what happened, about what we did. For now, my love, just be with me. We survived. Let's treasure that."

She leaned over, kissed his hand, then set it in her lap and held it tight as she watched the hologram.

100

DISHES RATTLED. WOOD groaned. Tchotchkes slid around the coffee table.

As the lodge trembled slightly, Tim Feely stared out the window at the moonlit landscape.

"Colding, tell me you drugged my Sprite," he said. "Tell me you slipped me a tab of acid. Or maybe some DMT."

P.J. Colding, also staring out the window, slowly shook his head.

"Afraid not," he said. "You're seeing this."

Off on the horizon, a mountain range was rising. Edges as well-defined as a brownie sliced from a pan. Were it not so dark, Tim knew he would be able to see strata as clearly as he'd seen them when he'd visited the Grand Canyon many moons ago.

Colding pulled his cell phone out of his pocket. He held it up toward the horizon.

"Get video of this," Tim said.

"Wow, good idea," Colding said.

The mountain range continued to elevate, lifting smoothly, steadily. It was impossible. *Impossible*.

"If I'm not on acid for this, I should be," Tim said. "Fuck sobriety. Lianna, you bring any drugs with you?"

She walked up to the window, raised a pair of binoculars to her eyes.

"Drugs aren't really my thing," she said. "Never a dull moment with you boys. First, a thousand-pound killer pig, and now this."

The mountain—no, *several* mountains; one thought of them as individual peaks only until one saw how their roots were one and the same—rose up completely out of the earth. A rectangular chunk. *Miles* long. Higher and higher.

He could see *under* a miles-long chunk of *mountain*.

Finally, it stopped. A mile above the ground? It hovered there, unmoving.

"Neat trick," Lianna said. "Pretty sure I'll never see anything crazier than this."

From the gargantuan hole, in the moon shadow of a floating mountain, something rose up, something *huge*, almost as long as the floating mountain above it. A cylinder of some kind?

"Turns out I was wrong," Lianna said. "I do believe that's a space-ship."

Colding glanced at Tim. "You think Klimas and Otto could be in that thing?"

As crazy as it sounded, Tim hoped it was true. If they had gone inside that mountain, Tim didn't see how they could have survived any other way.

As he watched, the ship moved forward. It slipped out from beneath the mountain's shadow. Tapered at both ends, like stubby bullets. The massive ship gleamed in the bright moonlight.

"Lianna, try calling Klimas," Tim said. "And keep at it. If he and Otto are on that ship, maybe they can hear us."

The mountain began to descend, going straight down just as it had come straight up.

101

SAM CHECKED TOMMY'S pulse again.

Fainter than before.

Far fainter.

Even if they could get him to a hospital at that very second, she doubted he would make it. Mullet and Klimas were far more experienced with death than she was—they had already given up.

Slowly, carefully, Sam placed Tommy's hand on his chest.

Through his scratched, dirt-smeared visor, he smiled up at her.

"Did we do it, Sam? Are we clear?"

The man's words were mere whispers, made audible only by the comm's amplification.

Sam glanced at the hologram. It showed the mountain lowering back into place—a rectangular peg in a rectangular hole—and the ship itself, floating above the surface.

"I think so," she said. "You did it, Tommy. You saved them."

His eyes were half-lidded. His smile was radiant.

"*We* did it," he said. "We all did."

Mullet squeezed Tommy's shoulder. "You got that right, buddy."

Sam heard a deep grunt of pain, saw Bertha helping O'Doyle walk closer. His left arm hung limp, streaked with blood, droplets slowly falling to the floor at his feet. The man looked as bad off as Tommy. But O'Doyle was not dying. That wasn't how the world worked — O'Doyle's greed was behind all of this, yet he would live while Ramiro was gone, while Tommy would never see another sunrise, while the rocktopi had to abandon their hiding place and once again risk extinction.

Because life wasn't fair.

"Tommy," O'Doyle said.

Tommy's dreamy smile widened.

"Looks like we did it," he said.

O'Doyle nodded. "Looks that way."

Silent tears rolled down Bertha's cheeks.

O'Doyle put his hand on Tommy's shoulder.

"I'm sorry," O'Doyle said. "I really am. For all of it."

Tommy closed his eyes. "You didn't make anyone do anything. And you gave me the greatest experience of my life. I love you, brother."

O'Doyle sagged. Bertha had to adjust to keep him from stumbling. Now he, too, was crying.

"I love you too, Tommy," O'Doyle said.

Mullet sniffed. Tears lined his cheeks.

"Y'all crying like a bunch of pussies," he said.

Klimas stood and walked over, touched Tommy's hand.

"You're a tough sonofabitch, Worm," Klimas said. "The greatest shooter I've ever seen, and I've seen a lot."

Tommy nodded, the motion barely perceptible. "Sorry you lost your partner. Right before he died, he said he was going to see Margo. That mean anything to you?"

Klimas choked back a sob.

"Otto's been looking forward to seeing her again for a long time," he said. "I hope he gets to do that."

Klimas patted Tommy's hand, then stepped back.

Sam heard a faint squeak, subtle, the rocktopi equivalent of someone clearing their throat. In the room's oval opening, Whitey, with a few rocktopi behind him.

Gray symbols flashed on his pale skin. She understood them almost immediately.

"They want to let us out," she said. "We're supposed to follow him."

Sonny stood up like a shot. "No shit? We're getting out of here?"

He didn't care about Tommy? Well, Sam couldn't hold that against him—Sonny had been through a lot. They all had.

"All right," Mullet said. "Help me get Tommy up."

Another squeak, sharper, louder.

Whitey flowed into the room. The leader stretched out a long extrusion, rested it on Tommy's chest.

The message was clear.

"It's okay, Kevin," Tommy said in his dreamy voice. "I'd rather lie here for a little while. You guys go."

There was no agreement, no cajoling to change his mind. Everyone knew the score. If Tommy wanted to die here, then that was his way.

Klimas walked to the shield lying on the floor. "We'll carry O'Doyle out on this."

Mullet squeezed Tommy's shoulder, then joined Klimas.

"I'm sorry, Worm," O'Doyle said. "I hope they have books in Valhalla."

Tommy laughed, winced. "Of course they do. You know those Vikings loved a good story."

Bertha helped O'Doyle to the shield, helped him lay down on it. Two rocktopi flowed in, tried to lift the shield-turned-stretcher.

Mullet held up a hand. "We got it, my squishy bros. We got it."

He and Klimas lifted the stretcher.

"Christ's curly pubes," Mullet said, "Ender, you're heavy enough without adding fifty fucking pounds of metal."

Bertha led them out of the room, Sonny right behind her.

Only Sam and Tommy remained.

She grabbed her pack, took out the horribly warped copy of *The Call of the Wild*. She put it on his chest.

"In case you want to read a little, before…before…"

Tommy reached up, held her hand, placed it on top of the book.

"I want you to have it," he said. "To remember me by. And why would I want to read now when I'm living out the greatest tale of all time?"

He sounded so calm, so serene. Sam couldn't stop her tears, but she took some small solace from him. Someday, she, too would die—and when that happened, she could only hope to move on with the grace and acceptance this man showed.

"Goodbye, Tommy Strymon."

He smiled again. His eyes closed.

"Goodbye, Samira Jabour."

Sam bent, touched her helmeted forehead to his. She wished with all the world she could kiss him, just one time.

But life wasn't fair.

She turned and walked out of the room.

TOMMY STRYMON TRIED to open his eyes. They refused to comply.

He still hurt, but in a different way. A dark, *cold* way.

Death had come for him. It hadn't taken him away, not quite yet, but Tommy knew, with full certainty, that his time had come.

He forced his eyes open. He beheld a wonder—*angels*.

Brightly colored, gleaming, fluorescing.

Dozens of rocktopi arms stretched up to the curled rungs in the ceiling, latching to that strange spinal column as it passed by overhead. He was being carried deeper into the ship. No impacts, no jarring, no shaking.

It felt like floating on a pillow of light.

Below him, in the corridor, more rocktopi than he could count. They all pulsed with their fingerprint-specific patterns, yet the colors were almost uniform—subtle variations of a soft, warm turquoise. As he passed over, they reached up tentacles to him, tips connecting with him, stretching as they followed along before dropping off, as if the aliens wanted to touch him for as long as they could before he was gone.

He understood. He didn't need language. They were saying goodbye. They were saying, *thank you for your sacrifice.*

Tommy felt the sting of tears.

His own nation had dismissed him with a kick in the ass and a warning to keep his mouth shut. These people—people from another race entirely—wanted him to know they understood what he had done, what he had given up.

Tommy knew he could never make amends for the things he'd done. He could never fix what happened at Bandah. He couldn't shake the never-ending guilt of having taken the lives of …

… of …

Well, wasn't that something?

He couldn't remember how many people he'd killed.

The angels carried him on.

102

On the surface

"DST THREE TO DST TWO," Lianna said into the phone. "I repeat, DST Three to DST Two."

Tim waited.

Colding stood at the window, looking out with the binoculars.

No response from Lianna's phone.

"Keep at it," Tim said to her.

"DST Three to DST Two. Come in DST Two."

Tim knew that he, Colding, and Lianna weren't the only ones who saw the ship. The thing was a half mile in the air. It was dark out and the ship had no lights, which would help, but anyone still awake in El Chaltén who happened to look west would see it.

Who was he kidding … after those tremors, *everyone* in El Chaltén was awake.

Tim put it at an hour, tops, before a pair of Lockheed Martin A-4AR Fightinghawks roared in, looking for the strange, *large* radar signature.

"You need to call your guy at State," Colding said.

Tim nodded. Yes, he did need to call that man.

How the hell could this be explained to the Argentinians?

Lianna kept calling.

"Hey," Colding said. "I think something came out of the big ship."

A tiny point of light … real, or Tim's imagination?

"DST Three to DST Two," Lianna said. "Come in DST Two."

"*DST Three, this is DST Two. I forgot I still had this thing.*"

Tim grabbed the phone out of her hand.

"This is Feely! Otto, you there, buddy? Come in, over!"

A pause, just long enough for Tim's heart to sink, knowing the bad news was inevitable an instant before he heard the words.

"*This is Klimas. I'm sorry, Director … Otto didn't make it.*"

Didn't make it.

Clarence Otto … gone.

Tim didn't even want to *think* about the things Otto had survived. Now he was gone.

"DST Two," Tim said, "are you in a … well … shit, are you in a goddamn spaceship?"

"*Affirmative, Director. In a little bitty one now, though. Where are you? We can come to you. We're not in great shape.*"

"DST Two, we are at the lodge rented by Patrick O'Doyle," Tim said. "Do you know where that is?"

A pause.

"*Roger, DST One, we are en route to your location. DST Two, over.*"

103

Among the stars ...

IN THE END, Tommy was not alone.

Eyes closed, he tried to soak up every sensation.

He enjoyed the ride.

They carried him. They touched him. They celebrated him.

He felt so weak, so cold.

And yet, so *happy*.

He'd done things he never thought possible. He'd tasted dreams that seemed to belong only in fiction. He'd discovered, finally, that man was not alone in the universe.

The stuff of boyhood fantasies.

He heard a door open, a hiss of pressurized air.

He was lowered, but not all the way to the floor. They rested him against something, something that angled backward. Tommy had a vision of the shitty recliner back in his shitty apartment. Whatever he rested against now was flat and hard. No cushion—why would creatures with boneless bodies ever need cushions?

It wasn't the most comfortable place in the universe to die, but Tommy could think of places that were a whole lot worse.

Tommy opened his eyes. Even that was hard to do.

He was facing a concave wall. Before him stood Whitey, Siren, and two rocktopi he didn't recognize. The two rocktopi mashed together, their colors melding, then pulsing in time.

Tommy knew what came next.

The twined alien flattened. Colors flickered. On that flat space appeared the image of a naked man, lying flat on a metal floor.

A naked, *broken* man.

His right hand, swollen like a gnarled club.

His left foreleg, broken, a piece of bone slightly tenting out of the skin above it.

On the floor around him, smears of blood.

The floor...the *curved* floor.

The man was on the ship.

Red hair. So small.

Tommy realized it was Angus Kool.

"No armor now," Tommy said. "And they even took your KoolSuit. Sucks to be you."

Whitey came closer. Gray symbols flashed on his white skin. Tommy thought he recognized some of them, but just as quickly that recognition faded. Even if he knew the symbols, he couldn't focus on them long enough for them to make sense.

"I'm sorry, Whitey," Tommy said. "Afraid I'm not much for conversation right now."

Exhaustion washed over him. Tommy's head lolled forward. He had to fight to look up again.

When he did, the rocktopi were gone—all but Siren.

"Jesus," Tommy said. "You look awful."

He hadn't noticed before. Siren looked pale, almost as pale as Whitey. Globs of thick, dried clump-bandage dotted his skin, the edges ringed by yellow blood both wet and dry to the point of flaking off.

And then, Tommy understood.

Siren was dying. Just like him.

Both of them, wounded so badly in battle that there was no recovery.

They would not burn out, but rather, gently fade away.

Together.

"Your luck finally ran out," Tommy said. "Sorry, my friend."

Siren let out a weak sound, a low, mournful whine.

He was sorry, too.

The alien flowed toward Tommy, moved slower than Tommy had ever seen a rocktopi move before. Tommy had learned that some things transcended the language barrier. Things like bravery. Things like honor. Things like pain.

Siren moved to Tommy's left, and there he stopped.

A tentacle budded outward, hung in the air, waiting.

Tommy reached out a hand and took it. The tentacle wrapped around his fingers.

The curved wall before them shimmered.

Shimmered, then became transparent.

Tommy's breath froze in his chest.

Earth.

He was looking at his planet.

He was *in space*.

"Thank you," Tommy said. "Thank you so much."

At the end, at the very end, Tommy Strymon's lifelong dream came true.

His eyelids fluttered, closed.

With a smile still on his lips, Tommy Strymon's light faded away.

104

DUMBFOUNDED.

That was the only word to describe how Tim Feely felt.

The alien ship—Tim could only assume it was alien, unless the Argentines had been some seriously sneaky bitches—lifted up from the shore of the little blue lake. With almost no sound, it rose, and then it took off like a silent shot, vanishing into the night sky.

It left behind six people on the shore: five standing, one lying on what looked a rectangle of thick metal.

"That's Klimas," Colding said, running toward them.

"Hold on," Tim called after him. "They could be irradiated! Or have alien microorganisms or something!"

He'd had more than enough experience with alien microorganisms, thank you very much.

If Colding heard the warning, he paid it no heed.

"Come on, chief," Lianna said. "They got wounded."

"Colding's face could melt off. You don't know."

She sighed jogged after Colding, leaving Tim alone.

Even in the faint light filtering from the lodge, Tim knew five of the six people on sight. Paulius Klimas, of course, and then three he recognized from the intelligence photos provided by André Vogel: Kevin Bliss, one of the NoSeeUms that served with O'Doyle; Bertha Lybrand, O'Doyle's wife and co-organizer of this insanity; and Sonny McGuiness, a consultant who had worked for EarthCore at the Utah Camp.

And, of course, the man on the sheet of metal, a face that Tim would never, *ever* forget—Patrick O'Doyle, former governmental assassin turned rogue fortune seeker.

Awesome. Fantastic. Just peachy.

Tim looked to the sky again. The massive, mountain-sized ship was gone. He had a hunch that no radar system anywhere would show the slightest blip. The shuttle—if that's what it had been—had probably flown up to join it.

Lianna and Colding helped O'Doyle up, got under the big man's arms. They walked him toward the lodge. Klimas, Bliss, Lybrand, McGuiness and the young woman Tim didn't recognize limped along after.

All of them looked like they'd been through hell.

"Shit," Tim said.

He jogged over to help.

105

PATRICK WANTED TO sleep. *Needed* to sleep. Blood loss. Exhaustion, to the bone. His body had given up on him, from his back to his wounded shoulder to muscles that simply no longer complied with his wishes. Physically, emotionally, spiritually, he was a two-dimensional sketch of the man he'd once been.

He didn't just feel old—he felt like a *corpse*.

But he could not allow himself to sleep. Not quite yet.

Everyone had gathered in the lounge, as if this was nothing more than a weekend meeting of neighborhood friends. Patrick and Bertha sat on the couch, the same place Skylark, Hatchet, and Curveball had sat days earlier. Sam and Sonny stood behind the couch, Sam with a cup of coffee, Sonny with a fifth of Jim Beam. The old man wasn't bothering with a glass. Patrick hoped there would be some bourbon left by the time all this business was finished—he needed a drink like he needed to breathe.

Klimas and Mullet were at the picture window, side-by-side, both of them eating from bowls of soup. Mullet had ignored everyone and everything, gone straight to the kitchen and microwaved two cans of chicken noodle. It smelled impossibly delicious. After three days (or was it four?) of eating warm paste through a tube, just about anything would taste amazing.

Even though they were on the surface, safe from the geothermal heat, no one had taken off their KoolSuit. Not even Sonny. Even damaged beyond repair, even drained of the coolant fluid that gave them their special ability, no one seemed quite ready to believe that things were *over*, that the suits were no longer the difference between life and death. Masks were retracted—that was about as far as anyone was willing to go.

Tim Feely sat in a chair across from the couch. Tommy had sat in that same chair.

It felt like a tense mafia meeting from a bad movie: Patrick, Bertha, Sam and Sonny, facing off against Feely and the two people standing beside his chair like consiglieres: P.J. Colding—Patrick remembered him as well, but only vaguely—and a tall woman named *Wilkerson*.

Throw in a severed horse's head, and the gangland vibe would be complete.

"That," Feely said, "is one hell of a story. Anything else to add?"

Klimas had given the shorthand version of the days' events.

"Plenty, Director," he said. "But you'll get it in my final report, I've given you all the major points."

Feely looked around the room, making eye contact with Patrick and the others.

"All of that, and the only thing you brought out was a slab of platinum alloy. That's *it*? No tech? No samples?"

Patrick had met Feely once before, seven years earlier. A helluva time that had been. Patrick had shoved down memories of those difficult days, blocked them out like he had so much of his past.

Maybe it was time to stop doing that. He'd trained himself to not think about Bandah, about the NoSeeUms, about Black Manitou Island. Where had that forced forgetfulness gotten him?

He would remember what had happened beneath Mount Fitz Roy.

He would remember Skylark, Hatchet, Worm and Sleepy.

He would remember Clarence Otto, the man who had given his life so that Bertha and the baby might live.

He would remember Slash, Axl, Whitey and Siren.

He would remember Angus Kool.

He would remember Utah.

He would remember Veronica, Sanji, Randy and Mack.

And he would *never* forget about Connell Kirkland.

"Seriously," Feely said. "Not one goddamned thing?"

Patrick had met Feely once, briefly, years earlier, on Black Manitou Island. Patrick had worked for the Department of Special Threats, the same department that Feely had, somehow, become the director of.

Patrick hadn't liked the man then, and he didn't like him now—especially considering how much Feely reminded Patrick of one Doctor Angus Kool.

"Back off," Sam said to Feely, an edge in her voice. "People died back there. Not that you give a shit about that, you officious little prick."

Tim leaned forward in his chair. "One of the people who died *back there* was a good friend of mine. Someone I've been through a lot with. So, yeah, I *do* give a shit. Save the pity party for another time. We need to get this shit sorted out pronto."

Sam stared for a moment, then looked away, her shoulders sagging. Maybe she'd put the last of her energy into that little outburst. Or maybe she was just as dead inside as Patrick was.

Feely sighed. "At least we have that sheet of metal. Maybe something good will come of it."

"*You* don't have it," Patrick said. "*We* do. It's spoken for."

Feely raised an eyebrow. "*Spoken for?* I know you're all Billy Badass, O'Doyle—or at least you are when your back isn't jacked up like you belong in a nursing home—but that metal is the property of the United States of America. We're taking it."

"If you want it, buy it," Patrick said. "Sonny, what's it worth?"

Sonny looked around. "Anyone got a calculator?"

Feely was getting pissed. He smiled, his expression angry yet confident—he thought he held all the cards.

"So you people want to play games," he said. "Okay, here's a fun game, I call it *Rot Away in a Secret Argentinian Prison*. You smuggled in weapons. You violated this nation's sovereignty. If the Argentinians figure out what actually happened here, they're going to blame you for losing the greatest resource ever found on their soil."

He leaned further forward.

"I am the Director of the Department of Special threats. That's like being the Director of the CIA, only with aliens, mutants, science gone horribly wrong—shit like that."

"I know what the fucking DST is," Patrick said.

Feely nodded. "I know you do. I know a lot about you, Pat. Mind if I call you *Pat?*"

"His *friends* can call him that," Bertha said. "You can call him *Mister O'Doyle*. Or, if you like ... *Ender*."

"*Ender?* Like in that book?"

Patrick couldn't remember, exactly, where Tommy had got the nickname, but knowing the man, a book was the only place it could have come from.

"That's right," Patrick said.

Feely nodded. "From what Longworth says about you, I suppose that's fitting. Yeah, I know some things about you, and your team. I know about your service. I know how they shut you down after Bandah."

Patrick almost winced at the very sound of that word, an ingrained reaction, but the wince didn't come. Bandah had been a tragedy. He hadn't been able to save those people, but he *had* saved another group of people.

He and the NoSeeUms had saved the rocktopi.

The scales had been balanced.

"I got it," Sonny said. "Figured it out in my head. That slab of metal weighs about fifty pounds, give or take. That makes it worth roughly eight hundred and forty grand. Considering where it came from, I think it's fair that you pay us one million bucks for it."

A *clink* as Mullet dropped his spoon and raised his hand, a long piece of white noodle hanging from his mouth.

"Yes, Kevin," Bertha said, "that is *US dollars*."

Mullet nodded, went back to eating his soup.

Feely's nostrils flared. He slid his hands across the tops of this thighs.

"Money," he said. "I lose my friend, and you want *money?*"

"It's not for us," Patrick said. "Three quarters goes to the daughters of Marie Dunlop. One quarter goes to the Church of the Holy Signal."

He had promised Marie and Doug millions. He'd promised *everyone* millions. This was all they had left to give. It wouldn't replace a missing mother, but it was something. As for Doug's church? Hopefully, a quarter million would do some good.

"Others died as well," Feely said. "Thomas Strymon. Anders Keeley. Carson Wampler. Nothing for them?"

Worm. Curveball. Hatchet.

Five members of his old squad, gone forever.

Patrick would never forgive himself for their deaths, but at the same time, they were soldiers to the bone. They had died doing the right thing. That *mattered.*

"Keeley and Wampler had each other," Patrick said. "That was about it for them, we believe. As for Strymon … I don't think he had anyone. Anyone except us."

An *us* that now consisted of only Patrick and Mullet.

The last of the NoSeeUms.

Feely sat back, visibly tried to reel in his frustration.

"I can see that you all went through a lot," he said. "I'm doing my job here, but I'm truly sorry you lost your friends."

Pain in his voice, too. He'd sent Otto to Argentina; was Feely suffering some of the same guilt that Patrick felt?

The conversation stalled. No one knew what to say next.

In the silence, Patrick heard the distant thump of helicopter rotors.

Feely turned to Lianna. "That one ours?"

She took out a cell phone, turned away. Patrick heard her mumble something, then turn back.

"It's ours," Lianna said. "But we don't have long. The Argentinians have launched a response team. We can expect them here within the hour."

Feely stood.

"We're evacuating all of you," he said. "We need to get you out of the country. The helicopter will take us to Neuquen. We'll be in Florida by noon tomorrow. When we're stateside, you are all going to answer a lot of questions. You may have caused an international incident that people will need to manage."

"Hold on a second," Sam said. "Are you saying we're being *arrested?*"

Feely shrugged. "I know some of you have a skillset that lets you fade into the woodwork. I won't let you out of my sight, not until I get the information I want. What choice do I have?"

"A choice that doesn't ends with my boot on your throat," Bertha said. "You don't control us."

Colding and Wilkerson shifted slightly, reacting to the tension in the room, the sudden threat of violence.

Klimas cleared his throat.

Feely glared at him. "If you have something to say, Klimas, fucking say it."

Mullet leaned close to Klimas. "See? That's why I always raise my hand—no one likes getting yelled at."

Klimas stepped away from the window.

"Director, I think there's a way to get the cooperation you want that makes everyone happy," he said. "Otto's gone. The things he'd encountered made him perfect for the DST. He had experience with unpredictable, dangerous situations. So does O'Doyle. And Lybrand. Hire them."

Patrick and Bertha traded a look—like him, she just wanted to go home.

"I've been down that road before," Patrick said. "I don't think that's for us. We're getting out of the game. Time to do something else."

Klimas smiled a sad smile. "Like what, exactly?"

"We'll go back to EarthCore," Bertha said.

Feely huffed. "Not sure that's what you want. Barbara Yakely has announced her retirement. Harvey Dillinger has taken over, although with all the lawsuits pending from the Utah incident, in a year or so I don't think there will be anything for him to actually run."

Yakely, out? Dillinger … Patrick didn't trust that man, not one tiny bit.

"Working for the DST isn't boring," Klimas said. "And, of course, there's the healthcare program. It might come in handy for someone who's going to need extensive recovery surgery. Or—" he looked at Bertha "—for other reasons."

Healthcare? Patrick and Bertha had just dealt with killer robots, a lost alien culture, a missed chance at billions, *and* the death of comrades, and Klimas was talking about *healthcare*? Something so basic in concept … and yet, so needed. Patrick and his wife had come out of this empty-handed. His back was *shot*—how could they afford medical bills for him, let alone for Bertha's pregnancy?

What would they do when the baby came?

He would figure something out. He wasn't about to rely on the fucking government to help him.

He'd tried that before. Twice.

"That's a dumb idea," Feely said. "Otto is dead because of these people, and you want me to *hire* them."

Klimas nodded. "I do. And *you* want to hire them. Lybrand and O'Doyle have detailed information on not one, but *two* alien encounters. They can give a full explanation of what happened in Utah. You, Director Feely, would be able to go to your next budget meeting with definitive answers on what happened there *and* here."

Feely glanced at Patrick, then Bertha.

"I hadn't thought of that," the director said. "Our budget is … not what I would like it to be. Your knowledge would come in handy."

Patrick sighed. The healthcare and steady paycheck were enticing, but he'd worked for the DST once and it hadn't ended well.

The helicopter grew louder.

"I don't know," Patrick said. "I don't think it's for me. For *us*."

"That's because you didn't hear Director Feely's full offer," Klimas said.

Feely sat down again. "This ought to be good. I, for one, would love to hear *Director Feely's full offer*. Please, Klimas—educate us."

"You can hire them as DST agents," Klimas said. "Ensuring their full cooperation. As part of the hiring process, part of showing that Lybrand and O'Doyle's knowledge is vital to national security, you could use your position as director to influence certain people, people who can correct certain military records."

Patrick felt a rush in his chest—was Klimas serious?

"Records about Bandah," Feely said, quietly. "What is it, exactly, that you want me to do?"

"Get the NoSeeUms *recognized* for their service," Klimas said. "Our country fucked them. For twenty years, they haven't even been able to say they served *at all*. With your position, Director, you can find a way to see that Doug Rapson, Anders Keeley, Carson Wampler, Marie Dunlop,

Thomas Strymon, Kevin Bliss and Patrick O'Doyle no longer have to stay silent about what they did for our country. You can give them back the honor that was stripped away."

Patrick felt stunned. He'd never imagined such a thing was possible. He'd lived with silent shame for so long we wasn't sure he knew how to live *without* it.

Feely closed his eyes. He rubbed the bridge of his nose. He reached a hand out to Sonny.

"Fuck it," Feely said. "McGuiness, give me a goddamn drink."

Sonny walked around the couch, handed Feely the bottle.

Feely took three swallows so big they hurt Patrick just watching them. He lowered the bottle, eyed Patrick.

"Believe it or not, I think I can do what Klimas wants. I know a guy, so to speak." Feely looked at Mullet, raised an eyebrow. "How about you, Unfortunate Haircut-Name Man? Do you want in on this deal, too?"

Kevin grinned. "Does a horny bear jack off in the woods?"

Feely stared at him for a moment, shook his head, and took another long pull.

"I'm going to regret this decision, I know it." He wiped his mouth with the back of his hand, looked at Sam and Sonny. "And you two? Since the Uncle Sam gravy train appears to be leaving the station, you want in?"

Sonny laughed. "Work for the man? Not in this lifetime. I think I'll stick around these parts, maybe look through some old tunnels, see what I can find. Sam, you got more experience with the area than I do. You know how to integrate with the townies, how to avoid attention from local authorities. Maybe you switch your interest from archaeology to entomology, help me see what I can find."

Sam stared at him. "Are you saying you want me to help you find … *bugs*?"

"Might be some interesting species around here," Sonny said. "Valuable ones, even. The earthquake might have damaged some areas, but how are we going to know until we look? What do you think?"

A smile slowly broke over Sam's face. "Come to think of it, I do already have a place to stay. Partners? Fifty-fifty?"

"Fifty-fifty," Sonny said. "Just keep your hands to yourself, if you know what I mean."

Sam laughed. "All right, Sonny. I'm in."

Feely again stood. The helicopter was so close he had to raise his voice to be heard.

"If you two are done with whatever thinly veiled code you're using to talk about hunting for alien artifacts, let me assure you Uncle Sam will pay far better than the going rate if you should actually find any. I'll leave you a way to contact me. Anything you find, you call me first, agreed?"

Sonny nodded. "Nothing like getting paid in taxpayer money."

Patrick looked out the picture window, saw the helicopter set down, oddly, in exactly the same place the shuttle had.

"O'Doyle," Feely said, "Jabour and McGuiness only get that deal if you come to work for me. Exactly like Klimas laid out. You, Lybrand and Bliss sign on as DST agents. You give me any and all information I need about Utah, Mount Fitz Roy, and anything else I want to know. And not for a few weeks, either—if you sign up, you commit to five years. But I give you my word that if you *do* sign up, I'll clear you record, and the record of your squad mates. And, yes, I'll get you that million dollars for Dunlop's daughters and Rapson's church. Do we have a deal?"

Patrick didn't know what to think, didn't know how to feel. Could Feely really erase twenty years of total silence? Could he bring honor back to the memory of Sleepy, Curveball, Hatchet, Skylark, Bookworm and El Gato, the survivors of Bandah? And what about Landslide, Knuckles and Swampy—the soldiers who had *died* there?

Bring honor back to Mullet.

And…and yes, even to *Ender*.

Such a thing wouldn't have seemed possible.

Patrick had gone into this hoping to become rich—but some things were worth far more than money.

He couldn't make this decision alone. He looked to his wife.

"What do you think?"

She took his hand—with two fingers and one thumb, she squeezed.

"Let's do it," she said. "Like Klimas said, at least it won't be boring."

She smiled. He hoped their child would have that smile.

Patrick looked at Tim Feely.

"All right, Director—sign us up."

Tim nodded once. "Bertha Lybrand and Kevin Bliss, welcome to the Department of Special Threats. And Patrick O'Doyle—welcome back."

"ANGUS! GRAB IT!"

Randy's voice echoed through the ancient metal corridors. First his voice, then his screams.

I could have saved him…I could have thrown that thing into the river…I let Randy die.

Angus woke with a start, sat up in the darkness, chest heaving, heart hammering.

Randy's death. The silverbug driving that jagged blade into him. The look on his face. The *blood*.

Just a dream.

Oh *God* did his head hurt.

Just a dream.

All of that was in the past.

So dark.

Where was he?

Pain in his legs, his hands…

Angus felt at both, his brain trying to come fully awake, trying to make the right connections.

He needed his meds… he needed a shot, something, *anything* to deal with the agony in his hand, his legs. Had his meds worn off? How long had he been out?

His exosuit.

Where was his exosuit?

The suit… wait, he'd worn it in Argentina, not Utah.

Argentina…

The mountain.

The tremors, the falling rock…

Fuentes.

The ship, slowly rising into the air…

Where *was* he?

Lights blazed on, making his eyes shut tight. He held out a hand to block the light, but it was everywhere.

His legs, his hands… the pain…

Where was his suit?

He heard something, something *moving*.

"Hello?"

No answer.

A crawling sensation crept through him, that shiver one might feel from reaching out in the darkness and touching something cold, something *wet*.

He'd run through the falling rocks. Fuentes… Angus had ordered the man's death, then sprinted across that nightmare of stone rain… to the ship, and…

Colors flashing on his closed eyelids.

Colors…

He forced his squinting eyes open.

Rocktopi… dozens of them… in every direction.

Angus tried to stand—his legs wouldn't support him. He scooted backward until his back hit something solid. He felt at it, turned and looked…

Glass?

He looked around.

He was … he was in a bubble.

Outside that bubble, rocktopi, flashing colors, so many *angry* colors.

Except for one … one of them was white.

"Where am I?"

The rocktopi made no sound.

Angus's breaths came shorter, faster. He would ask the question again, *had* to ask it again, but he already knew.

"Where the fuck am I?"

As if in answer, the white one extruded a new tentacle, a sickening thing to see, a boneless white worm squeezing out, becoming longer.

Pointing. It was pointing to the wall, the concave wall …

The material there shimmered.

The ship … Angus remembered crawling through the door as it almost crushed his hips …

He was on their ship … no, this couldn't be happening … he couldn't be on their ship …

The wall vibrated, then the shimmer faded away, became clear.

It was small, so small it took him a second to recognize it.

Out there, in the black, smaller than his balled fist, a ball of green and blue and white.

Earth.

Growing smaller.

"No." Angus shook his head. "It's a trick. Computer graphics or something. You drugged me. This isn't real."

Smaller still.

But it was real.

He knew it.

Outside the bubble, the slight waver of a heat shimmer.

Smaller, and smaller, now the size of his thumb …

In that moment, he knew he would never leave this ship.

Angus Kool began to scream.

BIBLIOGRAPHY

Allison, M. Lee, ed., and Sharon Wakefield, ed., *Energy and Mineral Resources of Utah*. Salt Lake City, UT: Utah Geological Association, 1990.

Carter, William, *Ghost Towns of the West*. Menlo Park, CA: Lane, 1971.

Langewiesche, William, *The Chaos Company*: Vanity Fair, 2015.

Lamb, Susan, *The Smithsonian Guides to Natural America: The Southern Rockies*, Washington, D.C.: Smithsonian Books, 1995.

Lees, Will, *Argentina vs Chile: The Fight Behind Claiming El Chaltén*: Culture Trip, 2018.

McKenna, Luke, and Johnson, Robert, *A Look At The Largest Private Armies In the World*: Insider, 2014.

Moore, George W. and G. Nicholas Sullivan, *Speleology*. Trenton, NJ: Cave Books, 1978.

Prados, John, *Notes on the CIA's Secret War in Afghanistan*: Journal of American History, 2002.

Shawe, Daniel R., ed. and Peter D. Rowly, *Guidebook to Mineral Deposits of Southwestern Utah*. Salt Lake City, UT: Utah Geological Association, 1978.

Turse, Nick, *America's new golden age of black ops: Inside our secret global war abroad*: TomDispatch, 2015.

Vogel, Shawna, *Naked Earth*. New York: Plume, 1996.

Watkins, T. H., *Gold and Silver in the West*. Palo Alto: American West, 1971.

Wharton, Tom and Gayen Wharton, *Utah*. Compass America Guides, 1993.

Whelan, J. A., *Geology, Ore Deposits and Mineralogy of the Rocky Range, Near Milford, Beaver County, Utah, Salt Lake City*, UT: Utah Geological and Mineral Survey, 1982.

Williams, Guy., *Fatal climb inquest: 'We know the risk'*, Otago Daily Times, 2020.

www.ingramcontent.com/pod-product-compliance
Lightning Source LLC
Chambersburg PA
CBHW072005180726

48291CB00001BA/4